WOLF-DREAMS

1: Wolf-Dreams

Figures approach through the clouds. She runs. There's an eye where the moon should be. Watching – no, looking for her. Not yet. Not yet – she hides. It isn't time yet.

'Easy girl.'

The figures pass overhead. The pride of Odin – the Valkyries – on winged wolves . . .

A hand on her breast, another on her brow. They are damp.

What?

'You're safe here. Be calm.'

Wet all over, she shakes. Her head throbs. She opens her eyes; a white brilliance stabs through, forcing her eyelids shut. She tries to sit, but the pain knocks her back. She feels something at her lip – water. She opens her mouth and the cool liquid makes her tongue tingle. She drinks and feels the water rush down her parched throat, burning, caressing.

'Easy! You'll drown.'

Water. She remembers: the boat, the ocean, the numbing cold after the storm. Relentless. *Am I dead?*

She remembers more. 'The sword! Astrid's sword!' Thyri tries to sit again; the pain doesn't let her.

'Shhh.'

The hand is soothing and the voice almost purrs. 'It is here. Safe. Try to rest.'

She rests. She wanders back into the clouds. She looks up at the eye. It still can't see her. It still isn't time.

WOLF-DREAMS

2: Nightreaver

Thyri looked up. A pale wash of white hailed the coming of the moon. Her eyes opened wide as the silver orb broke the horizon, and her legs went weak. She looked down and watched the white coat of the beast sprout through her skin and cover her lower body. Her breasts caved in as the rippling white coat grew up to her neck. Claws sprang from her toes, and her bones wrenched, forcing her to her knees. Pain flared through her, clouding her vision until the transformation was complete . . . and the white wolf had come fully into the world.

WOLF-DREAMS

3: Bloodfang

Thyri's heart beat faster as the trail twisted, doubled back, and twisted again, back onto the shadow-path. When the world suddenly shifted she barely broke her stride, and then only to make sure she didn't rush headlong off a cliff or into a pool of fire. Instead, the shift dropped her at the *bottom* of a fifty-foot cliff, and her senses urged her upward. Thyri grinned and cursed; if she didn't push her body to its limits she'd lose all the time she'd gained. Still cursing, she attacked the wall of rock, ignoring the screams of her muscles, racing haphazardly ever upward.

At the top, she found a field of barley. The ripe crop filled her nostrils, as did the tang of magic, but she didn't lose the fresh scent of her quarry, and she kept on its trail, her muscles fatigued for the first time all day.

Ten steps into the barley, the earth erupted in a shower of black and silver that fell on her, wrapped around her, and lifted her into the air. She struggled against the sorcerous grip as it tightened, and through gaps in the sorcery's claws, she saw her prey floating level with her, another ten paces ahead.

Also by the same author, and available from NEL:

MERCEDES NIGHTS

About the author

The son of an Air Force officer, Michael D. Weaver spent his early years in various parts of North America and the world.

He lives in Danville, Virginia, with his wife, where he works with computers. His first science fiction novel, *Mercedes Nights*, was published by New English Library to great acclaim. He is currently working on his next novel, *My Father Immortal*.

MICHAEL D. WEAVER

Wolf-Dreams

Nightreaver

Bloodfang

NEW ENGLISH LIBRARY
Hodder and Stoughton

First published in the
United States of America
as three separate volumes:

WOLF-DREAMS © 1987 by
Michael D. Weaver
Published by Avon Books in
1987

NIGHTREAVER © 1988 by
Michael D. Weaver
Published by Avon Books

BLOODFANG © 1989 by
Michael D. Weaver
Published by Avon Books in
1989

First published as an omnibus
edition in Great Britain in
1989 by New English Library
Paperbacks

British Library C.I.P.
Weaver, Michael.
Wolf-dreams.
I. Title
813'.54[F]

ISBN 0-450-49477-2

The characters and situations in this book are entirely imaginary and bear no relation to any real person or actual happening.

Printed and bound in Great Britain for Hodder and Stoughton Paperbacks, a division of Hodder and Stoughton Ltd., Mill Road, Dunton Green, Sevenoaks, Kent TN13 2YA.
(Editorial Office: 47 Bedford Square, London, WC1B 3DP) by Richard Clay Ltd., Bungay, Suffolk.
Typeset by Hewer Text Composition Services, Edinburgh.

1: Wolf-Dreams

for Elric

BOOK I

YOUTH

My name is Gerald; I'm sure of that much now.

Earlier today, I turned the key to unlock the door to this chamber I had not entered in nearly a year. I admit, I entered the darkness only after an interminable period of time during which my will waged ruthless battle with my fears of this place. On the threshold of Hell, I thought then. In my mind, I imagined all the screams of the damned echoing silently, maliciously within these walls, waves of the most terrible sound kept at bay by the fragile dam of a single beating heart. My heart.

Somehow, my will forced me across to the room's sole window, and I threw open the shutters.

Everything should have been caked with dust, encrypted as it had been for so long. But no, it was as if time had stopped here. As if, within these walls, the passage of time is measured solely by my presence. My desk – all my work – as if I had left yesterday.

And the pool – Satan's Chalice, as I have come to think of it – lay still, its surface like a gleaming sheet of polished red metal.

The sun had long since set. I have worked by candle-light for many hours now, reading all that I previously wrote. What I once thought masterfully penned now seems flawed, disjointed, a shadow of what it might be. I will borrow from it and begin here a retelling of this tale which you have but begun to read but which I, in ways I will not yet reveal, have lived. Even though this is not *my* tale.

It belongs to Thyri Eiriksdattir, sometimes called Bloodfang.

21: Homecoming

The homeland was cooling and the summer leaves dying, beginning to fall. She liked the smell. It promised winter and a rest from the fighting – warm fires, warm mead, warm companionship. A cold wind blew from the north, and she tightened the sash of her cloak. She looked at Astrid, who rode next to her, her gaze distant, her lips curled slightly in an unthinking, natural smile born of simple contentment, a smile at peace with its mistress.

The autumn feastings were over, their tales all grown stale as the fact of another winter grew apparent. Two days ahead lay Thorfinnson land, the family homestead. They had both left it long before, but in recent years they had wintered there, away from Ragnar's army. It was home, peppered with lazy, comfortable memories: the touch of walls touched since memory began, visions of Mother's young beauty and Father's unfilled early beard, smells of family brews and family cooking. Thyri had no more argument with it than Astrid.

They rode silently, stopping at noon to eat. They didn't speak: they rarely did when alone – they knew each other far too well. Thyri could usually tell what her cousin was thinking by watching her eyes, her smile.

A thick bank of clouds blocked the sun's cold light as the afternoon progressed. Thyri thought of winter again: not so long now. Another year of war and bloodshed had ended. In the cold, no one would fight. The sword bows to ice.

The sky cleared before the pale northern sun sank below the horizon. Streamers of delicate, fibrous light washed down from the north like a false otherworld dawn, filling the night with an eerie brilliance. The moon had already risen. The land hardly darkened, and they continued to ride. The night air was fresh, and Thyri realized how different it felt to be away from the heady smells of Ragnar's drinking hall. She retreated again into hazy, pleasant thoughts, losing time itself until her horse balked, drawing her outward.

Astrid had stopped. Thyri listened to the wood, hearing naught but a lone owl's hooting in the distance. *Men?* They had passed the last homestead near dusk, and none but the king laid claim to the stretch of land they currently crossed. It was too rocky, too treacherous for crops. Soon, the winter would make even the road impassable with neck-deep snows concealing crevices and encroaching roots. In the spring it would be worse as the forest reclaimed its own. Few traveled here. In time, Thyri guessed, there would be no road at all. Ragnar had carved it during the early years of his reign while repelling invaders from farther north. Now he had the ships to move his men in proper Viking style.

Astrid dismounted, drawing her sword. Moonlight streamed onto it, caressing strange purples and blues from runes near the hilt. The blade rose like a flame from her silver gauntlet.

Loki whinnied and Thyri leaned forward to stroke his neck. She drew her sword – a sister to her cousin's. Moving slowly, she took the reins of both mounts in her free hand and whispered happy things in their ears. Then the silence pressed in on her; even the distant owl had stopped. Wolves, she thought. The wind came from the north still – no predators in the wood there or the horses couldn't be calmed. She concentrated on the trees to the south and Astrid's progress west, up the road.

After fifty paces, Astrid paused. She retrieved a dark object from the ground and started back. Her face was grim. In her hand was a bloodied boot. She held it out to Thyri. One long red strip of flesh dangled from the top.

'He was horsed,' Astrid said. 'His mount panicked and turned back for home.'

A thin crescent was imprinted in the boot's leather. Thyri gasped.

'Yrsa's mark!'

'My sister's work has traveled far from home,' Astrid said, her eyes searching the forest to the left of the road. 'It went north.'

'Just one animal?'

Astrid nodded.

'Why didn't it go for his horse?'

Astrid shrugged and attached the boot to the saddle. 'It dragged the rest of the man away,' she said, mounting. 'If it has tasted human blood, it will desire it again. We should catch it before we make camp.'

They followed the trail of blood into the forest. The size of the wolf's paw prints disturbed Thyri but she said nothing. Astrid had eyes of her own. The procession through the trees themselves made her uneasy; the silence was unnatural, and she sensed something watching them, something dark and hiding from her scanning eyes. The short search ended in a pulpy mass of bone, gore, and small bits of flesh.

We should have found it still feeding, Thyri thought, eyeing the mess detachedly. Darker thoughts rose up: *We should have found it among a pack.* One wolf could hardly cast such a spell of silence over Nature.

Overhead, the clouds had returned. Tracking grew more difficult. As they turned to follow the wolf's tracks, it began to snow. A glade away and the visible trail lost, they dismounted. They still had its scent. They could continue on foot or simply wait and draw it to them. Whatever it was, it was canny. Better to meet it in the open, without branches hindering swordplay. Thyri untied a flask of ale from her saddle and paced across the glade, drinking thoughtfully.

Astrid stood by the horses, sword in hand, staring moodily into the trees. 'It is close,' she said, tucking a slender braid of forty-two knots behind her right ear. 'It has been close all along.'

Thyri took the flask from her lips, wiping her chin with the back of her gauntleted hand. She nodded absently.

Astrid touched her mount's ear. 'Stay alert, Yrafax. You let us know if –'

She stopped, shifting the grip on her sword. Yrafax tensed and pawed at the hard ground. He neighed, then bucked.

Thyri looked up. Astrid's gaze followed. A white shadow in the trees fluttered and blurred, streaking toward her. She whirled away from it, her sword swinging around, tearing shallowly along its side.

Spray of blood, Thyri noted. No phantom but mortal. *It bleeds.* Ale forgotten, she crossed half the glade while the wolf landed and turned, striking at Astrid again with blinding speed. Thyri saw all in acute detail: sword point parting moist white fur, blade glinting as it sheathed itself between ribs and angled for the heart while the beast writhed into the attack, fangs dripping and eyes blazing with a fire too intense and furious to be of this world. Wolf, Astrid, drawing closer. Astrid falling back. Wolf embracing. Fangs on throat, tearing away flesh. Drops of blood, arcing slowly, relentlessly, through the air. . . .

Astrid had missed its heart. Screaming, Thyri was on the wolf, driving her sword into its shoulder, spraying its blood over white fur and the ground's patchy carpet of powdery snow. It lashed out, grazing her thigh. She backed off, readying herself for a more thoughtful strike. Astrid's fall had unnerved her, spoiled her reasoning. She concentrated on the wolf. It snarled at her, its muzzle crimson. It leapt.

So huge, she thought. It's so impossibly huge. Keeping her sword steady, she threw her weight into the attack. The blade entered next to Astrid's. To reach its heart? She felt it smashing through the beast's ribs. Her boots gripped the ground, then slid for a moment before she fell with the wolf. All through the fall she watched her sword sinking into flesh, probing deeper, closer to *something* that had to be vital. Her back hit the ground – it still lived. Its hot breath struck her face. She shifted her shoulders, wrenching her blade to the side with all her strength and drenching herself in the thing's blood as she ripped its chest open.

Die, dammit! Die!

Pain flashed through her as fangs dug into her shoulder; then she wrenched her blade again, found at last the wolf's heart, and felt its weight crash lifelessly on top of her.

For a very long time, she could see nothing beyond Astrid's bloodied face and the gaping hole in her cousin's neck that had appeared so suddenly, so unbelievably fast. She cradled in her arms truly half of her life, a part of her that the best swords of the North could not have taken in fair combat.

She felt fear rising within – irrational, a terrible feeling that all her past, all her life, was a lie. How else could Astrid, who had not been *scratched* in combat in the past three years, have fallen with such lack of ceremony, with such ease? The panic gripped her, and she fought it with savage, primal fury. *A warrior cannot seriously flirt with any fear and expect to live.* Yet the wolf had killed her friend, cousin, and lover, and she could not believe it had happened. She lost herself, emptying thought, taming her churning emotions before allowing them to consume her. Grief and rage. If anyone or anything had come upon her then, she would have killed blindly, without thought. It was only when Yrafax stamped and snorted demoniacally that she became aware of more than her grief and Astrid's torn body.

She shot a fiery glance at the horse and snarled, then jerked her gaze in search of whatever had alerted him:

Where the wolf had fallen lay the bloodied corpse of a man. His chest was torn from side to side, and the rune-blades stood up in a V-shape from the wound that closed even as Thyri watched.

She laid Astrid gently on the grass, rose, and pulled the swords from the body. Its face grimaced. The man's features were gaunt and gnarled. Hauntingly pale skin sported a scraggly, two-day growth of beard.

Thyri screamed and brought Astrid's sword down across

his stomach, cleaving through his spine and part of his hip. The upper torso flinched and went still.

Turning from him, she built a fire of the tent and bedding furs. She threw the halved body onto the small pyre and watched the flames enwrap it, then she lifted Astrid's body onto Yrafax and mounted her own horse. Tears still streaming down her cheeks, she set off for the road.

The night was long and full of ghosts. Astrid rode before her, draped across Yrafax's saddle. He somehow knew where to go; they reached the sacred vale just before dawn. It stretched out before her, crusted with wind-brushed snow. Staunch evergreens fringed its northern edge, some bent low and twisted from years of enduring winter gales. And below the hard ground the dead of centuries past; ancestors whose lives had been spent laying claim to the unforgiving soil.

She spent the morning in the wood, slashing and hacking at a fallen tree, venting her grief while building a pyre for Astrid that stood to her shoulder. She made it wide and strong, driving its stakes deep into the ground. At one end she built a ramp of tilted logs. The last flurries of snow passed as the noon sun drew overhead. The clouds were breaking, and the snow on the ground dazzled in places with blinding brilliance. The horses lingered on the edge of the wood, scratching at the ground in search of clumps of still-green grass. Thyri called Yrafax to her.

He came, gazing at her with large brown eyes. She scratched his forehead. 'You must follow my cousin,' she said. 'Keep her from harm, Yrafax.'

She brought her sword around then, slashing through Yrafax's neck. Severed arteries sent streams of red across the snows. The horse's gaze remained fixed on Thyri's until his legs buckled and he collapsed, the impact raising clouds of powder that danced over him like spinning, glittering ghosts.

Harnessing herself like an ox, Thyri hauled the dead horse onto the pyre, the strain taxing her strength to its limits and igniting fiery agony in her wounds. She lay, after that, next to Astrid – resting, weeping anew. Then she placed Astrid carefully on the pyre and arranged her lover's cloak, trying in vain for a while to scratch stains of blood from the green cloth. In the field, among her ancestors, she chose a spot and dug out a wide plot a foot in depth. In late afternoon she set fire to the pyre and watched it burn.

The ashes she scattered in the grave under moonlight. Before covering them with a low mound of dirt, Thyri laid Astrid's rune-sword over the charred, flame-shattered fragments of Astrid's bones.

'Serve the gods well, my love,' she whispered. She filled the grave. Standing back, she screamed wordlessly at the night, her fingers probing the swollen, throbbing holes in her shoulder.

She drew her hand away, looked at the blood, and shivered. She felt – I don't know – the dead buried in that sacred vale reaching out to her? Or her own fears animating the death of that place in her mind? The feeling, whatever it was, wasn't pleasant.

She was twenty-one that night, though she was hardly innocent or unpracticed. She had survived four campaign seasons, and she had risen to share with Astrid the command of a Viking longship.

10: Changes

Thyri's tale. It begins with the woman, but the woman begins in the girl.

The crops had taken and flourished, heralding summer. She ran through the wood, feeling the crush of soft leaves under her feet. Her nose filled with a scent of burning pork; the wind blew it from where Gyda, her mother, offered up parts of their dinner to Thor and Freyja. *Freyja to feed us, Thor to protect.* It was the way – so said her father. Thyri ran until the smell was gone and only those of the trees, the flowers, and the sun on the moss remained.

She had a spot by a bubbling stream where she liked to go alone, to dangle her bare feet in the cool current or just think. The spot was under an aging willow. A crescent of white rocks formed a bridge that went halfway across the stream, and the water directly under the willow was calm, lapping onto a sandy beach. She sat on it with her knees to her chin, flexing her toes in and out of the sand. Looking out onto the rocks, she imagined Astrid there: grinning, kicking her long legs in and out of the water; laughing and diving into the deep pool at the end of the bridge. Summers ago, they had shared that private spot. Only one other had been there, during Thyri's ninth summer – Skoll, a wild boy who had taught her how to kill birds with a sling. She counted him her friend second only to Astrid. He was dirty and lanky, with bright eyes and a way of mocking Gyda's calls that always made Thyri gag with laughter. He had taken his name from the wolf that chased the sun; Thyri guessed he had never had a real one. Two springs before, she had fared out into the wood expecting to find the boy. He'd promised to return; he didn't keep that promise then. He hadn't still.

Recent years had been lonely with Erik, her brother, still too young to satisfy Thyri's sense of companionship. She had grown in the company of many older than she – two older brothers and two older cousins. She thought nothing of the three years that separated Astrid and herself, but Erik's six years and Thyri's ten were worlds apart.

Astrid had left when Thyri was seven. A tall, cloaked stranger had arrived at the homestead to talk with her father and uncle behind the closed doors of the hall. A long, fiery conversation had followed, with Thyri and Astrid pressing their ears to the outside wood; they could hear their fathers raging, but not clearly enough to pick out words. From the visitor they had heard nothing. At the end, the stranger had left with Astrid, and Thyri's father had threatened to beat her should she not cease her crying and her attempts to follow. Her tears had been tears of fury: no one would tell her where Astrid had gone. No one would tell her even why Astrid had gone. She still didn't know. But she would soon learn – with not even a snapping twig to warn her.

She felt a hand firmly in the center of her back, and suddenly she was rolling forward, sputtering and thrashing about in the shallow water. She heard light laughter and frantically swept wetly dripping clumps of hair from her eyes.

Her cousin's blond hair had grown long and silky with a thick, three-knot braid on one side. She wore a thin cloak of forest green cotton and carried a bow and quiver on one shoulder with a battle-ax on the opposite hip. She had breasts, and she had grown tall. She towered, a lean giantess awash in patchy sunlight filtered through willow leaves. Her laugh mellowed into a wide grin as she helped Thyri from the stream.

Eirik, Thyri's father, was the first to notice them. His calls brought excited shouts from his brother and their sons in the fields. Outside the hall, the family gathered around the two girls, firing questions mingled with laughs of joy. Eirik opened the doors and led them in.

Astrid set her bow and ax by the door and Egill, her father, gave her his seat at the head of the long-table for the telling of her tale. Thyri sat next to her, and Astrid took her hand beneath the table. Thyri's mother brought mead.

'I'm happy to see you, Father,' Astrid said to Egill, 'but I cannot stay long. You know where I've been. You sent me with Scacath, and much of what she promised has already come to pass. I have come now for Thyri. She is to follow in turn.'

Thyri's nails bit into the back of her cousin's hand. Astrid did not wince; she continued to smile placidly at her father while the color fled from her uncle's cheeks.

'No,' he said. 'Not both of you.'

'When Scacath came for me,' Astrid said, 'you thought her crazed. She offered a bag of silver for me. You refused. She needed her magic.' She paused, smiling sadly at her father as the disclosure brought tears unbidden into his eyes. 'It's all right, Father,' she continued. 'She cast a spell to persuade you to part with me, but it was *meant* to be. I am happy. She told you she would teach me the ways of the warrior and that this was my Destiny. I have come to prove this. And to take Thyri that she may learn what she herself must learn. You know she desires nothing of the normal ways of women. I bring no spells for her, only myself as proof of Scacath's teaching. And another bag of silver of the same weight as the last.' She reached inside her cloak and brought out a pouch that clinked as she tossed it toward Thyri's father.

Eirik looked at his brother, drained his flagon of mead, and slammed it on the table. He glared at Astrid. 'Spells and silver! Odin's beard, girl! You're nearly a woman! How can you speak of wielding a sword?'

'I can and I will.'

'And Thyri as well? You're mad!'

'I can prove that you are wrong.'

'You can, eh? How?'

'A test of ability and prowess. You may name it, though

you cannot name the sword for I have not yet begun my training with that weapon. We will wager, yes? Should I lose, Thyri and I shall stay here and do your bidding.'

Eirik scowled and fell quiet. Egill leaned over and whispered in his ear.

Thyri spoke, breaking the tension: 'Father, I *want* to go!'

'Silence, child!' Eirik snarled. 'You Astrid, who would think yourself a Viking, do you dare to wrestle with arms your strong brother Halfdan?'

'I requested a test of ability and prowess, and you suggest a test of strength. I would dare, but I could not win without deceit and the possibility of dealing grave injury to my brother whom I dearly love. I would wish that you name another test.' She smiled at Halfdan, then turned back to Thyri's father. 'But if this is what you require, and you will name no other test, I will respect your choice as a cunning one.'

Eirik chuckled. 'You have learned to use words, girl. I will name another test. Wrestle to the ground with Halfdan if you wish to give me proof.'

'To the long pin, the short pin, or just the fall? The long pin, Uncle, is another test of strength, and I would deal more harshly with my brother than I would wish. But if this is what you require, and you will not say the short pin or the fall, I will respect your choice as a cunning one.'

'By Odin, girl, you begin to sound like a saga,' he said wearily. 'The short pin will do.'

'Very well.' She looked at Halfdan, her elder by four years and but a summer from adding his strength to his king's army. 'Brother?'

He nodded and rose from his seat. Astrid squeezed Thyri's hand before rising, then the siblings moved to stand several paces apart in the open space between the long-table and the fire over which Gyda's hog boiled in a large iron kettle. Astrid glanced at Thyri, then looked to Halfdan.

As Thyri watched them, she grew fearful. Astrid was tall – nearly as tall as Halfdan's six feet – but her brother bore the muscles of the field on his arms and was twice the weight of his sister. Yet Thyri's fears did not reflect in Astrid's eyes. Assuming a relaxed, poised stance, she taunted Halfdan with her eyes and the sway of her hips. Halfdan tucked his beard to his chest and stalked toward her. He lunged, and Astrid stepped aside, bringing one knee up against his chest. In the same motion, she cupped his chin in her hand and swung around behind him, pivoting to land solidly on his back.

Thyri's heart raced. Astrid threw her hands over Halfdan's eyes and moved her legs so that they scissored her brother's apart, twisting his body and upsetting his balance. He fell back and Astrid swung away, still holding him by the head. Halfway through the fall, she pulled herself in, reaching across for his far armpit. By the time he hit the floor with a loud thud, she lay across his chest.

Thyri looked at Astrid, amazed, only partly believing that she did not dream. She had seen men wrestle – she didn't know girls could. Not, at least, against men. And to defeat one almost a Viking?

Astrid leapt quickly to her feet and reached down for her brother's hand. Halfdan gave it, grinned, then yanked her down to him, hugging her and burying his head in the flowing mass of her blond hair. 'I shall hate to see you leave again, Sister,' he whispered. 'But if you must, may Thor protect and guide you.'

They embraced, then rose to face the others. Astrid looked solemnly at first her father, then her uncle. 'Well?' she asked.

Thyri watched Eirik's eyes as he looked to the others around the long-table and the old ones who sat in the corner next to the pot. She had never seen her father's gaze so helpless, so unsure. 'My daughter will learn *that*?' he asked at last.

'That,' answered Astrid, 'and more.'

'And the sword?'

'Eventually.'

His hand went to his chest, to the iron symbol of the Thunderer's hammer on the strong chain around his neck. He fingered the pendant and looked curiously at his daughter.

Thyri looked back with pleading eyes. She went to speak, but he signed her silence. Eirik stroked the pendant and stuffed it inside his tunic so that it rested on his skin.

'Then so be it,' he said, looking from Thyri to Astrid. 'Stay the night. We have a hog to eat.'

Astrid smiled warmly.

Eirik laughed. 'And take back your silver. I do not wish to sell my daugher.'

'You are not selling her. It is the way. If you do not take the silver, then Scacath will not take Thyri.'

'Take the silver,' Egill said.

Eirik nodded grimly. 'Gyda! More mead! We shall drink to rival the gods this evening!'

Astrid sat, smiled at Thyri, and took again her hand.

Late that night, Thyri led her cousin through the dark to her room behind the hall. Years before, they had shared it between them. Thyri felt this night the last she would ever spend there. Though it was dark, she pictured everything in her mind, wanting suddenly to capture forever every small detail. In fact, it was simple room, with its soft bedding on the sleeping ledge and Thyri's white chests and her chair next to the table with the mirror of polished steel. The room's sole decoration, the miniature hammer symbol of the Thunderer that her father had forged for them long before, hung on the wall above the low entrance where it had been for as long as Thyri could remember, long before Astrid had first left.

Astrid pushed her, and she fell giddily onto the ledge. They had drunk of the mead – Thyri overly so because her father seldom allowed her the privilege. Gyda's light snoring purred from a room beyond, and Eirik's bellowing laughter occasionally reached them from the hall, where he and Egill and his sons continued to drink, their tales and songs growing both louder and longer as the night wore on.

Thyri crawled to the corner of the ledge and reached out for Astrid, only to find her sitting on the far end. Thyri rose then and groped on her table for a candle and tinderbox. The yellow light showed her cousin smiling thoughtfully, her eyes distant. Astrid's fingers fumbled with her braid, which terminated, Thyri noticed, in a large bead engraved with runes much like those she had seen drawn by the *volva*, Asta, her father's mother's aunt. Astrid undid the braid and began to reknot it.

Thyri watched her spin one, two, then three, and finally four knots before she affixed again the bead and tested its grip.

'Why did you do that?'

'Do what?'

'That – with your hair. You looked so far away. Like Asta looks when she's casting, or when she's sleeping with her eyes open – it's hard to tell.'

Astrid's eyes lit up and she laughed, stroking the braid with one hand, fingering the bead with the other. 'It's true that my thoughts were elsewhere, but not like Asta. The braid and the saga-bead are symbols. Each knot recalls for me a battle, either within or without myself. Each is a valuable lesson learned or a tale worth retelling. My braid is humble. I will tell you my knots at another time when they will mean more to you. Scacath's braid, I think, has as many knots as the sky has stars. She never wears her hair unbraided and I have vowed that neither will I. But you needn't do the same. Sleep now, Thyri. You will learn much more later.' Astrid blew out Thyri's candle and pulled her back onto the ledge, where the two girls curled up together and slept.

Late the next afternoon, Thyri stood next to Astrid and faced Scacath across the short space of a small glade in the wood. The ground sloped gently down before her to where a lively brook wended out from the wood to touch on the edge of the glade. The sun burned into Scacath's hair, which gleamed in the way only the blackest of blacks can gleam. The woman's braid, terminating in a stone bead like Astrid's, appeared little more than a thick strand of hair from where Thyri stood. But when the sun struck it right, it scintillated, its twistings casting reflections in all directions like a gem of countless facets.

For moments Scacath merely looked at them, a knowing

half-smile touching the corners of her lips. The look made Thyri nervous; she likened the smile to that her mother wore when tasking her, refusing to entertain her protestations. But the face was different: her mother's was thick, while Scacath's was thinly triangular with a sharp chin softened only by the transcendent quality of her skin – pale where the light struck, dark and shadowy where it did not. Her eyes loomed large over a pert, childlike nose. They were silvery blue and fathomless. Beneath the triangle of her face, a contrast of frailty and strength continued. She was lean, yet her breasts stood out proudly against the fabric of a green cloak held together by a round clasp engraved with runes much like those on the beads. Beneath that, she wore nothing. In those shadows, Thyri sensed terrible power.

Scacath's smile bloomed, dispelling Thyri's unease. She looked first at Astrid. 'You had no difficulties then?'

Astrid laughed. 'Only in giving him the silver.'

'Well, we expected that.' She turned to Thyri. 'Welcome, little one. Do you know why you are here?'

'To become a warrior, like my brothers.'

'No – not like your brothers. Your fate is both darker and grander than theirs, and for this you will need strength and skills much greater. You will leave here such that your Thunder God would deem you a cunning and worthy opponent. Or you will leave here not at all.'

To that, she could find no words. She could only look into Scacath's eyes in wonder.

10: Magic

Scacath sprang from the blood of an ancient race of the Northlands and the darker woods of the South, though it later made its home in Erin. Lugh Long-Hand of the *Tuatha de Danann* was her father; her mother was a goddess who had ridden from Southern lands in the hunt of a great stag, twenty hands at the shoulder, which she slew outside of Lugh's hall.

The huntress had stayed with Lugh for two years after Scacath's birth, then Lugh had raised his daughter alone until she herself had left home, taking with her much knowledge, for Lugh had great skill in all the arts known to men and gods. Because of her mother, Scacath had ever felt removed from her people. She'd desired to know her mother and to see the many things she'd imagined she could not see among the children of Danu. She went to Manannan, the son of the sea, and she gave him her body. In return, he taught her the *feth fiada* – the spell of hiding and shape-change. Scacath thanked him, transformed herself into a great raven, and flew off into the worlds.

She spent many years 'observing the denizens of all worlds, observing them at work, at love, but mostly at war.' She flew over the battles and duels of all, and she watched and she learned. She witnessed the battles of the Tuatha de Danann and the war between the sons of Odin and the sons of Njord – wars in which great powers had raged, tearing asunder the very fields on which they had fought. When her father's people fell to the sons of Mil, she remained free in Midgard while many others fled. And with her freedom, she witnessed the passing of her mother's race as the cult of the One God ripped Olympus from its roots on Earth.

Later, during that time when the Tuatha de Danann still concerned themselves with the affairs of men and they came to favor the sons of Ulster in Erin, they asked Scacath to train for them a hero. She did so, and the hero, Cu Chulainn, performed feats worthy of legend. Thyri would learn of this tale only after many years, and from the sorceress, Megan Kaerglen, not from Scacath.

After Cu Chulainn, when Scacath learned of Odin's hanging by his own hand on the world-tree and gaining thereby his first eighteen runes, she went to him, entering Valhalla in the guise of his raven, Memory. She stayed with the All-Father for three nights, and she gave him her body. In return, he taught her the rune that turns away missiles from one who bears it. This rune she cast upon the blade of her sword and upon the blades she forged for her students.

Thyri had grown with a love for those stories of the gods of the Northlands, but she'd always sensed qualities of the unreal within the tales. They'd added glitter to her secluded life, but they hadn't *described* it. She had never seen a giant, or a dwarf, or an elf, much less any of the Aesir with their great halls, their fiery passions, and their battles. Though she'd been told that Asta possessed magic of a sort, she had never *seen* it. Thus she'd never fully believed.

Scacath, however, showed her very early that magic was real. And Scacath's teachings made the gods real – Thyri's gods, and those of many others as well.

From the road, before taking the twisting series of paths leading to Scacath's grove, Thyri had seen the smoke of fires in the near distance, as of a hall or a small village. She never saw these from the grove, even when she fared out into the woods in the direction she thought the fires must have burned. Scacath told her that she had, in coming there, stepped sidewise away from the world in which she had grown. Only those with great power of their own could come into the grove against Scacath's wishes.

Within it, around the glade to which Thyri would go each

morning for water, were many other small clearings, some grassy, others worn to the light brown of packed earth by years of use. In two such clearings were huts of a strange construction: walls and roofs of soft, resilient furs and skins laid over a sparse framework of curved branches tied tightly where they met in the center of dome-shaped roofs. Thyri hardly expected the structures to withstand the rigors of winter, and she first entertained the idea that winter might not come at all to Scacath's world. But she found soon that the seasons did indeed turn as usual, and her hut, which she shared with Astrid, wintered as well as her father's hall. Better, in fact, for here a fire could be built in a depression in the center of the earthen floor, and she could sleep as close to it as she dared.

The floor of the hut sloped down from the fire pit so that the furs that covered it would not become wet with water flowing in from the outside. The roof was capped with a cone-shaped panel of hardened furs that could be lifted with a braced pole to allow smoke from the fire to exit. Furs of marten, sable, mink, fox, and rabbit, sewn together in such a way that they provided both carpet and bedding, covered the floor. Two large chests for clothing and some smaller boxes were arranged to one side, and racks for cloaks and other things (Astrid's sword greeted Thyri from its place on one) hung about the walls of the other side. Wet things could be dried near the fire on hooks swung away from the walls.

Thyri never saw inside Scacath's hut; the students were forbidden to enter. She would idly wish later that she'd dared, but by then the fantasy could not harm her, the world of Scacath having become like a dream, as it certainly seemed to her while she learned its ways.

Between the two huts was the common, a clearing where food and drink were stored and where they ate and occasionally passed time in talk, though always with a purpose as Scacath would never converse idly. She was ever the teacher. This clearing remained grassy year-round and stayed open to the sky as well. Here, the weatherlessness that Thyri had contemplated for the entire area prevailed. Not even a breeze would blow unless Scacath wished it to fan the flames or clear the smoke of fires. When it rained or snowed, the clearing remained open to the sky, and even in the darkest weather they could see the stars above as clearly as on a moonless night. For a long while, Thyri would have little time to think about this, for before her first day had passed, Scacath began her training.

Shortly after a dinner of berries, goat's milk, and duck, two great ravens flapped into the common and lighted on Scacath's shoulders. Astrid excused herself, and Scacath smiled at each bird, stroking them in turn.

'They are called Hugin and Munin,' Scacath said, 'after the ravens of your Odin. They are my friends, and you will see much of them while you are here.'

Thyri looked at Scacath and the ravens. She could think of nothing to say or ask, so she did not speak, only smiled as best she could. She noted that the ravens' eyes did not stray. They did not dart about after the usual fashion of birds, and she felt intelligent purpose in them. She decided then that it would be unwise to assume anything at all about Scacath and her grove.

'You say nothing,' Scacath said. 'Good. It means you are thinking. The way of the sword begins in the mind and in the senses. The mind must always be such to expect the unseen and the dangerous, and the senses must be sharpened so that they might tell the mind that such exist. The greatest of warriors, even gods, may be slain by a mere scratch of a thorn if the proper poison has been applied to the tip. A missile may be dodged, if one anticipates its coming. Prey, animal or human, may be tracked over almost any terrain if one knows how to perceive. Battles are won and lost in the mind and senses, not in the sword, which is but one of countless instruments capable of dealing death. It is useless in and of itself.'

Scacath paused; when Thyri said nothing, she stroked the ravens again and continued: 'Foremost also in the mind of the warrior must be the understanding that the concept of *friendship* may conceal an enemy. One is lucky to find in life even one true friend. Most find none at all, though they think and tell others they have many. A friend, a true friend, is one to whom you can entrust your life in any situation you might imagine with never a possibility of this trust being betrayed. Think hard on this and remember it well. A warrior is wise never to take a friend out of loneliness and expect devotion in return. A warrior should never make a pretense of friendship unless it be to attain a specific goal, and then a warrior must remember the nature of that friendship at all times and not allow herself to believe otherwise. You will build relationships on rank and loyalty to king and custom, for trust and compromise are among the ways of men. But so are wars and deceit. Lieutenants have poisoned captains while drinking in friendship. Your life is all you truly have, so you must be sure that when you entrust it to another, that trust will see it safely back into your hands.'

'Is Astrid my friend?'

'Yes, little one. The bond between you is as strong as any I have seen in all my years. But even this bond may be sundered by sorcery.

'I am not telling you to trust no one, nor am I telling you to be afraid those you do trust might betray you. I am telling you to be aware and observe. I am not telling you never to love. Indeed, life is hardly worth living without love. But a warrior will never perish by the deceit of another because she will always be aware of where and how deceit might lie, and she will notice its presence before it strikes. Train yourself to see things as they are, not how you wish them to be.'

Thyri did her best to take these things to heart and ponder them often. At first she felt confused, but as time passed and Scacath told her more, teaching her to watch things carefully so that when they changed she would know and be aware of the change, her labors began to bear fruit, and she began to understand.

She had come expecting to spend her time fighting and learning to wield weapons of all sorts, but she spent most of her first year in training thinking, watching, and trying to understand the things Scacath told her. The tasks set for her seemed odd. Scacath once had her sit for an entire day in the grove, asking her later to tell of everything she observed, both within and without herself. Another time, Scacath struck her, violently enough to bring tears to her eyes. While Thyri rubbed her cheek, Scacath asked her to go to the grove and return either when she could describe exactly how she felt right after the blow or when dusk came and the smell of fires reached her nostrils. Thyri did not return that day until dusk; she had been unable to form her feelings into words that she thought her teacher would accept. Scacath explained at dinner that this was because emotions dwell more deeply inside than words, which are truly but tools of the heart. Sometimes, when the emotions are very strong, they are unable to make the tools do what they require; Scacath likened it to a man trying to build a castle with but a shovel and pick. She told Thyri to be wary of her emotions during such times, for they could as easily harm as aid her. Thyri thought deeply on this one, but much time passed before she felt she understood.

Such was the nature of Thyri's first year of training. When she asked Astrid of it, Astrid would say that such had been hers as well, but the older girl always refused to give Thyri any answers, though she might occasionally ask questions that Thyri found helpful. Astrid would tell her nothing about the training to come except that, when Thyri worked with Scacath, she worked with Hugin and Munin. When Thyri questioned this, Astrid smiled and said no more. It was the way of the teachings that all things should be uncovered in time – only when the student was prepared. Later, Thyri accepted this and asked of Astrid less knowledge and more companionship; this her cousin gave as freely as she.

So the seasons passed. The leaves of the grove turned as the sun grew colder and the days shorter. Astrid killed an elk then, and Scacath took it into her hut from whence she would bring portions of the animal throughout the winter. As the first frosts came, Scacath drew runes on a piece of ground in the common and spoke strange words over it while her students watched. A spring bubbled up out of the ground, and Thyri no longer had to go to the stream each morning for water. When the snows came and the days grew shorter still, Scacath continued the training unabated, and though Thyri grew accustomed to weathering the biting winter winds, her thoughts in the day often turned to the evening when she and Astrid would lie in their hut, wrapped in furs and whispering quietly by the crackling fire.

In the spring, when the snow and ice melted, Scacath dispelled the enchanted well and Thyri had again to go to the stream for water. It pleased rather than irritated her. The wood along the path grew greener each morning and the dewy landscape, full of vibrant color and a multitude of fresh, newborn scents, excited her. The short trip made her feel very alive. The days grew longer, and as the day that marked the anniversary of Thyri's arrival approached, Scacath began to teach her the basic stances and movements of weaponless combat. After breakfast on the day itself, Scacath gave Thyri her first test.

The morning was warm and the sky clear. Thyri sat with Scacath, Hugin, Munin, and Astrid in the common. She waited, again patiently watching Scacath stroke Munin. She had learned to tell the birds apart: Hugin was slightly larger than his brother and a small patch of gray touched his feathers just above the shoulder of his right wing. Finally, Scacath looked at her carefully and said, 'The time has come, little one.'

Thyri smiled at her teacher but said nothing.

'Very well,' Scacath chuckled. 'Go to your hut and bring me your comb.'

Thyri looked at her curiously. 'What about the test?'

And Scacath smiled.

The path from the common to the hut showed Thyri nothing out of the ordinary: just her tracks, Astrid's tracks, and the marks of various small animals. She checked it several times, then she did the same with the other trails to the hut – the one from the stream, the ones into the grove – but she found them all as expected. Nor did she discover anything unusual in the surrounding wood. When she finally dared to approach the door and inspect it, she found small scratches in the bare skin along the frame. Birds, she thought. *Ravens*.

She went out into the wood and found a branch fallen from an aging oak and measuring two arm-lengths. Standing to the left of the door and as far as she could from the hut, she worked the branch into the opening and flung open the panel. Nothing happened, and she heard no movement from within the hut. Still, she waited several moments before approaching.

The hut's interior seemed as it should with everything as she and Astrid had left it that morning. She looked about, carefully tapping at the furs, paying special attention to those between herself and the small vanity box that held her hair things: her comb, a few wooden pins and clasps, and the leather thong with which she sometimes tied back her blond mane. The box itself sat atop her chest of clothes, and she avoided disturbing it or its perch while probing with the branch. When she had satisfied herself that nothing out of the ordinary lay among the furs, she stepped carefully onto them.

Well inside the hut's entrance, she noticed a subtle difference in the air. She felt a tingling on her skin and smelt a tangible sharpness that she felt she knew but she could not place. The sensations grew stronger nearer the box. She stooped to look at it, standing slightly to one side in order not to cast her dim shadow in the way of the diffuse light that permeated the hut through the thinner patches of the walls. She tried from several angles until she found the scratch marks she sought.

A claw had barely touched the wood of the chest, and the corners of the box on that side bore minute pits where she guessed the bird had taken hold in order to lift it. The pits were on the wrong side for opening the box – the hinged side. She searched her memories for the one that would tell her exactly where on the chest she had left the box. The exercise succeeded only marginally – she only *felt* that the box was placed improperly. Her real success came primarily through the poignant reminder that she needed to be more aware of these things in the future. She decided that it had been lifted, something placed beneath it or something done to the bottom before it had been placed almost as before.

Thyri sat back on the furs and thought. If something had been set beneath the box, she needed merely to open it very carefully and remove her comb. If the trap had been set to fire upon opening, then this was her worst approach since the trap would spring with her just where it would expect her to be. To avoid that, she could topple the box with her branch, setting off the trap in the first case, and probably even in the second. And she might not be able to get the comb if she made a mistake. . . Because she'd found the claw marks on the hinged side of the box, she decided to anticipate the first danger, but she took care and reached up from far to one side before lifting the lid, very slowly and very carefully. Nothing happened.

She stood and backed away, then approached and peered in. Her comb lay there, just on top of the thong, right where she had left it. She smiled, reached in, lifted it out quickly, and dashed out of the hut.

Scacath's luminous eyes cheated the sun's reflection as they absorbed its light, stealing it, taking it somewhere further inside her. She took Thyri's comb in her hand – a long, delicate hand with thin fingers, immune to the calluses of the sword. 'Did you learn the nature of the trap?'

Thyri looked at her curiously. 'No. That wasn't part of the test.'

'No.' Scacath grinned brightly. 'It wasn't. You felt it though, didn't you?'

Thyri thought back to the sensations – the tingling and the smell. 'I think so.'

Scacath turned her lips to Munin and whispered. The raven flapped away, toward Thyri's hut. 'You did. Munin has gone to remove the danger. You did very well, little one. You sensed the magic. We placed a rune under your box – a simple one, but you would be sore now had you disturbed it.'

Astrid laughed. 'Sore! My arm burned for a week!' She smiled at Thyri. 'I'm proud of you, cousin. You have earned your bead and first braid without injury. When I took the test, I got the comb, but I couldn't resist tapping the box from a distance to see what would happen. My first braid will forever remind me of that mistake.'

'Your path will grow more difficult now, little one,' Scacath said, 'but do not fear it. You have proven yourself worthy of the training. Do not forget what you have learned so far.' She reached inside her cloak and brought out a rune-bead, holding it and the comb out to Thyri.

Astrid stepped forth, took a thick lock of Thyri's hair in her hands, and slowly separated three strands. While Astrid fashioned the braid, Thyri held her bead next to her cousin's and learned that the runes were the same.

'What does it mean?' Thyri asked. 'The rune?'

Astrid paused. 'It means blood,' she said softly.

21: Ghosts

She sat on the sand, staring at the scattered snowflake patterns on the ice that lay like a veil over the surface of the pond. Everything was still, the forest around her like a cavern that swallowed all sound. Swallowed her thoughts. Her nightmares.

'I knew I'd find you here,' Erik said, crashing through the underbrush.

She thought of early summer in the land of the Franks, the sun warming green, rolling hills, painting her lover bronze. Birds overhead, swimming in the clear blue. Cool grass. The reflection of a solitary cloud in a dewdrop.

'You did everything you could, Thyri,' he said, squatting next to her.

Astrid wrapped in Thyri's sables on a cool autumn evening. Long legs stretched teasingly over the warm earth near the fire. Lips moving slowly, a low voice whispering secretly, passionately of tales she'd heard, things she'd dreamed. The sables sliding ever so slowly over her skin; the voice trailing off . . . a breast, beaded with sweat, shining in the firelight . . .

'She's in Valhalla,' he said, putting his arm around her. 'It was meant to be.'

She wanted to push him away and hold him at the same time.

'Odin must have sent those wolves for her, Thyri. No mortal could have killed my cousin.'

She couldn't speak, couldn't tell him.

'Are you sure she wasn't ill?' he asked.

Dumbly she shook her head. She wasn't sure of anything.

'I remember when I was little,' he said, 'and Father would

tell that my sister and cousin were special, that they would be the mightiest of all the Vikings in the land. That they would spit in the faces of princes and break the hearts of kings. That they would love gods, Thyri. That you and Astrid would love gods.' He started to cry. 'I would see you both, and I'd want to be like you. Why did she have to die?'

Like a fountain in the garden of Despair, she rose. 'Come, brother. You have a life to live of your own.'

He stood slowly. Straight, he towered over her. As tall as Astrid, his long hair almost as light, his eyes crying for her.

And Thyri saw him laughing, hanging off the edge of her ship with his sword out, skimming the surface of the waves. He had joined her crew the past summer. His sword had followed hers into battle, and she suddenly realized that it had been but a game to him. Once, Thyri had asked Scacath to take him into training after her. Her teacher had refused without explanation. Thyri now thought that she understood why.

'She died,' Thyri said, 'because everything dies some time. Flowers die. Trees die. So do warriors. And gods.'

As she led him back to the family hall, he told her that the king's skald had arrived that afternoon and had spoken long with Eirik and Egill. She fell silent again, wishing she could leave, disappear into the forest and never return, never see another human face. But her legs kept moving surely in the wrong direction.

Inside, the chatter of voices assaulted her like knives streaking through the air for her heart. The skald had lifted the cape of mourning from her family's shoulders. He had captivated them with tales of the king, of southern lands, of ancient prophecies and innocent love. Gyda had kept their flagons full, and her father and uncle laughed idiotically at the skald's every word, every gesture. The old ones huddled in their corner, giggling. Only the volva and Yrsa next to her remained solemn. The volva's gaze fell coldly on Thyri.

'Thyri!' Eirik said, approaching her when he noticed her

presence. 'Come! Sit! The royal skald himself has composed for you. It is a song fit to be sung in the hall of Odin!'

'Or the hall of his slaves,' the man said, feigning modesty.

'We'll let Thyri decide! Sit, daughter.' He turned to the skald. 'Sing!'

Without ceremony, he began. 'The Lay of Astrid and Thyri.' He began with their exploits under Ragnar, blown out of proportion so that they struck Thyri's ears like empty legends. She'd heard them all before. On a few drunken nights, she'd told them all before. The ache inside of her grew.

And the skald sang of Astrid's final battle. How a hundred hunger-crazed wolves had risen out of Niflheim and fell upon Astrid and Thyri as they'd slept. How the two of them had gained their feet, swords in hand, and laid into the wolves, killing three or four with each stroke. Then how a wolf so ferocious that he must have been spawned by Fenrir himself had dealt Astrid a mortal wound even as she'd killed him. And how Thyri then slew the rest in her rage, seven with her bare hands, three with her teeth. . .

Slowly, she forced the song, her family, her memories, and her thoughts out of her mind.

She wished that she'd had the strength to tell them about the *were*-beast, to tell them the truth.

She wanted to die.

11: Changes

In her second year with Scacath, Thyri's training began in earnest. Her teacher intensified her work with wrestling and the way of the hand-foot strike, which also involved the learning of those parts of the body most susceptible to pain. Thyri learned quickly, but the process brought her many aches and bruises. Astrid, instructed by Scacath, helped. In the evenings, she taught Thyri the ways to rub, at least in part, the soreness from the body. Again, Thyri grew quickly used to the changes in her routines; they made her feel happier, they proved her progress. She enjoyed, too, falling asleep to the rhythm of Astrid's gentle, knowledgeable fingers.

The months flew by and summer turned again to fall. Thyri learned the use of the bow and the ax, and she began to hunt with Astrid. Scacath began to show her all manner of weaponry to make her familiar with the ways these things – the spear, the crossbow, the dagger, the dirk, the staff, and many others – could be used. She only *showed* Thyri their uses; she did not teach them yet. In time, Thyri would learn to wield a great variety of weapons with skill, but her first real tasks were the bow and the ax.

And she learned the traditions Scacath had developed over her years of training others. The rune-bead and braid were most important, for they served to remind the warrior of herself and of all valuable things learned: the victories and defeats, the hows and whys. When Thyri asked why Scacath wore hers always, her teacher told her laughingly that it would take her days to rebraid it.

'Others,' Scacath said, 'make a ritual of braiding only before battle, remembering each trial as each braid is fixed.'

The sword, Scacath told her, was the end to which all her training tended. The way of the rune-sword. Scacath showed Thyri her blade and the one she'd forged for Thyri:

It was late fall, the morning of the winter's first snowfall. Scacath unsheathed the two swords and laid them on the light powder of the glade. The morning, painted crisp and white, carved itself vividly into Thyri's memory. She wore a brown cotton shirt and trousers, the latter tucked into soft, pliant boots lined with the fur of a rabbit she had slain early the past summer – her first bow-kill. The light crushing of the powder under her boots made her more aware of all her movements, and she noticed for the first time the strange sensations she felt in her stomach when her breasts rubbed against the fabric of her shirt. Scacath, dressed the same, with the addition of her green cloak and its rune-clasp, had never seemed more elegant, more ethereal, or more darkly, primally omnipotent. Like a dream, Thyri thought. Like a dream she'd had and forgotten long before in which gods had fought gods, taking and dealing blows that could rend mountains in two. A dream she'd lost in the daylight – until now. The glade, with its sheen of early winter, sparkled in time with the cold tinkling of the icy stream. Thyri and Scacath were alone there; Astrid, Hugin, and Munin were elsewhere.

Thyri looked at the blades. Neither showed any sign, any mark, of battle. All edges were razor sharp. The hilts were identically plain, built for strength and function, not show, and they had cross guards of thick, squared metal. The flats, however, told quickly the differences between the two. Though unscathed, Scacath's had the stain of age. Runes marked it from hilt to mid-blade. Thyri's (and Astrid's, she knew, for her cousin had spent many evenings honing its edge) looked fresh and bore no runes.

'The runes. Are they magic?'

'Very,' answered Scacath. 'Can't you feel it?'

Thyri tried to sense the tingling and the tang. She had

come to notice it more often – in the common, around the ravens, occasionally around Scacath. She could not feel it here. 'No.' Her answer was uncertain, but Scacath smiled.

'You are honest, and I am glad. The magics for iron have a more subtle flavor as they must have, for the metal is strong. Had you said yes, I would have known you lied. The magic can be sensed, little one, but you might train yourself to hear the footfall of a cat, or the breath of a fly, and yet never feel the magic in iron. Remember this.'

Thyri looked at the unmarked sword. 'This is mine?'

'Not yet. This is that toward which you work.' She paused, drawing from her cloak a thin, flexible gauntlet of silver, like Astrid's. She held it out to Thyri. 'Pick it up if you like, but put this on first.'

Thyri took the gauntlet and fitted it on her hand. The tips of her fingers did not quite reach the ends of those of the gauntlet, and the whole thing felt loose. 'It's too big.'

'Of course. It is yours – for your hand two summers hence. You must become used to thinking of the gauntlet and sword as one.'

'Why?'

Scacath smiled. 'Because the gauntlet is fashioned for the sword. Because your sword will one day bear runes such as mine. Their magic is strong, and once you have grown accustomed to it, it cannot harm you. But even then, certain sorceries can turn the blade against the wielder. The gauntlet guards against this. Were you now to touch my sword, unused as you are to its power and without the gauntlet, possibly even with it, it would kill you.'

Thyri nodded silently and reached for the hilt of the unmarked sword. She grasped it and picked it up clumsily, holding it before herself and inspecting the blade. A moment later, she set it back as it had been on the snow.

'You did not test it as a weapon,' Scacath said. 'Why?'

'I think,' began Thyri slowly, 'that I will remember this moment often between now and the day the sword becomes mine in truth. I do not wish to remember the feel of wielding it wrongly, as a child.'

Scacath smiled her half-smile, took back the gauntlet, picked up the two blades, and whirled, leaving Thyri alone with her thoughts.

Thyri learned other things that year, other twists of Scacath's teaching that blended rune-magic with the way of the sword. Scacath once said that she might, if she wished, teach her students the way of the runes alone. But this she did not wish. The runes she gave were presents, symbols, not teachings, for the magic of the runes was bound to the destiny of the gods, and the destiny of the gods was the sword. 'When the runes will fail, the iron will not': these are the words Scacath said to Thyri. As such, neither Thyri nor Astrid would be taught the runic ways, though it came to pass that Astrid learned much through observation alone due to a gift of magic that Wyrd had granted her at birth.

The rune-gifts of Scacath were four: the bead, mostly symbolic with a slight charm of remembrance; the clasp, a talisman of presence and restraint, attuned to the mind of the bearer who, in battle, might cast clasp and cloak aside with but a thought; the fifth rune of Odin, which sends missiles astray of their mark; and the twenty-third rune of Odin, the rune of sharpness: the sword that bears it need never be honed and will leave battle with the same edge that it held at the start. These last two gifts came, respectively, at the ends of the seventh and sixth years of training. The clasp came also at the end of the seventh – a parting gift from teacher to student.

Scacath told Thyri much of that which was to come: how she would learn more of the weaponry she might one day face, both visceral and sorcerous; how she would conquer fear and detach herself from herself so that she might use fear's energy to defeat its sources; how she would learn the sword with first two hands, then one, using in her freed hand another weapon for parrying rather than a shield for hiding behind; and how she would learn of many other methods, inferior methods, Scacath told her, which opponents might use.

As Thyri learned all this, the seasons turned and in early summer she took her second test. Scacath showed her a pale lizard but three inches long in the palm of her hand and set it loose to scamper off into the woods. An hour later, she sent Thyri and her bow out after it. For another hour, Thyri tracked it. She found it hidden in the bark of a tree, its color changed somehow to match the bark. Smiling, Thyri impaled it there with a single shot, then took it back to the common where Scacath and Astrid waited, Scacath for the lizard, and Astrid to tie the second knot in Thyri's braid.

Thyri's third year with Scacath was by far the most hectic of the first three. It was the year that Thyri learned to fight with the staff, and a year during which Scacath told her so much about so many things that she often spent long hours in the evenings lying back on her furs, calling up first one curious thing heard during the day, then another, turning them over and over in her mind and trying to patch them in with the rest of her knowledge. She felt as if she worked on a puzzle that would suddenly transform and grow into yet another picture just when she thought the first almost finished. And the new puzzle was always more complex and disjointed than the one before. Scacath told her that this was life, and it was good that she saw it thus at such an early age. So Thyri would build the pieces again into an almost-picture, only to watch them crumble while trying to fit the last few into place. So it would go on forever.

The third year was also the year she entered womanhood. During her thirteenth summer, she could feel her breasts growing and her hips widening by the day. The transformation scared her at first but by midsummer she had come to enjoy the new, sensuous feelings that accompanied the changes. And she had other things, happy things, to think about then: she would shortly gain her sword, and her growing body, as she accustomed herself to its feel, would be much more powerful, more suited to the demands of strength and fluidity that the sword training would require. And she would look also at Astrid and see how strong and beautiful her cousin had become, and she would think that soon she too would be thus. The cold nights of that winter played the backdrop for Thyri's first flirtations with passion. She and Astrid began to add the sharing of their bodies to the sharing of their thoughts and hearts.

When spring turned again to the grove, Thyri began to spend many hours thinking of her next test. She did not ask the others. She knew they would not answer. But she thought on it just the same. It came on a cool morning, defiant of the bright pastels of the season's flowers and the verdant green legacy of the spring rains. An overcast sky of patchy gray hung motionlessly over the grove, threatening a storm that would not come until late that afternoon. Over a breakfast of goose eggs and goat's milk, Scacath explained the task.

'Today, little one,' she began, 'you must go to the place where the stream issues from its underground course. It is a cavern, dark and fraught with danger. In the back, you will find an object that you must return to me. You will know what it is when you see it. Bring it back, and you will have your third braid and your sword.'

'How far must I journey?'

'Maybe a day there and back, maybe a lifetime.' And Scacath smiled.

Thyri went to her hut and fashioned a torch from a thick piece of wood, a torn shirt, and the stub of a candle. After securing the wadded, waxed shirt to the wood with a length of copper chain from a necklace, she set about transforming another old shirt into a pack into which she placed her tinderbox, some dried pork from the cache in the common, and a hook with a long piece of twine. The last she added as an afterthought; she seldom fished, but she would be traveling along the bank of the stream.

She put on long pants and her boots and her green cloak, fastening it with a plain bronze clasp. She attached her hand-ax and a short dagger to her belt, slung the pack over one shoulder, her quiver and bow over the other, picked up her staff, and left the hut. At first she started for the common; she could hear Astrid's light laughter there. But she hesitated after a few steps, paused, and turned confidently toward the glade and the stream.

Picking her way along the bank, she had often to stop and cut away patches of the thick growth that flourished near the water. Her bow would snag, but she resisted the temptation to cast the weapon aside; she could regret that action later in the day. Before noon, the forest thinned and the ground grew hilly. These were new sights for Thyri, and she had to push herself to keep moving. It helped when she thought of the reward for success.

She reached the cavern early in the afternoon. The closer she got, the stranger it smelled. A thick, odious musk lingered in the heavy air. Huge paw prints marked the ground all around the cavern's mouth, which was four times as wide as it needed be to provide an exit for the stream. Two sizes of prints – two bears. So much for simple traps, Thyri thought. And it was summer; the pair probably had cubs. As if in answer to her thoughts, a high, light squealing issued from the cavern's mouth, and a lower grunt followed.

Thyri knew bears, or, more properly, she knew of them. She had never seen one, but she could construct a picture of one from the size of the tracks and droppings, and she could imagine their enormous fangs and claws. She and Astrid had once come across the mutilated carcass of a doe, the victim of a hunting bear who had mysteriously been drawn away to leave its prey half-devoured. Scacath had told them that few bears ate meat, but there were some who, once having tasted blood, made a habit of it. Thyri wondered if these bears were such animals, and if, indeed, one of them might have been responsible for the doe. She sat for long moments trying to separate the smells of the individual animals. She did her best to recall the scents around the slaughtered doe, but the effort rewarded her not.

She wondered if she should wait for them to leave, then decided against it. Listening carefully to the sounds from the cavern, she learned that only two of the animals were home

– one big one and a little one, presumably a mother and her cub. If she waited, the father could very well return and she would have more bears to face than she cared to think about. The thoughts made fear real to her for the first time. She had never felt so alone, and though Scacath had often said things that Thyri had felt in her stomach, her teacher had always awed her more than anything else. This was different – no matter what Scacath said or did, Thyri felt she could trust her. The bears were real, and if she was caught by them inside their cavern, they would surely do their best to kill her. She became aware of her age. She had turned thirteen the past winter. If she did not succeed, she would never turn fourteen.

But she couldn't turn back. She knew this and felt it so deeply that the very thought of forsaking her sword, the meaning of her future, for a fear of fang and claw, however sharp, sickened her. Throughout the past year, Scacath had stressed the importance of containing her fear and she realized now that she must do this to pass the test. In essence, defeating fear *was* the test. A part of her stepped back then, watching, learning, and calculating, while the rest of her being trembled.

The stream issued from the cavern's mouth against its left ledge. Thyri saw no possibility, at least from the outside, of reaching the back of the cavern along any path across from the bears. She had to go straight back.

The water was cold, though she knew this even before she dipped a curious hand into the current. On the hottest days of summer, the stream by the glade was not a place to linger long in bathing. The waters near the surface were pleasant enough, but the cold briskness below made feet and legs numb, and traversing the stream by walking along the bottom was dangerous not because of any particular threat of drop-offs or sharpened rocks, but because of the cold – a cold that attacked the nerves, creating sensations that lied to the brain.

Thyri didn't waste time worrying about freezing. She

didn't plan on staying in the water any longer than she needed to reach a point deep enough in the cavern to avoid the bears. She got as close as she could while still keeping some undergrowth before her, then she took off her bow and quiver, her pack, her cape, and the rest of her clothing. Gathering several short but solid bits of branch and bark, she fashioned a float from her pack. After satisfying herself that it would work, she made a bundle from her shirt and secured the torch and tinderbox within. She tied it with the length of twine, then tied the pack to the float. She checked the structure once again in the water, making sure it still worked; she had no desire to be caught in the darkness of the cave without light and warmth. Before she entered the water, she tied her belt with her ax and dagger tightly around her naked waist.

She stayed underwater as much as she could, staving off the cold with thoughts of her alternatives: to walk boldly into the lair or to lie in wait, hoping to get clear bow-shots on each of the animals. The latter option could take days. As she entered the cavern, she began to wish that she'd made a harness to drag the float along behind her, freeing the hand she was using to guide it. As she stroked deeper and deeper into the darkness, her thoughts were of warm winter evenings with Astrid, and fears of losing her torch by snagging it on a ledge or, worse, by a curious swat of a bear paw. Or by an unseen foe attacking from below, forcing her to use both hands, freeing the float to the whims of the current that would push it back into the gray daylight without her.

The cold was numbing. She clambered out of the stream at the point where she first, while gasping for breath, smelt a lessening in the musk that pervaded the area around the lair. Trembling, she pulled the float from the water into the darkness. Clasping it to her breast, she staggered away, first finding a wall, then following it. The ground under her bare feet was soft, as of a silt laid by the stream over the cavern's rocky floor. For that she was thankful; her blind groping brought her toes against enough sharp things as it was. She wondered if the bears had noticed the man-smell invading their domain.

After several minutes of following the wall, she realized that a coldness close to that of the water had enveloped her. Unless she soon got warm, she would die as the cold worked its way into her heart. She found a niche in the wall, collapsed into it, and forced her trembling hands to part the bindings of the pack. Her heart raced as she drew out the torch; it was damp in spite of her precautions. She laid it on her lap and groped for the warmth of the tinderbox. The little clay vessel sent fire into her numb fingers when she touched it. She uncapped it, finding the embers still red and hot. After several frantic moments, she managed to set the shirt she had waxed alight. It sputtered uncertainly at first, then blazed as the wax took hold of the wood and the flames boiled the moisture away. Thyri planted the torch in the silt and warmed each part of her body with its heat, heedless of the poppings that sent bits of fiery cloth and wood against her skin. She almost welcomed the burns.

She would have liked to linger there longer, but she soon took up the torch and continued on. The light would not last forever, and she knew neither how much deeper she needed to delve, nor whether she had, in following the wall, taken a turn away from the main passage that led to her goal. If such were the case, she would have to backtrack and start over again, possibly having to face the bears. For now she pressed on. In the cavern along the stream, she saw many beautiful sights – things that glittered with all the colors of the rainbow. They hung from the ceilings and rose from the floors. Some met, creating columns of grandeur fit for the halls of the gods. Perhaps, she thought, some god *did* dwell here. Perhaps this was the road to Niflheim. The glittering pillars would give way to fanged beasts of dark rock, and the rivers of Muspellheim would cross the stream, and she would pass their fires to reach the great gates where Loki's son, Garm, lay chained, awaiting the end of all things.

At the end, she reached a chamber past which she could not fare. The stream poured from the far wall and but a handspan separated its surface from the rock above it. By the opening, on a low pedestal of the rainbow-stuff, rested a thin, silver gauntlet and the sword that Scacath had shown Thyri six seasons past.

Thyri took the gauntlet and pulled it onto her hand. It reached to her mid-forearm and glittered in the torchlight along with the rainbow-stuff. She smiled – it fit now. She took the sword by its hilt and, with it in her right hand and the torch in her left, turned back to seek the daylight.

Legend might have it that Thyri slew the bears as she left: that she, unversed, wielded her new weapon with the skill and grace of one who had studied its art many years. That this day she became a warrior. This did not happen. She left the cavern as she had entered it, with the tinderbox secured on the float. She did, however, hold the sword above water as she swam, not wanting to tarnish the blade.

21: Changes

'You should at least learn the making of a stew!'

Gyda stood, hands on her ample hips, glaring at Thyri. Thyri glared back at her mother, saying nothing. She ached – her heart ached, her body ached, her shoulder throbbed. She didn't care – the last few weeks had buried her pain much deeper.

'You chose that life,' Gyda said, throwing her hands up and returning to her work. 'I have lost two sons, a nephew, and now a niece. You think we don't mourn with you? You think we don't feel some fear when you, Halfdan, and Erik leave here with swords strapped to your sides and blood and plounder burning inside you?'

Gyda went to her, bending to one knee and placing her hand on her daughter's arm. 'Why, Odin, do you pain us so? I ask it of him every day. And every night I sleep without reply.' She looked pleadingly into Thyri's eyes. 'Put away your sword, Eiriksdattir. Marry. Bear me grand-children.'

Thyri sat, shoulders hunched, staring blankly at nothing. Gyda sighed, rose and brushed off her skirt.

'You are my impotent son,' she said distantly. 'Unable even to sow our seed among those people whose lands you rape.'

Only Erik's company had been bearable, perhaps because she saw in him an innocence that she'd lost. But her love for her brother could not lift the shadows from her heart. He'd known Astrid too well. He could not cease his speculations on the reasons for Astrid's fall: a sickness that she had concealed from Thyri, the snagging of her blade on the root of a nearby tree, the failing light, the snow. . .

Thyri could only nod and shrug dumbly at each successive explanation. But the ache Erik's words brought her burned fiercely, and she desired only to run from it.

Then there was Yrsa, Astrid's sister. Yrsa was not like them. She was shy, mousy, and skilled with her hands, spending most of her time alone fashioning cloaks, shirts, and boots for sale and trade with the spring merchants. To Gyda, she was the daughter that Thyri had never been; Yrsa's mother had withered and died shortly after her third childbirth. When not sewing leather, Yrsa's only interests were Asta and the mysteries of the runes. Thyri saw little of her, and for that she was thankful. Neither Yrsa nor the volva had eyed her kindly since she'd brought word of Astrid's death.

She found herself mourning anew for Astrid each day, each moment. She couldn't get it to make sense. Astrid was Valkyrie; she wouldn't be coming back. The entire world had changed, darkened, in the space of one fatal moment.

She rose unsteadily, going to the door of the hall. She opened it, heedless of the icy winds gusting in. The first hint of moonrise tainted the horizon, and she slammed the door shut. Somehow, she could still feel the moon outside, rising. . .

She ran to her room and huddled on the ledge. Her mother yelled something after her but the words lost to the rolling thunder in her head. Her shoulder began to throb terribly.

'No!'

The scream issued from her unbidden. Her door opened, her mother's frame filling the space.

Agony gripped her, tearing at her every nerve. Bile rose to her throat, and vomit spilled out onto the bedding and the floor. She heard Gyda's voice again, then her vision went red.

She killed her mother in a blind, dispossessed rage on her way out of Egill's hall. It was her first taste of human blood.

Over three nights of the full moon, Thyri roamed the countryside, feeding.

Her house was in turmoil. Yrsa found Gyda in time to look from the hall and see the white wolf bounding away across the snow. Of Eirik: his wife's death turned his heart black and folded into itself. His face fell devoid of expression. He did not speak. He did not even weep.

Egill, however, listened to Yrsa and Asta with growing horror as they told him the lore of the *were* and the dark runes that served it. Loki's spite – his warping of a light elven lady into a malevolent, vampiric beast in the image of Fenrir. She had denied him his pleasure. Aelgifu was her name and dark was her Destiny. She had loved a mortal prince whom she tore near unto death as they lay together under a rising moon. From there she ran, and she took her own life the next morning when the beast left her. Her lover, however, had survived. This unknown prince had spread the curse. In Asta's eyes, that curse had found Thyri.

Halfdan was sent for. Egill raged through those days, stomping about the hall with his father's war-ax gripped tightly in his fist. On the first day he battered Erik senseless, smashing his nose and cracking several ribs when the boy refused to join in the hunt for his sister. Eirik was abed. Asta and Yrsa stayed locked in the old one's chamber, casting and recasting their family's fortunes among a house of whispers but for Egill's furious railings.

Halfdan arrived on the third day and he and Egill set off immediately into the wood with bow, sword, and ax. They did not find her until after moonrise. She saw them and ran. They tracked her too well, boxing her in among boulders and rocks. They rained arrows upon her, putting three in her side before their quivers were spent. Then Egill sent Halfdan against her.

Thyri killed her cousin, part of her full of ecstatic fire at the taste of his blood, another part loathing and screaming out to some god, any god, for mercy. Then she killed Egill, who had forced Halfdan's death, rending him as she had her mother.

By day she cowered in a small cove that looked out over the sacred vale of her ancestors. She would cry out her pain to Astrid and be answered by naught but silence. She would look from her cave's mouth and see the sun warming the ground over Astrid's rune-sword. She would think of that blade and how easy it would be to unearth it and bury it in her breast, spilling her own blood over Astrid's ashes. But she was too weak for that crossing into the field in daylight. And when night fell, so came the hunger, leaving her no time to think of the oblivion waiting buried for her in the earth.

After the third night, when she slew her uncle and cousin, Thyri stayed in the cave for two days. That second night, after the setting of the moon, she crept out and went slowly across to Astrid's low mound.

Her fingers clawed at the frozen earth which fell away in unwilling clumps until she grasped that which she sought. She drew out the sword and planted it point first in the soil before her. The light of the stars caressed it as she wiped away the dirt. The wetness on her cheeks streaked with brown as her tears caught cloudy dust from the air. The blade clean, she drew it slowly from the ground. She gripped the cold iron and set its point to the flesh just below her left breast. She closed her eyes, breathing deeply.

'Thyri.'

She looked up.

Astrid stood before her, ablaze in silver armor. A winged steed pawed at the frozen ground behind her, tossing its head. He looked at her and she recognized his gaze. *Yrafax*, she thought. Her eyes filled with new tears, and all the pain, all the horror of the past month leapt into her mind. She tightened her grip on the rune-sword. 'I will join you now, my cousin.'

'No, my love. Do not do this thing.' Astid's words were like music, her voice no longer of Midgard. 'You must live for both of us. You must love for both of us now.'

'But it is not right! I have become as your slayer! I have tasted the blood of our kin!' Sobbing wracked her body.

The point of the sword pierced her skin. She hardly felt it, such was the pain in her heart.

'You are strong, Cousin. You will learn restraint. You must leave Hordaland. Go far from here and begin another life. Your sword will see you through. And when the moon sets upon you, be one with the wolves. Don't fight your Destiny. Prey will come easily; you needn't kill men for food.'

'Don't leave me, Astrid! I cannot – ' Her words failed in her sorrow. She knew she asked the impossible.

'I serve the All Father now, Cousin.' She stepped forward and lifted Thyri from her knees. She smoothed the tangled hair from Thyri's face and kissed her gently. 'Do not fear, Thyri. Your day will come to enter Valhalla. But that day lies ahead, not here.'

She pulled Thyri's head from her breast and brushed away her tears. 'Take my sword. I no longer have need of it. Perhaps with it in your hand, you will feel me near.' She parted from Thyri and went to her horse. 'Farewell, little one.'

Astrid and her steed faded away with a mist that descended on the field, then went as suddenly as it came. Thyri stood there, naked under the stars but for the blade jutting out from her clenched fist. Along it, starlight danced. The dead of the field called again to her but she hardly heard them. She turned slowly and started east, toward her home.

13: Departures

'Hello, little one,' Hugin said. 'We have waited these three years for you. Astrid has reached her final year, and Scacath must take her beyond that which is our ability to teach.'

Thyri tried to smile. It was the day after her third test. Scacath had told her to follow the ravens to the glade. They had reached it before her, and when she'd arrived she'd found not two birds but two young men, generously muscled and black as night. One stood as tall as Astrid; the other was shorter. Both wore nothing but scant breechcloths of green cotton and belted scabbards for their swords. Their heads were bald, and ivory white teeth shone from their mouths as they laughed at Thyri's astonishment. She'd known immediately that they were the ravens; their eyes hadn't changed. The big one was Hugin, the smaller, Munin. Mind and Memory.

'By your eyes, your cousin never told you of us. That shows her strength better than ever her sword arm might. We know how close you are.'

'She told me,' Thyri said, 'that you trained her. But she told me not how. I might have guessed had I had the time.'

'But you hadn't.'

Memories of the past three years rushed into her mind – all the things she'd learned and wondered upon. 'No,' she agreed. 'I hadn't.'

Astrid spent a week that fall at Egill's hall and brought back news from the world of men. Erik was now a strapping youth of ten summers and helping his father work the smithy. It was then that Thyri asked her teacher to take him next.

'He shall be trained,' Scacath replied, 'after the fashion of the Vikings, and he shall reach Valhalla by virtue of that teaching, not mine.'

Ragnar of Hordaland had a daughter named Gyda who was born on the same day, some say the same moment, as Thyri. The princess had grown very beautiful and powerful. An entourage of men from the Kingdom of Vestfold had come to Hordaland that summer. Their king and leader, Harald, son of Halfdan called 'the Black,' had led the entourage. From what Astrid knew, the king was but a boy, perhaps no older than she, but all said that he possessed that air of a great leader and warrior, and Asta had told her that his mother had dreamed a great prophecy of his Destiny – of a thorn driving itself into a tree as great as Yggdrasil, drawing blood from it that covered the trunk but left the upper branches white as snow. He had come to Hordaland seeking Gyda, who he had heard was the fairest of all maidens in Norway.

He had stayed at the hall of Ragnar for two weeks during which he could constantly be found at Gyda's side. After those two weeks had passed, he'd proposed marriage to the princess. It is said that she laughed and replied, 'To think that I should marry such a petty kingling as you!' He bore the insult with grace, and he did not strike her. He'd left, vowing to conquer for her a kingdom worthy for her to rule as queen.

Neither Thyri or Astrid knew the princess, but the story rooted within each of them a dislike for the girl and her capricious ways. They discussed the portent of Gyda's act for the homeland, and they wondered whether Ragnar would have them fight against the armies of Harald, whom they thought terminally stupid for his fascination with Gyda. The talk was prophetic, and it came to pass that the only lasting enemy of their years together under the banner of Hordaland was the southern kingdom of Vestfold.

The following summer, Thyri took her first test with her blade, and Astrid gained the fifth rune of Odin for hers. Scacath gave Astrid her rune-clasp on the day she left.

The glade lost half its light for Thyri when her cousin walked away. They had endured the preceding weeks well, laughing often and talking of the great things they would do together once Thyri's training was complete. That training intensified after Astrid's departure, and Thyri hardened her heart and welcomed it with renewed vigor.

That fall, when the sword training extended beyond stances and strokes and began to batter her body, Munin offered to aid Thyri in tending her wounds. She refused his offer and retired to tend to herself, thinking of Astrid's hands and wondering where her cousin slept that night.

Eventually, Thyri accepted the friendship of the ravens if only to fill some of the emptiness left by Astrid. She accepted Munin's in particular. It happened on a day the following spring when the sky was bright, the breeze soft, and the pastels of the flowers against the ubiquitous green were laughing at her solemnity. Her dark thoughts of the past winter were forced to the back of her mind to dwell with her first glimpse of Scacath, Skoll's laughing eyes, and other early experiences that were part of her and yet part of another – a child, not *herself*. Memories, she had found, could be cast aside, at least temporarily.

They had taken rest under the shade of an oak on the rim of the glade next to the swift stream that bled from the earth through the cave of the rainbow-stuff and the bears. Hugin changed form – a nearly instantaneous phenomenon with but a faint aura of magic shrouding his figure just before and just after the change. He flew off to seek his mistress.

A large welt high on Thyri's left arm oozed redly where the flat of Munin's blade had pierced the guard. With a dirk, she could have parried the blow without training. As it was, she had used her sword two-handed. She was quickly learning the limitations of that technique even though her wrist was not yet strong enough for a one-handed style.

Munin inspected the wound and applied a salve to it, bandaging it with strips of cotton that Thyri wore so often that she felt them almost a part of her normal clothing. After tying the bandage, Munin's hands fell on Thyri's breasts. She sighed. When she did not pull away, he bent over and kissed her lightly. He lifted her up and pulled her shirt over her head.

They began slowly, and Thyri accepted the new sensations with hesitation. His touch was light, but not as light as Astrid's. But she liked it, even though she wasn't sure that she wanted to. His caress was insistent, clouding her thoughts. She gave in to the waves of pleasure that followed. She felt the aches of her body melting away, much as they had when she'd lain with Astrid.

Munin freed her hips and legs from the loose leather skirt she wore. She found her hand moving under his breechcloth, discovering that uniqueness of man that she had seen but never felt.

Neither spoke until Munin rolled on top of her. She gasped at the sudden feel of his weight. 'It will hurt at first,' he whispered. 'I will be gentle.'

'Don't,' she gasped. 'I want to know how it really feels.'

So Munin drove himself deep within her. She screamed, and that moment was the first time she managed to fully forget how lonely she was without Astrid.

Thyri sought Munin's company from time to time during her last years with Scacath. The teacher was aware of it as she had been aware of Thyri and Astrid and even of Astrid and Hugin (of which Thyri learned only through a later admission of Astrid's). Scacath would speak little of these things, but she made it clear that, in the arena of love, their bodies were their own. In the arena of battle, of course, things were quite different.

So Thyri went to Munin as she felt the need for comfort, and Munin was always there to fill the need. She came to love him in her way, though no one could ever completely fill the spaces in Thyri's heart that her several partings with Astrid left behind. And Thyri knew that when she left Scacath, she would return to Astrid, thus leaving Munin. He belonged to Scacath body and soul.

The seasons turned, and the following winter Thyri was tasked with the letters of the dead empire of the Romans, the onetime rulers of all the lands to the south of the world of the Vikings. She studied scrolls and books in the evenings next to her fire as Astrid had in years past, though her cousin's studying had had little meaning then. She found in the script a comfort, as if it added not another complication to her puzzle of the world, but the promise of a thread that might aid in holding the pieces together.

So passed Thyri's last years in training. Scacath cast the rune of sharpness on her sword so that she might spend less time in the evening on it and more in thought and study. This gift came at the end of her fifth year – one year early. She asked Scacath of this; her teacher told her only that traditions were meant to be broken.

Thyri took her final test and earned her seventh braid in a battle of first blood with Scacath. The teacher won, but Thyri lasted a full minute before catching a thrust in her left shoulder. She knew she had done well to fend off Scacath's attacks for so long. While Scacath inscribed the fifth rune of Odin on her blade, Thyri bade farewell to the ravens.

At parting, Scacath smiled her half-smile and handed Thyri her rune-clasp. 'Farewell, little one. You are leaving with but a fraction more than that with which you came, though you may not think so now. You came here with your heart, and you leave here with your heart.

'The world of men will bring you pain, and though I cannot be there to guide you, I hope that I have given you the tools with which you might bear it well. I took you from loyalty to home and crown, and to that I now return you.'

Scacath said these words in the glade where Thyri had met her seven years before. The sky was bright, and a light breeze blew from the north, calling Thyri to the road. When Scacath finished, the ravens took their places on her shoulders, and she turned. As she walked away, her form grew hazy, and by the time she reached the far end of the glade, she was as transparent as the still surface of wine in a goblet. Thyri could see through her to the trees beyond. And above the branches, she saw thin wisps of smoke, as of the cooking fires of a hall or a small village. Into the trees Scacath stepped, then she was gone.

21: Homecoming

Thyri was naked but for Astrid's sword that final day she returned to the family hall. Her hair was laced with ice and separate strands chinked against each other like light, ethereal armor when she moved. Her feet were numb, then burning, as she stamped on the floor of the hall and slowly, agonizingly, approached the fire.

All the old ones but Asta huddled in the corners, staring at her, whispering. She paid them no heed. Not a glance to even acknowledge that she knew where she was. There were no other sounds but those of the winds outside and a high keening that came from beyond the hall, from Asta's chamber.

When she was warm she turned for her room, sword before her, her hair dripping a wet trail behind. Her things lay in disarray over the cot, nothing important missing but her own blade. On top of the heap was an old, worn scroll. She took it up and unrolled it, her eyes scanning words they had first read five years before, in her sixth year with Scacath. Hugin had brought it to her from the world of men. The script was Latin:

Dearest Cousin,

Many times have I tried to write you, but always things have come in the way. Sometimes it has been a task assigned me by the king, sometimes the need to practice all the things I have learned (much of which you will know by now). And sometimes it is my loneliness for you, which runs so deep that I cannot draw on the words to speak it, much less work laboriously with this quill to write them in this strange tongue. Perhaps it is best, for now you will have had time to learn this writing, and you will not need Scacath or the ravens to read my words to you. I write to you, not to them, though I miss them as well.

Among Ragnar's men I am thought of highly for my skills, though it was not so at first. I earned my ninth braid after being here but a week. The king took me in, for Scacath had informed him of my coming and convinced him of my skill long before (perhaps by her magic? There is a rune she uses that persuades. I could never figure it out; its magic is much too refined for my clumsy talent). But Ragnar took me into his hall and gave me a room by the hall of the women, not, he said, because I belonged there, but that there I might avail myself of the baths and not be required to use the stream with the rest of his warriors. At first I thought this unnecessary, as well you might be thinking as you read this, but I assure you that a woman has enough problems gaining the respect of a male warrior without adding the allure of her body to his already-wrong thinking.

The hall is huge! We could fit five of ours into but the main room of this one, and Ragnar has another larger still for the small army he barracks between here and his fields, though most of the warriors are often absent – to their homes or to battles where they carve their way to Valhalla. In my two years, I have already fought and killed so often that, without the aid of the braid and the bead, I would have lost track long ago.

In the hall, I often have to match the arrogant gaze of Gyda. I still do not like her. A young boy, not even of ten summers, once came upon her by accident as she bathed with her maidens in the river. She made Ragnar kill him and send his head in a sack back to his father. I am not to question my king, but that hardly seems a wise way to rule. Ragnar is a good man, as strong and brave as any of his warriors, but his daughter is his weakness. I have thought idly of slaying her, but I think she knows of my disdain as she no longer stays long in any room into which I enter.

I have heard that Harald of Vestfold has just begun his campaign for her heart, though I have not had occasion to face his forces in battle. I think that it will not be so for long. I don't think that Ragnar will sail openly against Harald, but I can easily imagine him sending his warriors to the aid of those kingdoms against which Harald turns his strength. He does not wish to lose his daughter. If he were wise, he'd send her to Harald bound and gagged. The girl knows no humility.

As for me, I have fought against marauders from the North, mostly homeless men whose fathers' halls came into the hands of older brothers. All they seek is land, and for that they cannot be blamed. But when they seek it in the realm of our king, they show their lack of inspiration. They would do better to fare into the lands of the Saxons or the Franks, where they would not be facing Viking blades.

And I have fought the Danes at sea as well, though it makes no sense that they would come north into our waters while there is such plunder to be had in the South (I know, for I have been there as well!). It would seem that we Norse have not a direction, but only a lust for battle. I have seen men reach *berserk* fury and die with laughter on their lips, welcoming the call of Valhalla. Thus it is, though I think, perhaps out of ignorance and inexperience, that it need not be thus. We are of strong blood; you cannot imagine it but must see it in the faces of our foes to the South. And we are many too. I have seen the sea covered with our sails, while each ship is bound for a place different from the next. Were all to sail together, we could crush the legions of Surt! But this, for reasons beyond me, we do not do. Instead, we fight each other as well as the rest of the world.

It is not a bad life, and it births such tales as you never hear men tell except at the drunken feasts that follow the slaughter of an enemy host. Still, I often imagine you and I at the front of an army that would cause the Thunderer to pause, but though the men will accept me as a warrior, the problems confronting a leader are great and varied, and I do not think myself equal to the task. At least not yet.

Perhaps Harald of Vestfold is a leader who might unite the Vikings. But he is yet young, and his unity may come too late. The strength we have is now, and misuse now may make it impotent twenty years hence. At any rate, I should soon find myself on the battlefield with him, my sword against his, and not by his side. In the end, it doesn't matter. The ways of the warrior, all the ways of the warrior, lead to Valhalla – to serve Odin until Ragnarok.

My braids are twenty-one now. I will not tell them here, but will wait until we are again together, and make each a story for a separate night when, our passions spent, I will carry you into the realm of dreams with my words.

I miss you Thyri, little one, and await your arrival at Ragnar's hall with such longing that you cannot imagine. I know that you must have labored long to read this (as I have in writing it!), and I do not wish you should spend your evenings fashioning a reply in a language you do not yet know well enough to use. Your coming here one year hence will serve as your reply.

Astrid

After reading the scroll, Thyri stared at it, her dripping hair smearing the ink and destroying the delicate parchment she had taken care to preserve for so long.

'Father's dead.'

She turned, crumpling the parchment in her hand.

Erik stood in the doorway. His hazel eyes were blank, empty of emotion. 'He came here yesterday and took up your sword. I watched him. He gripped the hilt and would not let go until the sorcery killed him. I have the blade hidden. I will get it for you if you wish.'

She wanted to smile at him – at his bravery, at his failure to condemn her. She cried instead. 'Take it, Erik Eirikson. Fashion for yourself a gauntlet of silver and bear my sword into battle. Perhaps then you shall remember your sister as a warrior and not as – '

The words caught in her throat. Through swimming tears she surveyed her possessions arrayed before her. Asta's keening grew more intense, more malevolent.

'The volva tries to purge the evil from our blood,' Erik said. 'She and Yrsa have not stepped from her room for two days. They work magic to slay you.'

'May they succeed.' Thyri picked up a leather shift and pulled it over her head, then sat to pull on her boots. She gathered together her belongings in silence. Clasping her cloak, she stepped past her brother, out of the hall that was now his, and into the snows.

For two nights she prowled the shoreline in search of a sea-worthy craft for one. She settled on a fishing skiff with a single mast and locks for eight oars. She wrapped Astrid's sword in oilskin, stocked the small boat with food and drink, and set sail. She followed the Valkyrie's belt star – the one that whirls from one end of the sky to the other over the course of a night. Thyri didn't know where it would lead her. She didn't know what she would do if the winds died. She didn't really care.

BOOK II

THE ISLAND

I proceed with some misgivings. Ten times as many words might be written to bring me to this point, and many things which I have mentioned only in passing could be discussed here at great length. But then, when I think of it, little might be gained, and much lost. The Twilight is of central importance, and its roots lie in Astrid's death.

I apologize to my reader if the haste with which I have told this tale thus far has created confusion. Many of the characters I have presented must seem little more than names, and though several are important, particularly Gyda of Hordaland, Harald of Vestfold, and Thyri's brother Erik, I will not ask that they be committed now to memory. Their importance will become apparent in due course. My only excuse is that I have tried to cover twenty-one years of a woman's life in this space, and those years were far from ordinary. I pledge here to proceed in greater detail.

Other volumes, I suppose, could be written of the exploits of Thyri and Astrid during the four years they were together after Thyri left Scacath's grove. For the most part, they were happy during this time, but they did little more than live and love from one battle to the next. Astrid gained, over time, a moderate degree of competence in the runic ways. I wonder yet if that might not have been what slew her. Perhaps, confronted with an unnatural foe, her thoughts turned for a moment to consider her sorceries. And in that moment she would have lost the advantage of her sword. It would, ironically, be then that the runes began to fail the iron. Astrid need not have died, and Thyri need not have felt the fangs of the wolf. Without her curse, Thyri would not have come to affect the lives of so many men and gods alike, and Lif and Lifthrasir might now be molding the ashes of Midgard to their liking, perhaps making the same mistakes as we who came before.

I will mention now that I do not profess to understand the majority of that which Thyri learned under Scacath. I am no mean swordsman, and I have lived my life on the strength of my sword and my wits, but the techniques of Scacath get caught in my imagination. And they were not taught to be thought on; they were taught to be practiced with repetition so exacting that one would hardly imagine the end result to be a free, flowing, and impossibly powerful style. I am able, then, only to write *of* it. Perhaps someone, if not myself, may glean from it the essence that made it so effective.

And still my researches have not shown me why two girls from a young barbarian kingdom warranted the attention of one such as Scacath. Perhaps there is no answer. I can imagine the Norns sitting in their dark cave, weaving their tapestry of life. Perhaps near the end of their work they grew bored and wove in Thyri and Astrid to make their final days more interesting.

Lastly, here, I paint a final picture thus far only sketched: Astrid had the type of beauty that has always reminded me of spring. Her blond hair was long and silky, grown to just above her waist before she died. Her eyes were sky blue. Her face was full and round and little-girlish with that delicate Aryan symmetry that gives the Norse such presence.

Thyri stood a head shorter, and her hair was streaked with dark and reddish gold. It was thicker hair, and it splayed over her shoulders like the mane of a lioness. While Astrid was tall and gracefully lean, Thyri was a small, compact bundle of curves and muscle. Her face was more animated than Astrid's; screwed into a mask of rage, it was the face of a cornered wildcat. Full of joy, it was a face of innocence that could break the stoutest of hearts, even with the jagged, inch-long scar that ran down from the lower lid of her left eye. But that scar is another story. Her eyes were deep hazel, and the scar ran down from the one like a permanent tear.

Magic

Figures approach through the clouds. She runs. There's an eye where the moon should be. Watching – no, looking for her. Not yet. Not yet – she hides. It isn't time yet.

'Easy girl.'

The figures pass overhead. The pride of Odin – the Valkyries – or winged wolves. . .

A hand on her breast, another on her brow. They are damp.

What?

Wet all over, she shakes. Her head throbs. She opens her eyes; a white brilliance stabs through, forcing her eyelids shut. She tries to sit, but the pain knocks her back. She feels something at her lip – water. She opens her mouth and the cool liquid makes her tongue tingle. She drinks and feels the water rush down her parched throat, burning, caressing.

'Easy! You'll drown.'

Water. She remembers: the boat, the ocean, the numbing cold after the storm. Relentless. *Am I dead?*

She remembers more. 'The sword! Astrid's sword!' Thyri tries to sit again; the pain doesn't let her.

'Shhh.'

The hand is soothing and the voice almost purrs. 'It is here. Safe. Try to rest.'

She rests. She wanders back into the clouds. She looks up at the eye. It still can't see her. It still isn't time.

'I found you among the rocks,' she said. Her body was lean and firm, rippling supplely in a black cotton shift as she sat on a stool next to Thyri's cot. Her skin was pale olive, and she had dark eyes and full, friendly lips. Thyri judged her about twenty-five. For a moment, Thyri almost believed she was with Scacath.

Her long black hair was pulled back over slightly large, delicate ears, then fell freely down her back. Thyri sat and her vision blurred as the blood rushed from her head. She blinked; her eyes fixed on a small mole decorating the slender line of the woman's neck. Her mouth filled with saliva and she felt a dark, hungry stirring within her.

No!

She smacked the side of her head with her fist. She opened her eyes again. The woman shimmered, then grew solid. She smiled. Candlelight ignited black, playful flames in her eyes.

Thyri looked around. They were in a small earthen hut with clay jars and pale green plants cluttering shelves lining the walls. Skins covered the floor and braziers burned in the four corners, perfuming the air with enticing incense. Another heady aroma came from a larger pot warming over a gentle fire by the door.

'You are not Norse,' Thyri said, looking back to the woman.

'No. I am not.'

'You speak my language well.'

Her awareness grew. A long stream of sunlight cut through a slat in the hut's door to lose itself in the candlelight. A fireplace, its embers cold and gray, was cut into the opposite wall. From outside: the bleating of a goat, the occasional cluck of a chicken, the mating call of a grouse in the far distance. The dull roar of the sea nearby, pounding against a cliff. Invigorating, moisture-laden air. There were no sounds of men. The hut faced west – were it the morning sun beyond the door, the birds of the morning would have been singing out their greetings to the day.

The woman smiled. 'Thank you. I try to learn all that I come across. The mysteries require it. I could not have healed you otherwise.'

'You are a witch?'

'I have been called that.'

Mystery in those black eyes, Thyri thought. *Mystery and dark, knowing mirth.* 'I was dying?'

'You were not well.'

She looked longingly at the pot. 'Where am I?'

Light laughter. Shadows deep as moonless black dancing in those mysterious eyes. 'You're hungry, aren't you? Not surprising.' She got up and ladled a bowl of stew from the caldron and handed it to Thyri. 'You are on Kaerglen Isle,' she said. 'It's just off the coast of Erin. The name can't mean much to you. We're a very petty kingdom.' She paused. 'Kaerglen is the name of the ruling family. My name is Meg.'

Forcing her hands to steady themselves, Thyri tipped the bowl to her lips. Small, fresh chunks of rabbit meat and little onions stung and tantalized her tongue.

Days, she thought. She had tasted nothing for days. Licking the spoon, she grinned at her hostess. 'Thyri Eiriksdattir.'

'Do you speak Irish, Thyri?'

'No.'

'Then I must teach you. It will make your convalescence pass quickly.'

'How long have I been here?'

'Four days.'

'I should be well soon?'

Meg nodded. Thyri tried to remember the sea. She had left Norway two days after the last full moon. She had been on the sea three days before the storm hit, and she could remember three days after that. But then . . . ?

With twenty-five days between one full moon and the next, she could account for twelve. But how many lost at sea? 'The moon,' she asked. 'How full is the moon?'

Meg laughed. 'Eight days yet. You needn't worry.'

'About what?'

'That the moon will call again before you can leave me. You do not want to kill me.'

How did you know?

I am a witch.

The shadow eyes smiled. 'I know many things,' Meg said. 'I tended you for four days. To heal, I entered your dreams. You're afraid, aren't you? You have not been this way long.'

'No.' Thyri lowered her eyes. Less than a month; it felt like forever. And suddenly something in Megan's gaze made her feel warm, loved. She felt that tang of magic, but she felt it comforting her. Healing her yet.

Megan had bewitched her.

The charm was probably in the broth that she poured down Thyri's throat until she could stomach no more. Or perhaps it was only the eyes; they have caused many other, more impressive things to come to pass.

Still eating, now on her second bowl of the stew, Thyri spoke of Astrid and how they had found the *were*-kill on a lonely Norse road. She spoke of the tracking and how the beast then set upon them. She spoke of Astrid's death and of the wolf's transformation. She spoke of her first change, when she had killed her mother, and she spoke of the trauma of the ordeal – the agony of the changes, the three days of fear and blood and hunger, the slayings of her uncle and cousin.

And she told Meg how Astrid's shade had stopped her from slaying herself and had bid her leave – to seek a life in the world apart from the Vikings. Thyri spilled her heart, hardly aware that anyone listened. Once started, she had to get it out. She had denied and lied to herself about the truth for too long. It was burning a hole in her soul.

'This Astrid was very special to you?' the sorceress asked when Thyri's words finally gave way to muffled, wracking sobs.

'We fought many years side by side. She was my cousin and – ' She stopped, gazing into the shadow world in Megan's eyes. Nymphs danced there, whorls of black pleasure trailing up and down their thighs.

Lover?

Yes.

Meg drew a long bundle from among the skins at her feet. She unraveled it. A faint violet light played along the edge of the rune-blade. 'This was Astrid's?'

'Yes. Do not touch it. It may kill.'

Meg smiled at her obliquely. 'I have touched it already. It is very strong.' Her fingers traced over the runes, and Thyri wondered what powers she commanded. *She's a witch . . .*

'This is no normal weapon,' Meg said. 'The lore of these runes has been lost to most for many years.'

The shadow gaze fell on Astrid's sword. Thyri felt a darkness rising within her, as if only those eyes kept her sane. She shook her head, casting away the tendrils of madness. 'Why did you save me, Meg?'

'Why not?'

'You do not know me, but you see into my nature. I would have let me die.'

'I am not you. Astrid told you to live on: heed her. The stars favor you. I tried to cast your future and learned nothing. The mark of Chaos shelters you, and that in itself hints at your Destiny. You bear a blade from the realms of Twilight, and I know of only one who brings such weapons into this world. Besides, you are Norse, you are fair, and I have little company and few friends. And your soul is not black.'

'Nor is it white.' Thyri squinted, noting the casual way Meg handled the weapon. 'What do you know of Scacath?'

Meg tested the rune-sword in the air. 'Little, but enough. Do not lose this.'

Thyri smiled, watching. 'When you slash from side to side, don't reverse like that. Do it like this.' She traced a loopy, upside down *T* in the air with her finger. Meg tried it; Thyri advised further, but the sorceress shook her head, smiled, and handed Thyri the sword.

"'I am not a warrior,' Meg said. 'If I must kill, I prefer subtler methods.' She sat down on the edge of the cot and brushed the hair off Thyri's cheek. 'You are very beautiful.'

The sorcerous grip of Meg's eyes faded suddenly. Thyri

looked into a face of mortality, of woman. Meg's neck taunted her, scant inches from her face. She remembered the wolf, deep inside, stirring in its dark lust when it had first looked out on her savior. And she thought also of Astrid.

She turned away.

The witch smiled distantly and rose. 'Would you like more stew?'

'No. Thank you. I feel tired again. How long before I am well?'

'A few days. You must learn much in that time. I can aid you with spells, but you are too weak yet to begin. Sleep now. We'll start in the morning.' Meg turned.

'Meg?'

Traces of shadow mirth again, flitting in the doorway. 'Yes.'

'Thank you.'

Meg shrugged and left. Thyri lay back, closed her eyes, and cried herself to sleep.

She woke the next morning alone. Near silence from without: the sea was calm, only swallows called to each other in the distance. She rose and staggered to the hut's door. A morning fog was lifting, the sky overcast but still.

She stepped out. An unkempt path ran from the hut's door into a stand of wood a hundred or so yards to the south. Meg's home was built into an embankment, shielded from gales coming off the sea. The ground to either side was muddy, scattered with straw. A fenced-in garden stretched along one side of the path and several hens scratched at the ground nearby. From beyond, behind the hut, sheep bleated.

Thyri looked down at herself. She wore a short shift tied loosely at the waist – lighter clothing than she'd worn at sea. And it had a clean smell; Meg had dressed her. A breeze teased her bare thighs. She heard laughter nearby, shrugged, and started toward it through the mud that squished pleasantly between her toes.

Meg faced away from her, hands on hips, facing off a

goat that had caught itself in a thick patch of the muck. The witch still laughed. She wore a shift like Thyri's and calf-high boots. One hand held a coiled rope.

Thyri trudged to her side.

'The storm you weathered at sea did not direct its fury at you alone,' Meg said, still watching the goat. It gave up its struggling and sat back on its hauches with a vulgar plop. 'They grazed this stretch bare long ago, and a good rain can leave the ground here like this for weeks.' She waded to the goat's side and tied her rope loosely around its neck. 'I could perhaps repair it' – she glanced at Thyri – 'but this sort of thing has a certain primitive charm.' She stood, smiling brightly and wiping a lock of hair from her face with the back of a muddy hand, streaking wet brown along on her cheek. Thyri laughed. The goat stared at them blankly.

Meg stepped back, breathed deeply, and started to pull on the rope. Thyri joined her, and together they hauled the animal out onto firmer ground. Meg untied it and it scampered away toward four sheep that grazed along the edge of the southern wood.

'Well,' Meg said, eyeing the splotches along her forearms. 'Shall we bathe? There is a hot spring a short way into the wood.'

The spring bubbled out of a rocky outcrop into a pool ten feet across, which itself ran into a briskly cold stream. Meg fell on the grass beside it and pulled off her boots, then took them to the stream where she knelt and forced them into the current.

Thyri looked up. Swallows swooped back and forth through the treetops above. A rabbit burst through a bush, hopped toward the spring, then noticed them and shot out of sight.

She sat at the edge of the spring and eased her feet into the water, brushing the mud away with long, critical strokes. The downy hair on her legs seemed lighter than usual, almost white.

The sorceress carried her dripping burden to the spring.

'Peaceful, isn't it?' she said, sitting next to Thyri. 'This is where I come to think.'

'Isn't it lonely?'

Meg laughed. 'You mean living here? By myself?' She dipped her boots next to Thyri's feet, than laid them aside on the grass. 'What is loneliness, Thyri? She rose and pulled her shift over her head. 'I have a peace of a sort in my heart.'

Thyri looked up. Meg's hair dangled freely around her waist. Her nipples tightened under the caress of the open air.

Thyri's senses heightened, responding to the nearness of Meg's pale flesh. The sorceress moved then, thrusting the triangle of soft black hair between her thighs into Thyri's view. She dived into the spring, leaving Thyri's senses reeling, her mind raging chaotic war with itself. She closed her eyes and saw her hands touching those lean thighs, probing their secrets. And she imagined her claws springing forth, gouging to the bone, spraying the morning red.

And then, without warning, Megan's eyes . . . a feeling of calm, peace.

You fear for nothing, little one.

A hand on her foot, tugging playfully, then forcefully, pulling her off the rocks and into the hot, steaming water.

Your body is ever your own, except when the moon comes.

She found herself floating, her hair tickling her face. Deft hands slid her shift over her head.

And even then you are lost only if you believe it so.

Thyri surfaced. Meg's playful smile fell away. Hesitantly, she reached out and traced the inner curve of Thyri's shoulder with her fingertips. She kicked forward, melting their bodies together. 'Let go of your fears,' she whispered. 'Your curse cannot touch us here.'

Later, Thyri lay back on the grass, watching the clouds break overhead, picking out shapes of eagles and bears and watching one cloud transform itself from the profile of a warrior with shield into the laughing face of an impish hill giant.

She lay where Meg had placed her, her head in the center of a circle of squat, gray, undressed stones. She could still feel the wetness of her hair behind her ears. The tang of sorcery filled her sixth sense – Meg's spell, to teach her Irish.

The sorceress sat before a small incense brazier behind Thyri's head. Flowers and shallow bowls of oily liquids were set around her. She hummed softly, occasionally touching damp fingers to Thyri's forehead. In her lap was a small harp. She built her hum into melodious song and her fingers danced lightly on the harp's stings. The music gripped Thyri, possessing her until the sky grew dreamlike and the ground under her giving, as if made of down rather than earth. Meg's song had no words, but it spoke of bright truths: of happiness shared among men; of the warrior with raised, open palm and friendly eyes.

Of moving lips. Of lips moving.

The perception of a mouth.

The pictures grew. Red, moving lips. Sentences returned: *She had moving, speaking, lips. She-lips that moved and spoke had . . . Lips moving had she (waving tongue and voice in her throat – she spoke) The woman spoke . . .*

Vision grayed, the lips fading to crimson-limned shadows, the last sentence echoing: *The woman spoke, spoke, woman spoke, spoke, man spoke, woman spoke . . .*

The thought-language wasn't Norse. Not any language. I have no tongue, she thought. The lips were solid again and they smiled. *Move to her ear! Speak softly of the beauty of sunrise in no tongue, in every tongue.*

Language if given, only speech changes.

The lips grew, grinned, and opened, swallowing her. A melody – not Norse – of a farm boy cursed with the love of a lady weaved in tragic tempo through the altar halls of the sun. She heard it; she cried. Her tears filled with honeysuckle and moonlight. They fell through her, and she dreamed.

Departures

'We are on the north side – here.'

Megan pointed to a nondescript spot on the parchment map of Kaerglen Isle over which she and Thyri bent. The island was roughly pear-shaped with a short peninsula in the southwest. 'In the southeast corner is Castle Kaerglen. The isle is well populated within a day's ride of it. With a good horse, you can get there in a day and half.'

'Why do you live so separate from them, Meg?'

Two days had passed since Thyri had first wakened. She already felt strong; she had managed some fair sword-practice that afternoon.

'I do not enjoy their company, and they fear mine.'

'Why?'

She smiled. 'I'm a witch.'

'But your skill can be of much use to them. Surely the king can use you?'

Thyri spoke carefully, in Irish. To her amazement, Meg's spell of the day before had worked, as if it had opened a room in her mind that craved to be filled with new words, new ideas. Meg had explained that the spell had provided a structural basis upon which they needed only add vocabulary, and this process had been aided by further sorceries. Thyri felt she already knew Irish better than Latin, and she'd spent years laboring to master *that* tongue's script under Scacath.

'The king distrusts sorcery. He has his reasons. On the peninsula, here, in the South,' Meg said, pointing again to the map, 'lives Pye, the wizard of the Blue Moon. He is Kaerglen's cousin – once was his adviser. Now they are bitter enemies. The wizard desires Castle Kaerglen, and one day, I think, he will take it.'

'Why?'

'He is powerful, very cunning, and his soul has turned black. He has no army to speak of, only what beasts he conjures from time to time, but he has repelled every one of Kaerglen's attempts against his grove. Or his army's attempts – he rarely involves himself in military matters. I've tried to offer him my aid, but he refuses it.'

'Why?'

'He has advisers who tell him to distrust all mages, whatever their power or motive.' Meg took the parchment map, rolled it up, and handed it to Thyri. 'Take this with you. You will need to know the lay of the land six days hence.'

'I will stay with you, Meg, if you wish. You saved my life.'

She laughed. 'Stay? While your body screams out for blood? You are a warrior, and every part of you wants to seek service for your sword. Kaerglen, though not very bright, is an honorable man. He rules with a gentle hand; it is his advisers who lead him astray. But you can aid him. You want to aid him. You also want to dangle the point of your sword before Pye and force him to tell you the nature of the Moon Mysteries. Tell you how you might be rid of your curse. His assumed title mystifies you, doesn't it?'

Thyri looked down at her hands.

'I'm sorry, Thyri. Don't think that I'm reading your mind, because I'm not. You intrigue me, and I see well the people who intrigue me. I asked the last question for another reason – a warning. Do not let him tempt you. There is no cure for the beast within you.'

'No . . .'

Meg smiled at her sadly. 'You can leave tonight. I will conjure a gate for you. There is an inn at Kaerglen called the Blooded Boar. In stepping through the gate, you will step through the front door of the public house. You should find the Captain of the Kaerglen Guard there – a man by the name of Cuilly. Impress him, and you will find service for your sword. It will not be easy; the sword is a man's toy here.'

'So is it elsewhere, with a few exceptions.' Thyri placed her hand lightly on Meg's, then ran it slowly up her arm.

Megan Elana Kaerglen. If ever I encountered one as enigmatic as Thyri, it was she. I have no proof, but I doubt Thyri would ever have seen Kaerglen's shores were it not for the sorceress. Whatever her ultimate purpose, Meg drew her here.

Wildfire

Thyri forced her way in through the crowded tavern tables. She wore her sables over a light leather jerkin, and she wore the boots she'd lined with the skin of a rabbit she'd killed long ago. Her sword swung prominently at her side. The inn was full of noise, but all of it died by the time she reached the bar. The innkeep stared at her questioningly.

'Mead,' she said.

'Let me buy for the costumed whore!'

A loud, adventurous voice behind her.

Several men laughed. Thyri turned and laughed back, the torchlight casting a dark shadow in her teardrop scar. 'Save it for the goats,' she said.

She took her mead and paid the innkeep, then turned back to the crowd. Most in the house were soldiers. She scanned them, looking for Cuilly by Meg's description. She found him in the corner, drinking with whom she guessed were two lieutenants; he watched her like the others. She smiled coyly when their eyes met.

A large man, goaded by the others, rose and approached her. 'Are you the one with the mouth?' Thyri asked.

'You have no manners, girl,' he said, stopping in front of her. 'I'm going to teach you a lesson.'

Thyri laughed and glanced at the blade at his belt. 'Won't you use your sword?' She placed a hand on the hilt of her own.

'Against a whore?' He lunged, barely managing to stop as Thyri whipped her blade from its scabbard and leveled it at his throat. He backed away slowly. The men behind him jeered.

'Draw your sword, goatherd.'

The fear of what he saw in Thyri's eyes had not yet overcome his bravado. He went for his blade. As he brought it up, she smashed hers down, landing a crushing blow on his hilt. He winced in pain. He lowered himself for a lunge, but a hand fell on his shoulder from behind, and Cuilly pushed him aside.

'Who are you, woman?' he asked, glaring.

He was tall and brawny. Thyri knew the type: fairly levelheaded, she could see it in his dark blue eyes. A commander by virtue of wit *and* ability. But only so much ability – he hadn't taken this wizard who afflicted his king.

'Who wants to know?'

'I am Sean Cuilly. I command these men.'

'Well, then, Sean Cuilly. I am Thyri Eiriksdattir. I wish to join these men.'

He laughed. 'Where did you get that sword, wench? If the smith put you up to this, I'll personally flog him.'

'You're not very quick-witted, are you, Sean Cuilly? Can you not see that this blade is finer than any your men bear?' She waved it in his face.

He eyed her distrustfully. 'Leave, girl. I'll not have you disrupt my men.'

Thyri matched his gaze and shifted into a relaxed fighting stance. 'Perhaps you would like to throw me out?'

Cuilly touched the hilt of his sword, then glanced at the man he had pushed aside. He was on the floor, still wincing, nursing his hand. 'She knows what she's doing, Cap'n.'

Cuilly laughed after a moment and looked back at Thyri. She smiled, saluting him with her blade.

'Do you really want to live with this rabble?'

'I have some silver. I shall stay here.'

'We muster at dawn each morning.'

'So? I'll be there. I will enjoy teaching your rabble how to spar.'

'Will you?' He laughed. 'Come, let me refill your mug. You can tell me how a girl masters the sword.'

They drank and talked of weaponry and war. She told him of longboat raids into Germany with Astrid. They spoke of technique and strategy, and Cuilly's respect for her grew as the night wore on. But she would speak only of battles and courage. Of her presence on Kaerglen Isle, she would say nothing.

That puzzled Cuilly. Outsiders seldom found the mist-shrouded island. The legends said that the mists could foil armadas. He had grown up believing them. The only merchant vessels that could find the isle easily were native. But now this woman with laughing eyes and a blade that looked forged in some hell pit had simply shown up out of nowhere.

And the blade was well trained. Its mistress floated in his mead-laden vision, speaking of experiences that paled anything he had seen on his island. Before the night was up he offered her the wage and barracks of a lieutenant. Even if she couldn't fight, he reasoned, she surely talked a great battle.

What else were lieutenants for?

Dawn was hazy with the light rising in bands of deep red coursed with orange rivers, teasing the paling blue overhead. Thyri breathed in the air and stomped about the traning field, getting the feel of its earth into her feet. She drew her blade and tested it against the morning.

On the crest of a hill high above her she could just see a corner of the castle – the seat of the island's power. She wondered if the royal family had risen as early as she or if they lay still in their down beds, dreaming the dreams granted only those born to rule.

The practice field was skirted by barracks on two sides and the quarters of the officers on another. The side facing the castle was left open for parades and demonstrations. For the moment, the field was hers alone. She danced around it in a system of attacks and parries, imagining a formidable foe as fast as she. She imagined his sword longer than hers. She imagined his strength greater.

Men began to emerge from the barracks, yawning, rubbing sore eyes and heads while their stomachs rebelled and vented foul fumes into the air. They watched Thyri's sword-dance. Some laughed. Most watched her dully through glazed eyes, occasionally looking away when the rapid flashings of her blade grew painful.

Thyri fought on until she slew her invisible foe. She eyed the disordered ranks of the men before stamping off to lean against the officers' barracks, gathering in her sables against the cold. For a moment the men continued to watch her, then the door behind her creaked open and the field sergeants barked their charges into line.

Cuilly came out while his lieutenants marched through the ranks. He stopped next to Thyri and squinted into the morning haze.

'I will not help you,' he said, rubbing the stubble on his chin. 'They must see you for themselves. There are those among them who feel that strength of sword alone should make them commanders. Others are wiser. But you start at a disadvantage with them all.'

She scratched idly in the dirt with the toe of her boot. 'I have commanded men before, Captain.'

'Yes,' he said, starting away. 'But it was never easy, was it?'

His small army settled, Cuilly announced with deadpan seriousness his recruitment of Lieutenant Thyri Eiriksdattir. The ranks rippled with comments and muffled laughter. Thyri sought among them the man she had put down the night before in the Blooded Boar. He laughed along with the rest.

Cuilly surveyed them. His command voice boomed out, loud and strong: 'Those among you who have something to say on this – come forth and speak your minds!'

The men were for a moment taken aback. They shifted; their captain's gaze was hard and icy. Those of uncertain conviction began to fall silent.

'Respec'fully, Cap'n.'

A short, brawny swordsman sidestepped from the sergeants' line. His eyes were alert, his features patiently intense and scarred by many years in his chosen profession. 'Even if she's more'n she looks,' he continued, 'as I heard went on at the Boar last night, she can hardly be expected to stand well in the field. Few fancy moves is one thing. Womens got no stamina. Can't keep a good hilt grip for more'n a minute at a time.'

The sergeant drew raucous approval from his men.

The captain smiled wryly. 'Well voiced, Duagan. Step farther to the flank.' He turned to the others. 'Any who think the same and are prepared to back their thoughts with blood may join this man!'

The declaration further disrupted the assembly. When all motion had stopped, eleven men stood behind Duagan, some as scarred and seasoned, others young and arrogant.

'Well met,' Cuilly said to them. 'We shall spar this morning. He who defeats Lieutenant Eiriksdattir shall gain a week's liberty at the brothel of his choice.'

Smiles behind Duagan. Moans from the massed ranks – a few tried to break and join the contestants; their sergeants forced them back into line.

'I'd rather bed the lieutenant, with all due respect, sir.'

A broadly grinning youth among her foes. Thyri placed him at twenty, maybe a year more. He was tall and lanky, sporting a disheveled blond mop. His gestures were lazy and slightly clumsy. Her gaze fell placidly on his. He grinned, but Thyri's unblinking pressure shortly turned his eyes.

'You may petition her first for that privilege, soldier,' Cuilly said.

'Duagan oughta be first!' someone protested.

'She oughtn't get to use that sword, Cap'n,' another said. 'Switch says it glows evil. Says it's what beat 'im last night.'

'What matters a woman with *any* sword,' Cuilly countered, 'to a week with the best port whores, paid by the king's gold?'

The men laughed heartily and Thyri broke her long silence: 'Let you each choose your weapon, it matters not to me except that we are matched. I tire of this foolish chatter.' She looked them over slowly. 'But let each of you say now that, should you lose, you will consent to my command.' She glanced at Cuilly. 'Any who refuse this should be returned to the main ranks.'

Cuilly appraised her anew. Of all things, he hadn't

expected this. The challenge had attracted the worst, the most headstrong, hardened, and foolish of his men. Eight of the twelve had been before him to answer for incidents requiring his disciplinary hand – stolen chickens, brawls in both city and port. Duagan himself had once led a drunken band of soldiers against the crew of an English merchantman that had rested overly long in the port.

And she wanted to command them? 'Well?'

Slowly, each man nodded. None refused Thyri's demand. Cuilly looked at her. *Who are you, woman? Where did you come from in truth?* 'Each battle,' he shouted, 'to first blood or submission by mace or staff! Fall out!'

Thyri unclasped her cloak and stepped forward into the spreading circle of men. The youth who had spoken out moved to face her. She raised an eyebrow.

'Swords,' he declared. 'I am afraid of no blade.'

Thyri shrugged, drew Astrid's sword, and closed on him. He charged. Iron clanged against iron as she met his blow. She brought her knee up sharply, into his stomach. He bent in pain.

'You are careless, young warrior.' She smashed her pommel down on his sword hand and the weapon clattered to the ground.

Thyri backed off. The youth straightened painfully, glaring at her.

'Submit,' she said.

He grunted. 'First blood,' he muttered, grasping his blade. 'So said the cap'n.'

A moment later he retired from the field, a long, slashing wound across his right breast, just over the nipple.

The next man fought with knives. She marked him in the same place as the last and then it became a game to her – marking each man in turn on his right breast. None declared an unedged weapon against her. As the morning wore on, the crowd began to cheer. Some of the soldiers, however, grew afraid. Whispers of sorcery surfaced anew.

Duagan was the last. He swaggered out to face her, drawing his sword in salute.

'Will you wear my mark as well, Sergeant?'

'Aye, mistress. I'll spar w' you.' He looked to Cuilly, then to the awed soldiery. 'But not for any whore or e'en the crown on yon hill! These eyes never seen a blade worked so well or so quickly. And eleven men afore me! Woman's got stamina more'n the lot o' you!' He grinned at Thyri. 'I'll be yer right hand. Be you woman or demon, I'll die for you if ye'll have me.'

She faced him, her stained blade lowering. He looked like a tough, wildly grinning bulldog. Tears rose to her eyes.

Duagan charged, swinging wide. 'No tears now, woman,' he grunted as he closed. 'Ye'll lose all ye've gained.'

She recovered and faced him again. Grinning yet, Duagan ripped away his jerkin and bared his chest. He drew a knife from his belt and put the point to his flesh, drawing it slowly up and around. He cast Thyri one last bemused look before turning on the soldiers.

'What're you staring at? Game's over – move your legs! Been slouching all morn. Ye're going soft.'

From the side, Cuilly looked on. He watched Thyri take up her cloak and clasp it; then she approached him, with Duagan, marked by his own blade, at her side. Cuilly began to wonder just what it was he'd done.

For the next few days he could hear her from dawn through dusk, shouting at them, laughing with them. Cuilly left her alone. As long as she returned them to their barracks too worn to cause trouble, he didn't mind.

It was the king who truly troubled him. The full moon approached and Pye's power would reach its height. Already, the steady sorcerous onslaught kept the king abed. If the wizard's hold did not break soon, Coryn would die, leaving the island to either the wizard or Queen Moira. Neither prospect sat well with the captain of the guard.

Since the king's cousin had retreated into his groves, Cuilly had managed nothing. When he fared into the wood, demons rose from the ground to slay his men. The wood would not burn. Those who lived to return from it came always with no news of Pye's exact whereabouts. What good then was his new lieutenant and her tamed maniacs?

Blue Moon

'. . . an' that's the whole of it, mistress.'

Duagan sat back and took up his flagon. Thyri sat across from him, drawing patterns in spilt mead with the point of a dagger. She drained her flagon thoughtfully.

'Among that wood,' she said, 'I can find him.'

'An' kill him? He will not meet us with iron.'

She hailed the innkeep to refill their flagons. 'I do not fear death, Duagan. In many ways I desire it.'

'Then we'll tell the cap'n. He'll be ready to try anything now. Moon goes full night after t'morrow.'

'No. He would lead us all in. Even should we succeed, many would die. And I doubt we'd succeed. A smaller force will carry with it surprise, and that is what we will need.'

Duagan grinned. 'Won't none of us fail you or betray you, mistress.'

Fresh mead came and Thyri paused to drink deeply. 'Can't all go. Some have to stay and make noise tomorrow morning. Can't let Cuilly catch on too soon or he'll do something stupid. And fewer travel faster, more quietly.'

'Ye'll not leave me behind.'

'No.' She smiled at him warmly. 'I never thought that. You I want, and one other. Modraig – the youth. He is very good with a bow.'

Duagan grinned and grunted. 'Modraig it is. I'll rail at the others to keep in line while we're gone.'

Thyri reflected on the past days as she supped alone that evening. She had garnered loyalty such as she'd never dreamed under Ragnar. In time, she thought, she could command them all.

The food went bland in her mouth. She'd nearly forgotten those last nights in her homeland. Amid fighting men, their swords, their boasts, and their brawling, she could almost believe all was well. It took her back to her days with Astrid. Before her curse.

I don't have time, she thought. *Unless Pye can help me, I don't have time.*

There is no cure for the beast within you.

She drained her flagon and spat. She went to her vanity box for her hair things and combed meditatively for a while before taking up her bead and starting to braid. Her knots were twenty-seven now. She did each slowly, eyes distant and reflective. And all the while she hoped that the night would, in one way or another, kill her pain.

They left an hour after nightfall, Duagan leading the way, with Modraig following and Thyri keeping rear guard. They went on horseback until far into the western forest; then they tethered their mounts and continued on foot.

Away from the steeds, Thyri stopped them and sat among shadows under a great elm, extending her senses into the land around her. She detected the calls of distant birds, smelt the passion fragrances of distant blossoms. She searched until she located what she sought: a faint but definite taint of sorcery. She rose, and led her party on.

Pye's grove was a dark, gnarled stand of oaks around which the surrounding forest was stunted and lifeless. Thyri stopped them in the last stand of healthy trees, beside a wide, lazy stream that passed along the edge of the desolation around the grove. All was silent within–no lights, nothing. The waxing moon peeped at them over the grove's top edge. Thyri forced herself to look at it. Though two days remained before its power would take charge of her form, she could already feel it calling to her, lovingly, menacingly. She sneered at it.

A thick, evil-smelling stretch of water issued from the

grove and joined the wider stream at which they had stopped. It was up this that Thyri led them into the oaks, her sword out and ready. Duagan and Modraig both carried light crossbows. Thyri held a small throwing ax in her left hand. From within, a discordant singing erupted. The wizard, Thyri hoped, casting his spell against Kaerglen, unaware yet that his domain was invaded.

She tried to think of a better plan than simply seeking out the voice, but further ingenuity failed her. She had no real estimate of Pye's talents (would that Meg were here! she thought, cursing herself for failing to ask more about the wizard before leaving). She could imagine them: trees with eyes, trees whose branches would come to life and strangle anything unrecognized, alien. For this reason she had chosen the stream. Foul as it was, she doubted it held anything more than filth. Filth could not kill, and it seemed logical that the stream would be less protected than the rest of the grove. Pye's powers had to have limits, and she hoped that he would think the stench of the stream deterrent enough.

They rounded a bend and Thyri bumped into the first body. It lay across her path, strangely bent, its bloated face evilly grinning up at her in the moonlight, its stench assaulting her nostrils full force. Its feet were caught up in the roots of a tree, and Thyri halted the others. She felt carefully around the morbid obstacle. Bits of flesh fell off bone and caught in the dead man's trousers – leather like Cuilly's men wore. Eventually, Thyri found what she sought: the man's right leg was bound against the roots with heavy rope. She smiled grimly. Pye had placed his guard there – a guard with nothing sorcerous about it, a guard of fear and revulsion.

She freed the body and pushed it around behind her. It floated slowly away with the current. Farewell, my friend, she thought. *You have served the wizard long enough.*

Modraig gagged as the rotting carcass that had once been a man went past him. When he fell silent, Thyri led them forward again.

They came on no more bodies until three more windings of the stream. The bed fell away under Thyri's feet, and she started to swim, then paused. Ahead, dimly visible in the moonlight, something loglike obstructed the surface of the water. Two more decaying human bodies lay end to end along the surface.

She tested the flow of the water. It still moved, slowly but relentlessly, its source probably a spring somewhere ahead. The bodies were being held by something. Between their lengths, they nearly spanned the stream. She signaled the others to wait, then silently pulled herself out of the water onto the bank.

She stood, dripping and squinting at what looked like a human dam. Behind the two, others were packed, floating facedown with the ones in the back bobbing lazily against the others. Most looked newly dead; she was glad that, except for one of the closest two, whose open eyes stared blankly downstream, they lay in the water the way dead should: facedown.

She was about to signal the others out when the water behind the dead men stirred and a thick, snakelike thing slithered over a body in the back and pulled it under. A moment later, several large bubbles broke the surface. Something was in the water – some pet of Pye's. The stream was probably blocked by a net that kept its food within easy reach.

Putting a finger to her lips, Thyri signaled Duagan and Modraig onto the bank. The singing increased in volume, keeping the same discordant, pulsating pace it had had before. Still unaware that we're here, she thought. She hoped.

The dark trees rose about them like sinister, silent ghouls. Thyri sensed magic everywhere now, its overpowering sensation a welcome but alarming change from the reek of the stream. A soft blue glow came from the direction of the voice. When Thyri moved, every step snapped twigs and crunched the leaves, setting her nerves on edge. Again, she signed for the others to wait, then set forth along the bank toward the lair of the thing in the water.

The trees suddenly gave way to a well-worn path that ended next to the human dam and wound away back toward the source of the light. It widened by the stream, and a short brick altar stood on the opposite side. Five decaying human heads stared out at her from niches in the altar's base. Thyri shivered. Shafts of moonlight cast shadows in the small clearing and on the stream. She didn't look up.

She went back for the others even though she'd begun to wish she'd come alone. They had gotten in so easily; she'd anticipated some sort of physical resistance. But they hadn't reached the wizard yet.

Before they gained the path, something cut the air behind them. Thyri spun and saw a dark shape sailing down through the trees at Modraig. She threw her ax and heard a satisfying thud as it bit into flesh. The thing fell to the ground, gurgling, weakly flapping leathery wings. She speared it with her sword, then freed her blade and ax and took to the path, hoping to reach Pye before encountering any more of his grove's denizens. As it was, the path went only a short distance before opening into a clearing that was the source of both the light and the singing.

The wizard sat there, his song unchanged, the blue light steady. He wore black robes, and his bald pate did not shine under the moonlight. They couldn't see his face because they were behind him. The blue light sprang from a ball of energy that hung crackling in the air before him.

She wished again that she'd come alone: she'd have put her sword to his neck, roused him from his trance and forced him to aid her. By herself, she would risk only her own life if she failed. Now she risked those of two others – not just any two, but two who had entrusted their lives to her. She hesitated only a moment before putting a hand on Duagan's shoulder. He raised an eyebrow, then bent quickly to one knee. He leveled his bow on the wizard and fired.

The bolt flew true, but before it could reach its mark, a

flare shot out of the blue globe and deflected it. It veered off and fell lifelessly to the ground a short distance away. Modraig shot. A flare caught his bolt and incinerated it in mid-flight.

Thyri cursed and charged. Pye's head turned slowly. She could hear crossbows hitting the ground behind her as the others followed, drawing their swords.

Pye's left hand came up and Thyri felt the air in the grove close around her and hold her back. She stuggled like a wildcat, making her way slowly forward, not caring that it wouldn't be fast enough. Pye rose from the ground, still in lotus. His body turned to face them. The blue fire lit his eyes.

He raised his hand again and it began to glow bluish silver, as if absorbing the moonlight. The ball sent flares out to the hand and it sucked them in, growing brighter still until the ball was no more and there was nothing there except that hand, shining like the moon. Light streamed out and flew past Thyri. Modraig screamed. She turned her head and watched flesh peel away from his skull under the hellish onslaught.

Another bolt and Duagan died.

The light turned on Thyri. She screamed, but it didn't destroy her. The agony stripped away her reason and she lost all thought of bargaining with Pye. Power coursed through her limbs. Her blade fell from her hand as pain shot up her sword arm. Silver links on the back of her gauntlet chinked lightly as they snapped. Her bones wrenched and warped, and the beast rose from within. Pye's face went white with terror.

Thyri grinned, her vision red and her soul wracked by consuming hunger. She leapt forward – fangs bared, dripping with saliva – and tore out the wizard's throat.

And then she fought herself. The beast, this time, did not have the fullness of the moon above it. From somewhere within, she lashed out and smashed it back down into oblivion.

Moaning painfully, she forced herself up to her hands and knees. Several hours had passed. Sunlight beat down on her; the chatter of morning in the forest was ominously absent. The grass around her was smeared with a pulpy redness. She moaned again as her stomach rose up in her throat and spilt red bile onto the ground.

Pye lay a short distance away, his body twisted, his head lying impossibly back along his shoulder. Two blackened, still-smoldering skeletons lay beyond him.

She staggered dizzily away from the carnage, finding a path opposite the one that went to the stream. It led her to a strange structure with walls formed of closely twisted yet living trees. Its ceiling was tightly woven of green branches. Braziers burned in it giving off noxious smells. She forced herself in and toppled the braziers onto the grassy floor. Hot fat leaked out and singed the grass. But it didn't burn; it only smoked blackly, making it difficult to breathe. Thyri pinpointed the tang of magic and snatched at it before leaving.

A pouch – three small gems inside of an aqua luster she'd seen nowhere before but in the sky. She tipped them back into the pouch and reached down absently to attach it to her belt, remembering only then that she was naked. She forced herself to return to the sight of the night's slaughter.

Her shift was in tatters, torn fully along the seam of one side. Behind it lay her cloak, apparently unscathed. Her gauntlet had a thin rip along its back. One of her boots had a wide hole in its side, the other was scratched up but untorn. The leather ties of her weapons belt had snapped. Swords and crossbows lay scattered where they had fallen. She tossed the pouch next to her cloak and turned back toward Pye's hut.

Inside, she groped with one hand, pinching her nostrils shut with the other until she found a long strip of leather. She went back to her things and sat to repair her shift and belt. Finished, she cut a thinner strip, spun it until it was like a stiff, thin strand of wool, and slowly threaded the links of her gauntlet back together. At noon, she set herself on a northeast path out of Pye's grove and into the forest. Against her thigh bounced a heavy sack containing the wizard's head.

Near evening she came to a road that paralleled the northern coast of the peninsula. She trudged along it, and slept settled into bushes alongside it that night.

The next day she entered farming land and saw a few travelers who eyed her strangely as she passed. She didn't speak to them; their field-hardened faces and bent backs recalled the grim realities that had been taken from her by Scacath. She watched a willowy young girl who labored under the weight of two buckets of milk. Milk splashed as she walked, making white spots that faded slowly into the dirt. There was a desperate, unforgiving defiance in her eyes.

Thyri watched her approach and saw herself as she might have been. Without my sword that is all I am, she thought. *All I would be. Wed, probably to a brawny, simple farmer. Happily, maybe – but no, never truly happy like that: enduring such hardship for the fleeting pleasures of nightly passions and too many children.*

Laboring under her load, the girl stumbled and fell to one knee. Thyri rushed to her, steadying the buckets before helping her ease them to the ground. Those defiant eyes glared at her. Thyri lifted one of the buckets to her lips, drank deeply, and walked on.

At noon she approached a farmhouse, showed the peasants Pye's head, and offered them a silver coin given her by Megan if they would feed her. It was more money than most of them had seen in one place. They fed her well, and one young man set off to inform the capital of Thyri's deed.

After eating, she set off north and stole a horse from the stable of a wealthy landowner. She ran it near unto death as she sped northward, seeking haven with the sorceress before sundown.

'I changed.'

'Early.' Meg poured water from a flask onto a rag to wipe

the grime from Thyri's face, then lifted her head and sloshed the remainder down her throat. She set the flask aside and glanced at the bloody bundle at Thyri's belt.

'The wizard's head,' Thyri said. 'He attacked me with magic born of moonlight.'

'His mistake.'

Thyri smiled darkly, then coughed. 'He had some gems in which I sensed power. In the pouch on my left side.'

Meg took the pouch and opened it. She examined the contents, then leaned down and kissed Thyri's forehead. 'Thank you.'

'I hoped you'd be pleased.'

'The beast didn't stay long?'

'Long enough to remind me how horrible it is. You cannot imagine its hungers.' *And the power it promises in return* . . . 'It took much from me to keep from feeding on the wizard's carcass.'

'It will be back tonight.'

'Yes.'

'Do not stray far. You will find plenty of game in the forest and there are shepherds a few hours to the southwest. Go there if you must, but stay far away from Kaerglen. Come back here after moonset. I will care for you as best I can.' Meg rose. 'Rest now, Thyri. I will wake you an hour before moonrise, then leave.'

You do not want to see it.

No.

In time, Thyri slipped thankfully into oblivion.

The three nights of the wolf came and went. Thyri roamed the countryside, killing and dining, all the while fighting with and hating herself and the menacing eye of the moon that glared down at her, watching, smiling. By day, she slept fitfully in the cool darkness of Meg's hut, her dreams full of blood and death.

Near the final dawn, she crept into the hut and onto the cot, the wolf feeling an agony as great as that she felt when she became it. The world began to swim, darkening before

Meg's touch drew her out. The sorceress leaned over her, brushing the hair from her face and pressing a damp rag to her brow.

I can't bear it, Meg.

I know.

Last night was the worst it's ever been.

It's over now.

Only for another month. I must do something. I have to go away again.

Why?

Because I can hardly control it. I could have hurt even you had you been here for the changes. I couldn't bear that. I have to find peace with it or rid myself of it entirely.

Where can you go? There is no escape.

West. West where the sun goes.

The moon goes there too.

But the change only works at night. I can hide in the sun.

She looked at Meg, crying, 'I have to try! Don't you understand? I have to!'

'Hush! I understand. Stay tonight. I'll gate you back to Kaerglen in the morning. If they won't give you a ship for killing Kaerglen's cousin, come back to me. I'll help you bring that castle down around their ears.'

Thyri smiled a shaky smile. *I'll come back.*

Kaerglen

She strode onto the practice field amid murmuring silence. Activity stopped, then suddenly all rushed into line at the shouts of their commanders. Cuilly came out of his quarters and saw her. When he reached the front of the formation, she awaited him, a wild madness in her eyes, a taunting slant in the way she stood. Her hair seemed longer, reaching far down the sables on her back. And it gleamed brightly under the sun and was streaked in places with fiery red and snowy silver.

A burlap bundle, stained with washed-out blood, hung at her side. She untied its string.

'The king is well?'

'Improving. Where have you been? We found the bodies days ago.'

'Long after I'd left. My men did well.' She smiled and looked for them in the formation. They were together, undispersed as yet. They stood to one side, and Dearen, a veteran of ten years, appeared to have taken Duagan's place at the front. He winked at her and smiled broadly. Tears for fallen comrades shed and dried. It was the way . . .

No!

She drew the head from the bag and dangled it before her, clumped hair gripped twisted in her fingers. She drew her sword and held it above her.

Heedless of their commander, the Kaerglen guard broke ranks and cheered.

Later, she sat inside his quarters. The raucous noise outside had faded to a bearable level. Cuilly was tired, worn somewhat by the celebrations of the past days. He'd had to disperse the men to calm them – set them free on the city. They *did* deserve it. Before, they had merely the knowledge that the wizard was dead. Now they had his slayer back among them.

He didn't share their joy. Deep inside, he feared her who sat at his conference table. To that, he could not admit. So he blamed his age: he was thirty-five that day.

He filled two finely wrought silver goblets from a glass flask and handed one absently to Thyri before sitting across from her.

She sipped: wine, certainly imported from lush valleys of far southern lands. The taste made her wish to someday go there and smell the air, the grapes growing fat and ripe where sun and soil were much kinder than in the North.

Cuilly downed one goblet and started on another. 'Where were you?'

'Lost. Wandering the woods. He cast some sorcery on me. I did not remember who I was until this morning.'

'You wandered for days with that – with Pye's head?'

She shrugged. 'It was a clue. I couldn't just throw it away.'

He filled both their goblets anew and sat back. 'I must take you to the king. He wishes to see you.'

'I want a ship, Cuilly. I have to leave.'

A light flickered in his eye. He no longer wanted her around. He didn't need her – not, at least, among his men. She would disrupt things. Especially since there was no foe left to fight. Deep inside, he feared for his command. But she would leave? 'What?'

'I want a ship. The fighting here is over. You don't need me anymore. Kaerglen must honor my demand.'

He smiled weakly. 'We shall speak to the king.'

Castle Kaerglen is old. Situated as it is upon the edge of precipitous cliffs that sink into a tumultuous sea, restricting approach from the south and east, it has long proved a valuable stepping-stone for military campaigns onto the mainland. The city lies to the north, at the foot of a steep slope. A gentler decline leads to the port in the west, itself protected by rocks and cliffs on either side.

A wall, ten yards high and eight thick, lies between the city and port, linking circular, slotted towers as ancient as the deepest shadows of the keep. Passage from one side to the other is conducted through two fortified gates. The guard was seldom present. The only archers vigilant in the purely defensive sections of the wall were the ghosts of those who had died defending it, or such is the story that a young woman from the city-side might have heard in dock-side haunts from sailors who didn't wish her to leave before morning.

From the libraries in the keep, this much can be gleaned: Kaerglen was touched many times during the ancient invasions of Erin.

The central structures of the castle were built by the Fomhoire who came first. They erected the brochs of the wall, filling the spaces with earthen ramparts. The defensive gesture was needless on their part as their conquest of the mainland was complete nearly before the final stone of the keep had been set in place.

Those Fomhoire who remained on the island later fell to the dark sons of Nemedh. These new invaders augmented the central works with rooms of their own before following their predecessors onto the mainland. They left a detachment which, after a period of time, abandoned swords and maces and cleared the woods in the south and grew barley. Yet even so, they did not forget the ways of battle. Twice they held the island against successive invasions – once after the Fomhoire intensified their bid for the mainland and again when new enemies, the demonic Fir Bolg, tempted their shores. Hastily constructed ramparts about the waist of the island thwarted assaults from the north. A few score archers placed in the towers consistently held ten times their number at bay. Both tribes, in the end, decided it wise to leave the sons of Nemedh alone. By the time the magic of Erin had spawned sorcerors and witches capable of aiding their armies, Kaerglen Isle had been forgotten.

Nothing changed until the Tuatha de Danann smashed the

Nemedians in a single, crushing blow. Manannan, son of Lir, lifted the sea up under the keel of *Wavesweeper* and battered the keep, drowning all within and cracking the foundation on the port side. Nuada and the other great lords washed over the island on mystical steeds shod with silver and bridled with gold, crushing all resistance. The island secured, they restored the keep and completed the wall. Most followed their predecessors on to Erin, but Manannan and his wife, Fand, came to call Kaerglen home. He augmented the ramparts and built the port wall. It is said that, in his time, the dark halls of the keep shone with a light of their own.

All things must pass. Over time, the children of Danu lost the mainland to the sons of Mil. Manannan, Fand and the others who had stayed on Kaerglen passed into – *otherworld* is the only fit name – with their kin. Yet Manannan cast enchantments still – when the sons of Mil later tried to reach the island they found only fog. So Kaerglen remained until Coryn Kaerglen's grandfather, Coryn mac Fain, arrived four score and seven years before Thyri Bloodfang set foot on the island. His story yet reeks of legend. It happened when the links between Midgard and *otherworld* remained strong:

Fand was wife to Manannan and among the fairest of all the Tuatha de Danaan. Her beauty – and her caprice – rivaled that of Edain. It is she whose heart truly illuminates Kaerglen.

Mac Fain was young, strong – a leader of that tribe in Western Erin named Connachta, a tribe that warred with itself as often as not.

It was Samhain Eve. The druidh were in their groves. Young virgins aspiring to sorcery had withdrawn into Erin's wild embrace, hoping in their passions to open gates that would bring them *otherworld* lovers, *otherworld* lords. They would dance naked under the moon, or drink arcane potions and swim in witch pools – many girls often drowned by this practice.

On this night, Fand walked the shadow paths along the edge of our world. She was a goddess with a goddess's heart. And in the way of deities before her, she saw mortal man and lusted. She appeared before Coryn mac Fain in flowing silks and the fairest flowers of *otherworld* spring in her hair.

He had wed the daughter of a neighboring chieftain. On that first night with the goddess, he abandoned his wife. Bloody war ensued. Manannan aided mac Fain's enemies and many mortals died.

And Fand grew enraged. She stole the great ship *Wavesweeper* from her husband and welcomed mac Fain and his people aboard. They fared west, and she gave unto mac Fain the island he named Kaerglen. None had touched its shores since she and Manannan had left.

Something must be said for the goddess. She stayed with the king she'd appointed, and she bore him five children before he died in 826 by the reckoning of the One God – after thirty-seven years of peaceful rule. Perhaps she indeed loved him. He, by his writings, worshiped her.

Had Thyri known this, she might have understood the island's strangeness. No man's roots in it extended past Coryn mac Fain's first step upon it. Before this, the strongest of the field and wood had ruled – the bear and the wolf. In the first ten years of his reign, the warrior from the mainland had purged those predators from his shores.

From the city, the castle is but a half-concealed edifice among the rocks above. The dark battlements are best found by running the eye along the edge of the port wall, then veering, at the end, a moon-width to the left. One might then see the kitchen tower over the crenellated, ballista-pocked battlements of the Nemedh. In good light, one can see a corner of the keep within. Little more.

The ground at the top of the slope rises first before falling to the level of the fortress. The port wall would, even without the natural barrier, block the seaward position of the castle from eyes in the city. Thus the view of the fortress does little to breathe fear into the hearts of enemies below whose major obstacle would seem to be gaining the crest of the hill – a fleeting goal, mist-eshrouded as often as not. The only road that leads there is on the seaside of the port wall.

To there, the Kaerglen Guard followed Thyri.

Cuilly had ordered an iron housing for the mutilated head of Pye. The cask was layered by tradition of the druidh with leaves of the sacred oak. Thyri's men bore it proudly as they rode through the city.

And a crowd of common men gathered, lining the road. They cheered, and they stared and whispered. Thyri sat proudly atop a dappled mare. She'd tied her hair back but otherwise it fell free, stirring, rippling in a lightly gusting wind. Her gauntleted hand rested on the pommel of the rune-sword, and her cloak parted at the side to let the scabbarded blade swing freely.

Through the port wall, she saw the eclectic fleet that formed the core of Kaerglen's sea power. She saw vessels with Norse lines: three merchantmen and two longships. Raiders, she assumed, that had strayed into the mists that hid the island from the rest of the world. Other ships dominated the force, strange ones both like and unlike the clumsy vessels of the Franks and Frisians – the handiwork of Kaerglen's own shipcraft. Many bore doubled masts, a feature Thyri had seldom seen and one which, in her mind, caused more trouble than it was worth: for scant increases in speed and maneuverability, the captain would pay dearly in manpower and would need more than one mouth to control the crew in battle. But Thyri watched them in the bay. They held some promise; they skimmed the waves nearly with the grace of longships, and this she had never imagined in a ship not built in her homeland. Her eye fell on one of the larger ones. It had two decked cabins – she would not need to remove the captain from his stateroom to give her the privacy she desired for the journey.

Next to the road, between it and the port, were the homes and hovels of sailors and fishermen. All were out to see her. She smiled at them and waved her silvered hand. They sang out to her, but she answered none save one: a little girl broke from her mother's grasp and ran in front of Thyri's horse. 'Look, mother!' she squealed. 'She has a sword!' She looked up at Thyri and tilted her head, squinting her eyes.

Thyri pulled up her horse and laughed, halting the procession. Cuilly's steed stamped restlessly next to hers.

'Is it real?' the little girl asked.

'Yes, little one,' she answered, 'it is real.'

The girl's mother screamed for her and Thyri bade her hear with a tilt of her head. The little one paused before she turned, beamed brightly, and scampered away. She'd been no older than four or five. For the remainder of the trip, Thyri called up the days of her youth and thought how like herself the little girl had seemed. And the girl's mother, too, like her own mother – impatient, demanding, assured that a woman's place is the home and that swords belong elsewhere. She felt a bitter sorrow even before her thoughts turned to the wolf, telling her that the sword had brought her a burden greater than ever a kitchen blade might.

The crowd followed halfway up the keep road, then Cuilly turned and bade them return home. He sent his army back as well, continuing only with Thyri and Dearen, who bore the iron cask containing with wizard's head.

At the crest of the hill, the castle thrust suddenly and fully into view. It caught Thyri up – the battlements spoke of ancient might and ancient fire, ages of perseverance. It stood there, pocked by ballista and catapult, yet ominously solid. She had never seen such an edifice, so forbidding a keep, so scarred a fortress. Not even the Franks and those other Southern peoples who claimed the dead heritage of the dead empire – not even they could boast of building walls so suited to discouraging assault. They built only with wood and earth – however impressive, their works held no light to Castle Kaerglen.

Riding closer, she saw the extent of the damage – the ruination left by the coming of the Tuatha de Danann. Though patched twice over, the battlements were a jigsaw sewn by ribbons of mortar, which crisscrossed back and forth without design. Once through the unguarded gatehouse, she saw the crack that marred the port side – the wound inflicted by the battle fury of Manannan. The stone had shifted several inches along the seam of the crack, reminding Thyri of the fault lines she and Astrid had discovered in the caverns the Dane Ottar had used during his short campaign against Ragnar (but that's another story). Some god, she thought, had built the fortress; another or the same had cracked it. No man could design such a structure in stone; no human force could cause such damage.

As written, they entered through a vacant gatehouse unchallenged. A lone thrush sat perched like a silent sentinel on the ramparts left of the gate. Thyri felt uneasy. This place, more a palace for gods than a dwelling of men, cried out for the singing of metal on metal and the raw bellowing of commanders testing the vigilance of their charges standing watch on the battlements.

Yet it was undefended, its army based on the outskirts of the city. So it had been throughout the 'war' with the wizard. The combatants had fought with weapons beyond the crudeness of the sword.

And she had won in a way that Scacath had never taught her.

Pye had never once left his grove. Never once sent a demon army against the capital. Thyri felt sorrow for Cuilly and his months bent to a task he could never execute. She felt sorrow for Meg, who probably could have done what she had by . . . *subtler* methods. She felt sorrow for the people of the island; they were probably as confused as she by the whole affair.

She thought again of the little girl, her innocent freedom that could only fade away, simmering slowly in a stew of ignorance and toil, waiting for the winds of time to take pity on her pain and carry her into oblivion. Even on this lost island that everywhere seemed, like Scacath's grove, to reach beyond Midgard, the lives of men proceeded unchanged. The soil kept its divinity secret, hidden from all she'd met except Pye and Meg.

But the king must have felt this, too. How could he not – he who ruled from this fortress built for gods, he who'd endured a power such as Pye's? Why on earth had he refused Meg's help?

The road into the keep, at least, showed signs of use. The occupants of the fortress still needed wares from the city and port. Thyri thought on this, realizing how popular a rule Kaerglen enjoyed, excepting the rebellion of his cousin. Merchants could, like she, come to the keep unopposed. Kaerglen did not fear his subjects. She asked Cuilly if he had ever trained his men to defend the fortress and he shook his head.

So why was it there?

Thyri shrugged off her questions and assumed that the keep was guarded in some manner, most likely as unbelievable as its actual presence.

A tethering bar, out of place in the general design, stood next to the main portal. Thyri cast her eyes about for a stable among the disused buildings littering the area between the battlements and the keep. She saw one that must once have housed horses, but it hadn't in recent years. Weeds had claimed the ground around it and the wood had rotted through in more than one place.

The three riders dismounted and tethered their steeds.

At the great wooden doors of the keep, Cuilly turned and signaled Dearen to hand Thyri the box.

A brass knocker shaped as a coiled serpent was set on the left of the double doors. Cuilly lifted it once and let it fall against the brass stop. The clang resonated deeply and Thyri listened to the echoes bouncing through the corridors within. The door swung open, revealing a slender, dark-haired woman with a delicately precise carriage. As old as Mother, Thyri thought, or as old as she would have been. But she showed little of the signs of middle age. Thyri doubted she'd gained a pound since her thirteenth birthday.

The woman stepped forward, allowing diffuse rays of sunlight to touch her face. Thyri adjusted her estimate of age more in the woman's favor. The creases beside her eyes had not fully taken root. Her skin had that dull pallor of those who seldom fare into the sun; its lack of color amplified the doughy indistinction of her features. Her eyes were a dull gray.

She flashed Thyri a formal smile, then looked to Cuilly.

He cleared his throat. 'I have brought her, my queen.'

The broken silence forced Thyri fully into the present, and the woman looked suddenly *too* erect, as if her poise required conscious effort while her shoulders fought to bow under the weight of years.

'Good,' she said, smiling again in the manner of those both used to decorum and despising it.

Thyri smiled back. She could not fault the woman for her curtness – Thyri herself held the customs of men born of position in contempt. Through ritual and decorum, one needed never to think or feel for oneself.

The royal smile warmed a little, acknowledging Thyri's response. 'You are welcome here. My husband will be pleased to speak with you, woman of the cold lands.'

'Thyri Eiriksdattir, Queen Moira.'

'Very well, Thyri. Come in.'

She entered. Cuilly followed and began to close the door.

'Bring your man in, Captain,' the queen said. 'You and he can keep the wine company while Thyri speaks with Coryn. He would speak with you after, but he would first meet his cousin's slayer alone.'

The castle was lit where needed by candles held in brackets set in the walls. The queen took one from its place and quickly led Thyri past the entrance into darkened halls. Cuilly stayed in the first room, which was furnished with couches and cabinets displaying the rare elixir of the South, decanted after the fashion of those wealthy peoples whose smiths fashion glass. Once away from Cuilly and Dearen, the queen began to speak. Thyri's concentration flashed between the words and her wonder at the internal architecture of the keep – and she was counting the openings passed as well.

She had never imagined such a structure in stone. She had never set foot in any but the most meager of stone buildings though she'd heard much of great works far to the south among the debris of the old empires. Vacant monuments in the scattered necropoleis of the centuries. In Castle Kaerglen she felt strength – the strength of the bones of Ymir from which Odin and his brothers had grown the mountains. She felt also strength in the spaces, in the air, the realm of Thor and the Valkyries. As she set each foot down on the stones, Thyri set it into two worlds.

And she sensed other things as Kaerglen's queen led her deep into the keep. She felt a familiar tingling rise and fall, ebb and flow. And the tang was powerful, permeating the castle. She knew not whether it came from the stones themselves or from things hidden in the spaces between them. She hadn't, since departing the glade of Scacath, felt the presence of such powers so strongly – not around Meg, not around Pye.

Along with the counting and the sensings of magic and dichotomous existence, the words of the queen came relentlessly to Thyri's ears, flowing with scarcely an interruption:

'I hope the halls are not too dark for you, though I think your eyes should soon adjust.

'We could have more light if we wished to employ one to tend the flames, but I enjoy tending them myself.

'I prefer to think this place a home, a house for the family rather than a fortress. But there is so much space beyond our quarters. All this . . .

'I think someday I'll have Coryn convert this entire wing into a chapel so that Brenden might do his work in a place that mirrors His glory. It's either that or a cathedral in the city – out of the question, I think, due to a lack of strong backs.

'Brenden wants to start a monastery in the North, but I keep telling him that this island is not like Erin and England. It is small and contained and as such can be consecrated from shore to shore to His glory.

'I think he's depressed – Brenden, that is – because in all our years here we are little further than we were before we began. But that was mostly Coryn's cousin's fault, and you killed him, didn't you?

'Oh, but I forget you are heathen. I *did* know that. Sean

told me you are Norse and I know something of your ways. You worship the Wodin or something, if I remember correctly. It's a pity – we should talk deeply on this, but that's something for another time.

'Those are the children's rooms down that hall there, and beyond are a few more I keep up for reasons I can no longer explain. We have guests so seldom.

'I wonder that we don't hear Tana and Seth at play. But no, that's right – they'd be in the garden with Brenden now, learning their letters. Very important, that. Necessary for understanding His word. I think Coryn should destroy all those pagan writings he keeps in his library, but he insists on having them. And who am I to command the king?

'Down that hall are the rooms of Coryn's mother's sister and brother. They keep to themselves mostly. I really don't think they like me much, my being from the mainland.

'Just up here are our rooms. Ah, here we are.'

As the queen spoke, Thyri began to understand her. The words lacked ceremony and were like the idle ramblings of one common wife to another (an extreme comparison, but valid, regardless of the occupations of the two women involved). Thyri's hostess was concerned with showing the details of her life, but these intricacies soured in Thyri's ears, both for their triviality and for the queen's zeal for the Cult of the One God. Behind the talk, Moira sought a confidante – one whom she felt she could find only in another woman (in spite of the sword at Thyri's side and the severed head of Pye in the box). To this desire, Thyri attributed the queen's sudden change of mood. Nothing else could have given rise to such an outpouring.

The king was abed, convalescing. His cheeks were bright, and his eyes had begun to shine with health – if still with lassitude as well. A matted mane of long brown hair fell from his head and spread about his shoulders and the silken pillow against which he rested. The room had yet the odor of illness and medicine; Thyri knew this before entering, for the smell permeated the outer corridor.

When Moira ushered her in, Kaerglen's gaze was fixed on that point outside the world where the seen is but a reflection of the mind of the seer and the world carries on around it as if a dream. The king did not look up at her entrance; it took Moira's voice to shatter his reflections.

'I have brought the one who killed your cousin, Coryn.'

'What?' He looked at Thyri. His face was not overly creased. He was fifty-five that day. Awareness came slowly, but he smiled.

'Thank you, Moira. Leave us.' He paused, allowing his wife to nod and exit. As she did, Thyri opened the lid of the box and lifted out the wizard's head.

Kaerglen grimaced, motioning her to put it back. 'Yes, that was once my cousin. No more.'

The room was furnished moderately, with the bed and several chairs to the side as well as a large wardrobe carved of oak and a table upon which doubled candles granted the king light for reading. Beneath the candles lay a book. Thyri squinted at the worn cover but found that no title graced it – just an ornate gilt design with no meaning to her.

The king watched her. 'It is Moira's. She insisted I have it by me, as if it could protect against Pye's magics. It was quite useless. Please, have a seat.' He indicated a chair by his bed.

Thyri put down the box and sat. She reached for the book, letting it fall open where it may. The script was Irish. She recognized it but could not read – Meg had not taught her written skill in the tongue. She shrugged and set the book back, looking at the king. 'The lore of the One God?'

'Yes. Does it interest you?'

'I know nothing of it.' She paused. 'I think not – not in a direct sense, though I find its effects interesting in a way.'

'I can see that I needn't try to educate you. This is good,' he said, smiling more brightly. 'I know nothing of it.'

'The One God is not your god?'

'No.'

'But he is your queen's?'

'Yes.'

'And you allow that? Is this how his influence spreads? How he wars with Odin in Midgard?'

'Perhaps. Perhaps it is good.' He sighed. 'I do not know. I am sure of little anymore except that I love my wife and see her goodness. And the gods of my family here – Dagda, Brigid, Lugh, the Morrigan, and the rest – they have brought curses upon us, though it was through them that my grandfather came here and came to rule here. Perhaps through Moira and her god my children will be spared my pain.'

'But not you. You know nothing of this god.'

'No, he is not real to me. I know only the children of Danu. I have seen them, or those few that yet remain near our world. They grow wild, and the One God has driven them from the mainland and they grow bitter with hatred. They cannot fight him, so they take their pain out on my family.'

'I do not understand.'

The king reached out and laid a hand on Thyri's. 'You cannot understand as I do because you are from the cold lands and your gods are yet strong. Mine fade, and I am given the task of helping them do so quickly so that my people do not suffer as greatly as they might.'

Thyri thought of Meg and thought how the sorceress wielded powers such as Scacath had. They did not seem powers granted by fading gods. 'I think you take it upon yourself. The One God and his cult can be fought. They must be fought.'

'If so, you killed one of the more serious threats to his domain. Had Pye killed me, he would have taken the throne and grown armies here with which to assail Erin. Many would have died, and Kaerglen Isle would have fallen to the wrath of those who hold power in the East. And then the little magic that remains in these rocks would go away.'

'Is that not what you want – to help it go away quickly?'

'Yes, but without great suffering. Pye's way, because he did not see the inevitability of our defeat, would have caused indescribable pain.'

'So the pain of war is a greater evil than the pain brought by the slow passing of your gods. Wars end, but it would seem to me that forsaking the future is eternal.'

'I do not forsake my future. But the Tuatha de Danann yet fade.'

The king grew distant, silent.

'It is war that is eternal,' Thyri said.

'Because you are a warrior, you see through your sword.'

'No, I see with my eyes. I see men with my eyes, and I see war in the eyes of men.'

Kaerglen smiled oddly. 'And in the eyes of women. You would have sided with my cousin had you known more of the stakes of our conflict?'

'No,' she said. But not, she thought, for any of the reasons he had given. It had been Meg's tasking – her desire that he have aid. If not from her then from her friend.

'Then why the disagreement?'

'Perhaps I only wish to learn the heart of the man I served.'

'You still have a place in my guard. You might *become* the Guard in time.'

'I am a warrior, but the wars of your island are done for me now. I have a quest of my own.'

'And?'

'I must go west,' she said. 'I must follow the sun.'

The king's eyes grew distant again. 'To Bri Leith, where the Tuatha de Danann go now to dwell – but no, you will no longer find that isle in this world.' Then he smiled at her. 'Take any ship in my harbor. But no more than three.'

'I need only one. Fully manned.'

'It is yours. But not until spring, woman of the cold lands. I will not give you men to take into winter. You cannot survive a week on the seas as they are now. Any crew I give you knows that. They would kill you before straying a day from my shores.'

Thyri had known this in her head, if not in her heart. It struck home then – the realization that she had to endure four, probably five, more cycles of the moon before she could begin to seek a haven. She felt Kaerglen's eyes on her and imagined he could see the beast under her skin.

But he still smiled in his way – a sad smile, one vacant of the potency to promise comfort. She lowered her eyes.

'Your quest must be urgent,' he said. 'The edge of your words hints at urgency as if you wished to leave tomorrow and forget the seasons. You do not appear one who would neglect such details.'

'You have great insight, my king.'

He laughed now. 'I am not your king. But I may be a friend. Call me Coryn. Your sword has given you that right. All that I have is yours.'

The loaded but necessary pledge from the saved to the savior – Thyri understood this and knew its traps. *All you have? Your island, my king?*

What she did not desire . . .

Rather she would ask him to raise the dead and purge the foul blood that burned in her veins – two things she knew were beyond him. 'Just the ship. The largest of your merchantmen.'

'You ask little. You will need a place to winter. Stay here. This place has more to offer than might first seem.'

'I have a friend on the north end of the island. She saved *my* life. She talks like she knows you. She calls herself Meg.'

He picked up the book and looked at the cover, absently tracing the faded design. 'Yes, I know that name. Megan. She yet lives alone? She is still beautiful?'

'Still beautiful, but no longer alone. At least for the winter.'

Kaerglen looked up, setting the book back on its table. 'I see. Well, stay the night at least. I have a library. You read, if your interest in Moira's book is any indication. Greek? Latin? Your own people have no writing, no?'

'We do of a sort. I can't read it.' The runes, she thought. 'I read Latin.'

'Then my library contains much you may find of interest. Translations from Greek: Plato, Aristotle, Euripedes – many others who wrote a millenium ago. Many wrote of the gods, the ones the empire took into itself. The ones that fell first to the power of the One God.' He paused. 'You are free to seek knowledge and comfort here. As you are free to come and go as you please throughout the winter.'

'Thank you, Coryn, I will stay the night. I would like to see your library.'

'Good. Moira!'

The door swung quickly open and the queen entered. Thyri guessed she'd heard, her ear to the door, all that had passed. 'Yes?'

'We have spoken. Prepare a room for this woman for the night. And anything else she desires, perhaps a bath. Show her the library as well.'

Moira nodded and beckoned for Thyri to follow her out. At the portal, Thyri turned back to smile at the king. 'Thank you for the ship.'

He shrugged. 'Thank you for my cousin's head. Take it with you. Have Cuilly burn it.'

Patrick

After taking Thyri back to the entrance hall, Moira led Cuilly in for his audience. Thyri gave Dearen the cask and asked him how fared the men. Well, he told her. He could think of little more to say, and Thyri volunteered nothing. The queen returned shortly to take Thyri to the library.

Walking again through the halls, she wondered further on the source of the magic and wondered if Meg knew. The witch *did* know Kaerglen. Kaerglen knew her, knew about her.

The library did not contain the answer – at least not in a form that she could read. The books and scrolls were arranged within three oaken cabinets, each covering a wall of its own. In the center of the room was a large desk with several candles that Moria lit for Thyri before leaving her alone. Between the candles Thyri found a neat stack of parchment and a quill pen. Looking at them, she thought of Astrid and the letter Hugin had brought to her while she was still under Scacath's wing. Burned now, in the fires of her brother's hall. Or perhaps Erik had saved it.

Many strange scripts marked the bindings of most books on the shelves. From those she recognized, she chose Aristotle's *Metaphysics*. 'All men, by nature, desire to know,' it began, and the ancient sage proceeded to tell her what to know.

She scanned the pages rapidly, realizing that, if the book were any indication, the gods of the dead empire were killed not from without by the Cult, but from within. She had no interest in pursuing the argument presented once she'd found this fault at its heart. She put the book back and took a survey of the empire's gods from the shelves. In this book, she spent the afternoon.

Late in the day, Moira interrupted her reading to say that dinner would be soon served and that she would send her son for Thyri when the hour came. In the few minutes left her, Thyri took up quill and parchment and wrote:

Dearest Cousin,

I make, at last, a reply. Would that you could read it. My blood burns for the past.

Thyri Moon-Cursed.

She folded the parchment and set it between the pages of the book in the section that told of Diana the Huntress – the mother of Scacath, by Astrid's reckoning. The link to Astrid was slender, imagined more than real. Yet to Thyri, those pages between which she folded the parchment bore her own sadness in their words. The note was her message back through them – to Astrid, to Scacath, to those gods who had reigned before Odin. She mourned them, those whose immortality seemed to her as fleeting as the lives of those paying homage to it. After closing the book, she set it among its brothers on the shelf and waited for Moira's son.

The boy was slender like his mother with blond hair and blue eyes that fell on Thyri with an unpleasant arrogance.

'Mother sent me,' he said in the crackling voice of a young man losing his childhood.

'She told me you would come.'

'Well!' he demanded. 'Let's go!'

'Why do you glare at me so? You do not know me or even my name, and I do not know yours.'

'I am Patrick. Mother named me after the saint. You are Thyri. See, I know your name. Mother told me. She also told me you are heathen and a warrior. You kill without His blessing.'

'And this is worth your malice?'

'You are evil.'

She laughed. 'But your mother who tells you so much of me welcomed me into your home.'

'Mother does not see things as clearly as I.'

'I see.' Thyri approached him, her hand on the hilt of her sword. The boy was far from becoming a man in truth; she stood taller than he by several inches. She stopped before him and laughed as he backed through the doorway. 'You are prince of this island, are you not?'

'Yes.'

'You would do well to think longer on my *evil*. Your *people* are heathen, as you call them. They are also peaceful. But Christian words that sting cause heathen swords to be unsheathed. Swords cannot cut words, but they can separate the heads of princes from the shoulders of would-be kings.'

She smiled coyly and cupped his beardless chin in her gauntleted hand.

Patrick's glare faltered and he spun away, leading her quickly through the hall to the dining chamber.

The dinner party consisted of Moira, Patrick, the priest/tutor of the children named Brenden, a shriveled old man named Rath, and the twins Seth and Tana, aged five. The king was not present.

The meal was served by a common woman. Thyri guessed she had cooked it as well, a remarkable feat judging by the spread of the table: roast pork, beans, peas, little onions, fresh milk and butter, and pies of apples and berries. The food Thyri relished, but she enjoyed more observing those with whom she ate.

Moira played hostess as well as she could, obviously trying not to offend Thyri's beliefs while speaking often of her own.

Patrick was mostly silent and the fire had left his eyes. He lowered them each time Thyri looked his way. At least she'd caused him to pause. She decided to be wary of the prince. It was doubtful that she'd changed his thinking with so few words. More likely, he would soon fall back into his black-and-white perception of the world and, in doing so, would count her a threat to his future.

The twins and their tutor ate silently, watching her with a strange intensity, remarkable on the parts of the little ones who should have been fidgeting in their seats and slopping their food about with the abandon of the young and undisciplined. And the priest: Thyri thought he must have been trying to fit her into his own picture of the world – she from far lands who carried the sword that had slain a wizard too powerful for his god to banish. She doubted his task would be very simple. For the priest to condemn her as Patrick had, he would need also to condemn her deed. And his nature would demand that he resolve the question. *All men by nature desire to know.*

The old one also watched her throughout the meal, smiling in secretive fashion as if seeing something in her, some purpose and meaning beyond the visible and known, and wishing to tell her he knew, that he approved. Thyri smiled back graciously.

In the words, predominantly between Thyri and Moira, little of interest was said. Only one subject brought reactions Thyri did not anticipate. It surfaced partway near the end of the main course when Moira mentioned Thyri's refusal of their hospitality for the winter.

'As I told the king,' Thyri said, 'I have a place in the North where I wish to winter. A woman who lives there saved my life. Her name is Meg. Your husband seemed to know her.'

Patrick started then, spewing milk over the table. He looked at his mother, who turned to him suddenly, glaring. Patrick took the corner of the tablecloth to wipe his chin, and Moira turned to Thyri and smiled as if to excuse her son's manners. 'No,' she said. 'I have never heard that name. I doubt Coryn has either.'

'But he told me – '

'You must remember that he is yet very ill. When it was worst, he would rant throughout the night about all manner of strange things unknown to him. This was the wizard's doing. Brenden thinks the spells carried my husband into a world where his dreams became fact within his mind. In this world brought by his cousin, he could be made to believe anything. Including such things as this woman of whom you speak.'

Thyri dropped the subject. She knew Moira had lied, but she had no idea why. She shrugged and nodded in agreement. It didn't matter – nothing would after she'd left in the spring. She had her own worries, those same worries that plagued her anytime she grew inactive or reflective. Her torments – she needed things to do with her body, with her sword, because she could rarely face her tormentor. And that tormentor was inside of her, a *part* of her. The tainted blood that ran in her veins could never in truth command her. It could only grant power to that devourer lusting from its cage beneath her will. And then when the power subsided, she had to live with destruction caused both by her and in spite of her. Better to forget, to immerse in sensation: the pleasure of a lover, the sheer synchronicity of mind and body in mortal combat. With neither present, her sense of doom could make the problems and trials of others petty.

The constant turmoil she attracted, indeed encouraged, could stem only for a time the tides of her emotions; keep them from flooding inward to smash mercilessly against the heart of the little girl she had once been, the little girl who had worshiped passion and battle in the arena of her gods, where the line dividing the light and the darkness was, if not clearly drawn, then removed from her own existence. Not that Thyri the woman was incapable of lucidly analyzing the subtle complexities of human strife (this is far from true), but she always would tend from it as a drunken man tends to sleep to escape the increasing waywardness and confusion of his mind. She would see to a point, then fail to see further, especially during the early days after Astrid's death when she had not even begun to accept her altered nature. She had no wish to see further because careful thought would force her to place herself into context and, in doing so, she would be forced to judge herself along with the problem. She had passed that judgment already, on the vale at Astrid's grave with the point of her cousin's rune-sword poised to taste the blood of her own heart. But Astrid had stopped her.

So Thyri answered and forgot those questions surrounding Megan's connections with the family of Coryn Kaerglen. She concluded that they knew Meg, some or all of them, and that her friend had, at some time, fallen from favor in Moira's and Patrick's eyes. Megan, most likely, had once been mistress to the king and later, for reasons that no longer mattered, she had been cast aside.

Thyri saw in Megan a possible replacement for Astrid. If a rift existed between the sorceress and a former lover, so much the better.

After the meal Moira showed Thyri the baths and left her there. They are sunk under the ground floor of the castle, and a window looks from them out into the garden that grows in a space at the center of the keep.

The sun was setting and so the garden was already full of dark shadows, it being dependent on light reaching over the surrounding walls. Thyri spent several moments taking in its beauty.

Strange, intricate trees whose leaves shone green even in the absence of the sun were arranged artistically around the central fountain. Flowers of red and white dotted the ends of the branches, and the fountain's waters bubbled blackly, streaked with silver where the sunlight reflected on them from metal in the keep's walls.

Thyri sensed strong sorcery in that peaceful place.

As for the baths – the sunken pool filled the room, leaving but an arm's length all around the walls.

Steam rose from the surface of water heated by fires beneath the stones below. Towels hung on hooks by the door. She stripped and hung her cloak, clothes, and sword on one of the hooks. She tested the water with her foot, then slid into the pool. It was hot, though not overly so; she found it soothed her as bathing had never done before. Her baths were often rare – not because she felt it evil, as many claim, but because she seldom had the chance, and actually preferred a quiet pond or lonely stream. But she'd never seen baths such as these. Those in Ragnar's hall had been caulked wooden basins filled with water heated over fires. They'd been barely large enough to sit in. Here, she could swim!

She basked in the luxury until interrupted by Patrick, who entered unannounced, stripped, and dove into the pool without ceremony. He didn't even look at her. She noticed his presence but said nothing and closed her eyes, a part of her mind keeping track of his location by the sounds of his movement, another part soaking with her body in the soothing warmth of the water. After a time, she felt the prince draw closer to the place where she lounged on a sunken staircase.

Silence.

A hand on her shoulder, gliding down, brushing against her breasts.

'I want to show you that I am a man, not a boy for you to laugh at.'

His voice. The hand on her breast again, uncertain.

She jerked away and spun down the edge of the pool. Tossing her head to throw her hair from her eyes, she laughed. 'A man thinks like a man, sees things like a man.'

She placed her hands on the edge and vaulted out, turning to look down at him with water still cascading from her body. 'You wouldn't know what to do with me if I let you!'

She danced away while his face turned red and his eyes burned. As he came out of the water, she relaxed against the wall, eyeing his erection. 'My prince!'

He dove at her, pinning her arms against the wall. She smiled. His eyes burned with rage then. 'Stop laughing at me, you heathen bitch! I'll – '

With a jerk and twist, she reversed their positions. 'You'll what?' She grabbed him between the legs and squeezed. 'You are nothing, little boy.'

He gasped and she felt a stickiness splatter against her wrist and forearm.

She smiled. 'You see? My sword is stronger than yours. Do not tempt me, Patrick. I am not your subject.'

Thyri pulled him off the wall and threw him back into the pool. She bent and washed her arms at the edge before going to dry herself. Patrick watched her silently as she ran the towel over her body.

She dressed in her tunic and leggings, pulled on her boots, took her cloak and sword from their hook, and left the baths.

Magic

Moira put Thyri in one of the rooms beyond those of her children. If the queen had any knowledge of the events between Thyri and her son, she did not show it in her manner. Just as well, Thyri thought. She'd already begun to look to morning when she would leave the place.

Her room contained one of the larger beds she'd had the opportunity to sleep in. The air was musty with age and disuse, but the bedding was fresh and she collapsed on the mattress, willing the tensions from her muscles. As tendrils of sleep closed about her mind, she welcomed them, not bothering to undress, much less crawl between the sheets.

She awoke thereafter, she knew not how long, to the sound of faint scratching at her door. Patrick again, she thought wearily, rising and unsheathing her sword on the way to the door. The opening, however, revealed not the prince but the pixie-sized Princess Tana.

The little girl placed a finger to her lips and slid through the narrow opening. Thyri could read nothing in her eyes – as if she looked through a window opening upon a vista without form. The girl's hair was dark and silky, almost veil-like – like Megan's. She wore a plain white cotton nightdress.

The princess moved quickly, genuinely surprising Thyri. She reached out and touched the rune-blade before Thyri could move it away. She ran her small fingers meditatively along its bared edge. Thyri held it firmly; movement on her part could do the princess grave injury. When the girl took her hand back, Thyri quickly sheathed the sword. She backed up and sat on the edge of the bed.

Tana pointed at the sword. 'With that you kill?'

'Yes.'

'My cousin?'

No, Thyri thought. 'Yes.'

'I could feel – coldness in the metal.'

'Metal is cold.'

'No, not like that. I mean like – well, more than that.'

Thyri eyed the princess, this girl who had touched her sorcerous blade as if it were a toy. So young, Thyri thought – sensing, perhaps, things she could not put into words?

'Sometimes,' the princess continued, 'I see things that my brother doesn't.'

'Brothers. You have two.'

'No. Patrick is not really my brother. His father is not mine. My mother brought him here with her and then I was born. Me and Seth, the same night. Seth is my brother.'

Thyri reflected. Kaerglen had not fathered Patrick? But he was still prince, next in line for the throne, if indeed Coryn viewed it that way. It seemed so. It reminded Thyri that she was on foreign soil; in Norway only a father's son could take the place and property of the father. Only, in fact, the firstborn. The younger ones had to find room and home of their own.

'So you see things that Seth doesn't see.'

'Yes.'

'And you feel things, too?'

Tanna nodded.

The girl *does* have magic, Thyri thought. Coryn's blood? He certainly hadn't special defenses against Pye's attacks. Tana, however, had been raised within the confines of the castle. The magic that permeated it might have found a home in the child. That seemed possible. It also seemed possible that the princess was mad. Except for the fact that Tana had touched the sword and lived.

Thyri tried and failed to perceive the flavor of sorcery about the girl separate from that in the walls. Her failure meant nothing; she'd seldom felt the tingling *at will* around Meg, Scacath, or Astrid, and she knew all three possessed ability in the art. Madness too was an elusive quality, often hidden far beneath the surface of the one afflicted.

'Why did you come here, little one?'

'I – ' The princess paused. 'I want to show you something. Ask you something.'

'Ask.'

'I have to show first.'

Thyri moved off the bed and onto one knee, closer to the girl. 'What do you have, little one?'

'Not here. You have to follow me, and we have to be very, very quiet.'

She smiled and stood. Tana gave her a hand, then fumbled at the doorknob as a child does when only one small hand is available for the task.

She led Thyri from the room and to the left, farther away from the main corridor that Thyri had taken to the king's chamber earlier that day. The candles lighting the hall ran out before they reached their destination; Thyri halted Tana long enough to detach one from its bracket. The princess would have led her into the darkness without light. Thyri's eyes were extremely sharp, and sharper still since her first change, but she had little hope of seeing in the inky blackness that prevailed in the unlit areas of Castle Kaerglen. Not without a candle, anyway.

The floor of the hall soon betrayed extensive evidence of disuse. Dust covered it in thicker and thicker blankets. At one point they came across the skeletal carcass of a dead rat. Cobwebs grew plentifully in the places where wall met ceiling. The dust on the floor was broken only by the tracks of small feet, going both ways. Tana or Seth or both, Thyri thought. No adult, not even Moira, had such small feet.

At last Tana stopped. They had come to a door, of oak like the others, but this one was bound. It stood ajar, and Tana pushed it open. After pulling Thyri in, she returned the door to the position in which they had found it. 'Don't close it,' she whispered. 'For a long time Seth and I couldn't get in. Until Rahne gave him the key. It locks when you close it.'

Thyri looked back at the door, then detached a pouch from her belt and set it on the floor in the opening. She had no desire to be trapped in the room should the door be shut on her by Patrick or any other dark agent the castle concealed. Judging by the magic that still assailed her from all directions, she couldn't discard the idea of the door shutting itself. She had seen stranger things.

The room at first appeared a bedroom much like the one given her. In addition to the bed there was a table beside it, a chest in the corner, and a wardrobe next to it. The walls looked strange; closer inspection showed them covered with disjointed chalk markings, some seemingly purposeful, others abstractions whose designs, if they existed at all, escaped Thyri completely. She sensed an increase in the level of magic in the room as a whole. And something else, vaguely familiar.

'Who's Rahne?' Thyri asked, inspecting the markings.

'Father's aunt.'

One of the old ones Moira had mentioned living in the next corridor.

'Your grandmother's sister or your grandfather's sister?'

The princess didn't answer and Thyri turned finally to look at her. Tana stood, innocently reflective. She focused on Thyri. 'Both,' she said.

'Both? How?'

'I don't know. But it's so. She is both of their sister.' She paused. 'They all used to play together here.'

That, Thyri thought, made the king a son of incest – if Tana could be believed at all. It was not the first she'd heard of such things in old, powerful families. She didn't suppose it would be the last. She shrugged and went back to examining the markings.

The princess gripped the tail of her shirt. 'I saw a lady here once. She looked familiar, but I still don't know how because I remember her from nowhere else. I could – see through her. She was looking for something, but she went away – disappeared when she saw me. She didn't find it.'

'Didn't find what?'

'The box under the bed. Seth and me, we – '

Thyri dropped to her knees and drew an object from beneath the bed with her scabbarded sword. The box was carved of walrus ivory – a stange thing in Southern lands. A silver cross lay balanced on the lid. 'Was the cross here when you first found this?'

'Yes.'

Thyri removed it and tossed it back into the dust under the bed. She lifted the lid. Inside lay a ring, a plain gold band streaked with silver. She took it out and almost dropped it. Her palm quivered under its weight.

Sorcery!

Never before had she felt the tingle of magic in metal, not even in her sword. She felt it in the ring. She set it carefully back in the box and closed the lid.

'The lady was beautiful and sad,' the princess said. 'I heard my mother once talking with Brenden. I think the woman was Megan. Then at dinner when you said her name – I had to know.'

'Yes,' she said softly, taking the box and hiding it inside her cloak.

'You know her?' Tana asked. 'What is she like?'

What can I tell her? Thyri asked herself. 'Beautiful, as you saw her. She is kind. She is – ' Thyri hesitated. 'Do you believe in the One God of your mother and your half brother?'

'I – I think so. I'm not sure.'

Thyri smiled and touched Tana's cheek. 'You have much to learn, little one. If only there were one to teach you.'

'Can you?'

'No.'

'Can Megan?'

'I don't know. Perhaps. Talk to the old ones. Ask them about – ' Thyri recalled her conversation with Coryn. 'Ask them about Dagda, and Brigid. The children of Danu.' Thyri drew the princess closer, brushing her cheek. Tana pressed her face against the metal of the gauntlet. 'But,' Thyri continued, 'be sure to ask them in secret. Away from your mother, your teacher, and Patrick.'

'Seth,' Tana said. 'He can know, too.'

'You are very close? You and your brother?'

Tana smiled dreamily. 'We know things *nobody* else knows.'

Thyri laughed lightly and the princess giggled along with her. 'Be sure he knows that no one else is ever to find out, okay?'

'Okay.'

Thyri stood, but Tana tugged at her shirt again. 'Was Megan looking for the box?'

Thyri smiled and went to the door, bending to retrieve her pouch. She attached it to her belt while keeping a foot in the opening before turning back to Tana. 'I think so. This was her room.'

That was the other thing that Thyri had sensed behind the magic – a musty, year-worn scent of habitation. Faint, to be sure, yet distinctly Megan's. 'Come,' Thyri said, 'We must not be missed.'

She latched the door and set her sword at bedside before disrobing and sliding between the sheets. She half expected more visitors, but none came. She thought for a while that Coryn might come, then she remembered how ill in fact he remained.

The emptiness inside her almost prompted her stealing out again to seek solace in the arms of – beneath the bulk of – the king. The desire was rooted not so much in an attraction for the man – still far too weak to be of any real use – but in an urge to goad Moira to anger, even violence. Thyri resisted it; the queen could hardly be blamed for what she was. And she would more likely fall apart than grow enraged in discovering her husband with Thyri.

Not like Gyda, Thyri thought on the skirt of dream. The treacherous bitch still lived, using her poisoned body to work the warped designs of her mind. Under Ragnar, Thyri had been as impotent as Astrid against her then-princess. Next time, she thought, things would be different.

When the darkness finally welcomed her, her dreams

would not let her rest. She stalked under a red sky, her paws stained red, dripping with blood – blood from the river she stalked along. Hungry. Everything was red: the sky, the river, the horizon, her coat. Not even a wisp of white broke the splotchy crimson that covered her body. And then the river rose up against her – an amorphous creature of blood, falling upon her. Smothering, squeezing. She fought. Her fangs found bone and crushed it. The creature fell away, but the victory did nothing to sate her hunger. She stalked on.

She left the next morning at sunrise after breaking fast with Moira. The queen talked; Thyri didn't listen.

Cuilly came for her with the dappled mare; the journey through the port into the city was uninterrupted and silent. She rode past the barracks of the Guard. Dearen and the rest of her men bade her come drink with them. She told them the celebrations, for her, had ended. Her mood that morning didn't invite argument.

Meg awaited her the following night, as if expecting her return.

'He granted your wish?' the sorceress called out.

Thyri only smiled until she reached the hut. 'I must stay until spring.'

Here?

Yes. Thyri dismounted. 'I have something you desire.'

'Several things.' Meg laughed.

Thyri laughed with her and dashed for the door of the hut. She whirled there and Meg crashed into her. She threw her arms around Meg and buried her hands in dark, silken hair. 'Those things and more, Megan,' she whispered.

Later, over dinner, Thyri gave her the ring. The sorceress touched it as if it were not real, then slid it onto her finger.

'You went to the castle,' Thyri said, 'but you couldn't find it?'

'No.'

'Someone had placed an amulet of the One God on the box.'

'Oh,' Meg said.

'The One God's symbol is that powerful?'

'In some ways.' Meg examined the ring, smiling crookedly. 'There is an irony here. Had I this ring on my finger while I sought it, I would have found it, crucifix or no.' She looked up at Thyri, smiling warmly. 'You have returned to me a part of my soul. It was made for me in the forges of Andvari. It is to my magic as your right hand is to your sword.'

'Andvari the dwarf crafted your ring?'

Meg smiled mysteriously. 'The children of Danu and the sons of Odin do not dwell in separate universes, Thyri. Your gods dwell in Asgard, mine in your Alfheim, dwarves in Svartalfheim, and so on, as sages have spoken.' The shadows consumed her eyes softly, sparkling. She turned her gaze on the ring.

Silver wisps bled from it, spiraling and twisting around Meg's hand and fingers. The wisps grew and flowered out, rising before Thyri in a sheet that suddenly transformed into a window that looked on another world, a dreamlike, dazzling snowscape of white and silver. It enveloped her and she felt it probing, delicately lighting on every part of her being. She felt a darkness slip further away. A mournful symphony of impossible beauty came teasingly to her ears – her own song of sorrow, given voice by the caress of the sorceress. Thyri laughed and cried as the music filled her, purging her misery. She became a part of it, melting into the sparkling lover around her.

And she was flying, miles above the earth. Mountains became crinkles in a mottled patchwork of green and brown. Rivers and streams were like the veins of leaves. She dived down, faster than an arrow, faster than thought. And then she flew through the peaks of a mighty range, alighting only on the highest mountain-top where she sat, satisfied, surveying the raw magnificence around her.

She stretched blissfully and yawned, then peeked out of one eye. Meg smiled, almost modestly.

And so began Thyri's winter with the sorceress. Thyri told her also of the Princess Tana but Meg showed little interest and would always grow reticent at mentions of Kaerglen's family. Whatever lay behind her past at the castle was something she didn't care to revive with words. Thyri let it lie.

The days passed. The weeks passed. The moon came again and again, relentlessly demanding of Thyri what she did not care to give. Without Meg to care for her those three days each month, she would not have lived to see the flowers of spring. If not slain by the cold or the swords of Cuilly's men who came to the Northlands to investigate wolf-kills, Thyri would have taken her own life. But none of these things came to pass, and the breaking of winter carried her southward to Port Kaerglen and her quest for the sun.

Though asked, Meg would not go with her. Whether the refusal came of sorrow – knowledge of the futility of Thyri's goal – or from some deep bond Meg yet felt for the island of her birth, I know not. Megan's heart, in this and all other matters, eludes me.

BOOK III

SUN, MOON

Such were Thyri's first days on Kaerglen Isle, this place I now call home. I feel as if I've been here forever.

The room in which I work is warm, comfortable – quite plain in appearance, if not in nature. The walls are of unadorned stone broken but in three places: the doorway to my sleeping chambers, a fireplace, and the small window through which I may look down upon the city by day and up at the stars by night. For furnishings I have my desk, its chair, a couch, and my stacks and shelves of books and chests of parchment. In the center of my disordered haven is the pool.

It is a perfect circle, measuring thirteen hands across. Filling it, to a depth of which I am uncertain, is human blood. Some of it is mine. Some of it I obtained from – other sources. All of it I am responsible for. Satan's Chalice. In this pool I have seen all of which I have written thus far.

To see through Thyri I have but to drink and concentrate upon memories of her. From there I may direct my perspective whence I wish – to her childhood, to her years with Scacath and Astrid, and so on. A greater draught of the blood is required to see through another, and then only some are open to me at all. One of these, Bryn Kearn, was the man chosen by Coryn Kaerglen to captain Thyri's ship across the western seas.

Kearn was an odd man. He'd run from his father's farm when he was nine and had worked the sea ever since.

He knew his trade. He had accepted Thyri as passenger because he *wanted* to fare west. He didn't think she would find what she sought – the sun – but he'd desired since first watching the sun set at sea to follow it, to see what lands lay beyond. The idea scared him as well, but not enough to discourage him. His crew was another matter. Thyri, however, would help; all knew she had slain the wizard Pye. In her powerful manner and foreign beauty, many would worship her. Thus they would do what she wished. Thus they wouldn't mutiny. She would keep their fear in line.

As for Kearn's seamanship, he was one of Kaerglen's best. Beyond that, the man had his vices, and he habitually practiced them within shouting distance of his ship.

The main docks of Port Kaerglen are all reached through tangled streets that pass through that part of the port called Morrigan's Palm. It is the heart of port commerce, and its main avenue passes straight into the Street of Smiths on the city-side. The seaside ridge of Morrigan's Palm has been, since mac Fain's day, dotted with taverns and the brothels from which most sailors take their wives. Some of these places are said to carry the curse of Manannan. I've heard that when hostile foreign vessels dock, their crews are attracted into these brothels by faerie demons and succubi, never to emerge. I suggest this in the spirit of those lusting spectral archers in the shadows of the port-wall.

The docks are splayed in front of the main row of brothels like two legs of Euclid's triangle.

The afternoon before he was set to sail, Bryn Kearn drank in a dock-side tavern and met a strange blond man with broad shoulders and hypnotic eyes. They talked. The stranger offered him powders – sorceries he said made women placid, silent, and yet when touched they would thrill and love with the passion of goddesses. Perfect in close quarters at sea, the stranger suggested, his eyes glittering in the light of the tavern's lanterns. Bryn bought the powders for three pieces of silver.

That stranger had called himself Ragnarok. His real name was Loki, and he'd intended the powders for Thyri. It was a joke that Kearn had not the knowledge to understand.

Departures

Actually, she was six and a half – seven now, but still a little girl.

Her name was Elaine, after the tragically beautiful Queen Mother. Elaine had never seen her; she'd died shortly after King Fiann's death, twenty years before. But Elaine's mother had told her many times of the tall, shadowy queen of her youth. One thing was certain in Elaine's world: she would grow beautiful as had that sad queen of long ago.

This she thought as she lay hidden within a coil of rope among gear next to the Tuathan merchantman named *Black Rabbit.* She's been playing on the docks after helping her father unload the day's catch. Something had taken her, lifting her spirit with the fresh smell of the sea mingled with spring. She'd run from her father; she'd hidden. Then she'd danced through Morrigan's Palm to see the king's ships. While there, she'd heard and seen the northern princess coming down Shipwright's Row. That was when she'd hidden in the coiled rope behind the nets.

Thyri who had saved the king was with a man – the nice-looking kind with fancy clothes, the kind of man her father didn't trust. They were talking together. The man smiled a lot and scratched his beard. Thyri with the sword never smiled. She walked past Elaine, gazing at the ship, frowning. She looked at the pile of gear where Elaine hid. Elaine ducked before she was seen; she listened to them talk.

'Dawn,' the man said nicely. 'It will be as I told you before.'

'Your men will be worthless. They drink tonight – they haven't even loaded. Look at that pile!'

'Those are last minute acquisitions, milady. They will be on board when you arrive. We – the entire crew will be on board when you arrive.'

'Snoring like hogs.'

'With respect, milady, this is last night ashore. They must – satisfy their passions for a long time. It is tradition. We will ship without incident. It has been done many times before.'

The princess didn't answer. She looked at the man impatiently, then strode away.

Elaine waited in the coil of rope for the man to leave. But he didn't. He stamped around for a while, then walked toward her. She squeezed down into the bottom of the coil. Be small! she thought. *Be small!*

She heard him whistling. A big bluefly buzzed into the coil and around her head. She wanted to slap it, but she bit her tongue. She was afraid. She didn't want the man to find her; it could spoil her game.

The buzzing stopped. She felt the fly walking lightly on her ear. She held her breath and flinched away. The movement sent small, sharp slivers of wood from the dock's deck into her bare legs. She winced. The sound came involuntarily from her lips.

'Well, what have we here?'

She opened an eye; he was smiling down at her.

She murmured her name.

'Elaine, is it?' He lifted her out of the coil. 'You are not in a proper place for a little girl. You want to go across the Great Ocean?'

His smile and his friendliness began to calm her fears. She liked the wild adventure that lit his eyes.

'Is that where you are going? To the end of the world?' That was what her father said was there. *Sail out,* he had once said, *to the end of the world and you fall into the downy fields of Hy Brasil, where the gods dwell.*

He looked at her strangely. 'Beyond,' he said distantly. 'I am the captain. The end of the world is mine to give. Would you like to see it, Elaine?'

See it? she thought. *All the gods in their silver palaces?* She didn't believe it, but his eyes didn't lie. She smiled shyly.

He laughed. 'Yes, say your eyes. Come.' He carried her up the plank to the deck of his ship.

The *Black Rabbit* set sail the next morning with Elaine sleeping the sleep of the gods inside a trunk in Bryn Kearn's cabin.

Thyri's cabin was next to Bryn's. She might have detected Elaine by the noises that came at night, but she saw, on the first evening out, the captain retire with his young aide – a boy of about thirteen, the youngest on the ship. Thyri watched them go in and close the door. It brought dark laughter to her lips. She ignored the sounds at night. It was, after all, Kearn's command. And from what she'd seen, the boy had invited his attentions.

She spend her days in dark, brooding vigilance on the foredeck, staring for hours on end at the horizon beyond the prow. At the beginning she had brief, pointless conversations with the captain on the matters of seafaring. After a time she avoided those talks – Kearn was hopelessly ignorant of true naval combat. He was a merchant.

As for Elaine, Loki's powders worked. The emotions that passed through the girl had nothing to do with her own.

So the days passed.

Changes

The storm had raged all day, pelting the ship with freezing rain and threatening to crack the hull. Bryn Kearn sniffed at the air. He scowled at the thick blankets of cloud above, even as cold northern winds whisked them away with each passing moment. He looked at his passenger, the brooding woman from the land of the reavers. Like he, she had weathered the storm while the crew had stayed relatively dry below deck. Her cloak and her hair still dripped wetly. In her way, she was beautiful, her golden mane framing a face with but one mar – the little jogging scar under her left eye. And that in itself was almost alluring. Piercing hazel eyes.

'What now?' she asked. She spoke Irish well. Excepting her dress, her manner, and her sword, he might have taken her for a native, at worst, of the mainland.

'Hoist the mainsail,' he said. 'Follow the storm.' His first mate climbed the ladder to the prow. Kearn glanced at him briefly. 'Get the men. Hoist the mast.'

'Aye, Captain.'

The wind blew strongly, pushing the storm ever southward while the *Black Rabbit* tacked along behind it, cutting across its wake. The reddened sun rested just above the horizon. Soon, its setting glow would color both sea and sky. The woman would always stay with Kearn on the prow until the sun's last rays had died.

The moon, full, rose behind them. The night would not be so dark.

She looked at him, the sun reflecting in her eyes and tingeing her hair red. She spoke seldom; and when she spoke now, the words were so soft that he imagined them, at first, the wind.

'I am going to my cabin, Captain. Whatever happens, do not disturb me tonight, nor allow another to do so.'

She left quickly. Strange, he thought. *Whatever happens?*

He watched the sun descend into the sea – at first a double sphere, one real, one reflected. Later a single orb, formed as the two became one – two halves of a whole.

Let the woman do what she wants, he thought. He pulled his cloak tighter as the northern wind intensified, and he thought of what he would do with his children that night.

Thyri closed her door and locked it with trembling fingers. She threw off her damp sables and wiped her brow. Her hand came away wet with perspiration. She went to her locker and got out the bottle that Kaerglen had given her. Whiskey, he'd called it. She unstoppered it and drank deeply. The liquor burned her throat, making her choke. But it calmed her. She took another, longer draught.

Odin, she thought, *I hadn't counted on this.* She dug into her locker and frowned at the small cache of dried beef and mutton at the bottom. It isn't enough, she thought. *It has to be enough!*

Bloodless.

Do you think of me, Astrid, when the moon turns full over Valhalla?

When you look into the sky tonight, Meg, when you remember the girl you nursed to health, will you remember her as the woman or the wolf?

She tipped the bottle again, and the liquor's bite felt weaker. A sharp pain stabbed at her neck.

It begins.

She tried to get up and push the locker in front of the cabin's door, but her legs wouldn't let her.

She screamed.

'Gods!' Kearn gasped.

'It's Thyri!' the mate shouted, racing to her cabin.

The scream had drowned out the wind, chilling the blood of the entire crew. Several deckhands followed closely behind the first mate. He reached her door and tried to open it. 'It's locked, Captain!' He slammed into it with his shoulder.

Kearn bounded from the prow. 'Wait! She said – '

The sound of wood giving way to bone split the air. Thyri's door flew open.

Kearn started through the throng of sailors before him. Another unearthly scream and the men went chaotic, many trying to back away through him. He pushed them aside, and he saw it.

It stood over the corpse of his first mate, blood dripping from its jaws and staining the snowy, bristly whiteness of its fur. It growled at him.

'Back, demon!' He stepped toward it. Foolishly. It lashed out with one great paw. The claws raked his chest. He moved reflexively for his saber, remembering too late that it rested in a locker in his stateroom. The huge wolf backed away, still growling deeply. It dragged the mate's body back into the cabin and nudged the door shut with its bloody snout.

Kearn stood there long in silence. Slowly, he became aware again of the pounding of the sea and the sting of the wind. The men stood by him, also silent. He looked down at his rent cloak, at his own blood. He turned to the nearest man: 'Get boards, and nail that damned door shut.'

He lay in his cabin and listened to them. The sunlight shone through the crack under his door. He had no desire to go out; even that little bit of light was too bright. After seeing the door well boarded, he'd retired to his cabin, cleaned up, bandaged his wound, and gotten very, very drunk. He had poured extra doses of Loki's powder into the little girl's mouth and left her locked up in her trunk, sleeping the sleep of sorcery. Hours before dawn, hell had broken loose in the cabin beside his – *she* was in there, throwing herself against the barrier of her crude prison and against their shared wall.

He hadn't slept much. The voices of his men hurt his head.

He listened to wood crack as the boards came away from Thyri's door.

Morosely thoughtful, he touched the bandage about his chest where she had scarred him. The scabs itched. He wanted to scratch and tear at them to make them go away, make the darkness go away – he knew well what his wounds might mean.

The entire crew would go after her with their knives now. A greater fear had replaced that of her sword. He doubted even he, their captain, could stop them. He wasn't sure he wanted to.

Thyri sat on the edge on her bed, head cradled in her hands. She listened to the sounds on the other side of the door and cried. She looked at the bloody pile of bones on the floor and felt the bile rise again and again into her mouth. The cabin already stank of vomit. She had been sick as the *were*-beast had left her, and again when she'd first surveyed her cabin.

And she was weakened. The wolf had grown hungry after devouring the man. It had tried to break free. She'd fought it. It could easily, otherwise, have torn its way to freedom. The wood around her door cracked painfully.

'Rise, little one,' she said, getting up slowly.

Time to die.

She went to her trunk and donned her cloak, fixing its clasp with trembling hands. She lifted out the long bundle wrapped in oilskin. A moment later she stood, Astrid's rune-sword held tightly in whitened fingers and pointed at the door.

A final crack as the last cross-board came away. The door flew open.

She slashed through the throat of the man in front and leapt out, dodging to the side to get her back to the wall. One man lunged at her; she gutted him with one swift stroke. The others held back for a moment, spreading out. An animal rage filled their eyes. The sun glinted menacingly off long knives. Shouts of 'Rape her first!' surfaced from the back.

Maybe, she thought. *I may kill half of them, but one cannot stand against fifty for long*. Not even with sword against knives. Not even with a wall to her back. *Not, anyway, after last night.*

They closed slowly, then the slaughter began. Bodies fell all around her as her sword flashed first to one side, then the other. But they were maddened, fearless; their knives found her as well. Within seconds, she bled from wounds in her belly and shoulder. She wondered briefly why she fought at all. She wouldn't win, and death would cure her pain.

But she couldn't let them take her. She was a warrior.

She winced as steel found her kidney. She slashed back with berserk fury, removing her attacker's arm just below the shoulder. His blood sprayed from severed arteries, splashing her in the face, stinging her eyes. Another blade found her stomach. Suddenly, her shoulder blades wrenched. 'Not now,' she screamed. 'Oh, Odin! Not now!'

She dropped her sword as the emerging claws broke her skin. Leather snapped, and her gauntlet slipped to the deck. Her rune-clasp unfastened at her bidding, and she stood before them, momentarily a demonic blend of naked woman and primordial beast. She could smell fear as they broke to run. She liked the smell and threw herself among them.

She'd slain seven with her sword. She killed another twelve; the rest jumped ship. Near the end, Kearn came from his stateroom, a maniacal fury in his eyes. The torn body of his aide lay at Thyri's feet. The captain charged her, and she killed him as well.

She paced the creaking deck of the desolate vessel.

Everywhere she looked, she saw corpses through her tears. She wanted to pitch them all overboard, but she couldn't bear to look at them.

She went to Kearn's stateroom and looked at herself in his mirror. Her hair was tangled and grimy with blood. The rest of her naked body looked clean, but it did not feel that way. She bore no scars – no reminders of the blades that had pierced her flesh. The wolf's body had healed itself.

She found rags, drew fresh water from Kearn's private cask, washed her hair, and scrubbed at the intangible uncleanness of her skin, rubbing her flesh raw. She felt the ship jerk beneath her, its sail filling with a brisk, southwesterly wind that sent it skimming over the waves. A wind from Valhalla, she thought. With no crew, the gods were pushing her westward. *Odin, just let me die!*

And then she smelt life – faint, but there, nearby. The smell of the captain's aide – but no, she'd just killed him, and his scent had been – different.

She searched for the source, and found it lying on top of Kearn's nightgown in an ornate mahogany trunk at the foot of the captain's bed. She looked down into a face she knew: it was the little girl from the procession to Castle Kaerglen.

Elaine lay there, still. She thought nothing; she felt nothing. She didn't wake.

Thyri stared at her. Innocence, she thought. *Innocence in this dream of blood to torture me.*

She closed the trunk, went back to look in the mirror, then smashed the mirror with her fist, heedless of the bite of the glass. She stepped from the cabin and gazed up at the full sail. Beyond it, the sun shone merrily down at her.

Thyri snarled at it.

She locked herself in her cabin and finished the bottle of whiskey Coryn Kaerglen had sent her as a parting gift. When the wolf came to her that night, she fought it – fought its rage with one of her own. She wouldn't let it out of the cabin. She forced it to eat only the dried meat in her trunk. In that, it won a small battle. It ate well over half.

The night left her barely able to move at sunrise, and she slept well into the afternoon. When she woke she heard Elaine's scratching and sobs. The powders had worn off. Thyri slowly made her way to Kearn's cabin and opened the trunk.

Elaine launched herself instinctively into Thyri's arms. She was thin, like a loose sack of small bones. Her eyes were hollow. Thyri comforted her without real compassion; her heart lay wounded, deep in the void within her.

She held the girl for a while, then pried her away. Elaine curled up on the captain's bed, weeping uncontrollably.

Thyri left and locked the door. She looked at the sun. It hung low on the horizon.

The moon was already up.

Sun will set, Thyri thought. *And soon.*

So little time.

She looked at the deck. The blood had dried and cracked in places, baked dark as mud during the day. Bodies still lay about in odd, grotesque shapes.

She wandered among them, unable to believe that she was responsible for the slaughter. Slowly, she picked them up and threw them overboard. Two bodies she found without faces – men unknown, unrecognized. These she dragged into her cabin before locking herself in to await sunset.

She sat there, staring at the dead men heaped inside her door. One had a scar on his arm – he'd worked a hoist on the mainsail. His face leapt into her mind. Hard-eyed and smiling, with a bent nose, full lips, and short bristly beard. And through the stench of death now she smelt the other man's scent. She knew him too.

She wept and was ill again. She couldn't throw them out. If she did, the wolf would win.

She saw Elaine's terrified face. Fangs sinking into her neck. Her small, bloodied body enraging the beast further. Even it would not be enough.

She wanted to drink, but all the ale and whiskey left was in the other cabin. And it grew darker outside.

Perspiration poured from her. Her vision blurred. She started for the door, for the whiskey, but the beast came then and another night's battle began.

Impervious to Elaine's sporadic wailing, Thyri didn't waken for a day and another night. When she finally did rise, she got up groggily and unlocked the girl's cabin. Elaine grew quiet and backed away from her, staring, a wild terror in her eyes.

Thyri turned and set to washing what blood she could from the deck.

She spent her days gazing into the depths of the great sea. She had no desire to look up and watch the inevitable progress of the sun and the moon. They mocked her, and she could not touch them. Nature and the gods had conspired against her – to keep her alive, to torture her. The steady wind never abated, and she hated herself for not slashing the sails from the mast. She could only let the days pass, eat from the ship's stores, and drink from the kegs in Kearn's stateroom. She drank much.

They had plenty to eat. After a time, Thyri tolerated Elaine's presence in her cabin in the evenings. The little girl would watch her with dull eyes as she drank Kearn's whiskey and his wine. On those nights, Thyri would sometimes begin to talk, to tell Elaine stories of gods, elves, and giants.

Elaine never spoke. She had withdrawn deep within herself. Thyri's words came to her more or less, sometimes coherent, other times garbled music. The girl was like a shadow, her soul stolen far away. It was not surprising. She had eaten of a drug designed for wills far more powerful than her own.

Thyri would chuckle sadly as she told her stories; the ironies of the gods no longer glittered, no longer made her yearn.

When she sighted land, she did nothing. She let the ship run aground.

Wildfire

With her sword, her sables, and a pack containing the few other things she possessed, she dragged herself out of the freezing water and onto the hard, rocky beach. Elaine lay there, sputtering and coughing where Thyri had thrust her before her.

She glanced back and saw the *Black Rabbit* sinking slowly where it had hit the rocks. She coughed out a mouthful of the briny water and collapsed. When she wakened later, it was night.

She looked up at the waxing moon. So little time, she thought. The slaughter of the *Black Rabbit's* crew burned still in her mind.

She shook Elaine. The girl moaned; her eyes fluttered. Thyri dragged her to her feet. They staggered ashore together.

Beyond the beach, a forest beckoned with its dark branches, the embrace of a foreign land. The sounds of night welcomed them, and they wandered forth into the darkness and slept that night on a bed of pine needles.

In the morning Thyri scouted. The new land was blooming, and the life around her quelled for a time her inner turmoil. In her homeland, late spring was beautiful. In the new land, its magnificence soared past the old bounds of her imagination. And most of the life was new, different from any she'd experienced.

She discovered the tracks of other men. She found a small, dry cave and moved her things into it – the last thing she wanted was confrontation. She wanted naught but to be left alone. The cave, she hoped, would hide her fires from them.

She wondered what to do with the girl. She couldn't leave her; she didn't want to keep her. She put her in the cave and told her to stay there.

Midmorning. She watched a pair of bright red birds alight on a bush of strange berries to gorge. After a time, she scared them off and ate of the berries herself until her stomach refused more. Then she picked a large handful for Elaine, who consumed them greedily.

As the sun loomed overhead, Thyri cut a sapling, settled under a shady tree, and lazily set to work on a bow. She strung it with gut from her pack. Just before dusk, she tracked and killed a buck. They ate well that evening, but when she slept she dreamt of blood.

The new dawn brought restlessness and unease. Leaving Kaerglen, Thyri had been driven by the hope that somehow she could free herself of the moon's curse. After the full moon at sea, she had returned to that same, haunted unreceptiveness she'd courted after Astrid's death. Her hope of refuge hadn't died. It had been buried under malaise and self-hatred. She awoke still thinking dully, *West – catch the sun*.

Outside the cave and watching the dawn, her awakening vitality killed that hope. To continue west would but torture and deny her yet again. The sun had grown no closer; it would continue to set. The new land had sprung out of nowhere, and if west had brought her to it, it was all west had to give.

She gazed at the land's beauty and sat. She felt the earth beneath her and smelt strange foresty scents in the air. She closed her eyes and reached out with her other senses. Yes, she thought, *grown out of nowhere, but nevertheless real*.

Throughout the morn she sat, melancholy, contemplative, seeking a reasonable course of action whilst trying to forget that the moon in two nights would again be full.

Chill winds blew that night and she added several dried branches to her cooking fire before sitting before it on her sables. She rubbed grease from the fat of the buck into the leather of her boots, and she carefully sewed new patches of fur into the lining where it had worn away and where the emerging beast had torn it.

That afternoon she had taken Elaine by the hand and led her out to see the world. She'd begun to worry; the child's silence was unnatural. As the new land teased Thyri's senses, it awakened her compassion. They had bathed in the waters of a clear forest lake, cleansing from their bodies the lingering smell of the sea. At times, Elaine had smiled.

After finishing her boots, she set to combing the tangles from her hair – combing until the blond, silver, and red strands glinted in the firelight like a silky waterfall about her shoulders. Elaine watched her distantly.

Thyri braided – thirty knots now. She looked at Elaine as she affixed her rune-bead.

'Well, little one,' she said. 'What am I to do with you?'

A hint of fear crept into the girl's eyes. Thyri saw it, and it wrenched at her heart. This innocence was in her hands. What would she do, she wondered, when she was not herself?

She smiled and ran her fingers through Elaine's wispy hair. Suddenly, her other hand was on Elaine's ribs, tickling. Elaine giggled just a moment, then her eyes grayed over again.

'If you talk, little one, I can help you.'

Nothing.

Thyri sighed. 'If you talk, I can teach you to forget.'

Elaine coughed. She looked at Thyri a last time, then curled up on the ground and closed her eyes.

Thyri laid her sables over Elaine and went to the mouth of the cave, breathing in the night. She knew already that sleep would elude her. She set to the task of binding again the tear in her gauntlet.

An hour later, the chanting began. It lilted over the forest to the cave, pulsing, hypnotic in its repetition. Thyri peered out into the darkness. The cave was set in a hillside facing a short, narrow valley. Through the trees below, Thyri made out the flickerings of other fires. A pounding of drums, thrumming and resonant, added itself to the voices.

Men, she thought. Neighbors, if she chose to stay.

She'd avoided thinking of them since her discovery of the tracks; she'd merely restricted her short travels to the wilder areas of the wood, in and around the hills. Too much else had weighed on her mind. But they'd gathered this night. She could watch them. See them and learn of them without being seen.

She pulled on her boots and set out for the valley.

They sat in a huge circle – the chanters – with the drummers in a short arc beyond. Within, an old man led the group. In the center, three young men sat facing outward. They were naked, apparently oblivious to the evening chill and the beating of the chant. Streaks of yellow and black pigment marked their skin. Their eyes seemed intent on that other world, the one beyond reality.

A rite of passage, Thyri concluded.

She had climbed a tree well outside the clearing, far enough away to avoid discovery yet high enough to give her a perspective over the intervening foliage. The resulting view made her think of Scacath's ravens and what it must have been like for them to see from the top of the world.

For a moment hope flared. Hugin and Munin shape-changed through sorcery, sorcery Thyri felt certain came from Scacath. If she could only –

But that was an old, abandoned option. Suggested, considered, and abandoned during her winter with Meg. She hadn't seen the goddess since leaving her grove. She and Astrid had tried to find her there more than once, but the pathways into Scacath's world were gone. Meg had done a casting – Scacath was not in Midgard.

Don't snatch at dreams, little one.

Thyri settled against the tree's trunk and watched the ceremony below.

The people were dark-skinned. They dressed in soft brown leather, the men in shirts and leggings, the women, who sat among them rather than apart as Thyri had seen in many societies, in jackets and skirts, a very few of woven cloth patterned with flowery designs. The men wore their hair long in the middle and shaved on the sides, a styling Thyri had never seen before. She wondered if it marked a man a warrior, since the three young ones in the circle wore their hair unaffectedly, shorn at the shoulder and held away from the eyes by leather thongs.

Beyond the gathering was their village, a collection of conical structures covered with hides and bark that reminded Thyri much of the hut she had shared with Astrid during their training. To one side of the village, and she guessed behind it as well, stretched clearings in which the people farmed whatever crops the strange land yielded. On the other side ran a narrow river.

Of weaponry, Thyri noted only bows, spears, and throwing axes – no swords. That would help if it came to a fight. With Astrid's sword she would be immune to the arrows and axes. But a few good spearmen, capable of using the reach afforded by pole-arms to their advantage, could prove more dangerous than twice their number with swords. Best, she reflected, to avoid ever finding out.

She watched as the chanting grew in intensity and finally stopped. The old man ladled three bowls of something from a pot borne into the circle by a trio of maidens. He handed one each to the young men, and they took the bowls and tilted them to their lips. It was the first time Thyri had seen any of the three move. After that, the circle dispersed, and the three sat motionless again. Thyri waited awhile, then slipped from the tree and returned to her cave.

The next day she took Elaine near the village and left her there. She watched from a distance as the girl's abandonment resulted in incoherent wailing, drawing attention from the natives. An old woman, washing clothes nearby, reached Elaine first.

The woman approached cautiously. Elaine fell mute. Others came and stood around her, staring. Eventually, the old woman took Elaine's hand and took her among her people.

Thyri sighed relief and turned away. She'd gambled. Better, she'd thought, to risk the unknown hearts of the villagers than risk the girl in the wilderness alone at night. Aside from herself, there were other predators. She'd already heard the howlings in the distance. And she'd seen the tracks of bears.

She spent the day reluctantly steeling herself for the change that would come at sunset. She ate nothing – her human body's hunger seemed to wane during the days before, during, and after the transformations. Near dusk, she retreated far back into the cave and lay down, naked, on her sables.

It was less painful, or perhaps her mind had begun to block out the bone-wrenching agonies. The snowy white beast arose and entered the new night.

She roamed farther into the hills, away from the valley and its people. She thrilled to the scents and sounds of the new land; her wolfen form's senses exceeded even the perceptual acuity she possessed as a woman. She almost lost herself, then she heard them again – heard their howlings, their calls to one another. And they called to her; they sensed her. The realization of this sent chills of longing and dread along her spine, raising her fur. The *were*-wolf bounded toward them.

Woman fought desperately. Her mental anguish caused her great pain, but it finally slowed, then halted the beast. She turned it from its brethren and sought the wildest, most desolate crags to prowl. The experience filled her with fear of what might happen if she met the other wolves and lost control of herself. She'd yet to face that eventuality. She'd been the only wolf on Kaerglen during her months there.

An hour later she was stalking a doe. The droppings she'd discovered at the pool were fresh, less than an hour old. The scent grew stronger now with each step. She could already taste the warm, sweet blood, feel it staining her fur and washing down her throat.

The trail led her to a small glade, to the doe grazing, unaware. And another scent . . . She hesitated, downwind. Something was wrong, the doe grew skittish. She leapt as it moved, and her claws but grazed its flank. When she turned to attack again, another had joined the battle.

He'd fallen from an overhanging branch, right onto her prey's back. He wore only a breechcloth and streaks of paint, and his hand was a blur as he brought his axe down into the animal's skull. They wavered together, hunter and hunted in the final steps of their macabre dance, then the doe hit the earth. He landed crouched, the blooded axe still gripped tightly, his body facing Thyri.

She looked at him. He was young and muscular – one of the three, she was sure, who had sat in the center of the circle of chanters the night before. His stance was relaxed, wary. His eyes, though, and his scent, showed no fear. He watched her as she did him. She growled.

No more human flesh!

Suddenly, he smiled. He touched his ax, then ran three bloody fingers across his chest, marking himself as if wounded. He turned his back on Thyri and quickly left the glade.

She listened to his retreat until the smell of blood overpowered her and she tore into the doe.

For the rest of the night she could smell him, sometimes near, sometimes far. She did not try to track him, or at least that part of her that was woman did not. And the woman, for the night, had already won. An hour before dawn, she began to run, tracing, retracing her trail in hopes that she would lead him away from her cave. But even when she entered it just before the first rays of hard sunlight breached the horizon, she had little confidence that she'd succeeded. The wolf left, leaving her exhausted and shivering in the dark depths of dawn.

Around midmorning she forced herself to rise, dress,

and strap on her belt. She reached the mouth and leaned unsteadily against the wall. The grass about the front of the cave was littered with lily white blossoms. She had not lost the young warrior the night before.

She squinted her eyes, scanning the forest from underbrush to treetop in search of him. Her efforts rewarded her not. Cautiously, she fared out and into the forest, to the lake, to wash the night from her skin. After that, she returned to the cave and slept away the remainder of the day.

When she emerged that evening a freshly slain buck lay on the carpet of white. And *he* was there; she smelt him before she saw him sitting cross-legged at the edge of the forest. She approached the buck, sniffing it, pawing it. It smelled clean, untainted. Her hunger grew ravenous, and she dined.

Finished, she eyed the warrior and growled, deeply, threateningly. He smiled as before, then retreated into the woods. That night, as she prowled, she caught no scent of him. No sign.

The next morning she found fresh blossoms and wreaths of red and yellow flowers set about the cave. There were three large basins of scented water and other containers, one full of drinking water and one of a heady, invigorating potion. She considered ignoring it all, but she knew not what that might mean to the warrior or his people – for surely he had told them of her by now. They must have sensed some connection between herself and Elaine. What if they killed the little girl?

Suddenly, she smiled at her worres and the indignation she felt at the warrior's assuming manner, whatever he meant by it. Another day she would rather have bathed in the lake; today she wasexhausted. For the basins she could feel some real gratitude. She used them and slept.

She was greeted, on the last night of the wolf that moon, by another fresh deer and a semicircle of the new land's people – ten of them inall, warriors, including the one who had found her. His hair was shaved now on the sides like the others.

When she emerged the following afternoon as a woman, rune-blade at her side, she followed them into their village. Thus did Thyri Bloodfang join for a time the people who called themselves *Habnakys*.

The village was arranged in a roughed seeeries of concentric semicircles: paired northern and southern halves. The hut they offered Thyri was in the center of the south side. Facing hers, to the north, was the hut of the Habnakys chieftain.

The structure was taller than that she had lived in long before. Inside it was much the same, with basketry mats covering the floor rather than furs and skins. A charred depression in the center marked the fire pit.

The warrior entered the hut with her. He smiled, nodding as he looked around. Then he left her alone; she heard the villagers outside disperse.

That evening she emerged and found him awaiting her, squatting patiently outside her door.

She smiled and he stood.

She held her hand out at her waist, touched her skin and covered her mouth with one hand, bulging her eyes out.

He frowned.

She made little weeping noises and repeated her other gestures.

Light flickered in his eyes and he started away, motioning for her to follow.

They came to a hut on the eastern skirt of the south side. He parted the opening and Thyri looked in. An old woman with scarred hands and yellowy bright eyes looked up from where she sat skillfully working strands of straw into a mat with those aged hands. An old man sat next to her, grinning with carefree pleasure as he flicked a string around in the face of a very young little by. The boy giggled and snatched clumsily at the string.

Other children – five in all – roamed free in the hut. The older ones looked up at the intrusion. Elaine was among them. She looked at Thyri blankly.

Thyri smiled tearfully at her, then turned to the warrior and nodded.

They left.

She spent the night alone.

In the morning, an array of offerings lay about the entrance of her hut: cakes of meal; bowls of young, tender roots; legs and sides of deer and elk – far more than she could hope to eat in a month, never mind the morning. And the warrior sat there among it all.

She motioned him into her hut.

He looked into her eyes nervously. 'Thyri,' he said, then something else in his curious, lilting tongue.

She imitated his words and he frowned. She pointed to herself. 'Thyri.' She pointed at him.

'Akan,' he said with a broad grin.

'Akan,' she said thoughtfully. She picked up a finely wrought bow, one of the many gifts she'd received. She looked at him inquisitively, and he gave her its name. She repeated it and continued on with other things, working into the alien language.

She saw Elaine that evening with the old woman. Their eyes met; Elaine smiled. Some of the villagers commented softly but Thyri could not understand their words. The old woman kept Elaine among the other children. She was yet withdrawn, but the children were friendly to her and Thyri felt for the first time a deep satisfaction for something she'd brought about. Elaine might have been scarred, but she would live. And for two terrible nights at sea, she had been the sole target of the wolf's lust for hot blood. Thyri had stopped it.

Akan

For a week, Akan came to her each morning and stayed until dusk. He was the one she'd first met; the tribe seemed happy to let him handle her for a time. And she noticed something of a fear of him among the others. She began to assimilate his teaching at a rate almost as remarkable as her conquest of Irish. Megan's spell, Thyri decided, had been far more powerful than the sorceress had ever intimated.

Akan arrived one afternoon after Thyri had spent the morning bathing in the lake and enjoying a time of solitude alone in the forest. She was naked, stretched out dreamily on her sables, not thinking of Astrid, of Meg, her curse, or anything else in particular. He entered, she rose, and he started to leave.

'Akan,' she said.

He paused, keeping his eyes averted.

'Akan, come here.'

He approached her, still looking away. She took his hand and lay it on her breast.

'What is your word for this?' she asked, smiling playfully.

He looked into her eyes, and she saw his surprise and shock.

'What is it?' she asked, more seriously. 'What have you in your hand?'

'Thyri,' he stammered, then he said those other words of his greeting.

She repeated the phrase, making it a question.

Akan took his hand away and began to wave both in the air. He said the words again, then, for lack of other words, he waved his hands above him. And suddenly she realized.

She locked eyes on his.

'No,' she said firmly. 'No, Akan, I am not *akiya toyn.*' What did it mean literally? she wondered. Sorceress? God? Goddess? *Wolf-goddess?*

'I am woman.' She took his hand and placed it again on her breast, pressing it firmly this time, looking at him. 'What is your word for this?'

He told her.

She reached beneath his breechcloth. 'And this?'

Akan told her. He tried feebly to back away; she said again that she was a woman. She pulled him down to the sables and kissed him. 'And this?' she asked. He told her the word nervously. 'Is it bad magic,' she said, 'to kiss akiya toyn?'

'Yes, Thyri.'

'I am not she,' she stated. She kissed him again, roughly. This time he didn't resist.

Thyri grew capable of holding longer and longer conversations in the Habnakys tongue as the weeks passed. Akan remained her most constant companion, but the elders of the village began to take greater interest after the first time she unsheathed her runeblade and attempted to show them its function. The tribe knew nothing, in fact, of metals. For Thyri this was exasperating – she knew well the techniques of forging iron, but she knew little of the methods of extracting it from the earth. Without that knowledge, the rest of her skills were useless.

Elaine, during this time, had a new mother and father. They were old and wrinkled, and they talked funny. They laughed with her and let her play with other children who talked as funny as they did. She was happy. She began to wonder why she couldn't understand what anybody said to her. She knew she was in Port Kaerglen no longer. The princess Thyri with the sword who saved the king was with her though.

Elaine wondered how they got there.

Any who might have doubted Thyri's divinity lost that doubt during a festival held a week before the next full moon. It celebrated a successful planting season, and the tribe's hunters had killed three bears, eight deer, and scores of wild fowl for the occasion.

It began solemnly, in the hut of the chieftain, a warrior named Tokaisin. Thyri felt a sense of honour in her presence there. Though they'd welcomed her and obviously thought her of super-natural origin, she had yet to spend more than brief moments in the presence of the chief – then only when summoned, and then only to stand while he watched her silently. She knew she interested him; she guessed he preferred to await a time when they could communicate on the dignified level of speech. He no doubt knew much of her already; Akan was his son.

They sat on finely woven mats of native straw. Thyri's place was to the left of Tokaisin; Akan's was to his right. The rest of the village elders, fifteen in all, sat with them in a circle. From a pouch of soft leather, Tokaisin produced a long wooden tube with a receptacle in one end. Into the receptacle he pressed a small wad of dried vegetation, then he placed the other end of the tube to his lips and set fire to the plant fiber. He breathed in, drawing smoke into his lungs through the tube, which he then passed to Thyri.

'Welcome,' he said, 'Thyri akiya toyn.'

She took the tube and placed it to her lips as he'd done. She breathed in, and the smoke entered her throat as if attacking, trying to choke her. Mentally, she fought the desire to cough, then slowly she breathed out. Withdrawing the tube from her lips, she managed a smile. She looked at Tokaisin. 'I am honoured, *haiki sen*.' She handed the tube to the next elder in the circle.

After Akan breathed in the plant fiber, Tokaisin declared the festival begun. It consisted of feasting and gaming, and it lasted for days. At least, Thyri thought as it began, she knew how to react. *If only they knew the brewing of ales and meads . . .*

There were dances and songs and contests of all sorts. On the first day there was an archery competition. Domahandi, a tall warrior of thirty summers by Thyri's reckoning, put three out of five arrows into a sapling at fifty paces. Before honoring him, Tokaisin insisted that Thyri try.

Laughingly, she tested the bow they had given her and the one she'd made when she had first arrived in the new land. She chose her own. As hastily constructed as it was, its feel was familiar, and the Habnakys bows were too short for her tastes. But she'd hardly fashioned a competition weapon. She strung it, however, and obliged the chieftain. Even with the oddly feathered Habnakys arrows, she hit the thin trunk four times out of five.

In the martial tournament the following day, she defeated eleven others, including Akan, and, at the end, Tokaisin himself.

At the end of that day she cursed her pride. No degree of insistence could now make them see her as less than their goddess. They had no women warriors at all, much less one a match for the best of their men. And she wasn't sure anymore that she wanted to convince them otherwise. She knew too little of their customs. She did not wish to damage the warriors' pride by showing she was a normal woman. Assuming, of course, she could show that in any way at all.

At least of all the things Thyri Bloodfang was ever named – *kin-slayer, demon, murderess,* and more – *akiya toyn* was by far the most pleasant. It caused her problems, but she lived with it for a time.

After she'd convinced Akan that she did not need food enough to feed an army, her meals had diminished to portions she could accept.

Around half of one side of her hut she had arranged the many other gifts given her: weapons, small wood carvings of people and wolves, a collection of beaded leather bands she had taken to wearing on her brow after the fashion of some of the women. And clothes – they had given her many soft doeskin jackets and skirts, even a few shirts after she'd indicated to Akan that she desired them. At first Akan had laughed; shirts were apparently for men.

He sat across from her now. He had entered moments before and words had not yet been spoken. Thyri smiled at him and he returned the smile warmly. Sweat glistened on his coppery skin; the sun that day had been hot. She gazed at him, admiring the tone of his muscles, his smooth, hairless chest, his inky black hair, and the innocent playfulness in his eyes.

'Tonight,' she said, 'I will change.'

'That is your way,' he said, 'Thyri akiya toyn.'

'Akan, please – I am not she.'

'You came to me in my dream-life.'

She looked at him and sighed. That night when they'd faced each other across the fallen doe, he had been on a dream-quest, under the power of mystical herbs given him by the tribe's lore-master. It has been a test of manhood: to meet his demon and defeat it. Thyri – akiya toyn – had been that demon. He had subdued her with kindness, but he'd subdued her just the same. Other Habnakys warriors whispered enviously when he passed by. Most of them had defeated less tangible monsters.

Thyri had heard of such practices from Scacath. Rites of passage, ways capable of bearing good fruit. In interfering, Thyri felt that she'd somehow cheated the young warrior.

'She will come,' Akan continued. 'It is said. She will come and her hair will glow like the burning sun and her skin like snow under the moon. She is like the earth and air and the warriors of the stars. She is one with the wolves and the land. And she is like wildfire – the toyn from which no enemy can escape. We are like you, akiya toyn, we are free. We are few, but we are free. We are honored to be your children. I – I am honored to love with you.'

'Is that what *toyn* means, Akan? Wildfire?'

'Wildfire, yes.' He flexed his muscles. 'Fury to make the

Great Bear cry out in fear. *Akiya* means she who is mother, lover, life; she who is the dawn and the spring.'

'That is a very pretty name, Akan.' Her eyes watered. *If only it were so.*

'It is you. Thyri – akiya toyn. Who else might have your pale beauty? Who else might run with the wolves and be one with the earth? Who else might defeat our mightiest in battle?'

'I – ' She paused, losing her thoughts as emotion welled up within her.

'Go now, Akan,' she said. 'Leave me. You must not be here when the sun sets.'

'That is your way.' Smiling still, he rose and left.

When she emerged from her hut, they awaited her – all the warriors of the village. She growled at them. She feigned charges. She fought the beast inside her with all her will – she could kill them, devour them, she realized, and they would probably let her. And that she could not allow. They were like children – they worshiped her, trusted her. Snarling, she bounded away into the forest. And the warriors, as best they could, followed, making a game of it – a test. They tracked her, and she would lose them only to later encounter them, out of breath, their faces grinning, their eyes joyous.

And she couldn't bear it. Midway through the night, she began to run. Westward ever, toward the sunset horizon and away from the Habnakys at such speed that they could not hope to match her, over terrain it would take them days to pass. The beast within her thrilled at her flight and took over. Suuch was her mood that she let it. And in a valley far from the eastern shores of the new land she met the pack.

Its hunt-master was called Gowrraag – he-who-fangs-the-wind. Seven hands he stood at the shoulder to Thyri's six. He had slain Klaawooor, the buck who'd killed his father, the father also of eight of the pack's seventeen adults. Gowrraag was young, strong, and proud, and he had never known defeat. When Thyri burst into his pack, fangs bared, white fur turned brown and splotchy gray by her journey, he challenged her, the other wolves growling and cowering behind him.

She faced him – all wolf, the woman long fled to dark corners within. Yet her awareness remained, and she watched in horror as she leapt and sank her fangs into his neck. Before landing, she twisted, tearing flesh from bone. Gowrraag turned on her, not yet aware of the fatal wound. Thyri leapt from his path. He landed, spun, then fell. Thus did Thyri come to lead the family-that-lives-by-the-fast-water-and-cares-for-the-deer.

Near dawn, she claimed the den of Gowrraag as her own. After the change, for the first time since the moon had claimed her, her body felt strong, stronger even than normal. And despite the fears and sorrows within her, she felt strangely at peace. During the day, the pack still recognized her. They looked to her for direction. They looked to her in fear and in simple, unaffected devotion.

After the third night of that moon, she stayed with them. She fashioned another bow; she led the hunt as woman. She learned to speak in growls and howlings – it was a simple tongue, without the abstract ideas and terms that make men so full of self-importance – and so potentially evil.

The hunt, for the fortnight she stayed, was good. But as the moon began to wax Thyri grew fearful, afraid that she would lose herself entirely to the beast. And she had left her sword with the Habnakys. She began to feel its pull.

There was a great howling on that eve of her parting from the family-that-lives-by-the-fast-water-and-cares-for-the-deer. Thyri howled with them, sang a paean to Odin, and promised she would return.

That which the wolf had traveled in a fraction of night took Thyri two days and part of another to cover on foot.

There were mysterious signs in the land. Confused flights of birds heading west. On the morning of her third day, as she drew close to coastal lands, she saw black plumes of smoke dotting the expansive horizon.

She grew afraid – for Elaine, for Akan. She found herself listening for the beating of hooves on the earth, then remembered seeing no horses at all in the new land. She waited the afternoon in the foothills overlooking the coastal valleys. The distant fires before her stretched out toward the north, where the valleys rose up sharply into the dark, craggy mountains.

She noted the position of each fire while awaiting nightfall to cover her approach.

No sentries hailed her on the fringes of the Habnakys domain. Chirping insects reigned in the valley air.

Thyri smelt the village before she reached it; half of the huts had burned. Bodies, spears and arrows sprouting from necks and chests, littered the streets. Death, pungently more than a day old, filled the air.

She ran for her hut; it was intact, unscathed, but only luckily so. The attack had come from the north and there was the damage; the Habnakys had apparently turned the attackers outside the hut of Tokaisin. Thyri could not see the haiki among the dead in view.

She paused, cursing herself, realizing what pain life without her rune-blade would cause her. Not that she'd had much recent need for it, but its ways were as much a part of her as the air she breathed.

She threw open the entrance flap of her hut. The interior was neat and clean, scarcely changed from the day she'd left. Except for Akan's body in its center. He lay faceup, his expression frozen midway between ecstacy and terror. His open eyes stared at her. Insects swarmed over his face and neck, entering and exiting his mouth and a small red hole they had dug in the side of his left eye. No other wound marked his skin.

Thyri understood too clearly what had happened: across from Akan, half in, half out of its scabbard and glowing softly in the ambient light of the hut, lay Thyri's sword. Akan had come to take it, and it had killed him.

Her vision swam – went red. She threw her head back and howled, her voice cracking, tortured. She could have been a demon then, screaming at the sky, staining the new land forever with the memory of her curse and her grief, unleashing terror in the hearts of all living things that heard that horrible sound. Pain stabbed through her chest, and she began to shake. Her lament softened and swelled and then was answered, her brothers and sisters in the wood mourning with her from afar. And as suddenly as she began, she stopped. The silence caved in on her, resonating through the hollow black caverns of her soul.

She stood naked over the cold body of her lover and cried, the beast finally giving way to the woman. And, after a time in that haunted domain of man, she grew aware of her nakedness. She took first her gauntlet, pulling it on, flexing her fingers before her eyes and feeling all the while that they belonged to a woman not herself. She donned the soft doeskin garb of the Habnakys. The leather caressed her skin, its sensous feel drawing her further into herself and intensifying her dark humour. She gathered up the rest of her things and left the hut. Moments later she started a small fire by rubbing dried bits of wood together as Akan had once showed her. She threw the hot brands onto the matting inside the hut, then sat before it, watching it burn until the supporting poles collapsed and naught remained but smoldering ash.

Later, in the forest, they came to her – the wolves she had run with and more. They arrived throughout the night, and the next morning her pack numbered three score and five. She led them north.

Wooorg – he-who-was-born-under-thunder-and-rain – found Pohati first. She was slight and young, no more than thirteen. She was Habnakys – her coal black hair nearly able to melt her into the shadows. Fire filled her eyes and her small fingers gripped the hilt of a knife chipped of dark rock. Wooorg cornered her and held her at bay. He would have killed her had Thyri not stopped him.

'Do not fear, little one,' Thyri said to her. 'I am an unfaithful friend, but still a friend. We will not harm you.'

The girl's face, which might have been beautiful were it not covered with grime and twisted by fear and rage, betrayed scant recognition at first: snarling, she looked at Thyri; then her almond eyes softened, filled with tears, and she dropped her knife.

'It is you,' she said. 'Tokaisin said you would return to us. Many did not believe him. I – did not believe.'

'You are Pohati, daughter-of-autumn?' Thyri remembered her; she possessed a great deal of presence for one so young. Even warriors would shy from her at times.

The girl nodded.

'Tokaisin – where is he?'

Pohati's tears welled anew and Thyri went to her and took her in her arms, resting her head on her breast and stroking her hair in silence, taking the girl's sorrow into herself.

'He died the same night,' Pohati said, 'though his bravery saved us all. He killed many of them. They were *Arakoy* – a raiding party. Tokaisin feared an army would descend upon us next. He led us to a haven east of here, by the great water. We did not know he was dying. He breathed his last promising your return, akiya toyn.'

'What brought you here?'

Pohati drew her head from Thyri's breast, looked up into her eyes, and smiled. 'I am *amazi* now. I am swift and strong. I am a warrior. Like you, akiya toyn.'

Odin, no, Thyri thought. *Is this how they have paid for my treachery? Have they made their children and women warriors now? To send them out to die?*

'We can make them pay, can't we, Thyri akiya toyn? We can kill them like they killed my brother, my mother, and my sister.'

Thyri nodded. She recalled what knowledge she had from Akan of other tribes. 'The Arakoy,' she said, 'are not sister-tribe to the Habnakys. They are from far.' She waved, indicating the northern mountains.

'Yes.'

'Why do they come?'

Pohati shrugged. 'The lore-master says they have not done

so in two lifetimes. But he says that our land gives more than theirs. That is perhaps why.'

Thyri wished again she had been in the village for the battle. In so many ways could the tragedy have been averted. Akan, Tokaisin, all the others – none of them need have died. 'Who is haiki now?'

'Tokaisin said you are.'

Thyri released Pohati and turned to the pack. She crouched and purred to them, her voice gravelly and deep.

Wooorg, Growaaag, Awwwwrgawoow. Take five scouts each and go north under the mountain shadows. Observe what the two-legs do there. Find out where they are, and how many are at each place. Tell the families there that we shall make blood with the two-legs soon and that they may join us as they wish. Tell them to make safe their cubs. Stay with them, but send a scout with news to me each night. Go.

Pohati watched the three great hunt-masters go among the pack, choosing their scouts. Moments later, they were gone. 'Who are they, Thyri, that you make speech with them? Are they of this land?'

Thyri nodded. 'They are friends. And they are amazi now. Like you, little one.'

Duguru

Wolves can think. They have a shallow awareness and they have speech quite effective in expressing ordinary desires and thoughts. Those of keener intelligence know of the ways of man and avoid his domains. They became hunt-masters and care for their packs, and thus they reach a harmony with the land and their own. This leadership and protection is the purpose they perceive, and toward this end do they consider their actions.

Thyri could enhance that purpose with something more; she added hate for the invaders from the north. She added love for her. She made them like shadows of men, fiercely loyal warriors to die for her.

For the wolves, the communion was rapture.

Wrrgr came upon the two-legs and approached cautiously. They were not of his land; the smell around their encampment was *wrong*. He watched them until he heard Growaaag's howling in the distance, then he turned to the east.

Growaaag was hunt-master, Wrrgr his finest hunter. When the pack had stalked the demon-who-had-slain-Weegaar's-cubs, Growaaag had cornered the huge buck, and Wrrgr had brought it down. Wrrgr had been ready to challenge Growaaag for the right to lead the pack when akiya toyn had disrupted the normal order of things. Now, Growaaag's howls charged from afar that he, Wrrgr, should care for the family while Growaaag went north to carry out akiya toyn's will. A moon before, Wrrgr would have had to slay Growaaag to gain that privilege.

A new order had indeed arisen. The gods had come to

lead the families once more. Akiya toyn, and another as well. Another whose presence told Wrrgr that life, in many ways, was changing.

Thyri silenced Pohati's increasingly eager chatter as the pack parted for the huge brown male who came barreling in from the west. Wrrgr stopped before them, panting, his yellow eyes full of fear and insensible glee.

'Two-legs,' he grunted at end.

'How many?'

'Half as many as the suns between the bright moons.'

'What do they now?'

He pulled his lips back in a leathery grin. *'Sleep.'*

Thyri touched Pohati's shoulder. 'He has found warriors. Twelve, thirteen of them.'

Pohati tensed under Thyri's hand. 'We must kill them.'

Thyri laughed dryly. 'We do not know they are the murderers yet.' She turned to the pack. *'Come,'* she growled. *'The hunt has begun.'*

She ran next to Wrrgr, Pohati following, struggling to maintain their grueling pace. When Wrrgr finally slowed to indicate that they neared the camp, Thyri fanned out the pack, sending arms of wolves to embrace the Arakoy. They closed the circle slowly, Pohati pressing tightly against Thyri's arm, her stone knife absorbing the night at the end of her other fist.

The glow of a small fire in the distance began to grow with each step.

Prying Pohati's fingers from her cloak, Thyri unslung her bow and peered into the wood before them. Pohati followed her gaze and saw only blackness while Thyri notched an arrow and sent it whooshing softly ahead. A few paces on, Thyri paused and pointed up. Wedged among branches above was the limp body of a man. A small ax dangled from a thong at his wrist. An arrow jutted from his throat, just below the chin.

Next to Pohati, a short bow lay across the top of a bush;

she fingered it for a moment, then Thyri led her on. Wrrgr stopped then; the women continued alone.

They stopped at a ridge that looked onto a clearing through a short stand of trees. The tents centered on a fire. One man huddled over it. His hair was tied back in a bunch, revealing thin, sallow cheeks. Streaks of ochre curved along his jaw. Perspiration on his face and body cast orange reflections from the fire.

'He looks ill,' Thyri whispered.

'He is Arakoy,' Pohati spat. 'Our land rejects him.'

'But not his friends,' Thyri offered sourly. 'They sleep – do you not hear their snores?' She lifted her head and let out a strained, mournful howl.

Kill the sleepers!

Hell erupted from the wood. The families fell on the tents, trapping those within. Claws tore at matting and flesh. Thyri was among them, stalking slowly toward the warrior who sat transfixed, in mute horror, the attack only just registering on his brain. Pohati stood stiffly on the ridge, listening to the screams with her knife clenched tightly in her fist. She tried to push herself into the fray, part of her lusting for its release, another part still a child and cowering behind and from the fierce sorcery of Thyri's sword. By the time she forced a foot forward, the battle was won.

Thyri held the point of her sword before the man's eyes. The fear there was uninhibited; his trousers clung to his leg where a wetness seeped down from his groin. He babbled rapidly, the words familiar to Thyri's ears but their structure foreign. Once, Thyri realized, the Arakoy and Habnakys had spoken the same tongue. She slowed him with a snarl and twitch of the end of her blade.

'How many?' she asked.

He stared at her, terrified.

'How many *are you*?'

'Hu-hundred. Four or five.'

'Camped further west?'

He nodded nervously. 'And south.'

'Why are you here?'

The warrior swallowed hard. Thyri's blade flashed, cutting deep into his cheek.

'The *haiki nagara,*' the man screamed. 'He comes.'

She turned to Pohati.

'The chief of chieftains,' Pohati said blankly. 'They are of the old days when enemy tribes from the west fled from the burning sun. A haiki nagara unites all children of the land. He gains the allegiance of each haiki. Or he kills him.'

Thyri looked into the warrior's eyes. 'How many are you? Under this haiki nagara?'

'Like the stars in the night,' he said, his lips quivering into a weak grin.

'And when does your warlord come?'

'Soon,' he said. 'Very oon.'

He fainted shortly after that. When he wakened, Thyri forced him at sword point toward the Habnakys haven in the east.

Duguru was the Arakoy's name. As Thyri prodded him through the rest of the night, his thoughts dwelt mostly on matters surrounding his personal survival. He felt himself in the clutches of demons, for wolves did not do what they had done in his camp that night. But be she demon or no. Duguru had no desire to oppose Thyri. His haiki nagara, for the moment, was very far away.

The Habnakys haven was a long grassy depression fenced into the side of a wooden hill by rock outcroppings on two sides. A cave at the foot provided access to an underground stream. The mouth of the depression flared inward, making the position easily defensible.

They arrived near dawn. Two warriors on watch woke the survivors, who struggled out of bedrolls to line the sides of the haven as Thyri entered. She pushed her captive before her still.

The Habnakys had been halved and but three score warriors remained, along with a handful of young women and boys whose fire – if not whose skill – matched that of their elders. A hollow ache filled Thyri as she entered the small camp; they should have hated her, these children she had abandoned to flame and arrow. Pohati went among them, telling them how they had captured Duguru. She told them how akiya toyn commanded the wolves.

In the faint moonlight, Thyri saw Elaine clinging to the skirt of the old man. The other children gathered at his feet. The old woman was not there; Thyri learned later that she'd died over the body of a little boy. And then the Arakoy had murdered the child.

At dawn, the tribe sang a song to Thyri of love and the sound of rain against stone. Before seeking the solitude of sleep, the families sang another song to her of other things: of her legend, of the fury of her namesake, of her beauty and her terrible wrath.

Within that joyous camp, surrounded by the Habnakys and her brothers and sisters of the wood, Thyri almost began to believe them. Though she had known nothing of the prophecy before arriving in the new land, her skills, the sorceries in her blade, and now her communion with the wolves had made her into the image of the Habnakys goddess. And wherein, she wondered, lay the difference?

Wildfire – you grow mad, little one.

Later that day she wakened Duguru and set the point of her sword against his chest. He told her more of the tribes called Arakoy and of Aralak haiki nagara.

The Arakoy peopled the forests and plains of the northlands, beyond the snows of *Hagara Kohn* – the teeth of the Great Bear. During Duguru's childhood, the tribes had warred with themselves, until came Aralak. He was a giant, standing a head again as tall as any of his warriors. He fought with a great battle-spear – blessed, Duguru swore, by the Earth Mother herself. Aralak was her servant and her herald. It was she, Duguru claimed, who had directed the warlord's attention southward.

In his fear, he grew incoherent then. Thyri had to await his recovery before continuing her questioning. His raiding party, she learned at end, consisted of scouts. Aralak planned to follow later, before the end of summer, with a full-scale invasion.

Thyri let the warrior live. Around his information she developed her strategy. First, she would stop the raiders from returning home.

That evening came scouts from the North with news of survivors and another splinter of the Arakoy raiders. The survivors belonged to the *Konanci* – a sister-tribe to the Habnakys. Thyri sent warriors to rally the surviving Konanci around their northernmost village, then she ordered death for the Arakoy scouts in the Konanci lands; Domahandi led two score warriors and two dozen wolves against them. He rejoined Thyri two days later, successful, his arrows having tasted the blood of men for the first time.

She sent Wrrgr and his family north into Hagara Kohn to spy on any Arakoy there. Scouts in the West had discovered the main mass of the Arakoy raiders; she sent another family there to watch over the foreigners and keep her informed of their movements.

The Habnakys survivors she led slowly north. She wanted to block any retreat the raiders might be depending on. She was counting then, without reservation, on Konanci loyalty to her cause.

And she sent emissaries to other sister-tribe warlords, the haiki to the south and west, whose people spoke tongues akin to the Habnakys'. She sent word from akiya toyn – this she hoped would be enough. She could think of no other method of threat or persuasion that might gain their allegiance in so short a period of time. She sent emissaries also to the more distant families. They, she knew, would come.

Sentinel

The moon, high overhead, lit Wrrgr's night like a lover leading him to paradise. The ancient one's howling danced through the trees, and fireflies flashed along the sides of the trail as he raced to answer the call.

The journey was rapture, its end Woraag Grag: one of seven legendary sons of *Worrr*, the Great One. *Grag* – 'of the blood' in the Habnakys tongue.

Two score other hunt-masters sat transfixed with Wrrgr, though all eyes were filled with the ancient one alone. No growl, no howl broke the silence of the night. He spoke into their hearts with a speech beyond words.

He had come as had akiya toyn. He had summoned them to tell them one thing: she wasn't to know.

Al'kani

'Teach us to ride, and them to carry us,' Pohati said suddenly.

Thyri wiped the stringy strands of hair from her eyes. They sat in the shade of a great conifer, their bodies still pouring sweat onto the bed of soft brown needles.

On the northward trek they moved only in the morning. Many of the Habnakys were old or frail, unable to walk further. Thyri had been teaching Pohati single combat with war-axes since noon. The girl learned quickly, but she was careless – too quick to strike, too vulnerable to feints. She was a natural fighter with long, agile legs and strong hands, but Thyri feared her youthful zeal would cost her in battle. She was too young to understand what was at stake. But Thyri couldn't bring herself to tame the young amazi: she wouldn't understand. She would think her cruel. Her spirit shone like the evening star, and Thyri needed that light to keep her own spirits high. And, she reasoned, they would all most likely be dead by winter, skilled and unskilled alike. Better for Pohati to die a fiery youth than a broken foot soldier.

'Too heavy,' Thyri said finally.

'I'm not. At least for the big gray ones. But there are others, smaller than I. The wolves can carry us quickly behind the Arakoy. We can slay more before they arrive.'

'Those are deadly missions for men. Only the wolves can attack swiftly enough, then retreat in time to survive. And with riders they would be less agile.' She spoke of her plans to terrorize the invaders as they passed through Hagara Kohn. She hoped also to garrison archers along the last leagues of whatever pass Aralak might choose. But for that she needed more men.

Pohati smiled weakly, lifting the wet leather of her shirt away from her breasts and flapping it, bringing cooler air in against her skin.

'Your idea, little one,' Thyri said thoughtfully, 'is still good. After the scouts, we'll have an invasion to meet. If we ever get enough men I want to fight a retreating battle. We can kill them, then fall away before them like ghosts. That's why I have so many warriors spending all their days cutting arrows. To do that best we need to be in many places. But we are weak then, one group unable to let another know how it fares. The wolves can travel swiftly, but they cannot bear messages as I am the only one who understands them.'

Pohati smiled. 'The wolves could bear children to bear the messages.'

Thyri returned the smile. 'You are rested now? We will see who can ride and who can bear another time. Today I am teaching you something else.'

She snatched up her ax and yanked Pohati to her feet.

So went things early that afternoon.

When Al'kani, the eldest of Konanci lore-masters, entered the camp, ushered by three warriors, Thyri and Pohati were at rest again. Pohati had a shallow cut along her upper arm from which blood trickled freely.

Al'kani walked erect like a young warrior. The wrinkles on his face, however, told the truth. His grin was gapped, and it linked the lines around his mouth to the lines of alert, steady eyes. Behind him were three Konanci warriors. Thyri rose and belted on her sword. The meeting was brief. Al'kani had with him the sons of dead haiki. They wished vengeance on the Arakoy. They wished to join forces with akiya toyn.

The lore-master did all the talking. His tone was lilting, peppered with the lazy, insensible humor of the aged who live on the brink of death. Or so it sounded. His eyes shone at Thyri as if he spoke of the greatest of jokes. The two boys stood silently, staring with dumb grins and starry eyes, as if her mere presence had charmed them.

Still boys, she thought. *They look out into dreams – my reputation does not aid me*. She smiled slightly at Al'kani. 'If you come to join me against the North, lore-master, you are welcome. I do, indeed, ask the aid of all Habnakys sister-tribes.'

'You are haiki nagara now?' he asked, his grin driving the wrinkles further into his cheeks.

'No,' she said. 'Just a warrior like all my people.'

'Not aikya toyn?'

A flare of anger dimmed Thyri's eyes. She felt the heat of the sun on her hair and heard the buzzing of flies as silence rippled through the camp, awaiting her reply. 'I am who I am. These valleys face a threat from the North – a haiki nagara among the Arakoy. You have seen what a *scouting* party has done, lore-master. I wish the peace of these lands to return. And I lead this tribe because they have chosen me and because I can do it. If you can show me how this is not true, then do so.' She growled lowly. Seven wolves bounded from the wood and gathered around her. One of them nuzzled up to Pohati, licking the blood from her arm.

Al'kani watched the wolves without losing his humor. 'I cannot show you that,' he said.

Thyri laughed. 'Join us, lore-master. We shall dine soon.'

He nooded to her, his eyes still insane with mirth.

They had camped along the banks of a river that ran from the mountains in the North. The evening was cool and pleasant as hunters brought in two deer and women with nets reaped three baskets full of fish from the river before the evening fires were started. Small groups of children danced in circles around rocks and trees as the horizon began to glow red and the call to dinner rang out.

Thyri sat next to Pohati in the great circle's place of honor. Al'kani sat to Thyri's other side. His young haiki sat beside him, still silent, watching passively and occasionally swatting away insects that lighted on parts of their bodies still wet from a swim before dinner. The Habnakys elders and warriors arrayed beyond spent much time talking of battle, arguing over bravery and the better ways to defeat an Arakoy. The latter debate grew heated and hilarious, lasting through the meal. Some preferred staring the enemy dead in the eye and insulting his war paint. Most liked the idea of hiding behind a bush and whooping like a female moose during mating season.

Not far away, leashed by ropes tied to deep-driven stakes, was Duguru. He was the object of thrown bones. They hurt him, but he salvaged and gnawed on them in between attacks. Thyri felt a sadness for him, the way she would for a hog that knew somehow it was to be slaughtered. Such hogs, she had observed in her youth, would often carry out their days as usual and go placidly to their deaths, nothing revealed of their pain but a certain pleading in the depths of their eyes. She had seen it often as a child. But her family had needed to eat then. The necessity here was one of leadership, stance. Duguru was the enemy, and war, after all, was war.

She made it a point to smile detachedly when any warrior or elder looked her way during the talk. Her thoughts were elsewhere: on the coming battle, her lack of strategies for it, and the fear that whatever she might come up with just wouldn't be enough.

And she thought also of Elaine – laughing, dancing, eating with the other children now as if she had grown up with them and never set foot on the *Black Rabbit*. Something in the girl had finally given, letting her life shine out again. As she ate, Thyri could hear her painfully struggling to talk with her friends. Elaine would try new words, make new sentences, and those around her would listen raptly and giggle when her attempts entered into linguistic absurdities. Elaine would giggle with them and try again.

There was much Thyri could teach her now. Much she could tell her . . . To what end? To tell her that her new life was a lie? It was not. To tell her how she had arrived among the Habnakys? Better left forgotten.

And remember, Thyri, that you were part of her nightmare.

Pohati's hand fell on her shoulder.

'You grew distant,' the girl whispered. 'Al'kani has suggested we celebrate this night with the mists of life. You, as haiki, must answer him yes. We are deep into Konanci lands. They are the children of the Great Eagle and we must partake of his *kouga*.'

Thyri glanced at the lore-master. He held a long smoking tube out to her. She smiled and nodded. The dried plant fiber was already pushed into the bowllike receptacle. Thyri took it and lit it with a brand Pohati handed to her.

The smoke rushed into her mouth, her lungs, with a different taste, a different feel, from the time before. She felt her scalp tingle and a warmth spreading through her torso from below her stomach. She exhaled and smiled oddly, handing the pipe back to Al'kani.

She turned to Pohati. The girl's face looked bright, almost made of crystal. 'This is strange,' Thyri whispered.

'It can be,' Pohati said with glittering purple rainbows lying on her hair where the setting sun hit. 'It is kouga, the mist of life. With it we may share ourselves with the spirits of the land. Tonight with the Great Eagle. Can you feel him?'

Thyri breathed in deeply. The warmth flooded through her body, then shot up her spine and exploded inside her head. Pohati grew hazy and solid again. 'I feel something,' Thyri said.

'It is he. He tests you. You are the daughter of his brother.'

'His brother named Eirik?'

Pohati wavered. 'I do not understand.'

A breeze of discord whooshed through her abdomen. 'I am not sure, little one, that I like this.'

Pohati squeezed Thyri's hand and raised an eyebrow. She turned to her right to receive the smoking tube. It had passed fully around the great circle.

Pohati inhaled the smoke, tightening her short vest. She shivered and leaned closer to Thyri. 'It is not to like, akiya toyn. It is to feel.'

Around the circle, several warriors sat now with chins against chests. Thyri looked at Al'kani. The wrinkled lore-master grinned brightly. Thyri counted the blank slots in his teeth. One, two, three . . . two, thr –

The boy haiki behind him smiled at her, opened his mouth wide, and croaked hoarsely. He smiled again. The boy behind him sighed and fell sideways with a dull thud. The thud rolled like thunder and boomed.

Pohati bobbed and flopped limply against Thyri's side. The young amazi's face swam around in her lap.

'There are further testings, akiya toyn,' Al'kani said through his grin. 'You should not pretend at what you are not.'

The last pursed lip of sun parted with the horizon and sucked away the sunset, a tide of darkness claiming all, shutting out even the moon and stars . . .

. . . the ground turned black, flat, and suddenly cracked at her feet. The earth rumbled and a cliff rose up, scant inches before her face.

Silence.

. . . three, four –

The rumble, low. Distant splashing, like the sea on the shore.

. . . seven, nine, si –

. . . and the river of blood crested the cliff, descending lazily onto her head. It lifted her and smashed her back into its jaws. She felt the claws breaking through her skin.

'You are not a warrior, Eiriksdattir akiya toyn.'

The voice – again, speaking the same again. 'Eiriksdattir has lost herself.' Laughing, leering. It came from above, without. But it came also from within; she grasped at strands of light and for her sword – her hand clutched it.

. . . sdattir, lost . . .

. . . eight, nine te – ten.

Desperately, she fought against the current and pulled herself panting from the river. She sneered at the black wasteland before her.

'What am I, then?'

'You are this!'

The beast exploded from its dark, hidden cage. Its fury overwhelmed her and let her sleep . . .

Moaning, something slapping at her leg. She grunted and rolled. Pohati, almond eyes yet glazed. Lips pursed in dreamy pleasure. Beyond her, the warriors crawling around, dazed.

'No blood,' Pohati said. 'No blood – like he wasn't really here.'

Thyri shook her head. Her senses opened. Something behind her croaked. Her face lay against clothing – with a scent familiar but vague. A scent smelt only in another time, among others. She tried to place it in vain.

Something on Kaerglen.

Through Elaine's eyes I watched the beast take Thyri and fly at Al'kani. Before she struck, he and his warriors blinked from existence, leaving behind only that which they wore. And, in the boys' places, three large toads.

The wolf left her a moment later.

It was again surely Loki. Again being careless. Or perhaps the trickster was weakened in the new land – a land whose people thought Thyri a goddess. If she did truly defeat him then, the questions of Faith's power grow deeper and more complex.

Unless Loki had merely been testing her.

The event caused, by the words of those who had witnessed it, Thyri's legend to grow. They proclaimed her *akiya nagara*, a title which she stubbornly refused, and they sent heralds further west and south.

Time passed, and Thyri founded a permanent camp under the shadow of Hagara Kohn. A few days after she solidified her position, the Arakoy raiders tried to get back through to the mountains. They had dwindled to three hundred, yet a formidable force and nearly equal in numbers to those able warriors Thyri had at hand at the time. But she had also the wolves.

She met them on a field, when she could have laid traps and finished them with little danger. But her warriors needed experience. Rune-blade in hand, she fought at the head of a wedge of twenty archers. The fifth rune of Odin deflected Arakoy fire and protected the wedge, and no spear could breach the whirling death that was Thyri's sword. Warriors of the families protected her flanks while Konanci archers lay concealed in the surrounding wood, raining arrows among the Arakoy. And then the might of the pack attacked from the rear.

Three hundred Arakoy died that day.

Togarin

They surveyed the wolves, the great grays of Hagara Kohn. Pohati wiped the sweat from her forehead and looked at Thyri, smiling, a little nervous.

Thyri raised an eyebrow, turned, and started back through the small throng of restless, excited children. 'Don't worry, little one,' she called over her shoulder. 'They know what you want them to do.'

For a while, Pohati watched Thyri recede. Neither of them had expected her to test her wolf-riding idea alone, but Thyri's life had become one of constant interruption, this morning by Togarin, a newly arrived haiki from among the peaks.

One of the little boys grabbed hold of her hand, and she tried to cast off the nervousness that seemed to grip her more tightly each moment she remained silent. Forcing a sigh, she turned to the children. 'Right,' she said. 'Who wants to be first?'

In the sea of small eyes and hands, excitement began to fade. The wolves watched her silently. Pohati felt her control of the situation rapidly slipping away, and she reasoned that no choice was left her but to boldly step forth, grab one of the animals about the neck, hop on, and hold on for her life. But as she started forward, the wolves grew restless. She eyed them. She could have sworn that they'd all been gray a moment before. But one of the beasts in the back looked dark, almost black, and he moved toward her, the others parting to make way for him.

As he drew closer, Pohati decided that it must have been a trick of the light; the wolf was indeed gray like the others.

Up close, what struck her most were his eyes – deep blue. She could almost believe they were laughing at her. The wolf reached her, then walked past, stopping before a boy a year younger than Pohati named Kuorok. The wolf licked the boy's hand, then nudged him with his muzzle.

Uncertainly, Kuorok saddled the wolf. He tucked his feet up and, a moment later, he was in the middle of the pack, still mounted, smiling at Pohati and the other children.

'Look,' he said proudly. 'Nothing to it.'

Pohati sighed. The other wolves were moving among the children now, choosing their riders. The largest approached her, gazing at her with sad eyes, as if he had witnessed her failure of leadership, had understood, and wished to console her. She smiled at him graciously, patted him on the head, and climbed onto his back.

As Thyri came upon the fringes of the camp, she realized for the first time just how much it had grown over the past weeks. She truly had an army now. And the tribes still trickled to her command as her word continued to spread. In a way, she was glad that the influx had tapered off. She'd grown tired of demonstrating her skills, and she hoped she wouldn't need to with Togarin.

All activity came to halt as she walked among these people she'd adopted as her own. She did her best to smile at them and not look too preoccupied, though her mind constantly turned on the confrontation ahead.

At first she'd planned to form a war council, bringing together the haiki and the best warriors of each tribe to discuss tactics. But she'd found quickly that more dissension arose from the meetings than anything else. Those who would agree to follow her would rarely agree to anything else. Their pride demanded rivalry between them. Only their faith in Thyri's divinity and the threat of the Arakoy invasion held them together. Thyri thought it wise to keep internal bickering over petty matters to a minimum. So she had quartered them separately and had begun to choose as best she could the most defensible sites for each haiki according to the tactics he proposed. She prayed that Pohati and the other children would succeed with the wolves: establishing a fast, dependable method of communication took on a greater importance as the days passed. In weaker moments, she wished for horses, but none in the new land seemed to know of the beasts she described.

She found it difficult to shake off a sense of impending doom; she had revealed to no one the exact details of the reports the wolves had brought her: Aralak had turned his forces finally into the mountains, forces so vast the wolves could not tell numbers, only such things as 'like the sea' and 'like the mouthfuls in a river.' But the families had bought her a little time. After discovering scouting warriors mutilated by wolves, Aralak was proceeding more cautiously, trying to keep his men safe in larger groups.

To her advantage and smug satisfaction, Aralak had no idea of what awaited him: none of his scouts had gotten far enough to see anything and live to tell of it. Facing the wolves, the Arakoy might now believe that the land itself had turned against their warlord. Only in this did she begin to think she might yet emerge victorious.

Domahandi intercepted her as she neared her destination. Since his victorious confrontation with the Arakoy scouts, he had become a trusted, if somewhat distant, adviser.

'What do we know about this haiki?' she asked him. She hadn't forgotten her encounter with Al'kani; it had made her somewhat more cautious during her introductions with the leaders who had since come to her.

'Haiki and lore-master,' Domahandi said, trying to match the rhythm of his pace to hers. 'His people are few, but their knowledge may greatly aid us. They are children of Hagara Kohn. The haiki is also *shaimn*. Very wise.'

Entering her command hut, Thyri breathed a short prayer to Odin before turning her full attention on Togarin.

He smiled at her. He seemed quite young to have been called wise by Domahandi; perhaps it felt odd because only the ancient in Hordaland were ever said to possess wisdom.

'Welcome, Haiki,' she said, seating herself across from him. Domahandi took his place behind her.

'Welcome, akiya toyn,' Togarin returned. 'I have heard of you. It will be an honor to stand at your side against the marauders from the North. Too often in the past, my people have had to face them alone.'

'These are not marauders,' she said. 'This is an army like you have never seen, commanded by a haiki nagara.'

He shrugged. 'It is fortunate, then, that you are uniting the South to stand against this haiki nagara and his army.'

'You will aid me then?'

He burst into laughter. 'Would you rather I challenged your right to command me?'

'No,' she said, laughing with him. She looked to Domahandi. 'Have some food brought,' she said. 'We have much to discuss with this man.'

Habnakys women laid a feast before them. Thyri ate ravenously, but Togarin ate little. Thyri wondered if he would have eaten anything at all if he'd felt it wise to refuse the hospitality of her table. Over the meal, she learned much: Togarin's people had lived for generations under threat of Arakoy wanderers, and they had repelled bands of the foreigners more than once during his lifetime. It seemed the Northern lands indeed were arid, less desirable than the fertil lands of the Southern valleys. Togarin knew how the Arakoy fought, but he warned her that he had little to offer in stopping a flood of the Northerners.

After eating, Thyri lifted one of the mats from the floor and scratched at the hard earth underneath with a throwing ax, trying, as best she could, to map out the mountains and Aralak's position among them.

Togarin watched her, rubbing his chin, then he sat down next to her, took the ax, and began to make corrections and fill in details she'd left out. As he worked, he began to smile mysteriously. 'The path the haiki nagara has taken runs like a river,' he said. 'Through here, here and here.'

'Then perhaps we can ambush him,' Thyri said, eyeing

how Togarin had carved a trail all the way to the lip of the Southern valleys.

He nodded. 'We should not let him reach open terrain. His people fight well there.'

'So do ours. Still, we can never match him in numbers.' She sat back, brushing her hair away from her eyes. 'But we can't hide our whole army among the peaks either. If we go in, he'll discover us, and if he breaks through, we'll have no hope of stopping him.'

Togarin still leaned over the map. His smile hadn't faded. He moved the ax back among the first tall peaks. 'There is a place here. *Hagara Bod* – the Great Bear's heart. Huge caverns where we could hide five times your army and more.'

'Perfect.'

'Perhaps he will let you inside for a time.'

'He?'

Togarin raised an eyebrow. 'It is his heart. Most who have entered have never returned.'

'Have you?'

'Yes, but I am not an army.'

'Perhaps there is no danger. Perhaps it is only legend.'

'Oh, yes, it is legend. It is also real. You must ask him before you lead your people there.' He sat back on his haunches, still smiling. 'Otherwise, he might swallow you all.'

When she saw Thyri returning, Pohati laughed and raced on wolfback to greet her. The other wolves followed, some retaining their riders, others not, as many children, already covered with scrapes and bruises from the day's work, fell to the ground. Pohati herself bled from a gash on her thigh from when she'd lost her balance and landed on a sharp rock.

'You were right, little one!' Thyri exclaimed as Pohati leapt to the ground.

Thyri bent to speak with the wolf. When she stood, she looked again at Pohati. 'He says he has enjoyed the day greatly. His name is Daargesin.'

Pohati mimicked the half-growl. 'Daargesin. Thank you, akiya toyn.'

And then the other children swamped Thyri, all wanting to know the names of their wolves. Thyri went among them, and she gave names to them all. Lastly, she reached Kuorok. While Thyri spoke with his wolf, he looked on proudly. 'I already know,' he said.

Thyri rose. 'You do? Well, then, tell me.'

'His name is Woraag Grag.'

'Good,' Thyri said. 'You are very perceptive. You will make a fine warrior, Kuorok.' She looked to Pohati. 'I want you to take over here, little one. The time has come for me to go ahead, into the mountains, and see where we might face the army when it arrives. I will speak with the other haiki, and make them aware of my plans. Togarin and I leave in the morning.'

Pohati's smile fell away.

'Do not worry,' Thyri told her. 'I'll be back.' She waved her hand out over the wolves and the children. 'You are now a commander, Pohati. You have work to do, as do I.' Briefly, Thyri gripped Pohati's shoulder, then she turned back for the camp.

Homecoming

It took Thyri and Togarin a day to get to Hagara Bod. On the journey, Thyri did her best to enjoy the beauty of the foothills while Togarin spent his time telling her the names of the plants and animals they saw, their uses and their dangers. She asked him once of the nature of Hagara Bod, but he changed the subject.

They entered the peaks in late afternoon, and just before dusk Togarin announced that they'd reached their destination. Thyri had guessed as much several minutes before he'd spoken: dark shadows dotted the mountainsides around them like so many hollow, vacant eyes.

The half-moon peeked out from behind the clouds above; Thyri stared at it, somberly reminding herself that scouting reports predicted Aralak's arriving in the valley in which she stood during the next full moon. No later, even with the wolves slowing him down.

'We should camp here,' Togarin said. 'There is a pool behind there,' he said, indicating rocks ahead, 'if you desire to swim before sleeping.'

'What about Hagara Bod?'

'You do not wish to await the morning?'

'Why? Is a cavern not just as dark during the day as at night?'

He shrugged. 'As you wish.'

'What should I do?'

'Go inside and ask his permission to bring your people here.'

'Where do I enter?'

'Anywhere.'

Thyri looked around, suddenly thrilled by the danger that seemed to lurk in every crevice, every shadow. She took a torch from her pack, lit it, and started for the nearest opening in the rocks. Halfway there, she paused and turned to look back at Togarin. 'If I don't return,' she said, 'you must stop the haiki nagara.'

She turned her back on him before he could reply.

Fifty paces into the darkness, she lost her torch. She hadn't dropped it; it had simply disappeared from her grasp. She started to speak, but the space before her mouth swallowed her words and her ears heard nothing but a low throbbing ahead in the distance. She stumbled toward it, feeling her way along the wall of the passageway.

She rounded a turn and met her mother, a shimmering ghost with sad eyes and a torn, bleeding throat. Gyda held a hand out toward her; crying, Thyri reached for it, but her fingers clutched at empty air, and the ghost faded. Another turn, and Astrid lay before her on her pyre, her lips curled into a empty smile, her skin tinged blue by the cold wind, crystals of ice glittering in her hair. She closed her eyes shut, but Astrid remained there, silently blocking her path.

'Why!' she screamed, her words, echoing this time, caving in on her. 'Why?'

She fell to her knees, and the world swam about her. On a dark, misty plain she sat. Featureless, nothing as far as she could see, then the ground before her shuddered and the beast rose up, a tower stretching up to the clouds.

'Why do you bring your pains inside of me, pale one?' boomed the sky.

'My warriors,' she said. 'We desire your shelter under the next full moon.'

'Warriors? Why?'

'Because you are our only hope. These are your mountains, are they not? Do you not feel the danger invading you from the North?'

'I feel it. But why should I aid you?'

His words crashed down upon her, battering her into

the hard soil, clouding her mind. She felt the beast rising within herself, and she fought desperately to contain it. 'Akiya toyn,' she spat through clenched teeth. 'I am akiya toyn.'

'What lies at the heart of war, akiya toyn?'

She felt as if a mountain rested on her back. She couldn't move, couldn't breathe. *'Peace,'* she croaked, then blackness gripped her mind, and her thoughts fell away into the void.

Togarin pulled himself out of the water and let the cool winds dry his skin. He listened to the night, wondering how she fared. Well, he hoped. He had no desire to take her place before Aralak. He half thought that he'd go off among the peaks and live his years out alone instead. With the deaths of thousands on his conscience.

He looked up at the stars, losing himself in the black depths between them. When his skin had fully dried, he trudged away from the pool for his clothing.

Next to them, next to his pack, she lay sleeping soundly. He smiled, and wondered what it was she had seen in the caverns. During his own initial encounter with Hagara Bod, he'd thought he'd died. Only to find himself waking the next morning, refreshed, naked under the sun.

Thyri lay before him now, her skin shining softly under the moonlight. Her sword and other belongings lay scattered on the ground next to her.

Togarin covered her with her cloak, settled on a blanket next to her, and fell asleep.

'What did you see?'

Still shaking her head, she sat up, squinting against the dazzling brightness of the morning sun. She blinked her eyes and saw Togarin there, solid, real. He asked her again what had happened and she told him.

At end, he sat, thoughtfully distant.

'Does that mean we will be safe here?'

'You are sure you asked of him what you wanted?'

'Yes.'

'Then we will be safe here. Had he refused, you would not now be alive.'

They made it back to the camp that evening, and Thyri got on with modifying her strategies to include the caverns. However weird the experience had been, she grew increasingly sure that she needed the advantage of ambush to stand a chance at all.

Her outlook on the coming battle began to improve as the days passed. A few days after Hagara Bod, a small army of children and wolves terrorized the camp, the children screaming with delight and, most important, staying mounted. Pohati assured her that they could not only ride, but that a few of them could also wield short bows, adding a new dimension to her original idea.

Pohati's council with Thyri remained constant in other areas. She made herself interested in Thyri's concerns over the overall defenses. At her suggestion, the task of fashioning arrows was given to the women, thus freeing warriors for training that many sorely needed.

Under the sun, Thyri met with her haiki and her warriors, making sure that all kept busy. Under the moon, she rested in her hut, Pohati at her side. So the days passed.

Aralak

Aralak's eyes fluttered. He could sense the old man over him, watching, ready to act should something go wrong at the end of the dream-walk. The old man's face was scarred by antiquity and a lifetime of seeking the *other* paths. But his eyes, piercing steely needles, could lay bare a man's soul. Aralak smiled and his body responded. He was haiki nagara; he feared no one. But if he were to fear, he would fear the old man. Non Sai, eldest lore-master of the Arakoy nation.

Non Sai's eyes softened, a twisted smile touching at his lips. 'Well, young friend?'

The visions, their majesties, their terrors, their death. 'As before. Men in shiny coats that turn our spears. Cities of gold far to the south burning. I heard the screams of children, smelt the stench of death. But it felt so far away this time.'

'In time, it could be near or far or never at all. She has chosen you to see that it is never so.'

'I must unite the land and take those cities into our nation. And then what? How long until the pale ones threaten our people? Do I build serpents to carry our warriors over the sea to them, serpents as they use in the dream? Those serpents are of wood, I am sure of it. I could draw them, show them to the woods-masters. But they are so huge, and the art is so strange.'

'Your dream-walks will show you the way. You are chosen.'

'Yes,' Aralak said, sitting up, his brow tense, casting deep furrows across his forehead. 'Chosen, but by whom now? The Earth Mother has not joined in my walk since we entered these cursed mountains. And now her children, the wolves, have turned upon us. We are entering the realms of other gods, Non Sai. We will lose our power.'

'No! You must carry it with you.' Non Sai's eyes darkened. 'She is strong and she is proud. She will help you banish these other gods from men's minds. The bàttle is never easy, but it can be won. You must keep her close. You must have faith!'

Aralak looked up. Non Sai's worn face was a shadowy yellow mask in the tent's firelight. 'It is dark. My walk was long.'

'Longer than most. A mist has risen, blinding the eye of the moon. It cannot see us, even with its lid opened full. It is a good sign.'

'It is only the moon, old friend. Some lore I can accept, but I have seen too much to think that the moon concerns itself with my conquests. It has glared at me often enough while I've killed. And done nothing.'

Non Sai rose, his withered limbs waving, his gnarled fingers clenched in fury. 'It was your birth-dream,' he seethed. 'To war with the moon. I saw it myself. You would do well to beware of it. To walk with caution along its paths.'

'If I feared the moon, old man, and hid myself away from its sight, I would not have united the tribes. We would not be here!'

Aralak rose, suddenly filling the tent with his bulk. Non Sai before him stood firm, dwarfed though his ire yet raged. 'Do not cast me aside, haiki nagara. You do not understand the forces you face.'

'And you, old man, do not understand that I would not *be* who I am if I trembled before your constant intimations of doom!'

The lore-master smiled. 'That's it! Draw your strength from within. I warn you not to make you tremble but to make you wary. Be wary of the moon. Be wary of her light and those who thrive under it. And keep the Earth Mother close to your heart. Without her you are nothing.' He sat, indicating a blackened leg of deer resting on a mat by the fire. 'Eat. Enforce your strength.'

Aralak snarled and snatched up the leg. He sank his teeth

into it, stripping a huge chunk of meat from tendon and bone. The greasy fat dripped, smearing his chin and the broad expanse of his chest.

Inside, he seethed. Though the mountains had turned against him, he would not be denied. Some enemy, some sorcery had fallen upon the wolf packs. When he found its source, he would crush it. He had faced sorcery before and emerged victorious. He was haiki nagara. He would spill the blood of an army of demons and tear teeth from the jaws of the Northern Bear before his dream-song was over.

Later, he stood outside his tent and leaned on the great spear from which dangled the tail feathers of the eagle king he had slain as a youth. The spear was as thick as his wrist; only *his* hand could encircle it. In battle it never left his hands. Its original tip had long since dulled; both ends were now sharpened like stakes. He could not remember the count of those whose blood had stained its wood.

The weapon was hardly a spear at all, though Aralak thought of it as such. In use and appearance, it most resembled a battle staff, a weapon Thyri had mastered before ever wielding a rune-sword. Aralak knew how to use it. The technique was new to the Arakoy yet many warriors had fashioned such staffs under the direction of their warlord. Aralak himself was shown the staff and the methods of its use by the Earth Mother, in a dream long past. Her training had not been unlike Scacath's. But it was faster – more primal, more furious.

He felt the feathers resting on the back of his hand. They did not move; no breeze had arisen to disturb them or the blankets of mist over his camp that hid him from the full, open eye of the moon. He spat – the mists had covered them each night but one since entering the mountains. It was the way of Hagara Kohn. The moon had nothing to do with it.

Around him, hidden from view, his men told stories and laughed; they had gathered together in small groups, eating and resting from the day's travels. But their laughter sounded clipped, strained. He could feel it. The wolves had touched shadowy places within them, unfettering their imaginations and fears. He would drive them hard the next day. Drive the fear of wolves from their hearts and replace it with a fear of himself. He yearned to breathe free of Hagara Kohn, to embrace fairer, more hospitable lands.

So he stood there in silence as the mist laid its burden on his hair and skin until he glistened darkly like a statue in the fountain of night. He leapt forward only when a scream disrupted the uneasy tranquility.

Some of his warriors yelped out of surprise, others held their tongues, hoping that silence would hide them from the unseen foe. They moved little; the scream had frozen them in place.

Aralak stalked forward, his spear ready and his eyes darting about, trying to pierce the white blindness. He stopped, sensing Non Sai at his side. They advanced together and found, after ten paces, the body of a sentry. Blood covered its chest, eerily stained pink by reflections in the mist.

'Wolves?' Aralak whispered.

'No pack could have infiltrated so deeply without alerting – '

Non Sai paused, looking down at the torn body.

'Wolf or demon.' Aralak grunted.

'Shhh!'

Aralak froze. He had heard it too: a footfall as undetectable as the sighing of grass to lesser ears. His eyes scanned the mist. For a moment he saw other eyes – red, piercing holes in the wall of white. They stabbed into him, then they were gone.

'She has challenged you, haiki nagara.'

Aralak squinted at the lore-master. 'Who?'

'The moon. I should have sensed her before.'

'She ran from me.'

'She challenged you. She possesses great sorcery.'

'Can you battle her?'

'I will try. But at dawn, after the moon has set. Double the perimeter guard. That should keep her from returning.'

'She appeared in the center of our camp, Non Sai.'

'No. If you look, you will see her tracks. She passed among

our warriors like a ghost. Double the guard, then she will not return. She has all the time in the world to choose her moment to strike.'

'And what have we, old man?'

Non Sai placed a hand on Aralak's shoulder. 'We have tomorrow, my friend.'

Wildfire

She breathed in the morning air, not quite believing that it could smell so sweet, so rich. The change had seemed little more than a twinge; she had felt no pain. She had not whimpered in agony. She was not now curled up in the corner of a dark cave or the dark cabin of a ship, pouring with sweat, her thoughts pacing dark corridors of self-denial that led to an oblivion barred only by an unstable acceptance of Astrid's desire that she carry on. On this morning during the height of the moon, Thyri did not wish to die.

Pohati slept still. She lay among the furs, smiling; Thyri wondered briefly at what. Stooping to wash in a basin of rainwater, she shrugged and thought back to the night. She remembered little, and that like snatches of dream. She remembered a harmony, a song full of beauty and horror and light. But the horror in the song was still music. It could not torture her. It caressed her. It embraced her like her destiny; she had run and slept that night in the arms of the land. Its song still filled her, holding her close.

She remembered seeing him. Like a cornered bear he was – confident, yet ready to strike out in the only way he knew how. A clumsy way. She had danced with him. He had not danced back. She could have killed him; she'd had the chance. Instead, she'd laughed.

She splashed clean water from another basin onto her skin, leaving the air to dry her body. She tingled all over. She'd never felt so insanely happy, as if all the world were reaching out to her, telling her it would right itself in the end. She didn't think about it – she let the sensations flow.

She stepped out and greeted the mountains; she'd moved

her army within two hour's march of Hagara Bod. The air was fresh, vital with late summer. She breathed in deeply, then returned to lounge lazily next to Pohati. The girl rolled and stirred, rubbing the sleep from her eyes.

'Akiya toyn, it is like the warmth of the Great Bear's heart to find you in the morning.'

'And the song of the stream to find you, little one,' Thyri said, completing the customary ritual. 'You slept well?'

Pohati stretched, yawned, then smiled sadly. 'I was worried for you, Thyri. Once I slept, I slept well.'

'And I too.'

Pohati's smile grew confused.

'I slept,' Thyri said. 'I dreamed.' She smiled warmly and fell silent. They lay back, losing their bodies in the softness of the furs.

At first Pohati was aware only of a chill in the air. She had fallen again into the pleasantness of hazy dream. But the chill felt wrong. As she grew aware, a sharp breath seethed through Thyri's lips, as if she'd been hit or stabbed. Thyri's eyes were closed, but they moved frantically, making the lids ripple.

Pohati shook her, and she screamed. Her eyes still did not open. Pohati looked at her and shivered; the air in the room was very cold. Thyri's skin was streaked with sweat.

Covering Thyri with a thin blanket of furs, Pohati dashed from the hut in search of help – from a lore-master, from anyone.

The river of blood passed under a gateway of mutilated men caulked with raw, oozing flesh. Arms reached out to her from the writhing structure, pleading for aid and clutching at her; their fingernails were fine sheets of steel, the edges honed as sharp as Bloodfang. They cut her; she passed them and continued on.

And the eyes that watched her from the shore. They were pools of madness, mirrors of black tortures and maggot-infested infants with hollow, vacant, dead eyes. And then the riverbanks moved. They rose out of the water, and a sudden gap marked the space between the sea and an endless expanse of blood that reached to the horizon. With a crash louder than thunder, the gap closed, sending whirlpools streaking across the sea's surface. One neared her. She dodged, then dug her claws in the riverbed, riding out the hellish turbulence.

The banks fell again. Blood covered her, filling her eyes and mouth. She desperately held fast. She tried to cough and blood flooded into her lungs. Her eyesight went gray.

Snakes, she thought as her lungs spasmed, crying out for air but receiving only more blood. Snakes in the Great Ocean – or two coils of Jormungard himself.

But you stand on a riverbed, there are no riverbeds in the sea.

Her lungs cleared and she could breathe. The riverbanks were as before – tangled morasses of roots and snake beds.

Playing with my mind, she thought. Trying to make me afraid. Trying to kill me.

An eye rose from the river. Its pupil was gold and it burned into her like liquid fire.

You have no mind, it said.

I have no mind, she replied. She stalked on.

Eternity passed.

'Who are you,' she asked.

'I am your self,' it said. 'I am the shadow within you.'

'You are the woman.'

It laughed. 'I am far darker than she.'

It rolled away, melting into the multitudes along the banks. Then the banks faded again.

Around her – colors. Bloodred to orange on her left, shades dark, unsettling, and alien to her right. The blood grew thick, like quicksand. Painfully, she pressed on.

The current lessened, and the river ran dry. She walked on polished ruby, her paws clacking heavily, throwing discord into the symphony of stars above her. She defied them to match her tune. Her ruby highway stretched on to infinity.

Cracked, Gjall, the horn of eternity. It lay where the yellow met the green, yards from Heimdall's outstretched fingers.

She loomed over the dead god. He looked so small. In the distance, Fenrir called to her.

Cracked, she thought. But it never sounded.

The Plain of Vigred shifted, and the Rainbow Bridge fell away.

It never sounded! It is not time!

Colors swirled about her. She smelt it – the scent of sorcery!

Get out of my mind!

A huge beast rose before her. Its head was of a wolf, fangs dripping, scorching the dry grass where it fell. Wings sprouted from its huge shoulders. Great wings, leathery like a bat's with veins as thick as tree trunks – they battered at her, but she refused to fight them . . . The beast faded.

A pale red sun lit the veldt.

Get out of my mind!

Out of my!

My mind!

Out!

'Out!'

She collapsed and felt hard ground tear across her cheek. She tasted dirt, then sunlight attacked her brain.

Pohati stood for a moment, limned in the doorway by a setting sun. 'Thyri!' She reached her side, lifting her from the floor.

'We thought you were dying, akiya toyn. We could do nothing.'

A face, strained and confused, appeared next to Pohati's. It belonged to Kon, eldest of the Konanci lore-masters. 'Nothing,' it repeated. 'You dreamed-walked, akiya toyn.'

She moved. Her nerves screamed, but she felt her body return. The knuckles of her right hand were white, cramped. She gripped the hilt of her sword; somehow she had risen from the furs and found it. And clung to it. Slowly, she released her grasp. The sword fell to the earth.

Pohati bent to retrieve it.

'Pohati, no!'

The young amazi looked at her.

'Akan,' Thyri forced from her lips. 'It killed him. Don't – touch.' She felt her vision dimming. The effort of speech had tapped her meager reserves of strength.

'Found me,' she murmured as Pohati and Kon carried her back to her bed of furs. 'Found death.'

'Go, Kon.' Pohati eyed him levelly.

'I am lore-master,' he said. 'I cannot go.'

'You cannot stay. You could not aid her in her need. You could not even see danger in Al'kani. She rests deeply now. She no longer needs the aid you cannot give.'

Her words were cold. She'd spent the day in fear and despair. By the time she had found Kon and returned to the hut, the chill inside could have challenged the might of *Wookaela* – the winter wind. Thyri herself had poured constantly with sweat. Kon could work no magic in the hut; his chants froze; his spells dissipated along with the misty breath that bore them. And it had grown colder such that none could stay inside. Only when Thyri had yelled out had they entered and then, as if it had never been, the freezing air was gone.

But it had taken all day. The lore-master had been useless.

'I cannot go,' he repeated.

'Get out!' She glared. 'When the sun sets she will be healed. We do not need you. We do not want you here!'

Kon looked at Pohati. Her fists were clenched, but her eyes held back the fury of the lightening. He shrank before her anger. Turning to exit the hut, he was vaguely aware of a softening of those eyes as Pohati knelt down and laid a concerned hand on the yellow-haired, white-skinned she-wolf. Then he was out in the clean evening air, though the day's memories would haunt him for many nights to come.

Duguru

Duguru moaned and rubbed at the rawness of his wrist and hand. Blood oozed from scrapes along his thumb and knuckles, but his hand was finally free.

Night had fallen. Those in the village had gathered together in the center – the women and children, chattering and playing. He could hear them not far away. Making arrows to kill his people. The white witch was already in the mountains.

He looked down at his bound foot. He glanced at his sleeping guard. The young Habnakys warrior snored lightly.

Bones and filth littered the area around Duguru's stake. Full of fear, he took up the jawbone of a deer and began to saw through the leather binding his ankle, all the while watching his guard warily. It seemed like forever, but his foot finally came free.

His guard hadn't wakened. For a moment, Duguru hesitated. He could have killed the guard, gained his revenge.

But the guard might have screamed, attracting others. No, into the night.

He turned for the forest, west – then he would turn north. Everywhere around him he imagined wolves. Howling near – far. He began to run. The forest loomed menacingly about him.

Wolves, he heard them closer.

To the north, he thought. *Must warn Aralak.*

Snarling, right in front of him. He screeched to a halt.

Dark green and shadows. He peered cautiously, trying to calm his racing heart. One step forward – a deep growl from nowhere, everywhere.

Duguru screamed and sprang to his left. The ground gave

way underneath him and he fell free for a moment, then sharpened stakes pierced his neck and torso. His scream still on his lips, he died.

Wooorg loped from the bushes and looked down into the pit. The two-leg, eyes to the sky, still twitched, still slid slowly down the stakes. The wolf howled and turned back into the wood.

Aralak

In the beginning there was no Earth. The Bear sat with the Wolf and the Eagle and long did they debate. They were all proud and could decide nothing. Then the Bear suggested they cast the ancient spell of time-power at the same time, in the same place. The result would be part of all of them. They would let it decide.

So they gathered in the emptiness and performed the casting. Great and terrible powers poured from each of them. Their sounds – the Bear's roar, the Wolf's howl, and the Eagle's scream – split the sky like the Ground Thunder. And in that rift there grew a light, and it gave off warmth. Brighter it grew, then brighter still until none of the three could stare into it any longer. They named it Sun.

The three released the last of their powers and scattered them like silver snow across the sky. Thus were born the stars. The Bear, Wolf, and Eagle agreed to leave Sun and fare out among the stars, there to await Sun's own creations, untainted by any meddling they might have engaged in if they'd stayed. So they left Sun before he was aware of them, and Sun was alone.

Long did he gaze into the splash of stars around him. He called to them with his own brilliance, but try as he might he could not reach them. So he gathered himself into himself and created Moon. But Moon turned out cold and envious. And Moon was like and unlike unto Sun. It was she-who-is-like-he. She/He defied Sun, and Sun banished her to darkness, starting the cycle that tortures her, opening her eye wide so that she can see the world's magnificence only to close it again, repeating her pain.

Thus did Sun leave her. He tried again, and he created the Earth Mother. She was beautiful, and her beauty shown out from within. Trees, mountains, springs dotted her brow. Her love bore her the children who play in her hair: birds, fish, all creatures of earth, air, and water. She created the Arakoy.

Moon has always loomed over her, hating her, torturing her with seasons. Moon brings the lightening that brings the wildfire that rages in the Earth Mother's hair. At night she/he whispers terrible secrets to the Earth Mother when Sun cannot hear.

Aralak had learned the details of the Arakoy lore before he was five. The Earth Mother had come to him first when he was thirteen to prepare him for his dream-walk. She had told him she needed him. She had told him also that the moon would try to kill him. This he had never told Non Sai. The life-dream seen at Aralak's birth was fuel enough for the lore-master's sense of doom.

Privately, Aralak felt little importance in omens and prophecies. He had defied many in uniting the Arakoy, and he could almost believe the Earth Mother's fear of the moon an illusion – a fear of her own. For was she not, in reality, a woman? She sought in their dream-walks a comfort not in his reverence but in his arms. Were those actions not like those of mortal women? What law denied her the ways of mortals? And if her fears were like those of mortals – unfounded, as often as not – they could be defeated by his strength.

As it neared dusk that day and he gazed down into Non Sai's pale features, he felt only anger. The lore-master lay, overcome, breathing uneasily. Earlier that afternoon he had nearly died. He had told Aralak no more of the spell he was casting than he had the night before. Aralak did not know what he had found, nor did he know what had defeated him. He'd only heard Non Sai's howl of agony. The old man had not wakened since.

For a moment, the lore-master's eyelids fluttered. But the eyes they revealed looked through Aralak, past him. And in those eyes the haiki nagara saw confusion and hopelessness. Gone was the fire, the ominous danger at the core of Non Sai's spirit.

Aralak cursed, set his jaw, and waved a clenched fist to the wind. Demoness, he thought, or goddess – *I will crush you!*

He stepped out of Non Sai's hut and its smell of stale air and age. Around him, the shadows grew. He stood with his back to the sunrise and watched the open eye of the moon peek over the craggy horizon. In the distance, a howling began.

That night he led the perimeter guard in a chasing of phantoms. The howling had grown, reaching the camp from all directions. He sent out units to find the wolves; his men either returned with no news or were found later, mutilated, their throats ripped out. Or so it was with most. It puzzled Aralak. Two of the dead had been shot by arrows. And these among those obviously slain by fang.

Who was he fighting?

Who could do battle beside the untamed beasts of the land?

By midnight he had lost five bands of warriors, a total of three score men. His men's fears grew more real. Reports – or rumors – had surfaced of a great white beast running within a pack of grays. On the back of one of those grays rode a *fofaarl* – a changeling demoness who walked among men wreaking destruction. She with the bow?

Aralak changed tactics then, ordering a spear-and-bow formation around the entire camp. It seemed to work; the howling continued, but the wolves and their unnatural leaders did not dare the defenses. It was little more than he had done the night before, and he grew more angry. Those of his men whose hearts had begun to fail, those who let their imaginations and fears run wild, he put to death. Their heads were carried through the camp with his unspoken message: *Fear me, not the enemy. Over it, you can prevail.* The example fostered a change of heart among the remaining warriors.

But problems yet remained, problems Aralak intended to solve or avoid while still in Hagara Kohn. The most pressing was the rumor of fofaarl in the enemy camp. If the Earth Mother could not enter the mountains, neither could her dark children. Near dawn, he discovered the rumor's source. A survivor of one of the lost patrols had made it back to the camp. Instead of reporting to Aralak, he had hidden, terrified. His fellows had protected him and kept his return secret for a time. But they had told others of what he'd said he'd seen.

The warrior's name was Totka. Aralak first slew those who had given him sanctuary. Totka then died slowly, after telling Aralak all he wanted to hear.

And then the sun cracked the horizon and the howling ended. Suddenly the dawn was deathly silent.

He marched his forces without compassion that day; in a few more, he hoped to be rid of the curse of Hagara Kohn forever.

Progress was good. He camped, according to old scout reports, between two peaks whose gateway marked a straight line into the foothills and the most fertile of valleys. Once in that terrain, wolves or no wolves, his warriors would be invincible.

He had met with his commanders en route and discussed arrangements for the details of the watch. Six strong warriors had died on the road that day; the rest neared exhaustion. They could not afford another chaotic night. The perimeter defenses were made tight, watch assignments were given, and silence was ordered in the encampment to quell rumor and encourage sleep.

Outside of his rage, Aralak may have felt doom. Things weren't right. Things hadn't been right; he'd yet no word from his advance scouts. This was not the way to fight a war. But he was being toyed with, and that thought – the realization that his enemy was somewhere out there laughing

– consumed all others. For a while though, all seemed well. He was nearly asleep, then the howling began.

He listened to it, shrugged it off. It intensified. It began to pound in his ears. He thought he heard disorder in the camp, but he wasn't sure – the howling buried other sounds, chased out other thoughts. He rose and went among his men, bellowing like the thunder of Mjolnir. His face grew dark and the powerful muscles and tendons in his neck swelled. He stood under the moon, naked but for the thin warp of leather about his waist, thrashing out with words but still more beast than man. The Arakoy cowered before him. He stormed through them, howling over the wolves and waving his great spear about until all of his men – all in that vast encampment were in their bedrolls or back at their posts. And then he focused his rage on the darkness about him, challenging the wolves, defying them and overwhelming their war cry with his own. Only when the pain in his lungs grew so great that even he could not ignore it, did he stop. Then he sought out his lore-master, storming into the heavy air of his tent.

'Old man. In the name of the Earth Mother! Wake!'

The boy's, the young warrior's – no, the war chief's face hovered over him, swimming in the mist. Heavy hands shook and picked him up.

Red rivers of blood.

'Non Sai, old friend! You must cast a spell of silence! The men must sleep!'

Eyes of ancient dead bearing into timeless evil – go home.

'Non sai!'

'Kneel to her,' the lore-master said. His word/thoughts echoed.

Kneel to her.

She is power.

'Old man!'

The hands smashed him down; the face swam away. He tasted blood in his mouth. Water of life, he thought, then returned to the darkness.

Sentinel

The white wolf padded softly through the trees until she could see the line of Arakoy through the mist. All stared out, looking for her, blind eyes passing over her position and scanning on, faces masked by fear and fatigue. Aralak's angry bellowing rang distantly behind them, demanding their vigilance.

A spearman leaned on his weapon, his eyes shutting against his will, his mind unable to shake off the tentacles of warm, forbidden sleep.

They would be worthless the following morning when Aralak would march them mercilessly into the valley flanked by Hagara Bod. Her army slept there, awaiting the battle.

She crept away to rejoin the pack that hid in a glade a short distance away. She reached it and mounted a rock to look over them: six score wolves, Pohati, Kuorok, and several other wolf-riders. Pohati yawned; another of the children lay curled up on a bed of moss, watched over by her mount.

The night burned inside of her still, but her forces felt the weight of sleep as did the Arakoy. They had done well; they had spread death and terror among Aralak's terrified, exhausted, and unprepared warriors. She had begun the attacks in earnest shortly after midnight. By then the families had exhausted the variety of their laments.

A patchy mist had risen, complicating the terrain and providing her pockets of invaluable cover from which she would spearhead a tightly formed group of fifty of the largest, fiercest grays in her command, followed by Pohati and Kuorok, who had grown amazingly adept with the

Habnákys short bow. They would choose weak points in the Arakoy defenses and strike, Thyri and the first rank of grays punching a hole aided by the children who would flank out and concentrate fire on preset targets, then taunt the adjacent defenders. Those foolish enough to pursue them had fallen to other wolves who had lain in wait.

It had been easy to avoid direct confrontation with Aralak; his roars had preceded him wherever he went. She had been free to strike like lightning, wreak havoc, and punch her way out again at a point where the children and an auxilliary command under Daargesin would be ready to give their aid.

She had lost only a handful of hunters, and the children had never really been in danger; they had had orders to avoid close confrontations once the initial surprise of each encounter had worn away. Only once had any of them been in threat of serious harm, when a lost Arakoy patrol of ten warriors had come upon Kuorok and another child from behind. Kuorok's mount, however, had killed them all; Thyri had seen the carnage afterward, unable to understand how Woraag Grag had done what he did quickly enough; or as viciously as he'd done it: two of the Arakoy had fallen with little more than skin still attaching their heads to their bodies. Ever since, Thyri had paid closer attention to the huge gray, but she'd noticed nothing out of the ordinary. She'd grown determined, however, to satisfy her curiosity before the night was done.

She leapt from her rock into the pack. She would send them to rest, but first she desired a last inspection of Woraag Grag. She stopped before him, and Kuorok backed away instinctively when she directed her gaze briefly in his direction. Woraag Grag watched her passively.

'It has been a good night,' she growled, locking her eyes into the blue depths of the wolf's.

'Many two-legs dead, hunt-mistress of hunt-masters,' he agreed.

She couldn't see it, but she could sense it now: something deep inside him denying her, laughing at her. She growled again, lowly, wordlessly, then leapt back onto her rock and ordered all back to Hagara Bod. She watched them slowly depart, something inside her seething, responding primally to animal threat, as if Woraag Grag's mere presence now defied her will, her leadership, her control of things.

While she quietly raged, Kuorok and his mount gained the point of the pack and led it off into the night.

Pohati nudged Daargesin to Kuorok's side and rode there next to him. Exhausted, grimly aware of the realities of the night, the children remained silent, Pohati trying to shrug off the echoing screams of the dying, those men who had fallen by her bow.

As they neared Hagara Bod, Woraag Grag stopped suddenly, his nose held high, attentive. Without warning, he started off north.

Pohati looked frantically after Kuorok; the boy didn't even offer her a parting glance. Woraag Grag began to run. Quickly, Pohati turned to the nearest child and ordered him to lead the others back to the caverns, then set off after Kuorok, aware that some, if not all, of the others had disobeyed her.

Woraag Grag picked up his pace. Pohati turned Daargesin then, and screamed at the pack. Daargesin joined her, and the others retreated from them. She glared at the children a moment longer, then Daargesin turned again and sped north, Pohati clawing at his neck, desperately trying to keep her seat and praying that no harm would come to them as they drew dangerously close again to the Arakoy army.

Thyri stopped when the trail of the pack lost its regularity to sudden, chaotic confusion. She skirted the mass of directionless tracks, discovering that, ultimately, only Kuorok, Pohati, and about ten other mountless wolves had left the others to travel north as fast as they could possibly travel.

She growled and raced after them.

The trail drew within a bow-shot of the Arakoy perimeter, and as she neared it, she could hear Aralak nearby. She slowed, torn by the need to follow Pohati and a burning desire to taunt the haiki nagara further. For the latter, she required only a moment's effort; she turned for the Arakoy. She would catch up to Woraag Grag soon enough.

Aralak screamed his rage, stamping along behind his defensive perimeter, waking the sleepers, battering several of them senseless.

The night would not defeat him. He glared defiantly into the mist. 'Demoness,' he screamed. 'Come to me! Face me here! Face my wrath!'

He paused; he sensed her nearby. He screamed for her again, then one of his warriors shouted, pointing at a nearby ridge.

Aralak looked up. There, on that ridge, she stood, a white ghost with those same red eyes bearing into his own. He charged her, drew closer, and threw his spear. It flew true, but she disappeared and it clattered against the rocks behind where she'd stood. A moment later he reached the spot and stooped, eyeing the tracks there, reassuring himself that he fought a physical, mortal foe. Then he picked up his spear, stood, and began to scream for her anew.

Daargesin ran until he collapsed to the forest floor, panting rapidly. Pohati fell with him, then scrambled to his side. She looked down into his eyes and began to cry. He licked her face and struggled to his feet, still looking ahead. Pohati followed his gaze and saw Kuorok standing in a glade ahead. Gripping Daargesin's fur, she continued forward. At the glade's edge, she stopped and looked on:

Kuorok stood next to Woraag Grag, but it was another there who filled Pohati's eyes: a tall, incredibly beautiful woman whose skin glowed green under the moonlight. She was naked but for a silver staff clenched in her right fist. She stood facing off Woraag Grag, who growled at her deeply.

'You aid his enemies,' the woman said to the wolf. 'You cannot stand before me. You cannot deny my right to gain his side.'

Woraag Grag growled again. Pohati sensed other wolves gathering behind her – the few who had followed against Daargesin's wishes. She looked around and saw all eyes fixed on the confrontation. She wished she could speak to them, learn what Kuorok's wolf had to say to the green woman.

'We will battle then,' the woman said, 'alone.' She waved a hand, and Pohati watched Kuorok fall to the ground; then her own vision clouded over and her knees buckled. She slept before her head met the earth.

Thyri reached them and stopped over Pohati's body. In the glade, she saw Woraag Grag and the Earth Mother facing each other, motionless. She snarled and dove for them but a force threw her back.

When she gained her feet, she saw the goddess fading, the Woraag Grag stood there alone. Again she attempted the glade; this time she succeeded.

Woraag Grag turned to her before she reached him. *'You should not be here,'* he told her.

'Who was she?' Thyri asked, still consumed by anger.

'One who would have been your death had I not stopped her. You are very powerful, akiya toyn,' he said, *'but you are yet mortal.'*

She looked at him silently, seeing him now for what he was, her realization banishing her fear of his threat.

'I involved myself in your battle tonight to save the life of a child,' he said, indicating the still form of Kuorok. *'My action invited her to join her own champion. So the wheel turns.'*

Kuorok stirred, and the wolf turned for him. Thyri heard Pohati and the rest of the wolves beginning to return to life behind her. *'Why are you here then, old one?'*

'These are truly my children,' he said. *'You have only adopted them.'* He looked at her again. *'You are chaos, woman. You have come , but you will go, and I will remain. Think on that when the blood flows tomorrow.'*

Kuorok groggily gained his feet and, as if in a trance,

climbed upon Woraag Grag's back. The ancient wolf set off with his burden toward Hagara Bod.

Thyri watched him go, then motioned the other wolves and Pohati to follow. After they'd left, she shook off the echoes of the encounter and cast about herself for the scent of prey so that the wolf could sate its hunger a final time before sunrise.

She chose a secluded spot at the north edge of Hagara Bod for the transformation. Becoming woman again, she rose and stood at the lip of a short ridge alongside a mountain stream. Nearby, she heard the bubbling of a small waterfall. There she went to swim. The chill waters braced and invigorated her.

She thought again on the night. With Aralak, she had accomplished all she'd desired and more. With Woraag Grag, she felt less certain. The images of those moments in the glade where a god had faced a goddess began to fade from Thyri's memory like dreams; she fought to retain them. She had involved herself in things that she realized she knew nothing of. Not only with Woraag Grag, but with Hagara as well: that experience yet haunted her when she felt the rock of Hagara Bod surrounding her. She was glad he had granted her wish – at least, thus far no harm had come to her people inside the caverns – but she decided then that she didn't wish to understand any of it. The Bear slept, enduring her fleeting presence; Woraag Grag posed no threat to her own life or her control of the upcoming battle; nothing else mattered.

Aralak would enter the pass within an hour. Or would he wait? Try to retreat?

No, Eiriksdattir. He will come after you. He will come whether an army marches behind him or a thousand demons block his path.

Her thoughts turned to relish their upcoming confrontation. He would fall by no other hand. She wouldn't have to order it; she doubted any in her command could stand against him. The thought of the test warmed her, fueling her longing for it. The darkness inside her was a treacherous, spectral foe. Today, she had something real, something she *knew* how to handle. She smiled at the feeling. *Let it build.*

Within an hour. For all her efforts, the warlord's host yet out-numbered her own forces. In the end, she had gained the allegiance of a mere fifteen tribes – less than a fourth of the original Arakoy number. And all her guerrilla tactics had done little to equalize the overall imbalance. The wolves cut her disadvantage in half, but she was still the weaker commander.

In numbers, the caverns gave her advantage. Once in the pass, the bulk of Aralak's forces would be caught in the middle, unable to aid their comrades at either end. There, a direct confrontation would be even, and drastically in her favor due to the state of the Arakoy warriors. And the maze of passages her wolves had mapped out gave her many openings: many small, concealed strongholds from whence brief, terrible assaults could be launched. Force placement had been relatively easy. A command of two tribes would emerge from the caverns behind the Arakoy, joining with a legion of wolves under Daargesin and Pohati. Tribes under Togarin's command would man the caverns and their openings, and Thyri herself would lead the Habnakys and the remainder of her warriors against the point of Aralak's army and the warlord himself. But what if he would not meet her? What if he turned to face the weaker forces to his rear or to his flanks? What if he had surprises of his own?

Thyri realized that she feared not for her plan. She feared for Pohati and the other children. Should Aralak turn on them, he could well wipe them out. But she could not bring herself to suggest safer, less deadly tasks – especially to Pohati, an amazi at heart now. At the time of the formulation of her strategy, Thyri had still considered her overall chances slim at best. Over the nights of the full moon, things had suddenly changed. Now she felt victory within her grasp. She felt a need to avoid risk. She felt as if she could defeat Aralak and all his forces alone.

Too many people, ones she cared deeply about, had

died. She feared the thought of adding Pohati to the list. She wanted her safe, waiting for her at battle's end. The back of a front-line hunt-master in a battle with men and arrows was not a safe place. But even then, Thyri could not think of ordering Pohati from the fray.

Even if she loved her . . .

Like Akan? Like Meg? Astrid?

Aralak will come to me, Thyri thought. *I will scream for his blood until he stands before me. He will not face the children. He will not ignore my call.*

'Our forces are placed and ready, akiya toyn.'

Pohati stood at the entrance of Thyri's command tent. She smiled at Thyri, and scratched Daargesin behind the ears. He growled softly in approval.

'And mine,' said Togarin from his seat as Thyri entered.

A group of lore-masters huddled tightly in one recess, bickering and speaking in frantic half-whispers. They debated the nature of their threat: the sorceror who had laid his curses upon akiya toyn from afar.

Thyri nodded to Pohati and Togarin. So easy, she thought. 'Go then,' she said softly, looking squarely at Pohati. 'Go and stop them. We must do it here. Today.'

Thyri went to a cavern at the end of a short series of winding, upward passages. It afforded the perfect view: from the bottle-neck Aralak would enter to the gauntlet in which she would squeeze him. Warriors under her direct command lay hidden in farther caverns and the crags and splashes of wood at the southern end of the pass. Awaiting her command to seal it. But she had plenty of time to get there. Plenty of time to watch. She watched and she braided – forty-one knots.

She wondered again if Aralak would simply march into an obviously indefensible position. He had to be a canny leader. No fool could have achieved his conquests. But he was enraged, and he hadn't slept, Thyri supposed, in days. He would enter her trap. He had no other way to go.

Akiya Nagara

Aralak, indeed, attempted the pass. Thyri watched, meditatively working the knots of her war-braid, until he was nearly beneath her, then she raced to her command post to give messengers last-minute instructions for her lieutenants. When she heard Daargesin's howl, signaling that the last of the Arakoy had entered the pass, she led the front line of her defenses onto the field. Aralak stopped a hundred paces from her.

She smiled. He towered over his warriors, and even at the distance she could see the great muscles banding his chest ripple and tense. He held up his staff and stared at her. Her hand rested on the hilt of her sword.

'Stand aside,' he bellowed. 'I am Aralak, haiki nagara of all children of the Earth. Stand aside or you will die.' His words came from a cross section of the Habnakys and Arakoy tongues. The mix sounded stranger than either tongue alone.

She laughed. Bloodshed already consumed her thoughts, though none had yet spilled under the morning sun. Her sword whispered from its scabbard. A short battle-ax appeared in her other hand.

'I am your nightmare, haiki nagara,' she returned. 'Do you not recognize me?' She raised the needle of her sword over her head. 'I am akiya nagara. I am mistress of the moon. I have led the mountains against you, and I deny you the valleys of my people. Turn now and take your men back to their women. You will not get another chance.'

For a moment he simply stared at her, his body rigid, only his eyes betraying his mounting rage. And from where she stood, Thyri actually *felt* those waves of fury. The part of her that was woman fell away. Her awareness expanded in all directions, noting everything from the scents of flowers to the positions of her men and the angles of their weapons.

Aralak's bellow of rage split the air and echoed off the walls of the pass. Thyri responded with a war cry of her own, a howl to call her forces to the attack. A shower of arrows fell on the Arakoy host as archers rained death from concealed positions along the cavernous sides of the pass. Daargesin returned Thyri's battle cry from afar, signing that he had sealed all escape routes.

The distance closed slowly as the commanders stalked toward each other. Turmoil raged behind Aralak, his warriors panicking under the sudden fire and new screams of death and a howling of wolves from the rear.

Under the sun, amid mounting cries both of bloodlust and death, they met. Metal crashed into wood, but the wood did not shatter. It had been blessed by the Earth Mother who, though far away, did still exert at least that much influence over her champion.

Thyri's attack had been deflected, but between her sword and ax she remained ready to block any of Aralak's possible counterblows or offensive combinations. He, as well, left no immediate opening. Thus did they join. Thyri's forces quickly pushed the remaining Arakoy back, stranding Aralak behind her lines. Though he surely must have been aware of this, he did not seem to care. The combat between them, they both knew, was all that mattered.

They fought – Aralak with amazing speed for his bulk, but Thyri with more. It hardly aided her. Aralak's greater reach and longer weapon neutralized her slight advantage in quickness. And, blow for blow, he was stronger. Thyri's thoughts began to turn to certain martial attack sequences, lessons learned in the very last of her seven years under Scacath, methods she had scarcely kept honed through experience. They were of a mystical nature, and they carried within them dangers to the user. Those dangers included death, if too much strength were tapped too quickly. She had never had actual cause to tempt fate.

She found herself shifting instinctively into what Scacath had called mind-of-the-tyger, a series of stances from which the warrior could begin combinations leading to the death strike. She retreated, fighting defensively, observing the patterns in Aralak's style. One of them even surprised her. Feigning an overhand blow, he shifted grip on his staff and swung wide, catching her in the side. She rolled with the blow, getting out of range before closing her guard again quickly to protect her cracked ribs.

She fought on, amazed at the feeling in her side. The pain she could shut out easily, but she'd never before faced an opponent as deadly as Astrid or Scacath. And them she had fought only in mock battles, tests of skill. With Aralak, she fought to the death.

She gritted her teeth and allowed him a seductive smile. 'Come to me, haiki nagara,' she whispered from the mind-of-the-tyger.

He lunged, and she turned his attack into one of her own. The sequence ended in an overhand death strike. Her blade met Aralak's staff at the point in front of his left hand. It sheared through the wood, and a demoniac wail pierced the air of the battlefield as whatever power the staff had contained was suddenly released. Fingers of pain fired up Thyri's arm and stabbed at her through the flaws of her gauntlet. The blade continued on, splitting Aralak's hand between the two middle fingers and traveling through hand, wrist, and forearm before exiting through his elbow.

Aralak's other hand dropped the shards of his staff and grabbed at her, catching her hair. He lunged forward, nothing in his eyes revealing any awareness of the mortal wound she had dealt him. Blood poured from his rent arm like heavy, crimson rain.

He threw Thyri back, though she got the point of her sword between them. As he fell on her, he fell on the sword. Still, his good hand struck her solidly on the side of her head, momentarily clouding her vision and blurring her thoughts. When she could see again, she looked into dead eyes.

'May Odin see you this day,' she whispered, staring up into those eyes, 'and find you worthy of Valhalla. He might hold at bay forever the forces of Ragnarok with warriors such as you, haiki nagara.'

She rolled him off herself and looked to the field. Her warriors had gained much ground. Arakoy dead covered the space between them. Shifting her sword in her grasp, she closed the gap.

Pohati

Pohati loved Thyri. If that is possible to say – if it is ever truly possible to say that one loves another – it is true. As she was light and laughter to Thyri, so was Thyri mother, lover, and mentor to her. Her fears for her mentor during the battle were actually as deep as Thyri's own for her. Pohati had seen Aralak. She had seen the man Thyri had to face. She wished they could battle him side by side.

When she joined the battle, those fears shifted to the back of her mind but they never left her. She had tasks at hand, and she worked with Daargesin, and Kuorok and his wolf, to coordinate all the activities of the families with those of the human warriors at their sides. For a time, all went well. The Arakoy were confused, and most were hardly in any condition to fight. The number of allied casualties remained remarkably low. They had smashed the Arakoy rear guard and had turned on the trapped masses within.

And then the cry went up: Thyri had slain the Arakoy warlord. Her armies cheered, rejoining the battle with joyous fervor, victory seeming imminent. The Arakoy panicked: they panicked in Pohati's direction.

For several minutes, the wolves kept them contained. The fear of Aralak, though, was suddenly lifted from the Arakoy; their fear of his killer grew. They lost all sense of reason, and fingers of them broke through Daargesin's lines. The fingers quickly became arms, the attack formations suddenly bursting apart like dams under the onslaught of rivers fed by mountain storms. The Arakoy had tapped their last reserves of strength, and they were using it to retreat.

Daargesin's howled orders might yet have contained them,

drawing in further lines of defense from his reserves, had not a stray arrow caught him in the neck. It came amid a shower of arrows, ironically from his allies above, who were wildly directing their fire in a useless effort to stop Aralak's stampeding forces. Another arrow bit deeply into Pohati's side. They fell together. Pohati scrambled, as best she could, away from the fray.

Danger, however, drew ever near. A band of fifteen Arakoy charged straight at her. Just when she thought she would die, Kuorok flashed to her side upon Woraag Grag and yanked her to her feet; the pain she felt then nearly overcame her. Out of immediate danger, he helped her onto the wolf's back. She was only vaguely aware that it was not possible that the wolf could carry them both. And then the lines before them truly shattered.

Woraag Grag dashed across the battlefield, seeking the sanctity of Hagara Bod. He reached it, but not before several Arakoy noted his flight. He took Pohati and Kuorok into the caverns, still followed by the enemy.

Once far in, Kuorok halted the ancient wolf. He listened (or Pohati saw him listen – I could see only through her eyes), and he heard the sounds of pursuit. He and Pohati counted footfalls. Five, maybe six warriors. Kuorok had seven arrows – Pohati had none; her quiver had emptied during her fall.

She collapsed against the wall of the cavern. She was dying. Her blood spurted out along the arrow's shaft in ever-increasing amounts. Kuorok tried to pull it from her side, but the pain of his touch sent flares of agony into her mind.

'Tell Thyri,' she gasped, 'not to mourn.' Her eyes closed, and her breathing grew shallow.

I viewed this event twice. I departed here the first time, then I thought on the presence of Woraag Grag. I returned to Pohati. She never actually died. After her eyes closed, I felt a rough wetness on her cheek – the ancient one's tongue. Then I felt Pohati drawing away. But she wasn't dying. She was entering the body of the wolf. Try as I might, I could not follow.

Departures

Near dusk they brought Thyri Pohati's body. She had been ready to call off the families – they had been tracking down the surviving Arakoy all afternoon. Seeing yet another lover, her skin flushed white by the absence of life – seeing Pohati with, of all things, an allied arrow in her side – changed her mind. Let them fear the shadows forever, she thought. *Arakoy! Your blind allegiance to him whose ambition caused this – I am your doom!*

Near the end, Thyri had lost much. Countless among the families had fallen by Arakoy spears during the retreat. Thinking that, Thyri doubted she could command the wolves to desist at all. Not those who had lost mothers, fathers, sisters. And Thyri estimated a full third of her human warriors dead after those last moments of fighting. After fighting to maintain her own spirits all afternoon, Pohati's thin, silent lips finally turned Thyri's victory sour.

She lifted the girl from her fur bed and held her to her breast. Thus did she sit, motionless, her eyes staring off into the sky.

Togarin, behind her, shifted nervously. 'She was in the darkness, deep. Kun, with his wolf-friend who humbles my best trackers, found her. There was a battle there, akiya toyn. I saw it myself. Six Arakoy laying lifeless, four wearing Habnakys arrows, two with torn throats. Beyond them, Kun found her. She was truly amazi.'

Slowly, Thyri shook her head. No, she thought. She looked at Togarin, her rage filling her eyes with tears. '*Your* archers killed her, haiki! Can't you tell the feathering of your own arrows!'

Togarin, his face full of sadness, stepped back. He tried to speak, then turned from Thyri and walked away.

She glared about her, and the others left as well. She was suddenly, for the first time since that morning, alone. The cold, lifeless girl in her arms could not comfort her.

It was an accident, little one. Togarin mourns for you as well. You died as all true warriors do – in battle.

No one heard from Kuorok for many days after that battle. He and Woraag Grag had disappeared after their skirmish with those last Arakoy warriors.

For Thyri, the pursuit of vengeance quickly lost its edge. She slept little that night, and the next day she apologized to Togarin. She even sent word to the families to plead for the last Arakoy lives. There had been enough bloodshed.

While she rested, allowing her rib to heal, they named her again akiya nagara. She smiled weakly under the shower of presents that followed, but she moved through the festivities only barely there. I can liken her frame of mind again only to her condition following Astrid's death. Events went on around her. She would be part of them, but then she would not.

A fortnight later, the chieftains that she theoretically ruled persuaded her to take half the army through the mountains into Arakoy lands to exact tribute from the defeated. She agreed to go, but not for that reason. She had begun to see in all the Habnakys the ghost of Pohati's spirit. And the Arakoy did need her. Without some sort of strength in the North, neighboring warlords had an open door, and the entire cycle could start over again. She desperately needed a change.

She left after enduring the next moon. For the most part, she avoided the other wolves. They had lost many while under her leadership, and she told them that she must make that calm within herself, and that she could do that only alone.

She roamed that summer through the Northern lands.

They saddened her; women and children were starving even as the crops began to ripen the fields. They had lost many hunters. Aralak, it seemed, had driven his people like slaves.

She found no evidence anywhere of foreign threats. If there were people further north, they were few and free. When autumn neared, she founded a new capital for the Arakoy, made a young Habnakys named Hoorantas haiki, assigned to him an army, then ordered the rest of the Southerners home with a request to give Togarin her right of leadership. She stayed to see Hoorantas test his reins of power, then left before first frost.

And so I reach that point at which I dropped this work some thirteen months ago. Some of that which you have read I have left untouched these past weeks. Other sections have exhausted me in my attempts to separate fact from my own fantasy. But you will not know what I mean.

This work demands much of me, more than I was, at one time, willing to give. It began with Akan.

He was a simple, beautiful savage; in seeing him through Thyri's eyes and feeling the things she felt, I found myself fearing, for the first time, the loss of my own identity. Thyri's lovemaking with Akan was animal in its fury. Always before, when I'd dared to enter the moments of Thyri's passions, they had been rooted in emotions, loves and fears *she* felt deeply, and I had felt like an unclean intruder, an observer unseen but nevertheless unwanted. When she first took Akan, Thyri did not love him. She later grew to care for him, but the first time she sought only release. The power of that release left me shaking and afraid, ending that day of my work and haunting me through another day, the first day my work on this task was disrupted.

My memories of that lost day are still hazy. I remember stealing through the streets of the city, somehow aware of pathways that I had never previously taken. I went into taverns. I drank heavily. Of that evening I have no memories at all. I awoke in my chambers near dawn. My sword lay unsheathed at the foot of my bed, and the rusty brown of dried blood stained its edge. I felt nauseous and became ill; the bile that rose was stained red. I do not know whether the blood in my stomach came from Satan's Chalice or from somewhere else. I have not tried to find out. But I have dared the city streets since, and none have eyed me any more curiously than usual. The guard did not attempt to arrest me.

Two other things I must mention of that night. The moon was not full. No reports surfaced in the city of wolves.

Whatever I did, I did as myself.

For a brief time then, I considered abandoning my work, to spend what years are left me away from my fellow man and my past. I felt I was losing myself to her. But I realized that I had done that long ago. My decision was never really in doubt – the past called me back then, just as it has now.

Things got worse. My talent can deceive me, for I have felt at times that I am like unto a god. Such powers this pool of blood grants me! And yet they are treacherous sorceries, denying me those I most crave to see inside: Astrid, Scacath, Megan.

Aralak's was perhaps the strongest mind besides Thyri's I have managed thus far to enter. His tongue was not too unlike that of the Habnakys and the other Southern tribes. Even his gods were similar. Earth Mother – akiya toyn. Like Aphrodite/Venus and Ares/Mars of the first and second great Southern empires. But there were differences. Akiya toyn was, by legend, one with the land of her children. The Earth Mother was thus also, but she desired more. And in desiring more, she lost a part of the beauty at her roots. Her people were never truly happy, never at one with themselves.

Once I dared to look into those dream-walks with Aralak's goddess. His thoughts turned to them often enough, and the idea that she appeared to him as a woman in need of physical pleasure and comfort intrigued me. Not, I think, because the idea was unique – far from it. But I wondered just to what extent she exerted her will over his. In truth, I wondered if she existed at all. And if she did, I wondered if she possessed power enough to release Thyri from her curse. Beyond that, I wondered at her motivations – what moved her to seek more? To push her followers out of her bosom, to conquer realms she seemed to desire in much the same way a child desires the stars? So many other gods have taken such paths – I sought for myself an insight into their ways.

I didn't gain it. I learned, in fact, very little except that she did exist – as Pohati saw her: tall, with large eyes, a long face, and a sad beauty that paled the splendor of life around her. And she *did* wield power. I saw her but for a moment; then a force more ravaging than the sea against a cliffside struck into my mind. I am not a cliffside that might prevail against such a force. I am made of flesh, bone, and blood – not rock. The impact hurled me from the side of my pool and smashed me against the wall of my room. I think for a time I lost consciousness; I do not remember (unconsciousness seldom carries lasting visions).

I have not since attempted my art upon a deity unless one counts Thyri herself among the grouping. I have little desire to do so in the future, but I cannot write that I'll never try again.

I felt some trepidation the morning I arose to research that battle in *Hagara Kohn*. I was gazing already into a phase of Thyri's life about which I knew nothing, about which I scarcely had clues. I *had* been with her in battle before, but not when she had been so in tune with her brethren of the wood, and not when I had no idea of the battle's outcome and the nature of the events that would immediately follow. For instance, I've assumed, all along, that Thyri will survive – all events thus far covered precede my initial encounter with her. But where I knew for a fact that Kaerglen Isle would not sink during Thyri's battle with Pye, my *personal* experience of details in the new land extends out of ignorance at only one point, that being my acquaintance with Kuorok, another being closed to me, and another like Thyri to whom past reflections do not come easy.

Seated by my pool, thinking these things, and preparing to

partake of the blood that would give me vision, I dwelt again on the episode with Akan and how I had nearly lost myself and the strength of my purpose in those brief, fantastically intense moments. A full year still separated my researches from that day I would meet Thyri in a Danish port far from the new land. The Thyri I met resembled little the *akiya toyn* of the new land, and whatever her memories of these events I now relate, they were not such that she wished to speak freely of them. To my present knowledge, she never spoke of them openly to anyone – and only to Megan, in any way at all. Deep within me, I feared for her.

I sensed that the battle in *Hagara Kohn* contained within it the seeds of her future misery and anarchistic fury. If a great tragedy had befallen her that day (and I imagined I might see her entire army perish and Thyri reduced to slavery or worse by Aralak's wrath), I did not want to be within her when it happened. I feared what that might do to my own sanity.

So I took extra precautions that morning. I quaffed two full cups of blood, hoping I would thereby acquire strength far exceeding my usual. I observed Thyri after the change, then sought a perspective.that would grant me safety as well as a view of the battle. I chose a bird – one of the bright red ones that are alien, as far as I know, to other shores. Its thoughts were extremely simple, and I found that, to some degree, I could exert my will over it by suggesting, for instance, that wherever I wanted to look was where it should look for the possibility of food. I found also, however, that its visual apparatus differs greatly from mine – things are much flatter through a bird's eye, colors are far paler, and a sudden movement tends to appear as little more than a threatening or edible blur depending on its size and speed.

The bird was useful for observing the overall direction of activities, but useless for details. I found myself that day jumping my perspective into and out of Thyri, Aralak, and a few others, ready to retreat back into the bird at the slightest sign of danger. Due to the diversity of events, I was required to observe sometimes the same span of time through different eyes so that, in the end, I had lived the battle fully twice, and certain parts of it five times.

And this day, I concede, consumed me, terrified me – for Thyri knew I was there. It was just before she joined battle with Aralak: no sound or movement escaped her; she could detect, for instance, the unnatural breathing of a nearby bird.

I had left it there, of course. I had desired to experience with Thyri the seemingly harmless moments preceding the conflict. But I hadn't dared to remove myself from it entirely. I held it still in my grip with tenuous strands of my consciousness. My meddling in this manner had somehow affected its metabolism. And Thyri felt the tang of sorcery! When her cold, deadly gaze fell upon the bird, then did my nightmares truly begin. Thyri's perceptions had exceeded, through her newfound harmony with her dual existence, any level that had previously held them, and the power that flowed through her was so heady, so intoxicating, that I feared complete loss of myself to her if I let go of the bird. But if I remained exactly where I was and she felt a need to kill it?

I retreated completely into the bird and forced it into the air. I have yet to experience death within a psychic host. I have more than passing reason to fear that Death's fingers might yet reach me through my voyeuristic endeavours.

I must write that I observed later those same moments from fully inside Thyri. The rushes of power the second time were not so intense, and I think that I might overcome in time those sensations of subjugation by practicing this art of mine on particular instances of Thyri's time line. I have yet to pursue this speculation in depth. At any rate, I stayed with her the second time through my departure the first. I wished to understand the exact extent of her awareness of sorcery. It began the same time as it did the first. It ended just when I had first left. So, once I was back fully in the bird, she couldn't sense me. Yet I still fear that somehow she *might* have. Alarak's war cry at the same moment must have distracted a significant part of her concentration. I think that she might have been capable even of sensing the subtle power in her sword. She did not, but I think the only reason for that is this: her senses extended into that blade forged by Scacath. It was a part of her then. She had not trained herself to sense sorcery *within* herself.

This past week I have completed my investigations of Thyri's involvement in matters across the Great Ocean. What I offer here, however, is slight:

Thyri spent the remainder of her time in the new land wandering, keeping to herself. Her heart was dark, and it grew darker. Of the details of this new darkness I *cannot* write – the thought of doing so has kept me sleepless for several nights. And, I'm thinking, it has no bearing on the events I intend to relate.

But that's not precisely true. I expect I'll continue to lose much sleep dwelling on this decision. Perhaps, in time, I can find the words.

Last night my investigation took me into the new land of the present – the new land of today. I desired to see Thyri's legacy – her small empire, so long after she'd abandoned it. The empire still stands. Togarin is strong, and he has kept the legend of akiya nagara and her victory over the might of the Arakoy alive. The very pass in which they fought is now a north-south trade route, and both Habnakys and Arakoy feet tread regularly the ground upon which their fathers shed blood.

Kuorok also became legend to them. He is *haiki grag* – war-chief of the blood. It is said that Thyri has returned to him, and that he is shadowed everywhere by a huge, gray wolf. Among the Habnakys there is a new song that the children sing while in the woods. It calls out greeting to Kuorok, and it asks for his favor should a darkness arrive to harm them at play.

Of Elaine: she has become a warrior under Togarin. She thinks herself Habnakys and remembers nothing of her past on Kaerglen Island. She has not taken a husband. It is said that Kuorok loves her.

I must write one last thing – concerning Non Sai. He never truly wakened from his attempt to enter Thyri's dreams. He was found dead within the remains of Aralak's last camp.

2: Nightreaver

for Galadriel

BOOK IV

THE VALKYRIE

For three nights I have dreamed the same dream over and again. As I drift into sleep, I am joined by a cloud of leaves that swirl around me and catch in my hair. Beyond the leaves: eyes of red fire. My heart fills with hunger and I sing to those eyes, begging for them to feed me, to make me strong.

And then the world explodes in a blaze of bright, silvery light. Time slows, each moment maturing into a terrible forever before the shapes around me begin to steal back their forms from the silvery realm, and I recognize the feel of cold earth beneath my feet.

I open my eyes, and the leaves have settled, carpeting the forest floor. Before me, in place of those red eyes, she stands.

Her eyes still blaze; the red burns now along the edge of her sword. The silver world lingers around her, and she moves, carrying it toward me. She raises her sword.

Never have I seen a sight more beautiful, more terrifying.

I stand motionless; beyond her, around us, nothing seems quite real. *She* is the meaning behind every breath I take. Without her I am nothing.

She draws closer, and I embrace her. Above me, something flashes, and then iron bites into my neck.

Her sword.

Here, I wake. I have lost count of the times I have so wakened these three nights. And why do I dream this dream? The scene I know; I lived it first a month ago. The woman, of course, is Thyri, but I look out through the eyes of another, one who died by her hand.

Through my research into the life of Thyri Eiriksdattir, I lived this death. Since I last put down this pen, I have spent all my days looking into that part of Thyri's life of which I now must write. Rather, I have spent all my days in research but these last three, the three days of my dreams.

My task, it seems, will grant me no rest. And so I move on. I last wrote of Thyri's days in the new land over the ocean. An idea had propelled her there: the idea that she might somehow rid herself of the *were*-beast hidden beneath her skin. This had not come to pass. If anything, Thyri had grown more like her brethren of the wood; the beast had dug itself deep into her heart, her mind, and she had abandoned her battle against it.

Indeed, she had rid herself of the company of men, and she spent the winter after her victory over the warrior-king Aralak alone, sheltering in a cave from which she would venture only to hunt, or to challenge the occasional predator daring to test her control over her domain. She defended every intrusion into her hunting grounds fiercely, like an animal. Then, when winter lessened its grip, she left her cave and fared north, traveling without destination, letting instinct be her guide. In a dark sort of way, she was content, and she let the demands of survival fill her days and dominate her waking mind. This land had become her home, and she strove to gain peace with it. Thought of leaving seemed as absurd as thought of evading the wolf under the full moon.

Her past she had buried, and when she came upon the new land's people she would watch them from a distance and they would seem to her like strangers, even though she had dwelt with them the year before and they had named her a goddess. She was not a goddess, and they were not her people. Her past beyond that, she recalled only as one recalls strands of dream, the memories hazy and incomplete as if they rose to the surface of her mind like the final, weak gestures of a drowning swimmer.

One morning, a fortnight after she'd left her winter cave,

she came upon the trail of a small boar. The scent was faint at first, but as she began to track, she lost herself in the hunt and morning passed effortlessly into afternoon. When the scent grew strong, she left the trail, skirting to the east, downwind of her prey. Approaching, she sighted the boar as he watered at a quiet pool. Under the heat of the sun, she slew her prey with a single arrow.

As she ate, she noted another faint, familiar scent: that of the sea. After eating, she swam in the pool, but the salty breeze made her restless and she set off again to explore the surrounding area. Near the sea, she discovered something that pulled up those old memories, teasing her mind, drawing her slowly up, out of the darkness:

Departure

The evening grew cold. It had not been spring for long, and after the sun turned its face away, winter was quick to reclaim the world. The sky was cloudy, and a light mist fell on the ground, glistening on the moonlit grass that covered the low mound. A great stone towered out of the earth at its foot. Thyri stood motionless before it; she had seen such sights before.

The stone was almost a megalith. It would have taken five men to set it in place. Moss had grown over it.

She stepped forward and scraped at the moss. Her labors bared the rune of the warrior and the rune of Freyr, Lord of the Vanir. There were other markings that she didn't recognize, marks of other gods; but Freyr's she knew. He was lord of more desolate climes even than those that had borne her. He was ancient, once the enemy of Odin and his sons. Thyri had known, and fought, many of his followers. They dwelt in jarldoms north of Hordaland.

How had they come here, and how long before? Grass and shrubbery had rooted in the mound. The moss on the stone might have taken one year or a hundred to gain the ground that it had.

Somewhere beyond the stone, under the mound, was a Viking warship.

The prince who had captained the ship – he lay buried with it. Had he perished of some accident or illness, or by the arrows of hostile Arakoy? Thyri stepped onto the mound. The prince had not died alone; she could feel the lost spirits of the dead in the earth and air, and a great sadness wrapped about her heart. The dead permeated the mist and caressed her like whispers of wind.

They had died far from home. With the name of Odin on their lips? If so, he had not heard them. He was too far away. They had sought new lands for their gods, and the gods had abandoned them just as Odin had abandoned her. Now they were trapped, cursed to forever live as shadows. If they had died in their homeland, they would now number among the ranks of Odin's host at Valhalla.

If Odin could not reach them, how did her curse reach across the Great Ocean to touch her?

The phantoms circled around her; the mist danced, and a dam suddenly cracked in her mind, a cascade of memories gushing forth to take form in the heavy air. She saw faces: her mother's, her uncle's, Pye's, Pohati's, Astrid's. Astrid gazed at her with hollow eyes.

Thyri rubbed her own eyes. These ghosts of her own making did not belong. She peered into the mist, concentrating. Her mother's features vanished. Pye turned, becoming a small funnel of wispy chaos before fading. A misty tear fell from Astrid's eye. Her lips quivered.

You have felt much pain, little one.

'Astrid?'

Do not mourn for them. They were not worthy. They ran from battle with Halfdan the Black, Harald's father. Only luck brought them to these shores.

The Valkyrie grew tangible. She began to glow, the mist now resting on silver armor, on gauntleted hands, on the fine wash of silky blond hair that fell down on her shoulders.

Then, behind her, Thyri heard sounds she had thought lost forever: a snort, and a steed pawing at the ground. She turned and saw Yrafax. He looked back at her thoughtfully and tucked his black, feathery wings against his sides. Astrid's steed, as immortal now as his mistress.

'Astrid!'

The Valkyrie smiled. *Time to go home, my love.*

Astrid's appearance chased all other thoughts from Thyri's awakening mind. She hadn't seen Astrid since that time she'd set to kill herself and Astrid had appeared to her to stay her hand.

So long ago . . . Now the Valkyrie returned. Astrid had not forgotten her. The darkness in Thyri's heart melted away, her old love for her cousin surfacing anew, turning back time.

'How did you find me?'

'I have never truly left you.'

'My curse is over? You will take me to Valhalla now?'

Astrid looked at her sadly. 'No. Your work is yet far from over.'

'What work?'

'I – do not know. Have you not learned peace?'

'And forgotten it again. I have tried. I have known happiness, and in each case I have destroyed it. I know only misery now. I bear a burden of many lives.'

'Your knots are forty-five now?'

Thyri nodded, her hand moving instinctively to finger the long braid behind her ear. Each knot touched recalled briefly its own set of memories, pieces of her past that Thyri had all but lost.

'Then you have learned,' Astrid said thoughtfully. 'I think, my love, that happiness is not ours to have. I have wondered if any of our people can gain it. We are desperate in love, desperate in war. We live, in the end, only to war with Loki and his forces of evil. And that, I think, is a war we shall lose.' Astrid walked slowly to her steed. She reached its side and looked back to Thyri, holding out her hand. 'You have with you all you require?'

Thyri nodded. 'I have traveled lightly.'

'Then come.'

They spoke no words as Yrafax left the ground behind and carried them up through the clouds. The land below became patchy, indistinct shadows. In the distance Thyri recognized the teeth of Hagara Kohn jutting darkly up against the night starscape. She felt as if she dreamed. Being there, in the sky

– being with Astrid, these things belonged in the realm of dream. She had left her sadnesses behind in the realm of the daylight; during that journey, Thyri was truly at peace.

They passed over a great flock of birds. Thyri looked down upon them, wondering how they all knew their positions in the wedge formation. The wind whipped her hair about. Astrid's hair blew back into her face, tickling her cheeks and neck. She moved forward, wrapping her arms about Astrid and fitting her body into the curve of her cousin's back.

'Balder is dead,' Astrid said. 'The omens of the Sibyl are coming to pass. I was there at Gladsheim after Frigg gained oaths from all things in all the worlds that they would not harm her beautiful son.'

Thyri listened to her cousin's words. She absorbed them as if they were song, a beautiful melody unmarred by the darkness of the lyric. The lyric she all but ignored, though she would recall it later and reflect upon it with alarm.

'It was like a game to us,' Astrid continued. 'No pebble, no arrow, no sword could harm Balder. His skin showed no marks or evidence of any attack at all. I struck him, Thyri, through the mind-of-the-tyger. He did not even feel my touch.' She paused, looking back. Thyri saw stars reflecting in Astrid's eyes, and she thought she saw tears.

Balder's death, spake the Sybil, signed the coming of the end.

'Hod killed him,' Astrid said, looking ahead again. 'Loki tricked him; he gave him an arrow of mistletoe – the one thing, I think, in all the worlds from which Frigg failed to gain an oath. The arrow pierced Balder's breast, and the God of Beauty died.'

'But he's a god,' Thyri murmured from her dream of peace. 'An immortal should be . . . immortal.'

'He yet lives in Niflheim,' Astrid said, 'if one can be said to live in that place. Hermod went for him. Hel appreciated his bravery and offered that, if everything in all the worlds would weep for Balder, she would release him.

'Frigg again petitioned aid from all things – all trees, all illnesses, all animals, everything and everyone except mortal man who *cannot* be involved in these things. All wept save *one* – a giantess who named herself Thokk.'

'Could you not kill her?' Thyri asked. 'Then all things would have wept.'

'No,' Astrid said. '*She* – Thokk – was the Trickster. Loki has disappeared. None have looked for him. All of Asgard mourns Balder.'

Slowly, the weight of Astrid's tale forced the beginning of an understanding in Thyri's mind. *I meant you, Astrid,* she thought. *You are Valkyrie. You must have some power among the gods. Or are things so ordered, so set by the will of Odin, that you cannot stray from his tasks?*

'I stood at his pyre, little one.' Astrid paused, gazing up to look at the gleaming, starlit outline of the serpent. 'Among my brethren I am called Shield Bearer.'

'And what shall I be called, Astrid, when I join you?'

'I am no longer sure you may do that.'

'Am I to rank then among the warriors of Valhalla?'

Astrid pointed into the sky. 'Do you see that star, my love? It was once whispered among the Aesir that the One God's son, the Christ, fell from there. The All Father desired to know, so he sent me to learn. I flew up, out of the sky and into the stars. Into the stars of the One God.'

'Stars are but flaming embers from Muspellheim,' Thyri said, 'inlaid into Ymir's skull by Odin when he erected the sky over the Earth.'

'No,' Astrid said. 'They are much more. This one was huge. Larger than the sun. And the leagues I traversed to reach it through open, glittering space – Thyri, you cannot imagine the beauty of it!

'But that is what I have learned as Valkyrie, little one. Of your destiny, I know nothing. I was there when they laid Balder on a pyre on his ship, Ringhold. I saw the throngs of Asgard gathered in sorrow, watching the giantess Hyrrokin heave Ringhold into the water with her great strength. I heard Balder's wife, Nanna, gasp as life fled from her out of grief. I watched Odin leap from the shore and lay the great ring Draupnir on his son's body.

'Since then the All Father has spoken but twice. First to the Thunderer, who grew enraged when he learned of Loki's masquerade as Thokk and desired his father's blessing for revenge. Second to me, to return you to nearer shores.'

'Why?'

'I do not know. I have seen Scacath. She has taken counsel with Odin since my death. I spoke with her, but she would not tell me the reason for her visit.'

'Where will you take me?'

'Where do you wish to go?'

'A battle,' Thyri said. She crushed herself against Astrid's back. 'A battle in which I might die. I'm so lonely, Cousin. I wish that this madness would end.' She paused. 'What did you find in the heavens, Astrid? Did you find the One God?'

'No. I found only a star, a fiery orb in an emptiness. It had no Earth. There was no life there but the star's own. I felt it, little one. Slow, churning thoughts. Strength. I have never felt such strength.'

Little more passed between them during the journey. In the silent spaces, Thyri fell back into blissful half-dream. She couldn't imagine being unhappy in the presence of her cousin; she had yearned for her for so long.

Her wish to die was a wish to remain with Astrid. In the skies, all the tragic details of her life seemed far away. Only later would she place herself where she fit into the things Astrid said. Only then would she think it strange that Odin had handed her an undefined task, and only then would she curse him for it.

Astrid, however, knew where Thyri's thoughts would lead. As they neared the shores of Erin, she uttered one line. It was preceded, and followed, by silence. 'It is because,' Astrid said, 'you are the wildfire.'

Thyri was on the edge of sleep. The words carried her fully into dream, and she would never actually recall them consciously. They entered her, rather, in a much deeper way.

They landed on a cushion of mist with grass faintly visible about three feet below the mystical horse's hooves. Thyri kissed Astrid and dismounted without speaking. Her feet stopped on a level with the steed's.

'Take care,' Astrid said. 'Yrafax will take your ground with him when we leave.'

'Must it be so soon?'

Astrid nodded. 'I am tempting Odin's wrath now. We were a night and a day in the crossing. We could have made the entire journey at the speed of thought.'

'I will not say farewell, sword-sister,' Thyri said. 'We will meet again very soon.' She turned and stepped down from the mist. When she glanced back, Astrid and Yrafax were gone.

Wildfire

The camp, smelling of fires, pork, and warm ale, was easy to find. After eluding the watch, Thyri strode boldly among the tents, her head held high, her hand on her sword's pommel. One man groped drunkenly for her. She kicked him and snatched the flagon from his hand. She went to his barrel of ale, filled his flagon, put it to her lips, and drained it. Then she filled the flagon again. She leaned against the barrel and smiled.

There was grumbling among them. All eyes fell on her. Her smile blossomed into laughter. The ale hit her stomach and its warmth coursed through her limbs. It had been so long since she'd drunk, longer since she had walked thusly into a band of male warriors who saw her as a woman, not a goddess. She never failed to get the same result.

'In whose bed do you sleep, wench?' one of them finally growled. He spoke Thyri's native tongue.

She drained the flagon and again refilled it. 'My own. And I intend to be extremely drunk when I enter it tonight.' She contented herself with drinking and watching them for a while. Her words had turned them to bicker among themselves as to who would share that drunken bed with her. They obviously thought her no more than a wench – one who had presumably dressed in some of her master's battle gear for a lark. She thought it funny that they didn't seem to care just *who* her master was. Were their fantasies true, and if she'd belonged to some officer, the winner of the argument would most likely have ended up dead the next morning.

So involved was their argument that they almost forgot about Thyri herself until she drew her sword.

Those who saw the weapon in detail gasped. One man told her to put it away. Others went for swords of their own. Another whispered, 'Bloodfang!'

She glared at him. 'Why do you speak thus?'

'Because,' a voice came from behind her, 'that is how you are known. A name given by he who bears the sister blade.'

She turned.

'Thyri Bloodfang,' he said. 'The legend lives.'

He was tall and broad, with a stiff blond beard and deep blue eyes. His hair was tied back, and his furs bore the insignia of a field commander.

'I am Anlaf Olafson. I fought against you once, battle-mistress. In the sea off the northern fjords. You captained a ship for Hordaland. You captured the vessel on which I served.'

'I do not remember you.'

'No,' he said, laughing, 'I doubt that you would. I worked an oar. You battled a man behind me. When I rose to enter the fray, you struck behind you with your elbow as if you sensed me, and I went over, into the sea.'

She considered him, smiled and raised her flagon to him, then drank. 'I am pleased to meet you, Anlaf Olafson.'

'What brings you here, Eiriksdattir?'

'Where is here, my liege?'

His gaze grew scrutinous. 'Lands of the Saxons, woman. Do you not know where you are?'

'There is to be a battle here?'

'A battle, yes, but not here. We await word from Ubbi Ragnarson, who brings ships and men. Then we march south and crush the Saxon kingling, Alfred.'

Thyri reflected on his words for a moment but did not voice her thoughts. 'Then,' she said, 'I now know where I am. I will add my sword to yours, Anlaf Olafson, if you will let me.'

His smile returned. 'Come with me, then. Partake of my ale. It is far better than the urine my men drink.'

The remark drew mixed response. One warrior protested that he'd stolen *his* ale from Anlaf's brew. In fairness, it must be written that Thyri, in the end, could tell little difference between the two.

She followed him, and catcalls from half of Anlaf's men followed her. The other half, however, had already begun to spread whispered rumor among their fellows.

In Anlaf's tent, they rested on furs and drank. Thyri eyed him over the rim of her flagon.

'What do they know of me? Your men? That I slew my kin?'

He nodded. 'They know that, yes. Some claim to know much more. Last summer I learned that Hordaland had lost the twin battle-maidens whose names had begun to invoke fear among all Vikings not under Ragnar's banner. It was said that Astrid died, and that you slew half your kin in your grief. You are *berserk*. But wintering in a tavern in Jorvik, I spoke to a warrior who credits you with the downfalls of three Swedish kings.'

Thyri grew thoughtful. They did not know of her curse – that much of her, at least, was safe. If they thought her *berserk*, they would think no ill of her at all. The battle madness was a gift of the All Father, and those who died before it were considered poor, hapless souls unlucky enough to be on the wrong end of the gifting. 'I know nothing of Swedish kings. I have fought Swedes as I have fought Danes. None recently. Their king-slayer is another.'

Anlaf laughed. 'Dread of prophecies probably.' He made a deep, growling sound, then laughed again. 'The Swedes have not the strength of the Danes.' He looked at Thyri through his mirth. 'Or Norwegians.'

'What of Eirikson? He who gave me such – an unusual name?' *My brother*, she thought.

He frowned. 'He is no longer a boy. He commands five ships under Ragnar. His blade, your blade, is feared. It is said that he calls out to you in battle.'

Erik? Thyri thought. *You have tainted his blood, little one. As darkly as if you'd fanged him . . .*

'Who,' she wondered aloud, 'tends the fields?'

'Burned,' Anlaf said. 'Your house has no fields except those Ragnar will grant your brother when the whelp bothers to ask. Harald has grown mad – assaulting Hordaland last spring. All this war he brings – for the hand of a woman.'

How many more of my blood dead?

'Gyda,' she said blankly.

'Aye,' Anlaf chuckled. 'She whose name has spread as well. She yet denies him. Harald Tangle-Hair he is called now – he swears never to comb mane or beard until she consents to wed him. He has already gained much land. And burned more, mostly the land of his beloved. Or one of them. He already has thirty-nine wives.'

'Enough,' she said, draining her flagon. 'I owe my people nothing now.' She refilled and drank more.

'Well,' Anlaf said, grinning and raising his flagon. 'Here's to Loki's tits.'

Thyri laughed and pushed thoughts of home from her mind.

As they drank, they traded stories. Thyri recounted the sea battle in which they had both fought. Another humorous thing had happened that day: a warrior had plugged a rent in Thyri's ship with his body in an accident involving a Danish arrow and a grappling hook that had ripped a section of hull out from under the port gunwale. He'd gotten wedged in, and they couldn't free him until the battle had ended. His bellowing during the fighting, however, had been louder than all others'.

Anlaf heard the tale with relish. He remembered the warrior's screams that day, remembered watching him squirm helplessly. He'd been in the water and seen it all. For Thyri, it was humorous only in retrospect. Her man had taken in a lot of water during that ordeal. He'd nearly died.

Later that night, Thyri's stories grew wilder. Near dawn, she made up a few.

Anlaf, however, told her much. Even the fraction she

remembered when she woke to the call to arms was substantial:

He served under a King Oscetyl, who served in turn under the Danish Overking, Guthrom. They had been warring with the southern Saxon, Alfred of Wessex, for years. That January they had taken Alfred's capital from him. The Saxon had melted into the wood. He was somewhere south of them, rumored to be recruiting a new army. Guthrom was holding his forces back from further encroachment into Saxon lands until reinforcements could arrive.

Those reinforcements were expected under the Raven banner of the sons of Ragnar, on Ubbi Ragnarson's flagship. Ragnar's three sons were infamous among Vikings who sailed Saxon and Celtic waters. Thyri had encountered one of them, Halfdan, during her days under Hordaland. But she had heard little but rumor beyond that. Anlaf took particular pride in telling her their tale. He was related to them through a distant cousin who was brother to Ragnar.

Many years before, three young *berserks* – Ivarr, Halfdan, and Ubbi – had set foot on Saxon shores with a small invasion force behind them, the family Raven banner above them, and their aging, rotund father before them. Ragnar had been mad. He'd killed without mercy, spreading his forces over the land as if he'd expected the sun to stop rising, thus spoiling his fun. It is said that he had never slain more than a hog before leaving his Danish homestead. After a short, fiery campaign, an angry Saxon king had thrown him into a pit with a wild hog who'd torn out his insides with its tusks.

His sons, however, had fared better. They'd gone to Erin, eventually gaining control of most of the waters around the island. The son named Ivarr had made himself king there and reigned for a few years before falling to Norwegian reavers. Halfdan and Ubbi had survived him, controlling large tracts of land and sea for many years.

Halfdan had fallen in battle the past summer, about the time Thyri slew Aralak in that great battle in the new land. Ubbi, Anlaf thought, remained strong, and he was on his way to join Guthrom's army at that very moment. All expected to soon see the Raven banner – which had, amazingly, survived through all the years, passing from brother to brother – top the edge of the plain on which the Danes camped, then lead them all on a campaign through the forests that harbored Alfred.

The ironic undercurrent of the whole conversation was that Ubbi was already dead. Not even Guthrom knew it. This is what had happened:

A week before, Ubbi had reached England at a point farther south than he had planned – well inside Saxon territory. He had left his stronghold with a force of fifty ships. The seas, however, had been treacherous, and he'd arrived with only twenty-three ships in his command. Rather than risk more men and ships in traveling up the rocky coast, he'd landed upon his first sighting shore.

He'd marched into Saxon territory with a thousand men lusting for battle. They'd laid siege to a Saxon fort. The commander of the fort, named Odda, had waited for nightfall before sending his superior forces into the field. Eight hundred Danes had died, the rest had fled to their ships and returned home.

Ubbi, and his Raven banner, had been among Odda's prizes that day. Alfred was quite pleased with the whole affair.

Despite Thyri's wish, Anlaf had not finished with his news of her homeland. Harald's skalds traveled throughout the North now, singing his saga and the plights of all others involved. Much was in these songs. Thyri herself was in these songs; her brother was in them as well.

Anlaf told Thyri that Erik had pledged to take Gyda for his own.

Warriors

The cries and shouts early the next morning pounded into her skull, forcing her awake. She looked around, tangling herself in her sables – she had passed out without disrobing for sleep.

Not far away, Anlaf still snored loudly. Thyri struggled to her feet and kicked him. He grunted. She stepped out of the tent, seeking first the nearest trough of water where she could purge the malignant taste from her mouth. Leaving, she dully noted the sounds of Anlaf awakening in a flurry of thrashings similar to her own.

The Danish camp was in an uproar. The cries came from messengers rousing the sleepers from their tents. There were many groans and curses – more than a select few had spent the idle night in ale. After drinking a great deal of water and splashing more on her face, Thyri grabbed one of the messengers by the arm and learned the details first hand: Alfred marched on them. He was, in fact, scarcely more than an hour away.

As this information sank in, Thyri snarled and threw the messenger away from her. She stormed back into the tent, colliding with Anlaf at the entrance and pushing him back onto the ground.

She glared down at him. 'An hour away. The Saxons are an *hour* away! Half the warriors are still drunk. And you' – she pointed at him – 'could very well die today due to the wisdom of your so-called leaders!'

Anlaf rubbed his eyes and looked up, still dazed. 'Wh-what?'

'Go see to your men, Olafson. I require time to myself to prepare for the day.'

The bewilderment in his eyes gave way to a brief flash of

anger. But, for whatever reason, he rose unsteadily and left Thyri in his tent.

She sat down then, untied her braid of forty-five knots, and brushed the tangles from her hair. Slowly, she began the braid anew.

Despite her experiences in the new land, Thyri was not known to the Danes as a particularly capable commander. Given time, and perhaps feeding their idea that she was *berserk*, she felt she could mold at least a group of them into a weapon she could effectively wield. But she didn't have time. She had only her sword.

In the middle of an army, and still alone.

Her thoughts returned to Astrid – how it had been when they'd first entered battle side by side. Among the ranks, they had been as boisterous and insolent as any of their comrades, but none had ever quite understood them – only their competence.

Then, they had been alone together. Their aloofness had always gained them a cold sort of respect from Vikings they'd led. But even together that had always taken time.

'Thyri!'

She looked up from her meditations. Anlaf's voice had come from outside. She heard his footfall just before he entered.

'Thyri,' he repeated, catching his breath, 'we are to spear-head the left flank, beyond the shield-wall.'

'Are we to have cavalry support?'

'I didn't think. You will want to go in mounted?'

'No,' she said, smiling disturbingly. 'I want to be in the middle of it.' *I want to die.*

'Well, then.' Anlaf smiled. 'I want you to the left of me at any rate. In front.'

'Your men won't follow me, Anlaf.'

'Oh, they don't know they will.' His grin broadened. 'Ottar! Sokki, Horik! Enter!'

The tent flap opened and three burly young warriors timidly filed in. They stared at Thyri.

'These boys are brothers,' Anlaf said. 'Sons of *my* brother who died, entrusting them to me. They have brawled together since they were this high' – Anlaf motioned to his knee – 'and they're not bad. Last year was their first season. The older warriors let them take the point of one formation last time out, thinking they would die. They didn't. They'll make formidable commanders one day, but they need experience. If you fight next to them, and they follow you, then the men will follow you. They won't take much convincing, fantastic stories of your past kept many of them awake late last night.'

'If I am so infamous,' Thyri said, 'why haven't I been summoned by Guthrom? Doesn't he know I'm here?'

'No. He has sworn a blood oath with Ubbi against your people – against all people from the far Northlands. He feels, as do many of our kings, that too much blood has been spilled on our soil by Northerners too lazy to seek holdings in the South. I neglected to mention this last night.'

Her eyes grew dark. 'How, then, did you propose to keep me here!'

'I follow Oscetyl. He does not share Guthrom's hate for Norway. And we are left alone by the overking. He will not learn of you until battle, and possibly not even then.'

'You talk as if this is a game, Anlaf.'

He smiled, his teeth showing through his beard. 'Combat is a game, Thyri Bloodfang. The only one.' He bowed to her. 'I must return now to the rest of my charges.'

Anlaf left, and Thyri scrutinized the three Vikings who shifted nervously before her. Were they so believing of ale-soaked storytelling, she wondered, that they stood in awe of a woman they'd never seen before?

She did not like that prospect. 'Which one of you is Ottar?' she asked.

One cleared his throat and nodded.

She frowned at him. His face and eyes could have belonged to any who had seen her as *akiya toyn* – as a goddess – in the new land.

Now she was elsewhere – relieved of that burden and glad of it; she had never asked for it. She suddenly felt free, and she intended to remain that way until death – until the Valkyrie – came to take her away.

She smiled at Ottar, then she kicked him sharply in the center of his chest with the point of her toe.

He doubled up in voiceless agony.

Thyri stood over him. 'Look at me once more like I'm Aesir fallen from the sky and into your lap, and I'll kill you.'

She threw them out of the tent and returned to her braiding. Thus began the training of the sons of Gunnar.

Ethandune

Misty rain fell on the plain. The sky was a uniform gray except where the distant sun turned a small patch of cloud cover a dull, pale yellow.

Gusts of wind whipped her hair about her face and neck. The wetness had penetrated her hair, bunching it into thick strands that stung when they struck her cheek. She ignored it for the moment, forcing her attention to stay fixed on the thin, dark line of the horizon.

She stood at the point of Anlaf's left with the sons of Gunnar just behind her and to her right. She was vaguely aware of unease among the warriors in her ranks. But her thoughts had no room for them. At the moment, she was cursing Guthrom's choice of battlefields. He'd made hardly an attempt at defense – she supposed he knew no other manner of battle than direct, frontal assault hinged on the terror that Viking ferocity spread. And they were on ground that sloped away behind them. The slant was gentle, and she doubted that Guthrom had even noticed, but the rain had slickened grass and loosened mud. Footing would be treacherous. Their cavalry had more to fear in the way of broken legs than Saxon spears.

They'd probably get orders to charge as soon as Alfred's banners crested the hill.

Keeping her eyes on the horizon, Thyri tucked the wet mass of her hair behind her ears and bound it there with a leather band she wrapped around her head and tied in the back. She looked at Anlaf then. Sensing her gaze, he glanced at her and grinned. He, at least, knew something of battle tactics. His front line would act as a noose, with his wedge and Thyri's forcing attackers into the space between them, disorienting them and making them easy prey for the Vikings whose axes awaited. She would feed the sons of Gunnar many maimed, staggering Saxons that day. *If* she felt her own left and rear protected. She turned to Ottar.

'Who is the best among you?'

'Uh – I am, Bloodfang.'

Sokki thumped him on the back. 'Tell the truth, Brother.'

Horik looked at Thyri and stroked his thin beginnings of a beard. 'Sokki is, battle-mistress.'

'Sokki,' she said, 'I want you on my right. Guarding my rear. You are the shield-with-teeth-and-eyes. You must tell me if our line fails on your side. You must tell me if the far flank begins to crumble. You will never stray more than two paces from me. Do you understand?'

He nodded and took the position.

Thyri turned from Ottar and Horik, who strained to catch her words as she began to instruct Sokki on the proper stance for his position and the most effective counterstrokes he could use. He picked up a little – more, actually, than she'd expected. It was a responsible task she'd given him. It contained within it attitudes and combinations of sword strokes that only she and Astrid truly understood. They had developed and perfected the tactic, so the martial techniques involved in it were peculiarly their own. In battle, they had been capable of switching the two positions without losing the tempo of the fight.

She couldn't count on Sokki for that. If he fell, she would be on her own. The prospect didn't worry her; she was there to lose herself in the clash of arms and the blood. In the back of her mind, she still wanted to die. If the Saxons could kill her, perhaps Astrid herself would return to escort her to Valhalla.

Shouts rose in the distance, and the Danes echoed them with their own alarms. Shady figures on horseback began to break the horizon. Banners fluttered above the riders as their numbers grew.

Thyri drew her rune-blade and tested its grip. She took

a short battle-ax into her left hand, then the order came to advance. As the hosts drew together, she squinted. Over the center of Alfred's army flapped two banners. One was a prancing horse on a field of white; the other, a stylized raven on a field of red.

Ubbi's banner. The song of the sons of Ragnar had ended.

Angry shouts and disturbed recollections of prophecies rippled through the ranks behind her as the Danes recognized the banner and realized what Alfred's possession of it implied: Ubbi Ragnarson had fallen. It had been said that none under the Raven banner could enter battle and know defeat.

Thyri snarled and commended Alfred. For all that he was her immediate enemy, he showed canniness – he'd attacked the Danes already with weapons that cut far deeper than swords. The display of the captured banner would have the same effect on her comrades as her use of howling wolves had had on the Arakoy. She knew then that the battle was already lost.

Battle cries erupted around her and the Danish armies rushed forward. She cleared her mind of distractions, making herself aware only of the grip of her boots on the soggy ground, the feel of Bloodfang in her grasp, and the ranks of the men she would slay with it. There was no ceremony before the battle, no talk among the leaders. Shortly before her sword first bit into flesh, she realized that Alfred had somehow amassed a force far greater than Guthrom's.

Throughout the afternoon, the battle raged. For Thyri, it was a mechanical exercise in bloodshed. Sokki held his ground well, and Thyri's wedge suffered few losses at first. She was never aware of the awe her ability instilled among the warriors behind her; many of them were able only to watch her while waiting to fill breaches in the line. She never spoke to them, never had to rally them because she never faltered. She simply killed to her front and left and maimed to her right.

The Saxons faced her with a fire that almost made her

weep. As her wedge cleared away rank after rank, the Saxons would charge anew as if they also wished to die. She wondered if their gods offered them the same glory Odin offered his fallen warriors.

As dusk neared, a command of Guthrom's to retreat reached Thyri. The overking's entire right flank had been crushed by a pincer movement executed by Alfred's cavalry, which had finally obliterated the weaker mounted units of the Danes. The shield-wall defending Guthrom's archers in the center had failed after that, and the bulk of the Danish host was in disarray and fleeing. And falling before cavalry spears.

Thyri ignored the command and fought on. The Saxons pressed against her and they fell before her in greater and greater numbers until their onrushing tide faltered against the rising barrier of dead. She began to wade through them when Anlaf's wedge collapsed. Behind her she heard Sokki pleading with her to stop lest they find themselves surrounded, one unit against the entire Saxon horde. The flank beyond him was fleeing.

She glanced back briefly to ensure that he remained with her, then she turned to press forward again. That was when Sokki brought the shaft of his axe down on her head.

When she awoke, the skies had cleared and stars dotted the roof of the world. The moon still hid below the horizon.

She groaned and heard voices in response. Ottar's: 'She will kill you now, Brother.'

She shook the ache from her skull. Sokki's face bent over hers. 'Anlaf is dead,' he said.

'So are you,' said Ottar. 'She was *berserk*. She wished to carve a path to Alfred, then die with his blood on her sword. She desired Valhalla.'

Sokki's face twisted in rage. 'Shut up, you fool!' He brushed the hair from Thyri's brow. His touch was light, his soft brown eyes full of concern.

'We are camped?' she asked wearily.

'Yes. Guthrom re-formed the shield-wall, allowing our escape. Many warriors died, but we would have been routed had we all tried to flee. He has found an ancient fort to the north. The armies are to regroup there in the morning.'

Pursued, no doubt, by this upstart Saxon king. 'You should have left me,' she spat at him. 'You have much to learn, young warrior.'

Sokki grinned. 'Had I left you, I would now have no one to teach me.'

Thyri grunted softly, then sleep returned to her.

Ghosts

The second morning after the battle, a trio of warriors sent by Guthrom wakened Thyri and invited her to Guthrom's council. Grudgingly, she rose and followed them through the camp. Everywhere she looked, she saw the anguished faces of wounded and dying men.

Guthrom's warriors had little interest in speaking to her, and she thanked Odin for this small favor. As for the reason for Guthrom's summons, she didn't care. Whatever he wanted, it had to be pointless.

A large number of Vikings milled uncertainly about the entrance of Guthrom's command tent. None of these men bore wounds, and she wondered if they'd been similarly summoned. She stopped briefly, and one of Guthrom's men turned to wait for her. She studied his gaze; it seemed placid, but the corners of his eyes hinted at concealed desperation. Still, he said nothing to her.

She smiled weakly at him.

The other two warriors had continued on; now they turned. One of them barked back, rudely demanding that Thyri catch up. The Viking who had stopped with her tried to smile.

'They do not know to whom they speak, swords-mistress.' he said softly.

She started forward. 'And you do?'

'Aye,' he said. 'I have heard tales enough.'

'And who are you?'

'I am Rollo Anskarson,' he answered, turning away.

Shortly after they reached the others, all were ushered into Guthrom's presence.

Nothing decorated the inside of Guthrom's tent but the

heavy, sharp odor of human sweat. Guthrom stood with his commanders at the far end. The overking cut an impressive figure; he possessed nearly twice the bulk of the average Viking. His legs were thick enough to be tree trunks.

If he'd been gifted with a competent brain, Thyri guessed that he would be quite dangerous.

No one present seemed capable of lifting the curtain of melancholy that had wrapped itself around the army's heart. Guthrom's eyes scanned over them with no emotion apparent in his thick features.

One of his lieutenants began to speak without ceremony, and Thyri learned what she'd begun to suspect: they had been gathered to receive appointments as field commanders, to be formally granted the tasks once executed by dead comrades. She wondered how she had happened to be considered for the position. Had someone conveniently overlooked the fact that she was Norwegian?

Her mind began to drift back to her days with Astrid. The gods had conspired to keep her alive, and she and her cousin were not to be soon united as she'd wished.

She heard her name called then, and she looked up at the speaker and nodded. Guthrom spoke, asking his lieutenant if the men would follow a battle-maiden. Oscetyl assured him that they would and said that several of Anlaf's men had told him that morning that they would follow no other. Guthrom looked for a moment at Thyri and nodded, then Oscetyl went on with his list.

Thyri paid them no attention at all after that.

When the meeting had ended, Thyri roamed out to the edge of the camp; Guthrom had led them to a hilltop that towered high above the plain below. The hill's crest was broad and wide, and it easily held the remains of Guthrom's once formidable force.

She walked along the outside embankment, staring down onto the plain. Alfred's horde approached – like an army of busy ants, she thought. She stood long in silence, watching the Saxons' progress.

It was noon, and the sun was much warmer overhead though the wind on the hill remained fierce.

She began to wish that she'd spoken out in Guthrom's presence, told him what a fool she thought he was. But still, she wanted nothing to do with him. She'd never even been sure that she wanted to war with the Saxon king; he'd merely been her first excuse for an enemy. He seemed a fine commander, and Thyri preferred now to watch him and possibly learn from the experience. Silence at the council had been her wisest choice.

At least Guthrom's scouts had found him an appropriate place to mull over his defeat. The hill fort was old, but its fortifications were adequately defensible. The slopes to the south and east were virtually unassailable. Doubled ramparts had been built around the entire perimeter by some king from ages past. Alfred, she guessed, would first skirt them to the west, then camp his men on the north side of the fort – the one position granting him relatively level ground.

Thyri eyed the barrow that stretched for fifty paces through the center of the fort. Guthrom had pitched his tents next to it in an attempt to allay fears among his men of the long-dead king buried there. She doubted it would help. The fears of the Danes were beginning to consume them. They had never known such defeat as they had suffered at Alfred's hands.

Slowly, she wandered through the camp to the barrow, then walked over the raised mound of earth. As she stepped down, she almost smiled as she realized that even this place would work ill for Guthrom.

She looked back to the barrow, wondering at the nature of the sorcerous presence awakening under its earth.

Two days later, Alfred had firmly entrenched his army on the north side of the fort. He'd gained the ground under cover of night and a siege was laid with all possible escape routes sealed after only another day.

Thyri spent this time mostly alone, though she eventually agreed to Sokki's pleas that she instruct him and his brothers in martial techniques. And in the evenings she would drink with her men, seldom speaking, but listening moodily to their tales. Many were of Harald – his power grew and the swords of his men drank deeply of the blood of neighboring Norse kingdoms.

She brooded, and she watched. The men began to dream strange dreams. On the third night of the siege, Thyri herself dreamed.

It began before she was truly asleep. She sensed its unnaturalness. It tried to draw her into visions of black death and snake-infested pits. It pulled her toward burning seas and malevolent, necrophagous mires. She fought it and woke.

Stepping out of her tent, she gazed at the barrow. Not far away, Ottar and Horik drank with a few warriors who yet remained awake, or who were afraid to sleep.

All over the hill, in fact, pockets of men huddled around fires, sleepless though dawn was but an hour away. And every few moments, someone would moan or yelp, breaking the stillness and the quiet drone of hushed conversation. From far away – from the Saxon encampment – she could hear pleasant laughter. She joined Ottar and the others.

'It is the kingling,' Ottar was saying. 'He has a sorcerer who plagues our dreams.'

Horik began to answer, but he held his tongue when he saw Thyri.

She sat on a rock next to Ottar. 'The Saxons have no sorcerer,' she said. 'At least none who does this.' She threw her head back, indicating the barrow. 'There is your evil. We desecrate hallowed ground. You have dreamed of evil, ancient death, have you not? Of skulls housing snakes and spiders? You hear corpses scream in the night, then waken to find the voice of the dead emerging from the throat of the man in the next bedroll. Who died here? How *many* died in this place long ago?'

And why? And how?

Ottar laughed. 'The dead are dead,' he said. 'They do not dream.'

Thyri ignored him. She drew her sword and inspected its

edge, then rose and went to the barrow. Her men, including Ottar for all his bravado, did not follow her.

She had no trouble with the watch – it was far away and intent on Alfred. She circled the barrow, tapping it gently with the blade of her sword, looking for a weakness that would provide an entrance. She found none. She climbed to the top and knelt, driving her sword a foot, then deeper, into the soil. She felt the sorcerous presence ripple and intensify. She pushed her sword farther.

Why do you wound me?

The voice came from inside her head.

'I wish to speak with you,' she answered.

Why?

'You harm my men.'

They are not your men. This is in your heart.

'True. But you harm them. They are warriors. They fight a battle now, and you intrude.'

They intrude. They disturb my sleep with their lusts and fears. I disturb them with mine. It is fair. Their battle, is it worthy?

'What is worthy?'

Do they war with demons, as did I?

Demons yes, she thought. Inside themselves. 'No. They war with other men.'

Then they fight without cause. They fight without enemy.

'Demons?' she asked. And he showed her.

Suddenly, the sun was setting again. The Danish encampment was gone, replaced by a sole group of fifteen tall, dark-haired warriors. The tallest among them spoke – words that Thyri could not understand but only feel: desperate, terrible words.

They were all beautiful, more like gods than men. And then from under the sunset came their enemy – black hell-spawn with leathery, oozing wings and large, watery red eyes. The things fell on the warriors.

They fought, they died. All of them.

'Two races of would-be gods,' Thyri said.

Gods.

Thyri sensed deep contempt.

What are gods?

Thyri thought on that. The vision faded.

Now you have seen. Will you champion your warriors-who-fight-men against me?

Thyri grasped the hilt of her sword and drew it from the earth. 'No,' she whispered. She turned and started for her tent.

Changes

Over the next few nights, the atmosphere in the camp grew worse, heavier and more desperate. The warriors took to napping in the day and spending long nights huddled about their fires. The ancient king pounded into their sleep, and the Saxons began a game of answering with crude calls the cries that wafted through the night from the Danish camp. Guthrom seldom left his tent.

Over these nights, the moon waxed even larger. Thyri observed this with indifference. The pathetic lassitude enveloping the camp disgusted her. Guthrom's own indifference disgusted her; it was all *wrong*. She – in returning to this place, this battle, this state of affairs – felt as if she witnessed the castration of her race, as if Astrid had delivered her unto subtle torture. Why had Odin allowed this to happen? Why had the swords of the north weakened and faltered?

As she thought these thoughts, the fact of her curse at first grew insignificant. Her acceptance of it had pushed its influence over her into that three-day cage toward which she now moved, if not willingly, then obediently. The familiar feeling of its inevitability almost granted her comfort in that it was certain, understood; it possessed qualities that stood in sharp contrast to the wrongness that had infiltrated the Viking army. Hearing the cries of the men at night, realizing that she herself slept in the arms of defeat, the edges of her new reality grew indistinct. She did not feel as if she had taken refuge among her own people any more than she had felt at home with the Habnakys in the new land. All were strangers, and none could connect her significantly to her past and thus substantiate her present. Anlaf had, but he was dead.

These feelings manifested themselves within Thyri and began to crystallize. In a way, this strengthened the beast because of its certainty, its reality, and with this strengthening came a vague desire to let them see her, let them know her for who she was – for *what* she was. Let Guthrom feel terror, experience true defeat: death, or a fate even worse.

And so she let the days pass and the moon overtake her. Only in the darkness after sunset, just before moonrise, on the first night of the wolf, did she think through the consequences of her inaction. The moon tugged at her already though it rested yet below the horizon. The bloodlust assailed her mind in waves, and terror gripped her as she realized that she had, over the past days, idly courted insanity; throughout her stay in the new land, she had kept the beast from human prey. She had made peace with her nature, but the cornerstone of that peace she had fashioned by forcing herself to seek sustenance from sheep, from deer – not from men. If she changed that now, if she stayed and let the wolf take Guthrom, she would make the overking's defeat her own. She would lose all the peace she had fought so hard to gain.

She should have left that day, escaped the camp and fled to distant forests. She would have left long before had she had a place to go, but among these men Astrid had brought her; beyond them, she had no apparent direction, no purpose. The land of the Saxons was not her own, and she knew little of it.

Nevertheless, she had to get away. She had joined Guthrom's army wishing to die, but not to die as a demon impaled upon the swords of her own people. As these realizations came to her, she looked across the space before her, into the real world: Sokki's grinning eyes gazed back at her.

They had just eaten dinner: a dilute broth that smelled of horsemeat. Supplies in the camp had run perilously low. Thyri smiled uneasily at Sokki. Why had she let things come to this? She had to get away!

'Battle-mistress?' Sokki asked, concerned. 'You look ill.'

Thyri rose unsteadily, looked desperately from Sokki to the horizon, then turned for her tent. She walked quickly, then ran, not looking back to see if anyone followed.

Inside her tent, she gathered her things, stuffing them into her sable cloak. Where was her sword? Where –

'Thyri?'

She looked up; Sokki stood in the entrance of her tent. Beyond him, on the horizon, a pale wash of white hailed the coming of the moon. She could smell the blood in him, and her mouth filled with saliva. She remembered how, long before, her mother had once stood thus in a doorway as the beast had taken her. She remembered the taste of her mother's blood in her mouth . . .

'Get out!'

'But –'

'Get out!' she growled, then turned back to her pack. Hurriedly, she took off her shift and her boots and stuffed them into the sables. Where was her sword! She closed her eyes, calming her thoughts, searching her memory for the rune-blade. She found it – resting on grass, next to where she had eaten.

Thyri leapt for the entrance, but once there, the moonlight pushed her back. Her eyes opened wide as the silver orb broke the horizon, and her legs went weak. She looked down and watched the white coat of the beast sprout through her skin and cover her legs. Her breasts caved in as the rippling white coat grew up to her neck. Claws sprang from her toes and her bones wrenched, forcing her to her knees. Pain flared through her, clouding her vision until the transformation was complete and the white wolf came fully into the world.

Then she fought it. The smell of human blood outside was almost overpowering. But she couldn't let the beast out; she couldn't allow it even a howl. The battle raged quietly, interminably, until she collapsed to the earth, in control, but the hunger raged as never before.

Still, she had to get out. She rose. With a swipe of her claws, she tore open the cloth of the back wall of her tent; then she took the knot that bound her pack into her mouth, clamped down with her fangs, and clumsily tossed the pack up so that it balanced precariously on her back.

As she stole through the new exit of her tent, she saw no men, and without further thought she shot into the night, stopping only as she neared the southern rim of the hill fort. With Alfred camped to the north, the southern guard was sparse, but still present. Along the ridge, she could count five men standing watch. Two of those men slumped on their spears, asleep.

A small hare scurried past her, and she dropped her pack and dove on the hare, pinning it to the ground with her claws. Hunger surged anew, and she consumed the hapless animal greedily, thankful that Wyrd had granted her this one small meal – not much, but enough to give her strength for what she next must do.

Quickly, she licked clean her paws, took up her pack, and crept forward. She tried to remember the lay of the southern hillside. The grade was steep and laced with gulleys, but there wasn't enough cover to hide her completely from view. However, the two sleeping guards were separated by only one other. If she could take him out silently without alerting the others, she'd have a clear path down the center of the slope.

She neared the guard's back, then leapt forth over him. Retracting her claws in midair, she smashed one massive paw down on his head; she heard the dull thud of his fall as she continued to sail out over the edge of the hill. When she landed, she began to roll, and she didn't gain her footing until she'd rolled and tumbled down a full quarter of the hillside. After that, bruised and battered, she looked up and listened. No alarm had been sounded; no one had witnessed her change, or her escape.

She made her way more carefully then, keeping to what cover the hillside offered as she struggled to contain the wolf until she could reach the plain below and race for the distant forests where she could allow it to feed.

Sokki Gunnarson frowned as he looked around the bare interior of Thyri's tent. Even in the darkness, he could tell that she'd left nothing behind.

When he noticed the tear in the far wall of the tent, he stepped hesitantly inside. With this act, he grew uneasy; Thyri's presence still lingered heavily in the air, and thought of invading her privacy caused an aching fear to take root in the pit of Sokki's stomach. The battle-mistress did not take kindly to intrusions of any kind.

And yet his eyes told him that she had gone, that she had discarded this place and that she would not return. At the torn flap of the tent's wall, he peered out over the moonlit camp. She was somewhere out there – gone from his life. But why had she left? He thought they had grown close. For him, the battle with Alfred had bound their fates together for life.

True, she had never sealed their companionship in any overt way, but she *had* spent a great deal of her time in his company, and she'd always treated him with respect, even if she hadn't been as kind to his brothers. Over the past few days, she'd even spoken moodily to him, telling him tales, offering him advice on warfare and what she had named 'the way of the warrior.' She was ever detached, but he'd considered her detachedness an outgrowth of her experience, not an underlying aspect of her character. He'd not thought her actually uncaring – until now.

Tears welled in his eyes and he squatted down, idly brushing his fingers over the earth. A gust of wind blew open the flap, and his eyes fell on an ant struggling through a depression in the soil just outside. The insect labored under the weight of a small beetle several times its size. As the ant reached an upward slope its determination exceeded its talents; Sokki watched it gain two steps, then tumble back to the bottom of the slope and try again.

He resisted an impulse to crush the insect and end its excruciating labors. And then his eyes took in the nature of the ant's obstacle. He bent forward and examined the mark; the animal that had left it was huge – far larger than any of the dogs that scavenged throughout the camp.

He brushed his hand over the earth, smoothing it, smearing the print and burying the ant who struggled out from under the dirt even as Sokki watched. Sokki stood then, suddenly fearful that some nameless beast had stolen Thyri away. But she had taken with her all her things . . . And she had acted strangely earlier, a fact reinforcing the evidence for her voluntary departure.

A tear fell to Sokki's cheek and he reached up, unsure of the meaning of the wetness. The size of the paw print lingered in his mind, and he connected it with the tear. He was crying – had his tears caused the mark of a dog to grow? He stooped to examine the print again, but his careless defacing of it had made an accurate assessment of its size impossible. He crawled forward, out of the tent, searching for a similar mark, but the ground there was seldom passed over and remained covered with grass.

He stood again and stared off into the distance for long moments before turning away, going back through the tent, and walking slowly back to the fire he had earlier shared with Thyri. It seemed to him mere moments before that they had sat there quietly, eating dinner in each other's company. As he sat, he noticed Thyri's sheathed sword. As he rose to retrieve it, Horik approached.

Sokki looked briefly to his brother. 'She is gone,' he said plainly.

'Where?'

Sokki shrugged and bent, lifting the blade.

'She left her sword?' Horik reached out for the hilt of the blade.

'No!' Sokki jerked the blade violently away. 'Do you so quickly forget the lore of these blades? They are sorcerous – they kill! Only with a gauntlet of silver may a Viking wield such a sword and live.'

Horik scowled. 'Do you really believe such stories?'

'I believe what I see, and I have seen a swords-mistress

who might have proved a match for the entire Saxon army. Will you tell me now that she was not real?'

'Of course she was real,' Horik said, dropping his eyes to the ground.

'Then the rest of her legend is real until proven false,' Sokki said. He held the blade, hilt first, toward his brother. 'Will you prove it false?'

Horik's hand started up, then dropped. 'No.' He paused. 'I'm sorry, Brother. What will you do now?'

'I will keep this blade,' Sokki said softly. 'I will keep it, guard it, and wield it if I can find a way. For Thyri Eiriksdattir I will save it, and no man shall take it from me while I yet live.' He sat, clutching the blade to his chest.

'We should tell no one, Sokki,' Horik said, openly alarmed by his brother's oath. 'If you carry that sword you should sheathe it plainly and show it to no one you do not intend to kill. If word spreads, Guthrom himself might test your oath.'

'I don't care.'

'But I do. Swear to me, Sokki. Swear this a family secret!' Horik spoke quietly but passionately, his eyes darting around nervously for anyone who might have overheard their words.

Sokki looked up. Tears had returned to his eyes.

'Swear!' Horik demanded.

Sokki looked down. 'I swear.' He set the sword between his feet. 'Go get Ottar,' he said. 'And bring ale. If ever Odin intended a night for drinking, this is such a one.'

BOOK V

THE SORCERESS

In my visions, time is a river and the past the infinite streams that feed it as it strains to spill into the sea of eternity. Looking upstream, one cannot rightly claim that the most meager trickle – the single drop – may have entered at any point other than that point where it did. Choice is illusion; all streams combine to define the present, and the placement of each drop embodies a unique significance. This I see clearly now, for no other view of the past can give substance to the present, else we all exist as part of a possibility, an imagined reality no more real than the imagined worlds of poets.

If only I could look downstream, to the future as well.

You will know that, after a fortnight in the ancient hill fort, Guthrom surrendered to Alfred. Seven weeks later, he and his lieutenants traveled south to Alfred's capital and accepted baptism by Saxon priests of the One God. Then the overking, and his followers, were sent back to the North.

The surrender ended the Danish conquest of my homeland. Thyri had no part in it. She wandered for a few months, then she surfaced in Danish Jorvik in late summer. I was there as well.

Guthrom's hall remained the center of affairs in the city for all that its lord had been defeated. In times past, a young Viking would have brought down the overking and assumed his place. As it was, all knew Guthrom's despair; the Norse bloodlust had been denied too decisively, and its thrust had turned back upon itself, leaving it free only to pervert the inevitable absorption of the survivors by the land of Arthur.

If anything, life in the streets of Jorvik was wilder than it had been since the Danes had wrested the city from the Saxons some twelve years before. The defeated Viking armies populated the inns and taverns, and nightly boasting contests often devolved into small, family wars. During daylight, affairs hardly improved: crime against merchants flourished in the absence of a strong governing hand.

I was still quite young that year: twenty-one years to Thyri's twenty-four. My father was a Saxon; I know little of him except that he died by Viking blades when the Danes took Jorvik, and that my uncle, who reared me, considered him a fine man. When I was twelve, my uncle died in an early, futile attempt to oust the Danes from Jorvik. A friend of my uncle had me sent south, where I studied for a time under Alfred's scribes.

Those years I still view as the worst of my life. The food was harsh, the discipline worse. A few years before Alfred's successful campaign, I denounced the son of Mary, whom so many people have accepted so readily, and I returned north to the wild lands of my birth. Life there always felt more real; perhaps it was the bleak power of the moors, perhaps it was that part of my blood I owe to my Pictish mother. Perhaps both – I don't know and it matters little. Alfred was a fine man and a greater king – to we Saxons, it seems, as great as the legendary Arthur was to the Celts. But he was never *my* king. My heart is lawless, and strong kingship mixes with it poorly.

So I lost myself among friends on the moors, faring into Jorvik fairly often during that time when Guthrom and his army chased Alfred around the southern realms. The city offered a great deal then to any man with a modicum of wit. The Danes were tolerant of those Saxons there still alive, and the Norsemen themselves were far from an uninteresting lot – drinkers and braggarts all. Yet still men, for all that my countrymen named them demons and reavers. They loved tales, the longer and more fantastic the better. For two years I braved the taverns where their post-raid ale fests would sometimes run on for days. With stories of hauntings and intrigues on the moor, I earned my keep. And I earned it well! It was nothing to pry from a Viking his most precious loot once he'd entered the glittering, hazed halls of Dionysus.

The small hoards I buried then . . . Probably all still there, overgrown now with heather . . .

Thyri had taken a room near the docks at the Harp and Sword, an inn run by a Saxon named Aelgulf who looked more bear than man yet still treated the transgressions of the Norse clientele with diffidence and great patience, the only way, really, that Saxons in Jorvik managed to stay healthily alive. One might put down one Viking one day, and the next find his five brothers in no placable state of mind demanding blood for blood no matter what the circumstances of the original conflict.

The heat that summer was overbearing, and I seldom entered the city before nightfall because of the smell. I remember that I considered traveling farther north, but news of that region bespoke always small wars and the idea of forced conscription never appealed to me much. I might have gone anyway had the swords-mistress from Hordaland not become part of my story, and I part of hers.

Warriors

From her room above Aelgulf's tavern, she stared moodily over the crowded marketplace. The dull aching wake of the previous night's mead lapped at the edges of her vision; she was growing used to the feeling. She'd entered the city two weeks before, but she'd found little to interest her but the drink and the temporary release it granted her.

As the sun set over the marketplace, she grinned weakly. She wished that, somehow, she could make it *matter*. She thought idly of what it might have been like had she leapt from Yrafax's back as he'd carried her from the shores of the new land to the field of battle where she'd desired to die. Even there, the Norns had denied her. Some dark part of her contemplated killing Sokki for saving her. He had no right. He had no understanding of the nature of the beast he worshiped.

Nobody understood, Thyri thought. Not even Astrid – it seemed to Thyri now that her cousin had lost her own heart in her blind service of Odin. But that was the way of the Valkyrie . . . Perhaps it was really Odin whom Thyri couldn't understand. He was real; Astrid was proof enough of that. And *he* let her agony burn on. She worshiped him with her sword, and he shunned her. When the full moon came to call her, he granted her no haven. He would not grant her even an honorable death in battle; he'd let the Sokki's of the world save her so they could gawk at her, lust after her, and tremble before her sword.

Deep reds and purples scarred the distant, western sky. Over the new land, the land of Akan and Pohati. Thyri had known some freedom there before the darkness of war had stolen it from her. She'd even loved. And now the mere thought of love pained her because everybody she loved kept dying. Astrid, Akan, Pohati – for all Thyri knew, Megan was dead as well.

Her eyes turned to the street as an armed cadre of six men approached the tavern entrance. They were already drunk, and several wineskins passed back and forth between them. She recognized two of the men as members of Guthrom's personal guard. One was Rollo, the guard who had spoken kindly to her on the morning of Guthrom's summons.

As the group drew close, they balked, and as Thyri's eyes turned farther beneath her, as she realized what fixed their gazes, she recalled the full extent of her actions the night before for the first time since her awakening late in the afternoon:

Posted on either side of the tavern's entrance, on stakes rising from the packed earth, two human heads spoke a silent warning to all desiring entrance.

Just before sunrise, still possessed of a drunken rage, Thyri had pounded those stakes into the ground herself. The men to whom the heads had belonged had confronted her late in the evening to inform her that the tales of her battle prowess had spread and that Guthrom had decided to take a royal interest in her at last. They had come to escort her into his presence. She'd declined; they'd drawn their blades and then died.

As Thyri had carved the stakes from the building's rafters, Aelgulf had feebly attempted to dissuade her, citing the fact that rotting, decapitated heads outside his door would attract only flies, not customers. She vaguely remembered asking him how he felt business might fare were his own head placed such that it might greet every customer without exception.

He'd backed off. She was surprised, however, that he'd left the heads. She must have presented a fairly convincing argument. She decided to tell him he could dispose of the sentinels whenever he wished; they *were* below her window, and the smell of the city was already bad enough.

And her actions had already served their purpose: she

could see it in the faces below. She had no doubt that the men had either heard of their comrades' fate or had come to look for them. Whatever mystery had remained, the sight greeting them had dissolved. Guthrom's message *had* been delivered to Thyri Eiriksdattir, and she wasn't listening. Maybe the realization would save their lives.

One of the leaders nudged the other, and the group proceeded single file into the tavern. Thyri looked again to the darkening sky. Unless Aelgulf told Guthrom's men where to find her, she would meet them downstairs soon enough. Perhaps they would even manage to kill her.

She looked over to the sword by the door; she had stolen it from Guthrom's smith – a fitting act since her own rune-blade probably hung now among Guthrom's arsenal. Perhaps it would kill him, as it had Akan . . . as it had her own father . . . She choked off the onset of tears with a crackling, dry fit of laughter. Once she would have confronted an army of demons to regain her blade; now it hardly seemed to matter.

As her laughter died in a hoarse croak, another sound – a strange, clacking *whoosh* from somewhere out in the dusky sky – grew audible. She peered out, fixing on a speck too near to be a star and too light to be a bird. Slowly, the clacking grew more distinct, and the speck drew closer.

Thyri forgot Guthrom's men downstairs. Something new was amiss; she could already sense the odor of sorcery infiltrating the omnipresent stench of the city.

The speck took on form – a bird. Or what was once a bird. Nothing but bones, it landed on the sill of her window, its skeletal wings still twitching, its empty eye sockets gazing at Thyri over a cracked beak. A thin silver tube hung from its neck on a golden thread.

She reached out for the tube. As her fingers brushed against its guardian's wing, the creature twitched away from her touch, then crumbled into a pile of white dust on the windowsill. A light breeze began to scatter it back out into the night. Within moments, Thyri was left only the tube on its golden thread. It was unadorned, perhaps the diameter of the finger of a small child, and it was sealed at both ends. She shook it, and something small rattled inside.

Rising, she retrieved her sword and placed the tube on the floor. Testing her aim once, she brought her sword down and sheared off one end of the tube. Inside, she found a scrap of parchment and a small aqua gemstone. Scrawled on the parchment, in Latin, was a short message: *Crush the gem in a place of power and wait for me there.*

She rose, testing the feel of the gem in her cupped hand. She knew it; she had felt it thus before. She smiled.

She knew only one possible explanation for a skeletal bird bearing such a burden: Megan of Kaerglen Isle.

Gerald had entered the city shortly after midday. For the past month he had lived a leisurely life in the country as the guest of Othar Farfirson, an elderly Dane who had retired from battle young, modestly wealthy, and wed to the daughter of a Saxon merchant. The marriage had satisfied all involved: Othar had gained an alternative to warfare, and the bride's father had gained acceptability, and thus a profitable living, among the Norse settlers, for Othar had been a feared and respected warrior in his day.

In his later years, Othar had become an expert at *hnefatafl*, a game on which Norsemen were often inclined to gamble. Gerald had accepted his friendship hoping to gain enough skill at the game to supplement his income during his forays into Jorvik. At one time, Gerald had himself been expert at dice, but he'd given up that pastime after a band of rogues had accused him of cheating, stolen his money, and all but blinded him in the left eye.

And that explains why Gerald favored that side of his face as he sat in the Harp and Sword, drinking mead and occasionally laughing at one of Aelgulf's jokes about the heads staked outside the door. Often he would scratch at that scar as the heat made it itch. He scratched at it as Guthrom's six guardsmen entered the crowded tavern.

Aelgulf, at the time, was filling Gerald's flagon. Earlier, before business had gotten out of hand, Aelgulf had put away a large quantity of the mead himself while explaining to Gerald the tale behind the heads and how he feared they would be the end of him. Now, with the tavern nearly full and the clientele notably unswayed by the gruesome spectacle outside, Aelgulf was quite boisterously drunk. As the six men entered, Aelgulf winked at Gerald and hailed them, 'Come, brave warriors, you are pale! Have you seen ghosts?'

At that, the entire tavern burst into laughter. One of the leaders of the six looked at Aelgulf, snarling. 'We have seen no ghosts, man, but we shall see yours if you do not serve us obediently as a Saxon maggot should.'

Aelgulf muttered under his breath and scurried off to his casks. Gerald sat back and looked over the tavern, which was indeed nearly full though the sun had just set. The night promised to bring the Harp and Sword more customers than it had housed all summer. All due, of course, to the same severed heads that Aelgulf had feared would chase business away. Rumors of the previous night had spread like fire through the city. It had even been said that Guthrom himself would enter the tavern to exact revenge for the deaths of his men.

And these rumors had attracted Gerald as well. He had already heard something of Thyri. Few hadn't, as many survivors of that last battle with Alfred claimed that she had slain more Saxons that one day than most Vikings might hope to their entire lives. Gerald had felt it worth an evening to see this woman for himself.

When she descended the steps, when he did see her, he had no idea of the impact she was about to have on his life. She did not even strike him as beautiful at first; he'd expected a giantess, muscles packed in shining armor and rivers of flowing, silky hair.

The woman Gerald saw was short, her blond hair tangled and matted, her armor naught but a brown cotton shift and a skirt. Her gaze was thoughtful, distant. If not for the sword dangling from her belt, Gerald would have taken her for a tired servant. He could not see through to the pains she felt; he could not picture her at the front of an army confronting a giant Arakoy warlord. He had no comprehension of the strength in her sword arm or the skill hidden behind her hazel eyes. He did not know that she, of all living warriors, had received the training of a goddess. And he would never have guessed in a century that, for three nights each month, all that skill could not hide her from the curse of the *were*-wolf that burned in her blood.

He saw only a woman, no hint of anything more, until her eyes focused on the tavern and he noticed how intently they scanned the crowd, how they paid particular attention to Guthrom's six men, and how they passed confidently on, making him feel as if, somehow, she had seen through to each of their souls and knew already who would confront her first, who would shy from battle, and how each would fight. And that intensity in her eyes cast her face in a different light, as if, when he'd first seen it, it hadn't been fully alive.

And then she looked at Gerald and started toward him. During those moments, something came alive inside him; he could feel it rise like a vine up his spine, sending icy fingers of sensation over his skin. The stale, smoky air suddenly tasted clean, and he couldn't shake off the impression that summer had magically fled and that it was spring now that clutched the earth to its breast. Spring, the flowers and festivals of Beltane, the season of making. And what had inspired this feeling? A woman. Not the warrior inside the woman, but the nearly palpable completeness – the wholeness – of the woman's presence. This he hadn't felt since the death of his Pictish mother some years before. He had come to think that he would never again feel it. Power, and the power of creation.

She stood a mere arm span beyond the far edge of his table. That was when she smiled down at him and seated herself before him.

He looked at her, unable to speak. He realized that she hadn't had the choice of drinking alone; nearly all seats in the house had occupants. From the tales he had heard, he imagined that she could have easily demanded, and received, a table of her own, but she seemed to possess nothing of the primal bloodlust that the tales of her tended to suggest. He supposed that she could yet demand that he leave her, but she only looked passively past him, her smile contained, secretive. He found himself now failing to believe that this woman had taken two heads off the shoulders of Guthrom's handpicked guard and displayed them for all to see outside the door of the tavern in which she had committed the crime.

'I am called Thyri,' she said. She was speaking to him, and her words . . . they didn't break the spell of her presence, they expanded it and yet freed him from it, inviting him to enter, to become a part of it. And when she looked at him he felt as if she were giving him those hazel eyes like a lover would.

'I am Gerald,' he said.

'I greet you, Gerald,' she said. 'Pardon my rudeness, but I need a guide. You are familiar with this city?' Her eyes strayed back to survey the contingent of Guthrom's men. She had spoken to him in the Saxon tongue; her words had been peppered with a curious hesitation, as if she struggled absently with the language.

'Yes.'

'Then I can pay you well.'

He watched her face; at first glance it remained unremarkable, almost boyish. He wondered whose weapon had given her the scar under her left eye. It was the way her expressions flowed, one into the other, that captivated him. Every blink of her eyes, every slight motion of her lips, was natural, marked with amazing fluidity.

'Where do you wish to go?' he asked her finally.

'You must escort me to a place of power.'

As she'd entered the tavern hall, seen the looks on the faces of Guthrom's warriors, and felt the tension in the air, Thyri had felt a sudden urge to laugh, like it was all part of a dream deposited on her windowsill by a delicate, flying skeleton. Gone was the dark, brooding cloud that had engulfed her heart for longer than she cared to remember.

She had found Megan, or rather, Megan had found her. The sorceress was alive, and she still cared. This one act, this act of seeking, made Thyri feel loved as she hadn't since the death of Astrid. Not even the love of the Habnakys, the love of an entire race of people, could match this gesture, for of all she had met since the fangs of the wolf had tainted her soul, Megan alone had understood her. When she had sailed blindly from the shores of Hordaland, when the sea had overwhelmed her, Megan had saved her and given her life again. When Thyri had later, desperately, sailed west in hopes that she would thus purge the curse from her veins, she had sought Megan's companionship, but Megan had refused. Only now, with the promise of the sorceress burning inside of her, did Thyri realize how much that refusal had hurt her. And that pain now but sweetened the promise.

Eventually, she focused on Guthrom's men, and the blades they carried reminded her that she did not dream. *Crush the gem in a place of power . . .* She needed to get out. By herself, finding such a place presented no problem except time. Her senses were easily keen enough, but she felt impatient, and wandering without apparent direction in and around the city could only get her into trouble. She felt no desire at the moment for swordplay or death. *Megan*, she thought, *we can set each other free.*

She began to sift through the faces in the crowd, disregarding the Norse, concentrating on those of darker hair and skin. Most sat in rowdy groups; only one sat alone. Still thinking of Megan, she started toward him.

Rollo Anskarson was twenty-nine that night, and he had served Guthrom for more than twelve years. His sword had first tasted blood when the Danes had overrun Eoforic and named it Jorvik. Since then, he had lost count of his victories. And yet, for all that he had great confidence in his prowess, he couldn't dispel the terrible fear that there, in that very tavern, a greater warrior drank. He had no real stomach to face her though he had sworn to the old man that he would escort her, dead or alive, to his hall that night. If he did not succeed, Guthrom would very likely take his head.

Rollo looked around at the others, seeking some clue in their eyes that might tell him that his doubts about facing Eiriksdattir were not his alone. But whatever they had felt at the sight of their friends' severed heads had now turned to anger; vengeance, he knew, burned in their hearts. Somehow, he could not summon up the same emotion within himself. His growing respect for Eiriksdattir's prowess made the heads outside a simple matter of fact, not tragedy.

As Rollo watched Eiriksdattir descend from her room above, Thorolf, next to him, cursed under his breath: *'There she is, the witch!'* Her eyes fell on them; Rollo wanted to look away but found that he couldn't. She looked at him, and he knew then that he could not cross his sword with hers. To his amazement, the realization did not make him feel a coward. He had no *reason* to fight her. True, Guthrom had ordered it, but the old man was truly king no longer; he had lost that right to Alfred. Rollo could not see even how Odin could fault him. Guthrom had, after all, forsaken the All Father in accepting the One God's baptism. Even if he'd done it to save his kingdom, he'd done it nevertheless. And, Rollo reasoned, if his lord could do such a thing, so could he.

No, he would not fight her. He would live to see the morning. When she sat with Gerald, Rollo found within himself a real desire to join them. He continued to watch her while listening to the conversation among his companions grow more brave, more adventurous with each passing moment. When Erling, one of the youths, started to rise, Rollo reached over and put a gauntleted hand on his shoulder.

'*I* will go,' Rollo said. They were the first words he'd spoken since entering the tavern.

As he approached Eiriksdattir, he noted how casually her hand fell to the hilt of her sword. She did not watch him directly, but he knew she was aware of his every movement. Slowly, he raised his hands to rest them on his breast. The position felt awkward, but he hoped she would read in it his true feelings. She didn't turn away from the Saxon, nor did she remove her hand from the hilt of her sword, until he stood over her.

'Guthrom sent you,' she said.

'Yes.'

'I will not go to him, Rollo Anskarson.'

She remembered him – remembered their brief encounter in the Danish camp. He did not let his surprise show, but he chided himself for supposing that one such as Thyri would consider any meeting inconsequential. 'I know.'

'You will fight me now?'

'I will not. The others might.'

She looked past him, then she looked at Gerald. 'You agree to my request?'

The Saxon nodded.

'Go back to them,' Thyri told Rollo. 'Tell them I will accompany you, but I must go first to collect my belongings.'

Rollo nodded, and Thyri rose and went for the stairs; the Saxon followed. Rollo returned to his table. 'She will come,' he said as he sat. 'She saw our swords and knew that Guthrom's will cannot be denied.'

He looked at Thorolf, and his fellow veteran grinned wildly. 'She is ours then,' he whispered. 'Let's take her, Rollo! Let's lay that Norwegian bitch in an alleyway –' He paused, tilting his flagon to his lips, pouring a large quantity of the mead over his chest. 'Let's take her,' he continued, 'and let her feel the fires that burn in Viking loins.'

Rollo grinned back, striving to keep his betrayal hidden. 'We shall see,' he said. In Thorolf's eyes, he could see the scene just suggested played out. The idea was absurd, repugnant – unworthy of one named a Viking. With these thoughts, Rollo's uncertainty about Guthrom – for the overking was ultimately responsible for the attitudes of his men – began to turn to hate.

Still, Rollo kept his grin steady while his hate and disgust extended from Guthrom to Thorolf as well.

Magic

Upstairs, Gerald discovered that Thyri's room bore no marks of the riches he'd been sure she'd possessed. Other than a broken silver tube on the floor, the only evidence that the room even boasted an occupant was a large makeshift pack fashioned out of a sable cloak. Wordlessly, Thyri lifted the pack, tossed it to him, climbed out the window, and disappeared quickly onto the tavern's roof.

He carried the pack to the window and held it out. She whisked it from his hands, and he climbed out after her.

Standing on the roof, he looked out over the city, seeing it in a way he'd never seen it before. Rows of buildings snaked up and down hills like crazy, directionless rivers. For a moment, he forgot the reason for his lack of experience; when he remembered, he motioned for Thyri to crouch low. On the roofline of Jorvik, a man was a thief; and Guthrom's archers would not hesitate to fill them with arrows without ever seeing their faces.

Thyri maintained her crouch as she led him quickly away from Aelgulf's tavern. She reminded him of a cat, so easily did she pass over the most treacherous stretches of wood, carrying her pack as if it were weightless. After she'd stopped, it took him a full minute to reach her side.

'Well?' she said.

He bent next to her, panting. *Places of power* . . . If she meant the stone circles where the countryfolk still practiced the old rites in defiance of the orders of the One God, he knew of several, but most would be unattainable before morning without good horses. He knew of one in the city, on the property of a wealthy merchant, but it would be guarded heavily by the cult that practiced its rites there. Then there were the ruins, south by the river. The city dwellers never dared enter them; they had even built their roads around them. The ruins were said to be haunted, but Gerald had passed them several times and noticed fires within. An old woman once told him that Brigid was strong there and that the goddess had put the fear of ghosts in men's minds to protect her sanctuaries within.

Places of power . . . It suddenly stunned him – how easily he courted the thought, how easily his mind turned to places shrouded by tales of demons and other unspeakable horrors that awaited the uninvited intruder: the aching consumption of the Morrigan that could suck up the unwary Christian traveler, leaving no trace but the echoing wail of a devoured soul; the vengeance of neglected, forgotten gods; the sacrificial knives of the druid . . . It was *she* – Eiriksdattir – who allowed him these thoughts without fear. She, fearless herself, would protect him. He felt this with a certainty he had never felt before.

Rising, he decided the ruins a lesser risk than the merchant's circle of stones. Taking a final, deep breath, he motioned for Thyri to follow.

The buildings there, south by the river, must once have been grand. Now no roofs remained, and only a few walls stood here and there. The river had laid its silts over the area, covering any traces of floors. In places, huge intricately carved columns of stone rose out of the ground, some as thick as the chests of the mightiest of warriors. Those walls still standing were cracked at their base by the roots of nearby trees. Vines also dug into the cracks of stones once raised to the glory of Apollo and Mars and those other gods of the dead empire. More primal forces had since claimed the terrain: Thyri could feel them, their terrible strengths lacing the air, bringing to life her sixth sense.

Gerald stood next to her. She handed him her pack. 'This place is Brigid's, you say? I know that name.'

'She was life to the people of Arthur,' he said. 'There

is a rhyme of her that my mother taught me as a child: *Born under roof without walls, fed with the milk of a white red-eared cow, she hangs her cloak on the rays of the sun, and the halls of her house blaze with its fire.*'

'She is not a cruel goddess?'

He shrugged. 'All of the ancient ones are cruel. All have lost great powers in the shadow of the One God.'

Thyri started forward. When Gerald took a step, she spoke without looking back. 'Stay,' she said. 'Await my return.'

She stopped as she neared the river. The ground where she stood was marked by charred grass, burned in circles and other patterns. The power of the place swamped her senses. Rougher stones than those hewn by the Romans lay scattered around the patterns in the grass.

Sitting before the centermost stone, she closed her eyes, and the wind began to whisper to her. She tipped the aqua gem from its pouch into her palm. Starlight glittered at the edges of its facets. A tiny yellow flame burned now in its center. She placed it on the stone, whispering, 'I would make you an offering, Brigid of flaming halls, but I know not how.'

'Your wish is offering enough, daughter of Chaos,' the wind whispered back.

The reply awakened a deep mourning in Thyri's breast. *You are alive,* she thought, *yet you wither. Like Odin, whose sons have learned defeat at the hands of the One God's people. Whose sons have taken baptism and turned their backs on he who gave them strength.*

'I have strength enough, moon-cursed, though I have been named a saint of the One God. In time that will kill me, for I will not change. Perhaps it is your Odin who changes. Has he not abandoned you?'

Moon-cursed, Thyri thought. *I have been named that but once, and by my own pen. Is my pain so visible?*

'To those who may see it, yes.'

Is there no escape?

'From all the pains of life, there is but one certain escape.'

Death, Thyri thought. *But Death will not have me. Had it desired me, its chances have been many.*

'Then live. Work your magic and go.'

Thyri recalled Tana, princess of Kaerglen, whom she had told to seek knowledge of Brigid. The power in the girl was very strong. *'Wait, goddess,'* she whispered. *'Perhaps I can offer you something. There lives a princess, on an isle the far side of Erin. She is very young. She seeks you.'*

'Do not fear, she has found me. I am no dead saint yet. Work your magic. We shall meet again.'

'Tana,' Thyri said, crying now as she felt a grief she did not try to understand. 'Tana, goddess, her name is Tana.'

The wind, this time, brought no reply. Thyri looked down at the gem, and the yellow flame at its heart faded and then was gone. Still crying, she unsheathed her sword and brought its hilt down on the gem, which shattered almost effortlessly, laying rays of fine blue powder over the surface of the stone.

'Come to me, Megan,' she whispered. 'Come heal me again.' She cast about for the slightest hint of Meg's presence. 'Come to me, lover, I call you from the haven of your goddess. I call you with the heart beating in my breast; I call you with my eyes, my lips. Come to me, and let our love burn so brightly that eyes not our own must turn from it. Let us join and cause mountains to tremble. Let the thought of us breathe fear into the hearts of men. Let our love scorch the earth. Let the gods see our strength and know despair!'

First, a small, shimmering circle of silver and gold suspended in the air: Megan's ring. Thyri's hands ran over the surface of the stone. Minute shards of the gem dug into her palm; she pressed down hard against the pain and closed her eyes. *Come to me, Megan!*

'Hello, white-hair.'

Thyri opened her eyes and let Megan's beauty steal her breath away. Before her, cascades of black hair framed a face so serene and refined that the most masterful artisan of porcelain could never hope to match it. A plain dress of black silk wrapped her body from shoulder to hip, then flowed down with the breeze to tease her ankles over her bare feet. Her nipples pressed hard against the silk, thrilling with the ecstacy of the sorcery. Almond eyes shone through the night like stars. Rouged lips moved slowly, sensually, into a wide smile. 'Oh, Thyri,' she said, 'I thought you dead!'

Thyri rose. 'I have wished it, Megan.'

'So my bird found you at last? I cast a spell a mere week after you left me.'

'I found a great land over the ocean.'

'Too far for my magic to travel – I had guessed as much.'

'But not too long for your magic to last. Even after flesh abandoned your messenger, the sorcery survived.'

The sorceress smiled sadly at Thyri. 'You did not escape the moon?'

'No.'

Megan stepped forward. 'You must tell me all that has transpired.' She reached Thyri and took her into her arms. 'Why do you cry, little one?'

'I – I do not know. I have missed you.'

'I too have missed you. I was wrong to let you leave alone. I'm no longer even sure why I remained on Kaerglen. Only after you had left did I realize what I had done. Now we are together, and my heart is healed.' She looked down into Thyri's eyes; Thyri saw a tear streak down her lover's cheek. 'Shall we leave this place?' Megan asked.

Thyri sighed as she felt the sorceress shift in her arms. She let her hand fall lower to rest on the curve of Megan's hip. She reached up and tore at her shift, ripping it down between her breasts and spreading it open so that her own nipples stood free and aching in the air and magic of Brigid's haven. Slowly, she eased her body back against Megan's, sliding her nipples over the silk, inviting a white ecstatic fire to grip her body and consume her mind. And then she felt Megan's hands gripping her breasts, nails digging into her skin, then one hand sliding around to the small of her back, and the other pushing her down onto the grass. 'Not yet,' she heard herself sigh. 'Let's not leave yet.'

She felt lips dancing lightly on her neck, then moving down over her breast, the ache in her nipples suddenly fired anew by the grip of teeth. And then she felt the sorceress everywhere, sliding over her, silk setting her body effortlessly on fire.

Gradually, she forced her hands and her mouth into motion, slowly returning every caress she received.

From high above, the waxing moon shone down, lighting their bodies and the grass and stones around them. In four nights, it would be full.

Avalon

For centuries, the void had consumed her tortured cries, returning her naught but silence. Silence from which her only escape had been sleep – dreamless, as formless as the void.

Still, she'd slept. In sleep, she didn't remember. In sleep, she would allow a generation of Man to pass, then she would wake to test the void anew, to strain futilely against unseen chains, to curse the darkness she had once served, the darkness that now trapped her.

Sleep without thought. Yet now, she woke, and the void stretched out before her.

'Merlin! Release me!'

Silence; the wizard was dead, but his spell remained.

She cried out again, calling upon agents far darker than her captor.

Warriors

'Odin's beard, man,' Thorolf bellowed at Aelgulf. 'What do you mean, "She disappeared"?'

'Jus' what I said,' the taverner slurred back. 'Sh'ain't there. Go look for yourself if you want. Naught there but this,' he said, dangling the silver tube before his eyes; Rollo snatched it quickly from his grasp.

Thorolf leapt to his feet and reached over the table to clutch at Aelgulf's shirt. 'You drunken lout! I'll kill you!'

Rollo reached up and grabbed the Viking's arm. 'Sit down, Thorolf. It isn't his fault.'

'Whose fault is it, then?' Thorolf seethed. 'Yours? You let the bitch escape us!'

'If so, I probably saved your life.'

Thorolf let go of Aelgulf and turned on his companion. The taverner scurried quickly away. 'What are you saying?' Thorolf roared. 'That a wench with a sword is a match for Thorolf Godfredson?'

'No,' Rollo said, anger exploding inside him. Under the table, he unsheathed his long knife and placed it on his thigh. 'I'm saying that Thorolf Godfredson is a fool to think that Guthrom still wields power enough to command warriors who owe him loyalty no longer.'

Thorolf's face went red, and his hand began to funble at his sword hilt. As the blade began to slide from its sheath, Rollo gripped his long knife and buried it in Thorolf's chest. The Viking stood up straight, blood beginning to stain his hairy chest. Rollo pushed him back, then jumped up, drawing his sword.

The four young Vikings with him stared dumbly at Thorolf's

limp body. 'It is a sad day,' one mumbled, 'when a Viking kills a Viking over mead.'

'It is a sadder day," Rollo said, 'when a Viking kills more than one Viking over mead. Leave me! Go tell Guthrom that Eiriksdattir has abandoned Aelgulf's tavern and that I, Rollo Anskarson, will seek her. Tell him that if she desires him, I will bring her, but tell him also that she will not desire him, and tell him that Rollo Anskarson wishes that Thor would piss in Guthrom's flagon to teach him the folly of the One God's baptism.'

The four looked on, still stunned. Rollo waved the point of his sword before their eyes. 'Go!'

Fumbling, the four rose and scrambled out the door.

Rollo sat, glaring about in defiance of the stares of the other customers. 'Aelgulf!' he shouted. 'Quick! Another mead. I can not remain here long.'

Sokki made an effort to maintain the confidence in his stride as the four guardsmen came toward him. Still, his had fell discreetly to his belt, and he casually flexed his fingers inside the gauntlet lined with thin silver links. He kept his gaze on the four steady, steeling himself for a confrontation, but they passed him by with scarcely a glance.

Puzzled, Sokki walked on toward the tavern that rumor said housed Thyri. After a few steps, he paused and glanced behind him. Guthrom's men had already rounded a turn; they were nowhere in sight, and Sokki realized that the anxiety he'd felt that afternoon for Thyri's safety had been unnecessary. She had vanquished already her foes of the evening – at least the first wave of them – and she'd done so without the rune-blade. Not that this minor detail mattered much: the perfection of Thyri's mystical weapon could only enhance her ability, it could never define it.

His hand fell onto the hilt of the sword, and he felt a brief flash of envy. For him, the blade had been a heavy burden. Not that he'd have done things any other way, but the temptations had nearly torn his soul asunder. Though he possessed a legendary weapon he could wield it only in secret, and he could tell no one but his brothers of its lightness and perfection of balance. He had not had the chance to use it in battle, but now he was glad of that fact. Even without the attachment that battle would have brought, it had taken him all afternoon to overcome a persistent, nagging desire to keep the sword, to discard the opportunity he now had to return it to its rightful owner. He'd finally forced his hesitation to dissipate by reflecting long on that experience they'd shared on the field against the Saxons. In his memory, his respect for Thyri could only grow, and, searching his heart, he'd realized that he'd do anything to regain her companionship, a prize next to which her sword was a trinket of no real value. *She* was the legend, while he, though skilled, was but a novice. And after her, he knew that he could accept training under no other warrior. His mind already dwelt constantly on the past, dissecting every memory of her words, her actions.

Sokki eyed the tavern's sentinels only briefly before pushing his way inside. The chatter of excited conversation enveloped him, but most present were Saxon, and he could understand few of the words. As he looked around for Thyri, he noticed the body of a Viking sprawled on the floor. Near the dead man, another Viking sat, calmly belting down a large flagon of mead. Both men bore the colors of Guthrom's personal guard.

As Sokki tried to fathom the meaning of the scenario, the living guardsman rose and brushed roughly past him and out the door. The Viking's brusqueness confused Sokki more than angered him, and this confusion grew as a drunkard claiming to be the innkeep staggered up to him and forced a flagon into his hand.

Before the innkeep moved on, Sokki grabbed his shoulder. 'Where is Eiriksdattir?' he asked softly.

'Dissapea'd,' the innkeep said, grinning wildly. 'Gone! Poof! Dissapea'd.' He laughed, breaking out of Sokki's grasp and gesturing wildly at the other customers. 'Poof!' he declared loudly, and the tavern burst into laughter.

Sokki stood still for a moment, then glanced at the dead man on the floor and suddenly realized that the Viking who had just left might be his only hope of a straight answer. He turned and dashed out the door, but the man had already vanished from view.

Sokki sighed and fingered the hilt of the sword before setting off for the room near the docks that he shared with his brothers. Inside him, turmoil raged. Had he not wavered in his decision that afternoon, he would not have missed Thyri. But even if he had found her – what then? She had abandoned him once already. At least now, he still had her sword . . .

So ran his thoughts, around and around, throughout the duration of his walk.

Rollo searched through his mind, trying to recall details of the village off the north edge of the city. He wished he'd drunk less. The roads between the dwellings had surely changed . . . Why, by Odin, wasn't there enough light for him to see? His fingers felt cramped; he realized that he had hardly eased his grip on the small silver tube since he'd found it on the floor of Eiriksdattir's chamber.

Now if he could only find Fandis – she whom the Saxons named 'the river witch.' He knew she dwelt nearby. Exasperated, he slammed against the door of the nearest hovel and felt the latch crack under his weight. He burst into the one-room shack and thought he saw a figure moving on the far side. Instinctively, he drew his sword.

'Don't kill me! Please don't kill me!'

It was an old man's voice. 'I won't kill you,' Rollo said. 'Tell me where I can find Fandis!' He decided to leave his blade bared, hoping it would persuade truth from the man.

The old man spewed out a stream of directions, and Rollo had him repeat them more slowly. When he felt sure that he had the directions memorized, he sheathed his sword and fared back into the night.

Gradually, the shadows grew less menacing, more familiar. Around each turn, a memory seemed to linger, a memory waiting to catch him up and carry him back to that night years before when they'd plundered the village on their way into the city. He'd been young then, with a young heart. He'd seen his companions laying into the villagers as if those armed with broomsticks were warriors. He'd spent most of the night staying the hands of others. That was the night he'd found that part of himself that could command men. He'd been foolish: if the nascent leader within had not been strong, he would surely have died.

He wondered now that he had survived this night. Before that battle with Alfred, he could never have defied Guthrom. No Viking could have done so. To Guthrom and Odin they had pledged their very lives. It was Guthrom who had betrayed that trust, not Rollo Anskarson. His anger swelled; under Guthrom the Danes would become like their enemies. They would cease to be free. They would be turned back from the gates of Valhalla.

So why did he not call on that leader inside of himself? Why did he not raise the call to arms anew?

Because it was too late. Because *she* had not done so, and if she hadn't, then that dream – the dream of Norse rule over the Saxons – had ended. If she would raise her banner, then Rollo would follow her.

Fandis did not sleep. When Rollo entered her hut, she moved not at all, and her eyes stared blankly past him. She sat, her back straight, her head held high and tilted back slightly. She looked much older than he remembered her. She hadn't been young then; she could almost have been his mother, but she'd still been beautiful. Now her painted cheeks bore the lines of age, and the skin of her neck sagged, folding in grotesque flaps. Three candles, two black and one white, burned on a small platform before her. A small frog squirmed under the light where she had pinned it with slivers of iron.

The smell in the hut, and the sight of her, made him gag. Over the years, he had thought of her often as he'd drifted into sleep. Over the years, she'd grown more beautiful in his memories, not less. Now he felt his loins shrivel, recoiling from the fantasies, the many thoughts of her that had once set them on fire. Two dreams now had the night taken from him.

'Fandis!'

She stared past him. He thought that she began to smile.

'Fandis!'

Still, she did not respond. He started forward; then, slowly, she raised her hand. He paused; when her palm fully faced him, he felt something grip his mind. *Wait*, he heard a voice say. It was a voice he'd heard but once before in truth, and countless times in reflection. This time there was but the one word; before there had been many. That night he saved her . . . that night when five Vikings had held her pinned to the ground, and he'd preserved her virtue with his sword. As he'd lifted her from the ground, he'd heard her voice: 'My thanks, man,' she'd said, 'but I never thought I'd be thanking a Dane. Return to me when I am well, and one boon I will grant you. One boon alone, for I owe not your people much.' With that, she had swooned, and he'd returned her to her hut where he'd discovered the tools of her trade. From a villager outside, he had gained her name, then he'd gone on to the city . . .

As her grip on his mind relaxed, he began to wish he'd forgotten her. But no – he would have his boon. Her hand had dropped, but her eyes still stared past him.

He looked around the hut; it hadn't changed much. In one corner was her dingy cot; everywhere lay scattered the talismans and other wares of her witchcraft. Opposite the bed, a bag of grain lay on its side. He watched a rat scurry from the shadows into the bag. There, he kept his attention, preferring the shadows and the sound of the rat's scratching to the decaying ghost of his fantasies working her magic on the floor at his feet.

'A new power has entered the land this night,' she said as she came out of her trance.

He grunted, still listening to the rat. 'I care not of that,' he said.

'Look at me, Dane,' she said. 'I must see your eyes.'

He turned.

'Ah!' she said. 'I remember you now!' She smiled; his stomach churned again as he saw the rotting mass of her teeth. She burst into laughter. 'So! You've come for me at last, have you? Here, on the floor? Or can you contain your passions long enough to reach the cot?'

He felt his face grow red, and his hand gripped the hilt of his sword. 'I do not desire that, witch!'

Her laughter subsided into a cackling, rheumy cough. 'But you once did,' she forced out between spasms. 'I can see it in your eyes.' She paused and spat into the dirt next to her. 'The years have not been kind to me, my young savior. Why have you come to me?'

Slowly, he bent forward and placed the silver tube in her hand. 'A woman abandoned this thing this night,' he said. 'She hails from Hordaland, and she is called Eiriksdattir. You must help me find her.'

Fandis stared down at the tube, then looked to Rollo, amazement kindling new life in her eyes. 'You came by this? Were it not you asking, I would slay you.' She sighed. 'But I am no longer young, and I owe you one boon, and the river witch keeps her word.'

'So – where is she?'

Fandis closed her eyes and fell silent again. Rollo waited; two rats now milled about in the grain. After a time, he began to feel his own weight dragging on his shoulders, and he sat, resting his back on the creaky framework of the hut's walls.

'She moves,' the witch said finally. 'I can give you no direction this night.'

He stared at her.

'If you wish,' she said, 'you may sleep here. Perhaps on the morrow, I can aid you.'

He started to protest, then grunted agreement. Even if she could have told him where to go, he wouldn't have been able to make it there. Sleep already clouded his mind. He slumped over onto his side, and he listened to her rise and shuffle to her cot. She still mumbled to him, he strained to hear her words: '. . . there are powers so bright they burn, my young savior.

'. . . let not the hunter become the prey . . .

'. . . *beware her fangs* . . .'

Wildfire

At the edge of the ruins, with Thyri's pack for a pillow, Gerald drifted into and out of a fitful dream. In this dream he was lost in the heart of a blinding snowstorm. A roaring, bitter cold wind pounded ceaselessly against his aching ears. He could feel nothing in his feet, even his legs, but looking down he could see them moving relentlessly, propelling him forward, against the wind.

Cold – such as he'd never felt before. Cold, stinging his face, his eyes, biting through to his heart.

And the wind . . .

A woman's voice, distant, urged him on.

The wind – something terrible hid in the wind. It twisted the swirls of snow into faces, demonic images: a cat-faced warrior with five arms; a hideous, shapeless mass of flesh with a thousand eyes; a monstrous wolf with fangs of ice.

Nightmares in the wind.

A woman's voice . . .

. . . a strange tongue. Familiar – his mother's?

He opened his eyes. Thyri emerged from the ruins, a dark shadow at her side. She spoke – that strange tongue; the shadow grew.

Gerald sat and shook his head. When he focused again on Thyri, the shadow next to her had taken form: another woman, draped in dark fabric. From a distance, the woman's figure brought thoughts of his mother rushing back into his mind. As the pair drew closer, the woman's beauty swiftly brushed away the wisps of memory. She stood half a head taller than Thyri, and her light skin almost seemed to reflect the starlight beaming down from the heavens. She walked with the carriage of a goddess, and Gerald wondered if Thyri had done nothing less than persuade Brigid to enter into the world.

They approached him. Their speech grew clearer, and he grew certain of its alien familiarity. It *was* his mother's. Or close.

Had this night suddenly thrust him into the affairs of the gods?

Did he still dream? Would that snowstorm arise from the ground without warning to again engulf him in its fury?

For a moment, he felt sure that Thyri and the woman would pass him without a glance. Their conversation seemed absorbing enough to shut out all else, but then Thyri drew next to him and stopped. Her companion, upon closer inspection, appeared no less fantastic.

'Gerald,' Thyri said, 'this is my friend Megan.'

He felt his head bob in acknowledgment. Meg raised an amused eyebrow in return.

Thyri smiled and spoke to him again. 'She's a witch,' she said. She bent for her pack and threw it over her shoulder. 'Is there a place nearby where we can eat in peace?'

'A bed would also be nice,' Meg added in Gerald's tongue.

Gerald cleared his throat. 'Country tavern?' he forced out. 'Probably no Danes though.'

'Perfect,' Thyri said. 'Shall I pay you now, or will you lead me further, Gerald of Jorvik?'

He almost told her that she need pay him nothing at all. 'I will lead,' he said, turning for the road quickly in an effort to hide his confused smile.

As they neared their destination, Gerald's thoughts, ironically, turned from the wild gods of his mother's people to tales he'd heard at Othar's of increased wolf-kills in the local flocks. The country people thought it an ill turn in the land, and many whispered of coming famine and pestilence. A few, he'd heard, had even invoked the ancient idea of evil man-wolves in explanation. Such talk was common, and Gerald knew that it could occasionally lead to persecution and death of strangers. For a moment, the thought alarmed him; then he recalled the near legends he'd heard told of Thyri's sword. Farmers with pitchforks would present no threat to his companions. Still, he would have felt more comfortable entering the tavern with Megan looking a little less – conspicuously sorcerous.

And little did he realize, as he opened the tavern door for the women to enter, that she with the sword was the source of the countryfolk's fears. For two months she had hidden in the nearby forests; for two moons she had dined on the local flocks.

A wicker talisman in the shape of a wolf's head – folk magic to ward off the curse of the *were* – hung over the tavern door. Thyri passed under it, Megan followed, then Gerald entered and swung shut the door.

Inside, Gerald counted ten customers, but only a few looked up at their entrance. Most of the others sat captivated by the peaceful meditations of a lutist working his trade on a raised platform in one corner. The night was no longer new, and the movements of all present seemed lazily slurred. One of the customers lay collapsed over the table before him; as Gerald led Thyri and Megan through the tables, this tableau didn't change. His fear of some sort of confrontation began to ease.

They had taken seats before Gerald became aware of the change in Megan's appearance. Gone was the black garb of the witch. Gone was the flowing, black-as-night hair. The witch now sported a disheveled brown mop, and her clothes were also plain brown and covered with the dirt and grime of the fields. He blinked, and Thyri too changed. She looked older, her sword transformed into a walking stick, which she propped against the edge of the table next to her. He looked at Megan and her eyes smiled knowingly back at him. She was a witch . . .

A tavern wench brought mead. 'A leg of lamb,' Gerald

said. He smiled up at her nervously, hoping that she hadn't noticed the sudden changes. When he smiled, a look of disgust spread across her face.

'Filthy old man,' the girl said, backing away.

Gerald looked down at his hands and saw that they were wrinkled, bony, and covered with warts.

Thyri giggled. 'Careful, Meg,' she whispered. 'Too much and they'll refuse us beds.'

'That could easily be fixed,' Meg said.

'Yes, but why waste the effort?'

Gerald sat back, watching them, awed, again wondering whether he sat in the presence of a goddess. Or goddesses. But he felt no fear. With Thyri especially. She had been kind to him all evening. Even now, though she seemed preoccupied with Megan, she did not shun him; she hadn't bade him leave. And until she did, he had no desire to stray from her presence. She was, after all, the reason he'd entered Aelgulf's tavern that afternoon.

Over the lamb, the two women fell to conversing in their strange tongue – Irish, Gerald later learned. He'd begun to feel nervous that his part in the affair would soon end when Thyri looked at him suddenly and asked, 'How well do you use that sword?'

For the first time since watching her descend the stairs, Gerald remembered the blade he wore at his own side. He looked down to see it; it had transformed into a cane. The sudden shock of it all made him laugh. He smiled at Thyri. 'Well enough,' he said. 'But I daresay my blade is no match for yours, swords-mistress.'

'Call my Thyri,' she said.

He nodded.

'I have been called many things, Gerald, least among them demoness and kin-slayer. Do these things scare you?'

He looked into her eyes; he could see nothing of those names in them. 'No,' he said.

'Will you serve me? Follow where I lead?'

Anywhere, he thought. He felt a cool tingle slide across his scalp, a sensation he related to the taste of a rare, fine wine, or the first hesitant touch of a repentant virgin. He felt very wise, but he was still a child.

The Warrior

The smell of boiling pork lured Rollo from a vague, uneasy dream of misty waters and the haunting voice of a songstress whose body hovered distantly in the mist. He rolled over, and his cheek bit into dusty, packed earth.

'Good morning,' Fandis said behind him.

He turned and looked at her. She was slumped over, tending a small caldron over a fire of coals. In her other palm rested the silver tube he had brought to her. 'I thought you would sleep through breakfast,' she said. She looked up. In the morning light, she simply looked old, or perhaps it had been his fantasies laying a veil of revulsion over her features the night before. Those fantasies seemed less real now in daylight. He remembered Thyri. Had she been unreal as well?

No. The question couldn't be asked. She had brought him here. Over her, he had slain Thorolf.

He grunted and sat up. 'Smells good,' he said.

'I knew pork would get you. Never knew a Norseman who could resist it.' Fandis smiled weakly, then looked down at the silver tube.

He sighed and rested back against the wall, letting the aroma of cooking revive him slowly.

'I have performed your casting,' she said flatly.

'What did you learn?'

'Many things. The winter is coming.'

'What winter?'

'*The* winter.' She gave him a curious smile. 'Your winter. The winter that will end all things.'

She spoke of the *fimbulwinter*, he realized. When the gods would battle on the Plain of Vigrid. 'How soon?'

'Not soon,' she said, tossing him the tube and taking two bowls from a shelf behind her. 'But not long either.'

'Did it – did the vision scare you?'

'No. I will be already dead.' She paused, holding the bowls in her lap. 'Did you know,' she said distantly, 'that with the stone that vial once contained, I could have spelled myself young again? Why could you not have come into it a mere hour before you did?'

He didn't answer; he felt his stomach rumbling and restrained himself from grabbing for Fandis's caldron. His impatience made him rub his back roughly against the wall. 'Where is she?' he asked gruffly.

Slowly, she began to ladle her broth into the bowls. 'South of Jorvik,' she said. 'A small inn where Guthrom's men can't find her.'

'Can you tell me the way?'

'Aye,' she said, holding one bowl out to him. 'But first you must eat.'

His stomach reminded him that he hadn't eaten since noon the day before; he hadn't lingered long enough at Aelgulf's to dine. He took the bowl from Fandis's bony hands and tipped it to his lips, pouring the hot broth down his throat, pausing only occasionally to chew the small chunks of pork that slid onto his tongue from the bottom of the bowl. When he finished, he handed the bowl back and nodded for more. Eiriksdattir could wait a little longer.

The blazing sun rose higher in the sky as Rollo walked south, skirting the city. The heat had already begun to coax moisture from his skin, causing the woolen shirt he wore to stick and itch. He thought of the *fimbulwinter*, idly welcoming it if it would bring the summer to a rapid end. Most Danes preferred the climate of the Saxon lands to that of their homeland; Rollo, however, often found himself wishing for the vast expanses of snow and ice that he'd known in his youth. Even during the depths of Jorvik's winter, such sights were rare. His father had once told him that it was the winter that gave a Viking his strength; perhaps that explained Guthrom's failure. Perhaps that explained all the failures of the Norse in southern lands . . . failures presaging the end of all things.

His mind raced, whirling back to the oracle of the river witch: *fimbulwinter*. Three years of snowstorms descending like armies on all lands, north and south. Warfare possessing all, pitting father against son, brother against brother. Women deserting their men for the spawn of their own wombs . . .

Lokki freed from his chains . . . But did the Trickster not first need to be fettered? Had this already come to pass? Had Balder already fallen?

Rollo tried to discard the questions. Were Fandis's words true, no power within his own mortal grasp could break the final, fatal threads of fate's tapestry. And if the terrible wars were indeed coming, he could think of no master he'd rather serve than she whom he now sought. Whatever she would command of him . . . His every thought of her came tinged with mystery, legend.

As he passed a field where goats grazed, a small swarm of flies discovered him. He stripped off his shirt and flailed it about to discourage them. The sun bearing down on his bare back, he left the flies behind.

Ghosts

Gerald rose midmorning as was his habit. He went to the window and relieved himself, then drank a portion of the water he'd brought up in a pail the night before. The last of the water he poured over his head, soaking his long, black hair.

He left his room and went down the hall to the door of the chamber Thyri shared with Megan. He listened, hearing no sounds from within. After a moment, he backed away; he'd almost reached the stairs when he remembered the spell Megan had cast to conceal their true features. He looked down at his hands; they were clean, young again. For him to wander freely in the inn, they needed to be diseased and gnarled.

He scowled and returned to his room. He sat on his cot for a while, wishing for a quill and parchment though he had no clear idea of anything to write. After he conceded the fact that wishing would achieve nothing, he lay back down, stared at the rafters, and slowly drifted back into dream.

Fandis felt the riders' approach before she heard the hooves in the distance. She knew they would draw closer. She *knew.*

So soon, she thought. She hadn't expected this so soon . . . Still, the night before, when she'd looked up at Rollo, death had lurked beyond his shoulder. Just as death had intruded into all of her castings of late, watching her silently, patiently.

She rose and went to her chest, taking out a small, neglected mirror covered with grime and dust. She polished the metal with the cloth of her robe, then peered in, at her face. The sight made her gasp; she had grown so old. She raised a bony hand and ran her fingers over the creases in her skin. So this was what Rollo had seen the night before: this old, decaying face. Where had her beauty gone? Stolen by the lonely years . . . and the magic.

She had been a fool. The warrior who had come to her – she could have had him; she could have lived out her life with him, in the arms that had saved her. Perhaps she could even have used her talent to maintain her beauty.

After that night long ago, she had so often wondered how long it would take him to return to her. After a year had passed, she'd begun to regret the harshness and brevity of her words to him. Still, she'd waited; her pride would not let her seek him out herself. If only she could turn back time.

'You're a fool,' she muttered at her reflection. 'An old fool.'

She had chosen magic over love. She had sacrificed her body for power – the power to see into distant places, into the future. It was the only real power she had. It had shown her Guthrom's defeat. It had shown her, the night before, the entrance of Megan Edain into her world. It had heralded her own death.

So be it, she thought. If one could not accept one's own demise, then wasn't one living a lie? Yet truth could bring such sorrow. Her savior *had* returned – far too late. And his life had bound itself to another's. Not hers.

She had seen truth in Rollo's eyes. Truth: the secret love he'd bore her all these years. Truth: the horror of her appearance, the horrible cost of her sorcerous dealings.

After it seemed that he would not come to her, she'd given herself to the power greedily. She'd often thought that, if she would not court a man, then she would court death. Death was a lover ever faithful once won.

And now death returned her affections. How ironic that the man had shown death the way.

The pounding hooves had grown ever closer. Now, even as she eyed her reflection, they stopped. She heard boots on the earth, the crack of wood as someone burst through her doorway. A hand on her shoulder, whirling her around to gaze into cruel eyes, the same cruelty she had seen over and again the night she'd been raped.

Yes, raped. Rollo had been too late. He'd merely halted the last of three assaults.

Now, as she looked deep into the cruel eyes, she saw something else. Death again, but not her own. That death – her death – hung in the air. She smiled.

'Where is he?' the Viking demanded.

'Death,' she said. 'You do not want to know.'

'Where is he?' The man shook her.

She smiled again.

'Beat it out of her, Einar!' came a voice from outside.

She looked deep into the Viking's eyes, past his glare, into the impish, mischievous glint of death. She closed her eyes for a moment, seeking the death's nature.

A heavy hand smashed against the side of her head, and she fell to the floor. She struggled to sit, but the Viking pushed her down, thrusting his face in front of hers. 'Where is he?' he seethed.

She smiled at the death in his eyes, then she told him where to find Rollo.

Ahead, a cart approached, laden with barley; perspiration streaked the driver's face as he fought to keep his unruly mules on the road. His daughter, next to him, held on to her seat, frustration creasing her forehead.

Rollo acknowledged the mules' protests with a wry smile. The day before, he'd been no better than they. No, he'd been less: they cried out; he'd wanted to, but instead he'd shied from the bite of Guthrom's reins and obeyed in silence, in shame. On that day in spring, in that battle with Alfred, Rollo had lost something, become like a living ghost: the ghost of the already-dead, the listless spirit of lifeless motion, Guthrom's tame mule.

No more. He laughed, softly at first, but his mirth grew, blossoming into a sound that rang out over the fields. As he passed the cart, he noticed that the girl had relaxed and now took the jolting ride as a simple matter of course. She gazed at him in soft-eyed amazement; he didn't fully realize what that look meant until the cart had passed. On another day, he could have stopped the cart and taken the farmer's daughter at sword point and she would have thanked him later and offered herself to him as a wife. She would have loved him and followed him anywhere; he could see all this now in his memory of her eyes. She had young eyes, eyes that had not yet lowered permanently to the level of the ground just beyond the edge of the milking pail. Her eyes could see dream in the daylight; they could turn a man on the road into a hero with the power to give the world itself as a gift.

The look, directed at him, felt strange; it wasn't a thing he'd experienced often. Perhaps she'd seen through his laughter, seen through to the rebirth of that thing he'd lost in the world of Guthrom and Alfred, his awakening at the gateway to a new world, the one *she* offered.

Could the girl have seen him even more closely, she would have seen that he was like her. What she had seen in him, he had seen in Eiriksdattir. His mind turned, picturing the girl abandoning her father and racing back down the road in search of the laughing hero who had passed her by. The absurdity of her chasing him while he chased Thyri made him laugh again. He forced her back into the cart, next to her sweating father. She would stay chained to her life, thinking of him in the darkness of night much as he had dreamed of Fandis. Or perhaps she would remember him only briefly one summer morning years hence when the sound of his laughter would ring anew through her mind. And she would wonder what it had been that had made him laugh. And she would long for him again for a moment before bending down under the cow and reaching for a teat . . .

Maybe the farmer had been destined for Jorvik. Maybe Rollo had gifted the girl with the strength to test her chains, to escape into the city.

As Eiriksdattir had gifted him with the strength to escape . . .

Rollo stopped suddenly, realizing that ahead, just off the

road, sat his destination. His walk was nearly done; within the wooden walls of the distant tavern, Thyri would be. The cart in his mind had fueled his journey, consuming the miles. He strode forward.

And then, behind him: pounding hooves. The sound grew rapidly, and Rollo cursed, throwing himself into a patch of bushes at the side of the road. He looked back and counted twelve riders. Einar Godfredson, Thorolf's brother, rode at their head. Rollo knew all of them; the day before, he had been a leader among them.

Cursing again, he prayed that he'd hidden in time. The riders drew near and he steeled himself, but then they passed, reining in their steeds only when they reached the tavern. He watched a figure step out into the yard, a woman with hair like the sun and a blade raised high over her head. *Thyri!* He crawled closer.

The riders remained mounted and circled her. They produced a net and stretched it out. She went for one of the riders, but the net caught her, and he saw her sword fly out of her grasp as the net battered her to the ground. And then six of the twelve descended on her, forcing her, still netted, into a large burlap sack, which they lashed around with many lengths of thick rope.

'Rollo!' Einar bellowed. 'Where are you? Where is the maggot that killed my brother!'

The words stung Rollo's ears as they stained the air that he had filled with laughter. He wanted to lunge out and call Einar to him; he wanted to free Thyri, killing them all if he had to. All twelve . . . *Twelve swords, mounted.*

Seething, he stayed hidden. The ghost of the already-dead cackled in his ears.

Guthrom's guard milled about outside the tavern, then eight came back toward him. They passed, Eiriksdattir still bound, her cloth cage attached by rope to three of the horses and bouncing along in the rear.

Einar had stayed at the tavern, had started for its door. He had with him now only three others. With surprise, Rollo could take them . . . *But they were killing Thyri!*

Abandoning everything but his sword, Rollo leapt to his feet and raced toward Jorvik after the riders.

Thyri ducked underneath the edge of the window and giggled up at Megan. 'That was beautiful! How long do you think it will take them to open the sack?'

Meg eased down next to her, starting to giggle herself. 'Probably not until they get where they're going. They're dragging you with three horses, so they'll never notice a sudden loss of weight.'

Thyri choked back her laughter at the thought of Guthrom's guard proudly dumping a heavily bound chicken at their ruler's feet. She looked over at Meg, but a distant glaze coated the sorceress's eyes, and shadows still danced around the ring on her finger. Not all of the riders had departed, and Meg yet worked her magic.

Thyri rose slowly and went for her sword.

Einar Godfredson grinned as he stooped, lifting the blade from the dust. He tested its grip and smiled. With the witch's blade, he would kill Rollo.

Motioning for the others to follow, he kicked in the door of the tavern. A room empty of all but tables and chairs greeted him. He ordered two of his men to the kitchen and waited until they emerged with three people, an old couple and a young girl.

He started up the stairs. 'Rollo! The Valkyrie lust for your blood!' He reached the top and smashed in the first door. Gerald looked up out of his dream and saw Einar, a hulking shadow that filled his doorway. The shadow backed out.

Einar knocked down the next door – and there, before him, impossibly, stood Eiriksdattir. He struck at her with the sword in his hand even as the blade disintegrated into a shimmering mist.

Thyri allowed the Viking time enough to draw his own, real blade before she killed him. She stepped out to confront the last three who tried to assault her in unison. They attacked wildly, swords biting into the wood of the restricting walls. She reacted mechanically, and each fell within seconds.

Gerald emerged from his room and looked down at the bodies littering the hall. Blood still ran down the edge of Thyri's blade. She glanced up at him briefly before walking back into her room.

Warriors

It took Rollo twenty minutes to reach the city. Along the way, he found several short strands of hemp – twists of the rope with which the riders had bound Thyri. He carried the strands in one clenched fist; in his other hand was his sword.

Thyri was dead.

Among the last stand of hovels before Jorvik's south gate, he stopped, panting heavily, a wildness burning in his heart. His lungs drank in the air and begged for more. The blade at the end of his arm twitched, and anger flared through his mind in waves.

Thyri was dead! She had to be; she couldn't have survived. The rocks on the road had splintered every bone in her body.

She would be avenged!

He would slay the riders, and Einar when he returned. And Guthrom. Especially Guthrom, for it was he who held the reins that commanded all the mules, ruly and unruly alike; all but the one who had broken free.

And Rollo would find Thyri . . . She deserved the burial of a queen.

As he caught his breath, he realized that some instinct had stopped him short of storming the gate. Caution hadn't occurred to him. He felt strong enough to defeat Guthrom's entire army with his sword. He felt like trying, but something deep inside him, beneath his thoughts, had remembered that the gate guard had arrows in no short supply. That something had saved his life. If only it could have saved Thyri's as well.

Slowly, he grew aware of the people around him. Most were women whose husbands slaved away in the city for a day's worth of bread for their families. He spotted a couple of old men in the crowd, and small children ran everywhere in packs. He looked around; if Jorvik were ever assaulted, these people would be completely at the mercy of the attackers. But they had nowhere else to go; the city was already overflowing the walls built a short ten years before.

He knew the people watched him, though they turned their eyes when he stared back. He shut them out again. Sheathing his sword, he moved along the face of the last building and looked around:

His eyes grew wide in horror, and again he almost stormed Jorvik in *berserk* fury. High on a stake next to the gate was another human head, one with dark hair, one he recognized with certainty even at a distance. His vision blurred with tears, and he slumped to the earth.

Two deaths played through his mind: Thyri Eiriksdattir's, and now – Fandis's. Guthrom's men had done to the river witch what Thyri had done to their comrades-in-arms. Why? Because Rollo had gone to her. He couldn't believe that he had been followed. More likely, they had learned of his movements from those who had seen him pass. The old man who had directed him to Fandis? He would have been all Einar needed.

Before she died, Fandis must have told where she'd sent him and that Thyri would be there. And then they'd staked her head outside the city as if they thought it a game that they could win against Eiriksdattir. As if they thought they could defeat someone such as her.

But they had been victorious . . . Rollo cursed Odin for these cruelties – all dispensed in less than a full passing of the sun. As the curse passed Rollo's lips, he realized that all that had passed had its cause in him. His actions had led to Fandis's death. *He* had led Eiriksdattir's killers to their prey.

He looked up, and the stares of the people suddenly accused him and condemned him and his betrayal of the two women. In one child's eyes he thought he saw Thyri's gaze cursing him for his meddling.

Guthrom had won.

No.

She lived, and she would have her revenge. As long as he could wield his blade, she could not fully die.

As he rose, his anger consumed his mind, forcing his thoughts down to where reflection and introspection cannot follow. His senses sharpened; in a way, he became much like the beast that took Thyri under the light of the full moon. Low, menacing growls escaped through his teeth as he turned toward the river to seek a more accessible path into Guthrom's city.

'We need a ship,' Thyri said softly, twisting a blade of grass absently around her fingers.

Gerald watched her. A beam of light filtered through the leaves above had caught in the thin scar under her left eye. Thyri looked as if she cried, and the sun itself was providing her tears. Gerald found his hand moving automatically to touch the scar below his own left eye.

'I know little of the sea,' Megan said. She stood under the low boughs of the old oak. Gerald and Thyri rested on the grass near the trunk. Beyond Megan, the afternoon sun scorched a heavily grazed grassland. Against the light, Megan seemed little more than a dark, shapely shadow.

She turned and looked at Thyri. *Except that the sea brought you to me.* She smiled and looked away again.

Gerald did not hear Megan's voice. Thyri heard it in her head, as clearly as if it had been spoken. Gerald did not yet suspect that the two women could communicate without words. 'I know nothing of the sea, either, swords-mistress,' he said. 'But I do not fear it.'

'That is good,' Thyri said, smiling at him.

They had left the tavern within minutes after Einar's death. Megan had given the old couple who ran it a gold coin to compensate for the trouble of the corpses.

Gerald had had no idea of their next destination (beyond the oak tree) until this talk of a ship. 'Guthrom has many ships,' he said, trying to present an idea that would justify his place in the odd trio. Already, after seeing Thyri in action but once, he found it difficult to consider himself a swordsman. And what had he to offer on the level of Megan's sorcery?

And it certainly didn't seem as if he could offer either of them anything as a man. Only a fool could see them together and not *know* . . . Only a fool would dream that he could somehow give Thyri what Megan could not.

And yet, deep within Gerald, that fool lusted. Gerald refused to acknowledge this, but it made him no less insecure.

'Precisely what I was thinking,' Thyri said. 'Guthrom has more ships, in fact, than he needs.'

'Arise, little sleeper!' *answered the void.*

'Merlin!'

'No, Morgana, I am no mere wizard. I am the binder of light. I have sired beasts with power to crush this earth. I am Balder's bane, and I am the darkness. I am the ending of that which you began.'

'Me? Then you are *my* son, and I command you to free me.'

The void laughed. 'You do not command me, and I will not free you. I will remove but one layer of your prison, and you must do the rest. I return to you your sorceries as well; you are no good to me without them.'

'No good for what?'

The void laughed again, then it smashed down upon her, thrusting obscenely through every defenseless pore of her being. She felt icy fire ignite within her; the laughter crawled up her spine and into her mind, possessing her, filling her as no man, mortal or demon, had filled her before. She growled, struggling against it even as the fire spread and grew hot, burning her. Waves of ecstatic pain crashed onto her, into her, through her.

'More!' *she screamed.*

'Free yourself!' *it demanded, vanishing, leaving her achingly unfulfilled.*

'More!'

Silence, but the void turned gray and laced itself with seams. Rays of light streaked across the gray . . . stone. Sunlight – no, the light of the moon. Hesitantly, she moved, gritting her teeth as a painful creaking sound split the air. She sat, brushing the dust from her white, fleshless limbs. Bone clacked against bone.

'I live!' she shrieked. *She held her skeletal fingers before her eyes and laughed insanely.* 'I live!'

She crossed the chamber to the window and gazed out at the moon. Below her, surf pounded against the cliff at the foot of her tower. It made no sound; she yearned to feel the freshness of the sea breeze, but the air around her was still.

She turned, her hollow eyes falling on the pedestal near her altar. A patch of darkness spread out from the pedestal's center. She approached it. From the center of the darkness, a black orb beckoned to her as if it were alive. She approached it hesitantly, watching her reflection on the orb's surface grow more distinct.

The orb of Babd? Had Merlin been fool enough to leave it within her grasp? Or had he used its power to trap her? No, such humor was not in his nature . . . Nor would he have left it for her in the tower. Had she known of its presence, she could have freed herself. And she had tried that aeons before.

No, the presence in the void had returned the orb to her. She owed much to whatever wizard or god had freed her. 'Free yourself,' *he had told her. One layer of her prison now was gone. Through her sorcery, and the power of the orb, her spirit could be free, outside the tower as well as in. Merlin's curse on her physical form, however, was more permanent, unbreakable. Should her body ever leave her tower, her soul would perish. She knew the spell well. Of course, if her spirit found a new home . . .*

She picked up the orb and let its power surge through her. In her thoughts the void assumed a form of masculine perfection; she had been given no hint of his physical shape, so she shaped him in her mind: a muscled, golden youth with eyes of fire. She twisted the vision carefully until it resembled her son, Mordred. She began to feel a terrible aching for her flesh.

Her mind filled itself with the memory of the presence's

laughter. She looked down at the bleached nakedness of her bones and imagined the laughter the moon's.

She sneered. The moon would not laugh long; nay, it would lust for her!

She turned to seek out the darker chambers of her keep.

Vishnu and Ra lay curled around the pedestal of her scrying stones. She set the orb of Babd among the crystals and stooped, lightly touching the leathery, shriveled skin of the hounds. A dark brown substance came away on her fingers.

'We shall be free, my pets,' *she said, reaching up for the orb. Over Ra's head, she squeezed it, conjuring tendrils of darkness that oozed out between her fingers and flowed over the hound's mummified form. Beneath the black magic's caress, Ra's hardened flesh began to grow supple. As it darkened to its natural black, the orb's magic spread to Vishnu as well.*

'Free,' *Morgana muttered as Ra's eyes fluttered open. His irises were orange, like fire.*

She reached between his legs and he growled at her. She dug her fingers into his scrotum, pressing her palm down hard against his penis. She felt it harden, and she stroked it until its semen spurted out and up, along her arm – where her arm should have been. The white liquid hung suspended in the air, an inch from her bones; as she watched, it began to flow slowly down the imaginary curve of her flesh.

Chuckling, she reached for Vishnu and awakened him as she had his brother. When she was finished, she stood and spread the semen over her body until her own flesh began to take form under her fingers. Then she took the orb and held it over her head, bathing herself in its magic, completing the spell.

She lived.

She returned to the chamber of the moon with a silver mirror and sat on the stone platform on which she had slept for centuries. In the mirror she gazed at herself, using the orb's magic to adjust her features until she became satisfied with the perfection of her own dark beauty. She grew thick, black hair until it reached to the pale smoothness of her thighs. She let it dance there, reveling in the feeling of her flesh, her fingers slowly probing between her legs as she sought to quell the ache that the presence in the void had left her.

Vishnu and Ra watched their mistress. Vishnu tried to force his snout between Morgana's legs, but she kicked him away.

Screaming, clawing at her breasts with one hand, she brought herself to orgasm. When the waves of pleasure had subsided, she still felt the ache.

She sighed and went to the window, the hounds padding along behind her. The surf was still silent, and her hair hung limp; the air about her remained still.

Ghosts

A place known as Reaver's Haven stretched from the south wall of Jorvik to a point midway between the city and the ruins to which Gerald had led Thyri for her summoning of Megan. It was a lawless place where Guthrom's ruling hand was seldom felt. Merchants could avoid tariffs by dealing there, and thieves, beggars, and whores lay in wait for these merchants in every dark corner and alleyway. Dwellers of the city proper were likewise considered fair game by the Haven's denizens.

The name might suggest that it was a safe place for Norsemen; it was not. In the Haven, the Saxon still ruled. It gained its name from the thieves who plied their trade there. They named it thus to goad the Norse to enter.

Guthrom, of course, could have eradicated the problem with a single, crushing blow. He hadn't done this because he'd had other problems, one of which had been Alfred. But even if Guthrom had been an unambitious ruler, it is doubtful that the Haven would have had much to fear. Too many of the overking's men had been captured by the women there. The Vikings were the first to take the thieves' bait, and the first to swear on the Haven's innumerable, exotic virtues, even though most who braved the Haven's paths exited significantly less wealthy than they had been upon entrance.

Such a place is not unique; any city of modest size has its own Haven, its place where the generally understood, established order of things does not apply, where one can witness the depths of human pain and cruelty, or experience pleasures unimaginable in safer surrounds. Sometimes, it is a small place; at other times it spreads itself like a disease over entire countrysides. In Jorvik, it took the form of an outskirt that rubbed up against the city wall like a playful bear.

In Reaver's Haven, Rollo Anskarson had fulfilled, from time to time, some of the fantasies he'd built around Fandis over long, sleepless nights. The fact that he'd sought such fulfillment in the arms of nameless whores had often bothered him. For hadn't Fandis been waiting for him to ask his boon? Couldn't she have been his for the price of an evening's walk? And yet, deep inside, he'd understood his inaction: Fandis had been his promise of perfection, a mirror in his mind into which he could gaze to judge his own thoughts and actions, to measure himself as a man. And into this mirror, Rollo would often look and despair. Even before Guthrom's defeat, Rollo had felt somehow *wrong* in doing the bidding of this man whom he saw as just that – a man. But he was a warrior, and warriors served leaders. He had had no other leader, had known of no other way to live.

And so he'd felt unworthy. And with that feeling, he could not shake the fear that Fandis would reject him, even laugh at him when he approached her. After all, he was Norse, and she'd made it painfully clear that she bore no love for his people. And if she'd – if his *perfection* had laughed at him . . . No, it had always been better to leave the mirror in his mind unblemished, uncracked. At least until he'd felt worthy.

Now Fandis was dead. If Rollo had not been consumed by grief and anger that day he last entered Reaver's Haven, he might have sensed something significant in the way that Thyri's entrance into his life had erected a new, more polished mirror in his mind next to Fandis's. But Thyri was dead as well.

Fandis, before she'd died, had been old. Now, in his memory, she was young again, forever youthful and beautiful. Thyri had never been old. Both their mirrors blazed behind his eyes, they had become twin beacons urging him forward on his mission of revenge. Somehow, despite the knives that the day had buried in his heart, he had never felt more alive.

As dusk gave way to night, the beacons in his mind began to burn more brightly still. Some weak but victorious fragment of his wisdom had urged him to stay in the shadows until the sun could no longer betray him, until he could count the night his ally. He had hidden in an abandoned shed, but now the night called him out, and he followed.

On the streets, he set himself on a course for the city wall, to a section that he knew would be unguarded. Beyond the wall, he would find Einar and Guthrom and the others. On the way, he dimly realized that the beggars were letting him pass, as if they sensed in his gait that he would cut them down out of his path before proffering a coin. The whores were less empathic, and he had to brush them aside. Several times, however, his eyes unwillingly met theirs. Each time, he found the ghosts of Thyri and Fandis staring out at him, demanding blood for blood.

As Rollo stole over a dilapidated section of wall into Guthrom's city, Thyri, Megan, and Gerald entered Reaver's Haven from the south. The women had donned long, black capes with hoods that hid their features. The capes were real, woolen; they had bought them on the road from a traveling merchant. Megan had provided the money. She'd also offered to provide disguises again, but Thyri had cautioned against it, pointing out that hoods would achieve the same objective, and abuse of Megan's sorcery could likely place them at added risk. If Guthrom had enlisted the aid of a sorcerer or wizard – and the fact that they'd been ferreted out at the country tavern hinted at just that – then their very disguises would give them away.

That thought had sobered Gerald somewhat. He'd found it quite easy to lose himself in a sort of numb-minded euphoria in Thyri's presence. He couldn't picture her failing at anything, and in a way he felt just as safe with her as he had as a boy with his mother. Talk of a sorcerous opponent, however, had rekindled the feeling that he was suddenly in over his head, involving himself in a conflict in which he would have never imagined himself on his own.

With this thought, he entered the Haven. He had enemies there; their faces passed briefly through his mind as boisterous singing reached his ears from the first inn they passed. There was the high-priced harlot who called herself Ramona; Gerald had once cheated her of a night's pleasure by posing as a Frisian prince (he'd not known the language then, but neither had she). But hers was the most attractive of the remembered faces, and she posed no great danger to his life. Ogbert and his organized band of thieves and mercenaries was another matter entirely.

Years before, he'd been foolish enough to play dice with the uncrowned lord of the Haven. Ogbert had only just begun then to consolidate his power, and he'd still spent much of his time on the streets. Fate had brought Gerald in contact with him. Fate had blessed Gerald with an impossible run of luck that night.

He'd been lucky to get out alive.

Now he felt naked, acutely aware of the fact that he wore no disguise and that he hadn't had the presence of mind earlier to take his past into account.

Here he was, without even a hat, looking exactly as he had when Ogbert had slashed his face with a knife. Except now he had the scar . . . He tried to convince himself that Ogbert and his friends had probably forgotten him. After all, they had known him for but a night. And the number of small-time hustlers they'd stepped on over the years was surely vast.

As they passed a band of about ten men and women holding an impromptu party in the street, Thyri asked Gerald if the Saxon people always enjoyed life so thoroughly, or if Guthrom's defeat still contributed to their high spirits. He told her that Reaver's Haven didn't care who controlled the city as long as there was a city off which it could feed.

Thyri laughed at that, and her laughter chased his fears away. Suddenly, he found himself hoping that he would find Ogbert and that the thief would confront him. With Thyri, Gerald could gain his revenge.

So strongly did this feeling grip him that he changed his

plans. Thyri wanted a ship, and for a ship they'd need a crew. He'd flirted with a vague notion of picking up men in the city on the strength of Thyri's reputation or Megan's sorcery. Upon reflection, effort expended in that direction directly under Guthrom's nose was likely to attract the overking's attention. And there was an establishment in Reaver's Haven where one could engage in such an activity as manning a ship and go quite unnoticed. Besides, Thyri had said that they didn't really need a crew until they started downriver for the sea. She hoped to remove a vessel from Guthrom's harbor without his knowledge, and that would require slow stealth, not the speed afforded by a dozen oarsmen. If they could hire men to meet them downstream, they would be better off. And in Reaver's Haven, they were already downstream.

The establishment, which Gerald had thought of bore no formal name. It was called, simply, Ogbert's.

He had never been there; it hadn't existed two years before. But the place was almost legendary, and he'd heard that word of it had spread already to the ends of the earth, even to the far south to the ears of the descendants of the dead empires. It was a gambling house, and it was a brothel, and a menagerie. In it, he'd heard, one could see creatures the likes of which one could see nowhere else. And the women – some were said to have skin the color of night, others the color of the sun.

Ramona probably sold her wares there now as well.

Thyri stopped abruptly as she reached the end of the entrance hall and took in the view. The building was circular, built in three tiers with an open center. The ground floor was crowded, and the noise of human voices was almost deafening. At the banister of the second tier, a row of women garbed in colorful silks motioned and moved seductively for the men below. On a raised platform opposite, a dark-skinned woman danced erotically with a serpent. Those men not caught up in drinking or gawking at the spectacle of female flesh were gathered around a railing in the center of the floor, looking down; there was some sort of pit at the building's core.

Megan drew next to Thyri and gasped. 'Incredible,' she said after a moment. 'I never thought such sights existed in this world.'

Thyri smiled; she didn't share Megan's wonder, yet the nature of the place excited her because its pleasures were tainted, attracting the cruelest and most heartless of men. Within these walls, she could sense the demons that lurked in the darkest corners of the human spirit. She did not necessarily enjoy the company, nor was she wont to seek it out, but experiencing it provided an ironic comfort. Here, in such a place, she could almost feel clean.

Gerald led them to a table near the pit and ordered mead. Thyri asked him what the pit was for.

'Cockfights,' he replied, hoping that what he'd heard was true. He started to look out over the crowd, searching for people he knew from the city as well as those faces from his past. He didn't see Ogbert; it seemed sensible that the proprietor would spend his time managing the finer details of his business in a place removed from the noise. In this Gerald felt relief. His boost in confidence had begun to wane.

As Gerald looked around, Megan glanced at Thyri, rose, and walked to the edge of the pit. A young girl with circles cut in her shift to reveal her nipples stopped briefly at the table to deposit three large flagons. Thyri took up one of the flagons and drank, eyeing Gerald over the rim.

He started to speak, then felt a hand on his shoulder. Ogbert! he thought, his hand moving to the hilt of his sword.

'I thought you didn't like this place, my friend,' said a thickly accented voice.

The voice made Gerald jump. He turned and looked up into an exotic, olive-skinned face with a flat nose and dark, almond eyes. 'Rui! I thought you dead!' The sight of the familiar face swept away Gerald's unease; he laughed, rising to embrace the newcomer.

'I have often thought that myself,' the man said, smiling warmly. 'May I join you?'

Gerald looked to Thyri, who nodded almost imperceptibly under her hood. The man sat, and Thyri pushed Megan's flagon toward him. Gerald signaled for more mead, then turned to Thyri. 'This is an old friend, though I hardly expected to find him here. His name is Rui; I cannot pronounce his surname.'

'Taichimi,' Rui said.

'He's a merchant.'

'No, just a traveler. I no longer have anything to sell.'

'Are you elven?' Thyri asked suddenly.

Rui looked at her, openly surprised that the voice coming from the hood had been female. 'No,' he said uncertainly, 'if you mean Fairie as Gerald's people call that race. I was born in Nippon, the land of the sun.' He turned to Gerald. 'Who is this woman dressed like a man in the company of harlots?'

'Thyri Eiriksdattir,' Gerald said.

Thyri pulled back the rim of her hood, revealing her face to the traveler. He could see restrained fire burning behind her eyes.

Rui laughed. 'Eiriksdattir? I did not intend my words to insult you.' He paused, looking at her carefully. 'I am honored. It is said that you deny the lord of the city.'

She nodded, then retreated into her hood. 'You are a traveler? That means you know ships?'

'I know them enough to stay alive on them. If I knew them well, I would not now be so far from home.'

'Rui,' Gerald said, 'I have brought Eiriksdattir here with her companion to find men like you. They plan to steal one of Guthrom's ships tonight.'

Rui raised a dark eyebrow. 'Companion?' he asked after a moment's silence.

Gerald tilted his head in Megan's direction. Rui looked. Megan's back faced them; her slender ankles and bare feet were just visible in the shadows beneath her. And then she turned, starting back to the table. She sat.

'Who's this?'

'Rui Taichimi, friend of Gerald's,' Thyri said. 'He says he is not an elf.'

All fell silent then, and it seemed to Gerald that even the noise around them backed off into the distance. Rui could not see Megan's eyes, but he nevertheless felt the weight of her gaze.

'He isn't,' Megan said softly.

Rui smiled. 'I hope not.' He indicated the pit. 'Did you enjoy the game?' he asked.

'No,' she said, 'It seemed cruel.'

'It is cruel,' the traveler said, 'but so is life at times.'

'We seek a crew here,' Gerald said.

'That can be arranged. You have money?'

Megan reached across the table and dropped a handful of silver coins into Rui's hand.

He tested their weight and began to stand.

'Wait,' Gerald said. 'Pay them half, and tell them to meet us at the first landing south of the ruins.'

Rui nodded, then disappeared into the crowd.

'He can be trusted?' Thyri asked.

'As well as any,' Gerald said before he realized that Thyri's question had been directed to Megan.

'He seems a strong, honest man,' the sorceress said. 'Very calm inside.'

Gerald asked them if they'd like to see more of Ogbert's. Thyri considered the idea briefly; exploration hung implicit in the air, such was the nature of the place. Falling prey to the temptation, however, was not a part of the strange comfort she'd found there. She declined.

After that, they drank in silence. Gerald began to feel foolish that he'd ever feared confrontation with the master thief and his minions. He watched Thyri, realizing that this old fear of his – this defeat by Ogbert that haunted him – no longer carried weight in his reality. Thyri had carved him a new reality, one that could free him from his fears and make him whole. In her, he saw no trace of fear. He saw now that he and other men cherished fear and labeled it caution to justify their cowardice. The caution – the cowardice – chained men as surely as the strongest iron, but beyond these chains, didn't death lurk? Were the chains not necessary? A week before, he would have answered smugly, fatalistically, in the affirmative. Now the fact of Thyri's existence proved him wrong.

He threw back his head and drank deeply, trying to drown the convoluted contradictions in his thinking. To his relief, Rui returned, providing reason to turn his mind to the matters at hand.

The traveler sat. 'It is done,' he said. 'Eight men, though I would not stake my life on their worthiness.'

'Can they work oars?' Thyri asked.

Rui nodded.

'Then let us go.' She stood.

'Eiriksdattir?' the traveler asked hesitantly. 'May I join you now? I would much like to see how you do what you plan, and I am no novice at battle.'

She paused, then nodded silently. They rose and started for the door. Rui stopped them there and retrieved a large bow and its quiver from a nearby storeroom, then they exited into the streets beyond.

Nightreaver

Thorir Ulfson wearily dismounted and stamped his feet on the packed earth, trying to shake the ache from his legs. He had been riding since shortly after sunrise.

Painfully, he led his steed to the water trough and cursed loudly when he found the trough empty. Still cursing, he went to the nearby well, brought up two bucketfuls of water, and dumped them into the trough. He tied his steed where the beast could reach the water, then he started for the barracks. He would stable his mount later, after the muscles in his legs unknotted.

Starting up the barrack's wooden steps, he smelled smoke and stopped in alarm, standing motionless until he realized that the smoke emanated from his own clothing. He stank of the day's business. Behind his eyes, the country tavern ignited again and the flames reached up to the heavens. So would Einar Godfredson's passing be remembered forever.

With this thought, Thorir entered the barracks. Buri and Askold, two of his fellow guardsmen, looked up at his entrance from the table where they had just dined. A half-devoured leg of hog sat on a plate in the table's center. Thorir silently went to the table, tore off a chunk of meat, and started to eat even before he had sat. When his behind touched down on the wood of his chair, new spears of pain shot up his spine. He winced and tore into his dinner with new vigor, trying to ignore the pain.

'Eiriksdattir is still free?' Buri asked him.

Thorir looked up impatiently. 'Had I found her, do you not think you would have known before I entered this room?'

Buri averted his eyes. 'Einar should never have slain that

Saxon witch. If she could find Eiriksdattir for Rollo, she could be finding her for us now.'

Askold slammed his fist down on the table. 'Buri! You tempt evil omens by speaking the name of Thorolf's slayer without cursing him in the same breath!'

'Evil omens have found us already, Askold. Seven of us dead in the space of two days. We used to be called Guthrom's best. We used to be feared, but now we are laughed at.

'And I tire of your talk of evil omens. You said it would be an evil omen if we untied Eiriksdattir before we reached Guthrom. You said it might free her! If we hadn't done what we did, if we'd presented Guthrom a chicken, *he* would probably have slain the rest of us!'

'How do you know that we didn't free her? Perhaps she worked some sorcery upon us!'

'It was a dead chicken, Askold!'

'Then perhaps Eiriksdattir is dead. Perhaps –'

'Tell us who killed Einar and Erling and Gorm and Haki Fjolnirson then! An evil omen?'

'The maggot-spawn, Rollo!'

'And how do you explain the report that Eiriksdattir was seen in a field south of the city early this afternoon?' Buri scowled. 'Rollo's sorcery?'

Askold grew distant. *'Fimbulwinter,'* he said softly. *The Saxon witch had spoken of fimbulwinter* . . . 'Evil stalks all the Norselands now.'

As the room went silent but for the sound of Thorir's jaws, something heavy smashed into the rear wall of the barracks. A low growling came to their ears from outside.

Buri jumped up. 'Dogs,' he said. 'Now we have dogs trying to get to our food. Is there no end to this madness!' He rose, unsheathing his sword. Askold followed. Thorir started to rise as well, but Buri told him that two of Guthrom's best swords ought still to be a match for hungry hounds. Thorir shrugged and tore off another chunk of ham.

At the bottom of the steps, Buri stopped, then he signaled Askold around the other side of the building. He waited a moment before he himself prowled down the building's edge.

At the corner, he looked around and saw nothing. At the same time, he heard Askold scream.

His heart suddenly beating in his ears, Buri raced toward the sound. He turned the far corner to find Askold curled on his side, his fingers clutching at his chest where a stream of blood still poured out onto the ground.

Then something bit into Buri's leg. He jumped back, agony flaring in his mind. Dimly, he saw a blade retreat under the building. On that side, there was almost a two-foot gap between the earth and the barracks floor.

'Eiriksdattir!' Buri thought, desperately trying to limp farther away.

Rollo snarled as he crawled, blade first, from under the building. He locked his gaze on the wounded Viking and stalked forward, wild power surging through this limbs.

Buri's face contorted in a soundless scream as Rollo drove his sword into Buri's heart.

And then Rollo turned back for the barracks, running until he reached the steps. He started up. The door was ajar, but he kicked it violently open. Inside, there was only one to face him. Blood dripped from his blade onto the floorboards as he moved to face this last opponent.

Thorir stood, his back to the far wall, his eyes wide in disbelief and horror. Once, he had called Rollo friend . . . 'You!' he said. 'Rollo, you've gone mad!' He tightened the grip on his sword and wished again that the pain would leave his legs. With the threat of death before him, the throbbing only grew worse.

Growling softly, Rollo closed the distance between them. From ten feet away, he began his charge, smashing his blade down upon Thorir's.

Thorir felt the hilt of his sword disappear from his hand, then heard it clatter to the floor. As Rollo brought his blade down again, Thorir closed his eyes. And that is how he died. He had been twenty-six that day.

Rollo backed away, then slipped silently from the barracks and started for the hall of Guthrom.

As Thyri's small party passed along the edge of the grounds of the royal hall, a scream split the night's silence. Thyri commanded Gerald to halt, and she led them slowly toward a breach in the wall. At the breach, she stopped and looked in.

Guthrom had taken residence in ruins much like those south of the city, though these remained largely intact; the central structure possessed a quiet grandeur unequaled by that of any building Thyri had looked upon during her travels. To those ancient dwellers of Ebaracum, it had been a temple, a monument to the dwellers of Olympus, and a sanctuary dedicated to reflection. It yet radiated its architect's desire for unity; its pillars mirrored the heavenward thrust of the trees growing in its garden, and its strong, subtly curving lines granted an illusion of growth from the very rock of the earth.

Even so, motion in the garden gave its serenity a menacing, indistinct cast: shadowy figures moved away from Thyri across the grounds; she could see the needles of their swords shining in the moonlight.

Thyri needed to move on to the docks, but there, at the breach, she hesitated. Guthrom claimed ownership of all she saw: the ruins, the bushes, the trees of his garden. These things he did not deserve, and she possessed the power to take them away from him. And yet, his death had not been part of her plans . . . Events had moved too quickly, and were she now to seek Guthrom's downfall, she would place the lives of those who accompanied her at grave risk.

Still, she had almost stepped through the breach when she heard Megan's voice in her mind:

We need a sentinel here, white-hair, said the voice of the sorceress, ***and I am the one most suited to the task. Call to me when you have secured your vessel. I will hear you.***

Megan's clipped seriousness surprised Thyri. She could find no words with which to reply as Meg brushed by her into Guthrom's garden. The sorceress looked back; her eyes told Thyri firmly that her friend understood what Thyri had been considering, and she was not going to allow it. There remained the threat of a wizard now working evil at Guthrom's side.

Thyri turned away, quickly leading Gerald and Rui on. As Gerald passed the breach, he looked in to see Megan moving cautiously toward Guthrom's hall. He paused then, watching the sorceress. After a moment, Megan seemed to turn and melt into the air, leaving Gerald's eyes naught but the moonlight glinting off the garden's grass and trees.

As they reached the docks, Thyri took cover and scanned the harbor, quickly choosing a slender oceangoing Norse vessel with a deck and cabins. The ship would require twenty oarsmen to attain speed in still waters, but she would worry about that later. For now they needed only to drift downriver. After that, Rui's crew of eight would give her oarsmen enough for a time.

As for Guthrom's guard, Thyri could see but four lone figures along the docks. The task would be easy.

A ridge composed of rigging provided her ample cover as she led her party to a point behind the guard nearest her target. From there, she moved forward alone, drawing her knife and flipping it so that she held it by its point. Ten paces from the guard's back, she stopped, raising the knife.

She paused, studying the guard's back – she knew the man, and she could not bring herself to kill him for all that she had cursed him the night before. After a moment, she stamped her foot on the deck and the guard turned.

'Sokki Gunnarson!' she whispered loudly, pulling back her hood to reveal her face.

Sokki's eyes widened. 'Thy – ' The greeting was cut short as his eyes took in the raised knife. He stepped forward, lowering his sword. In the moonlight, Thyri recognized the blade. 'Thyri,' he whispered excitedly. 'What are you doing here!'

'Stealing that ship,' she said, pointing with her knife at the vessel beyond.

Sokki glanced over his shoulder, then his eyes returned cautiously to Thyri. 'You were going to kill me?'

She nodded. 'I may still, unless you join me. But I do not desire your blood on my hands.'

Slowly, Sokki fell to his knees. 'I have failed you, Thyri,' he said. 'Through my own inaction, I failed to return to you what is rightfully yours.' He looked up into her eyes, nervously turning Thyri's rune-sword in his hands so that he held it out to her hilt-first. 'I have kept this blade for you these months. Please take it back.'

Thyri smiled at him, shifted the knife to her other hand, and took the sword. As she gripped the weapon, she felt a part of her old self returning, as if the blade gifted her by Scacath now made her whole. 'Thank you, my friend,' she said softly. 'I did not expect this.' She looked down at Sokki, seeing in his eyes a reverence that once offended her. Now she understood how much she owed him. He had saved her life once, and now he willingly returned to her one of the few possessions she'd ever truly valued. When she had given up hope, this man had taken that hope into himself and provided it a haven.

She studied him silently. 'You will remain in Guthrom's service?'

Memories of that day on the field against Alfred rushed through his mind. He could almost feel Thyri next to him, feel the power of her battle fury surging through his own veins, making him feel invincible. And invincible they had been until Guthrom's retreat . . . 'No,' he said. 'I will follow you.'

'Where are your brothers?'

He pointed to his left.

'Call them,' she demanded.

'Ottar! Horik! Come quickly!'

Thyri looked right long enough to be sure that she knew the men approaching through the night, then she turned left to watch the approach of a third figure, the guard whose identity she did not yet know. For a moment, she thought the Viking would not stop before he reached her.

'Thyri!' Horik Gunnarson exlaimed behind her.

At that, the fourth guard stopped, fear spreading across his face. Thyri watched his sword start to rise, then fall again. This one would not fight her alone. He started to turn to flee. Before he could turn his face away, Thyri threw her knife, burying it between his eyes. The Viking still moved, his legs turning him back in the direction from whence he'd come before he fell face-down on the dock.

She turned back to the sons of Gunnar, glancing over their shocked faces. 'I'm sorry,' she said, 'but I have a friend who must soon join us. I will not risk her life unnecessarily by allowing an alarm to be sounded.' She fixed her gaze on Sokki's while signaling behind her for Rui and Gerald to join them. The two emerged shortly from the shadows.

Briefly, Thyri closed her eyes. *Megan!* she called in her mind. *Join me now!* She waited for a reply, but none came. From the direction of Guthrom's hall, however, a war cry suddenly erupted, and Thyri's enhanced senses picked up a distant clash of arms.

An intense fear wrapped itself around Thyri's heart, and she fought to keep it hidden. Megan was all right. Megan *had to be* all right.

'Just do as she says!' Sokki whispered to his brothers. Thyri opened her eyes and glanced at him again as she stepped by him for the ship.

'Come,' she said. 'We have much to do.'

During the same moment that witnessed Thyri, knife poised, realizing that friends, not enemies, stood between her and her goal, a sixth man, a Viking named Arnulf, fell by Rollo's sword. Rollo, however, was not keeping count. An army stood against him; numbers didn't matter. The only thing that mattered was victory, victory and Guthrom's death.

He had fought his way onto Guthrom's grounds. Silence filled the night around him, but he knew they were out there, hunting him now. But they were mules hunting a fox more deadly than the fiercest of wolves. They could kill him, but first they'd have to catch him. And that he could not allow until Guthrom's blood had stained his sword.

He heard several sets of footsteps approaching, and reason forced him to melt into the shadow of a tree next to the wall of Guthrom's hall. The overking would be somewhere beyond that wall. Rollo could almost smell him; in his mind he could picture the unworthy ruler lounging in the luxury of his governing chamber, being tended by a stream of Saxon servants while reveling in his defeat of Eiriksdattir. Perhaps Guthrom now displayed Thyri's head at his side.

The footsteps of his enemies receding, Rollo scaled a pillar and reached the stone roof above. In the center of the ancient building, adjacent to that room centered on Guthrom's throne, was another small garden; Rollo had seen it often, though Guthrom's guard was forbidden to enter it. All close to Guthrom knew that the overking often spent hours alone there, and Rollo had heard, during one such time, the overking's voice imploring Odin not to forsake his chosen conqueror.

In places, crosshatched boards patched holes in the roof; Rollo fought the *berserk* madness inside himself, forcing his body to its hands and knees to crawl carefully along the seams of the roof toward the central garden. After what seemed an interminable time, he reached his goal safely, then dropped down to the grass.

Immediately, he sensed movement. A hulking form behind him shadowed the ground at his feet, and he spun around in defense. But the form was a statue, a rendering of the god the dead empire named Jupiter. Again, he sensed movement, and this time he dove. The singing sound of an iron blade split the air behind him.

Rollo landed and rolled, raising his sword. A human form now blocked out the moonlight from above. Metal clanged against metal; Rollo's grip held, and he kicked up at his attacker, rolling again after his feet connected with flesh and the shadow backed away.

He gained his feet then, and he glared over his blade at Guthrom. The overking stood in Jupiter's shadow. For a moment, the two Vikings did not move, then Guthrom stepped out into the moonlight and relaxed his stance. He wore only a wrap of fur about his waist, and a sheen of sweat coated his skin with a silver glaze. He stood taller than Rollo, and the muscles of his arms and chest rippled as he shifted his grip on his blade.

'You,' Guthrom growled softly. 'You disappointed me, Rollo. I have waited for you here.'

Rollo didn't reply; he flew at Guthrom almost before the last words passed the overking's lips. His attack pressed the larger man back, and Guthrom thudded into the statue's base. Rollo attacked again, but Guthrom moved quickly, and Rollo's blade hit into stone. He jerked it free and turned in search of his opponent.

Guthrom stood under the moonlight again. Blood streamed down his sword arm where Rollo's last attack had grazed his shoulder. The overking bellowed, his battle cry shaking the night. Rollo returned the bellow with one of his own and braced himself to turn back Guthrom's charge.

The overking's weight crashed into him, and Rollo felt the force of the attack surge down through his legs. He stood his ground, and threw Guthrom back. Guthrom fell, and Rollo let him rise before he charged anew, his sword whirling in the night, forcing Guthrom's retreat with each blow. So consumed by the fury of the battle was Rollo that he scarcely noticed that Guthrom had backed out of the garden and onto the pillared landing that edged the throne room.

Within the throne room, a growing audience – ten already of Guthrom's guard, Rollo's former peers, and an equal number of Saxon servants – watched the two combatants. Still, Rollo pressed the attack into the throne room, oblivious to the presence of all save the sweating, faltering Viking he had once sworn to serve with his life.

In the end, Guthrom said nothing of great note, and for all the overking's power, Rollo's *berserk* fury never allowed him even a weak counterattack. Methodically, Rollo pressed him all the way to the far wall, and Guthrom's guard watched, dumbstruck. Halfway to the wall, Rollo's sword bit deep into Guthrom's stomach, tearing it from side to side. At the wall, Rollo buried his blade into Guthrom's heart.

And then he turned. The rest of the guard moved uncertainly, their faces a mixture of awe and fear. Rollo glared at them, not recognizing any of the faces, seeing only enemies whose leader's blood still dripped from the point of his blade. Slowly, his enemies spread out, cautiously drawing their swords.

During that moment, Rollo Anskarson could have commanded the allegiance of the Danes of Jorvik, and none would have opposed him. He could have taken Guthrom's place, and he could even have taken the battle, once again, to the southern lands of Alfred if he'd wished.

Instead, Rollo attacked again, and ten expert blades rose up against his one. He killed one man, then another, but as he felled the third, he felt iron bite into his thigh, cutting through flesh and into bone. He looked down at the wound, stunned that he could feel no pain. He raised his blade against the man who had dealt the injury, then a blow of incredible power smashed into him, knocking him back, to the ground, into darkness.

Thyri grew tired of inspecting the ship's two cabins and stepped impatiently back out on the deck. *Megan!* she thought loudly. *Answer me!*

She looked anxiously toward Guthrom's hall. The clash of arms had ended. Horik passed in front of her, carrying supplies to Ottar, who packed them into the ship's small hold.

Rui appeared at Thyri's side. 'She is strong,' the man said strangely, as if he understood her thoughts. 'She will come.'

'Did you learn much, traveler?' she asked sharply, recalling his request to join her and reacting against his invasion of her anxiety. 'Did you learn much from my capturing of this vessel?'

'Certainly,' he answered.

She looked at him. 'And?'

'I learned that you know what you're doing.' He smiled at her curiously; the expression intensified the alien set of his features. 'It would be unfair to your friend if I assumed that she does not.' His smile faded before he turned and went to help Sokki and Gerald load the rigging.

Thyri looked up at the waxing moon and felt like screaming. If she had to endure the moon's curse again, without Megan awaiting her in the morning, she didn't know what she would do. The sorceress had given new meaning to her life; thought of losing her so swiftly terrified her. Guthrom had his wizard, and they did not know his power . . .

White-hair!

Megan! she replied uncertainly, fearing now that Meg's call could be an illusion of the night. *You're okay?*

Fine. But I'm not alone.

Thyri sighed relief. She wanted to ask Megan why she had ignored her earlier calls, but she'd known that all along: with Guthrom's wizard nearby, *any* exercise of Megan's powers – necessary or frivolous – placed them in danger. Rui had been right; she'd been wrong to speak harshly to him. On the other hand, Thyri knew Megan, and she knew that the sorceress had seldom, if ever, had to fight for her life. Powerful she was, but power was worthless against the unexpected; Astrid's death had been proof enough of that.

White-hair! You must concentrate deeply on a flat hard place near you.

She looked around, then raced by Gerald onto the dock. There, she stopped, looking down the planks before her. After a moment, the air ahead shimmered as two forms began to take shape in front of Thyri's eyes. Thyri restrained herself from leaping into Meg's arms until her nose verified the sorceress's complete materialization. Next to Megan, the second form collapsed onto the dock.

'Odin!' Thyri whispered. 'I thought I'd lost you again. Did you clash with Guthrom's wizard?'

'I saw no sign of him at all.'

'Perhaps he has fled.' Thyri dug her fingers into Megan's back before she stepped away and looked down at the limp form at her feet. She nudged it with her foot, bringing its face into the moonlight. The slow but deliberate motion of the man's chest assured her that he lived.

'He slew Guthrom,' Megan offered, 'but he would have been slain himself had I not intervened. He seemed a great warrior, and I could not bring myself to leave him.'

The man moaned and coughed, then kicked one leg spasmodically. Blood seeped slowly from a slender gash in his leg. Thyri bent and gripped him under the arm.

'Be careful with the leg,' Megan said. 'I did not have time to heal it fully. It was a dire wound.'

Thyri nodded, then lifted the man from his wounded side. His eyes fluttered open, and he looked at her dully as his other leg uncertainly tested the deck beneath him.

'Eiriksdattir,' he said softly. 'So this is death?'

'No, Rollo,' she said. 'Not quite.' Patiently, she helped the Viking onto her ship.

Magic

Rollo tried to sit and winced as pain flared up from his wounded leg. 'I *am* alive,' he said emphatically, then he collapsed back to the deck and looked at Thyri. 'I saw you captured! You could not have survived that ordeal.'

Thyri looked at him oddly, slowly realizing that he must have witnessed the events that morning at the country tavern. She should have suspected something then, what with the leader of the riders calling out Rollo's name. 'That wasn't me they captured,' she said simply, looking at Meg and glancing at Rollo's leg. The sorceress nodded and went to bend over the man.

'What of Fandis?' Rollo asked. 'Is she alive as well?'

'I don't know that name,' Thyri said. 'How did you find me this morning?'

Rollo propped himself up on one elbow while Megan examined his wound. Wincing occasionally under Megan's probing fingers, he told Thyri how he had sought to find her, how he had gone to Fandis for aid, how she had directed him to her, and then how he had seen her fall. And then he told how Guthrom had hung the head of the river witch at Jorvik's south gate.

The images Rollo painted with his words sobered Thyri; she couldn't help feeling that she was the source of all that had transpired. At least Guthrom had died . . . She glanced at Megan, who returned her gaze.

So here is Guthrom's wizard, the sorceress said silently.

Thyri nodded, and Megan looked down into Rollo's eyes. 'I can heal your leg,' she said, 'but you must sleep.' She passed her hand over his eyes, and the reflections off her ring fluttered about him, then began to steal away his thoughts. He didn't fight the magic.

As the ship drifted downriver, and as Guthrom's harbor receded into the distance, Megan remained bent over Rollo and began to sing. Gerald and the sons of Gunnar still worked, readying the mainsail, but the sound of Megan's voice stopped them with its beauty. Almost in concert, Sokki, Horik, and Ottar abandoned their task and sat back against the port gunwale; Rui and Gerald sat on the starboard side, balancing the load. And Megan sang.

She swayed over Rollo, unaware of how her lyricless, soaring song of healing enchanted the entire crew. Ottar heard in her voice the simple, pleasant comfort of childhood, and Sokki thought of tales he'd heard of the One God's angels. Megan's voice transported Horik to the shore of a moonlit lake, and Rui to a place half the world away where he'd once contemplated the beauty of a single drop of water on a blade of grass.

For Gerald, it was as if the song became part of the night, and the night the song, with the stars themselves dancing off each note, each phrase.

And when she finished, Megan looked up at Thyri as if time hadn't passed, as if the song that had passed her lips had been as natural and unremarkable as breathing.

'Do we yet require Rui's crew?' Megan asked.

'To man the ship,' Thyri answered, 'yes. Actually, we'll need more than that. This was one of Guthrom's best ships, and we'll need thirty oars in battle to handle it.'

Is that all? You've not been thinking of building a fleet? Raising another army as you did across the water?

No, Megan. Where is the use for that?

'What if I could provide enchantments to make this vessel obey the commands of four oars, even two oars?'

'Then we would not need the crew.'

'But you have already paid them!' Rui spoke out.

Megan turned to him, reaching into one pocket of her cloak. She withdrew a handful of corn and held it out for Rui to see, then she passed her other hand over the corn. She smiled; five pieces of silver now rested in her palm.

Rui creased his forehead and reached into his own pocket, withdrawing a handful of coins. Megan touched his hand, and two of the coins shriveled into golden grains.

Rui laughed. 'Brilliant! But dangerous – you risked mutiny.'

'Mutiny,' Thyri said softly, 'requires the demise of the ship's captain.'

Megan looked at Rui. 'Had we the money, we would have given it gladly. But we are not rich. They would have been paid in the end, just as you shall be, if that is what you desire.' She took the grains of corn from his hand.

Sokki chuckled. 'So where do we go?' he asked.

'Let's go back, depose Guthrom, and make Thyri queen!' Ottar offered excitedly.

'Guthrom's dead. Rollo killed him.' Thyri pointed to the deck where the Viking snored softly.

Ottar dropped his eyes, feeling as if his mother had just admonished him for failing to strap up his boots.

'Then it will be that much easier, Thyri,' Horik said, 'to make you queen. We can make the Danes follow you! We can take the war again into Alfred's lands!'

'Do you not think, Brother,' Sokki said to him, 'that the Danes would have already crowned Thyri had she wanted that? Any true Viking who witnessed – '

'Enough!' Thyri said. 'I do not want that. I do not feel like a queen.'

'Then where shall we go?'

'Anywhere.'

'And what shall we call this vessel bound for anywhere?'

'Nightreaver,' Gerald said. It was his first word since they'd pushed off the dock, and even as he said it, he wondered what had inspired the sudden utterance. But since they'd shipped, he'd felt incredibly at peace with the night around him, and Megan's song had carved the atmosphere into the stony cliffs of his memory. And reavers – that was what they

were: Norsemen, reavers – at least five of the eight of them. Reavers of the night.

Thyri grinned. '*Nightreaver.* So be it.'

Thyri had indeed chosen one of Guthrom's best vessels. *Nightreaver* was a war boat, crafted in Vestfold where Harald had collected the most talented shipbuilders in all of the Norselands. Guthrom had come by it as a battle prize, and he would have made it his flagship if he hadn't abandoned the sea for the conquest of land.

Under normal circumstances, Thyri should have had a crew of sixty-odd. As it was, the six men on board faced a near impossible task in manning the sail in rough winds. The ship stretched seventy feet from stern to bow, and it could achieve speeds, under sail, exceeding ten knots.

With only eight people on board, Thyri could almost picture them as ants bent to the task of managing a horse. But the presence of Megan added her sorcery to her strengths. And if they picked up a crew of nameless faces, men whom she did not know, as she had not really known the crew of the *Black Rabbit* . . .

That slaughter came back to her, acute in every detail: the screams, the blood . . . The hunger, and Elaine's pleading eyes . . . She would not allow it to happen again.

And so they drifted south down the river. Ottar and Horik retrieved a keg of ale from the hold, and Rui told all a long story of a warrior of his homeland who had once challenged the fire-breathing god of the mountains and lost. It was said that when the molten rock spilled out of the earth near the warrior's village, the warrior's face could be seen in its surface, twisting in pain as it flowed slowly down the mountainside, destroying all in its path.

Midway through the story, Rollo awakened. He felt dazed, and the strangeness of his company, and the fact that his leg bore not even a scar, fueled a nagging doubt that he yet lived. But if this was Asgard, then Rui might be Aesir, and Rollo did not care to interrupt a god's tale to ask where he was. Groggily, the Viking rose and went to the cask of ale, keeping his silence.

As Rui finished his story, Megan took a small leather pouch from her cloak and tipped its contents into her palm. Two small gems – twins of the one she had sent Thyri for her summoning – fell onto her skin; from where Gerald sat, he could see little beyond a faint blue glow until Megan took one of the stones from her palm and held it up under the moonlight, where it became, for the others, a glittering new star. When the sorceress lowered her hand, the gemstone remained fixed in the air before her. She closed her eyes and began again to sing.

This time, the others could *feel* her song; it became part of the night. Megan's ring began to sparkle, then shine, its light brighter even than the moon's, its beams reaching out to engulf the ship. The aqua gem's brilliance grew to rival the ring's; sparks flew from it, streaking the ring's silver light with scintillating greens and dark blues.

Gerald felt the deck become like clay beneath him while Megan's song and the light wrapped about him, holding him. And the clay beneath him flowed and stretched. Behind the sorceress, the deck rose up and two additional cabins began to take shape. Near the bow, benches for oarsmen began to melt under the ring's power, and the prow stretched out, a ghoulish shape wrapping about its length like a demon caressing it in the night.

The little gem exploded in a blinding shower, and then the night itself fell on the ship, painting it black from bow to stern. Megan's singing abruptly ceased. No one moved until she opened her eyes. She smiled weakly.

'Odin!' Rollo gasped. He *was* dead.

Gerald wiped his forehead in amazement and gazed at the sorceress, only dimly aware that the wood beneath him was solid again.

Megan reached down for her ale-filled cup and brought it up to her lips. 'Now,' she said, 'I can relax and enjoy this.' She looked at Thyri. *The talismans of power you gave me, my love, are strong, are they not? This last one we shall keep for the future.* She tipped the remaining gem back into its pouch.

Thyri smiled at her, but concern lurked at the corners of her smile. *You look pale, Megan. You should have rested first.*

Megan chuckled, smiling warmly. *I am always pale.*

Thyri scolded her briefly with her eyes, then Sokki moved, capturing her attention. The man rose and went to the prow, his hand hesitantly reaching out to touch the hindquarters of the beast Megan had shaped. Thyri followed his actions. *You cannot escape it*, she heard Megan again in her mind, *but now you command it.*

The beast shaped around the prow – the sight that would first confront any enemy they approached – was a huge, black wolf. It had only to move to seem alive.

Throughout the remainder of the night, the only thing that felt real to Gerald was the ale. Drunkenness was not normally his habit, but that night he welcomed it. The others were in a similar mood; this became apparent when Ottar and Harik launched into a series of drinking songs without considering the presence of two women in their midst. Rui and Gerald soon added their voices to the noise.

Thyri didn't mind; she drank quietly, said little, and felt simple contentment inside, as if she dreamed a pleasant dream that no longer threatened transformation into nightmare. Her only concern was Megan; the others couldn't notice, but the sorceress had expended much in her last casting. Megan's ever-erect carriage slumped when its mistress grew careless, and fatigue lingered behind her eyes. What concerned Thyri was not so much that her friend was exhausted, but that Megan tried to hide the fact and did not seem of a mind to sleep it off – a small thing, perhaps, except that they did not know what dangers might lie ahead, nor how soon they would have to confront them.

Still, all was peaceful. And the sorceress, after all, had embarked on a new adventure of her own. Thyri guessed that the present circumstance had summoned up the child within her, and this suspicion was confirmed as Megan began to pick up on the choruses of the others' songs and join in, adding her voice without inhibition to the otherwise raucous cacophony.

Gerald watched Megan also, finding the joyousness of her expression difficult to believe. He did not yet know that she had spent her life on a relatively small island, among people who either loathed or feared her. She hadn't been treated casually since she'd been a girl, and the ale and the night and the songs had brought something to life inside of her that had not lived in years.

As dawn began to tinge the eastern horizon, Thyri staggered drunkenly to Rollo's side. The Viking's silence had gradually come to disturb her, and she'd slowly come to guess at its causes. She took his cup, went to the keg to slosh more ale into it, and returned it to his hand. 'Look at me,' she said firmly.

Rollo's eyes met hers; she searched his expression, finding both tenderness and fear. It was the fear that she meant to dispel. She took his hands in hers and squeezed. 'You are alive,' she said. 'And so am I. This is not Asgard. If you don't say you believe me, I'm going to start punching you.'

A faint smile spread across his lips. 'I believe you – I think.'

'It's true, Rollo. When you die, are you not to go to Valhalla, to Odin's hall?'

'So it is said.'

'And does this ship seem to you like a hall?'

'No.'

'And how does one get to Odin's hall?'

'The Valkyrie.'

'Have you seen Valkyrie this night?'

'No,' he acknowledged.

'Listen, Rollo! While you slept, while you healed, these Vikings suggested I return to take Guthrom's throne. That throne is rightly yours, and you have but to ask and I'll turn this ship and we'll go back and make you king. If we do this, all the Vikings, these included, will be yours to command.' Thyri nodded toward the sons of Gunnar. Ottar had collapsed against the gunwale and already snored softly. Horik bent over his cup, all but asleep himself while Sokki was slurring something in the direction of Rui, Gerald, and Megan.

Rollo followed Thyri's gaze and laughed. He looked back into Thyri's eyes. 'Last night,' he said, 'I swore my sword into your service. If you will not be queen, then I cannot be king.'

Thyri smiled at him, squeezed his hands again, and went for more ale.

Megan had gifted *Nightreaver* with two extra cabins – enough space for all on board to live comfortably. This night, however, the ale tarnished her magic in its way, and sleep claimed all of them where they sat.

Avalon

In her tower, she dreamed, the orb of Babd clutched to her breast. Her physical form shook under the dream's violent intensity, and the beauty she had crafted in her face faltered, her features contorting into horrible grimaces, her fingernails cracking against the unyielding surface of the orb.

And yet, in her dream, she refused her body's limits. She pushed it, commanding its lungs to take in more air, commanding its heart to beat faster and faster, pumping its strength into the flight of her soul.

She had soared over the seas, seeking a means of escape. Her quest had taken her to the eastern shores of Arthur's kingdom. On a river there, she had found a vessel that had given her hope, and it was coming her way, into her waters, into the reach of her powers.

All on board possessed great strength, but it was Edain who had first attracted her attention. Or at least, the woman had felt like Edain.

Though she had been pressing herself on her quest for nearly a full day, Morgana refused to return to her body. Not yet . . . She couldn't yet; she needed to know more, and she needed to be sure that the craft would not dock before it reached the sea. Through the mortal hearts on board, she sought the answer to that question, and she felt a dark joy as she learned that all thought themselves bound for the sea.

Into the immortal hearts, she could see little. The one felt like Edain, and then not like Edain. If she were Edain, she possessed power greater than ever in the past. Morgana had little desire to confront such strength, but if it could grant her freedom . . .

In the next immortal heart, she found the darkness that she truly sought. This heart Morgana could persuade; this heart she could use. She studied it long.

When she finally left, she did not do so on the demands of her body, but on a growing fear that Edain would discover her presence.

She would learn of it soon enough, but not now . . .

Nightreaver

Throughout the morning, the crew of *Nightreaver* woke, shook off the ale, and made their way to the cabins. The sons of Gunnar elected to share one amongst them; Gerald found himself bunking with Rui, and Rollo had a cabin to himself. Thyri and Megan shared the captain's cabin.

Before she retired, and against Thyri's protests, Megan cast a simple spell to keep *Nightreaver* centered in the river, and then, for a few brief hours, none on board was awake to guide the ship. After she woke again, Megan took pains to shield the vessel from the eyes of those on ships traveling upriver for Jorvik, but during that time while all slept, *Nightreaver*'s dark, black lines and its wolf's head prow impressed observers as a demonic vessel; other captains on the river steered well clear.

In the light of day, Thyri couldn't bring herself to scold her friend for dispensing again her powers, even though Megan's fatigue had grown more apparent, and she looked as if she'd slept not at all. Upon reflection, Megan's spell did seem a wise one. Pursuit by Guthrom's armada could not be discounted, and in such an event, the invisibility Megan granted the ship could save it. And, after all, Megan *was* the sorceress and, as such, knew best her abilities. And Rui's scolding kept returning to Thyri's mind; against her better judgment – and her understanding of Megan's lack of combat experience – she kept silent.

Later, after all had risen, they ate from the ship's stores. They were wanting for nothing – Horik and Ottar had packed the hold full, and it was capable of providing for seventy men for ten days. With only eight mouths to feed, they could survive on the water for months without setting foot on land.

After eating, the sons of Gunnar and Rollo took up the ship's oars, and all were amazed at the speed they quickly attained. Thyri called Rui into her cabin, leaving Gerald to help Megan look ahead for danger. The sorceress perched herself on the small foredeck she'd created the night before, and Gerald stood next to her, feeling useless again as he couldn't imagine his eyes being more effective than those of the sorceress.

The cabin Thyri shared with Meg was, like the others, black inside as well as out. On one side, also like the others, a table extended out of the wall, and there were several chairs fixed to the floor about the table. In the center of the table was an oil-burning lamp, while brackets around the walls held several other lamps.

Unlike the other cabins, Thyri's boasted a large table for charts and one large bed instead of wall-bunks. This last fact did not surprise Rui; rather, it affirmed what he'd suspected about Thyri and Megan during those times he'd seen them together. In this way, the archer was much like Gerald.

One other item marked Thyri's cabin uniquely: over the bed, a large painting covered the major part of the wall. It was a scene of woodlands, with mountain peaks reaching toward the sky in the distance. Above the peaks, a full moon cast an eerie glaze over the landscape. Rui had never seen a work of art rendered with such realism; he assumed that the painting had decorated the cabin before Thyri had taken the ship. This was not so; Megan had created it as part of her sorcery the night before, and none of *Nightreaver*'s crew could have guessed at the purpose which it served.

Thyri sat at the table and had Rui sit across from her. She'd brought a bottle of wine in with her from the hold, and neither of them spoke until she'd uncorked it and poured two glasses. Rui drank with her; the wine was good, but after the night before he would have preferred a less potent brew.

Thyri stretched back in her chair and truly surprised the traveler for the first time since he'd first heard her speak. The surprise came in the form of a question, and the question was this: 'You said you came from the land of the sun, Rui. In this land of the sun, does the sun set and the moon rise?'

'Of course,' he answered. 'Does the moon not rise over all lands?'

'I suppose,' she said distantly; then she smiled sadly and looked into his eyes. 'That is not why I called you here. I wanted to ask you of your travels; I have been no farther south than the Frankish lands. I have heard of lands beyond – are they interesting?'

'Yes,' he said. 'There are places where winter does not come. Many strange sights. In one land, there are temples the size of small mountains, and no one knows who built them. In another, the people are wild, and they have skin the color of night. There is much to see in the South, if seeing is what you desire.'

Thyri had grown distant again. 'At the moment, my friend, I can think of nothing else.'

'You seem troubled,' he said. 'You should not be so. I have done many interesting things in my years, but the most interesting of all was joining you last night. You are a woman, but you carry yourself like the bravest of men. I've seen enough of your skill to know that I would never dare cross arms with you, and yet you are not arrogant. You are a mystery, more so than those temples, because you are alive. Are you a goddess?'

She laughed. 'Please, not again!' She paused and filled her cup. 'I am not a goddess, Rui.'

'Is Megan?'

She looked at him curiously. 'I do not know. Perhaps. Perhaps we are all gods in our way. What makes a god a god?'

'Immortality.'

'Then there are no gods,' she said flatly. She fell silent for a while, and when she spoke again, she told him to go, to tell the others to fare south when they reached the sea.

After he'd left, Thyri sat long in thought, staring into the painting over her bed, into the eye of the moon.

In two nights, the moon in this world – the real world – would be full.

They could be far from land at sunset.

She prayed Megan's magic would work.

Water

Later that evening they reached the sea; they raised the mainsail and fared out, away from the coast, and headed south. Then came the storm.

It had been a peaceful, starry night when clouds suddenly darkened the sky and the first giant spear of lightning streaked across the heavens. Thunder crashed, and just before the rains fell, the four Norse crewmen joked that, somewhere above, Sif had just accused her husband, Thor, of infidelity and now the Thunderer was breaking his hammer against her head (Sif's head being the hardest substance in Asgard). Rollo chuckled at the joke (it had started as Horik's, then Ottar had expanded the theme), but Fandis's prophecy of *fimbulwinter* darkened his mirth, suggesting more insidious objects for Thor's wrath.

Such was the banter as they lowered and secured the mast and stowed the sail; then the rains came and the sea rose up violently against them and all became more concerned with staying on board than with jokes and dark prophecies.

Thyri and Megan were in their cabin when the storm hit. Megan immediately sat up on the bed and fell into a trance; Thyri rose and exited, running to help Sokki and Rollo, who were struggling to close the hold. After that, she made sure that the crew all safely reached the cabins.

When Thyri returned to Megan, the sorceress opened her eyes, and Thyri saw fear now mingled with fatigue. 'This storm is not natural!' Megan shouted. She closed her eyes again and grimaced, as if she struggled with some powerful, sorcerous foe.

Thyri stood in the doorway and glared up at the sky,

heedless of the pelting rain that stung her cheeks. At that moment, the ship lurched violently, throwing her into the cabin, toward Meg. For a moment, it was as if the sorceress rushed straight at her. She twisted in midair, narrowly missing her friend, but now Megan moved as well. The sorceress's head cracked loudly against the bed's headboard.

Thyri braced her own collision with her hands, then scrambled to Meg's side. The sorceress was unconscious, but still alive. Thyri placed her hand under Megan's head and it came away beaded with blood. Anxiously, she turned Megan onto her stomach, took a knife, and carefully began to cut Meg's hair around the wound, revealing a large, oozing bruise. She tore off a piece of sheet and pressed it against the wound, then rolled Megan over and lay next to her, trying to brace both of them against the continuing, violent jerkings of the ship.

Across the room, the cabin's door flapped loudly against the wall several times before the ship lurched once in the opposite direction and slammed the door shut.

Nightreaver's crew had all gathered in Rollo's cabin and braced themselves against the walls. Conversation was difficult, and little was said (or shouted) until Rui protested that the storm should be no match for Megan's powers. This thought began to consume them all until Sokki finally volunteered to rise and check on Thyri and Megan. He went out, returning minutes later with the news that Megan had been hurt. After that, each fell into his own thoughts as they struggled to ride out the storm.

Gates of black iron, their portals shaped of intertwined serpents, rose up before the sorceress. Machinery ground beyond, and the metallic rumblings grew deafening.

Megan raised her hand over her head and called forth her ring's magic: that flame from the fires of creation gifted her by Fand of the floating gardens and bound into the metal by Advari the dwarf. The power came in spurts; she had tapped it too often of late. And she was tired, and a numbing pain threatened to blacken her vision. Where was she? What had happened to the ship?

She gritted her teeth and commanded more energy from her ring. The pain's grip tightened on her mind, then the power surged, and she forgot all else as she struggled to save herself from the fury of her own magic. The silver flames fought against her, and cackling laughter penetrated through to echo malevolently between her ears. A sibilant voice came in the wake of the laughter, its whispery hiss invoking names unspoken since the fall of Danu's children. They were old names – weak names – but even as Megan cast them out they tested her strength, forcing her to draw further on her reserves until the voice retreated into its laughter and then was gone.

Megan stood alone then, cloaked in her flames. Her anger swelled; her attacker had toyed with her with weak magics, and she had almost faltered. She took part of her fire within herself, soothing her pain, bracing herself for the next assault, but none came. For a moment she stood, eyeing the black gates solemnly. She took one step forward, then raised her magic high over her head and smashed it against the gates. Again, the effort sapped her strength; she could feel the straining tendons in her neck and hear the blood pounding in her temples. She sensed dark clouds lurking beyond the edge of her mind, swirling, prowling, seeking a weakness, a way in. The laughter lurked there, among the clouds.

As her magic spread out over the gates, the sorceress screamed, focusing the negative energy of her rage. She stepped forward again, and a resounding crack split the air.

The gates flew open, and Megan's silver surged through. The laughter rushed at her now with the roar of an aural army; she quickly drew back her magic to shield herself from the overbearing sound, then, slowly, she walked between the opened gates. As she stepped through, the laughter faded and the voice returned. 'Welcome to my world, child,' the voice hissed.

Megan retained her shield and said nothing. She did not know her attacker's voice, and its mystery nagged at her. She would ask of the voice its name, but to do so would show her ignorance, her weakness. She had been named a child. Young she was, but no child. And a match for her opponent? Time would tell . . . She had not lost yet; she yet lived.

The hiss fluttered a moment into laughter. 'I am Arthur's bane,' the voice said as if it knew her thoughts. 'I am Morgana, child. And you have already lost. Death is not the only defeat.'

Megan heard the gates slam shut behind her. She whirled then to see them shimmer and dissipate into wispy nothingness.

The voice laughed again, then left her in silence.

At dawn, the storm fled as quickly as it had risen. Thyri was first to gain the deck, and first to gasp at the scene that greeted her eyes.

Straight ahead, a dark granite tower blocked out the rising sun as *Nightreaver* drifted slowly into a quiet harbor. The island out of which the tower grew was small, almost impossibly so, but it was the tower that claimed Thyri's unswerving attention. Anger burned inside of her; Megan's last words rang continuously through her mind: *This storm is not natural.* She thought of her friend, still prostrate in their cabin; she seethed. She had no doubt that the tower's resident had sent them that storm, no doubt that the storm had drawn them there. If Megan died, she would bring that tower crashing into the sea before she would leave.

Rollo was first to reach her side. 'Odin!' he exclaimed.

Thyri looked at him a moment before going to her cabin for her sword. As *Nightreaver* eased up to the sandy beach, she strapped her blade to her side.

'I will get the others,' Rollo said, starting to turn.

'No!' she commanded. 'I will go alone. Stay here with Megan. Guard her with your life.' She turned without another word. *Nightreaver* ground to a halt, and Thyri jumped down into the waist-deep water and started for shore.

Fire

Off the beach, a path to the tower's door invited Thyri as if it were carpet laid at her feet. She stepped upon it, her anger forcing each step without caution.

As she neared the tower, she thought briefly of Castle Kaerglen, the only other structure she'd seen of similar, forbidding construction. The tower looked hewn of solid rock. High above, a solitary window looked out to sea. At the end of the path, a massive wooden door broke the seamless expanse of stone. Her sense for sorcery went wild. While she looked at the door, it swung open as if her eyes had pushed it in.

She never reached it; near the tower's foot, a mist rose up and enshrouded her, and her next step was upon stone.

As each moment transformed achingly into the next, a deafening roar filled the silence. It built slowly, heralded by the deep, persistent thumping of her own heart: the drumbeat orchestrating the flow of blood through her body, the wellspring of the roar.

Never had she felt so alone. Blackness had cloaked her since Morgana's departure, and she'd nothing but her own churning thoughts for company, thoughts that came and went, flitting through her mind like cautious butterflies pursued by the dragons of nightmare. At times, when she peered out, evasive white lights would dot the void, temporary pinpricks in the black fabric; nothing stayed. She could move – swim through the darkness – but reach nowhere, each place attained was ever like the last.

Then – after eternity – another sound; just a faint, distant whiff of a voice, but in the silence, it boomed like thunder, drowning out the sounds of her heartbeat and the blood rushing through her veins. She felt the pain in her head again, and she focused on it, gathering her other thoughts around it, fighting desperately to regain her will. As she fought, silver sparks began to stream forth from her ring. In the darkness, the silver shined like life itself. The sight heartened her, and she coaxed the magic forth consciously now until she stood in the void, bathed in the light of her magic.

She had not lost. Morgana could not hold her.

In a burst of brilliance, she filled the void with silver. The magic showered, exploding in the darkness. She poured it forth until she felt cold stone beneath her feet.

She looked down at the stones. Her feet were like mist, insubstantial, without flesh.

Her body was elsewhere . . . Still back at the ship? Never mind, she thought. For this battle, flesh would be useless . . .

A round chamber – how far up the tower, Thyri didn't know. On one side, a spiral staircase wound both up and down. In the center of the chamber was a large table, laden with a feast enough to feed twenty men. On the far side of the table was a woman. When Thyri's eyes fixed on her, the woman rose.

She was tall and slender, perhaps twenty years old, if that. Her gown was dark violet, and her dark hair spilled down well past her waist. She possessed great beauty, but her eyes were cold, impersonal. Thyri looked into them and drew her sword.

'Won't you dine with me?' the woman asked. Her voice was sweet – like honey. With the sound, Thyri felt a hunger consume her; her mouth filled with saliva, and the aromas of the feast on the table assailed her nose. The woman's eyes grew warm, and Thyri began to lose her sense of time.

She forced herself forward, trying to throw off the bewitchment.

'At least speak with me,' the woman said. 'You cannot kill me. If you do, you can never leave.'

Thyri stopped, she felt the tower's walls pressing in on her, crushing her, strangling her, suffocating her. She forced another step.

'I invited your entrance, and only I can invite your exit.' The voice was like nectar, intoxicating. *'Don't you see? Look at me. Look at my body. Is it not beautiful?'*

The woman filled Thyri's eyes. Thyri could almost touch her. Scents of honeysuckle and sweat danced in the air. Supple flesh moved sensually under velvet; breasts pushed themselves enticingly toward Thyri's mouth, then drew away, but the woman's soft eyes drew her in. *'I am in heaven, and heaven is yours. I will trade, my body for yours.'*

Thyri concentrated hard and forced another step.

Rollo turned on Ottar. 'If you suggest again that we follow her, I will kill you!'

'But, Rollo,' Sokki invervened, 'we must do something!'

'Guard Megan! Those were her orders! We do not know what we face here. You saw Thyri disappear as did I! How do you propose we follow?'

Sokki glared at Rollo, put one hand on the ship's gunwale, and jumped over the side into the water.

Rollo lurched forward and looked down as Sokki splashed toward the beach. He started forward, then felt a hand on his shoulder. He turned to see the face of the archer.

'No, Rollo,' the strange man said. 'The folly of one man should not tempt that of another.'

'Sokki!' Ottar shouted, rushing for the gunwale.

Gerald pushed his way to Rollo's side. 'Whatever happens now, Rollo, he shouldn't go alone.'

Rollo turned his eyes to shore; Sokki had gained the beach and headed inland without looking back.

'We can't all go,' Rui said to Gerald. 'This is a witch place. We may see no enemy now, but that is perhaps the greatest danger. Magic and danger fill this air, can't you feel it?'

Rollo looked desperately from Gerald's eyes to Rui's, then to the shore and Sokki. 'He can't go alone,' he said. 'I will follow.' He lifted his leg to the gunwale.

'No,' Ottar shouted, vaulting overboard. He landed in the water and struggled to keep his feet. When he finally stood, he drew his sword and held it over his head, then turned briefly, squinting up at the faces who stared at him from above. 'I will go,' he declared to Rollo. 'He is my brother.'

With that said, Ottar started for the beach.

'My body for yours . . . My body for yours . . .'

Thyri screamed as her bones wrenched. Her vision blacked out, then, suddenly, the river of her nightmare – the river of blood – stretched out from her feet toward the horizon . . .

'My body for yours! I will take your curse! I will take your curse and your nightmares . . .'

Megan stood before Thyri in the river. She held out her arms, but Thyri leapt, her fangs digging into Megan's smooth flesh, ripping into her throat.

'Yes!' she screamed. 'Take it!'

'My body for yours . . . My body for yours?'

'Yes!'

The river of blood disappeared, and the woman danced before her, drawing closer, into her. A cold darkness began to wrap itself around her heart.

Then a brightness flared up through the darkness, and the woman screamed. Thyri felt the clouds around her mind tear away. She felt her blade in her hand again. She opened her eyes, and the room, this time, appeared nearly bare. On the table, where once she'd seen a feast, she now saw only dust – the deposits of years of neglect. The enchantment had broken. Of all the room's ornaments, only the woman looked the same; her transcendent beauty alone had been authentic.

As for sorcery, traces lingered in the air. Streams of light, like errant moonbeams: Megan's ring magic.

Behind the woman, Megan stood, ethereal, silver. Thyri's attacker turned to face the threat of the sorceress.

She watched Megan and saw again the vision Morgana had shown her, the warping of her old nightmares. *I will take your curse! My body for yours!* She tried to press forward, but still couldn't move.

One moment before, they had come within ten paces of the tower's foot. Sokki could see the grain of the granite and its dull polish, the smooth sheen hewn by centuries of pelting, unrelenting sea winds.

Now, he could see only white. Fog cloaked them – they were under attack. He rushed forward for the tower's gate – or where he thought the doors had been. He met only the tower's ungiving walls. And Thyri remained inside . . . He had to help her. Keeping his hands on the tower, he began to move along its face, frantically seeking the feel of wood.

'Sokki!' Ottar called to him.

He pressed against the stone. The door had disappeared! Everything around him was white unless he pressed against the granite. An inch away from the gray stone, the walls were invisible.

'Sokki!'

He couldn't answer. Tearfully, he slumped against the stone. He had failed Thyri. She was lost inside.

'Hello, Morgana,' Megan said. 'You should not have told me your name!' She stared into the eyes of the ancient demoness, unleashing the remaining potential of her ring toward them.

Her attack was met by a sheet of fine red fire that sprang up inches from Morgana's face. The silver met the fire and, for a moment, seemed to penetrate the shield. Then, to Megan's horror, her magic began to spread out over Morgana's shield and dissipate harmlessly around its edges.

She dove to the side, using the fury of the conflict between them for cover. In that last blast, she had expended the last of her ring's power, and several hours would be required before the talisman could support even the simplest of castings. Frantically, she searched her memory for some knowledge that might aid her. During all the years she'd spent in study, she'd given precious little time to the contemplation of battle magics. She'd never considered the possibility that the ring's attack could be turned back! She cursed herself – her vanity – for giving the witch the chance to face her, the chance to turn. The first blast of her ring had been meant solely to command Morgana's attention; the attack had been weak, but it had surprised Morgana and bypassed her defenses. Her second, more powerful attack had not, and now she would pay.

Gaining her feet, she whispered a short charm of defense, then another of luck. As the last word of the spell passed her lips, Morgana's fire-shield fell away, and its mistress emerged from the flames. She smiled at Megan, laughing hysterically.

Megan kept her gaze steady on Morgana, though she strained to gain some view of Thyri. On the far side of the room, Thyri appeared now to be moving. She refused to avert her eyes; such an act would alert Morgana to the new threat.

'She knows my name!' Morgana declared, a huge mass of fire gathering around her raised hands. 'You know *nothing*, fool!'

The last thing Megan saw was red. It surged through her, consuming her. She had never felt such pain.

'Loki's tits!' Rollo cursed as a hellish shriek behind him tore his eyes away from the pillar of fog.

'Megan,' Gerald said softly, the blood draining from his cheeks as the shriek reached its piercing crescendo. He stared at Rollo, his gaze fixed, his legs unable to move until the big man grabbed his arm and pulled him toward the captain's cabin.

Inside, Gerald saw the sorceress, and again he froze with fear. Megan lay on her back, her hands awkwardly tangled on her chest. The blankets that had covered her lay half off the bed, half on the cabin's floor. Her body quivered spasmodically; her face was white, like ivory. As Gerald watched Rollo move toward her, she moaned painfully, and one arm flailed out to the side, bouncing twice on the bed before going still.

Rollo grasped her hand, then dropped it suddenly. 'Like ice,' he said to Gerald.

Gerald looked away, and the painting over the bed caught

his gaze and stole away his breath. Such was the artist's illusion that the full moon over the haunting landscape seemed to possess a light of its own. Gerald shivered and moved forward to help Rollo, who struggled now to get blankets back over Megan's body.

Anger and despair sent power surging through Thyri as Megan's wail filled the chamber. A scream came to Thyri's own throat, but she denied it a voice. She directed the new strength to her legs.

The woman's back faced her as she covered the distance between them with blinding speed. Only as Thyri began to bring her sword down on her target did Morgana turn, grinning wildly.

In an instant, Thyri watched the ecstatic smile melt into fear. Morgana tried to raise an arm in defense; fire flickered briefly in her eyes, and Thyri felt unseen fingers begin to wrap tightly around her sword arm.

But the rune-blade would not be stopped. It bit into Morgana's shoulder and angled it, snapping bones until it ground to a halt in the center of her chest. Black liquid spurted out, and Thyri jumped back, withdrawing her blade. As the shower of black blood struck the floor, fires sprang up on the stones, spewing out small clouds of acrid, choking smoke.

For a moment, Morgana's eyes seemed yet to possess life. Thyri turned from them; she had never seen eyes exude such hate. When she looked back, the woman had transformed into a black, oozing mass no longer resembling anything human. The black liquid poured ever more freely onto the stones, and the smoke that issued from this contact began to fill the chamber.

Thyri breathed a small amount and nearly gagged. She fought to quell the spasms of her lungs, closed her eyes, and pinched her nose shut as she raced for the side of the chamber, feeling along for the opening where she hoped she would still find stairs.

When the wall turned out, she paused. Megan had fallen in

this room. When Thyri had seen her, however, she had only *seen*. Her keener sense, her smell, had registered nothing but the tang of magic. She'd assumed that meant Megan had confronted Morgana unencumbered by her body. But if this were not true? If some sorcery in the place had confused her nose . . .

She remembered the assault Morgana had first waged on her, the scents that had filled her like nothing she'd experienced before. One with such power could easily have concealed Megan's scent. But would she have done so? In attacking Megan, Morgana had dropped her guard against Thyri.

Thyri could have answered the question surely but for the smoke. She dared not open her eyes now. She could *feel* the smoke against the skin of her face and hands, burning her like weak fire.

But if Megan remained there?

Then she was already dead.

But what if she wasn't?

As she stood there, the pain caused by the smoke grew until she felt as if her skin was aflame. Still torn by the question of Megan's fate, she turned into the spiral staircase and started down.

Halfway down, she was challenged. A growling – some beast – barred her exit. She pinpointed the growl and lashed out with her sword, feeling a dark satisfaction as her blade bit into flesh. The beast howled, and she attacked again. This time she heard a dull thud as the animal – whatever it was – collapsed on the stairs. She stepped over it, and quickly moved on.

Outside, in the fog, Sokki felt something that he imagined as the fiery breath of a fire giant blow through him before the fog suddenly disappeared as quickly as it had come. The sun above dug into his eyes, and he fell to his knees, feeling as if he'd wakened abruptly from a terrible dream.

Ahead, along the tower's wall, he saw the wooden doors that he'd failed to reach in the fog. A moment later, he heard a crash against those doors; as he rose to his feet, they burst open, and Thyri emerged, dashing out into the daylight.

Puffs of dark smoke followed her, then she slammed the doors shut.

'Thyri!'

She turned on him; by the look in her eyes, he felt as if she were about to attack. Her face was red like the skin of one scorched by the hottest summer sun. Blood, and some darker, fouler liquid, stained the edge of her blade. He stared at her, readying himself for death. The moments seemed to slow, then recognition flashed in Thyri's eyes, and her expression hardened into one of simple anger. She exhaled, then breathed in deeply.

'I told you to stay with the ship!'

He stared at her, unable to speak.

'Who else came with you?'

Slowly, he rose to his feet. 'Ottar,' he stammered.

She looked around. 'Where is he?'

His eyes followed hers. His brother was nowhere in sight. He looked back at Thyri. She stood oddly, sniffing the air. 'Never mind,' she said. 'I know. Follow.'

Without looking back at the tower, Thyri turned. She led him fifty paces from the tower's base where they found Ottar in a gully. Thyri ordered Sokki to carry his brother, then she raced ahead of him, back for the ship.

Thyri gained the deck, glanced only briefly at Rollo, who helped her aboard, then rushed to her cabin. Inside the door, she stopped, dropping her sword, staring at Megan on the bed, relieved that her friend hadn't perished in flames, but already aware of the chill in the air and the pale, deathlike mask over Megan's features. Hesitantly, she moved forward and pulled back the blankets covering her lover.

Megan's beauty brought tears to her eyes. Thyri bent and rested her head against her lover's breast. The heartbeat within was so faint . . .

'Odin,' Thyri wailed. 'Not again!' Sobs wracked her body.

She clenched her eyes shut and saw Megan, laughing that day Thyri had returned from Castle Kaerglen to winter with the sorceress. *I have something you desire,* Thyri said then. *Several things,* replied the sorceress.

Not death!

Oh, Odin! Not again!

Wordlessly, Gerald, Rui, and Horik gathered around Rollo as all tried to ignore the weeping Thyri did not bother to conceal. Rollo looked at them and frowned. For the time, there was nothing any of them could do. Nevertheless, the tension – the feeling that something *had* to be done – began to grow unbearable. Rollo himself had almost turned for Thyri's cabin when movement on the beach caught his eye and he looked to see Sokki struggling with the limp form of his brother.

Horik's eyes followed Rollo's and he gasped. He looked to Rollo, who nodded, then he jumped into the water to help the pair reach the ship.

Gerald and Rui, likewise, were thankful for the distraction. Together, they went to the hold for rope, fashioning a loose noose that could be used to hoist Ottar aboard. When they returned to the gunwale, the sons of Gunnar were waiting below.

A few moments later, they lay Ottar on the deck and knelt down around him. He yet lived, but showed no signs of reviving. Rollo felt around his scalp for wounds but found none. He looked at Sokki. 'What happened?' he asked softly.

Sokki shook his head. He didn't know.

Rollo stood and looked up at the sail, testing the wind. The air was all but still. He glanced briefly at the tower, cursing softly, then ordered the others to the oars.

As they exited the bay, the sky suddenly darkened anew and lightning flared.

'Ship the oars!' Rui shouted as a terrific wind smashed into the ship, filling the sail. The mast creaked and strained. Fighting sudden swells, they got the oars aboard and headed for the cover of the cabins. Rui alone made it; he tried to grab

Gerald on the way, but the ship lurched, throwing Gerald to the deck. Horik and Sokki had already fallen.

Rollo barely kept his feet, dove at the boom, gave slack to the sail, and *Nightreaver* shot out of the harbor into the sea. The rains came again, and lightning stuck dangerously near the ship; Rollo hung on desperately, praying that the spears of crackling energy would strike clear of the mast. His muscles screaming, he rode out the wind until the island and its tower became lost in the storm's fury.

And then, as before, the storm subsided as unexpectedly as it had risen.

Rollo unclamped his hands from the boom and fell to the deck. His head ached and his muscles throbbed; pain and exhaustion made every movement an effort. Groaning, he rose and looked around. Gerald, Sokki, and Horik lay flattened against the deck. Rui emerged from his cabin and limped out to the gunwale. Sokki got up and crawled toward his brother. Gerald groaned.

'How's Horik?' Rollo asked, looking up wearily at Sokki.

'He's alive,' Sokki said after a moment.

'Where's Ottar?'

Nobody knew. They searched the ship, but Ottar was nowhere to be found.

Avalon

She pulled herself from the water and looked down at her body, running her hands slowly over her chest and her hard, flat stomach. The muscles in her arms responded effortlessly, even after the swim. She felt as if she could rip a tree, roots and all, from the earth.

Already, she felt all her strengths returning . . .

Standing naked on the beach, she gazed musingly at the stark, inland tower where she'd been trapped for so long. Throwing her head back, she laughed. The deep, resonant boom that issued from her throat startled her. She paused, then tested the voice, singing a song she'd once heard voiced by Lancelot.

The poor, ignorant swineherd!

When she finished the song, she chuckled, gazing at the tower. She felt her loins stir; she looked down and smiled, hesitantly touching her rising pillar of manhood. The rippling sensation that flowed from the contact shocked her, and she moved her hand away.

She would have plenty of time to explore this new possibility later. She thought of Eiriksdattir, and her humor grew dark. She had come so close. The power of this male flesh was nothing compared to the prize she could have won.

She wondered if Thyri could have known whose soul had perished there, inside the tower. No, she decided, the wolf's friend might have understood, but she fought now a darker foe even than Morgana. The sorceress battled death, and had not the leisure to think of anything else.

Morgana suddenly gripped the twitching thing between her legs and hoped Megan would win. Even though this wasn't the body she'd wanted, it was quite strong enough for now. And Thyri's body could still be hers, in ways more varied than she'd previously contemplated. Revenge would be sweet.

Smiling again, she strode for her tower. When she opened the door, the black smoke of her near-death buffeted her. She coughed, then waved her hand to dispel the sorcery.

On the stairs, she found Ra licking the blood from Vishnu's seeping wounds. She looked at the beast and smiled; he looked up and growled at her, then began to whine painfully.

After a moment, the hound burst into flame. She watched her fire consume him and the body of his brother. When the flames died, she stepped over the carnage.

'You are no longer necessary.' *She chuckled absently, continuing up the stairs to the chamber where she'd slept for all those years. There, she went to the window that looked out over the sea.*

A gentle breeze blew in, caressing her cheeks. Merlin's spell was broken, and she was free.

BOOK VI

THE GODDESS

It's spring, and the warmth and sunshine taunt me with their gentle omnipresence. Looking up into the blue sky, I have asked myself why I do not set down this pen, why I do not lose myself in idle leisure. But I cannot; this task of mine may not be abandoned. But I have made it more easy, at least for a time. No longer do I work in the tower room next to Satan's Chalice . . . The atmosphere there is dark, unbearable at times. And there is a smell – of rot and decay – that will not let me write.

I have moved my desk and my notes to a room off the old library, a room that looks out into the garden with its sparkling fountain. The spring growth there is fantastic: brilliant blossoms dot the branches of every tree and bush; flowers of every color imaginable lie strewn over the yard like gemstones in the treasure trove of some ancient king. So I have great beauty before me when the words refuse to flow. Better than a circle of leering, mocking red. At times in the past, I have stared idly for so long at the surface of that pool that, when I lie down to retire, the red circle remains, hovering before my closed eyes, inviting me into haunted, disturbing dreams.

I no longer need that pool at my side, day in and day out. I write now, finally, of experiences I have lived through, and much of my research now involves recollection rather than sorcery. What questions I have for the sorcery to answer I now may assemble for brief excursions to the tower when they become absolutely necessary. Even then, I have come to question this necessity at times, for have I not reached that point in Thyri's life that captured my imagination completely when I could but see from the outside? Is there not sufficient wonder in that alone? And, in so many cases, such as the sequence of events that led to Rollo's inclusion in our adventures, do I not know enough from the tales of others to avoid sorcerous intrusions into their pasts?

Such are my thoughts now. In ways, what I write now is far less demanding of my spirit than what I have written in the past, for the characters I know, and the places I have seen with my own eyes. And yet I have encountered new difficulties for there seem to me so many ways to present this tale, so many interesting perspectives that conflict, yet complement one another. And I have such a wealth of detail at my command that the formation of *Nightreaver*'s crew might occupy this entire volume if such were my desire. But I cannot desire this, for my story, in fact, is still merely beginning.

I have written before of difficulties I have experienced in attempting my sorcery on those of great power, and within this context, I must admit that Morgana proved no exception to this rule. I desire foremost to achieve accuracy in my telling, but Morgana's entrance into the stream of events has always puzzled me, and it seems now that I may never learn with certainty the real reasons for her involvement. That she drew *Nightreaver* to her lair is fact; that she battled Thyri and Megan as she did is also fact, and that she was awakened or persuaded to these actions must necessarily be fact as well. She surely possessed the ability, at the time of the battle, to escape from Merlin's exile by taking the place of another, and I find it incredible to think that she might have endured four centuries of imprisonment in anticipation of this possibility. For could she not have drawn to her any vessel from the seas of Midgard, freeing herself at the earliest opportunity?

No, Morgana slept. Nothing else fits, and my instincts guided my pen as I wrote of her awakening. It is fantasy, surely, but if another scenario possesses a greater claim to accuracy, let it reveal itself to me. Where I cannot write what I know, I must write what I believe to be likely.

For purposes of clarity, I reiterate here that Megan Kaerglen remains closed to my sorcery. In relating the details of *her* conflict with Morgana, I needed only to draw on Thyri's memory for, in time, Thyri learned these details herself.

On the evening after the battle with Morgana, *Nightreaver*'s crew ate in silence. Thyri, in the cabin, had grown quiet. Rollo tried to take her food, but she ordered him out, telling him to do what he wished.

He emerged with her orders and looked out over the sea. He could think of nothing to do but wait until Thyri could contain her grief and give them direction. Grimly, he joined the others, resolved, simply, to get through the night.

Before I forge ahead, a brief word needs be given the old couple who ran the country tavern that Guthrom's guard burned the day they rode in search of Rollo and Thyri. This word is that they did not perish, but fled to the farm of the old man's sister's son shortly after Thyri, Megan, and I departed. They fled with curses on their lips for the Norse, and some slight fear of the *were*-beasts rumored to roam the vicinity. Passing under the tavern's threshold, the old woman snatched the talisman of protection and carried it with her. Later, she hung it over the portal of the farmhouse where she lived out her days, thankful, at least, that she had some protection from the dangers of the moors.

Ghosts

The morning after the battle fared no better than the night, worse perhaps, because Thyri's sobbing had again grown audible. While the others broke fast, Thyri emerged, red-faced, to fill a flagon with fresh water. As she stood at the barrel, bent to this task, Rollo hesitantly approached, laying a hand on her shoulder, half expecting her to flinch away. To his relief, she did not, but neither did she acknowledge his presence.

'She yet lives, does she not?' he asked her softly.

For a long moment, she did nothing, but in the end, she nodded. 'Barely,' came her coarse whisper.

After that, she returned wordlessly to her cabin.

Near noon, the inactivity grew unbearable. No wind had risen, so Rollo ordered all to the oars, and, for lack of a better direction, they began to propel the vessel eastward, where Rollo hoped they might reach Frankish shores. He didn't necessarily intend to dock, but sighting land might, in some way, break the monotony of endless seas that did nothing, at present, to boost morale.

At the oars, the amazing effectiveness of each stroke reminded all of the power of the sorceress, and the loss they now faced. And it caused them, also, to think of darker things. Each of them could not but help envision Megan as a goddess, immortal after the fashion of such beings. Yet now she lay near death, making the consolation of faith treacherous, insubstantial and fleeting. Even for the Norse, whose theology necessitated the deaths of immortals, direct confrontation with such an idea was unsettling.

Gerald found himself working an oar next to Sokki. Next to Thyri, the young Norseman appeared most affected by the battle. Gerald studied the man; it was almost painful to watch Sokki's eyes gazing ahead with resigned listlessness. He'd known the Viking for less than two days, but his first impression had been one of implacable vitality and optimism. It had been Sokki's optimism, even tainted by despair, that had propelled him ashore to help Thyri – his optimism that any dangers ahead were surmountable and, thus, not to be taken seriously.

From the sidelines, two nights before, Gerald had understood that Sokki knew Thyri, that Sokki, in fact, worshipped the swords-mistress with a fervor akin to that which Gerald felt within himself, perhaps even a greater fervor, for it had been Sokki who had, upon watching Thyri's disappearance at the base of Morgana's tower, felt compelled to rush to her aid. Such a reaction hinted at a greater feeling of loss, a more deeply seated fear of losing a companionship so recently regained.

And so he had defied Rollo and rushed to Thyri's aid. His brother, who had followed, had fallen, then had gone overboard, unconscious, and had undoubtedly drowned. Gerald suspected that Sokki blamed himself. In Sokki's eyes, Gerald saw something of the same things visible in Thyri's despair, sorrow, and anger without an object.

Watching Sokki, Gerald found himself fishing for words of consolation. He remembered the death of his mother. He'd been a boy then – eleven in years, scant months away from his uncle's death and his trip southward to join Alfred's scribes. At the time, no one's mere words had been able to ease the pain. He'd long thought that the experience had ushered him into manhood. If he'd remained a boy, he'd simply have perished with her. Only as a man could he accept the fact that life had to continue.

But how did one handle the death of a brother? He didn't know, he'd never had one. Drawing on his sketchy knowledge of Danish customs, he tried desperately to find something to say; the words that came out were stilted, peppered with uncertainty: 'He is happy now, Sokki,' he said, gripping the Viking's wrist. 'He is with Odin in Valhalla.'

Sokki didn't look at him. 'Perhaps,' he said after a time. 'But we do not know how he fell, even the nature of his enemy. We do not know that he fought bravely.'

'He was your brother,' Gerald said. 'He could have fallen no other way.'

Sokki grunted, but kept his eyes fixed ahead.

In actual fact, Ottar had not fought at all. Morgana had not given him the chance; in the space of an instant, she'd drawn him into her tower as she'd drawn Thyri, then she'd simply plucked his soul from his body as if it had been a grape on a vine. Her exit, after that, had been no problem at all.

Rui rowed with Horik, whose mood, in many ways, mirrored Sokki's. The archer, however, did not try to speak. Instead, he paid particular attention to keeping the rhythm of their oar constant, hoping, in this, to ease the Viking's heart with the consistent, meditative quality of their work.

Rollo, meanwhile, climbed to the foredeck and gazed out to sea. Resting his hand on the haunch of the wooden wolf Megan had carved there, his eyes scanned the horizon, searching for the slightest hint of land.

Near dusk, Rollo began to suspect that something was amiss. Solid ground remained as elusive as the heartbeat of a fly. He had not seen even a gull, something that struck him as strange the longer he reflected upon it. The birds were always a constant fixture of life at sea; now, he could not recall hearing their chatter since before the storm that had deposited them in the harbor of the dark tower. Once that afternoon, he'd thought he'd seen something in the sky in the distance. Yet, even then, it had seemed impossibly huge – far too distant to be a gull or any other bird he'd ever encountered. After rubbing his eyes, the thing in the sky had disappeared.

And the events of the day before, the battle that Thyri had obviously underaken in the tower, began to nag at him. For all that he'd assumed command of the crew, he still didn't understand why. Thyri had said nothing of her experiences. Nor had Sokki, for that matter.

With the sun setting on one side of the horizon and the waxing moon rising on the other, Rollo called the others to dinner. Over the meal, he watched Sokki and Horik. He needed to speak with Sokki, but he couldn't find words to broach the subject. The entire meal, again, was silent.

After eating, Rollo filled a large plate with dried pork, added an apple in the center, poured two large flagons of mead, and knocked on the door of the captain's cabin. After a minute passed with no reply, he cautiously pushed the door open and entered.

He shivered involuntarily; the inside of the cabin had grown unnaturally cold. He pushed the door fully opened and stoppered it, then stood there, looking at Thyri. She sat on the edge of Megan's bed, the sorceress's right hand sandwiched between hers.

After a moment, she spoke: 'Close it,' she said without turning.

He paused before answering. 'No, Thyri,' he said softly. 'It is like winter in here, and she needs warmth. The others will not intrude, they have sorrows of their own. Sokki and Horik have lost a brother.' He walked to her table and set down the plate and the flagons; then he sat so that he could face her.

Slowly, she turned to him. 'Ottar is dead?'

'We laid him on the deck when he was unconscious. After the storm, we could find him nowhere.'

She stared at him, her eyes distant, as if they looked through him. 'It has begun again,' she said sadly.

'You must eat, Thyri,' he said.

She focused on him slowly. 'How long? How long have I been here?'

'Only a day.'

'That's all?' She smiled weakly and rose, squinting as she looked out the open door.

He watched her, noting that, even burdened with sorrow

and despair, her every move embodied subtle grace. She tried to smile again when she sat across from him.

'She yet lives?' he asked, glancing at Megan.

Thyri nodded, tears welling anew in her swollen eyes. 'I do not know how to care for her, Rollo. I give her water, but her mouth never seems parched. I do not think she hungers. It's as if she is frozen, neither alive nor dead. Outside of time.'

'Perhaps she struggles within herself.' He reached out for Thyri's hand, turned it so that her palm faced up, and placed a chunk of pork in her fingers.

Thyri absently carried the morsel to her lips, chewed it slowly, and washed it down. 'Now and then,' she said, 'her ring flickers. I do not know whether she causes this, or whether some sorcery within the ring acts on its own to keep her alive.'

Rollo watched her, feeling relieved as her hand went on its own to the plate of pork. After eating another chunk, she looked into his eyes. 'You and the others should leave us,' she said. 'Abandon this ship. You are not safe with me. With Ottar's death, it has all begun again.'

He looked into her eyes, detecting, in their depths, a restrained, almost childlike pleading. He smiled at her. 'Not possible,' he said. 'I have sworn to myself to serve you, to follow you wherever that may lead me. I cannot speak for the others, but I'm sure they feel the same. And aside from that, we have found no land upon which to disembark. This vessel is more swift than any I have known, and we've propelled it ever eastward since the morning. No land in sight, and I can't explain it. We should have been scant hours from either Frankish or Frisian shores.'

She looked down at her hands. 'I feared as much,' she whispered. 'I have some sense for magic, Rollo, and things have felt slightly wrong since the onset of the storm that drew us to Morgana's island. We are not where we should be. It is possible that we are no longer on the seas of Midgard.'

Rollo lifted his flagon and took a long draught. Her words didn't really surprise him much; during the course of the afernoon, he'd begun to fear something akin to what she'd just expressed. On the other hand, he remembered the thing he'd seen briefly in the distant sky. If they *weren't* in Midgard, then he wasn't sure he wanted to speculate on the nature of that which he'd seen. If it *was* some sort of bird, he was glad it had flown no closer.

He voiced none of this aloud. Instead, he tried to turn the conversation to what he did need to know. 'Morgana?' he asked carefully.

Yes, Thyri thought. That was what Megan had named the woman when she'd entered the battle. 'Some ancient demon, I think. Powerful, I know. Perhaps Gerald can tell you more; I believe the Saxons know of her.'

Calmly, Rollo reached out again and squeezed Thyri's hand. 'What happened, swords-mistress?'

Thyri looked at him and brushed back a tear. She pushed another chunk into her mouth, drank deep of the mead, and related to Rollo what she'd experienced on Morgana's island. In speaking, some small part of her pain began to melt away, and something in Rollo's eyes almost made her tell him of her curse and how Morgana had tried to use it against her, how Morgana had almost won. But this she did not tell.

All of the rest, however, she poured out to him, hoping vainly that she would see some way that it had all been a dream, that she could blink her eyes, turn for the bed, and see Megan rise, smiling her old smile.

Later, after Rollo had calmed Thyri and left her alone with Megan, he went to Gerald and asked the Saxon about Morgana. He did not like what he learned. Gerald said that Morgana had an older name: the Morrigan, he called her. The bringer of death. Morgana was a name she'd earned only centuries before – the name she'd assumed when she'd single-handedly destroyed the golden empire of Arthur, whom Gerald called the greatest and most noble king ever to rule over a nation of men.

In the end, the bringer of death had learned defeat at the hand of the great sorcerer, Merlin of the Seven Groves, but even Merlin had been unable to kill her. He had, however, imprisoned her in a dark tower he erected on a small island, in a sea where normal men, by accident, could not fare . . .

After learning this from Gerald, Rollo sat alone for several hours, staring into the night sky, trying to prepare himself for what might lie ahead. Thyri claimed that she'd killed the demoness in her tower. But if Merlin could not kill her . . . Merlin was a legend among Saxons, but tales of his great power and deeds were such that they traveled far from Saxon shores. Rollo had first heard of the wizard when he was but a boy in Denmark.

His thoughts turned back disturbingly to the strange storm during which they'd lost Ottar, the storm that had raged *after* Thyri's battle. It had felt as unnatural as the storm that had drawn them to Morgana. His most optimistic explanation had Megan somehow, in her battle with death, creating the maelstrom.

This, he hoped, was the truth. If it wasn't . . . What meant a physical body to one who lived for centuries?

In the night sky, he vainly sought answers. Even after retiring to his cabin, sleep eluded him for most of the night.

In the morning, Rollo emerged early, hoping the sunlight would make his fears of the night before less real, less substantial. The sun on his face felt good, but the pleasant warmth seemed false, illusory. He found himself wondering about what sorts of monstrosities might lie below the surface of the sea, and what they might find on land, if and when they ran across it.

As he stood on the deck, he noticed that an easterly wind had arisen. With this discovery, he set to raising the mainsail, grateful for the opportunity to exercise his muscles rather than his mind.

Once the sail was up, he worked the rigging, fighting to keep *Nightreaver*'s course as straight as possible as the others began to emerge from their cabins. One by one, they joined Rollo at the ropes. So passed the morning.

With the sun high overhead, they had their first glimpse of land: another island. As they drew near it, Rollo left the sail to the others and went to Thyri, informing her that they'd sighted land and that he would take two of the others ashore in hopes of learning something of the nature of their situation.

Thyri agreed to his plan but expressed no desire to leave her cabin.

Megan's condition had not changed.

Warriors

Gerald stooped and examined the trail. It was well worn, but bore no signs of human feet or horses. In places, however, the earth was split by long gashes, two or three feet in length. He shook his head as Rui drew next to him.

'Claw marks?' the archer asked, looking down.

Gerald stood. 'I hope not.' He looked down the slope. Rollo had scouted to the north; he was still halfway down the hill and closer to the beach. Far below, *Nightreaver* rested an anchor in a shallow bay. Gerald caught Rollo's eye and waved to him; the Viking nodded and trotted toward them.

Gerald stooped again to examine the markings while Rollo covered the distance up the slope. He was shaking his head again when Rollo reached his side and bent next to him. The Viking ran a hand along one of the gashes. 'Perhaps the earth is weak here,' he said. 'Perhaps rains caused this.'

'They're not all downhill,' Gerald countered.

Rui had wandered to the nearby trees. After a moment, he called the others to him, and pointed out the condition of the lower branches. 'This can't be a wolf run,' he said. 'If it was, some of these would be broken. You'd find bits of fur.'

Rollo nodded. He stood up straight and rubbed the back of his neck. In doing so, his eyes traveled upward. 'Odin!' he gasped involuntarily.

Gerald's eyes followed his. High in the tree, several branches looked as if they'd been pulverized. It hadn't been lightning's work; there were no scorch marks, and the damage was nearly uniform from tip of branch to trunk.

It looked, rather, as if some great hammer had smashed into the tree from the side.

Rui had, again, wandered farther away. Gerald could hear him foraging behind a nearby bush. He approached the sound and parted the foliage. Rui looked up at him and lifted what first appeared to Gerald to be a large stick. Then the archer rose, turned, and stepped forward, dragging something behind him. Gerald backed away and waited for the archer to reach the trail. As he emerged, Gerald and Rollo gaped wide-eyed at his burden.

Trailing behind the archer was a white feather the length of *Nightreaver*'s mast.

'Birds?' Gerald said incredulously, looking at Rollo.

Rollo swallowed hard. Carefully, he began to relate to the others what he feared he'd seen the day before. He related also some part of the conversation he'd had with Thyri – the suspicion that they journeyed now in a world far different from the one they knew.

When Rollo finished, Gerald pointed out that the feather was white. 'Maybe they're just chickens,' he said.

Rui chuckled. 'And what,' he asked, 'do you suppose chickens that size might like for dinner?' He paused, his expression growing serious. 'If we're to explore this place further, we should do so well away from the trail.'

Rollo nodded, and turned into the forest. A hundred paces in, he turned north, and the others followed.

As they picked their way through the underbrush, Gerald reflected on the conversation he'd had the evening before when Rollo had asked of the gods of his people. For some reason, his mind had refused then to connect the conversation with reality, but he suddenly realized how he'd been a fool not to understand Rollo's curiosity, to understand why the Viking had dwelt on the Morrigan.

Now, after seeing the feather and knowing that no such bird could be real in the world he knew, he began to grow afraid. The dark tower leapt back into his memory, becoming Morgana's prison. *Her prison on an island, in a sea where normal men could not fare.*

But they'd reached her, and Thyri Eiriksdattir had battled not a mere sorceress, not a witch, but a demoness as old as legend. What amazed him was that Thyri had survived. But had she been victorious? The land upon which they now trod belonged, undoubtedly, to that sea where Merlin had exiled Morgana. And the sorceress that Thyri called friend – she lay near death back on the ship.

These thoughts all confirmed the feeling that he'd had before, the night he'd taken Thyri to summon Megan, the feeling that he'd entered the affairs of the gods. If they *had* battled Morgana . . . He could not now envision the dweller of the dark tower to have been anyone other than Arthur's bane.

So – they meddled in the affairs of gods and walked upon an island of giant chickens. What troubled him was that he, Rui, and Rollo had forged ahead alone, without Thyri at their side.

After an hour of slow, cautious progress, the sound of waves crashing against cliffs began to grow louder with each step. Shortly, the forest gave way to a grassy strip, about fifty paces wide, that led up to the cliff's edge.

Among the last stand of trees, they hesitated, looking out to both sides in search of danger. Only after several minutes did they venture forth, Rollo in the lead.

Even before they reached their destination, Gerald sensed something was wrong. Amid the crashing waves, he heard a sound he thought was thunder; in looking up, however, he saw barely a hint of clouds, just thin, insubstantial streamers of cottony white. Then, near the cliff's edge, a huge, branchless tree trunk thrust slowly into view.

When they looked over and down, they saw a ship: not a normal vessel – its mast stretched up, high over the deck and level with their eyes. Within its hull, one could fit hundreds of *Nightreavers*.

And further north, off the bay that harbored the ship, a huge hall constructed of wood and mud rose up from the ground. By its size, it could have been a hall of gods. Its slovenly appearance, however, could mean but one thing: the chickens had keepers.

Before Gerald could get past his amazement to scrutinize in detail what his eyes told him he saw, Rollo grabbed his arm and yanked him away from the cliff's edge. Without speaking a word, the trio dashed for the relative safety of the wood, then continued on in stealth and silence, each struggling with his own fears, each unwilling to voice even a disbelief of what he had seen with his own eyes.

In the end, all their caution, all their stealth, went for naught. Halfway back to *Nightreaver*, a deep, silly giggling roared across the sky. A voice followed.

'I smell little goodies,' it said.

Nearby, several trees cracked, and the ground shook under the weight of a heavy foot. Looking up, Gerald caught a brief glimpse of a huge, cherubic face above the trees. His despair brought tears to his eyes. At the same time, he almost felt like laughing. They'd been discovered not by a warrior-giant, not by a master-tracker giant or even an oversized wizard, but by a child.

When the giggle had first rippled through the air, they had frozen in their tracks. When the voice had followed – the words were Norse and thus understandable by all – they had looked up frantically for its source. Now, with the grinning child's face visible, they drew swords and began to run. The heavy footfalls followed, and the chase was hectic, but brief. A massive, stubby-fingered hand appeared suddenly before Rollo. Its fingers wrapped around him before he could dodge out of the way.

As the giant lifted him off the ground, Rollo brought his sword down, slicing into the huge thumb. The blade stopped when it reached bone. The earth shook as the child fell to his knees. The violent motion threw Gerald and Rui to the forest floor.

'Goody stung me!' the giant squealed. 'Bad goody stung me!'

The sound was almost deafening. Gerald watched agony crease Rollo's face as the giant began to squeeze the Viking.

Leaping to his feet, Gerald dove at the giant's wrist; his sword point met flesh, drawing another horrible squeal from above.

Rui, meanwhile, notched an arrow and sent it whizzing up through the branches. Glancing up, Gerald saw the arrow dig into the giant's eye. As Rollo fell to the ground near him, Gerald dropped his sword and covered his ears. The child screamed and fell back, the impact creating another bruising earthquake.

When the worst of the tremors had passed, Gerald crawled over to Rollo. The Viking sat, shaking his head; when Gerald helped him to his feet, he winced and clutched his side.

'Can you run?' Gerald whispered desperately.

'I'll have to, won't I?' Rollo grimaced. 'Let's go,' he spat out, 'before Daddy arrives and really gives us problems.'

Trying to keep close together, they ran for the ship. The ground they had covered stealthily in a half hour, they covered now in five minutes, though these minutes were among the worst Gerald had ever endured. Pain wracked his lungs, and, occasionally, he and Rui had to force themselves to slow so that Rollo could catch up. The Viking, all the while, clutched his side. Gerald didn't even want to guess how many ribs the young giant had cracked. As they ran, tree trunks snapped and the ground shook behind them.

Cresting the hill that led to *Nightreaver*'s harbor, they heard Rollo's fear realized: a voice, far deeper than that of the giant they'd battled, growled distantly behind them. The child had been found by an elder; as they raced down the slope, the rapid approach of their new pursuer sent boulders tumbling down the slope with them, and they fought to keep control of their descent. Below them, Gerald saw Sokki and Horik raising the mainsail.

When they reached the water, Gerald and Rui spun the panting Rollo around and dragged him in backwards, holding him between them as they swam for the ship. A moment later, the sons of Gunnar pulled them quickly aboard and drew in the anchor.

Nightreaver, at first, lurched for shore and almost grounded itself. Rollo, still clutching his side, staggered to the boom and pushed it around until the sail sagged. 'Row!' he yelled.

As Gerald ran for the oars, he glanced back. Above the tree line, a huge head appeared. Its eyes were like fire, and Gerald's heart nearly burst when those eyes fell on the ship. He gained the oars with the others, and, somehow, they managed to time their first stroke. Such was their desperation that *Nightreaver*'s hull creaked as it sped out of the bay. The ship jerked then as Rollo let the sail fill, and the easterly wind grabbed them and set them skimming along the island's southern shore.

They dug the oars in until their speed threatened to crack the blades, then they looked back. The giant raced over the island's southern terrain, but he appeared to be falling behind. Gerald sighed in relief, then moaned as their pursuer shifted course, gained the beach, reached out over the water, and smashed his massive hand down into the waves.

A monstrous swell began to rise up behind them. In unison, they dove under the benches and clutched at the braces as the sea tipped them forward. Gerald felt a painful popping in his ears as the sea lifted them high into the air. He braced himself for a jarring descent, but it didn't come. After a minute, he crawled cautiously from his hiding place, fearing now that he might actually find the ship flying through the air with no water beneath it. Instead, he saw something he'd thought he might never see again:

Thyri, grinning with wild abandon, worked one end of the boom, helping Rollo to keep *Nightreaver* balanced and riding the crest of the swell. The weight of the moment had somehow drawn her from her dark humor.

One by one, the rest of the crew went to aid them. Behind them, the island of the giants receded rapidly into the distance.

As Thyri worked, her fears of the coming night, as well as her fears for Megan, came and went. Meanwhile, the giants' great vessel took to sea and headed after them. Thyri glanced back occasionally to check its progress; there were moments during which she hoped the ship would catch them. Battle would force her fully into the present and chase the clouds from her mind. The huge ship, however, was slow. It gradually disappeared below the horizon.

The swell did not level off until late afternoon.

When their battle with the sea had ended, *Nightreaver*'s crew ravenously pillaged the hold. Thyri, uneasily eyeing the descent of the sun, could not bring herself to join them. Instead, she went to the stern, ostensibly to watch for signs of the giant ship emerging under the coming sunset. Rollo followed her.

Thyri looked at Rollo then and realized, for the first time, the wound he had sustained. He had shut out his pain during their flight; now, with the danger passing, the pain returned. He winced as he returned Thyri's gaze, his hand again moving involuntarily to his side.

'You were right,' he said, forcing a smile. 'We are no longer in Midgard.' He stepped away from the gunwale.

She forced herself to smile back. 'I'm sorry, Rollo,' she said. Behind him, a full moon began to rise from the sea. She glanced west again; she had two hours of the sun left to protect her, then it would go dark and the wolf would take her.

Desperately, she searched his eyes for consolation, but she found only his pain. A pure pain – physical, unlike that which tormented her. But beneath the pain, Thyri found hope.

'Come,' she said to Rollo, taking his hand. 'Those ribs need tending.'

On the way to Rollo's cabin, she ordered the others to tack north for a while; assuming the angry giant would be slow but persistent, she didn't want to take any chances.

She stopped Rollo just inside the cabin's door, turned him, and took off his shirt. Carefully, she felt around his injured ribs. The Viking looked down at her, gritting his teeth, refusing to voice his pain. After a moment, she stepped back. 'If you do not make any sounds,' she asked, 'how am

I supposed to do this?' She moved closer again; this time, as she explored his side, he let her know where it hurt.

When she was satisfied that she'd determined the extent of the damage, she smiled up at him. 'You've been worse off,' she said. 'If we bind you right, you'll hardly feel it.' She left his cabin then, returning shortly with several long strips of fabric.

Slowly, she wrapped the cloth around him. He held his arms out, his eyes never leaving her. On each turn of the bandage, when she moved closer to him to reach around his back, he could feel her warm breath on his chest. The sensation excited him, and it scared him as well. He had never thought of her as a *woman.* He had never thought of her as he had of Fandis. She was more than a woman; she did not deserve such thoughts.

And her lover – she lay, near death, in the next cabin.

Yet now . . . Thyri's breasts brushed against him. The hairs on his chest stood out as a chill swept through his body. Underneath the thin cotton of Thyri's shift, her nipples hardened, then her breasts brushed against him again. The pain in his side grew distant.

As her closeness to Rollo filled her senses, Thyri thought of the moon.

That morning, fear of the coming night had overshadowed the pains she felt when she gazed at the pale figure on her bed. Megan grew neither worse, nor better, and Thyri had become accustomed to the melancholy monotony of her vigil.

But with the approach of the full moon . . . Her monthly terror had gripped her. That morning, her mind had replayed each moment of her second change on the *Black Rabbit;* she had relived the death of each crewman, seen their faces, witnessed their fear, tasted their blood.

And when the rush of memories had ebbed, her reality had treated her no better. She would see Megan on the bed and remember the scene Morgana had shown her. She would envision her fangs sinking into her lover's neck, and she would jerk away, only to have the vision linger in the darkness of her mind, awaiting her next weakness, its next opportunity to surface.

Her only hope had been the painting over the bed. On their first night out, while they drank, Megan had whispered to her briefly, promising that the painting would aid her when the curse took her body. But how? It couldn't stop the beast; Megan would have told her that precisely if it were true. And it couldn't be true because otherwise Megan would have lifted the curse from her long before.

Thyri had spent long, idle hours gazing into the picture's haunting, dark corners. It looked so real – if she knew Megan, and knew her sorcery, then the painting would be her window, her gate into another world. A place where she could go . . . a place to hide her, and to hide *Nightreaver*'s crew from the beast's bloodlust.

All this she hoped. But what if the sorcery failed? What if it needed Megan, alive and well? What if it was incomplete, or if it required some specific action from her of which the sorceress had not had time to tell her?

What if she had to *do* something that she did not know how to do? And then – what if it worked, but not in full? What if she could not return?

That fear had kept her on board when Rollo had disembarked to explore the island. She had feared nightfall on land. She had feared her own crew discovering her dark secret and abandoning her, fleeing from her. Either way, trapped on land or trapped in the painting, she would be without Megan again, and that thought she couldn't bear. Not as long as there was hope . . .

Until Thyri could learn how to help her friend – if she could help her – then she could risk nothing. But tonight, she would have to. She prayed that the painting would grant her haven and a safe return. If she could overcome the fear of being trapped . . . But if she couldn't, she would lose all to the beast, and then Megan, Rollo – everyone – would die.

And then, if the sorcery didn't work – if she were trapped on the ship, in the cabin with Meg . . . She would have no choice but to leap into the sea, placing Megan in the care of the others. She refused to consider stocking her cabin with meat from the hold. She had managed that before and succeeded, but just barely. She *had* to be in the cabin *with* Megan to get the painting . . . if its sorcery failed, she couldn't bear thoughts of the conflict that would ensue. No amount of dried meat could sate the wolf's hunger when it smelled fresh blood. True, she had defeated the beast's nature before, but always she'd had assistance. On the *Black Rabbit*, she'd had walls between herself and Elaine, the ship's sole survivor. On land, she'd always had other prey. On *Nightreaver*, tonight, she would have none of this.

Whatever happened, she could not allow herself to destroy her whom she loved most. But would she have the strength to do whatever the night might demand of her?

Strength – it was strength she needed. And compassion. The darkness of the recent days had chipped away at her humanity, and she desperately needed that back.

The afternoon had restored something of her old vitality. At least it had made her feel alive. She needed to keep that feeling, she needed to make it grow.

She needed to feel *human*. Now she had her chance.

Cautiously, she reached behind Rollo for the end of the last strip of cloth. She tied it slowly, looking up into his eyes. He had a kind face; blue eyes sparkled even amidst his confusion. His cheeks were high and strongly defined.

'Is that all right?' she asked.

He nodded uncertainly. Thyri tried to decode the emotions hidden behind his features. She felt another flash of fear as she recognized something in his eyes – a something she had seen before, in the new land, in Akan's eyes – a sort of reverent disbelief, a denial of the intimacy she offered.

Rollo, like Akan, had thought her a goddess. He thought her above human love. The realization sent her thoughts racing. With Akan, she had overcome this. But she knew already that Rollo was stronger than Akan. He was as strong as any man she'd ever known. What if he denied her?

Never before had she so wanted to be touched, to be

held. For the first time in her memory, she grew nervous. She felt a warm wetness spread out over the space between her thighs. *Touch me,* she thought.

'Is something wrong?' she asked.

'No,' he said. 'Thank you for the bandage.' He made a weak effort to step back.

Her hand darted out for his. 'Sometimes,' she said softly, 'I wish I had never seen a sword.'

He looked at her oddly. 'But . . .' She turned his hand palm up, then ran her fingers over his, over his palm, to his wrist. 'Megan,' he gasped.

She looked into his eyes. 'She would understand,' Thyri whispered. 'More than you can. More than I can.'

She took his hand and placed it on her thigh. The contact sent shivers up and down her leg. Slowly, she moved his hand up, pushing up her shift, then she swiftly brushed it against her wetness. She pulled his hand up between them, the moisture of her passion shining softly in the cabin's weak light.

'I am a woman,' she said. 'Won't you love me?' She smiled at him, watching his eyes. She pressed his hand against her breast and closed her eyes. 'Love me, Rollo,' she said, 'Don't ask questions. Don't doubt.' She reached between his legs and massaged his awakening manhood. He grew harder under her touch.

Slowly, he squeezed her breast.

'That's it,' she gasped. She pushed him back, toward his bunk. Once there, she pressed down on his shoulders and he sat. She stood in front of him, moved closer to him, her breasts inches away from his mouth. 'Undress me,' she whispered.

Hesitantly, he reached out, unclasped the buckle of her war belt, and let it fall slowly to the floor.

'Undress me,' she repeated hoarsely.

He ran his hands up her legs, then gripped the bottom of her shift. As he raised it up, her breasts came free and she pushed them toward his face. She threw off her shift and moaned as his hands touched on either side of her waist.

His tongue danced lightly over a nipple and she dug her fingers in his hair, pressing him closer, feeling herself grow wetter as he took her breast into his mouth.

After a moment, she gently pulled away and pushed him back onto his bunk. She knelt, lifting his legs, her mouth hovering teasingly over him. She wanted to taste him, but the fire in her loins burned achingly, and his nearness only added to her desire. She forced herself to stand, then she moved onto the bed and straddled him, pressing her knees against his hips.

She bent down and kissed him, teasing his tongue into her mouth. She moved her mouth to his ear, he moaned as she brushed herself against him.

As she pushed back and felt the waves of ecstasy as he entered her, she bit him lightly on the neck. 'Slowly now, Rollo,' she whispered. 'Don't forget your ribs.'

Changes

A mist rose near sunset.

Gerald and Sokki stood side by side on the prow, peering out into the mist. The sea lapped hypnotically against *Nightreaver*'s hull, and both men lost themselves in thought long before. Their conversation had been pointless; Gerald tried but could not remember even the subject. They had spoken on everything but the one thing they both dwelt on. Each knew what the other felt; each had been unable to voice it. Meanwhile, time had passed with Thyri, alone with Rollo, in his cabin.

Once, she had cried out. The sound had sent chills up their spines.

For Gerald, what had occurred had been unthinkable. He had known, and understood, Thyri and Megan. Now he felt that he understood nothing. He did not even understand his own jealousy.

Sokki felt simple pain. From the moment he'd met Thyri, he'd seen the woman underneath the hard shell. It hadn't been a difficult thing for him; as a warrior, he'd known many men – commanders – who could cast aside the cloak of authority and become an equal among their charges. Thyri, however dark her moods, had proven no exception to that rule. And part of his pain was that he understood what she'd done, or at least he felt that he did. She mourned Megan, and, in her mourning, her need for comfort had grown unbearable. He had felt much the same since Ottar's death, but, while he had needed her, she'd been lost in her own sorrow. His heart had ached with a desire to go to her, to offer her comfort, but he hadn't known how to do that. Now it didn't matter.

He felt no hate for Rollo – neither did Gerald – but he cursed himself. His was a sorrow of lost opportunity, for the moment that might have been.

In all their churning thoughts, neither man could guess that the real reason for Thyri's actions floated before them: a silver orb behind the mist.

They turned briefly when Rollo's door opened and Thyri emerged. She glanced at them and smiled, then climbed up to the prow toward them.

As she approached, Gerald began to feel that all, again, was well. What had occurred in Rollo's cabin had not, in fact, occurred. Her smile was too real – too authentic. He shook the dark reflections from his mind.

When she reached them, she placed her hands on their shoulders and spoke softly. 'Rollo must rest,' she said, gazing out into the mists. 'Danger may lurk out there,' she whispered. 'Be prepared.'

She looked at Sokki sadly, then wrapped her arms around him, pressing him close. 'I'm sorry about Ottar,' she whispered in his ear. 'If I could bring him back, I would.' She pulled away and looked into his eyes briefly, then she turned to Gerald.

'I must not,' she said, 'be disturbed tonight. Under any circumstances. Please – if you do nothing else – heed me in this?'

Slowly, he nodded. She smiled again, then turned for her cabin.

They watched her until her door had shut, then they stared back out to sea.

Thyri threw off her clothes, crawled onto the bed, and looked down into Meg's face. In the shadows, the sorceress looked so at peace on the surface, but what did she feel inside? Anything? Did her serenity bode good or ill?

Thyri bent and kissed her, then crawled to the head of the bed. She rose up on her knees, placed her hands on the painting, and gazed in at the moon.

'Oh, Odin!' she whispered. 'Let this be real! Do not torture me tonight . . .'

A wave of sensation swept through her body. She felt the hairs on her arms stand out.

It begins . . .

Within the painting, the moon grew bright. Or was it just her eyes?

She blinked. A dull ache ran up her arms from her wrists. The moon drew away from her. Dew glistened on the grass before her eyes. She pushed forward, but the canvas did not give.

She began to cry. Through her tears, something moved. She wiped her eyes. A bird had appeared on the limb of a nearby tree; Thyri couldn't remember it being there before. She glanced down at Megan, then gasped as the claws popped out from the tips of her fingers. For a moment, they pressed into the canvas; she feared she would tear it, then she fell forward, and her hands met the earth.

Her body on fire, Thyri leapt forward. She rolled on the grass and came up on all fours. Pain flashed through her; she screamed, but the sound that escaped her throat was a thin, mournful howl.

She looked back at the place from whence she'd come: a cave in a hillside. Its depths were black, unfathomable. Her hunger was like that – it ached, clouding her thoughts.

She glanced up at the moon and growled. Around her, the forest beckoned.

Silent now, the white wolf turned for the trees.

Avalon

When the darkness came, she smiled. In the orb of Babd, she watched them and fed off their fears, their sorrows. Perhaps, over the next few nights, the chaos in their mistress's heart would show them the full extent of their folly. Mortals in Jotunheim!

She laughed.

No need to offer them an easy death now. Let them suffer. Let them mourn their dead brother . . .

He will return to them soon enough. And they meant nothing compared to the wolf and the witch. She would gain her revenge, however, in her own way.

Rising, she wrapped the orb in a swath of black velvet, then she placed it carefully into the burlap sack where she'd collected the few other talismans she'd felt worth keeping. With twine of twisted goatskin, she tied and bound the sack.

In darkness, she descended from her tower and walked slowly to the moonlit beach. There, she glanced back briefly at the spire that jutted darkly up into the night. She would not miss it.

She looked down at her naked body and ran her hands a last time over her muscled chest; then she whispered the incantation of feth fiada *in dark, menacing tones. Almost immediately, pain shot through her as her bones stretched out. As she felt her jaw push forward, a hoarse cackle bled from the half-formed beak.*

With the spell, she needn't feel pain, but that was the way she'd always liked it.

She screamed as the bones in her arms cracked and stretched. Her skin turned black, stealing the moon's light.

Down grew from her body like moss, then feathers sprouted from the downy bed. Within moments, the transformation was complete, and she stood, a huge, black bird-thing.

She tested her wings and opened her beak, sending a terrible, shrieking caw out over the sea.

In her talons, she gripped the burlap sack, and, with this burden, she took to the air, spiraling slowly up into the night.

Wildfire

In the night, she knew harmony. The forest was bountiful; the hunger – she sated it quickly, easily, and without anguish.

The old buck eyed her as she brought him down; in his gaze she thought she saw gratitude, as if he tired of battling the summer heat and the winter snows. Within her, he became strong again, lord of the trees and protector of his brethren from the fangs of the wolf. At least for the night.

After dining, she roamed. Her world knew no borders but the mountain peaks on three sides. Between them, a valley flourished, and mountain streams fed a river that flowed gently out to some distant sea. At the river, she drank deep; the water was cool and clean. Everything felt real, tasted real. And the smells – she'd never imagined they could all fill the air of one place. Some flowers: she knew them only from her childhood in Norway, but the pines recalled to her the woodlands of the new land over the ocean. Behind it all was a sweet tang – magic, but here it seemed real and proper, too, as if it had grown, with the vegetation, out of the fertile soil.

Beside the river, she lay down on a bed of moss. The magic was the earth itself; she could feel it. What small kingdom had Megan gifted her? She felt at home – at peace with the beast as she had not felt since . . . As she had never felt. Even now, with her lover neither alive nor dead. In the air here, she could feel Megan's love.

As she rested, she began to sense the presence of another: a familiar, friendly scent, but its identity eluded her, as if her memory of it had withered, buried itself under layers of other thoughts, other impressions.

She strove to peel back the layers, and as the memory came into her grasp, as deep sorrow wrapped suddenly around her heart, he stepped from the shadows.

Thyri, he growled softly.

She stared at him, into his ancient eyes. The wildness of the beast surged within her, but her sorrow was too great, overwhelming.

How came you here? he asked.

She didn't answer; she just stared at him, unable to believe that her past had so returned to haunt her. And it was a past in which she'd loved – all the more cruel because she could not lash out; she could not destroy it. She could only flee as she had before, except now she had nowhere to go.

He approached her slowly; she felt the warmth and sweetness of his breath. *I sensed your entrance on the pathways. I came here as quickly as I could.* He stopped, gazing at her.

In his eyes, she saw Pohati's. *Akiya toyn,* she heard in her mind, *it has not been long, but it feels like forever.*

The white wolf looked away from the gray. She wanted to run, but she could not move. On the bed of moss that edged the gentle river, the white wolf wept.

Here, my reader, I must intrude and admit failure. Though my heart bids me stop, I cannot omit this part of my telling for reasons that will, in the end, become apparent.

Yet, of the past events that might serve to illuminate this moment, I have written nothing. I had thought to spare myself the memory of what little I learned of Thyri's last, dark months in the new land, but my task has proven me wrong. By all accounts, I should set aside this section of my manuscript, return to the beginning, and tell it as it should have been told. Though this cannot be evident here, I have just spent an entire evening staring at this half-finished page, considering this thought. I feel no better for it.

I cannot go back. I cannot direct again my research to the days of Thyri's deepest pain, for I do not possess the talent to relate them well. Beyond that: beyond this scene with Woraag

Grag, those dark days need not be told. The pain Thyri felt then, she came to tame, to hide so well that it could not touch her, so that it could retain no hold on her life. She never thought of it outside those moments when the presence of Woraag Grag summoned up the cruel, treacherous winds of remembrance.

And still I digress. I have written how Pohati fell in Thyri's clash with Aralak, and I have written how Woraag Grag, the ancient one, took the young Habnakys battle-mistress's essence into himself. I have written that, after the war in the new land had ended, Thyri roamed, wintering alone and, near spring, shunning the company even of wolves. One who has read closely this history of mine must ask, 'Why? Why was it that she who had gained a peace with her curse, she who had found a new home among the beasts of the wood, would retreat into the darkest of her depressions, for that is how she is described that last day before Astrid's descent from Valhalla and her return to the lands of the Norse. Indeed, upon that return, she desired to die. Why?'

I have the answer, yet still I hesitate to immortalize it in ink. But I have come too far to turn back . . .

Woraag Grag, as written, was a god. Within him, the souls of countless fallen warriors shared his eternity. Pohati was but one of many.

But Thyri had loved Pohati. During Thyri's first changes after Pohati's death, she had sought out the ancient wolf, and they had hunted together, Thyri at peace with Pohati nearby. And, in the pale hour before sunrise one night, they had loved.

Three cycles of the moon past that, Thyri gave birth to three monsters, all dead.

There – it is written. No more! I will not go back to fit this event into its proper place, for it has no proper place. It is neither a fitting end to the tale of Thyri's life in the new land, nor is it a fitting beginning for her departure. It is only a sadness beyond words, and I am yet tempted to strike it from this page. Perhaps I shall do so. Have I not entered fantasy in my presumption to know Morgana's thoughts? Is not my tale already blemished by lack of truth? If Morgana, why not Woraag Grag? Why not leave Thyri at peace with the new land, in love with its people and the families of beasts that ruled its wood? Why not have her flee Astrid, and have her battle her cousin? Have Astrid subdue her and carry her against her will into that conflict with Alfred?

It is late, this night on which I write. By rights, I should sleep, but I know already that sleep will elude me. For now, I shall embrace that which my sorcery has known me to be true.

I move on . . .

Woraag Grag watched her silently as the tears trickled from her eyes, soaking her snout. He let her cry for a long while, then, finally, he inched closer to her, settled down on the moss, and gazed out over the river.

I never thought our union might have caused you such pain, she heard him say in her mind. *Such mortal burdens should not be yours.*

I am a mortal woman, she replied. *This form I wear under the full moon is a curse, not a blessing.*

So I have learned. Once I knew you to be mortal, but through Pohati's eyes you are akiya toyn *– the wildfire. Through the eyes of many others you are the same. Do you know that you age? Are you certain that this – this form you wear – does not shield you from the ravages of time? I have sought to understand much since your passing from my land. I sought you on the shadow-paths, to no avail until now. But I found others. I have counseled with your teacher, and she informed me of much.*

For a moment, Thyri felt as if time had suddenly stopped; as his words sank in, her mind caught fire as waves of excitement cut through her despair. *Scacath!* she thought. *You have spoken with Scacath?*

Yes, he answered. *Does this anger you?*

She rose, shaking her head, banishing the last, lingering phantoms. *Where is she? What did she tell you?*

She is where she is, just as you and I. You have not yet told me how you came to this place. He looked up into her eyes. As she studied him, she grew aware that he shared with her the sadness of their past, that he would, if he could, undo their tragedy. Love remained in those eyes. Pohati's memory lurked there as well. *Have you learned to walk the roads of the ancients? I always thought you knew, for by what other road might you have reached my distant shores?*

The shadow-paths, she thought. *No.* She remembered the certain turnings she'd taken to reach Scacath's grove during her years of training under the goddess's tutelage. She remembered how it had always seemed that she'd passed from one world into another, quite separate realm. *I think, perhaps, that I have done so without understanding how.*

It is not difficult, he said. *Some pathways are so open that they may be found by accident alone. Is that how you came here?*

She lowered her eyes. *No. I came here through the sorcery of a friend.*

She is a powerful sorceress?

Thyri nodded slowly. *But I fear she is not powerful enough. She lies near death, and I do not know how to aid her.*

He looked at her sadly. *Would that I were a healer. But I am not, and we are many worlds away from my own.*

What of Scacath? she asked. *How near are we to her world?*

Near, but I cannot promise she is there.

Take me to her, she said pleadingly. *Can you do that? Can you teach one how to find these shadow-paths?*

For a being of power, it is a simple task. But it can be demanding, at times very dangerous, for great evils know the pathways as well. Will you risk this?

Yes, she replied. For Megan, she thought quietly, she would risk anything.

As Woraag Grag led her downstream, Thyri realized that she had not pressed him for knowledge of Scacath's words to him. Now she did not wish to interrupt him with conversation. The night was no longer young, and from wherever he would lead her, she would need to return.

They did speak, or, rather, he did, from time to time pointing out to her the signs that he followed: the curious, unnatural twist of a certain twig; a certain change in the air that she perceived as an eddy in the ocean of magic surrounding them. They had not gone far when he abruptly turned toward the river and stepped off the bank into the air.

She smiled wryly as she watched him walk out over the current, his paws inches off the surface of the water. Fearing to think too critically of what she attempted, she followed him, smiling again when she discovered that she had not plunged into the water's depths. The air around her felt charged; her fur bristled up her spine and along her flanks.

At midstream, he disappeared. When she'd reached that point, when she saw him again, they were in another world.

They walked along a ridge, high above a golden city. A haze filled the air, and the full moon's light was paled by the burnings of countless candles below. Peering down, Thyri picked out roads traveled by what she guessed to be giant beetles marching rapidly in bizarre, chaotic patterns executed with an almost military precision.

Woraag Grag continued to speak, and she forced herself to tear her eyes away from the scene below. As she breathed the air of this new place, she noted many unplaceable scents; their impression overall was one of decay.

Strange trees dotted the ridges. They skirted them, but each time, the gray wolf quickly led the white back to the ridge's peak. He told her that he sought a specific tree and that she too should recognize it when they found it.

Indeed, she did. The overall tang of magic in the air had dispersed completely once they'd fully come into this world, but as they neared the tree of which Woraag Grag had spoken, the tang returned. She was aware of it several moments before he pronounced his discovery.

As they drew close to the next twisting in their journey, Thyri looked to her left and felt her heartbeat jump as she found herself face-to-face with one of the beetles. It was, at most, twenty paces away, and its eyes watched her dully. It smelled of metal, and it did not move. She could see into its belly; it had devoured two people, but they did not seem to care. They were – kissing.

She paused a moment and watched the people. As she did, they paused in their passion and gazed out of the beetle's stomach toward the ridge. For a moment, they did not see her, then suddenly the female's eyes met hers. A muffled scream split the night, and the beetle's eyes came suddenly to brilliant life.

At the edge of her vision, Thyri saw Woraag Grag step again out into open air. To her left, the beetle roared with a fury she'd never heard escape the throat of even the fiercest bear.

She bolted forward and dove into the air, following her guide.

Two worlds later they came to a forest that Thyri recognized immediately. She knew every tree, every trail. Years before, she had hunted here; she still possessed the boots that she had lined with the fur of a rabbit she had slain among these very trees.

Every step forward brought a new memory rushing into her mind: there, under that oak, she had loved with Astrid on a rare, lazy afternoon; here, on this very tree, she had once pinned a lizard of many colors and, in doing so, won her second braid. And, in the distance, she heard the tinkling stream that led to the bear cave full of rainbow stuff where she had won her third braid and her sword.

The memories engulfed her; the scent of her teacher filled her nostrils, and she raced forward, leaving Woraag Grag behind.

The smell of Scacath grew stronger, overwhelming her. She *was* here. All trails led to the common, and that is where Thyri found her. She sat in the clearing's center, her carriage erect, her visage dark, the embodiment of power.

Thyri stopped abruptly before her. Several moments passed before Scacath opened her eyes. 'Hello, little one,' spake the goddess.

Thyri, watching her, was no longer aware of her wolfen form. She was again the student, fearful of her teacher's presence, yet forever in awe. Only vaguely did she sense Woraag Grag's approach behind her.

'What brings you here?' The goddess's eyes burned like dark fires.

Knowledge, Thyri answered. *I must ask of you many things.*

You cannot ask many things, the gray wolf spoke in her mind. *If we do not depart soon, the dawn will be upon you.*

And Megan's sorcery may fail . . . Thyri looked at Scacath desperately. *I captain a ship now, teacher, and I have found love again, but she has fallen in battle and neither moves nor dies. Will you aid her?*

'I am not a healer, little one. But I fear that, even were I able to help you, I could not. Matters of grave import need attending; the balance of the major worlds is endangered; even now, Surt arms his legions.'

Ragnarok?

'Perhaps.' Scacath looked away and up into the stars. 'On what seas do you sail?'

Jotunheim, or so I believe. We have battled giants.

Scacath raised an arm, pointing to the western sky. 'Then follow that star,' she said. 'Under it, you will find healers. Do you see it. The left eye of the Great Raven?'

Thyri looked up. *Yes, teacher.*

Woraag Grag nudged her flank. *We must go,* akiya toyn. *Do not tempt fate!*

Thyri looked at Scacath; her teacher smiled at her – the mysterious half-smile she knew so well from her youth. Her mind on fire with fear of the future and fear for Megan, she forced herself to turn away. Woraag Grag quickly led her back through the wood.

During their return, Thyri found it impossible to concentrate on Woraag Grag's instructions, even though she knew it meant that she would be unable to make the journey again on her own. Her emotions, her fear that she would be unable to return to Megan before sunrise, spoiled her thinking, which itself turned constantly on one thing: her failure. She had failed to fulfill her dream, that dream she and Astrid had shared of spending idle time with their teacher as equals. She could never be equal to Scacath; the goddess had been as elusive as ever she was when Thyri was young.

Dawn licked the horizon as they passed through the world of the golden city and the beetles. Thyri began to fear she would be trapped in Megan's forest, unable to cross the final portal back into her cabin.

If the sun rose, perhaps Woraag Grag could still usher her back onto her ship. Then again, perhaps not . . .

When they gained the air over the gentle river, Thyri ran with Woraag Grag pacing her at her side. Near the end of their journey, he spoke with her, words she would not fully understand until later, when she'd time to reflect: *I will not seek you again,* akiya toyn, *for I understand now your pains, and I do not wish to deepen them with my memory. However, when you walk the shadow-paths, you may call to me. I will hear you, and I will come.*

She glanced at him only briefly before she dove into the dark cave in the hillside. She felt the wolf flee her as dawn exploded into the world, and she landed on her bed, naked, exhausted, the tentacles of sleep wrapping quickly about her mind.

Jotunheim

When she wakened, well after noon, the past night seemed to her like a dream. She recalled Woraag Grag, but his memory brought back only her pain in the new land, her memory of that night when . . . when . . .

She looked over at Megan.

Scacath pointing up . . . *'The left eye of the Great Raven.'*

Healers.

Woraag Grag.

Thyri shook her head, rose, and staggered out into the daylight. Rollo, at the prow, looked back at her and smiled. She remembered the evening before . . . She smiled back weakly. Odin! she thought. *What tortures we might suffer in one passing of the sun!*

She turned back into her cabin, to Megan. She spent the afternoon at her lover's side, trying not to think too deeply on the past day's trials.

As the day grew old, Rollo brought her food. She felt no hunger, and though she tried, she could not eat. He grew concerned, and when he touched her hand, sorrow filled her heart. She looked into his eyes and saw the love there. Part of her wanted to return it, to replay the evening before, the way the actors in a play repeat the same loves, fears, and agonies on consecutive nights. But she could not: Scacath had given her hope for Megan, and she had to cling to that now.

She told him she had had a vision, and she had found for them a haven. The experience had exhausted her, but he needn't fear for her because now she had hope. She needed only rest for a couple of days. He should explain this to the others.

And after sunset, he should set course for the left eye of the Great Raven. Did he know it?

Yes, he answered, then he left her alone.

As the evening grew dark, she fought the turmoil in her mind. Woraag Grag had promised to come at her bidding. The mere thought of that promise pained her. But – his presence again? Only his mention of Scacath had been able to overcome that agony.

She yet desired Scacath's counsel. Her teacher was wise; Thyri felt that she, of all beings, could help her sort out the tangled mass of emotions that her life had become. Only Scacath could tell her why . . .

Assuming she would.

But to find her once again, Thyri would need Woraag Grag. And if she called him once . . . If she weakened and let the part of him that was Pohati through again to her heart?

No. The risks to her sanity were too great. And Scacath had already told her what she most needed to know. Later, when the weight of the moment had lessened, perhaps she would try to reach her teacher on her own. Perhaps Megan could help her; perhaps they would walk the shadow-paths together.

When the wolf came, Thyri roamed Megan's valley, filling her night with the hunt. She ate her fill several times over, but, in doing so, resisted the temptation of a return to Scacath, an act that could leave her either inextricably bound again to Woraag Grag, or hopelessly separated from her lover.

The next day and night were much the same. Another two days passed before Thyri found herself able to endure the company of others. When she joined them one afternoon at the sail, she saw the joy in their faces as her mere presence uplifted their spirits.

She could understand their reaction – but then again, she could not. Looking into herself, she could not see what they saw. She felt dark and desolate inside. Pohati's face would often surface in her thoughts, and Thyri would realize the cruelty inherent in her rejection of the gray wolf.

All the while, Megan lay motionless in the dim, cold solitude of their cabin.

When Thyri had offered Rollo their new course, some small irony had lingered in the fact that, at top speed, they were yet just under a month from their destination. As *Nightreaver* sped eastward over the immense ocean, the moon waned and waxed again, growing ominously more nearly full with each passing night.

Of that journey, much could be told of small mishaps and near-adventures: near because they were avoided as *Nightreaver*'s captain grew obsessed with their desire to dock under the left eye of the Great Raven. One episode warrants mention, however, but for no reason other than that Rollo had dreamed of it that morning before he woke at Fandis's: On the mist-enshrouded seas, late one evening, *Nightreaver*'s crew fell under the enchantment of a solitary voice that called sadly to them through the mist. Rollo, at the time, recalled his dream and he turned *Nightreaver* for the voice. As they approached, they saw the woman, a wraithlike thing of skin and bones, but at the time, all thought her beautiful, and Rollo began to shout with Sokki, arguing over who should love her.

During that battle of words, Thyri emerged from her cabin, calmly took Rui's bow and quiver, and ended the siren's song with a single arrow.

All other events were minor and of no lasting consequence, even though Horik almost lost a hand during one of the battles with sea monsters. No, during that journey, only small happenings came and went. Sokki and Horik slowly grew to accept the death of Ottar, and the jealousy the others felt for Thyri's attentiveness toward Rollo faded as her seeming favoritism toward the affable Viking came to be accepted as part of the natural order of things. It was to Rollo that the others looked in times of danger, and the perils of the sea left no room for any childish defiance of his command.

And the matter never again grew pressing. Though Thyri occasionally favored Rollo's company while she drove them ever eastward, she remained chaste, and, thus, passing time allowed Gerald and Sokki to build their fantasies anew.

Rui, after his fashion, took all happenings in stride.

Their quest led them to land, the first sighting of any real size. After a brief, southerly diversion, they found a broad river and started inland. After a day and night of struggling upriver, they found what they sought.

Thyri, at the time, was painfully aware that the next night's moon would be full.

fi-Logath

Dawn brushed the eastern sky, painting a mural of red and violet over the city of crystal spires. Several ornately carved vessels, their lines cast starkly in shadow, floated in the waters at the city's foot.

Horik and Rui shipped their oars as the vision loomed larger, stealing their breath away. A spear of sunlight suddenly broke over the land beyond and struck one of the tallest spires, streaking the sky over the river with lights that flashed and flashed again: all the colors of the rainbow. Horik, as a boy, had known well the lights of the North; only against those subtle, interweaving light streams could he measure what he now saw. The rainbows above were brighter, more intense, more dynamic and alive, a concert of rainbow swords lashing out, slicing through the dawn.

As the sun rose, the rainbows settled into the spires themselves. Still, the two men found it difficult to look away. Several moments passed before Rui noticed the figures on the near end of the city's docks: five warriors, armored in gold, stood in a line, watching *Nightreaver*'s approach.

Rui nudged Sokki, pointing at the warriors; he rose, turning to wake the others. Moments later, all stood at the prow as Horik and Sokki brushed the oars lightly over the water, maintaining a slow, steady approach.

'This is it?' Rollo asked, glancing down at Thyri.

Gerald stared across at the golden warriors. Three were male, two female; their armor fit close to their bodies, its contours incredibly faithful; he wondered what smith might have dared such a feat: they looked almost towering, naked, golden youths. Even at a distance, their height was unmistakable; the shorter of the females stood at least a head taller than Rollo. Their hair, long and golden like their armor, flowed out from under silver, feathered helms. Each wore a sword in a jeweled scabbard; while the males posted spears, the females carried tall, slender bows.

Rui spoke softly to Gerald: 'Nothing I have seen – and I have seen much, my friend – could rival this.'

'Not giant chicken feathers?'

The archer chuckled. 'No,' he said, 'not even that.'

As he spoke, a rich baritone erupted over the river: a steady, wordless tone that suddenly modulated, then soared as if to dance among the clouds overhead. Just before the resolving note, a soprano joined the baritone, following in its steps, mirroring, two octaves higher, each breathless leap, each inflection. They sang in rounds, the melody at once simple yet beautifully ornate, the counterpoint majestic, as if a choir, not two voices, sang a greeting to the morning.

The song's beauty recalled Megan's casting, when she had remade the ship. The singers, if anything, were more exotic and fantastic than the sorceress. The male – the central figure among those on the docks – ended as he'd begun: holding his final note steady while the soprano at his side descended her scale before they jointly dropped off into silence.

Gerald watched the singer's eyes pass over each of them. The gaze was warm, but cautious, guarded. The giant (for he *was* so, in human terms) brought his eyes to rest on Thyri before calling out over the water.

'We greet you, Eiriksdattir,' he called. 'She of the hidden lightning advised of your coming.'

Gerald glanced questioningly at Rui; the archer shrugged. They looked to Thyri as she smiled back at the warrior.

'Then you know of our burden,' she called back.

He nodded.

'Can you aid us? I offer you anything in my power to give.'

He looked at her oddly, then bent as the woman beside him whispered something in his ear. When she'd finished, he stood straight and called back to Thyri. 'That will not be necessary. You are guests.'

Nightreaver glided ever nearer the dock. Gerald grew increasingly captivated by their hosts' appearances. At a distance, only their height had confounded their humanity. Upon closer inspection, their skin possessed a blue-gray translucence that seemed both youthful and aged. And their wariness nagged at him; he wondered what *she of the hidden lightning* meant. Certainly not Morgana – and Megan didn't make any sense. Brigid? Had Thyri communed with the goddess that night he'd met her? Much, on the other hand, had transpired since then.

Rollo tossed a rope to the dock; Thyri kept her eyes locked on him with whom she spoke. She too was wary, but only in reaction to the thinly disguised skepticism in the eyes ashore. It demeaned the value of their welcoming song, the beauty of which had been flawless, but, now it seemed, coldly so, offered as an obligation. What had Scacath told them? Threatened them with? Warned them of? If her teacher had not intervened, would these warriors have allowed *Nightreaver*'s approach at all? Surely they were powerful; they lived in a world of constant danger, of giants capable of crushing their fantastic towers under the weight of a single foot, but those towers stood and had stood, Thyri guessed instinctively, for centuries, if not millenia.

And Scacath had said they could heal Megan; there was power, surely, in that, and that thought kindled excitement in her heart. She had reached her destination!

She felt some surprise when a woman's hand was offered to help her ashore. Thyri shifted her gaze, looking up into an uncertain smile. The tang of magic washed over her. Abruptly, she grasped the hand and let it guide her forward. She looked into the woman's eyes and smiled warmly as she felt the magic probing her; she opened herself to it, hoping that whatever darkness it might find would not be one which they feared. She had to gain their trust. They *had* to help her; she hoped they would see that she desired nothing more.

As her foot touched on the dock, she spoke. 'I am Thyri,' she said into the magic. 'Please do not fear us. We come with peace in our hearts.'

The woman's smile grew more relaxed. 'You bear many burdens,' she said.

Thyri nodded. *But they are mine, not yours. I seek relief only of one.*

I apologize, Thyri, if your welcoming seemed less than joyous. These are troubled times when evil often bears a semblance of goodness and familiarity. Odin, himself, we would greet in the same fashion.

Am I evil, then? Or good.

The smile broadened into sad mirth. *Both, as are we all. But you strive to transcend the darkness, and that is all that matters, is it not?* She turned to the warrior next to her. 'Go,' she told him, 'and bring *helfin*, and a harnessed, canopied bed. The ailing Tuathan lies in the rearmost cabin.'

The man nodded, then raced toward the crystal spires. The woman turned then to the humans on *Nightreaver*'s deck. 'I am Arithea,' she said. 'We have sung you the ancient affirmation of goodwill. Welcome to fi-Logath.'

Slowly, Rollo disembarked and gained Thyri's side. One by one, looking up at their hosts, the others followed.

What can be understood by mere mortals of such a place as fi-Logath? Crystal spires rooted in the soil not by men, but by sorcery? They reached up into the sky, some straight, some at angles, just as smaller crystals grown by nature. But these were oddly cut, hollowed, melted in places where they resembled the spires and pillars nature fashions in damp caves. They possessed nothing of the symmetry men so value in their palaces and shrines, yet their majesty dwarfed anything envisioned by mortal architects or builder-priests.

fi-Logath was the essence of that which men strive to capture and edify. Man's works, at best, capture only some small facet of the divine.

Arithea's brother, the warrior with whom she'd sang and he who had spoken first with Thyri, was named Donalu. His eyes were like cool fires, their irises deep blue and flecked with red and orange. When he smiled, as he did now, they were warm, laughing eyes. As Gerald watched him, however, he found himself hoping that he would never have to face those eyes in battle. They had a sorcerous, hypnotic quality: a strange ability to externalize emotion, filling the dining chamber where they now sat with joy and peace. In battle, Gerald had no doubt that those eyes would send real, tangible fear into the hearts of Donalu's enemies.

The foods they ate – strange fruits, nuts the size of small apples, and a sweet, milky liquid – were borne to their table by rosy-skinned, muscular creatures half the size of normal men. *Helfin* Arithea had named them – the same creatures who had come to the docks and carried Megan to the towers of fi-Logath. 'They are like us,' Donalu had already told them, 'a people unto themselves. Their fathers were dwarves, but their mothers were of the fair race. They have some magics of their own, but they use them always in our service. We do not keep them here by force.'

His words had rung true. Gerald had watched the *helfin* engaged in their chores. Not once had he seen a face that had not smiled. They seemed to thrive on their work, performing with joy the tasks that human cultures often assign to slaves. Gerald had found this curious, but, in the end, he'd concluded that the relationship between the *helfin* and Donalu's people was a symbiotic one. The little folk found safety under Donalu's wings; manual work was a small price to pay under such circumstances.

Now they ate the products of the *helfin*'s labors. Each bite tasted more delicious than the last. Their drink was heady, like a wine, and it spread warmth through their limbs, yet did not dull the mind or senses. If anything, it made them stronger. Donalu named the liquid *abrosi*. Among the foods, there was no hint of meat or flesh of any kind.

Donalu and Arithea sat across from Thyri and her crew. The table was long, with seating for a dozen along each side. Donalu's people filled all the remaining seats. The chamber was undecorated but for the natural beauty of its walls and arches. In one corner, a trio of *helfin* harpists played sad airs, their instruments resonating hauntingly within the crystal walls.

After introductions had been made all round, it was Donalu, mainly, who spoke. His voice, in conversation, was much like it was in song: smooth, tranquil, and majestic.

'Two millenia past,' he said, 'when the men of the middle world were yet young, the fates of the elder peoples were decided here, in this world and on these plains. It was then that the sons of Ymir, fleeing some greater, growing evil in the fiery realm of Surtur, came here and did battle to lay claim to their newly chosen land. The wars cost all sides much, for the physical strengths of the giants were great. Only the most noble and powerful of the elder races survived the initial, crushing waves. The *Pharosia*, the eagle people and once rulers of all lands and worlds, were slain to the last warrior by the *fir-Jotun*, Surtur's own sorcerous children.

'They were wars of sorcery against muscle. In the end, the sorcery lost and won. The most powerful warlocks and sorcerers of the elder races cast terrible spells that tore the worlds asunder, thus creating new worlds into which they could retreat, leaving to Ymir's children all the ancient homelands. Into these new worlds fled the children of Danu, the children of Chronos, and of Bor and the rest of the ancient fathers. The homelands became Jotunheim, forever debased but for pockets of light into which lingering sorceries dissuade the Jotun from entrance.

'It is said among the *helfin* – the only race not dislocated during these terrible wars – that Herculon, then the bravest and strongest of the sons of Chronos, had defended this place from the invasions. Herculon alone of the elder warriors was a match for the Jotun. With his sword, he slew twenty of the giants without the aid of sorcery of any kind. In the end, Herculon fell. His blood soaked the earth, and from this joining, we sprang the following spring.'

At this Arithea laughed. 'So the *helfin* tell us,' she said. 'In fact, we are, like them, mongrels. We are called the faer-Jotun, spawn of hil-Jotun, the smallest of the giant races, and a few unfortunate daughters of Danu. We are children of those wars of which my brother speaks, and the blood of both sides runs in our veins. It is said among the children of Danu, whose word in this case I find more trustworthy, that our mothers, before our births, fled here and grew these towers from the earth to house us. They knew then that we could not live among their people or among the Jotun, for both races would see in us their enemies.

'As for the tales of the *helfin*, well, I fear they pity us. We are like them, but worse. True their blood is tarnished by a mixing of races, but their fathers were not ignoble. One cannot say that of ours. Our mothers all died in childbirth, and the *helfin* cared for us in our youth. I feel that, in their hearts, they yet see themselves as our caretakers. Their tale of Herculon I remember hearing first during my third summer. I have seen countless summers since then, and I feel somewhat wiser.'

Such was the tale they heard while dining at the faer-Jotun's table. They also learned that those eighteen faer-Jotun with whom they dined composed the mongrel race of immortals in its entirety. Once, they'd been twenty-five, but seven of their number had perished in various conflicts with the Jotun over the years.

And the faer-Jotun women were of infertile womb. Immortal, divine mules.

Changes

Arithea sat on the floor next to Megan's bed and laid her hand on the sorceress's brow. Thyri, standing next to her, whispered a short prayer to Odin, pleading to the All Father that Arithea would not tell her something she did not wish to hear. Megan *had* to be healed, otherwise Thyri herself would perish from grief.

The faer-Jotun, sensing Thyri's raging emotions, looked up at her after only a moment. *Do not fear, white-hair, she is not lost. Your friend is strong, and though her spirit is gravely wounded, she heals herself even now. In time, she will recover on her own.*

How much time?

Two centuries, maybe three.

We do not have that much time.

Arithea smiled. *I know. I can aid her return to this world. It will take a week, maybe less. You must leave me alone to do this.*

I could not stay even if you allowed me.

The full moon? I know – that is why you cannot stay. Otherwise, your love could aid me. I have seen into you, Eiriksdattir, and I know your pain. You must soon leave fi-Logath and be far from here by sunset. I trust you can fend for yourself no matter what your surrounds. Return when the fullness of the moon has passed, and perhaps, by then, your friend may greet you herself.

'What of my men?' Thyri asked aloud.

'They will think you here with me, will they not? Do not fear, they will be attended. But they are, in their hearts, loyal to you. I do not think that knowledge of your secret would turn them against you.'

'No,' she said flatly. 'That I will never allow.'

Arithea turned her gaze back to Megan. 'If that is your wish, white-hair, so be it.'

Thyri left the dining chamber with Arithea; Rollo, Gerald, and the others stayed. Donalu entertained them with further stories, some certainly half-true or less, of the ancient wars. Spirits among the men rose to new heights when a new, more potent brew was brought by the *helfin* after the eating was done.

After a time, Donalu tired of speaking and asked for a tale in return. The other faer-Jotun joined him in the request, all eyes eagerly settling on *Nightreaver*'s crew. Sokki found his gaze captured by a slender, seven-foot female with an obvious, seductive smile and streaks of red in her golden hair. He felt himself responding to her attentions, surprised that he suddenly could not picture Thyri clearly in his mind.

In their corner, the *helfin* ensemble had grown to ten instruments, and the music had grown wilder.

Rollo smiled. 'How can we tell you a tale that you do not already know? We know many tales of Odin and his sons, but I daresay you know them better. Perhaps we have a tale to tell, but she has left the room, and, in any case, she seldom cares to speak of herself.'

'You do yourself an injustice, Rollo!' Rui spoke out. 'What of your tale? How you threw off the shackles of the Overking of Jorvik?'

'What of it? That is *her* tale in truth, for without her it never would have happened, just as you would not be here, just as none of us would be here. Sokki's tale also, of the battle with Alfred, would be nothing without her. We are but facets of her more brilliant gem.'

Donalu laughed. 'Well put, my friend! But surely a gem of any worth may be appreciated facet by facet, no? My sister told us little before your arrival, hardly more than to be wary of deception until she was sure you were no Jotun trick. Tell us more.'

'I cannot tell without her,' Rollo said.

Gerald cleared his throat. He felt elation; the *abrosi* and its successor had more than gone to his head. 'I have heard, at least in part, all of our tales. If the others do not object, I will tell.' He paused, looking at Rollo. The Viking raised an eyebrow, then shrugged.

And so Gerald spoke. He told of the battle of Ethandune as he'd heard it from Sokki and Horik. He told of Thyri's beheading of Guthrom's guard and how that had drawn him to her, and he told how, later that evening, he had aided Thyri in her summoning of Megan.

Gerald told then of all that had followed, of Rollo and Fandis as the Viking had told it, and of Thyri's reunion with the sons of Gunnar. Then he told of the mysterious island where they had battled Morgana, and he finished with the confrontation on what *Nightreaver*'s crew had come to call the Isle of Giant Chickens, when Rollo's ribs had been cracked (it must be written that, though the Viking had suffered and had, by this time, healed for the most part, he had not shown pain in his features since that evening with Thyri).

Such was the air of goodwill around the table that, when Gerald finished, he was rewarded with spontaneous applause. The reaction brought a beaming smile to his lips.

That smile – his happiness, was, perhaps, his first real mistake.

Unnoticed by all, the morning had turned to afternoon, and the afternoon had aged, turning the crystal walls first a bright yellow that paled and split into oranges and blues as the sun hurried in its descent.

Unknown to them, Thyri had already departed to spend the last hours of sunlight scouting for possible dangers near the mouth of the cave she had chosen as her lair for the evening.

In fi-Logath, all save Arithea had grown consumed with joy and mirth.

Near sunset, Sokki found himself being led by the hand through crystal halls to the chambers of the faer-Jotun with the rosy lips and the red-streaked hair. Her name was Elinta, and his evening with her was long and memorable.

Later, the rest of *Nightreaver*'s crew found themselves similarly matched. For the time, thoughts of Thyri vanished from all their minds save that of one: Rollo, as the giantess's caresses reawakened the dull achings around his ribs, found that he could not shake the ghosts of that one evening with Thyri from his mind. Caught in his passion, he played it through, but sleep, afterward, was long in coming.

Late that night, Megan Elana Kaerglen heard a faint, distant voice calling to her from far above. For a long time, she listened to it, wondering what it was and what it meant. As she thought, she began to wonder who she was, and, then, what that meant.

After a time, she struggled upward and fell. The voice yet called her; she struggled toward it again.

Slowly, the voice grew louder.

Thyri hunted.

Game in this land was scarce. She'd not lacked sustenance, but the pursuit of small game had led her, by midnight, far from the region to which she'd intended to restrict herself.

She needed something larger than squirrels and rabbits to sate her hunger, but deer – in fact, all hooved beasts – seemed markedly absent. Thyri guessed that unseen, more menacing predators than she were responsible – several times already she had neared patches of the forest that stank of rot and disease, reminding her of the grove of Pye of the Blue Moon on Kaerglen Isle. These blemishes in the forest she'd avoided.

As the night wore on, and as the dark hungers within her grew more demanding, she nearly gave in to the beast, to let it fare where it would, into whatever dangers lay waiting in the forest's darkest, decaying corners. As this thought of resignation played through her head, she caught whiff of a faint, yet distinct scent that sent her thoughts racing anew.

Disbelieving her senses, she followed the scent until she

could believe only one thing: Scacath had passed through this wood a mere fortnight before. The goddess had been hurried, unconcerned with covering her passage. In places, Thyri discovered faint traces of footprints.

Her teacher had traversed this ground. She'd been alone . . . Why had she not used her sorceries to inform fi-Logath of *Nighreaver*'s approach? Thyri would never have guessed that Scacath's words to Arithea had been spoken face-to-face.

Unless – *Ragnarok*. Did the final, great conflict truly approach? The warnings she'd heard, from Astrid, from Scacath herself – they were real.

All the Norse knew that *Ragnarok* was the certain destiny of themselves and their gods. But to know that it came *now* . . . How soon? What forces had marshaled themselves for the conflict? Who would perish?

Her thoughts gained urgency. What if it were true? What if the fates of all worlds hung now in precarious balance? What if terrible forces would soon destroy all the lives she knew, even her own? And Megan – did Thyri seek her recovery only to offer her a brief life of warring and bloodshed?

She had hoped, in taking *Nightreaver* from Guthrom's harbor, to travel unburdened by loyalty to all save Megan, herself, and their crew, but this had not come to pass. She had already lost one man, and she'd almost lost Megan. She'd desired to avoid conflict, but now – perhaps conflict was her only destiny . . . perhaps there could be no end to the bloodshed and heartache.

And Scacath: she had spoken with her teacher and failed to gain the answers she so desperately desired. On the last moon, on those last two days in Megan's forest, she had failed to attempt the passage back to Scacath's grove. Now, here, Wyrd, the goddess of fate, had given her a new trail. But to follow it?

Now was the time. In her wolfen form, she could cover more ground in a few hours than she could hope to match in several days on foot. But what of Megan's recovery and her crew? They were safe. With luck, she would soon return to fi-Logath.

Such was the train of Thyri's rational thought. Beneath the logic, her emotions broiled in a chaotic caldron. Deep within, she knew she could not leave Scacath's trail unexplored. Her decision was never in doubt.

Doubling back on her tracks, Thyri raced to retrieve her clothing and her sword; then, with five hours left before sunrise, the white wolf headed north, away from fi-Logath, into the land the *helfin* had long before named *Atale* – the Reaches of Despair.

Warriors

Rollo wakened, blinking his eyes momentarily against the soft, white light of the room. Hints of silver and blue flickered in the walls; for a moment, he thought himself in a cage of ice, then he remembered the day before.

He sat shaking his head, expecting to feel the dull ache of a hangover. But his mind felt clear and his limbs strong. He felt softness beneath him and tested it with a hand: he had slept on a down mattress. He looked around the room; he was alone.

The faer-Jotun, Ingrit, had left him. Late in the night? No – the mattress next to where he had lain was yet warm, and her perfume lingered strongly in the air, pungent. The smell was sweet, enticing, but as the night came back, he hated it. What had they done yesterday? After weeks at sea, thrust suddenly into the company of a race of gods . . . What of Thyri and Arithea? How fared Megan? When Arithea had made a brief appearance in the early evening, she had told them that she might remain cloistered with Thyri and Megan for as long as a week. They were not to be disturbed.

But what Rollo needed right now was to see Thyri's face. To see himself in her eyes and reassure himself that all was as it seemed. He needed to see that she did not hate him. He knew that she loved Megan; he knew that Thyri could never be his, but he belonged to her nevertheless.

Ingrit, goddess or not, could never sunder that bond. But she had surely weakened it.

As if responding to his thoughts, she entered, bearing a tray laden with fruits and crystal goblets of *abrosi*.

In the morning light, he appraised her. She *was* beautiful, her face perfect, finely chiseled like those of the ancient statues in Guthrom's old hall in Jorvik. Her full, blond mane made him think of the Valkyrie, her lightly rouged lips of his old fantasy memories of Fandis. Flowing silks, violet and white, draped her figure, clinging to her around her breasts, which were full and – he knew – soft and unblemished though she'd told him she was, like the rest of her race, some twenty centuries old.

And yet there was no hint of that age in her eyes. As she gazed at him, offering the tray, she could have been nineteen, for all the girlish nervousness and excitement hidden in her expression.

Seeing her face, Rollo turned away, unable to watch or take responsibility for the pain that his rejection summoned into her eyes. The *abrosi*, the food and drink of these gods, had commanded his actions the previous day. For the faer-Jotun, and perhaps for the rest of the *Nightreaver*'s crew, this may have been right, but for Rollo Anskarson . . . Too much weighed on his mind. Danger still stalked them. Somewhere, out there in Jotunheim, Morgana brooded and awaited them. She could not have forgotten them. One amongst them, at least, needed to remember that.

'No,' he said to Ingrit. 'Today I shall fast. I wish to be alone.'

For a moment, she did not move, then he heard her turn and silently exit the chamber.

Sokki's reflection greeted him from every polished surface in the hall of sculptures, his blond hair and brown garb giving their color to each fantastic statue, each etching in the walls of the hall. And the art: nymphs reclined on the floor of a forest of crystal trees while dragons curled around the branches above; fish hung suspended in the embrace of a frozen waterfall; on one wall, a palace of fire and ice topped a distant hill; on another, Odin gazed out over all in the gallery from his throne while, directly before the All Father, empty suits of armor danced a frozen battle with swords and spears that floated free in the air, unmoving, yet unheld by any hand.

As he moved, the colors in the chamber changed subtly – a streak of red here, a patch of bluish silver there. On a low, crystal toadstool at the foot of a lounging wood nymph, Elinta sat, her eyes absorbed by his face, his sense of wonder.

'You're impressed?' she asked, smiling.

He nodded.

'Some pieces,' she said, idly looking around, 'were the work of centuries.'

'Who are your artists?'

She laughed, tilting back on the toadstool. 'These are all mine,' she said. 'We must have something with which to occupy our time. We can raise no children. You might say that we are willing prisoners of our towers.'

'Why can't you leave? Fare out into this world and conquer new lands?'

She raised an amused eyebrow. 'Why? What might we find that we do not already have? We are only eighteen, and can be no more. We are comfortable here, and we are seldom threatened. The *helfin* provide for our every need.'

'Have you never felt lonely?'

She leaned back, running a hand up the leg of the nymph. 'Sometimes. But great beauty can flow from loneliness. You do not like my work?'

She sat up straight, her arms against her sides, her hands pressed against the curve of the toadstool next to her hips. Her long legs stretched out over the floor toward Sokki.

'It's beautiful,' he said. 'Like she who created it.'

She smiled. 'Over the years we have had countless visitors, so loneliness does not concern us much. We are a haven for those of the elder races who occasionally pass through these lands. And we entertain each other. Most of us have galleries like this among the towers. I have two others, but this is my favorite. But we all do different things. Ingrit paints. Doranu crafts animate toys to entertain the *helfin* children, and Arithea carves figurines from black stones when she is not practicing sorcery. Did you know that every tune you heard the *helfin* perform yesterday was composed by Donalu? And he has written countless thousands more. You must ask him to play before you leave; he can be quite shy in the company of strangers.'

He looked at her distantly. 'Is that how you see me, Elinta? Another passing stranger? I have never had a night to compare with the one I have spent with you. Will you choose Rollo this evening, or perhaps Donalu? Surely, we mortals cannot match the passions of gods!'

She eyed him cautiously. 'We chose each other, Sokki. Have I rejected you? I too enjoyed last night. A moment ago, as I sat here watching you appraise these children of my heart, I thought of how it might be to capture a moment of our love in crystal so that, centuries hence, another might come here and feel –' She stopped suddenly, her eyes moving to the image of Odin she had carved in the chamber's wall. 'There may be no more centuries, Sokki,' she said distantly. 'This may be the last. Ours may be the last love fi-Logath sees before the first gusts of the final winter.'

Slowly, he approached her. Her words, tainted so with impending doom, did not disturb him. Instead, they added a desperate, romantic edge to his presence there. So much had changed in the last day! He stood in the presence of an immortal. He had loved an immortal.

He placed a hand lightly on her shoulder, caressing her skin, brushing back her hair. 'I am a man, he said. 'I am human, destined to die.'

'Yes,' she said, gazing into his eyes. 'But is your heart?'

With that question, Elinta brought tears into Sokki's eyes. She swam in his vision, her face softened by his sorrow.

For long moments, they stood thus, gazing at each other. After a while, she brushed away his tears and summoned a smile up through her sadness. She rose, and walked slowly to the floating battle of crystal swords and armor.

'We all have a little magic in us, Sokki, even those of us who do not often practice sorcery.' She glanced back at him. 'I have seldom desired to use enchantments in my art, but this piece would have been impossible without them.' Her voice again grew distant. 'In this lies the essence of warfare. There are no faces in war, only weapons and death. Without weapons, without armor, a warrior is naked, is nothing in battle. And even at the hilt of a sword, in the space within the armor, the life itself – by itself – is nothing. Formless, and too light to tip the scales of the balance.'

She reached out and grasped the hilt of a long, gleaming sword. 'To the Jotun, of course, that doesn't apply. Their weapon is their size.' She turned and strode back to him, holding the sword before her. 'Take it,' she said. 'It is a true weapon, the art would have been meaningless were this not so. It will aid you. With this, my brother Feron slew three Jotun before he died.'

He stared at her. 'But it was a sculpture,' he said, reaching out hesitantly to touch her hand where she gripped the sword's hilt. 'Part of a sculpture that you created.'

'No,' she said. 'Before the art, there was only this, in my brother's hand. He died thirty years ago, engaged in the very exploits you just so casually suggested. Only after that, after Donalu returned with Feron's sword, was the art born.'

He squeezed her hand and drew close to her. The night before, he had felt awkward when they'd first embraced. She had towered over him, pressing his face between her breasts. Now he longed for that embrace. He looked up into her eyes. 'I will take this gift, Elinta, but I will never use it. I will never leave you. I will make this place my home.'

'You cannot,' she said. As confusion swept over him, she smiled sadly. 'Oh, do not fear, we would never ask you to leave. I would never want you to leave, but leave you will. It is said among the *helfin* that no traveler may come once to fi-Logath and stay. For two millenia, that has held true. Something will call you away. When you go, take my brother's sword. Perhaps it will give you the strength to return to me.'

He brushed his lips lightly over her breasts. 'I have not left yet,' he whispered.

She bent down. As their lips met, Horik's voice echoed harshly in the chamber: 'Sokki!' came Horik's words. 'We have found you at last!'

He backed out of Elinta's embrace and looked to the entrance.

'Come,' Horik called to him, placing his arm around the back of his companion. 'Renta has just told me a remarkable tale of a battle between elves and dwarves! You must hear it as well.'

Sokki glanced back at Elinta and sighed. She laughed and pushed the crystal sword into his hand; then she grasped his other arm and led him out of her gallery.

Gerald carefully placed the scroll on Tuathan battle customs back into its slot and returned to the long wall of books stacked from floor to ceiling. He had exhausted the middle row earlier, searching in vain for a script that he knew. Even among the scrolls, he had found comprehensible only the one, penned in a curious mix of his tongue and – something else.

He had spent the morning trading tales with Donalu, and after a lunch as enticing as their feast the day before, Donalu had offered him free rein in his library. He hadn't thought then that this embarrassing clash of language would be the result, and his pride kept him from calling for aid.

And, aside from that, he felt good. The *abrosi* had filled him with warm contentment, and the monotonous results of his explorations through the faer-Jotun's tomes had made him laugh more often than not. He had had worse days.

Chuckling to himself, he reached up for another volume.

Rui squinted at his target – a distant tree – and scowled; his last arrow had struck wood, but a full six inches from the knot at which he'd aimed. He notched another arrow, then paused as he sensed someone approaching behind him.

He turned, and, momentarily, the towers of fi-Logath caught him up. They reached up into the blue sky, their sheer faces gleaming with blues and whites from the clouds and the sun's yellow light. The approaching footfalls came from behind a tall hedge; as they grew louder, Rui lowered his eyes. After a moment, Rollo rounded the hedge and stopped before him.

The archer smiled. 'So – you seek solitude in these gardens as well?'

Rollo nodded.

Rui turned, unleashing his arrow. This time, he hit his mark. 'You do not care for the pleasures offered here?'

Rollo thought for a moment before answering. 'I do not mind pleasure. This just does not seem the time for it.'

Rui turned back to him. 'Why? What's the point of life, my friend, if not pleasure?'

'These pleasures are illusion,' Rollo said distantly. 'We are hear to heal Megan; then we must go.'

'Back to the world we know? Because the sorceress can guide us there?'

'In time. But first, a battle awaits us.'

'What do you mean?'

Rollo looked at the archer and sighed. He had never laid out his suspicions about Morgana for the crew; before, at sea, he'd thought it for the best. Now, he wished he'd taken a different approach. The threat was too real. On the other hand, the conflict was Thyri and Megan's – they were the ones with whom the decisions rested. Perhaps they wouldn't leave fi-Logath. Perhaps, after Megan's recovery, she would seek out Morgana – for surely the sorceress knew that Thyri's victory could not have been final – with the faer-Jotun at her side.

In that case, perhaps he was unnecessary. In any case, with Megan healed, Thyri would not longer need him, for she would have again her chosen companion. Perhaps he *should* return to Ingrit . . .

But still that didn't feel right.

'Nothing,' he told Rui at last. 'Our presence here just does not feel right. My thoughts turn again and again to Ragnarok.'

The archer laughed, notching another arrow. 'A war between gods? Were it so, Rollo, we would do best to seek refuge far from the battlefield. There are lights too bright for mortal eyes.' He turned away and let loose the arrow, which bit into the wood just under his last shot.

'We can do,' Rui said cryptically, 'only that which we can do.'

'Who are you?' Megan asked as the beckonings grew louder.

'A friend. Arithea I am named.'

'I have no friends.'

'That is untrue. What of Eiriksdattir?'

The voice's words conjured images in the darkness: a face, a sword. A body, burnt by the sun, beaten by the sea. A hand on her breast . . . 'I know that name.'

'That is good.'

'Where am I?' She gazed up at the face of Eiriksdattir; the eyes were familiar, comforting.

'The edge of nowhere. You are close; you must come to me.'

'Very well.' The sorceress struggled upward. She felt as if she swam through molasses. 'It is not easy,' she gasped as she swam through the face.

The vision shattered, sending streams of color out through the darkness.

Thyri dove to the side as the giant lizard lashed out at her. She felt the hair on her legs bristle as the huge talons missed her by inches.

As she landed, she struck across with her sword, the blade biting through scale into flesh. The sound of cracking bone split the air, and the monster roared. Its head loomed over her; saliva dripped from its jaws, burning the grass at her side. She swung her sword up into the maw of the beast, slicing off a row of its razor-sharp teeth. She swung back and cut through its neck. Blood sprayed over her. She swung again and rolled away, coming to her feet as the monster crashed to ground.

Staring at it, she bent over, her hands on her knees as she caught her breath. She felt filthy; the day's battles had caked her arms and clothing with blood. She felt exhausted, but she knew the land would not let her rest. She had to keep moving, keep to Scacath's trail.

If her teacher could pass through this land, so could she!

She needed only to stay alive until nightfall; then the wolf would keep her safe, its speed capable of outdistancing any danger. At least any the land had thus far served up.

The afternoon wore on, and Scacath's trail twisted suddenly eastward. She followed the signs carefully, the scent more difficult to follow in the day than at night.

Near dusk, she reached the carcasses. They sprawled over broken trees, their bones green, covered with slime and moss. None were fresh, but the smell, to Thyri's heightened senses, was repugnant.

Giants. All long dead, some with impossibly huge swords clutched in bony, rotted hands. She didn't care to know what had slain them. Scacath, thankfully, had skirted the carnage.

Following her teacher's detour, Thyri felt a nausea take root in the pit of her stomach. Pinpricks of light began to invade her vision, and her sense for magic went wild. Something had again found her; she was under attack!

She cast about for signs of predators but found none. The sun rode low in the sky; the moon had already risen. It glared at her, beckoned to her. Soon it would take her, but what of the transformation? She needed safety if she wished to preserve her clothes and her sword. During those few moments, she would be vulnerable.

The nausea clouded her thoughts; she had to banish it, and soon. Swallowing hard, biting her lip to create a new pain, to distract her from the nausea, she rushed headlong for the magic's center.

Her nausea grew, and she fought the urge to collapse, to spill out her guts onto the forest floor. A wind rose up, and leaves whipped through the trees, into her face, but she brushed them away, forcing herself deeper into the heart of the sorcerous maelstrom. She felt her teeth cut through her lip and tasted her own blood mixing with the bile that had begun to rise on its own into her mouth. The leaves grew wilder, and she resisted an insane urge to battle them with her sword. Just when she felt she had lost, that she would surely die at the hands of this unseen foe, she reached the magic's source:

In a clearing, at the heart of the whirling leaves, it stood, a beast like a bear with tentacles and an extra pair of eyes in its forehead. It watched her placidly; it didn't move, though its tentacles flailed about absently at its feet. She felt an agelessness in its gaze, and the nausea flowed through her now in waves. She bit harder on her lip and rushed at it, bringing her blade down into its neck.

She met no resistance; as she charged, it simply gazed at her. As she cleaved through it, no blood escaped. The wind of leaves seemed to sigh, and then the beast collapsed, and the nausea, the magic, fell with it.

She stood there, panting over the bear thing as the sun began to set and the sky darkened. After a moment, she staggered away, stripped off her clothes and wrapped them about her sword, fashioning a blood-caked bundle.

During this last conflict, she had lost Scacath's trail. After nightfall, she would retrace her steps. Now, she waited for darkness, for the wolf.

Magic

Arithea squeezed Megan's hand hard as the eyes of the sorceress fluttered open. The faer-Jotun smiled; then something like white fire ripped through her and she screamed.

Megan feebly tried to break free of Arithea's grasp; the grip had tightened and remained so as the faer-Jotun's wailing subsided into wracking sobs. She closed her eyes and spoke to the voice that had summoned her from the darkness. *What has happened?* she asked. *What pains you?*

He has fallen, Arithea answered after a moment. *Our northern border is breached.*

Megan opened her eyes and looked around at the crystal chamber. Everything was white. She had no idea of where she was, or even, truly, who she was with. Where was the ship? Where was Thyri? And Morgana . . . Thyri must have defeated her. How else might they have survived to come here?

She waited for Arithea to calm, then she asked of her these questions. How came she here? Arithea, still shaken, told her how Scacath had come to fi-Logath and bade them receive *Nightreaver* and heal its fallen sorceress. So they had done so, though not without caution. Arithea had met Thyri and discovered her curse. As for Eiriksdattir: the moon was full, and she was out in the land beyond their towers. She would return the day after next.

Who was 'he' who had fallen?

He had no name – the guardian of the north.

How had come Scacath? Through sorcery, on horseback, or by foot?

On foot – the times were dark, and those of the elder

races who traveled did so at grave risk. Powerful sorceries enhanced that risk, so Scacath had come alone, on foot.

From where?

Arithea looked at Megan, tragic realization creasing her brow. 'From the north,' she said. 'Oh, Megan – the wolf was pupil to the dark lady! Would she have tracked her? Could Thyri have done this?'

Megan closed her eyes again. *Yes, Arithea. If she has found traces of her teacher's passage, she could only have followed.*

Even with you here?

Even then.

What have I done!

Megan squeezed the hand weakly. *Will you avenge this – this guardian's death?*

For a long moment, Arithea did not answer. *No,* she responded at last. *She could not have known. But the damage cannot be undone; in a way, it is fitting. Ragnarok approaches, and Wyrd has decreed that fi-Logath will not be spared the carnage.*

She rose. 'I can find no hate within myself for your friend, but I must leave you now. You are weak. I will send food and drink – you will be attended.'

'I owe you my life,' Megan said. 'If I can repay you, Arithea, I shall.'

The faer-Jotun smiled weakly. 'I must go. The darkness threatens us all now, and I must perform castings and assess the dangers. When I am done, I shall return.'

'What of Thyri?'

'What of her? She has chosen this path for herself. I cannot follow, and you are yet weak.'

Arithea turned then, leaving Megan alone with her thoughts.

Rollo stirred in his sleep, then started, sitting up suddenly on the bed.

After his conversation in the garden with Rui, his lack of sleep the night before had overcome him, and he'd retired an hour before sunset. Now – what had wakened him? He sifted through his thoughts, trying to find traces of what he'd dreamed.

Nothing.

He rolled over and clutched the downy pillow. Some ghost, he thought, had wakened him. Some ghost within these crystal walls.

He yet felt exhausted, but again, sleep was long in coming.

The white wolf howled as it circled again the spot where Scacath's trail disappeared.

In the distance, something roared, returning her howl. From another direction came a distant crashing of trees.

At the spot, Thyri collapsed to the earth, tears streaming from her eyes as she forced her own mind up through the fierce, instinctive presence of the wolf. And as she did so, as her senses came to the fore, she found hope:

Magic. In the air, lingering in the trees. Magic in a sheet draped over the space between two bushes.

Woraag Grag, she remembered. *The shadow-paths. Scacath knew them as well!*

Slowly, she rose, sniffing the ground before the sheet of magic. Yes, she thought, through this gate, her teacher had gone. Growling softly, she leapt into the magic.

Still she was in a forest, but now the night sounds were familiar, less threatening. She gained again Scacath's scent, and she followed.

As if in a dream, she found herself on the same path she had walked with Woraag Grag a month before. She passed again the trees she knew, the places full of memories of Scacath, Astrid, Hugin and Munin – the ravens – Mind and Memory. And as she rounded the turn to the common, Munin stood before her.

'Thyri,' spake the raven, smiling. 'Come, she awaits you.' Quickly he turned, leading her away to the huts, to Scacath's hut, inside which she had never set foot.

He entered it, and without pausing she followed. Inside, she found only darkness . . . and magic – it swamped her senses. Scacath's magic, and the magic of someone else . . .

Suddenly, from the darkness a figure stepped. He was young, fair of skin and hair and with dark, fathomless eyes. But for those eyes, she knew him. In his hands, he held a black orb, the source of the magic darkness.

Ottar! she growled.

No, he said without speaking. *I am Morgana.* He smiled, his teeth shining white with their own light. They looked like fangs.

She growled and leapt for his throat, but an invisible hand smashed her down to the bare earth. It crushed her, forcing the air from her lungs, and strands of darkness reached in for her mind. She gasped as they strangled her thoughts. Within her, the wolf growled, then whimpered.

Not again, she heard Morgana insert calmly into the darkness. Then – nothing.

Morgana stood over the still form and laughed. After a moment, she waved her hand, and Munin responded, lifting up the body of the wolf and carrying it back out into the night.

Atale

Arithea did not return to Megan until morning. Once there, she sat silently as the sorceress slowly wakened, and even after Megan opened her eyes, it was long before she spoke.

In her eyes, Megan saw thinly veiled fear, but when she spoke, she asked first only of Megan's health. The sorceress replied that she felt stronger; she had used some of her ring's magics to speed her recovery.

'That is good,' Arithea replied. 'We may require your skills. An ancient evil has passed through here to a shadow world where, even now, it works its dark designs. As I worked my magics last night, I did not expect this. We must marshal our forces against this threat, and soon. We must banish or destroy it, for if it discovers our weakness to the north and summons our ancient enemies, we will have no defense.'

Megan eyed her curiously. 'What is the nature of this evil?' she asked.

'The Morrigan,' Arithea said distantly. 'She is free, and nearby.'

Megan started, bolting upright, grabbing Arithea's shoulders. 'Thyri!' she said desperately. 'Arithea, she wants Thyri! We have battled your ancient evil, Eiriksdattir and I! It was Morgana who defeated me!'

The faer-Jotun eyed her grimly. 'And you lived?'

'Without Thyri, I would not have escaped.'

'I am afraid that your friend may not do so this time. If the Morrigan has found her, she shall perish. We must strike out, but we cannot ride into battle against such a foe. Our only hope lies in sorcery, in annihilation of that half-world where the evil has taken refuge.'

'No!' Megan shook Arithea. 'You cannot do that! Let me try! Take me to our men. We shall go after her ourselves. You cannot condemn her.'

'You will fall again, daughter of light. She defeated you once.'

'I *must* try! My body may be weaker, but my magic is not. My talisman possesses its full power, and in the last battle I blundered, I let her win. I will not make the same mistake again.'

'You will need speed, but you cannot spell yourself there, else she will be prepared for your arrival.'

'Have you the steeds of my people – of your mother's people?'

'Yes.' She paused. 'You ask much, but I will grant your wish. They will be readied.' She gripped Megan's arm and closed her eyes. The sorceress felt strength flow through her, charging her with energy. 'There,' Arithea said weakly as she moved her hand away. 'I give you that as well, though now I am weakened. You must leave within the hour. If I do not sense your victory by this time tomorrow, I will handle the matter after my own fashion.'

Megan smiled at her and stood. 'Thank you, sorceress of fi-Logath. Lead me to *Nightreaver*'s crew. We must waste no time.'

They gathered in the dining chamber where they had been welcomed by the faer-Jotun two mornings before. Sokki sat next to Elinta, sqeezing her hand, staring solemnly at Megan, who sat between Donalu and Arithea. Next to Sokki sat his brother, and next to Horik, Renta.

Rollo sat between Rui and Gerald. He was first to break the silence. 'Where is Thyri?' he asked abruptly.

Megan tried to smile at him and failed. Eventually, she lowered her gaze. 'She is in danger, Rollo. That is why we are here.'

Arithea placed a hand on Megan's arm and began to speak. She told them of what she had seen through sorcery the night before, how she'd discovered, unexpectedly, sorcerous traces of Morgana's passage through their world, and she told the faer-Jotun how she planned to deal with the evil.

'But first,' Megan interrupted her, 'I wish to find Thyri. I fear that Morgana seeks her, or perhaps she has found her.'

'But she was with you!' Rollo protested angrily.

'No,' Arithea said. 'She sought solitude in the garden two nights before, and she has not returned. We fear that she found traces of something that she could not ignore.'

'What?'

'Scacath,' Megan said. 'The name will mean nothing to you, but to Thyri it was once everything. From Scacath, Thyri learned her skills. Somehow, Thyri's teacher learned of our plight and came here, to fi-Logath, to plead aid for us from the faer-Jotun. She came on foot, and Thyri is well capable of identifying scents in the forest, even those months old.'

'So' – Rollo stared at her – 'you're saying that she left us here, to chase after this Scacath?'

'Yes.'

'Perhaps into a trap? Laid by she whom you battled on that island?'

'Perhaps.'

Rollo rose. 'Then let us follow her!' He glared down at his companions. 'Why do you not rise with me? Did you not hear!'

Slowly, Rui stood. 'I will come,' he told Megan, 'though I do not know what use I will be.'

'If you encounter the Morrigan,' Arithea said darkly, 'probably no use at all. You are welcome to stay.'

Rui looked at Rollo, then shook his head. 'I will go.'

'And I,' Gerald said simply.

Sokki glanced at Elinta, then, silently, he rose. His brother followed.

Donalu cleared his throat. 'I also will go.'

Arithea turned on him, glaring. 'No! You are our strongest warrior, and I will not risk your death in this. If the Morrigan emerges victorious over a foe with you among their number, she will turn her wrath on our people.'

'But – '

'No!' she said flatly, turning to Megan. 'You and your people must go alone. You have one passing of the sun to complete this task.'

Grimly, Megan nodded.

The Tuathan steeds awaited them in the garden: six great black stallions, bridled in silver and shod with gold. As they stamped the earth, the ground shook, and their fiery eyes fell on their riders with cold intelligence.

Twenty *helfin* milled about the horses' hooves, running their hands through the thick coats, jumping up on the horses' necks to whisper in their ears. Slowly, Megan and the others approached.

'They will take you where you wish, sorceress,' Arithea called from behind them, 'but they will not leave this world. If you abandon them, they will wait for you one half-day, then they will return here.'

Megan paused and turned. 'Thank you, Arithea. We *shall* return.'

'Perhaps,' the faer-Jotun said indifferently. 'Be wary of your sorcery. Let not the Morrigan sense your approach.'

But how might I track Thyri?

Your steeds will follow her path.

Megan smiled and nodded, then turned back for the others. Silently, they mounted. After all were seated, without a word, the horses carried their riders swiftly northward.

Gerald, like the others, spent the majority of his time clinging to his mount's neck. When he did look around, the land was little more than an alarming blur. At times, they were pursued by creatures he could not have imagined, even in his nightmares. But the Tuathan steeds easily outdistanced all dangers, and after a time Gerald began to fear more for the pains he would know when he dismounted than anything else.

Rollo's thoughts revolved around Thyri, and his rage came and went. He would not lose her! Not like Fandis! He would face Loki himself if that was Wyrd's demand for Thyri's life.

Sokki found his hand moving often to the crysal hilt of the sword he wore at his side. He thought of Elinta, then of Thyri. At times, he wished he had stayed at fi-Logath; and with that thought, he felt ashamed.

Meanwhile, the sun made slow, relentless progress on its westward trek.

Near dusk, Megan's steed came to a sudden halt. As the others drew next to her, she dismounted, examining the ground. She looked around desperately. Why had they stopped?

Wait! she thought. A gateway . . . Cautiously, she cast a minor magic, and a place in the nearby air grew suddenly substantial – a faint, silvery latticework, like a spider's web. Behind her, she heard the others dismount.

'What is it?' Rollo asked, shaking the stiffness from his legs.

She turned to him. 'From here,' she said, 'we must continue on foot.'

Horik kicked out the ache and felt spears of pain shoot up his back. He stamped his feet against the ground and staggered away from his steed, into the bushes.

As he relieved himself, the whispering began in his mind. *Come,* it said. *They do not need you. Come and rest.* To his horror, his foot stepped forth on its own. His other foot followed. Out of the corner of his eye, he saw a dark thing in the trees – a raven, watching him.

Come . . . His pace grew more rapid. He wanted to call out to the others, but his mouth wouldn't open. *Sleep,* said the voice. The sky grew dark, and his limbs heavy. He collapsed to the ground and felt something alight on his back, talons digging into his flesh, pulling him upward.

Sleep!

The darkness enveloped him, and his thoughts faded away.

As they gathered about Megan, Sokki looked about desperately. 'Where's Horik!' he whispered. 'Where is my brother?' He turned for the wood, but Rollo grabbed his arm.

'Quiet!' the Viking told him. 'He knows where we are – he will find us.'

'We cannot wait!' Megan said.

Sokki turned on her. 'We cannot leave him!'

'We cannot embark on a search either, my friend!' Rollo seethed in his ear. 'If some ill has befallen him, it would then find us, one by one. Your brother is a Viking, we will wait a few moments, then go on. If you wish to wait longer, here with the horses, you may!'

Megan closed her eyes and risked another spell. Sokki's brother, she discovered, was nowhere near. 'I do not sense his presence,' she said after a moment. 'Perhaps it is he who has gone on without us.'

Sokki lowered his eyes. 'No,' he said. 'He is dead. I have lost another brother.'

Rollo squeezed his arm. but Sokki shrugged him off and drew his crystal sword. 'Let us go,' he seethed. 'And let the evils of this place beware, for the last son of Gunnar shall not so easily be vanquished!'

Megan smiled sadly, then asked for each of their hands on her arm. As they clutched her, she stepped through the gateway, pulling them through behind her.

Ice

. . . into a raging snowstorm. The flakes pelted against them like tiny shards of ice; the cold burrowed through to their bones, freezing out the aches of the journey, replacing them with a duller yet more alarming pain.

'Fimbulwinter!' Rollo shouted over the whipping winds.

No, Gerald thought, as weariness flooded through him. It was his dream – that dream he had had that morning after he'd joined Thyri. It was all here: the snows, the cold, the weariness, and the feeling of eternal hardship. And Megan's voice now, calling to him, urging him to move forward. Something horrible, he knew, awaited them out there in the snow. He forced another step . . .

The sky was dark, the clouds and the storm blotting out the little sunlight that remained. Megan's voice came to him distantly. He hurried to reach it.

While the others rushed after Megan, Sokki heard Horik's voice calling him from the side. He turned for it, his mind filling with memories of his youth, of his long days in weather like this, playing outside the family hall, in the snows, with his brothers . . .

In the distance, he saw a figure. As he drew near it, the storm fell away, and his feet touched down on grass. In the waning sunlight, Horik awaited him.

The Viking stood, his blade drawn, smiling at him. 'Come to me, Brother,' Horik said. 'See what I have found.'

Sokki watched his eyes; they were hollow, vacant. They stared past him. 'Horik!' he cried. 'Look at me!'

'I am, Brother,' he said. His eyes did not move, did not focus.

Sokki raised his sword and moved cautiously forward.

'I have found Ottar,' Horik said. 'We are three again.'

'Ottar is dead,' Sokki said softly. He crouched, then lashed out at Horik's sword, seeking to disarm him. But their blades did not touch as Horik danced back, then whirled into an attack.

Sokki fought him silently, tears streaming down his cheeks. Horik had the strength of a demon, his attack forcing Sokki ever back, back toward the blizzard. At first, Sokki sought only to disarm; he was ever the better of both his brothers, but never had Horik possessed such strength! His attacks, even blocked by Elinta's crystal blade, sent waves of jarring pain through his arms. But the crystal blade held under an onslaught that iron could never hope to withstand.

Even so, Sokki could not force himself on the offensive. Horik fought demonically for blood, to the death, his eyes vacant of recognition. Once, as they locked blades, Sokki's cheek grazed his brother's, and the contact stung him, so cold was his brother's flesh.

Then, Horik's sword bit into his side. Sokki backed away, and the battle fury possessed him. Horik's face melted into a featureless head, and his body became a shadow. Only the sword in the air before him was real. At it, Sokki lashed out, matching his opponent stroke for stroke, Elinta's gift whirling, glinting with the sun's waning light.

And then – blood. Red streams flying off the end of the blade. He struck again and again until the lifeless figure before him collapsed to the ground.

Only then did the face again become Horik's. When Sokki recognized it, he fell to the blood-soaked grass next to his brother and cried.

A brilliant, silver explosion filled the sky before Gerald, and suddenly he could see.

No trace of the blizzard remained, not even snow on the ground. Ahead, he heard dark laughter. As the shower of silver faded, he picked out figures: Megan, Rui, and Rollo faced – something that vaguely resembled Ottar. Megan and the others had reached a clearing; Gerald raced to join them.

The thing that looked like Ottar had dark, scarred skin. Ottar's features were twisted by the demonic forces behind them. From the thing, came the laughter. In one hand, it held a dark globe from which writhing, black strands escaped like tortured, nightmarish snakes.

It spoke to Megan. 'You've come to try again?' it asked derisively. 'You did not learn?'

On the ground, next to it, Thyri lay. At first, Gerald thought she was dead, then, he noticed her head move slightly to the side.

On the western horizon, the sun began to set.

Rollo glanced from Ottar to Thyri, roared, and began a charge. As he moved forward, one of Rui's arrows whizzed past his ear; as the arrow neared its target, it exploded in a burst of flame. As Rollo flew at Ottar, an unseen force smashed him to the ground. Pain seared through his sides as his ribs cracked anew. But he kept his eyes forward, and he struggled to crawl closer to the thing that wore Ottar's body.

Megan answered Morgana's questions with her magic. With a wave, the silver streamed forth. This time, instead of fire, her assault met the black power of the orb of Babd.

From her ring, the silver flowed effortlessly, engulfing the black. She poured it out as resistance mounted.

You cannot defeat me, Morgana sneered in her mind. *I am eternal.*

So, Megan returned, *am I.*

Deep within her darkness, Thyri heard the summons of the moon. The beast joined her in her prison, howling in her mind, clawing her way out to the surface.

She felt no pain, but she pressed forth with the beast. Perhaps, together, they could escape the evil that had defeated them the night before. But, as she thought this, she didn't believe it. Only when the wolf opened her eyes, when she saw the cascading silver, did she know true hope.

Megan! she thought. Again, confronted with the evil from the dark tower, Megan had joined her side. Did she dream? No – Arithea must have healed her friend. Then, this was real. But real also was her inability to move. Before her, she was the whiteness of her foreleg. She looked up at Morgana; around the demoness, arrows flared and fell harmlessly to the ground. The archer was with her. The others as well?

She couldn't tell; she couldn't move.

Rollo heard his own silent scream in his mind as he watched Thyri's transformation. What had Morgana done to her? He pushed forward, every muscle on fire. Slowly, he inched closer to his goal.

Gerald watched the scene unfold with mounting horror. Megan's sorcery met Morgana's and the two forces clashed like juggernauts in the air. All the while, Morgana laughed. The demoness toyed with the sorceress, but Megan was undaunted. She fought back with fury, exploiting every opening in Morgana's black cloak.

Then flames began to spring up from the ground at Megan's feet, and the earth beneath her rocked and buckled. She dodged away from the fires, struggling to keep her footing. Streamers of black fire surged through the sudden gaps in the silver, and Gerald heard Megan gasp as a black flare lashed across her leg. His eyes opened wide as he witnessed Megan's blood flowing from her wound.

If the sorceress fell, he knew, so would they all. Drawing his blade, he dove into the fray; Morgana brushed him aside and down as if he were a fly. He found himself, like Rollo, pinned to the earth, unable to move, able only to watch Morgana methodically turn back Megan's weakening assaults.

And to watch, also, Rui exhaust his supply of arrows against Morgana's impenetrable shield.

Growls escaped Thyri's throat as what silver she *could* see gradually grew black. Megan was losing, and this time,

Morgana would not be careless, would not give Thyri a chance.

Still she struggled, and then a thought came to her – another hope. *Call to me when you walk the shadow-paths,* someone had once told her . . .

Scacath's world lay at a crossroad of those paths; this she had learned all too well. If ever she were to summon him . . .

Woraag Grag! she screamed in her mind. *Pohati! Aid me!*

She looked up at Morgana, wondering if she had heard. But no, the demoness, enshrouded in black, was too intent on her battle.

Thyri, trapped at her feet, was harmless.

Megan stumbled to the ground, quickly drawing her magic around her in a shield, using it to douse the fires that Morgana ignited constantly around her feet. And still the black fire pounded against her, consuming her silver. Though she had been careful to conserve, her ring had scant power left.

Especially if she desired to use it to attack. If she ever got an opening.

She crouched behind her dwindling defenses, desperately seeking another tactic, hoping vainly that Morgana's talisman would exhaust itself as had her ring before.

But there seemed no end to the black onslaught. And even were there one, Morgana retained all the other powers at her command.

Bravely, Megan rose to her feet and lashed out anew, drawing on the strength Arithea had gifted her. For a while, it would aid her. After that, she would have only what was left in her ring, and the simple magics that had proven useless in her last –

Suddenly, a howl erupted in the air. Thyri! Megan thought. She lashed out again, clearing the black from the space before her. The noise had startled Morgana; Megan could see her now, looking around for the howl's source. Thyri yet was pinned at her feet.

As Morgana looked away, a streak of gray flew through

the air behind her head. The gray met the source of the black magic; then a deafening scream split the night as the black orb, and the hand that held it, was ripped from Morgana's arm.

The gray steak landed. For a moment, Megan recognized it as another wolf, then the black engulfed it and a horrible howl emerged from the darkness to join in chorus with Morgana's scream.

As for the demoness, she looked at Megan, dazed. Motion erupted at her feet; Thyri dove at her, tearing out her throat with her fangs. Rollo's sword cleaved through her legs, and she began to fall.

Then began the true battle: Morgana, given a brief respite, would again escape. Megan poured her magic forth, bolstering it with the last of Arithea's gift. She wrapped her fallen enemy in a silver cage and squeezed it shut, trapping the horrible soul. Even now, it fought maniacally, and the battle raged on as Megan emptied her ring of its power.

The others watched in terror as agony creased the brow of the sorceress. Rollo struck the silver mass with his sword, but the impact did naught but throw him back to the ground. Morgana's struggling inside was plainly visible as the magic contorted and pulsated, and an eerie wail filled the night.

They watched, waited, and prayed.

Megan fell to her knees, and still they watched. Morgana's struggling grew wilder. Then, suddenly, another was among them; Gerald turned to see Sokki charging into the clearing, his crystal blade held high. He dove at the silver cocoon, slicing through it with the blade that had slain three Jotun before Elinta's brother had fallen.

The wail grew in intensity, and the contortions of the magic grew more erratic, but Gerald, watching Megan, saw her smile.

Sokki struck again. And again. Slowly, the wail subsided, and the silver ball shrunk until, at last, Megan squeezed it into nothingness.

The sorceress collapsed back then, panting, onto the charred grass.

For a while, all stood still. Gerald's eyes strayed slowly, from the spot into which Morgana had disappeared to the beast that, earlier, had been Thyri. The white wolf, whining softly, sniffed around the charred remains of what had once been one of its kind.

What had once been Pohati. What had once been immortal.

Thyri looked up into Gerald's gaze and whined again, then turned and bounded into the wood.

Thus perished Arthur's bane, and thus did *Nightreaver*'s crew learn fully of Thyri's nature. With the deaths of Horik and Woraag Grag, there was little cause for celebration.

Though we did not wish to stay in that place, we spent the night in Scacath's clearing, awaiting Thyri's return in the morning. She arrived among us as if it were she who had been defeated, as if *she* had perished in the battle the night before. And she mourned, as well, for Woraag Grag. Of all among us, only Megan truly understood.

Another appeared that morning as we prepared to leave. A dark-skinned warrior – Munin, with whom Thyri had trained in swordplay in her youth. He *had* been there; his appearance before Thyri (and his abduction of Horik) had been no illusion. Munin told her that Scacath had abandoned her haven two weeks before to join Odin's host in Valhalla, to await the coming of the end. He had returned only to gather the last of their things, but Morgana had surprised him and stolen away his mind.

From then, until this morning, he had thought no thought of his own.

Necessity bade us depart quickly, else the Tuathan steeds would be gone. Thyri said her farewell to Munin, solemnly covered the remains of Woraag Grag with a blanket of leaves, and came with us. The day's ride back to fi-Logath was exhausting, and, when we arrived, we spoke hardly a word, not to each other, nor to anyone else.

During our stay, the faer-Jotun treated us well, but they remained distant. True, we had defeated the Morrigan, but we also had drawn her there. And they all knew by now how Thyri had laid open their northern frontier. When Arithea told her what she had done, Thyri apologized, but the damage had been done. Thyri offered to stay and fight for them, but Arithea did not welcome that suggestion warmly.

Two mornings after that, *Nightreaver* set sail, Megan again at the foredeck. Once past the mouth of the river, into the sea, she spelled us out of Jotunheim, back onto the seas of Midgard, the seas which we knew.

By then, we had lost all the sons of Gunnar. Sokki, bereft of his brothers, remained in fi-Logath with Elinta. He shed tears the morning we departed, but the tears were as much for himself as for us. The burden on his heart was heavy, and long in lifting.

As for us – well, the world, for a time, was ours. Our new knowledge of Thyri's dual nature did nothing to sever our loyalty to her. Indeed, it made us stronger, for we were now able to understand her moods, to understand when she left our company at first light of a full moon.

Later, when we docked at a Frisian port, we learned that, while scarcely more than a month had passed in Jotunheim, several years had come and gone in Midgard. The year was now 884 by the calendar of the One God. Much remained to transpire.

Here, briefly, I set down my pen.

3: Bloodfang

for Tana

BOOK VII

QUEEN OF THIEVES

Sometimes I wish I could start over. Not with my life – that is too much to ask – but with this, with Thyri's story, my story. I've only had this one chance, and time is running out. Still, I fear I've failed in every way. I read what's already written and weep at my words; they haven't captured the *life* of it all. Immobile they are, dead on their pages of parchment, and so what use are they? Who will read them and understand? Whoever does will know Thyri only through me, through this work, as poor and lifeless as it is. I want them to see her smile, smell her hair, feel her presence, taste her agonies and passions. But I've been vain; I've stained her story by betraying myself in the words. Can you understand that? If so, you're beyond me, because I'm not sure I do. I only know that, so far, I've written selfishly; I've written, I realize, so that I, not you, might regain Thyri's world. Lifeless ramblings I've written, so I would start over and make Thyri more alive for you, but I can't. And if I could, my heart tries to tell me that I would fail, again. Words can mean only so much.

Have my years made me wise? I don't think so; I still proceed on this reckless course, racing for my destiny. I think, though, that I've learned love, if love is a wisdom. My wife – it is she who has lifted me above this thing I do – she lets me see it clearly, lets me see my selfishness and injustices, and helps me understand why I do what I do, even though it pains her terribly.

'And, Gerald,' she says, 'for good or ill, you must continue.'

For good or ill.

I continue:

Warriors

Thyri stooped to the ground and touched the grass thoughtfully. She was closer and gaining, only minutes behind. She tested the air for magic; it was everywhere, the air a latticework of subtle, shifting sensations. Given time, she might separate the peculiar qualities she sought, but she didn't have time, not if she wanted to keep gaining. Still, she took a moment to stand and savor the thrill of the chase, begun hours before in the early morning. It felt so good to be out of the city! And so close to her prize as well.

She wiped the sweat from her forehead, lifted her hair a moment to let cool air onto her neck, and started off again.

From the wood she was watched, her watcher full of fear and awe and reverence. Moments before, he had observed the chased; by rights – and orders – he should have followed then. But to be caught by the chaser, from behind and unawares? No, Ai'reth was a warrior and not that stupid.

This one – the chaser, the hunter – short by low-blood standards, but his first sight of her made him tremble. She was high-trained. Tuathan-trained by her stance, and she carried a dwarven sword, very *fei* and alarming, for why did she have it? How had she come by it, and what brought her here? The hunt, surely, but how could a low-born know how to follow? He would have expected a dragon of Svartalfheim, or Nidhogg himself – considering the darkness of the days – before this.

Still, this usurping of order could not explain his trembling, the way his hands had shook and his heart had thumped in his chest. That had come from a glimpse at the battle inside her, the clash of dark and light that afflicted all low-borns of Midgard – the Midgard curse the Sylvan jokingly called it – the playground of the High Gods, the mortal pawns the Creators had given the high-born to test their powers – the *yangyi* as Ai'reth had once heard it called by an initiate of the Ishtan mysteries.

The *yangyi* of the low-born, always before a joke whenever Ai'reth had seen it: so weak it was, so pathetic and dim, scarcely bright enough to power a beating heart, and so easy to twist and shape. Even when the light was strong, it could flicker out in the most simple magical breeze, or, on its own, with no help, continue its battle with the defeated dark, nurturing it, keeping it alive in a phantom battle that only the Creators could possibly understand. Ai'reth certainly didn't. His spirit was a bright flame, the last traces of darkness banished aeons before, in his childhood. He was a bright warrior, and no trick within himself could turn him. He knew this well because his sense for spirits – light, dark, or *yangyi* – was the finest he knew. Dark masquerading as light had never deceived *him*, and whenever S'kiri desired a second judgment, it was Ai'reth she summoned.

As the woman-warrior with the dwarven sword started away, Ai'reth still trembled at the memory of what had happened when he'd opened his sense to her *yangyi*. It had struck him like the fist of a giant; its light had burned his eyes, and its darkness had enveloped him so suddenly and completely that he'd almost lost control and cried out. He'd had to *fight* just to shut off his talent and regain his normal senses, and after that he could only look at her in wonder. This low-born of Midgard – for she certainly was that – turned the Sylvan joke of *yangyi* into a joke of itself. Her spirit was as wild and strong as any he'd seen in any realm. Her darkness made him fear for the strength of his own light. Her light urged him to fall on his knees and beg her to take him into her breast, but this he didn't do for she moved away too quickly.

When she was gone, he scrambled from behind his leaf-shield and into the clearing where she'd stopped. He, like her, touched the grass, then he bent close to it and sniffed, finding her strong, low-born scent. Before, it might have choked him, the way a forest-dweller might crinkle his nose in the midst of pigs, but now, after he'd *seen* her, he wanted her smell to be stronger, to surround him as if it might solve her mystery, as if he might find in it some clue to her presence here and what that could mean to himself and his people.

Some months before, he had heard it said that low-borns had brought down the great Tuathan sorceress Morgana, not merely capturing her, not merely defeating her, but actually *slaying* her, banishing her power and influence from all worlds. He'd laughed at the tale then; now he could almost believe it. This was his thought as, carefully, as silently as a cat, he became the hunter of the hunter and followed in the chase.

Thyri's heart beat faster as the trail twisted, doubled back, and twisted again, back onto the shadow-path. When the world suddenly shifted she barely broke her stride, and then only to make sure she didn't rush headlong off a cliff or into a pool of fire. Instead, the shift dropped her at the *bottom* of a fifty-foot cliff, and her senses urged her upward. Thyri grinned and cursed; if she didn't push her body to its limits she'd lose all the time she'd gained. Still cursing, she attacked the wall of rock, ignoring the screams of her muscles, racing haphazardly ever upward.

At the top, she found a field of barley. The ripe crop filled her nostrils, as did the tang of magic, but she didn't lose the fresh scent of her quarry, and she kept on its trail, her muscles fatigued for the first time all day.

Ten steps into the barley, the earth erupted in a shower of black and silver that fell on her, wrapped around her, and lifted her into the air. She struggled against the sorcerous grip as it tightened, and through gaps in the sorcery's claws, she saw her prey floating level with her, another ten paces ahead.

Megan of Kaerglen Isle smiled at her as the sorcery continued to flow from the ring finger of her raised hand.

Thyri fought fiercely, trying to swim through the air toward the sorceress, but the magic blocked her, and then suddenly, unexpectedly, the bones of her right shoulder wrenched and a dark hunger began to grow in her stomach. 'Stop!' Thyri screamed. 'Megan, please!'

The sorcerous grip loosened, and Thyri felt herself falling slowly. Still, her vision went red and her hunger grew as the beast within her struggled to break free. She glanced at Megan and felt saliva fill her mouth, and she screamed, spitting out, fighting to beat down the wolf's sudden rush of bloodlust as the magic laid her gently down among the barley and quickly retreated.

For a few moments, Megan hung still in the air, watching her friend on the ground as she shook and whimpered and finally let out a strangled howl before going still. Even then Megan waited a little longer, until Thyri looked up at her wearily, before descending.

'Goddess,' Megan whispered as she smoothed Thyri's brow. 'Can that happen so easily?'

Thyri felt tears rising to her eyes as she nodded. 'Not *so* easily though; only when I'm beaten.' Hadn't she told Megan about the other times? About the time on the *Black Rabbit* when the wolf had emerged in broad daylight and slain the entire crew before leaving her? *Oh, Megan – it would have killed you!*

'Never,' the sorceress said softly. 'Our love is too strong.'

'I'll be all right in a moment.'

Quiet! There's no hurry.

Megan stretched out and laid her head on Thyri's breast. The heartbeat within was rapid; she ran her fingers gently over Thyri's bare stomach until the heartbeat slowed.

'Careful,' Thyri whispered distantly. 'You're starting something.'

'Thyri?'

'Yes?'

'Did I do well?'

'What do you mean?'

'Did I practice well? Did I make any mistakes? If it were a real battle?'

Thyri laughed lightly, remembering herself that morning when she'd told Megan to play for real, to take it seriously even if it was a game, to start *thinking* like a warrior because if she didn't she was going to get herself killed one day. She'd gone on: *'Then next time we get in real trouble, I want you at my side, not near death and on your back and useless! Use your sorcery, but don't ever abuse it. Conserve it, don't throw it around as if it's boundless because it isn't.'* Megan had taken the hint. Aside from a couple of very subtle sorcerous attempts to throw Thyri off the trail, Thyri had encountered nothing of Megan's ring magic during the chase until the final confrontation. The sorceress had conjured no beasts to guard her path, laid no elaborate traps, and chosen her own field of battle, in a place where she knew Thyri would be weakened after the exertion of climbing a cliff. Thyri actually found herself wondering if Megan had purposefully slowed before the cliff, allowing her to gain so that when she faced the wall of rock, the need for swift climbing would be all the more urgent. Thyri knew that her friend hadn't climbed; the sorceress had floated, spelled herself fairly effortlessly to the top.

'Yes,' Thyri said finally. 'You did well.' She unclasped her weapon's belt, grabbed Megan's shoulders, and pushed off with her legs so they rolled and tumbled through the barley. 'You ambushed me!' Thyri said, landing on top.

Megan nodded, smiling. 'I did, didn't I?'

Thyri touched her cheek, traced her lips with her fingers. 'You did,' she said. 'And you caught me.'

Megan growled playfully. 'I'm glad.'

Ai'reth

He peeked through the tall stalks, watching the two women, glad the hunt had been but a game. He kept very still; he didn't fear discovery in particular – no, his charms would hide him from all scrutiny but the sorceress's ring. He kept still, rather, out of reverence for fear of shattering the beauty of what he saw. He watched power mingle with power, power caressing power, and, wonder of wonders, the powers were both low-born! At first, when he'd seen the sorceress race by him, he'd thought her Tuathan, but she had low-blood in her; he could definitely smell it now, and her *yangyi* – it was nearly as strong as the other's, though much lighter.

What had he found this day? What had he witnessed? Two powers at play while such darkness hung over all the worlds?

He watched awhile longer, dared to murmur a quick charm of following, backed away, and scrambled down the cliff's face while the two women lingered on their bed of barley.

Back in his familiar wood, Ai'reth wondered more deeply. The powers he'd witnessed – they were not low-born powers. And the white-haired one – so obviously Tuathan in style, in grace. Likewise the taller one of dark hair. Perhaps they were hybrid, like he and his people; women of high blood were wont at times to lay with anything it seemed. He'd once heard of elven owl-people . . . But more was amiss than that. He had to know more before returning to S'kiri with any news of this. Perhaps there were prophecies . . . So he wondered and wandered. The birds in the trees chattered of the dark armies; he shut them out and only thought of them again when the chattering stopped.

Instinctively, in the sudden silence, he froze, beaming out his talent in all directions. The cloud of darkness hung on a limb directly over his head. He shaped it; *vulture,* he thought. *Or dark raven? Scout or warrior?* He remained still, waiting for the flyer to move. It had to be a scout; a warrior would have fallen on him by now. But it was so high; if he attacked, he would surely miss, and it would fly back to its masters with news of him, or worse, stay high above and watch his every move. That thought burned in him; he would not be rendered powerless by a stupid bird!

Slowly, he began to look around, but never upward. He stretched his arms out, then plopped down on the grass under the tree and decided to eat, opening a pouch full of dried rabbit meat. He ate slowly, hoping the flyer would grow bored and fly away with nothing more than news of a hungry felnin. But the stubborn scout stayed high above, out of reach and unmoving.

Time for tricks! Ai'reth thought angrily. *Stupid tricks for a stupid bird!* He muttered a minor charm of making, and a white spell-mage leaped from the bushes across from him.

'Evil felnin!' he had the spell-mage shout at him. *'You face the great Zesthistedamir! I have slain dragons and giant armies, and now I slay you with but a click of my fingers!'*

The spell-mage clicked its fingers, and Ai'reth toppled, wide-eyed and motionless, onto his side. In a colorful explosion of smoke and fire, the spell-mage disappeared.

Now Ai'reth stared directly up at the giant raven. That's good! he chuckled silently. *Stupid bird now does two things. It flies away with news of the great Zesthistedamir, or it comes down for a closer look. Either way, Ai'reth wins!*

Ai'reth stared blankly; slowly, the raven flapped away. Ai'reth chuckled again; probably the raven knew him, his name and his greatness, for why would a scout of the dark powers shadow an unknown felnin? Now to all the dark powers Ai'reth was dead. He would teach them in the end.

He leaped to his feet, but before he could start away, a silver wall sprang up before him. He stamped on the ground. 'What now?' he cried out. Behind him, he heard light laughter and clapping.

He spun. 'Dryad!' he growled angrily. 'Take down wall!'

She was pretty with light brown hair and almond eyes and olive skin. 'You save me,' she giggled. 'You're so handsome! What is your name?'

She stepped toward him; he quickly pulled out a knife and waved it in the air between them. 'No time for dryads! Don't you know? Is war on all worlds!'

'But you ate in my shade! That means you love me?'

'Love nobody! Take down wall, or I slice your tree!'

The dryad burst out crying. 'Am I not beautiful?' she sobbed.

'Beautiful, ugly, who cares? Take down wall!'

He lunged at her, and she stepped back, merging into her tree's trunk. As the silver barrier began to dissipate, Ai'reth leaped through it and back out onto the path. 'Ravens and dryads,' he mumbled, brushing traces of silver from his vest. 'What did Ai'reth do to deserve such things?'

Now, he thought, calming down. Now what? Prophecies, yes; no more time to waste! He would seek the oracle.

She dwelt in a lake a short distance from Ai'reth's home. He reached her shores and summoned her: 'Klorista! Ai'reth the felnin calls!'

Only silence answered.

'She sleeps,' he sighed wearily. 'Must wake all the powers of Light? Is Ai'reth alone the ready one?'

He sat on the lake's mossy shore and took out his pipe, packing it carefully with his herbs of calming. Lighting the herbs, he began to will his angers and frustrations away. He exhaled the smoke out over the water, watched it swirl there and mix with the lake's light mist. He concentrated on the water's light lapping on the shore, then reached out gently with his magic and set the lillies below spinning, making a slow, dancing circle.

From his belt, Ai'reth took his finger drum and brushed it lightly a few times before starting into a rhythmic tapping.

He straightened his spine and closed his eyes, keeping the image of the spinning lillies before him, making them into a tunnel, and opening the tunnel into a world of light on the far side. *Klorista!* he beckoned. *Come forth!*

His drumming grew louder and more resonant. Light swirled at the end of tunnel. *Who calls?* she whispered.

It is Ai'reth, dear Goddess.

Ai'reth? What brings you, felnin?

I have seen low-borns of great power, and I do not understand such strong yangyi. *The great wars come, Goddess.*

Low-borns? Show them to me.

Ai'reth conjured up likenesses of the two women and sent them into the tunnel of lillies in his mind.

Ah, said Klorista. *I understand. What troubles you?*

Who are they? Why are they?

They are low-borns. One of Light, the other of Chaos.

But so strong!

The High Ones made them so.

Will they fight in the wars?

They do so already.

On whose side?

I cannot say.

Ai'reth sighed. *What now for me, then?*

Look to your people.

But the worlds are ending! All will perish! So spake the Sybil. Fimbulwinter *descends on Asgard!*

Ah, Klorista countered. *But not Midgard. What does that mean, little felnin?*

I do not know.

The One God grows strong there on Midgard, Ai'reth. He keeps the fimbulwinter away. He may yet keep the great war away as well. What if Surt burns all the nine worlds save one? Save Midgard? Will the One God then stay there and let the old mysteries be reborn from the ashes as the Sybil foretold? Will he allow his enemies to grow strong anew and threaten his hold on Midgard? I think if all prophecies come to pass, we will destroy ourselves and nothing more.

But Midgard is battleground! One God can't rule all!

All battles may be won, dear felnin. And the One God has his opponent, as Odin has Loki. And there are other gods against which we do not war, but the One God does.

What gods?

Do not think of them. Think of us. Think of the questions I have asked, for they are very good questions.

Tell Loki to think of your questions! Is his fault!

Loki is blind to prophecy. He feels he will cheat it.

Can he?

Perhaps. He is not all dark; he is part Chaos. Go now, Ai'reth. Look to your people and think. Act if you like; thoughts cannot save much.

But what of the low-borns!

He had no answer. The circle of lillies fell apart in his mind, and he was left on the lakeshore, staring out over the water.

The birds in the trees chattered again of dark armies, and Ai'reth cursed softly, wishing they'd be still.

Magic

'Aha,' Megan said, stopping suddenly near the trunk of a large oak. 'I think I've found one!'

'One what?'

'A *felnina*. The reason I brought you all the way out here.'

Thyri's eyes followed Megan's into the high, dense thicket beyond the oak. She raised a puzzled eyebrow and laughed. 'A *what?*'

'A *felnina* – a quest-house. Very witchy,' Megan whispered playfully.

Thyri nodded gravely, then they both burst out in a fit of uncontrolled laughter. The light sound filled the air as Megan pushed against the huge trunk and the bark gave way.

'Loki's tits!' Thyri laughed, then, 'Wait!' as Megan disappeared inside the trunk.

Inside, the old wood twisted into a stairwell that led up, then opened into a large natural chamber on the far side of the tree. The walls and ceiling were of interwoven polished hardwood branches, the walls stepping upward and outward in ledges like an ampitheater. A gentle creek flowed in from the far side, and it was blocked into a pool by an intricate circle of stones that both dammed it and guided it to drainage holes in the moss-covered floor. Moss, in fact, was everywhere, on the floor, on the ledges, even dangling down through gaps in the ceiling. In places, it was several inches thick.

Megan removed her boots and motioned for Thyri to do the same, then she dove out onto the floor and sprawled on her back, smiling with deep satisfaction. 'Yes,' she sighed, closing her eyes. 'This is what I wanted to feel again!'

Thyri knelt, pulling off her boots, then touching the moss thoughtfully. 'There's magic everywhere, more than outside. In the walls, the floor, even in that water,' she said, pointing.

'Oh, yes.' Megan's words were dreamy, distant. 'Very gentle magic. Magic to soothe, to refresh. Look – by the door there is food.'

Thyri looked. There were bushels of nuts and berries, and pouches of dried meat, even three small casks of mead. She stepped out onto the moss with her bare feet; its coolness washed upward, unknotting the tired muscles in her calves and thighs. When she fell next to Megan, it was almost as if the moss pulled her down into its embrace. She had never felt such sensations; she recalled the hut where she'd studied under Scacath, where she and Astrid would lounge on layers of furs. She thought of the pool in Castle Kaerglen, and of the other pools and quiet places she had discovered on her travels. Nothing compared to this.

The moss almost grew into her; it massaged her, staying ever cool. Its scent was like honey infiltrating her mind; the trauma of the afternoon – when the wolf had almost taken her over – grew distant, a memory years old, one that could no longer hurt her, or even one that belonged to somebody else, some other existence outside herself, a tragic existence with which she'd shared life for a time, but which she'd now abandoned for a future of simple, happy contentment. Suddenly, she felt she almost glowed. She felt infinitely safe. No danger outside could enter and harm her. She felt that even if the moon were to rise, her curse would not be able to take her here, to twist her body and mind in this peaceful place. The curse, perhaps, was not even hers . . .

'Where are we, Meg?' Thyri asked at last. The words bubbled out of her, as if rising from great depths. She heard them – the words of somebody else. Reason began to rear up and survey the unnatural peace within her.

'Alfheim,' the sorceress whispered. 'I led you all the way to the edge of Alfheim.'

'I mean this place.' There it was again, that alien voice. Thyri began to grow uncomfortable. All this peace began to hurt. Little voices began telling her she was good, pure, a servant of Light. She should forget her curse, the killings, the bloodlust – they meant nothing, minor failures of a past no longer hers. In the future, all was bright, love and light and soft moonlight. No worries at all . . .

'The *felnina*?' Megan rolled onto her side, placed a cupped hand on Thyri's shoulder, and rested her chin there. 'The quest-houses of old . . . they are everywhere, some older even than the Tuatha de Danaan. The felnin make them; I believe they live in them for a time, and then move on. But always they tend their old homes, keeping them fit for travelers who know how to find them.'

'Who are the felnin?' The little voices? No, the voices were magic, trying to deceive her, to make her forget. They were gentle voices, warm voices, the voices of spells meant to soothe, but they instead inflicted pain. They wanted her to *forget* the trials of the past, to look to the future; maybe for Megan that was a good thing, but for her now? Too much horror lurked within, too much terrible death, and she couldn't risk forgetting it, not in the complete sense the *felnina* demanded. She could never forget, because forgetting an enemy was the surest way to lose the battle. Maybe this place *could* shield them from the external world, from external enemies, but internal enemies? Thyri couldn't let herself believe it; her worst enemy was ever within herself.

'I don't really know,' Megan answered innocently, unaware of Thyri's internal conflict. 'An elder race, a light race. They are the unseen of the fair peoples, shadow-warriors. Those who have seen them say nothing, out of respect. They serve the forces of Light in their own way. Lore says the Creators made them, even before they made Buri and placed him in his block of ice.'

'Odin's grandfather?'

'I've told you before; common lore is seldom trustworthy.'

Later, Thyri gazed into the shallow pool. Little silver fish swam there, feeding off the moss that grew down over the rock. She touched the water with her fingers, and the fish, curious, swam up for a closer look. When she lifted her fingers out, the fish scattered, flashes of silver radiating out from the center like the flying points of a star.

She wanted to smile, but that *felnina*'s magic still taunted her. She felt shaken; she'd almost believed, almost let herself slip into fantasy and think her curse away, as if it were only one long, bad dream. And as she remembered that feeling, another part of her longed for it again, pleaded with her to submit to it, to be carried away into happiness. Hadn't she forgotten her curse at times before? Hadn't she loved and let the worries melt away? Wasn't that what she lived for? Yes, yes, and yes, but not like this, never so fully and disarmingly, never quite so euphorically.

The magic of the *felnina* made her feel helpless, like a child or a baby. It tried to force innocence upon her, an innocence she knew she couldn't keep because it wasn't real. For those who once lived here, perhaps for them, this was the most wonderful magic of all, so wonderful that they kept it alive for others, weary travelers, elven warriors, white sorceresses like Megan. For them, this innocent comfort could be transcendent, but not for Thyri. She couldn't accept the helplessness, but she couldn't help longing for the careless oblivion.

Yet she couldn't succumb. She would want to keep that feeling forever, to take it away with her and carry it wherever she went. Right now, the memory of *almost* having it hurt. She felt how she imagined a blind person would feel if suddenly given the power of sight for a few moments, only to have it stripped away again. Which would be the greater torture? To be blind, experience sight, and lose it? Or to be blind, never see, and long for it?

After a time, she realized she was crying. Megan slept, blissful in the embrace of the *felnina*'s gentle magic. She had brought Thyri here out of love and unknowingly caused pain. She looked to Meg, stared long at the mass of silky black hair splayed out over the green moss, at her breast which rose and fell on the slow tide of her breathing. Thyri looked and felt herself apart from her friend and lover as she never had before. Always, they'd shared everything. Most of the time, just being in Megan's presence elated her, making her feel whole and alive. It wasn't working now. Megan had brought her here, intending this place as a gift, and Thyri couldn't accept it. Neither could she bring herself to wake the sorceress and flee. For once, she couldn't see herself admitting her pain, even to her best friend. Somehow, she felt that that might destroy everything. Megan might finally see the darkness within her and hate her for what it was . . .

I'm mad . . . She knows me. She's seen inside me. We speak, half the time, from mind to mind. Why did she do this to me? Why didn't she tell me how much it would hurt!

S'kiri

The sounds weren't right.

As he approached his home, the birds no longer chattered. He cast about with his talent; above was no vulture or dark raven to silence them this time. All the trees shone white, a defensive, frightened white. The frogs near the water pined croakingly for their lovers, but the females didn't answer. No felnin maiden sang out the music of the night. No young felnin chased after rabbits in the bushes. The moon behind the clouds, even, did not moan of the Midgard tides.

'Dryads,' Ai'reth whispered. 'Dryads, what passes?'

No answer.

Stupid dryads, he thought. *Be silent, then! Ai'reth is friend! He asks; you do not answer, and he will remember.*

Outside the *felnina*, nothing stirred, not even the frogs. The Queenstone's light-magic on the stairs shone weakly, beckoning his entrance.

From his belt, Ai'reth took his sword and held it before him, then, step by cautious step, he ascended through the oak.

Inside, the tribe gathered, lying restlessly on the ledges, all eyes turning toward him. Across from him, beyond the pool, on the ancestral ledge of the queen, a blackness sat, a low-born blackness – another low-born bearing a dwarven sword! At his *feet* sat S'kiri.

Ai'reth smelled blood in the air. As the eyes looked at him, he looked at them, counting. 'Where is Ai'dana?' he asked at last. 'And Ai'pez?'

No one spoke. S'kiri looked fearfully at Ai'reth, her eyes rolling up, indicating the low-born. Ai'reth's gaze finally settled there, booring into the low-born blackness. The low-born smiled at him. 'The great warrior has returned,' he said, chuckling.

Ai'reth stared. 'Come here, wife,' he said softly to S'kiri.

'No!' the low-born commanded. The dwarven sword fell down heavily in front of S'kiri, barring her path. The man's gauntlet, silver mail, shone like the moon in the black of a starless night.

Ai'reth's eyes stopped on the runes near the sword's hilt. 'That is sword of Light!' he said angrily. 'You are not worthy!'

'But I am,' the man said. 'It was given to me. Have you seen such a sword lately?'

'No,' Ai'reth answered, half falsely, half truthfully. Two dwarven swords in one day . . . He'd never seen the woman-wolf's bared.

'You lie,' the man said darkly. 'Your tricks are up, Ai'reth. I know you were scout today. I know who you've seen.'

'Who's that, stupid low-born?'

'Eiriksdattir.'

Ai'reth shook his head. 'Low-born stupid. Low-born dreaming or drink too much.'

'You lie,' the man said calmly. 'I want you to bring her to me. Bring her, or I will kill your wife, and you, and everybody.'

Ai'reth glared around at the felnin on the ledges. 'Do you let him take your queen? Do you let him take your home and kill young felnin? Are you not warriors? Think Ragnarok is bad dream! Curses on you!'

'Silence, Ai'reth,' S'kiri shouted at him. 'He holds the Queenstone!'

The man behind her grinned and raised a fist. He opened it slightly, and the blue light of the tribe's ancestral talisman shone out from between his fingers. Passed down from queen to queen, only S'kiri's hands had touched it for the past millennium – until now. Its power had shaped their home, and all their homes before this one.

Ai'reth laughed. 'Stupid rock!' he exclaimed angrily. 'Just

stupid rock now, felnin. The worlds will end, and you mourn theft of stupid rock!'

S'kiri's eyes pleaded with him. How had the low-born taken it from her? Ai'reth wondered. Had she given it up willingly after he slew Ai'dana and Ai'pez? The Queenstone meant much, he knew; it was the source of all S'kiri's magic, and much of the tribe's itself. For all he knew, it could guard their very immortality . . . But Ai'reth felt the vast, impossible weight of Yggdrasil and all the worlds on his shoulders. The balance of Ragnarok – Klorista's words bespoke prophecy for the woman-wolf, and Ai'reth knew without asking that she was whom this man desired. Even would she let him, he could not deliver her to him and make himself the first traitor to Light in the end of all things. Next to the balance of Ragnarok, the Queenstone meant nothing.

Ai'reth took a knife from his belt, and returned S'kiri's pleading gaze, hoping she would follow his thinking. Then he flipped the knife in his hand and sent it spinning through the air toward the low-born. Ai'reth took a terrible chance. He hoped – he prayed – the man knew his sword. The runes – Ai'reth knew at first glance that one would deflect missiles. S'kiri had to know as well. At the same time, the man would have to *use* the sword, lift it, giving S'kiri one brief moment in which to escape.

Ai'reth breathed easily as the man watched the knife and grinned. He did know his sword; it came up to block the knife, and S'kiri leaped – but not away! She leaped for the Queenstone! Ai'reth watched in horror as the sword came around and bit into S'kiri's side and she screamed, her claws falling away from the hand that held the Queenstone.

'Flee, felnin!' Ai'reth shouted as he leaped forward. 'Flee for your lives!' Furiously, he grasped at spells. S'kiri was dying, and he had to have the stone now to save her. He glanced only briefly to make sure the tribe had obeyed him; then he whispered the power of Thor into his sword and struck at the low-born's dwarven sword with all his might.

The blow knocked the man back, and as Ai'reth hoped,

the Queenstone dropped into S'kiri's ledge as the man came forward, his blade now in two hands.

Ai'reth closed his eyes against the sight, held up his sword, and frantically whispered another spell. As the dwarven blade came down, Ai'reth, the Queenstone, and S'kiri all disappeared, leaving the man alone in the *felnina*.

Outside, Ai'reth caught his breath. His muscles ached and his mind was dizzy with fatigue from the powerful sorceries. Still, he pushed himself, taking up S'kiri and the Queenstone and running without pause until he reached Klorista's shores. There, he whispered a ward of guarding before laying S'kiri gently on the grass. 'Wife,' he said, his voice choking with sorrow. 'Hear me!'

He examined her wound; blood already soaked the grass, dark in the moonlight, red in his tears. He pressed the Queenstone into the wound, drawing on its magic, trying to heal her.

'Ai'reth,' he heard her whisper, 'you saved the stone!'

'Yes,' he said excitedly, looking into her face. 'I heal you!'

'Too late, my love,' she coughed, blood flowing out of the corner of her mouth.

She lifted her head slightly to look at him, then it fell, lifeless, back to the ground.

Ghosts

The points of the stars contracted, nibbling at her hands as she scooped water out of the pool and splashed it on her face. She drank. She looked back at Megan who still slept.

She thought of Rollo; on the seas of Jotunheim, when she'd faced a full moon at dusk with Megan near death on the bed in their cabin, he'd given her strength, strength she'd needed then, strength she needed now. She hurt all the more as she realized that it wasn't Rollo she really wanted, *just his strength*. She felt weak, helpless, besieged by this magic that pulled at her, taunted her, forcing her to see herself again and again as the wolf, as unclean and unworthy.

Megan sighed in her sleep, then moaned with pleasure. Did she dream of Thyri? Who embraced the sorceress in her dreams? Did she ever dream of Thyri and dream of the wolf? Was Thyri ever her nightmare?

Rollo was leagues away, worlds away in the city of the Franks. With Rollo were Gerald and Rui Taichimi, and under them some two dozen rogues, all ready – Thyri knew – to face death at her side. They'd built quite an empire since their battle with Morgana and their return to Midgard. They'd pillaged for a while, then taken *Nightreaver* up the Frankish river into the heart of Charlemagne's old empire, if empire it still was over forty years after the death of the great ruler's son. Chaos it was in truth, but amid chaos, Thyri prospered, thieving and drinking – that was her world. By herself, she was invincible; with Megan at her side, doubly so. It was a game, but one that kept Thyri's mind busy, one that kept her battle skills honed and deadly. In the city of the Franks, there was no end to the stream of swordsmen who sought immortality in her defeat, only to find their own. Assuming they could find her, but that was all part of her game.

Maybe she just needed to get back. This was only one night, really. One night that Megan had meant as a gift; she could endure it. In the morning they would return and find Rollo, Rui, and Gerald waiting.

Why had Megan brought her here? How had she known of this place?

Just a game it had been in the morning . . . Practice – a chance to get out of the city and test, at the same time, their skills, both in combat and in navigating the pathways between the worlds that Thyri had more or less avoided since the ordeal with Morgana. Who had suggested it? Megan? No, Thyri had, but the sorceress had quickly grown excited at the thought. Had she unwittingly played into Megan's hands, into the sorceress's desire that they be here, in a world she knew, rather than there, in the world Thyri knew?

Thyri touched the pool's surface again, attracting the fish, trying to turn her mind outward. Megan didn't deserve such doubts, even if she knew this place and had kept it secret from Thyri. Since returning from Jotunheim, the sorceress had not expressed any desire to be anywhere but by Thyri's side. Could Megan help it if she had a past? If she had been places of which Thyri had not even dreamed? Thyri never asked her friend much of the days before they met; she was too afraid to hear talk of lovers past, lovers lost. She'd suspected long before that Coryn, King of Kaerglen Isle, had once had Megan as mistress. If the sorceress didn't wish to speak of it, Thyri didn't wish to ask. But it left a void between them; Megan knew all of Thyri's pains, while Thyri knew virtually nothing of hers. Megan knew Thyri's sword-training under the goddess Scacath, while Thyri, again, knew nothing of how Megan had come to wield the power she did. Thyri didn't even know Megan's age – the sorceress looked scarcely more than twenty, but the ways of sorcery could hide century upon century of experience behind the face of youth. Only Megan's mistakes, her obvious inexperience in battle, hinted at the possibility that her appearance might at all approximate her age. And yet nothing guaranteed that a century of years need be a century of strife and battle.

So did Thyri's thoughts circle themselves, and so it was what she did not witness Megan's waking until the sorceress placed a concerned hand on her shoulder.

'Is all well, little one?'

Little one . . . What Scacath had named her, what Astrid had called her.

'How come you by your sorceries, Megan?'

Megan laughed lightly. 'By training, Thyri. There is no other way.'

'How? Why? By whom?'

'By the spirits of the air, as I called them. I puzzled for many years. The will of the gods, I think. Their will that I meet you, Thyri. That I aid you.'

Thyri turned, her eyes blazing with sudden anger. 'Then you are here for them! Not for love? You endure me by their command?'

No one commands –

'Use your tongue, your lips! I want it out loud!'

Megan lowered her eyes. 'No one commands me, Thyri. I love you for you, for the kindness that I know is in your heart. Because you love me, and you *do* need me, but I also need you. I was an outcast when we met, powerful perhaps, but very alone. You made me whole.'

'Then why all this talk of gods!'

'Because you asked. I was not *told* by Odin or Loki or Lugh or Brigid to find you. I know only that I was trained, and when I asked why, I received only laughter or riddles. "*Because the white needs the black, and the black the white*" – does that sound to you like the command of the gods? What I've guessed of their will, I've guessed only since I met you, and not before.'

Megan looked up, and the tears in her eyes and the words

that hung fresh in the air dispelled Thyri's anger, and Thyri fell forward, into the sorceress's lap. *Oh, Megan, I'm sorry! I did not mean to hurt you!*

Pain for pain . . . I was unaware of the hurt inside you.

It's this place! I cannot endure its magics. They pain me; they want a deep forgetting that I cannot give!

I understand. I'm sorry – I should have known.

May we leave now? Sleep out under the moonlight?

Whatever you wish, my love.

Thyri looked up then, and it was then that she noticed Ai'reth standing in the portal where the steps came up into the *felnina* through the great oak. The felnin was scarcely more than three feet tall. His face was animate, almost human, but his body that of an erect cat with thick, powerful rear legs and manlike hands. In one, he held a sword, in the other a large blue gemstone. A jerkin covered his torso; it, and one of his legs, was slick with blood.

The little creature looked at Thyri, then fell to his knees and laid his bared sword down on the moss.

Blood

'You must flee!' Ai'reth said excitedly. 'You are hunted!'

Thyri sat back up, 'I am hunted?' she asked. 'By what?'

'A man – a dark, powerful man. He took our *felnina*. He killed my wife!'

Megan crawled toward him. 'Goddess!' she whispered. 'Are you hurt?'

'Not Ai'reth. Came close; blood is wife's,' he said sadly, holding back tears.

'Come here,' Megan said. 'Wash at the pool and tell us.'

'Flee!' he said stubbornly, but he didn't fight the sorceress as she grabbed his arm and led him across the moss to the pool.

By the time he was clean, they had most of the story out. A man, searching for Thyri, had taken Ai'reth's people hostage to get to her. That made little sense, especially when the felnin insisted the man was from Midgard and had named her Eiriksdattir. Dark powers obviously were at work – dark powers that knew Thyri was here, in Alfheim.

'It stinks of gods,' Thyri spat.

'But why didn't this man come to us?' Megan asked. 'If he's strong enough to take a *felnina* – why didn't he just confront us?'

'Maybe because he'd first have to find us, and that might warn us, prepare us for danger. So he's strong,' Thyri continued thoughtfully. 'But not that strong. It still stinks of gods. Can you describe him, Ai'reth?'

Ai'reth nodded. 'Blond hair, low-born, very dark inside.

He wants to kill you, but you cannot be killed! Ragnarok comes! He is big and dark. Has dwarven sword.'

'Loki in disguise?' Megan wondered aloud.

'No,' Ai'reth said. 'Trickster fettered until the end. Was *man*! Low-born!'

'But possession and manipulations won't be beyond him –'

'Megan – wait!' Thyri interrupted gravely. She took up her sword and unsheathed it before Ai'reth's eyes.

The felnin gasped. 'That's it! Same runes, dwarven sword! Twins!'

'Oh, goddess!' Megan said. 'He is full of darkness, you say? Powerful?'

'Yes.'

Megan looked at Thyri, placing a hand on her arm. Thyri stared blankly ahead at the pool, tinged red by S'kiri's blood. 'That's my sword,' Thyri said distantly. 'I kept Astrid's and gave him mine, and now I've destroyed his life, too.'

'Flee,' Ai'reth repeated. 'You must flee!'

'No,' Thyri said, standing. 'He is my brother.'

As they traveled swiftly through the night toward Ai'reth's home, Thyri's thoughts spiraled backwards back to the days of Astrid's death, the terrible pain and misery when the wolf first took her and she tore out her mother's throat and wished for nothing but her own death. She'd left behind her a trail of blood, her family's blood, and now, Erik, the last relative she cared anything for, sought her death. And he'd murdered, murdered along the way, just to get to her.

How had he come here? What enemy of hers had adopted him and played him like a pawn against her, to torture her? The last she'd heard, he was fierce, a Viking – he'd come to hate her and called out her name in battle, but that hardly bought him passage out of his world, Midgard, into this one.

As Thyri ran, she screamed up at the sky, shuddering as the scream transformed into a high, terrible howl. Now, she thought darkly as they neared their destination, he knows I come.

Alone, she stalked silently up the stairs. Another *felnina* . . . Earlier, she'd wished never to enter one again. She stopped at the portal, her sword before her. Ahead, all was darkness but where the moonlight shone down through gaps in the ceiling. 'Erik!' she commanded softly. 'Show yourself!'

'Kinslayer,' came a lilting voice from deep in the shadows. 'Her mother is dead, her father is dead, their blood on her lips and her fangs and her claws! She is evil, like the dragon in the sea, like the hound at the gates, like the teeth in the giant's mouth.'

'Forget the rhymes,' she seethed. 'Show yourself!'

He stepped forward, a tall, lanky, shadowy figure in the moonlight. His eyes burned red.

'Why do you seek me?'

'I do not seek, sister! I have found!' His exclamations were obscene, orgasmic.

'I will not fight you, Erik!'

He laughed. 'She is here, but not to fight, that is good! Let us go then, to my master! I have a spell for you!' Strands of red light coiled out from his fingers and wrapped around her. Thyri fought against them, but they bound her, holding her still. How had he come by such sorcery! Erik stalked slowly forward.

'Erik, stop!' she cried. 'I don't want to kill you!' Already, she could feel the bones twisting in the back of her neck and shoulders, just as they had the day before, so easily did the beast emerge when all seemed lost.

'Kill me?' he laughed. 'I'm going to kill you!'

'Who commands you? Who did this to you? Who gave you this power?'

'Command?' he spat. 'Gave? No one! I traded!'

'What did you trade?'

He stood right in front of her now. She could see his face, see the young, innocent features of her little brother twisted now into something impossibly evil. As he raised his sword, she looked into his eyes, his burning, red eyes, and she saw herself there, all the murder and blood of her past racing up through time to consume her. In that instant, she again wanted to die, prayed for his sword to descend down upon her, even as the agony of transformation twisted her spine and the hunger grew inside her, devouring her thoughts, pushing her human awareness down to where it was helpless to do anything but look on in horror.

As Erik's sword came down, he whispered an answer: 'My soul,' he said. Before his strike could sink into flesh, the beast took Thyri and twisted violently out of the magic. Erik's sword only grazed her flank, and that wound began to heal even as she jumped away.

Now, the wolf stood before him. The red madness burned in his eyes, and he attacked again. The wolf leaped to meet him, heedless of the point of his sword. She fell on him, pushing him back to the moss, the sword piercing her stomach. Snarling, she writhed, pushing the sword through her body until her fangs reached Erik's throat.

Thankfully, the pain of the wound consumed the little awareness Thyri had left. She didn't see his eyes right before he died; she didn't see the red madness flee, and pure, human terror take its place before the wolf's jaws snapped shut.

Magic

In her dreams, she floated. Everything was white, and she wondered if she were dead. The sky was white, the ground white, nothing even moved, and then a terrible, freezing wind blew through her. The white in the sky grew solid, huge snowflakes falling around her, through her, like spears of ice through her body. In the distance, dark clouds lurked, and above, colors began to shine through the light – the colors of the rainbow.

The Rainbow Bridge. She fell next to Heimdall's foot. Dark armies moved across the distant snows. It was *fimbulwinter*, the coming of the end. She looked at herself, and she was the wolf.

She bit into Heimdall's big toe . . .

Megan sat, stroking Thyri's forehead as she slept. The sorceress's eyes were red, strained by fatigue. She'd traveled hard through the night with Thyri to reach this place before morning, and once here, she'd been unable to sleep. She still saw, in her mind, the terrible carnage she'd confronted when she'd entered the *felnina*: blood everywhere, the head of Thyri's brother torn from his body, Thyri herself, naked, half wolf, half woman, a sword piercing her stomach and emerging a full foot on the other side.

Ai'reth had helped her remove the sword, then she'd cleaned it and wrapped it carefully with Thyri's other things. She'd then set off immediately for home, using her sorceries to push her burdens before her. By the time they'd made it back to the city of the Franks, Thyri's body had healed, and she'd turned fully back into a woman.

Then Megan had cast her spells, tried to sleep, failed, and now waited for Thyri to wake.

Slowly, sunlight invaded the snowscape, and Thyri felt Megan's hands brushing over her skin. She opened her eyes and saw the walls of the large room they shared on the north side of the city. She creased her forehead. How had they come here? The last she remembered, she and Megan had loved, in a field of barley after a hot day's chase on the pathways between the worlds.

'What – '

'Hush,' Megan said. 'Everything's all right now.'

'But what happened?'

Megan smiled sadly. 'I've cast a spell, Thyri. I can't lie to you – it's my doing that you can't remember.'

'Odin!' Thyri said, bringing her hands up to her face. 'What did I do? Did I change? Did I attack you?'

'No, my love. You didn't attack me.'

'Then what?'

'I can lift the spell if you like.'

'Megan, I have to know!'

'I have done other castings,' Megan said quietly. 'He was not himself. He was made to hate you, twisted by a power he couldn't resist. I'm not sure what power, perhaps Morgana before she died, perhaps another. I just want you to know that.'

'Who's he?'

'Thyri, please. You don't know what you ask.'

'I can't spend the rest of my life wondering about it!'

Megan sighed, tears rising to her eyes. 'I thought you would feel thus. Do you want the memories back, or do you want me to tell you? Either way, if you ask quickly, I can renew the spell.'

'The memories, Meg, else I can't be certain of the truth.'

'You can trust me.'

'But without proof I might always doubt it!'

'Very well.'

The sorceress closed her eyes, took Thyri's head between

her hands, and began to sing softly. Thyri felt something sharp, like a knife stabbing inside her mind, then it all came down upon her, not only the memory of slaying her brother, but the anguished hours before then, in the *felnina*, the pain she'd felt there, and her resentment toward the sorceress for putting it upon her. All of it hit her at once in a huge, crushing, agonizing wave. 'No!' she screamed, struggling in Megan's grip. 'No!'

Megan's song abruptly grew louder, and suddenly Thyri was screaming and wondering why. As her scream faded, Thyri knew only that *something* had caused it, something Megan had again hidden from her. Anguished, she coughed, her body wracked by sobs.

Without, she heard a loud crack – the door to the room bursting open. Rollo Anskarson filled the space, his sword ready. He glanced, concerned, at the two women, his eyes meeting Megan's for a moment, then he nodded slowly and backed out, shutting the door.

'I still have to know, Meg.'

Thyri sat on the edge of the bed, her head in her hands. Megan sat across from her, cross-legged on the floor.

'Tell me, Meg,' Thyri pleaded. 'I'll trust you.'

Slowly, the sorceress rose, lifting up a bundle near the door. She took it to Thyri and unrolled it onto her lap. Two swords fell there; Megan unsheathed them, laying them side by side.

Thyri's hand moved to touch the two blades. 'Erik!' she whispered. She looked up, teary-eyed, at Megan. *Did I have a choice?*

The sorceress knelt, took Thyri's hands from the blades, and held her gaze. 'No, my love,' she said. 'You did all you could do.'

Gerald

In the city of the Franks, on the Street of Merchants, the high end, near the palace, an establishment called The Emporium peddled its wares to rich and poor alike. On its shelves one could find ancient scrolls and parchments in nearly all scripts known to men. Stone and wood carvings from the north sat in cabinets near the door. Bolts of fine silks colored the right side of the entrance hall, while statuary stolen from the old southern empires beckoned the visitor from the left. At the counter, one could request gemstones of all sorts, or fine scents from the far east, pendants and jewelry from around the world, or, in a back room, some of the finest swords and arms in all of the Frankish Empire. It should be noted that the average customer, more often than not, exited with a forgery of one of the above, rather than the genuine article.

Two other chambers, aside from the armory, led off from the main: two taverns, one of the wealthy, replete with silk-draped dancers and fine intoxicants of all sorts, the other for the common man and the servants of the wealthy, where one could purchase only mead or, if he knew who to ask, the services of one or more of the assorted rogues that lurked, by day and night, in the corners of this second public house.

In general, The Emporium enjoyed marked success, catering faithfully to the whims of all who entered. To some in the city, its success provided some small frustration as well as mystery. Thieves, it seemed, came away from attempts at penetration bruised and battered, or they came away not at all. No one, to anyone's knowledge, had successfully exited with anything for which he had not first paid, and two attempts at outright sabotage – midnight efforts to set the building aflame – had ended in equal frustration, the agents involved suffering similar fates to those of the thieves.

In some circles, whispered voices proclaimed The Emporium guarded by witchcraft; in that respect, they were correct. Sorceries permeated the walls and the wares, and much more went on within the building's walls than anyone uninitiated into its mysteries might guess at. No conversation held within, in fact, was safe from sorcerous eavesdropping. No freelance rogue hired from the second tavern left without primary allegiance to one or more of the establishment's generally unseen proprietors who lived in practice in the lavishly furnished rooms above.

One of those proprietors, the exception in that he was ever the most visible and often worked personally behind the establishment's central counter, was Gerald of Jorvik, the offspring of a Saxon and a Pict who had followed Thyri Eiriksdattir from his native soil to the seas of Jotunheim and back to here, the center of all European wealth, the heart of the empire conquered by the great Charlemagne, now ruled by a descendant lovingly known as Charles the Fat, King and Emperor of the Franks. With Thyri, Megan of Kaerglen, Rollo Anskarson, and Rui Taichimi, Gerald had thieved his way into part ownership of The Emporium, and now, with the others, he thieved from it.

Without a doubt, the proprietorship of The Emporium was a high point in Gerald's long, illustrious life. Though the establishment served many purposes of all involved, its day-to-day operations were managed by Gerald exclusively and his success as a trader provided him great personal satisfaction. He chose the wares to sell and marketed them to his customers, and he knew that they all could now live by his efforts alone. *His* efforts kept Megan and Thyri in silks, and himself, Rollo, and Rui in women and the finest meads and wines. He'd even commissioned a secret tunnel in recent months, overseeing the workers led blindfolded to and from their toils, in order to give Thyri safe passage from the city during the nights of the full moon. The week before, he'd presented this tunnel to her as a present, and he'd known by her smiles and tears that the gift was well received. In this, he felt great pride, for he knew that he'd accomplished a feat on the level of the sorceress, and moreover, he'd kept it secret until the gift was ready, and earned in the end the thanks of she against whom all other women paled.

Not that Gerald didn't have lovers. His business brought him the attention of many of the best women the city had to offer. He generally had his choice when he wished; he'd even spent a few glorious days with a pampered, *educated* great-granddaughter of Charlemagne himself. But he'd left even her, though he'd gifted her with a large sapphire fit for the crown of any queen in the world; no method of existence appealed to him more than the management of The Emporium, for only there could he remain close to Thyri and Megan, their beauty, and the greatness he perceived in them both. Even though he knew by now that he might never get close to Thyri, in the way that a normal man possesses a normal woman, he didn't care. Just serving her was enough, and he knew that Rollo and Rui felt much the same way. She had the loyalty of each of them, and it was a loyalty that knew no bounds. Only she could ask him to forfeit the luxuries he'd gained, but if she asked, he would do so willingly, without regret, and follow where she would lead, no matter if it were the seas of Jotunheim again, or the very gates of Niflheim itself.

On that morning Megan comforted Thyri, trying to help her friend face the pains of the night before amid the sumptuous furnishings of their bedchamber (if these were not described it was only because Thyri did not *see* them or perceive herself among them in the depths of her despair). Gerald worked below, entertaining a pair of wealthy travelers from Barcelona in their own tongue, just as he normally entertained Franks eloquently in the Frankish tongue. He'd grown fluent in all the tongues required for his dealings, Megan having cast for him and Rollo and Rui the same spell by which she'd once made Thyri fluent in Irish in the space of a few days.

Once, Gerald had had a quiet chuckle when overhearing a gossip state that the king would do well to hire the advice of The Emporium's proprietor because he'd had the finest education of any in all the land.

But to return: Gerald entertained the Barcelonans, showing them silks and fine scents when suddenly Thyri's screaming above echoed faintly in the rafters. Such were the magics in the building that Gerald alone heard the sound, and then only distantly, while his customers went on bantering cheerfully over the price of silk and the dangers of the far eastern trade routes. Gerald, meanwhile, lost the thread of their talk and grew fretful, his imagination racing wildly in attempts to explain the sound he'd heard. No one upstairs would ever scream so with no good reason – that he knew well. So, were they under attack? Had Megan or Thyri been injured or killed by some unknown assailant?

Gerald resisted the impulse to turn and bolt upstairs, heedless of his business. Rollo and Rui would handle it – whatever the problem was – and he wasn't certain what impression his sudden departure would make, or even that he was definitely the only one in the room to have heard the scream. So he stood, detached, before the Barcelonans until Rollo Anskarson came out of the door from the back stairwell and stood silently, nodding and smiling at the customers looking his way like an affable, friendly guard. Gerald glanced at him and felt relief that no emergency had transpired; at least Rollo didn't signal his undivided attention, but in another way, the scream grew more puzzling. Had Thyri's nightmares returned? What *had* happened?

One of the Barcelonans clicked his fingers in front of Gerald's eyes. Gerald looked at him, smiled and apologized effusively, then the Barcelonan shook his head, held up a handful of glass vials, and said, flatly, 'Two hundred.'

A real barterer, Gerald realized dismally. His response should have been abusive, followed by a firm declaration of 'One thousand, no less!' but instead he smiled weakly and waved his hand toward the door, 'Take it,' he said abruptly.

Now the man stood before him, insulted by Gerald's

refusal to carry out the game. To many, the act of bartering was as sacred as showing pity before an altar. Merchants, in fact, owed their existence to the tactical skills, the offers and counteroffers, involved in a sale. By not demanding four or five times the Barcelonan's initial offer, the traveler could only assume insult, that he'd drastically overvalued the merchandise he desired, or that he held in his hands something of a quality somewhat less than advertised.

Gerald saw the insult and hurriedly attempted to dispel it. 'No, just take it,' he said, smiling warmly. 'For nothing! Free! I've just remembered today's my birthday, and I must make amends to myself for forgetting.' He raised his hands, declaring loudly, 'All my customers! Today is my birthday, and I wish to celebrate! This place should be closed this morning, but you are lucky to have gotten in. Please, take what you have in your hands, as gifts from me, but leave now!'

Hearing the declaration, Rollo stepped forward to guide The Emporium's few morning customers toward the door. Gerald looked again to the Barcelonans and placed a hand on the one's shoulder. 'Please, my friend,' he said. 'Take my gifts. Come back another day and I will gladly relieve you of your money.'

Shaking his head in slight disbelief, the Barcelonan stepped back. As Rollo showed them to the door, Gerald heard them laughing, and at the portal, the one turned back and promised Gerald that he would, indeed, return.

After Rollo had gone to declare the same holiday in the taverns, he returned to Gerald, smiling. 'Don't forget this date, friend,' he said. 'You'll have to remember it in the years to come and treat it accordingly.'

'Just won't open at all,' Gerald said, searching the larger man's gaze for some clue to the events upstairs. 'It was Thyri, wasn't it?' he asked finally.

Rollo nodded, his dark hair falling down in front of his eyes, his hand brushing it quickly away. In Gerald's memory, the Viking was ever his natural blond, though Rollo had consented to Megan's cosmetic change after learning how unwelcome Norsemen remained in the lands of the Franks. Before Gerald could say more, Rui came down the stairs to join them. The archer appeared as always, his alien, exotic features, his flat nose and catty eyes, setting him apart from other men. Rui resisted any sorcerous disguising of his everyday appearance, conceding this principle only in the most necessary of circumstances. Instead, on the streets, he traveled cloaked like a monk, though he seldom went without his bow and quiver. At Rollo's side, he was usually left alone. Now, Rui came cloaked, though his hood was back, the concern on his face mirroring Gerald's.

'I don't know much,' Rollo told them. 'Thyri screamed, but she didn't look hurt. The witch was with her; I didn't ask any questions.'

For a while, they stood around restlessly, silently. Gerald knew they all thought the same thoughts: They all desired to ascend the stairs and learn first hand of Thyri's troubles. In that she was with Megan, they all felt powerless. They would learn what they would learn, in time and not before. Finally, Rui suggested they get out and wander.

'Take our frustrations out on some poor rogues near the docks, you mean,' Rollo chuckled darkly.

Rui looked at him calmly and shrugged.

On the streets, Gerald felt the weight of the sword at his side lift another weight off his shoulders. He'd almost forgotten what it was like to move free, anonymously, among other men. On his cloak he wore a pendant fashioned by Megan; to others he would not appear as himself, as the groomed proprietor of The Emporium, but as an unkempt ruffian on the right flank of Rollo, a giant of a man among the small Frankish people.

They did go to the docks, but they didn't find a fight. They found instead something else: A messenger for the king, fresh off his ship, sat at a table and drank, one mead turning to two, then more, and the mead loosened an otherwise confidential tongue. The messenger's news for the king was good.

A few weeks before, the city had learned of an invasion on the river. Hundreds upon hundreds of Norse reavers had started upstream in search of land. Much talk had centered on the outcome of the bold frontal assault, and the last anyone had heard the Norse only wanted to settle, and though the nobility was up in arms, King Charles in his detached and fatalistically cowardly way, was going to let them. Thyri and Rollo had had something of a special interest in the news, both feeling the bonds of kinship with the invaders, but the king's apparent lack of belligerence had pleased them and they'd been happy merely to watch.

Now, through the king's increasingly drunk messenger, Rollo, Rui, and Gerald heard a different story. Under pressure from the nobility, the king had secretly blockaded the river and, with his ships and armies, now held the seven hundred-odd Norse ships trapped and more or less helpless. At the king's command, the messenger told all the tavern, the Norsemen would be summarily slaughtered.

Hearing this, Rollo, Rui, and Gerald quietly left.

Thieves

Rollo watched Thyri closely as she and Megan came into their council chamber, a second-story room furnished with cabinets and a large oak table where they occasionally took their meals, but more often than not simply gathered to drink and discuss present and future plans. Few outsiders ever saw inside the room; when they met with others, such meetings were held in one of the taverns, or in some location well away from The Emporium. Here, Megan had covered the walls with wards and other arcane drawings, protections she claimed would shield their councils from even the most powerful sorceries. As Thyri entered, she looked at these wards and drawings; they were chalk, and Rollo couldn't know that they recalled for Thyri a room in Castle Kaerglen, to which the Princess Tana had once led Thyri, and wherein Thyri had found many such drawings, as well as a ring, a plain gold band streaked with silver, Megan's ring in Megan's old room. Chalk drawings on the walls, just like here . . .

Externally, Thyri showed no sign whatever of the wound she'd endured. She seemed her ever confident, calm self – except that her eyes took overly long to meet those of the others. She looked long at Megan's drawings; something about them bothered her. She felt as if she'd thought of them lately, or dreamed of them lately, but couldn't remember when. Was this memory, along with Erik's death, hidden from her behind the shield of Megan's spell? Two swords now stood in her room, where yesterday there had been only one. Chalk on the walls – Megan's past and present. She yearned briefly to know again, to have the sorceress lift the spell again, but they'd tried that once. *Let it be forgotten*,

Thyri heard in her mind. She glanced at Megan. *Let it rest.* In the sorceress's eyes, there was pleading and love. Thyri nodded imperceptibly, and saw Megan smile. 'What news have you?' she asked, turning to Rollo.

'Sit first,' he said, taking two flagons and filling them from a cask of mead.

Thyri and Megan sat, taking their flagons. 'What news?' Thyri repeated.

'Charles has attacked, and the seven hundred are trapped, awaiting death.'

Thyri drank, then set her flagon down. 'Then it's war,' she said.

Rollo eyed her closely, looking again for signs of her wound. Did she suggest, seriously, a frontal assault on the Frankish armies? A possible suicide, that idea, but he wouldn't refuse should she command it. 'Shall we prepare *Nightreaver*?' he asked carefully. 'Recruit the rabble?'

Thyri laughed, and in her laughter, and the sudden intense concentration in her eyes, Rollo saw that he'd never learn what had pained her that morning. The news he'd brought would now command her attention; in effect, it had already healed her, diverting her thoughts, making her look fully to present and future battles, not to past ones. And then he realized that she laughed at him, his suggestions. He failed to understand, though he realized that he had thought very little about the news before bringing it to her. Even after learning of the king's treachery, he'd worried most about Thyri. Now, in the light of Thyri's laughter, that worry felt burdensome, ill-placed.

'And what then?' she asked him, still laughing. 'Do we attack the castle? Burn the city? Have you been a thief this past year, my friend?' She grew serious. 'No, we must have a more subtle way. Those Norsemen seek only land, not war with this empire, or even control of it. If we make it war, we will be too few to win.'

Now it was Rollo's turn to laugh. 'With her sorcery?' he asked, nodding his head toward Megan. 'She could lift the king's palace and drop it on his armies' heads!'

Megan smiled at him, but she spoke calmly, 'No, Rollo. The One God is very strong in this land, but he slumbers and his followers do not know I am here. I have been very careful to conceal myself from them, for if they turn certain of his sorceries against me, in this land where his power is so great, I may well die.'

'Subtlety, Rollo,' Thyri said. 'Our people want land, and they should have it. All lands resist us now, ever more effectively. Once, I thought we might rule the world, but that seems fated not to pass. We must, however, survive, and this empire has no right to slaughter seven hundred ships full of men when it has land to spare them. If we fight incorrectly though, the Franks will not rest until all of Norse blood are cast out.'

Rui tapped his fingernails on the table. 'What,' he said slowly, glancing at the others, 'does the king value most? It is his decision, is it not? Whether or not to attack? Whether or not to wage war?'

'His throne?' Rollo asked, unsure.

'No,' Gerald answered, leaning forward, cracking his flagon down onto the wood. 'Not his throne, but his gold.'

Thyri smiled at the Saxon. 'Perfect. Now, how do we do it? With our wits alone? With sorcery? With the rabble? After this, I doubt we'll be able to stay here, but we should think first of a way to do it alone. I will entrust none of this to any Frank or cutthroat in this city. I will not have what we do undone, whether we stay or leave.'

Rollo stared at her, at the sparkle in her eyes, and his thoughts turned back again to the morning, when he'd heard her scream and seen her, deep in despair, with the sorceress. The questions still burned in him awhile, then the sparkle in her eyes affected him as, slowly, he thought and wondered on what she proposed. Eventually, he sighed and gave his mind over to the future, as she obviously had. Whatever secrets the morning harbored, it could keep them. Adventure beckoned, and the lives of Norsemen, his people, were at stake. And after that, she'd said they might leave, hadn't she? To be back out on the sea? That thought comforted him.

Thievery and this city had their good sides, but sometimes, and fairly often of late, Rollo had ached for the feel of a sword in his hand, for the anarchy of battle. He might not get that now, but with the sparkle in Thyri's eyes, and the promise of leaving, battle felt ever closer, as if she moved, and he with her, in a slow flirtatious dance to the sound of clashing swords.

Magic

The plan, in the end, rested mostly on Megan, and such a plan it was that Rollo found himself wondering on the sorceress's earlier words on the power of the One God. Surely this idea concocted by Thyri would tempt the One God's wrath, but Megan consented willingly, even laughing with delight from time to time and adding ideas of her own. It didn't amount to dropping castles on top of armies; in ways, however, it sounded worse.

Most of the time, the men simply listened, each of them thinking, as they all had in the past, on the incredible talents of the women they followed. They sat, smiling in amazement, as each new twist of the plan fell from Thyri's lips.

In the end, it sounded remarkably simple, assuming the One God would fail to rise up and strike them all dead.

Getting inside the palace was the first problem. Megan's sorceries would be sorely tested during the operation, and she didn't desire to use them except when absolutely necessary. So instead of a sorcerous approach, they decided on a covered one.

Gerald, Rollo, and Rui loaded a wagon full of The Emporium's finest wares, then all but Gerald and Rollo concealed themselves within. Once loaded, and its horses hitched, the wagon carried them quickly to the palace gates.

'I must see the king!' Gerald called out to the guard.

'Who hails the palace?' a man returned, opening the gatekeeper's hatch.

'It is Gerald of The Emporium. I wish to see the king.'

'Come back tomorrow. It is late.'

'I cannot,' Gerald said impatiently, 'for tomorrow is not my birthday – only today, and I have presents for the king on my birthday. I have presents for you, as well, if you will only let me in.'

'What sorts of presents?'

'Jewels and scents for your ladies,' Gerald said, holding up a handful of necklaces and vials. 'Surely you have ladies?'

'Aye,' the gatekeeper laughed. 'You must wait.' The man disappeared. A moment later, the gate came down.

Gerald drove the wagon across and stopped it where they were flanked by two dozen guards. Rollo smiled at them, hopped down, and threw back the canvas covering their load so all might see they carried no dangers for the king. As the canvas came up, it seemed to all that a light breeze descended from the sky, filling them with feelings of great warmth. A few of them look up and saw, high above the castle, a new star that shone as brightly as the moon itself.

That star was Megan's star blazing in the heavens; she had stolen it from the lore of the One God, from the tale of his son's birth. Rollo glanced at it and shuddered; they tempted great powers, and would do more before the night was through. And such powers he couldn't challenge with his sword. Seeing the star, and knowing that the earth had not yet opened up to swallow him, his confidence in Megan's judgment began to improve. 'The One God is not like our gods,' she'd told them. 'His mysteries are open, free to all, while ours are closed and sorcerous. Any man can become one of his priests, but in our world one must be born into the mysteries and then taught their secrets. We of power are closer to our gods, but those opposing us are far more numerous. Most important, though, he *depends* on his followers to carry his cross, the banner of his mysteries, into battle. They are but men and can be tricked, and they can't fight with his power unless they know there is a battle. We're going to trick them. We're not going to let them know.'

Rollo thought on it as he looked up at the star. Odin would never stand for such sacrilege. He hoped the sorceress was right.

Thyri, Megan, and Rui hurried across the courtyard, concealed by Megan's sorceries but nevertheless fearful of lingering. If the plan succeeded fully, they would have to beat Gerald to the king. Overhead, Megan's star beamed brightly, lighting their way. While running, the sorceress cast other spells, locating both the king and his gold. The treasury was underground, though it had a heavily guarded entrance on the palace's outer wall. To there they went.

The guards, four of them armed with sword and mace, saw nothing until a shimmering silver key materialized in the air, and the door behind them suddenly opened. Before they could shout out, Thyri and Rui appeared before them, but they did not see a short, fierce Norse swordsmistress and a strange archer from far off lands. Instead, they saw two tall figures clothed in white and bathed in white light. Behind the figures, sprouting from their shoulders, huge wings twitched in the air, and one by one the four guards all fell to their knees.

Improvising, Thyri smiled at them, then carried a finger to her lips and pointed up with her other hand, to the bright star over the castle. One of the guards actually began to weep with joy as streams of gold came through the air from behind him and seemed to pass through his chest before soaring up into a window high on the castle's walls.

Megan stayed only long enough to be sure the guards would not see through the sorcerous disguises of her friends, then she spelled herself to where she'd sent the streams of gold. She had, by the way, stolen nothing. All the king's gold remained where she'd found it; she'd wanted mostly to see it, to be sure of the reality of her illusions.

In the room where she went, she found a ready audience, a perfect audience, for he was alone. He sat on the edge of his bed, his mouth agape, his eyes fixed on the stacks of gold bars that had poured in through his window. He was a fat man, and, in a way, a very simple one. But he was also good of heart, and he'd first declined to oppose the small Norse invasion out of dislike of bloodshed, rather than fear of it. It seemed to him that his God, with his son The Christ, had meant to teach men something. Peace was one of those teachings.

As it was, Megan almost felt sorry for the king. She appeared before him, a small dark-haired woman draped in brown cloth. She looked at him sadly, but said nothing until he spoke.

'Who – who are you?' he finally stammered. His body quivered, his rolls of fat shaking with his voice.

She turned to the side and became a man, a bearded man with a crown of thorns on his head. 'I am your god,' said the man's voice.

'Wha – '

She turned and became the woman again. 'I am taking this from you,' she said, indicating the pile of gold. 'Seven hundred bars, one for each ship you offer Death.'

He stared at her, wide-eyed and speechless.

'You have nothing to say?'

'But, Virgin,' he said. 'You can't mean those godless pagans!'

'I can, and I do.'

'So you take my gold?'

'As a start, and a warning, yes.'

'A warning?'

She nodded. With a flick of her wrist, she started small, dark, magical fires in the corners of the room.

The king fell to his knees before her. 'No, please! I'll do anything!'

'Leave the ships alone, then. Let them ashore. They will fight bravely for you when the real wars come.'

'What real wars?'

'You will learn in time.'

'Oh, Virgin,' he cried. 'I'll do anything! I'll give this gold to those ships, if only you will let me! I will let them land, but please leave my life and my soul so that I may worship you forever!'

'You will give the gold to the reavers?' she asked, choking off amazed laughter at the unexpected twist of irony.

'Yes!'

'Then I return it to your treasury,' she said, flicking her wrist again, sending the gold streams back out the window. With another flick, she extinguished the fires, and then she stood over the king, looking at him with warm, motherly eyes.

'Thank you!' he said, crying, gazing at her.

'Your life is blessed,' she said, and she disappeared.

Downstairs, in the castle's entrance hall, Gerald began to worry, straining his ears for any hint of danger. From outside, the sound of great commotion sporadically reached him; Gerald couldn't be sure whether it was the continuing effects of the star above, or whether something more alarming was happening. He wished for his sword, but he had come unarmed as part of his character. If it came to battle, he could always take a weapon off of one of Rollo's first victims, not that they'd then have a much greater chance of getting out alive. He could see in Rollo's eyes that the Viking felt much the same.

He'd already handed out a fair portion of his wares just getting the castle's main doors opened. Once in, the powers inside the castle had directed him to leave the gifts and then depart. He would not have his audience. The point of his actions began to seem meaningless as he oversaw Rollo and several guards carrying statues and rolls of silk through the castle's entrance hall into the king's council chamber. He yearned to get outside, to find Thyri and see how the plan fared.

But then, as the men worked, King Charles, looking dazed and almost bouyant despite his great bulk, stumbled in. Gerald's heart began to pound in his chest; he watched the king from the corner of his eye. Charles called several men to him, gave them whispered orders, and they hurried off. After an agonizing wait, the king came toward Gerald.

'What's this?' Charles asked, watching Rollo and the guards come in with another huge roll of silk.

'Presents for the king,' Gerald said, forcing a pleasant smile. 'It is my birthday, and I have presents for the king!'

'Did she send you?'

'She – ' Gerald feigned surprise. 'Oh no, my king. I am not married.'

'No, I mean – ' the king stammered, looking confused. 'You mean you're bringing all this to me? Gifts? Not taxes?'

'Not taxes at all,' Gerald said happily. 'It is the night of my birthday, and a wondrous night it is! Have you not seen the bright star in the heavens?'

'Star?' the king asked in amazement.

Gerald watched, finally relieved and chuckling to himself, as the king bobbed merrily toward the door for a look outside.

That night, the proprietors of The Emporium laughed and drank until they collapsed under the weight of their merriment. Gerald talked at length of the king, of the rapturous look on his face as he'd started outside to see the star; as an afterthought, Megan had made it explode in a shower of silver before the king's eyes. In the midst of the spiritual euphoria that ensued, they'd have no trouble leaving. Charles, in fact, had commanded the gates be thrown wide so he might invite in his subjects and tell all of his divine visitation.

The story – and its absurd hilarity for Thyri and her friends – had grown quickly. Throughout the castle, it seemed every man or woman had been blessed or visited by all manner of angels and visions. As Gerald and Rollo had mounted their empty wagon, they'd heard three women proclaiming joyously that the Archangel Gabriel had come to them and blessed them all, simultaneously, with child. Departing, Gerald had heard the king's gardener describing in detail his vision of heaven's gate and how The Christ stood before it, kissing those who entered and showing the horrible wounds on his hands to those who were turned away.

Even in The Emporium's taverns and throughout the city the tales of angels and visions flourished. Thyri and the others finally retreated to the solitude of their council room for fear that their laughter and their own words might undo what they'd accomplished. It seemed the entire Frankish nation had been blessed along with its king.

Once alone together, they laughed until their sides hurt, all save perhaps Megan. She smiled and chuckled at the others' stories, but weariness hid behind her eyes, and occasionally, Thyri thought she saw sadness there.

Rollo, though, relaxed fully. At the height of the celebration, he went to the sorceress, lifted her up, and gave her a hug that threatened to crack her spine. 'You are fantastic!' he shouted out, then he kissed her sloppily above her breasts.

Gerald, at the sight, fell silent. It stunned him – the Viking's lips and beard touching Megan's flesh in such a way. When Rollo put the sorceress down, he almost expected her to back away and inflict upon the Viking some terrible, excruciating death. But this she did not do. 'Thank you, Rollo,' she said, then she sat back down.

Rollo's happy eyes darted about the room, settling finally on Gerald. Gerald stared; Rollo stamped his foot on the floor. 'What's wrong, Saxon?' he bellowed. 'Seen a ghost?'

Gerald blinked, glanced from Rollo to Megan, and smiled weakly. 'No, my friend,' he said. 'Just a vision.'

Later, near dawn, Thyri curled up to Megan and found her tense. She touched her cheek and realized the sorceress cried. 'You are troubled?' Thyri whispered softly.

'Yes.'

'Shadows on our victory?'

Our end I saw, Thyri. The end of our ways, the passing of our gods. Even you laughed at the idiocy, at the way the visions I started spread like wildfire from the castle out over the city. Yes, it was absurd, hilarious, and laughable. But behind that absurdity lurks the death of our way of life, the death of the natural spirits before the coming of the detached spirit of meaningless, nonexistent visions. See how they spread with all the people of this city so eager not to be left out? Instead of disbelieving the stories, ridiculing them, the hearer simply creates a grander one, or a more mysterious one, and they go on believing each other, interpreting these invented visions until they actually come to believe they had them. Tonight, my love, I have made the One God stronger and quickened the passing of those we know. I have been his miracle, and from this miracle, he spreads and gains even more strength.

Rollo feared his wrath, but why should he be wrathful? I have helped him, in a way he rarely helps himself. And I did it very well; I did it perfectly.

'But you saved the Norse,' Thyri protested gently, caressing Megan's breast.

Yes, but for what? So they might hear of the One God's miracles, forsake Odin, and follow the cross blindly with the rest?

'We will tell them the truth.'

Will we? How many will believe us, and how long before our truth fades?

Thyri sighed. 'We've long known of our gods' passing, Meg. Why such sorrow now?'

To know is one thing, to feel is another. Tonight I felt it.

Thyri lay silently, thinking. She pictured Odin on his throne, with the Thunderer at his side. How could they fall before any power less than that of Fenrir, Jormungard, and Surt? Nothing in all the worlds could withstand the crush of Thor's hammer, not anything real, anything that could be touched. Why didn't Odin and Thor take the battle out, confront the One God and destroy this disease of faith?

Megan interrupted her thoughts: *I fear, Thyri. I fear especially for you. I learned many things yesterday, from one who loves you, but one you will not remember.* Fimbulwinter *has come to Asgard. Do you feel it here?*

No.

'It is the One God,' Megan whispered, her voice cracking and stark in its sudden emergence. 'It is the One God who keeps it away.'

Thyri stayed silent. The talk of gods, the exhaustion of the day, and Megan's mention of the day before sent her thoughts tumbling into murky, disconnected images:

She was the Wolf, the Reaver. Odin's head grew small; Thor's hammer floated among clouds, writhing like a snake. Memories pulsed and burned, straining to break free from their cages of darkness. So were her thoughts as she drifted into equally disturbing dreams.

The next day, far upriver, the Frankish armies pulled away from the banks. Hesitantly, seven hundred ships weighed anchor and started for land.

Though they had no leader, the first Viking to step ashore was named Hrothgar Olafson. He debarked armed, but he did not attack the few Franks that remained near a sole, canvas-covered cart. Instead, he approached them cautiously.

'Hail, friend!' called one in the Norse tongue.

Hrothgar stopped. The Frank reached under the cart's canvas and Hrothgar saw something glint in the sunlight as the Frank stepped forward. At Hrothgar's feet, he dropped a bar of gold. Hrothgar stared down, unsure whether or not he dreamed.

With ceremony, the Frank pulled a scroll of parchment from his vest and read aloud. By now, several other ships had landed, and the Viking marauders had begun to gather behind Hrothgar. 'By decree of Charles, Emperor,' the Frank read, translating into Norse, 'I offer you land and welcome you among my people. For each ship, the King and Emperor offers peace and one bar of his gold. You may divide the land here among yourselves, except that land that is claimed and worked by another. In this, may the Lord God make you prosperous.'

The Frank lowered the parchment and looked up at Hrothgar, clearing his throat. 'You will, of course, pay taxes,' he added.

Hrothgar bent to the ground and lifted the gold, testing its weight. Behind him, cheers broke out among the Vikings as the Frank's words sank in and spread. As Hrothgar walked away, followed by his men, he felt a sudden weight on his shoulder and stopped. Turning his head carefully, his eyes met those of a bird, a small blackbird. He stared at it, and it spoke to him. *'Eiriksdattir greets her fellow travelers,'* the bird said, then it flapped away to a tree and sat there, watching until the next Viking came away from the rest with his gift from the king.

BOOK VIII

KAERGLEN

So it all now truly begins, and I only wonder why true beginnings stand so close in time to their endings. Events rush together, gaining momentum, shaking all the worlds in their calamitous joining. That calamity – its thunder – roars like death and life together. I suppose little Ai'reth knew it well, for this vision I have in my mind, of life and death at war, recalls the *yangyi* I have seen through his eyes.

Yes, my power grows; my vicarious sorceries nearly drove through Megan's shields last night. Nearly – but not quite. Ai'reth was easy, though very difficult at first. Once, Tana, daughter of Coryn, king of Kaerglen Isle, was closed to me, but attempting her of late, I've succeeded as well – a timely success as only now have I need again to write of the princess and her family.

Still, I do not understand why I gain strength, unless it be that I am a part of those events rushing to a common, fateful conclusion, gaining speed and power along the way. That is a thought, but I fear I am but an echo. I dream of darkness now in the night, dreams of nothingness so vacant I wake and turn restlessly until dawn, or I steal away from my bed and come to this work, toiling by candlelight. I've come to cherish the silence of sleepless nights, inasmuch as I can escape those dreams. To be aware, aching for light, for movement, but to dream only of this yawning void of darkness. Nothing moves in my dreams; nothing changes, but the dreams themselves feel eternal.

At first – or I should write *Long ago* – I wished to write of those days of chaos when we thieved and pillaged and built the small fortune that grew into The Emporium. It did not take long, not for Thyri, and especially not for Megan: goddesses crushing ants, both of them. I guess now that that is why I have not written of those times. They were times of diversion, akin to all the adventures of Thyri and Astrid before Astrid's death. I must stay focused on the Twilight. Why write of the hero's idle afternoons while the battles remain untold? And, as always, I do not know what time I have left. Satan's Chalice threatens, even now, to run dry before long.

So follow as the tale leads us onward and elsewhere. As events unfolded, we abandoned The Emporium anyway.

Ghosts

Her name was Tana, and she was just fifteen, the age when childhood still bubbles up unexpectedly through memory, as it now did for her. She was fifteen, with long nut-brown hair and green eyes, long, strong legs built like a doe's for grace and speed, and her breasts had already grown larger than her mother's. But she didn't feel fifteen. She felt about ten – no younger than that because until that age she'd never truly felt herself weak, a child. Until then, she'd felt only the magic; she'd felt almost ancient, a child of Brigid, a spirit as old and wise as the sea, as quick and strong as the wind, as bright as the sky. Until ten, her mother could not make her tremble with fear, and the night's mysteries never menaced or haunted or whispered of past evil. Until ten, she'd been more spirit than girl, with all the world her witching ground. *'Touch me,'* the rocks would say, and she would touch them and hear their sighs. *'Feel me,'* the wind would whisper, and she would, feeling more than the wind, feeling the spirits that rode on it, feeling the wind's age, seeing where it had come from and where it had been. Until ten, when the wind touched her, she could close her eyes and race with it over mountains and follow it from one world to the next – over the seas of Midgard to the glittering shores and golden forests of Alfheim; the majestic plains and halls of Asgard to the granite crags of Nidavellir. In dark Svartalfheim, she'd see her own light illuminating the twisted wood, and when dark spirits would join her in the wind, she'd feel a chill and then, simply, open her eyes . . .

To stand on the hill below the castle or on the rocky shore down from the secret grotto where the wind-dreams would come to her even when she kept her eyes open – oh, the ageless peace of it all! Sometimes Seth would be with her, standing silently, his hand hesitantly reaching out to touch hers. She'd look at him and search his face – his own ten-year-old face, for they were twins – and then she'd ask what he'd seen. 'Glimpses,' he would say. Glimpses of forest and lake, dragons at the edge of the sky that would transform into cloud as soon as he tried to focus on them. Tuathan gatherings – great bonfires that spit sparks like fiery, hellish eyes into the night. But always only glimpses; he could follow her, chase after her, strain to catch her only to lose her again, but he could never lead. The wind-dreams were Tana's, but she shared all she could, as she and Seth had shared all ever since they'd been born. Whenever her brother finished telling his visions, she would talk, completing them, placing the dragons in context, the lakes among mountains, the Tuathans in their woods, and the bonfires before the temples of the worlds. She would speak until Seth understood, until he assured her that he felt her wind-dream as his own, as if he had never left her side.

Which, in fact, he hadn't, at least not on Midgard. In her heart and mind she would fly, while he would watch over her body. It had happened first when they were six, exploring some forgotten corner of the castle. They'd found a door, and beyond it a passageway, which they'd followed, winding ever downward until it had opened into the grotto. He'd held her hand while the wind-dream had come and carried her away.

Now, Tana was fifteen and wanted that day back. She tried to find the six-year-old inside herself, her old sense of wonder, her elation when she finally *knew* herself and her strength. For years, she hadn't known what gave her those waking dreams. They would come when she wished, wherever she found herself, but always with effort away from the grotto. With tremendous effort these days . . . She'd lost the feeling; she'd been broken. When she'd first spoken with Brigid – when the sad goddess had finally revealed herself to Tana in the grotto late one formless, shapeless day – it had already been too late.

She still felt ten, the age her world ended, when the wonder within her bled from her wound as she'd found herself suddenly naked before all the world. Even five years later she couldn't fight it. To think brought it all back. To try not to think made it worse.

Autumn had come to Kaerglen, and now, near dusk, the full moon shone brightly down into the garden at the castle's heart where Tana slouched, limp in the wooden chair Finaan had insisted on bringing her. (Finaan – of all men it had to be *him* fawning over her, touching her face and hair, trying to comfort her with his vacant, treacherous smile! Finaan whose heart was black like coal, whose men raped her island, whose insidious sorcery hastened the end of all the beauty that remained in the world. Who – but, no, she mustn't think it . . . Too late already, though: Here she sat, her own father near death. And who did she think of? Her father? No, she thought of Finaan. And Patrick.)

There was a time – once, so long ago – when Tana's and Seth's world had nearly seduced their elder brother, nearly made him one of them. How ridiculous that time seemed now; Patrick was eight years their senior, and only their half-brother actually; King Coryn's blood did not run in his veins. And yet he was heir, and long ago – six years? Yes, they'd been nine and he'd been seventeen – they'd almost had him. It was after Rahne's death; something then had made Patrick morose, listless. Tana wondered what yearning within him had sapped his strength. It could not have been mourning, for the prince shared no blood with the ancient woman, she being the sister of the king's mother. Perhaps it had been simply the shock of death in the air, with Patrick finally mature enough to sense his own mortality hidden implicitly in the ugly, bone-white wrinkles of the corpse, in the blood-bruised skin of its impossibly thin arms. He had, after all, found her first, collapsed in the hall in a lump outside his door.

When Queen Moira had come at his call, they'd found a long, thin dagger hidden in Rahne's skirts. Was that it? Tana wondered (as she had countless times over). Was that dagger the key to Patrick's near-conversion? She and Seth had known Rahne fairly well; in fact, the old woman had informed them many times of her impending death. She and Seth had gained much of their knowledge of the castle from Rahne, and Tana had often seen that dagger – it was very slender and all of stone with a bird's head carved into the hilt. Rahne had used it in eating, in sewing, and Tana had known that she'd kept it with her always, hidden in her skirts. But had Patrick known this? If not, he might have imagined the dying woman seeking him out with the last of her strength, intent on taking him with her into death. She'd fallen before *his* door. That was slightly strange; Tana reasoned that she'd actually been trying to reach her and Seth. Only a few more steps, and she might have made it. What last secrets might she have told them then in the last moments before death?

Patrick with his deep voice and cruel muscles – even then she'd thought his physique obscene, as if he'd been shaped of muscle and bone, his maker regarding soft, simple flesh as unnecessary, carving only powerful but *cruel* lines, veins that bulged, sharp muscles that moved like snakes under skin, a belly crisscrossed with lines like the back of a tortoise. And whenever she'd seen him, his flesh had been wet, drenched like the coat of a work horse. 'Christ's champion,' their mother called him. But when he came to Tana – that day after Rahne's burial – he was crying.

She and Seth took his hands and led him deep into Castle Kaerglen, to where he'd never been, back past the rooms of the old ones and deeper still, down stairs and into a maze of halls covered in dust and debris. The castle had known better days; Tana now knew something of its history and its age, its roots in the many ancient invasions of Erin and how it once was home to Manannan – the very god of the sea – and his wife, Fand. Where she and Seth took Patrick – even Brenden the priest had never been this deep on his periodic missions of exorcism. So the magic remained ever strong, and they passed through it, to the tunnel, the winding stairs, and the most magical place of all: the *faerie* place, the grotto. Tana had her wind-dream while holding Patrick's hand, and through her he could feel the peace and wonder of it all, the power and strength of the winds that blew through all the worlds.

He cried then with tears of joy, and a week later, Tana and Seth led him again to the grotto and repeated the ritual, and afterward they showed him the exit to the rocky shore below, where one could look away overhead and see a corner of the castle at the top of the cliff. They ate there on the rocks and laughed together, Seth singing for Patrick old songs he'd learned years before from Rath, and the sea crashing lightly below them as if Manannan in his depths knew the tune.

A few days later, their cousin from the mainland, Finaan, arrived, and everything changed. When they went to Patrick, he and Finaan laughed at them, so that was that; the near-conversion ended, and Patrick remained unchanged, his cruel muscles yet moving like snakes beneath his skin.

In the grotto she'd had her defeat; Rahne's death had opened the treacherous door for her own compassion to shape it. It hadn't taken long – maybe a month at most. The days grew darker, Patrick's muscles more cruel, and she and Seth were too young to perceive the subtle shifts in the castle's atmosphere, so when Patrick and Finaan arrived suddenly, exploding in like nightmares to devour the grotto's serene magic, the twins had been paralyzed, unable to act as their world crumbled around them . . .

Tana shifted in her chair as she sensed Finaan's approach. Above, the full moon grew brighter and she gazed at it with helpless longing, as ever she did when it went full. This attraction was real in a way, for perhaps – if she could reach out and touch it – she might regain the hope that had fueled her one, failed quest. Forgetting the present, she closed her eyes and reached up, but her hand touched something rough – Finaan's face – and she quickly drew it back.

He stood in silence for a while, eclipsing her salvation, the moon's light casting him a dark shadow with the wild black hair around his head paled to dull, glittering gray. His eyes were like dark craters, unreadable in the shadows, the same shadows that turned his nose up, into a snout like a pig's.

As she watched, he moved his hand to his face, touching his cheek where she'd involuntarily caressed him. His other hand held a goblet toward her. 'I brought you wine,' he said.

The silver vessel flashed in the moonlight, a red liquid lapping over its sides. It made her think of blood, and she shook her head. 'Leave me,' she said simply.

Instead, he raised the goblet to his lips and drained it himself, then he squatted before her. She could see him more clearly like that. He wore a light mail shirt under his black silks, and the sword at his side made a scraping sound against the ground as he shifted his weight slowly from side to side. She almost laughed; the man went everywhere prepared for battle. As she thought about it, she couldn't recall a single time when she'd seen Finaan separated from his weaponry. He even wore his sword at the dinner table. With him squatted like this, she could see something of his eyes, and his nose looked normal, no longer like a snout. She idly wished he'd stand again and resume his demonic form with the moon behind him; the pig's snout would keep her aware of his true nature. But even as she saw him more clearly, she couldn't think him handsome, not with all the imagination she could muster. The servant girls (and she had heard their gossip enough to know this was true) – let them adore him and vie nightly for his bed. Let them save her the anguish.

'Can I get you anything?' he asked.

'Just leave me,' she said. There was no force in her words. There never was anymore; what difference did her words make anyway? He wasn't going to leave, not on her command. Finaan did what Finaan wished, and only that. Her very *lack of force* was her defense. Her defeat was her defense; it kept his passions subdued, at a distance.

And he did ignore her. He scarcely moved, save his slow

shifting from side to side. 'Anything,' he said after a moment. 'I'll do anything for you, Tana. If you would touch me again like that – if you wouldn't draw away, if you would sigh when I touch you – I would do anything.'

She grunted.

'You can't hate me forever,' he said. 'I will fight the darkness inside you until you love me, until you beg me to hold you. I will be a king one day myself, you know. My own father is old. When Patrick and I are kings, we shall conquer all of Erin. And I would do anything if you would be my queen.'

The darkness inside is all within you, my prince, she thought. But she found herself repeating his word, the word he offered her again and again. 'Anything?' she asked listlessly.

'Yes!' he said softly, inching closer to her. She imagined she breathed his breath – an acrid stench, the breath of his One God's hell.

'Then kill my brother,' she whispered.

He reached out and touched her knee; she jerked it quickly away, and he cleared his throat. 'I will when we find him. I will redouble our efforts, I promise!'

Inside, Tana erupted in a torrent of anguished emotion and unspoken words. She wanted to scream, to leap forward and take him by the neck and say, *'Not Seth, you fool! Not my twin, you idiot! Do you think I believe him the enemy of the throne as you do? Do you think that time has sucked me into your fantasy of Kaerglen, and that I have so forgotten the past that I believe in the one you've invented inside your head, instead of the one I know to be true? Do you not realize that Seth is the one person in all this world that I am sure I love? That Seth is the only one who has never betrayed me, that he is more a part of me than you or any other man will ever be?*

'No, Finaan, you are slave to idiocy. You are blind and ignorant. Were you to kill Seth, I think might finally have the strength myself to kill you!'

These words nearly gushed forth, nearly signed her own death. If she'd said them, she would have lost her last defense.

As it was, only the whites of her knuckles as she clutched the arms of her chair betrayed her true thoughts. At last, when she spoke, her voice was vacant of this fury, though the words it spoke made it cold and flat, shocking even herself with their dispassionate ultimatum. 'Not Seth, Finaan,' she said. 'Kill Patrick.'

The weight of her treason hung heavy in the air, dispelled only when Finaan rose and laughed, softly at first, then loudly, as if bristling with sudden, revealed irony. 'You would be queen!' he declared softly when he finally paused, then he laughed again. When his mirth subsided, he looked down at her and spoke softly again, his voice level and starkly sincere in the wake of his raucous laughter. 'If I could believe that would make you love me, my princess, it would be done.'

With that he left her, the echoes of his laughter still sounding in her ears. She gazed up at the moon, forcing back tears, cursing the weakness that had broken her resolve and allowed her to ask anything at all. And after all was said, Finaan still hadn't understood her request; he'd translated it into a lust for power on her behalf. Tana had no desire at all for the monarchy. She wished, merely, to be free of her ghosts, and she cursed herself again for uttering treason in the presence of Finaan, for she knew – inasmuch as he was the darkest of all who haunted her – that she could never survive the sort of alliance she might have intimated.

If he carried it through, she would have to kill him, or kill herself. She doubted she had the strength for either act.

She closed her eyes to the moon and went back again in time.

She was ten.

The grotto was the most magnificent place in all the worlds; even her wind-dreams had shown her nothing to equal its wonder. And this wonder began with its light, a light that had once illuminated the halls of the castle itself, a light which had spread from here in the happy days when Manannan sat on his throne high above and ruled over the waves and all creatures beneath them, when the mists around the island set it fully in Alfheim, and when the Tuatha de Danaan would gather here on Kaerglen for their feasts and songs and games and romances. And Fand had built the grotto for lovers.

It had kept its glory, untouched by the violence of the island's history. When she and Seth had discovered it . . . one entered from the spiral staircase that wound down from the castle. The stairs themselves had their own light, and along the way were niches and tunnels that led off to other chambers, mostly empty but some containing ornate chests – some empty, some still locked – and a quick eye might discover the dull flash of gemstones here and there buried under the dust, hinting at the treasures these chambers might once have contained. But the grotto – its treasures had remained intact. At the entrance, tinkling water sounded its greeting from the right where a cold, fresh-water stream issued from a flat gash in the wall. In this first chamber was statuary, birds and beasts carved of shining rock or shaped in crystal. Three quartz salmon leaped from the stream while a hungry fox watched, its amethyst eyes positioned so that no matter where one stood, they held the reflection of one or more of the fish. At the end of this chamber, a tree of brown stone leafed with green shells spread over the far wall, and beneath it a pearly white dryad posed, forever drawing one's attention to the next chamber, a shell-filled wonderland of dazzling reflective beauty. Beyond this was a mossy place (not unlike the *felninas* of Alfheim) where the stream gathered into a round pool and strange white flowers dotted the green carpet in patches and clumps. Further on was the passageway that led down to the shore.

The moss chamber was where Tana mostly had her wind-dreams. The grotto's peace was most meditative there, and even when the air outside was still, a gentle, sea-laden breeze always came up through the passageway. To there, she and Seth would escape – until the day when the living nightmares came.

How they made it up the passageway fully armed without alerting the twins was their secret. But they made it, bursting in with drawn swords, laughing, a hellish cruelty in their eyes. Finaan grabbed Seth by the arm, carried him through the chambers of shells, and tied him to the dryad. Seth's screams, coming a moment later, chilled Tana's blood and echoed and echoed until she slowly grew aware that some of the screams were her own.

Patrick was on top of her – her own brother. The coldness of his mail shirt pressed into her flesh. Her shift lay across from her, half fallen into the pool where Patrick had tossed it after tearing it off her in one violent sweep of his arm. She was only ten; her breasts scarcely larger than Seth's, the hair between her legs more tender than the first shoots of spring. But Patrick took her anyway, filling her with pain beyond her imagination, and all the while he whispered and panted in her ear: *'This is an evil place, sister, a pagan place, but I will save you from it. Even now I am saving you . . . Feel the power of God inside me. Feel . . . the power . . .'*

When he was done, Finaan – this demon in a prince's disguise! – came and did the same. Through the raging fury inside her head, she could hear Seth's sobbing from where he remained tied to the dryad. And Finaan's pounding against her was worse than Patrick's, for he had already sated himself on Seth and now had to heave and strain to have his full pleasure on her. Through her screams, she heard his voice, but unlike Patrick, he didn't even talk to her. He talked to Patrick who looked on, a broad, cruel grin spread across his face. As he heaved on top of Tana, Finaan looked at Patrick and said, 'I do feel it here, Patrick. That evil you mentioned – it must be cleansed.' And he went on talking and pounding against her. He never finished though, because, suddenly, another was on top of him and there was a flash of metal and Tana felt a gush of blood splatter against her cheek. Finaan quickly rolled away from her and gained his feet, one hand clutching the opposite shoulder where blood poured freely through his fingers. Seth had only just missed the veins of his neck.

Yet filled with pain, Tana turned to see her twin crouched beyond them, near the tunnel, his eyes alight with a fire she'd never before seen there. In his hand, he held a knife with a blade no longer than three inches. He'd carried it strapped to his forearm (as old Rath had once told him a knife should be worn), and he'd used it to free himself after Finaan had abandoned him and left him alone.

Now, Finaan howled in fury. 'I'll gut you, you little imp!' he howled, letting go of his wound and taking up his sword. At that, Seth looked desperately to Tana, then he fled, down through the passageway to the shore. Still howling, Finaan ran after him.

Tana tried to move, but found she could barely stand. When she did gain her feet, Patrick slapped her down, so she lay back on the moss and watched him, dark brooding on his face, as he waited for Finaan's return.

When their cousin came back, he had not caught Seth. He did, however, set to the grotto with his sword, prying out all the shells inlaid in its walls, gouging out huge chunks of moss and tossing them in the pool, hacking and screaming at the statuary until he'd shattered most of it before his sword finally broke. That was how Tana always remembered Finaan – full of animal fury, his eyes malicious pits, his muscles churning and his sword flashing and chips of stone and shell careening off surfaces that sparked and pleaded for mercy. And the louder their agonies, the more violent the punisher, his body wild, one arm painted crimson by his own pumping blood.

When Finaan finally rested, he and Patrick left, abandoning her to find her own way home.

The pain went on forever, though she healed – physically – within three months. But even with her body as evidence, Moira – the queen and her mother – refused to believe her tale. At least she wouldn't admit it; she wouldn't listen long to Tana's weeping. Ever since Tana and Seth had refused Priest Brenden's tutelage to the point of the man's exasperation, they'd grown wild in their mother's eyes. Though they'd lived their days as they'd wished, the queen had completely abandoned them to their whims and focused all her maternal devotion on Patrick alone. *Christ's champion* . . . When Tana spoke, Moira heard not the truth, but Satan, and she told Tana so.

King Coryn, Tana thought, believed her. But he would do nothing. He told her, in fact, that Patrick was prince and would be king, and if his God wished him to possess his sister, then as prince and future king, he had that right. The assertion brought tears to Tana's eyes, and she tried to flee her father, but Coryn grabbed her and held her close, speaking softly to her until she grew still. It was then that he told her of the fading of Brigid and Lugh and the rest of the Tuatha de Danaan; it was then that he tried to explain everything to her, even though she could hardly grasp it all. Coryn had foreseen the fading of his gods and the sure futility of resisting it. He had been defeated, and even the violation of his own daughter could not bring him to fury, so certain was his own defeat.

Tana couldn't understand it. She tried to tell him of her wind-dreams, but he wouldn't listen.

As for Seth, he had disappeared, and it seemed to Tana that she alone mourned his absence.

In the garden, the sky had grown dark but for the moon, and the night's chorus of insects enveloped her, drawing her back briefly to the present. She listened to the sounds; once she had felt only wonder here, the insects the very minstrels of life. Once she would have spent hours separating their songs, naming them all. Now they seemed alien, an obtrusive cacophony with no power left to awe or inspire. They went on, slaves in this castle to the powers that ruled it, caring nothing for the deaths of those who writhed and faded before the power of the One God's cross.

She had the sorcery – *she, Tana Kaerglen* – had the power of the ancients in her blood, as had Megan before her. So said Brigid, and so she knew it to be true. But all her sorceries failed before the cross . . .

She returned to the grotto a week after her violation. She found it *cleansed*, all the shells and sculptures broken out and removed. Only the tree remained, leafless and barren. And the moss, it persisted; though fires had blackened it in places, Patrick and Finaan had eventually decided it would grow back anyway. Then – finally and too late – Brigid had spoken to her.

The voice came on the wind. *'Do not despair, my child, for your power remains, if mine does not. I would have saved you if I could.'*

Tana fell to her knees and wept.

'*Sleep and dream*,' said the goddess. And after a while, Tana did sleep.

In her dreams, she saw Brigid in all her sad glory: a tall, pale woman with brown hair full of leaves and twigs. *'This is my world you dream, princess, and it is far from your own. I would now that we had spoken in brighter times, but I thought the wind-dreams would teach you all you needed to know. They teach power that comes from the heart, but your heart is now shattered, so you must learn normal spells. Would you have me teach you in your dreams?'*

Tana nodded, and so it went. From time to time, whenever she was sure of Patrick's and Finaan's absence, she would overcome her terror of a repetition of the past, and descend to the grotto, there to sleep and dream and learn spells, all of which worked, but none of which could harm her hated enemies, so surrounded did they remain by their faith and their talismans.

And even in these sorcerous dreams, the fading of the old powers haunted every moment. Brigid's voice came to her from far away, and of it, Tana could never ask questions; she could only listen and learn. When she asked, she would waken unexpectedly, as if a simple question strained the limits of the sorcery. She wanted to cry out to Brigid, to ask her how to overcome her brother and cousin, to ask what *would* work and where was Seth, but none of these answers could be hers.

In Tana's thirteenth spring, Brigid taught her the sorceries of the gate, and Tana set herself on a quest, imagining she had real hope for the very first time. Years before, there had come to the castle a wild swordsmistress named Thyri who had slain the druid Pye. From Thyri, Tana had learned that Megan yet remained on the island, and Tana imagined now that only Megan might aid her in breaking Patrick's hold on the throne. She began casting her sorceries, growing excited as if her heart soared again freely among the clouds of all worlds. Through her spells, she found Megan's home and gated there, only to find it disused and abandoned, a lonely hut in a field of mud, battered by the cold northern winds.

In the hut, she found a single clue to the events of the past. A small white tablet sat at an angle on a shelf, and it read, simply, *I, Megan Kaerglen, do forsake this island of sorrow, to seek my heart, and follow the moon.*

And that was why Tana, at fifteen, sat in the garden at the castle's heart and gazed in yearning at the full moon, while Finaan of Connaught – who had spoiled her life and that of her brother – came to court her heart.

Within the castle, Coryn – long since truly king – lay dying in his chamber. Patrick, his adopted heir, awaited the coming of death in anticipation of his own coronation and his destiny to be king of Kaerglen Isle.

Changes

That night was the third of the three nights of the full moon. Thyri spent it in a forest, far from the city of the Franks. In the wood, the changes came painlessly, and she almost enjoyed her days for the solitude they granted her.

The past weeks had not been kind. She felt wounded inside, and in a sense beyond healing. She had killed her brother, and knew that she hadn't the strength to face the memory. In the solitude of the wood, with the day paced by her own heart and labors rather than the bustle of the city, she was forced to face herself and tend to this wound. At least the wood gave her the peace to handle the task.

Erik was dead; she'd killed him – she knew that much. On Megan's word, she'd had no choice. She couldn't hate herself for it; maybe what bled inside her was that lack of choice. Why couldn't there have been another way? Why had the Norns twisted her life so that she had no choice in the direction of the thread? For instance, all might have been avoided had she not followed Megan into Alfheim, and yet the decision had been hers – she'd felt she'd needed an escape from it all, from the city, from the sweat and the smell, just as she'd come here alone to get away where the beast within her could run free in the night and feed and not fight her for its right to human flesh. If she hadn't followed Megan, then she wouldn't have killed Erik. But she'd followed blindly, and what was done was done. What law of the gods made it thus? What law allowed her pains, and her curse, and what law forbade her breaking the first?

It all seemed meaningless and cruel. She almost felt as if she'd lost all she'd learned from Scacath, all that had made her a warrior. In her mind, the will to fight had grown arbitrary, as if she could no longer choose her battles as all warriors should. She knew this, and yet she was propelled blindly nevertheless – to battle Erik, to battle the emperor of the Franks. What had spoiled that last battle? Megan's tears in the night. Defeat lurking like a viper in the heart of victory. No matter what happened, she couldn't seem to hold it together anymore, even with Megan. The love they shared was losing its power to comfort and heal. No longer was it good enough to seek out each other and forget the rest of the world, because the world kept intruding on a whim, haunting them, stealing their passion.

She had no desire to return to the city and try to go on with things as they were. At night in the forest she hunted and killed and feasted, at one with the beast. There was a harmony to it, a basic purpose in that cycle of hunger and death. It needed no explanation, no decisions, no consideration of any fact, whether it be the lives of the Norse, the battles of the gods, *fimbulwinter* on Asgard, the fading of the old ways . . . The cycle stood apart from all this, somehow above it; it simply was.

The cycle went on because it had to go on: hunger required food and food sated hunger. In the past, Thyri might have reasoned that peace required warfare, and victory in warfare brought peace. But much time had passed since she'd had to fight to guarantee her next day. And now, when the peace after victory did not guarantee her happiness – if it spawned only new vipers meant to torment her – then where was the meaning of her victory?

Over those days, Thyri decided she would find another battle, one in which she could believe. Instinct drove her ever farther from the city, and ever nearer to the land on the riverbanks that she and Megan had secured for the Norsemen of seven hundred ships who would have died but for her intervention.

When she arrived among them, the whispered rumors began and she wished them quick speed with a twisted inner smile.

Before the morning passed, she paid a man with a horse to take word to Megan, so that her lover might join her.

As for her welcome among her people, her name was well-known and it did not sit well with many. Though a powerful ally, she was berserk, and cursed. All wondered why she had come to them, and all suspected the worst. Fantastic things had happened; they'd been given land when they'd expected death, and they'd been hailed by a bird that had spoken, greeting them in the name of a berserk legend. Now, so soon after that, she was among them, and they could imagine nothing of her purpose but that she might demand payment for the honor.

Eiriksdattir greets her fellow travelers.

For the most part, they were tired men, weary of battle. They had in truth come south seeking land. Now that they had it, most had little desire for the sagas to continue. What legends they desired, they would keep for nights when, armed only with ale, they could tell them in safety and comfort in front of warm, crackling fires.

Magic

Ai'reth stopped short of the portal where the messenger went in. The wards laced the building in a mystical wall – the work of the low-born Tuathan? He would not assume such a thing, not in these dark days, not with him hiding a cat's breath from Midgard and unsure whether Loki remained chained.

But surely this would be her home; the wards shone white, and had he not followed the man ever since he'd left the white-haired one? The messenger had not strayed, had come straight here, and he wasn't a dark man, just a normal, pathetically weak one. The longer Ai'reth paused, the more sure he became that this was the home of the dark-haired power, Megan, his friend. If he wished to see, he would have to enter and trigger the wards. But what harm in that? It would only tell her of his coming.

Unseen by human eyes – but a cat's breath still from Midgard – Ai'reth plunged through the wall and the wards. Their magic twisted him fully into the world, and he would have laughed at the sorcerous subtlety had he not found himself plunged unexpectedly into a room of men. *She knows her tricks,* he thought wryly as he scampered silently across the floor, taking cover in a pile of cloth before daring to look around, to learn whether he'd been seen.

The place was a treasure trove of human wealth. Why would the powers be here? Were there not battles to be fought?

The messenger spoke with a man behind the counter. Another man – a large one, much stronger and brighter than most – came up as they spoke. The large man took the message and turned, starting up a stairwell. Ai'reth took a breath and ran low along the floor, around the counter, and up the stairs behind the man.

Chaos had drawn him to Midgard, Chaos and his own thoughts, his memories of the night his wife had died, his memories of power where power did not belong, in these two women who had brought death to his wife by their presence – but that wasn't their fault. S'kiri had gambled for the Queenstone. She had died brave but foolish. And during war, all blame fell on the darkness.

With S'kiri's death – after that night when he had followed Megan nearly to Midgard – he had wandered, the Queenstone his burden and his sole reminder of love. He had watched battles, and seen gods die. He had seen giants like mountains fall on Aesir, Tuathans, Vanir, Elohim, and all the forces of light. The end came – grew closer moment by moment – and all the while, Klorista's words tumbled again and again through his mind: *What if Surt burns all the nine worlds save Midgard? We will destroy ourselves and nothing more . . . They are low-borns, one of Light, one of Chaos . . .* What would come of it?

And then he'd realized what mattered. It was Chaos – the wildfire – the drums that changed heartbeats and the directions of the winds. So he'd wandered closer to Midgard, and at dusk, with the moon newly full, Chaos had burst like an eruption into the night. Through his talent, it had reached for him, and he'd followed and found her, the white wolf bitch of the elder legends, chaotic power in harmony, the power that the dark Erik had tried to steal, the power that had overcome. Yes, the elder legends – to them he turned. Common skalds declared a wolf-age before *fimbulwinter: 'An axe-age and sword-age starts the flow of blood, with a wind-age to staunch it, and a wolf-age to howl down the ice.'* What if the common lore was wrong? With Chaos so strong in the wolf-age, it could howl down the end of the ice. Or might it best the fires of Surt, and save the worlds' burning?

He couldn't know, but it had given him hope, and since that hope could be followed, then follow he did.

Megan opened the door before Rollo could knock. He eyed her oddly; something had her on edge, he was sure of it. She took the letter from him without a word, only smiling distractedly when he said it had come from Thyri.

In the doorway, she unfolded the paper and read it, frowning at first, then smiling again. 'I will be leaving today,' she told him.

'And Thyri?' he asked unsurely.

'She is with the invaders.'

'Will she be coming back?'

'I don't think so, Rollo.'

He grinned broadly and patted his sword. 'Then it is good news!' he said, turning away. 'We will follow tonight.'

She smiled as he left, then shut her door and let the letter fall to the floor. Some sorcerous presence had accompanied the message from Thyri; her ears burned with awareness of this. She closed her eyes and summoned the power of her ring, seeking out the intruder. She found him under her bed.

Ai'reth revealed himself just as she prepared an attack. He stood before her, trembling and smiling, his sharp teeth white in the curtained darkness of her room.

She relaxed and asked him how he fared. He answered her with hurried riddles and tales of the wars. Lugh had died, and it was said that Jormungard had swallowed Manannan whole. The legions of Jotunheim rampaged, awaiting Loki to lead them to Vigrid. It was all only a matter of time.

As to why Ai'reth had come to her, he couldn't say. Chaos had drawn him, and only in it did he see hope. He was glad now that he'd found her; he'd been afraid to show himself to Thyri, not knowing how she would think of him after her battle with her brother in his home. As he spoke, he pleaded with her, for her aid, for Thyri's aid – for them to join in the fight.

'How?' the sorceress asked. Her eyes were like small, dark fires, burning into him, almost hurting him. 'We are not gods! My powers pale before those of Scacath and Odin, never mind Loki and the dark kings of Svartalfheim.' Her light grew stronger, even as he heard her say these things.

'You have been dreaming, felnin,' she continued. 'In desperation, you look for miracles, and, finding flimsy wishes and groundless hopes, you take the fate of Ragnarok upon your shoulders and try to bend it to your will! Don't you think that if Odin wanted us, he would invite us himself? No – the battle is his and he must manage it. Look to him, not us. We are of Midgard – among my mother's people I am nothing, a trifling invalid!'

'You are wrong,' he insisted, flinching before the strength of her light. 'You do not know yourself.'

'You are wrong, Ai'reth,' she countered. 'I am just like you – a gnat that might bite a giant's toe or two before dying in vain. And do not go to Thyri with your wild stories – you should not show yourself to her at all. She does not have memory of you.'

He lowered his eyes to the floor. At his feet, the hilt of the rune-blade borne by the dark Erik jutted out from under the bed. He picked it up and unsheathed it, his eyes running slowly over its length, the iron once stained by S'kiri's blood.

'In this world,' Megan continued, 'you are in grave danger if you are seen by anyone. If you are caught, they will kill you.'

'Ai'reth knows that,' he said, looking up from the sword. 'But he must do *something*! Light succumbs! All is at stake!'

'Yes,' Megan said sadly. 'I agree you must follow your heart, however foolish it might be. If you are drawn to Thyri, then stay near her, but that is all. Watch over her. Protect her. If all is as dire as you say, then I fear in any case that we shall not avoid the battle.'

'Avoid it! You *cannot* avoid it! She is the hope, the wind-breaker, the wildfire and the Chaos!'

Megan eyed him darkly. 'How can you insist on knowing such things?'

He didn't answer; how could he explain to her his thoughts and Klorista's riddles? If she was a power, and couldn't see his mind, then his words would have no power to show her if they hadn't done so already. He *knew* – now more than ever – and that was that.

Megan sighed. 'I wish I could believe you.' She went to the window and opened the curtain, absently looking out. 'Do what you will,' she said.

When she turned back to look at him, he was gone, and with him went the sword Scacath had given to Thyri, the blade Thyri had left behind with Erik after taking Astrid's sword as her own.

Ai'reth passed out of Midgard, hurrying along the pathways to a half-world where he could sit quietly and think. He was troubled; he had expected Megan to summon Thyri and for them all to depart Midgard together, to build new armies to stand against the darkness. He had come away with but a weapon, and one he had stolen at that.

In a half-world of trees and waterfalls, he tested the blade. He could never wield it effectively; it was far too long. He sheathed it and brooded. If the armies were not to be, the hope yet remained. Perhaps Megan was right about now, while he was right about the future. Time alone would tell; Light – though wounded – had not perished yet.

So he would look over Thyri, he decided. He would stand as her guard until such time as she came to the aid of Light. He would not reveal himself to her unless he had to, and if the time truly came when all would perish without her aid, he might even be able to trick her into the fray. At any rate, he could not abandon his hope, not when it had grown so strong and not when he saw no hope elsewhere, no matter how desperately he looked.

Slowly, his dark mood lifted. If this was now his path, he had to be prepared. Beneath the waterfall, Ai'reth took up his finger drum and began tapping, conjuring up hazy and uncertain images of possible futures, seeking clues and omens of where it all might lead, and where he might need to be.

Reavers

'. . . And so we fled south, meeting army after army, even here,' Olaf Ulfson concluded, smiling at Thyri.

She eyed him thoughtfully, then looked beyond him, out of the canvas shelter and out to the fields where Vikings toiled, raising wooden houses from the Frankish soil.

'So Harald is truly strong now?' Thyri reflected aloud.

'Aye, swordsmistress. He rules all of Norway, even the coldest Jarldoms. And those Norse he does not rule, he slays.'

Thyri didn't respond. Her thoughts turned back to her days with Astrid and in particular, to a letter Astrid had once written her:

> . . . I have fought the Danes at sea as well, though it makes no sense that they would come north into our waters while there is such plunder to be had in the south . . . It would seem that we Norse have not a direction, but only a lust for battle. I have seen men reach berserk fury and die with laughter on their lips, welcoming the call of Valhalla. Thus it is, though I think, perhaps out of ignorance and inexperience, that it need not be thus. We are of strong blood; you cannot imagine it but must see it in the faces of our foes to the south. And we are many too. I have seen the sea covered with our sails, while each ship is bound for a place different from the next. Were all to sail together, we could crush the legions of Surt! But this, for reasons beyond me, we do not do. Instead, we fight each other as well as the rest of the world.
>
> Perhaps Harald of Vestfold is a leader who might unite

the Vikings. But he is yet young, and his unity may come too late. The strength we have is now, and misuse now may make it impotent twenty years hence. At any rate, I should soon find myself on the battlefield with him, my sword against his, and not by his side. In the end, it doesn't matter. The ways of the warrior, all the ways of the warrior, lead to Valhalla – to serve Odin until Ragnarok.

Time had passed, a decade for Thyri, even more including the years we lost while on the seas of Jotunheim. It was now the year 886 by the calendar of the One God. Viking strength had waxed and waned, and all that time, Norse had killed Norse while Harald of Vestfold had sought to rule all. They might have ruled all the southern lands, all the old empires, had Astrid's wish for unity come to pass. Now it was too late. The south knew them, feared them yet, but ever more often turned them away. The Norse remained as they had been, leaderless, without direction or vision while Harald hacked at their roots. He was a leader. He could have compromised, united, and conquered the south. Instead, he still conquered the north. Thyri blamed it all on a princess of Hordaland, her own kingdom. Gyda, she was. Years past, Harald had asked her to wed. She'd laughed and called him a petty kingling. He'd then set out to prove her wrong.

Hordaland had fallen to Harald. He'd made great enemies throughout the north. He'd won Gyda, but he battled still.

Thyri brooded, the ghost of Astrid – the Valkyrie – shadowing her every thought, making her ache anew for the past, for the days before her curse. Since she'd been a child, she'd borne a hatred for Gyda. Since she'd been a child, she'd known of Astrid's dream of the Norselands united. Since she'd been a child . . .

Astrid stood tall in her thoughts, laughing, her eyes full of joy as she spoke to Thyri of Scacath and the wonders of her teaching. Astrid, her cousin, her first love. Her purest love, before the curse, before Megan, Akan, Pohati. Her dream had not come to pass. The *fimbulwinter* had come to Asgard. All threatened to end. Astrid deserved her dream fulfilled. And Gyda, in Thyri's mind, deserved death.

Slowly, Thyri rose from her seat; Olaf watched her strangely, his hand falling nervously to the hilt of his sword. He didn't understand the distance in her gaze. She had drifted away from him, and while her thoughts had carried her back in time, so had his. He had recalled all the legends and whispered warnings of she they called Eiriksdattir, Bloodfang. He began to sweat, fearing she might attack him. Instead, she looked down at him, her gaze suddenly present and stern. 'Erect a tent, and summon all warriors. Tomorrow night, I will address them.'

'But swordsmistress,' Olaf protested, 'they toil on their houses!'

'Houses for which I toiled to allow them,' she added flatly.

'Eiriksdattir,' he said carefully, 'many do not believe that. We have heard tales of miracles – the entire land is alive with them – and the tales say the One God gave us this land.'

'Odin's beard!' she seethed, turning on him. 'Whether they believe or not, you take them my word! I desire a gathering place, a shelter for those who wish to attend. They may come or stay away, but have it built! I only wish to speak to them; I will command nothing!' With that, she turned and left.

Hope

Tana bent low to Coryn's ear and whispered. 'I am of your blood, father, and I despair. Tell me we may win! Tell me that all is not lost, even if it is a lie!' She backed away from him and looked into his eyes: dull, yellow, vacant mirrors. He coughed. 'Do not fight her, Megan,' was all he said, then his eyes closed, this shortly followed by a pained, croaking snore.

She stood to leave, looking down at his withered body. She had begged him, and he hadn't even known who she was. Whatever pathways he traveled in his mind, she couldn't find him. Thinking this, she fought back her tears. In a way, they were so alike, he haunted by his visions of his gods' passing, and she a victim of the same haunting. In days past, he would have loved her, cherished her every word, for in a twisted sort of way he'd been a noble king. He'd sacrificed his power to his judgment and his compassion for his people. Over the years, she'd come to understand him better, perhaps because her plight so resembled his: he'd abandoned the battle after foreseeing his inevitable defeat; in essence, that was an act of noble virtue, for why should he cause blood to flow and wars to be fought if it was true that the One God's followers would win in the end? What right had he to oppose it? Hadn't he married Moira and brought her and Patrick here specifically to hasten the end, to shorten the battle just where the old powers rooted in Kaerglen might have prolonged it for centuries? And wasn't Tana the product of this union of faith and power? She and Seth both – born of Coryn, King of Pagans, and Moira, Queen of Christ.

She looked at the old man and loved him and hated him in the same moment. Perhaps he was right and noble, but in another way he'd betrayed them all, betrayed them simply by being a man, by allowing seduction by his wife, by fathering children at all. By rights, Seth should gain the crown upon his death. Patrick wasn't even of his blood! Yet since Seth had disappeared, Coryn had scarcely uttered his name.

Coryn was already dead, Tana realized. He'd been dead before they'd suffered their first breaths in this world. He'd been dead from the moment he'd given up, and he'd been dead even when Thyri had slain Pye to save his life. Moira had ruled Kaerglen since she'd come there, so Coryn's death would mean . . . absolutely nothing, a senseless formality that would legitimize his entire philosophy, a philosophy he'd ensured by his own inaction, his own death nearly two score years before.

Such thoughts left Tana morose as she left her father's bedchamber. When he died, all hope would fall finally on her shoulders. And Seth's – if he were truly still alive.

Patrick would have her wholly in his power then, or he would kill her. She would be a fool to think differently.

Her thoughts propelled her from the castle, there to stand on the hill that looked down over Port Kaerglen. The sea breeze brushed against her skin, and the pale autumn sun only darkened her mood. She stood – forgetting time – until the sun grew red and the breeze cold, then suddenly it filled her with a chill and then a tingling and a rush through her mind like fire and ice, wind and rain, and she was torn away and . . .

Flying!

As easily as before, with no effort, no exhaustive hours of preparation, no strain on her heart like the talons of death! She flew . . . over the castle; from above it looked so small, a dark mountaintop with its deep green heart, the garden of the insects and Finaan and her brooding and weakness . . . She was free! The wind blew and the world shifted; a lush, deep forest spread below her, a leafy quilt over the hills split only by a mighty river that roared down from distant mountains, over falls and cascades, wending like a snake, dipping and meandering below her.

The winds blew her down, among swallows and hawks. Aerial harmony – the hawks picked fish from the river while the swallows sang and bats chittered beneath the waves of leaves. She soared over the water, racing for the peaks, up the waterfalls and on. And then she saw the fires and the smoke looming on the horizon. Huge tracts of gutted forest cropped up in the green sea like great wounds, their trees charred and scattered like twigs over blackened earth. And as the wind blew her, the leafy sea itself turned black as life gave way to death and she grew ever more near the fires that licked the edge of the black sea like great, monstrous tongues. And even farther away, she could see giant figures among the flames, figures to whom the trees were like grass and the river but a trickling stream – this was not their world!

Closer still, she saw the elven armies, crackling with sorcery, fashioning great spears of white magic to hurl into the fray. Here and there, acres of reeds lay crushed under fallen Jotun. The battle raged on; legions of arrows swarmed with deadly accuracy at the faces – the eyes – of the invaders. Clouds of smoke billowed in waves across the battlefield. The winds blew Tana down, and the roar of fires grew deafening. She tried to open her eyes, to return to Kaerglen, but the effort failed. The winds blew her down into the Tuathan host, to its heart where Lugh bellowed desperate commands out to tall, beautiful gods colored black with ash and grime and red with blood.

For a moment, Tana hung motionless, her eyes filling with the carnage. In every direction, she saw Tuathan dead, fallen gods. The wind, like animate breath, nudged her and set her spinning, pirhouetting through the ranks of her gods; everywhere was blood, desperation, and death. Slowly, twirling, she became the wind. The ranks parted, and she spun over Brigid; the goddess lay on the ashy grass, white and yellow petals spread around her in the rough shape of a leaf. Her dress was turned gray by the smoke, her pale face slackened and wan. Tana dropped down to her bosom, and Brigid smiled sadly. *'All ends now, little one,'* she said. *'I can teach you no more.'*

As the wind, Tana couldn't speak; she whistled mournfully through the petals, lifting them in small whirlwinds to dance around the goddess.

'*You must hurry*,' Brigid whispered into the wind. '*Go to your grotto, and close your eyes in the room of the dryad. In your mind, you can make it whole again. Spin three times and step into the water.*

'You will find Fand's haven, and talismans there you can use. Wishing stones full of blue power whose limits are but those of your dreams. Use them well, but hurry! The last battles have begun, and this is the last gift I might give you.'

Tana lingered over the goddess, weeping a light mist. She brushed over Brigid's cheek, kissing her, then rose high above the army, and opened her eyes.

Now it was night, so still that her dress hung motionless above the grass. From the chimneys of the port below, smoke rose in pillars that solidified in the moonlight, like long white arms reaching up for the stars.

Tana stood, looking out as if through new eyes, as if the tears on her cheeks had been cried by another, younger self. All she had just seen . . . Within, she felt a warm power – a tranquil strength – blossoming around her heart. Her wind-dream had reshaped Patrick and Finaan – so small they seemed now compared to the enemies her gods faced. What if they did spoil her sorceries? What if they had stained her island with the blessing of a god she did not know? The power yet lived, and if it failed, that did not make it weaker. If a spell shriveled and collapsed, it could not lose its *meaning*. Not if she persevered; not if she kept it alive in her heart.

As Tana turned away, she was watched. Far below, against the dark line of the port wall a solitary figure hid in the shadows, gazing up.

He was young and strong, his muscles shaped by sail and

rigging, by fish-laden nets and battles with the wind and waves of the sea. For years, he had fished and forgotten, seeking solitude on the water where the past could become a dream, or a wasteland like the endless blue expanse spreading out in all directions beneath him. On the sea, only what the fisherman brought up in his nets and kept mattered; the fish thrown back was nothing. On the sea of the past, it could be made much the same, the painful memories discarded, pushed back under the surface into the depths of nothingness. And so he'd lived his days discarding the past, naming himself Sean, an orphan. He'd fled to the doorstep of an old fisherman and been taken in, going out daily on the waters where he could forget.

Two years back, the old man had died, and he'd inherited the boat. The old man's wife, Maire, cared for him like a son, so after the old man's death, nothing much had changed – he brought in the catch to Maire, and she cleaned it and took it the next morning to market. Together, they survived.

But now his father was dying and he could no longer escape the memories. Rumors that the king might perish even before dawn had spread through city and port earlier in the day, and those rumors had greeted him on his return from the sea. At his side now, he wore an old rusted sword he'd won from the son of a blacksmith in a wrestling match. He'd taken the day's catch to Maire and left quietly, moving through the shadows, inching up the port wall, and stopping only when he'd spied his sister standing out on the hill. That sight had brought the memories flooding back, the good memories of their youth. She had grown, as had he, but in seeing her he realized how much love remained inside of him. He'd wanted to rush out from the wall and embrace her, to lift her into the air as she had done for him so often with her magic in the grotto.

He'd wanted to run to her, but he couldn't. He'd abandoned her and left her to face the aftermath of that fateful day in the grotto alone. For a few days, he'd gone back, hoping she might come so he could take her away with him. But one day he'd found Finaan's guard there, and he'd fled for the last time, alone. He'd become a fisherman, and fought his battles with the past on the sea; while from the port, he'd watched his homeland invaded as his mother brought architects, builders, and armies from Erin to raise churches and chapels all over the island. These men had come, the old, simple folk of Kaerglen powerless to stop them. The city and port had become very dangerous places, though ironically, the fisherman's village on the port's southside was his haven. He seldom dared to leave it. Over the years, he'd suspected the old man had known his true birthright, but he'd never been betrayed. When the guard had first scoured the port, the old man had told them he was his grandson. Seth had cropped his hair before they'd arrived, and the guard hadn't looked at him twice.

Since then, Finaan's search for him had not abated, but it had focused mainly – in vain – on the forests in the north to where more than a few followers of the old ways had fled. Bandits were there now, Seth knew. Bandits making travel unsafe on an island where all had been peaceful in the year of his birth.

So much had changed. He watched Tana disappear up the hill, and he began to grow afraid. What could he do now? He'd had no sword-training, while Patrick and Finaan were veterans with their weapons. All on the island knew of their mock duels and of a good number of foolish souls who had dared to challenge either or both of them.

What could he do? Tana had halted his progress up the hill, and now he was frozen in place, unable to take another step. His senses began to heighten, both within and without as fear took over him. Nightbirds cooed above him from their niches in the wall. Insects chittered all around, and he heard a roar in his head like the pounding of waves, like the sea of forgetfulness calling him back to its safe, constant bosom. Just then, he heard a dull thud behind him, and he whirled, drawing his blade.

At first, Seth saw nothing, but then his eyes caught on a band of darkness in the moonlit grass, just out of the wall's shadows. He approached it cautiously, until he saw that it was a sheathed sword. 'Who is here?' he whispered out into the night.

From the shadows, a voice answered. 'If my magics don't fail,' it said, 'then you be the true prince of this place.'

'What?'

'Is sword for you,' said the voice. 'Sword to befit a prince. Sword of Light.'

Seth peered hard into the shadows all around him, but he saw no one. He had frozen again, scarcely able to move. 'Who are you?' he asked.

'Just a felnin,' answered the voice. 'No more questions. Take sword, but beware. Is blade of power, so carry by scabbard. Go to where you are most strong, and only there unsheath it. It will test you. It might even kill you.'

In the windless night, Seth heard the faintest breath of movement. 'Wait!' he whispered desperately, but the voice had spoken all it would.

After a time, the young prince inched toward the blade resting in the grass. He gazed at it awhile, then picked it up by its scabbard and pressed it to his breast. Then, glancing up one last time toward the castle, he started back down the hill.

Magic

She could feel the ghosts in the halls, the aeons of intrigue, love, and battle that the castle had known. Dead and dying gods had thrived here. How often had the feet of Brigid herself touched these stones? How often had Manannan's laughter sounded out for all to hear? All present now were just transient visitors, fated to die, but the structure itself would live on.

Tana passed her mother who seemed pale, nonexistent – less real than the dead for whose memory she ached. She held them close to her heart, striving to keep them strong, drawing their strength into herself. For had she not seen them – even them – engaged heroically in a battle they seemed doomed to lose? How petty her own struggles seemed in comparison! She fought men, not giants. Simple, greedy mortals.

She walked in long, resolute strides, straight for the depths of the castle, to descend to the grotto. Her mother faded behind her, like a ghost into memory. Voices came and went; nothing phased her or caused her to pause until Finaan materialized in her path. She tried to brush past him, but he grabbed her and she spun away, backing up against the stony wall. The torch she carried clattered to the floor.

'Where are you going?' he asked abruptly.

She didn't answer. Torchlit from below, Finaan looked taller, a beast with a chin and deep shadows for eyes. She bent quickly and lifted the torch up between them. A sizzling crackle and sharp stench filled the air as the torch brightened, its fire catching on strands of Finaan's long hair.

He didn't back away. 'Please answer me, Tana. I didn't mean to frighten you.'

She laughed. He *was* small and petty, though she knew he had killed time and again, remorselessly, like a dog trained for violence. Yet in his eyes – she filled them. They softened with her reflection there. Perhaps she had misread him in the garden . . . With a word – no caress required – she could make him hers, her obedient servant. For the first time in her life, she felt within herself the power of womanhood. Before Brigid had renewed her, she'd been a child, and as a child she could only have submitted, not controlled. Now, all that had changed. This – this confidence that swelled her breast, that held her head high – made her someone she had never been before. She could take him, control him like a dog, pet him, make his strength a part of her own. These were evil thoughts, she knew. But the knowledge that she *could* was all that mattered. She was changed. She was a woman now, with the power to choose.

At first, Finaan shrank from her laughter, then anger flared in his eyes. 'Here, bitch!' he seethed. 'Be still, or I'll take you here.'

'No, you won't,' she said softly. He approached her, reached for her arm, but she skipped to one side. 'You won't because you wouldn't enjoy it. I would scream and bite you, and claw your pretty face.' She scratched quickly at the air with her free hand, smiling as his eyes locked onto the movement. 'You'd have to kill me and then settle for a lesser queen. You'd spend the rest of your life in agony, wondering whether I might ever have loved you willingly, hating your queen because she couldn't be me, feeling the worms of my death crawling around inside your head.' These abruptly unleashed words amazed her, so easily did they pass from her lips. A day before – even a few hours before – she could never have said them. Just thinking them in Finaan's presence would have paralyzed her – body and soul. But spoken now, they bolstered their own truth. Rage yet burned in Finaan's eyes, but he kept his distance, his mouth twisting into a feral grin.

'You acknowledge me,' he said, a maniacal warmth edging his words. 'For the first time, you've admitted that I will win.'

She shook her head. 'I simply spoke the truth – for the first time. You think that I don't know you, that I would love you if only I gave you a chance. But I do know you, Finaan; do you think I could not? How could I not come to know one who abused me and abused my brother and chased him away? I have watched you when you didn't even know I was there, when my soul ached with a desire to tear my eyes away from you, but my eyes refused to stray. And alone in the night, I have thought of you, much more often than I suspect you've thought of me. I've hated you and feared you, but I refuse any longer to chain my every waking moment to that fear.' As she spoke, she felt her body trembling, her recurrent waking nightmares pleading for her to stop, but it was too late now. Had she said too much?

Finaan stared blankly ahead, taking in her words. 'I was a boy,' he said distantly.

'You were a man,' she countered. 'I suppose you've all but forgotten it. But I haven't. If Seth is alive, neither has he. I hope he kills you.' With that, she turned from him and walked, ever deeper into the castle.

Finaan ran after her, grabbing her arm again and spinning her to face him. 'I love you, Tana,' he said fiercely. 'Why do you think me evil? I worship the most powerful god of all, and he is a just god.'

She laughed and clutched at the silver cross hung on the chain around his neck. 'Just, you say? Just leave me, Finaan. Go pray for your just god's forgiveness.'

'No, Tana. You have spoken your heart to me, and my own will have its say.'

'Will it?' she spat at him. *You mean I've drawn first blood,* she thought. *I've drawn first blood, and the warrior within you will not let you abandon the battle . . .* 'Come then,' she said, turning again, leading him silently ever deeper, down the stairwell to the grotto where all things for her began and ended.

In the chamber of the dryad, scant traces of magic yet

lingered; she could feel it when she could not before. With each passing moment, something was growing within her, a new strength, of womanhood. This strength – a pool of serenity swelled at its heart. She had rediscovered something she had lost long ago. She had come to where she had to be, to where the goddess had directed her. In the same act of strength, she had brought her tormentor to this ancient place that he had long ago defiled. What first? she wondered. She felt Finaan behind her; she turned on him, capriciously testing her power. 'Take it off,' she said.

'What?'

'The crucifix – take it off. This is no place for it. If you want to know my heart, you must take it off and feel what truly belongs here. And if I don't believe you know my heart, then I'll not listen to any words of yours.'

For a moment, she thought he might refuse her, but then, slowly, his hand went to his neck, and he lifted the chain over his head. She smiled and looked away from him. 'Do you remember this place?' she asked. 'How it looked before you spoiled it with your One God's iron?'

'A little,' he said uncertainly.

'Your blade is blessed as well, isn't it?'

'Of course.'

'Then you must drop it with the cross.' She half closed her eyes, gazing at the remains of the dryad's tree, slowly fitting each lost green leaf into its proper place in her mind. She didn't look back at Finaan; only when she heard his sword clatter to the rock did she turn. She smiled to herself; so easy this had been, after all the years of hopeless conjuring, of secret spell after secret spell, she had finally brought down his defenses in the most unmystical, mundane way she could imagine. And in this place, what she planned would require virtually no effort at all . . . She whispered a preliminary charm and crossed her fingers in the sign of the Sybil. Her eyes still half closed, the dryad began to take shape in the image in back of her mind. As she turned toward Finaan, she moved her hands, completing the spell. He stood before her, confused, misunderstanding the light way her wrists had brushed over her thighs, thinking the sudden hardening of her nipples betrayed desire, not sorcery. 'Come,' she said gruffly, and he approached her without thinking.

He came within arm's reach of her, and she disappeared. He looked around; the grotto had transformed, regenerated itself, the old glittering statues staring at him from all directions. And he felt smaller; his head was dizzy, his mind unclear. His sword and cross were gone, disappeared along with Tana.

Footsteps sounded behind him, and someone grabbed him roughly by the shoulders and lifted him into the air. He twisted to see the face of his attacker, and it was a face he knew well, his own face, his eyes leering, his mouth slavering like an animal's. One hand held him up, the other fumbled at his trousers, ripping them from his body. He was thrown violently against the dryad and lashed there with rope, then he screamed out in agony as his attacker entered him lustfully from behind. The pain rushed through him, filling his entire body. He could feel his own blood running down his leg.

When the assault ended, the pain came and went yet in waves. He began to breathe more easily, then suddenly the dryad faded into mist and he was on his back, fully naked with a terrible weight on top of him, a weight bearing the same face – his own face. This time, the pain was even worse, and his attacker wouldn't even look at him. He was looking at somebody else – Patrick, his best friend – and talking detachedly about evil . . .

Tana stared down at Finaan's jerking, weeping body and frowned. She *knew* what he suffered: every moment of her agony, and every moment of Seth's – double the pain even she had felt, but it was all pain that he'd inflicted. He'd claimed he was a boy. Perhaps she'd misjudged him; perhaps he had felt remorse in recent years. No matter – she'd ensured future remorse with this revenge, but it didn't please her the way she thought it would. The warrior looked so pitiful now, writhing and moaning, screaming out like a child, the child her sorcery had made him. Knowing what he relived made her remember again . . . Yet this was her victory. Now she could kill him; all she had to do was take up his sword and run it through him. Then he could never warn Patrick, never reveal to her brother how powerful she had become. Patrick might even be seduced by the same trick. He'd never hinted at any remembrance of that day, but she'd lately seen lust in his eyes when he'd thought she wasn't looking at him. She'd won a battle, and now victory of the war within her grasp.

She took one step for the sword, then realized she couldn't do it. She hadn't the strength to kill him – no, she *had* strength, but such an act would abuse and defile it, as surely as she had been defiled in this place five years before. The maliciousness of her sorcery – the pain she inflicted at the moment – already caused her grief. She wasn't an assassin; her power grew out of life, not death. That was why she'd been so weak all these years. The will to murder did not reside in her heart, and she'd interpreted it as weakness rather than strength. She'd made herself weak, without understanding anything.

The revelation settled uneasily, cleansing her spirit of the refuse of her darker thoughts, but leaving at least one doubt unresolved: If she couldn't kill now, with success assured, how could she possibly manage it later, when much more – perhaps even her own life – might be at stake? She looked away from Finaan and his sword and crucifix, trying to shrug off the doubt, forcing herself to remember Brigid and the words that had summoned her here. The gods were dying. Each wasted moment might spell disaster and deny her forever the talismans of Fand's haven.

She stood at the stream's edge and calmed her heart, continuing again to reconstruct the grotto in her mind. Green leaves affixed themselves to the branches of the tree behind her; the dryad smiled and bent slightly, offering her arm to guide all noble guests onward. A fox perched across from her, smacking its lips, then freezing, its amethyst eyes shining with the reflections of three pink salmon that leaped from the water to hang suspended in the air. Birds settled to the rock on all sides; she could almost hear the flutter of their wings as they settled stonily on their perches. Tana held all this in her mind and began to twirl – once . . . twice . . . thrice. She stepped into the water and fell forward.

Far away – nestled in a chamber high up in the rock above the grotto – he bent into the candlelight, his forehead creased, his eyes straining to follow the miniscule scratchy writing in the black volume he'd retrieved from the library. It was a strange book; as many times as he'd scoured the shelves of his father's library, he'd never seen it before today, the day, certainly, of Coryn's death. The day that would make him king.

So he tried to read, growing more angry each moment. He would decipher a word and move onto the next, but by the time he'd handled the second word, the meaning of the first would be lost. Beneath his right hand lay leaves of blank parchment, the topmost covered in illegible scribble, further evidence of his frustration. He'd sought to defeat the book by recording the meaning of each word as he discovered it. He'd thought it a worthy idea, what Arthur might have done confronted with the same puzzle. But when he looked back at his writing, it too had grown mysteriously meaningless. Something was wrong with the night. The day had brooded uneasily from dawn until dusk, but the night – the night had escaped its shackles of reason. What he did, perched here with this damnable book torturing him, made no sense. It was like a dream or a nightmare, except he was awake. He slammed the book shut, turned from it, and froze. Not two feet away from him, a pillar of fire rose up from the stone floor. He could feel no heat, and though the fire was bright, it illuminated nothing, nor did it cast shadows. The air in the room grew suddenly cold. 'You are betrayed,' said a voice that came from all directions. 'Betrayed on the eve of your ascension.'

Patrick looked deep into the fire and swallowed. 'You know who I am?' the voice asked, awaiting no reply: 'You have called to me after your prayers to Him. You've cried out to both of us without an answer, tears wetting your pillow as you've entered sleep with my name on your lips more often than His.

'What do I offer? Read again and you will see.'

Patrick fumbled behind himself for the slender black volume, never letting his eyes stray from the fire. He let it fall open on his lap: Connaught has betrayed you for your sister's heart, *read the opened page.*

'Now – what will you do about it?' asked the fire that offered no light.

Above her, the stream remained, flowing through the air like a living, watery bridge, a crystalline airborne snake. Beneath her, the ground felt soft, like velvet. She touched herself hesitantly; having passed through the water, her clothes and skin felt completely dry. She fought the urge to take off her boots and lie down on the velvety rock from where she might watch the stream moving above and let the softness below envelop her. Fand's haven was a chamber, of stone all around and but half as large as the dryad's chamber above, but the rock was soft and blue, dimly lit by some magic in the air itself and bathed in gentle, moving reflections off the overhead stream. If only she'd known of this place long ago! So often she might have escaped here. This was a place for thinking, and so soft! A place for lovers to turn an afternoon into eternity.

She raised a hand and touched the stream, feeling its wetness. A slight trickle – no more – ran down her arm. She lowered her hand and touched the water to her lips, then peered around, in search of the room's other secrets.

There was a place where the rock rose, as if to form a bed, and beyond this she found three chests, lying open, filled with dresses the beauty of which she might never have imagined. Among the dresses were candles and sticks, and a warm tinderbox – everything fresh and new. Fand's haven knew nothing of dust or time. She dug deeper into the chests, finally deciding to remove the dresses, which she piled reverently in neat stacks on the bed (If only these were happier times and she had a worthy lover!).

There were rings and necklaces, hats and scarves, boxes of powders and vials of lotions – what games Fand and Manannan must have played here! She could easily spend hours puzzling over each piece, but she had come here for a reason, and though she'd never seen the stones Brigid had bid her to take, she somehow *knew* she would recognize them when she found them.

This she did. They were stored in a plain leather pouch – a handful of large aqua gems. Poured into her palm, she could feel the tingling of their magic.

She left by reaching up into the stream until she touched rock, then pulling herself back up, through the water. In the chamber of the dryad, she found herself alone, her spell on Finaan having run its course and the foreign prince departed, gone to lick his wounds. She smiled sadly. She wondered what changes his eyes might reveal when next they would meet.

Ghosts

Yes, something was wrong with the night – even in the land of the Franks. The waning moon rose orange, and mists fell on the streets, coming in rolling banks off the river. Such was the atmosphere without as the followers of Thyri Eiriksdattir prepared their final departure. They walked the streets awhile after Megan left, Gerald filled with a deep foreboding sadness, Rollo boisterous and rowdy, his yellow mane and beard freed of Megan's disguises, and Rui, as usual, indifferent. By the time they returned to The Emporium, an abundance of wine surged through Gerald's veins, and it was a wine that added mysterious swirls to the mist and a curious waver to the moonlight. He wobbled through the entrance, and his eyes passed over all they had collected within. Rollo and Rui went upstairs for their packs; Gerald went alone into the room of armaments, for a task he'd put off until the latest of hours.

By torchlight, he gazed long at the rows of swords, weaponry, and mail, much of which he'd personally polished to perfection. With the wine dancing in his head, the armor seemed almost alive in the flickering light, a spectral army ready to leap away from the wall at his command. He knew the feel of each piece, its strengths and weaknesses. He walked along slowly, touching every one, recalling its origin, its memories. In reality, he wanted only a sword, and he chose, at last, a fine, Norse-forged sword, which he scabbarded and tied to his belt. As he waited for the others, his own pack ready under the shop's counter, he drew the sword and tested its weight, thinking grimly of the days that might come. He scarcely sensed their entrance.

'It is time,' Rollo said, recalling him from far away.

Gerald looked up at him and motioned at the rows of metal. 'Take what you like.'

Rollo shook his head and patted his belt. He wore his axe and his own sword, both heavier and finer than the one Gerald now held in his hand.

Slowly, Gerald turned away, leaving the spectral army behind. In the main chamber, Rollo had pulled several feet of material away from one bolt of cloth. The material lay there like an uneven carpet; Gerald approached it, lowering his torch. He staggered slightly as the wine in his belly shifted the floor beneath him, and the cloth became a flowing, elusive wave.

Moving quickly, Rui Taichimi caught him. From the archer's arms, Gerald looked up. 'I filled two sacks with gold,' he said, smiling wildly. 'In the tunnel; don't let me forget them.' The archer only grunted, correcting Gerald's balance.

Standing, the Saxon again lowered his torch. Errant threads at the edge of the silk shriveled and writhed away from the fire as if fleeing in agony. Tiny infernos sprang up at their ends and flew like sprites to collide with the rich eastern hues. At the cloth's edge, the sprites grew brighter and rose up, twisting, glancing at their brothers on either side before lowering their heads – as if in agreement – and growing longer, laying down on the cloth to merge into one unified wall of flame, a sprite army which then moved in unison over the silk, whose colors shone brightly a moment – a final moment of glory – before succumbing to the enemy's might.

Bathed in the bright light of this battle, the three warriors stepped back and watched as the wall of flame advanced, and the rolls themselves caught fire and burned.

He stayed until the roar of the flames filled his mind and the smoke left him teary and choking. Even then, it took Rollo to pull him away.

Through the tunnel he had dug for Thyri, they left, pausing briefly for him to retrieve his fortune. Laden with the heavy sacks, he thought of Thyri – over him, watching him. A week had passed since he'd seen her, since she'd left shortly after their victory over Charles the Emperor. During her absence, the full moon had come and gone with her away, deep in the Frankish forests, letting the beast within her run free. *What did she plan now?* He asked it aloud as they walked along the tunnel, the pyre of The Emporium fading to a faint, distant crackling.

Next to him, the Viking shrugged. 'Battle, I hope.'

Rui walked silently behind them until they reached the tunnel's end.

Through the ill-forged night, they skirted the city toward the river, and there sought a raftsman. *Nightreaver*, hidden by Megan's spells, stood at anchor a good journey downstream.

The raftsmen all lived in a small village of huts at the edge of the city. Rollo went in alone, leaving Gerald and Rui to gaze up at the stars and shift restlessly, awaiting Rollo's return. Behind them, an orange glow rose over the skyline of the city where The Emporium burned. Above it hung the orange moon, suspended in the night sky as if it had just ascended from the wreckage, risen from the rolls of silks and the vapors of incinerated perfumes, not a heavenly light but simply a child of their labors.

In the first hut, Rollo found a sleeping man. He nudged the raftsman with his foot; he didn't waken. The hut stank of wine. He moved quickly to the next hut, where he encountered the same thing: a drunk, slumbering raftsman. Exiting the hut, he cursed: 'Odin! Are they all drunk!'

'I'm not,' said a voice.

Rollo turned for the source. A tall, lanky man emerged from the shadows. On the streets, despite the man's ragged garb, Rollo would never have taken him for a river man. He was clean shaven with elusive, laughing eyes. Rollo gripped the hilt of his sword. 'You're not a raftsman,' he growled.

'But I am,' chuckled the man. 'I am pale, I know, but I am the night raftsman. I only work at night.'

'Why?'

'Because I love the moon? No – my friends need sleep. I allow them.' The man's eyes glinted in the light of Rollo's torch. 'Come, let me take you downriver. Your wish is my command.'

Rollo stared long at the man, then grunted. 'We are three,' he said.

'No matter,' the man shrugged. 'I make four, and my raft will carry eight. Please come.'

'We will meet you at the river,' Rollo said, turning away for his friends.

The light of the orange moon burned the river with flames of swirling mist. For a moment, the moon, the river, and the mists seemed all one to Gerald, mirrored reflections of the flames behind his eyes, the dancing, orchestrated sprite army. The raftsman found by Rollo moved slowly, whistling off-key, sending spears of dissonance into Gerald's melodic chorus of flame. Gerald began to wonder whether he dreamed; at any moment, he felt as if the entire vision might melt before his eyes, reduce itself suddenly to some uniform, limitless plain of fire.

Rollo's fingers dug into his arm, forcing him to move. The tall raftsman held out an arm, inviting them onto a large wooden craft. Sleep began to cloud Gerald's mind; he wanted to fall forward, embrace the wood, and let his dream of fire carry him away. As he staggered ahead of Rollo, Rui's arm shot out like a bolt to block his path.

'This is not right,' Rui said distantly.

Gerald gasped for breath. Flames leaped high out of the water like fountains of dragon's breath. His eyes turned to the archer; Rui's arms moved like liquid, the thin line of an arrow arching over his head, notching against bowstring, pivoting, eyeing the smiling raftsman, then dropping askance to target the raft. Rui loosed the arrow, and it bit deep into the wood. The flames Gerald saw on the water roared. The raft itself seemed to shudder, then its bindings snapped and it unraveled, the grain of its wood squaring off and turning to scales. Like a serpent, it uncoiled and raised itself, a hissing tower of darkness, Rui's arrow jutting out like a spike from its eye.

To Gerald, all moved slowly, like some play of fiery shadow. Rollo's sword sang out of its scabbard. Rui's bowstring rustled softly as another arrow fitted into place, then it too sang as the archer let the arrow fly. Before it could strike its target, the strange raftsman had disappeared.

Briefly, an odd laughter erupted around them, a laughter as unsettling as an off-key whistle, then all grew suddenly still. The laughter resounded faintly among Gerald's flames as Rollo's fingers wrapped again around his arm, and they moved quickly away along the riverbank. After a time, Rollo let go, and Gerald stumbled along on his own. Somewhere along the way – much to his later anguish – Gerald abandoned the sacks of gold as he fought to keep one leg moving in front of the other.

Away from the city, Rollo found a small boat tethered to the riverbank. Rui tested it carefully, then they boarded, Gerald's exhausted body falling down to embrace the planks. And then they were out on the water, speeding for their rendezvous with *Nightreaver*. Gerald bundled his cloak under his head and drifted off into dream. In the moments before sleep came, he glanced up; the moon now shone bright and white above them.

Water

It was a windless night – after Tana's flight, all the Midgard winds went still. On the sea, Seth's sail hung slack and limp, fluttering only with the motion that Seth himself created as he rowed out and away from the port, into Kaerglen's wall of mist and beyond, his eyes never straying from the strange weapon with which he'd been gifted, its hilt propped up against the stern gunwale, its length resting on his carefully folded nets.

Destiny had visited him on the hill. He knew not of felnins, but the blade before him was real, its hilt alone intimating its sturdy, fine quality. He had seen its like before, but he couldn't remember where; it was a simple, strong, leatherbound hilt with a Norse cross-guard. He gazed at it and rowed ever outward, under the stars, away from Kaerglen until all was sea around him, the island's mist but a distant band of white on the horizon.

When he shipped his oars, his little boat came to a halt, as if it had never moved. 'Go to where you are most strong,' the felnin had said. This was it – away and alone out on the water, on the calm seas where he had banished all the demons of his past. He knew every creak of his craft, even knew where to cast his net whenever a large school of fish passed beneath him and tipped the boat ever so slightly to either side. He knew no fears here; the sharks never bothered him, and when the great leviathans came near, he knew only wonder. When they rocked his boat, he called to them; in the past, they had never come too close, but if they had he might have leaped out, onto one's back to join in its journey. He'd dreamed of this – life on the back of a whale, knowledge of all the mysteries of the sea. He knew he could never survive such an act, but the thought so seduced him that death did not seem to matter.

Yes, he was strong here. He drew his strength up through the planks from the water. He smiled in his solitude and reached forward, grasping the felnin's blade of power by its hilt. With his other hand, he grasped the scabbard, then he slowly pulled the weapon free.

At first he felt little, a tingling that crept up his arm, a slight burning in his palm. A moment later, something exploded in his head and agony screamed in his every nerve; his flesh tightened around his skull. An unearthly wail parted his lips. He felt on fire, but he held tightly to the beast that tormented him, holding it over his head, then bringing it down, its edge cutting deep into the gunwale. There, he gripped it; in his mind it became the leviathan of his dreams, the monster of the depths that would reveal to him all its secrets if he could only stay alive, if he could only breathe the water and cling to its back and ride.

In his mind, the winds blew anew and the waves crashed. The beast writhed, trying to shake him. He dug into it with claws and teeth, locking onto its flesh, sapping its stamina, its fight. It burned him, but he kissed it while its fires grew ever more fierce. After an eternity, its struggling lessened, then subsided, and Seth rode the beast and gazed out in wonder. He breathed, his lungs like gills, pulsing in the ether of the sea. He saw the depths, the cavernous homes of great monsters and the palaces of sirens and mermaids. From the leviathan's back, he knew all, as if he were Manannan reborn.

Seth took in the beauty of his journey and cried, his tears flowing down his cheeks, falling to the deck of his boat to mix with the water of his dreams. After a time, he opened his eyes and looked along the edge of the sword, at the pinprick reflections of the stars above that danced along its length. He felt changed, gifted with more than just a sword

– gifted with the granting of his dreams, if only for a few wondrous moments.

The sword of power had given him this; it felt strong in his grasp now, a part of his body, like an extension of his arm. For a long time, he looked at it, bathing in its power, then he sheathed it and took up his oars, the mists of Kaerglen beckoning him now from the horizon.

They called him prince.

Reavers

Thyri squatted, moodily scratching the earth between her feet with a dagger as she eyed the moon riding high overhead. Megan stood next to her, dressed in the brown, drab garb of a servant girl. 'It is time,' the sorceress said. They could hear muffled grumbling coming from the direction of the hastily erected shelter a hundred paces on. Thyri rose, sheathed her dagger, and started forward without a word.

The Norse had assembled as she'd requested – at least a fraction of them had, maybe four hundred but no more. They sat on freshly felled logs and unpolished stumps, the best they'd been able to manage. One group leaned up against the hull of a small warship dragged that afternoon from the river. Kegs of mead were scattered haphazardly through the assembly, and to these Thyri pointed as she walked among them. 'Drink!' she shouted heartily. She slapped one man hard on his shoulder. 'Why is your cup empty, man? Go fill it – this is not a night for the weak at heart.'

Her words drew hesitant laughter, and she smiled at them as she stepped up to the small platform they'd built (as she'd commanded). She looked out over them and shook her head. 'They say in the city of the Franks that the Norse are a pathetic lot!' Angry eyes fell on her from all sides, and what grumbling had persisted after her entrance gave way to an abrupt silence. Thyri laughed. 'I see I have your attention! Well, I don't believe that. You're warriors – Vikings – all of you. Your teeth were cut on the points of swords, and your hearts carry all the fury of the north. No – pathetic you're not.'

'We know this!' shouted an impatient man in the back. 'What do you want from us? Why have you called us here?'

'Battle,' she said grimly, stamping her foot down on the wood.

'For what?'

'For your blood,' she answered. 'Is this your birthright – to beg for land of a king who knows not your tongue, your gods, and your ways? Are these the followers of Thor before me, or are they tired old men content to scramble like dogs for scraps fallen off the table above them? I want battle! I want the Norse united, and the deaths of any who stand in my way!

'I have had a vision, of Norwegians, Danes, and Swedes united. Of fleets that cover the seas from horizon to horizon, fleets to make emperors and kings tremble with fear.'

Someone laughed. 'You have no right to command us, Eiriksdattir!'

'I have no right?' she asked, letting her anger boil quickly to the surface. 'I have no right! How do you think you came safely to this riverbank? Why do you think you now possess half the treasury of the king? Was it your looks?'

'There were miracles!' The shout came from several directions.

'Yes,' she said. 'Miracles of my making!' she sneered. 'You'd all be dead without me.'

'And not dead with you, kinslayer?'

The assembly murmured darkly as Thyri's eyes fell on her questioner. The man's hand trembled, his fingers touching at the hilt of his sword. 'Draw it or leave,' she said coldly. The men around him pushed him forward, shouting at him to fight, their laughter and jeers growing louder with each passing moment.

'I suggest you leave,' Thyri said. She stared him down, watching his eyes as he weighed his wounded pride against his life. He glanced nervously around, then turned away, departing silently amid a shower of flying mugs.

'Anyone else?' Thyri asked them.

Megan looked on distantly, breathing a slight sigh of relief that the gathering had not erupted suddenly into bloodshed. Thyri dominated their fears, at least, but the sorceress didn't care to guess where Thyri's address might lead them. To Megan, the night was rife with futility; though they bowed to her will, these men resisted Thyri. She would not forge an army this night, and even if she did, what use could it be, with *fimbulwinter* in Asgard and Ragnarok looming over the future like a fathomless, inevitable void? And these thoughts – Thyri could read them in Megan's eyes. Thyri fought them, the sorceress watching her with all the rest. Perhaps Megan thought of Ai'reth, his words and his visions. Perhaps she thought of darker things, sensing something of the strangeness of the night, and the events transpiring lands away, on the island of her birth.

Thyri calmed them with a wave of her hand. 'I did not come tonight to command you,' she said. 'I do not ask a price for my part in saving you from death on the river. I ask for your homeland, and your gods. The lands of the north boil with the blood of our own kind. That is *wrong*! Don't you see it? You came south, many of you, in flight from that conflict! You should have come united! How else will the ways of our ancestors be preserved?'

'She speaks of Tangle-Hair!' a man near her whispered.

'Yes!' she shouted, seizing upon his utterance. 'Harald of Vestfold has sapped the power of the north. I mean to bring him down, and all who wish to join me may do so!'

'You're mad!' someone shouted.

'Perhaps,' she answered. 'But perhaps not. Do you know the name of Rollo Anskarson? He who slew the overking of Jorvik? Well he commands the warriors of my ship, and he brings it here even now. It will arrive this night, and in the morning it will sail . . . north. You may choose: stay here and forget your past, raising children off the wombs of Frankish whores, or come with me. If you are not with me now, then depart! I do not need a host for this – only a core of brave, daring warriors.'

Slowly, the assembly rose. When all had departed who would, only twenty men remained. In turn, they came before Thyri and knelt; she recognized several of them as veterans of the battle on the plain of Ethandune. One, a Sigurd Rolfson, had even been under her command. As he knelt before her, he lifted Thyri's scabbarded blade to his lips, then looked up into her eyes. 'No finer Viking lives,' he said, 'than she who wields this sword.'

She smiled at him, but it was a sad smile. She had but twenty men, off the crews of seven hundred ships. The rest – all weary of battle – had forsaken her.

Later, she and Megan lay awake in their tent, silent for long moments, awaiting the arrival of *Nightreaver*. What words they spoke were brief. 'Is this wise?' Megan asked once, stroking Thyri's hair.

'No,' Thyri answered, 'but what use is wisdom? It is needed; I fear I will be mad without it.'

'We could go alone,' Megan suggested.

Thyri looked up at her. 'We could. But then who will tell the tales of it? And after Harald's death, perhaps I shall have the fleet of Astrid's dreams. Perhaps the north can be united and made strong . . . What else am I to do, Meg? I am cursed with a life with no direction, no great battles of any meaning. I can no longer simply fight and feel glory in the thought of sending my opponents to Valhalla. I have had no real purpose.'

'And this is it – your purpose?'

Thyri didn't answer her; the words were causing her too much pain.

Rollo and *Nightreaver* arrived a few hours before dawn, and Thyri and Megan went to meet them. As she stepped upon the planks of the ship, Thyri finally felt the day's troubles slipping away, and she entered her cabin and slept.

Wind-Dreams

For the house of Kaerglen, it was likewise a long night, of no wind and little comfort. After Fand's haven, Tana retreated to her chamber where she laid the wishing stones before her and cast other spells that served up both excitement and ominous portents. For the first time, her sorceries found Seth – he *was* alive, and somewhere nearby. But she found also a dark cloud around Patrick, one that had not been there before. And as for Finaan, she could not find him; perhaps he had retreated behind his talismans and fled.

This was not true. Tana had become but a piece in a game, a game engineered by Patrick, a game that brought them all – just before dawn – to the roof of the east tower. Each felt suddenly compelled to go there, and each felt the thought come freely to his or her own mind.

Tana brooded, expecting Finaan's arrival either in fury or supplication, but it didn't happen. She wandered in her mind, wondering where it was taking her. After her vengeance in the grotto, she'd almost begun to yearn to see Finaan's face, how she might have changed it. And as her mind wandered, so did her feet. She found herself in the halls, climbing stairs, yearning to breathe the still air of the night. From the roof she might see more clearly, remove the confused emotions flooding her mind.

She reached the roof, but Patrick was there, his back to her, looking out over the battlements. She dashed quickly to the side and hid in the rubble of an old curtain wall of ancient construction. From there, she watched Patrick's back. He was there for a reason – looking for something.

Seth? Some other answers in the night . . . Tana fingered the wishing stones she held in her palm. What spell could she cast to kill him now, had she the need? By overpowering his talismans for but a brief moment, she could throw him over the edge of the wall, to a bone-crushing death below.

But new footsteps came and Patrick turned away from the wall, smiling; Tana had never seen such horrible depths in his gaze. His eyes shone almost red; she rubbed her own, fearing it was a trick of the night. When she looked at him again, if anything, the red in his eyes had grown brighter, more distinct.

The footsteps were Finaan's.

'How fares your father?' the one prince asked the other.

'You care?' Patrick returned.

'Of course.'

'For him or for me?'

Finaan laughed. 'For us, Patrick. Our plans of conquest.'

Patrick smiled, the red beaming from his eyes. 'Speaking of that, has my sister consented to marry you? Where is she anyway?'

'I – I don't know. Is something wrong, Patrick? You look strange.'

'Nothing's wrong except you, Finaan. When did you promise Tana you would kill me? Here? Now?' As Patrick said this, his blade whispered free of its scabbard.

Finaan took two steps back and quickly drew his own weapon. 'Must it be like this? I have not betrayed you, my friend.'

'Not yet,' Patrick laughed. 'But should I wait for your betrayal? Who do you love more, me, or my sister?'

Finaan held his sword before him, then launched into an attack. Patrick parried easily, effortlessly, then, before Finaan could set himself up for a counterstroke, Patrick's eyes flashed blinding red, and the point of his sword cut across Finaan's stomach. Links of chain armor screamed out their agonies to the ill-forged night, and the prince from Erin fell to the roof, howling in agony.

Patrick stepped back and laughed. 'Next!' he shouted, then he turned and resumed his post by the wall.

Tana watched, horror-stricken. This could not have been foreseen. She wanted to rush to Finaan's side, but the evil in Patrick's eyes had left her shaking and paralyzed. He had sorcerous power, and she had no idea of its source or nature. She had not been the only one who'd gained strength that day.

As she looked on, more footsteps came. This time, it was Seth.

How to defeat Patrick's new sorcerous alliance? Tana, frozen, watched Seth stealthily approach Patrick's back. She closed her eyes and warmed the stones in her hands with a slight charm; blue light bled from her fingers and she held her hand over her head, then sent a spear of the magic at Patrick's head.

Her brother easily dodged her attack and laughed as Seth challenged him with his new sword. Metal clanged loudly against metal as their blades met, and Tana sent forth another blue spear, forcing Patrick to dodge again dealing the inevitable. 'Run, Seth!' she shouted. 'Flee! He will kill you!' Her words were nearly buried under Patrick's laughter. Patrick's blade caught Seth's shoulder, and the younger brother fell to his knees. That was when Tana finally dashed into the fray.

She screamed as she charged, straight at Patrick. As she ran, she felt the wind and the sorcerous pulsing of the stones held in her fist. Patrick, smiling with his red eyes aflame, braced himself against her charge, but she stopped before she reached him, grabbing Seth's hand, at the same time letting the winds blow through her and calling upon all the powers of the stones. In her fist, she felt them crumble, and for a moment all went blue, then Patrick's red magic roared forth, and she felt herself falling – an eternal descent – slowly to the stone of the roof. As she fell, she smiled. She no longer felt Seth's hand in her own; she no longer saw him, his blood or his cropped hair, his sea-weathered muscles, his gentle face.

She had saved him. With her last act before her defeat, she had given him, mind and body to the wind. He would fly free where Patrick could not find him, and in the wind, he would learn and grow and perhaps one day return to seek vengeance for them all.

Tara

It was well into the morning when *Nightreaver* departed the camps of the Norse with its crew of twenty-five. Rollo herded the new recruits on board, then set sail without waking Thyri or Megan. The day was full of the sun, and the river burned blue now in Gerald's eyes – Gerald who spent most of the morning nursing his swollen head and recalling one after another of the puzzling incidents of the night before.

The wailing that filled the captain's cabin near noon was not heard outside its walls. In fact, Thyri herself could hear little more than a distant warbling cry, like the sound of a faraway, dying bird, its agonies filtered through leaf and branch in the forest. She woke, however, with Megan's fingernails digging into her arm.

'Bean sidhe!' Megan spat. 'I must leave, Thyri.'

'Why?'

Megan laughed wryly. 'A battle, one with meaning for me.'

'How long will you be gone?'

The sorceress looked at her calmly. 'I don't know. Come with me if you like.'

'To where?'

'Kaerglen. Thyri – please – abandon this quest of yours! Send Rollo back with the others; I fear there will only be death for them if they stay with us.'

'I can't, Meg!'

'Then I must go alone? Has our love weakened so?'

Thyri shook her head, her eyes suddenly brimming with tears. 'I don't know what's happening, my love,' she said softly. 'If you want me, I will go with you, but let the ship follow us. Cast a spell to speed its course . . . Will you do that for me?'

Megan looked at her long, then nodded slowly. 'It will be done. But hurry!' She was already dressed, and the silver sorcery of her ring began to flow out into the cabin, tracing the outline of a gateway in the air.

Thyri threw on her sable cloak and left the cabin, glancing back briefly at Megan – now fully intent on her casting – and wiping a tear from the corner of her eye.

She took Rollo aside and quickly whispered her plans to him, then she ascended to the ship's prow and spoke briefly to the crew. 'Something has happened,' she told them. 'We go first now west of Erin, and I must travel ahead. This craft will travel swiftly – more swiftly than any ship you've known, but do not fear. Stay aboard – Rollo Anskarson commands fully in my absence, and you must do whatever he says.' As she stepped down, she added a battlecry. 'Death to Harald!' she shouted. It had a hollow ring to it in her own ears.

After she'd returned to her cabin, Rollo was left to handle the grumbling crew. 'She goes ahead?' they asked.

Rollo smiled at them. 'Of course!'

'But how?'

'Have you noticed Eiriksdattir's companion? She of the dark hair and pale skin?'

'The servant girl?'

'No,' he laughed. 'The witch. Forget all you may have heard of Eiriksdattir, and sit and listen!'

So they did as *Nightreaver* suddenly lurched forward, speeding along the river at an incredible pace. Rollo, Gerald, and Rui sat across from Sigurd Rolfson and the other additions to the crew and began to speak, to weave the tale of the ship's origin in Jorvik, and the tale of the battle with Morgana in Jotunheim. They spoke long, and told all they knew except of their knowledge of the beast within Thyri, the beast that surfaced under the light of the full moon.

Rollo let Gerald tell them of their lives in the city of the Franks and how Thyri and Megan had set to saving the lives of them – the Norse invaders. So at least that tale became known in full among Thyri's people, if only for a short time.

When the tales were done, Rollo rose and, as if to prove all they'd said, showed them the empty interior of Thyri's cabin.

Thyri and Megan stepped out onto the crest of a hill. Below them, in all directions, a great, verdant expanse of grassland stretched to the horizon, bathing in the mellow warmth of the late autumn sun. Puffy white clouds hung above in the blue sky.

Thyri felt a sudden place within her breast, cleansing her of the heartaches of the morning. This place was power; she felt almost close enough to touch the clouds – their illusory solidity, the banks of mist as she knew them as Astrid had shown her. The eye deceived . . . The swan must seem a demon to the fly, and a mountain but an anthill to Surt, to be passed *through* as easily as she and Astrid had passed through the clouds.

She looked to Megan, wondering where they were; this place certainly wasn't Kaerglen, but the sorceress had said nothing since Thyri had left her to speak with Rollo and *Nightreaver*'s crew; upon Thyri's return, she had found Megan's castings completed, and the sorceress set on packing provisions.

Megan broke her silence in this new world. 'Coryn is dead,' she said softly. She looked fatigued; 'We are almost in-between,' she said. 'The one place in Midgard closest to all the other worlds. One foot in the world of men and, Mag Mor – Alfheim – just beyond our sight. Can you feel it?' Her voice grew strained; she sat even as she spoke, back against a great, undressed stone that stood rooted at the hill's summit.

Thyri nodded. The sorcery here was palpable; she stretched out her senses, finding in virtually every direction some hint of the pathways between the worlds. From here, she might be able to get to anywhere, perhaps even to Asgard itself.

Megan lifted a hand over her head and touched it against the stone. 'This is the Lia Fail, Thyri, the crowning stone of all of Erin. In earlier times, it wailed, sanctifying a king's coronation. The powers of all the worlds would meet here, hosted by a Tuathan council.

'Yes, this place was much stronger then. I have only been here once before, but it has grown weaker even in these few years. It fades; the One God's cult has diluted much of its power.'

Thyri looked off into the distance. She saw no signs of movement anywhere; were they still in Midgard? 'How far from Kaerglen now?'

'Far, yet near. We could reach Castle Kaerglen in an instant, but I should rest . . . No sense showing up exhausted for a battle.' She tore two chunks off the haunch of pork. Thyri sat next to her, unstopped a flask of mead, and set it down between them. So they began to eat. After a time, the sorceress spoke again:

'Long, long ago,' she said, her voice soft and distant, as if recalling something heard long before, 'Midhir, lord of the Tuatha de Danann of Bri Lieth won Edain Echraidne for his wife. Scarcely had she shared his bed before Fuamhnach, Midhir's lover before Edain, grew so jealous that she struck Edain with her magic rod and changed her into a pool of water, and then Edain caused herself to change into a worm, and from there into a purple fly, a form from which she could escape no farther. The fly, at least, reflected her earthly form; it possessed a radiant beauty, while the beating of its wings produced a music unimaginable by human ears and filled the air with the scents of spring rain and the passions of lovers.

'When Midhir beheld the fly, he knew without a doubt that it was his Edain. The fly stayed at Bri Lieth, and while it was there, he could not bring himself to bed Fuamhnach, for he loved Edain as the fly as deeply as he had Edain in her true form. So Fuamhnach consorted with her druids and created a magic wind which carried Edain away and buffeted her about over the Great Sea for seven long years. At last Edain managed to return, and she was found by Oengus, the son of Dagda and Boann, and the lord of the Tuatha at Brug na Boine. Oengus loved Edain as Midhir had, though Midhir had won her first; Oengus took her in, and created for her an elegant crystal sun-bower in which she could hide from the wind of Fuamhnach. At night she was able to attain her womanly form, and she and Oengus loved, deep in secret chambers of his sidhe.

'When Fuamhnach learned of the return of Edain, she stole away from Midhir and traveled to the sidhe of Oengus. The two spoke long, and in the end she convinced Oengus of Midhir's fervent love for her, and the wisdom of meeting with Midhir to smooth relations between them, as the one had long been distrustful of the other since the days when they had both sought the hand of Edain. Oengus left, and Fuamhnach snuck back and shattered the sun-bower, sending Edain away again at the mercy of her relentless magic wind. Oengus returned and learned of Fuamhnach's treachery; in his anger he chased her down and cleaved her head from her neck with his sword. The blow, however, did not dispel the wind, and Edain was forever lost to Oengus.

'Years passed, with Edain ever at the mercy of Fuamhnach's wind. Then one day the wind carried her into the home of Edar, a champion of the kingdom of Ulster, which lies north of here in the realm of men. She landed in the drinking cup of Edar's wife, and the woman swallowed her before she could escape. Thereafter, she was born as Edain, daughter of Edar, and grew up to be the most beautiful maiden in Erin.

'Midhir learned of this and knew indeed that she must be the Edain he had lost long before. He came to her while she bathed with her maidens, and he sang songs of her beauty. But Edain did not recognize her husband; he only frightened her, and in sorrow, Midhir went back to Bri Lieth and the loneliness of his empty bed.

'The King of Erin at this time was named Eocaidhe Airemh. His druids decreed that he should marry none but the most beautiful maiden in all Erin. He sent out his men for the search, and they brought back Edain. Eocaidhe

Airemh and Edain were wed right here, Thyri, in this very spot where we sit.'

Thyri watched Megan curiously. She started to speak, to ask about the story, but the sorceress placed a finger to her lips, signing silence while she paused to tear again into the haunch of pork. After tipping the flask of mead, she continued: 'Edain and Eocaidhe Airemh, as I said, were wed here. We sit on the Hill of Tara, the seat of power for all of Erin, all of Midgard. From here, the king may look out over all the lesser kingdoms.' Megan waved her hand out over the view of the plain.

'As Odin may view the worlds from his seat in Yggdrasil,' Thyri murmured.

Megan smiled, wiping the juices from her lips with the back of her hand. 'Just as. For years, during the Feast of Tara, the joining of Eocaidhe Airemh and Edain was reenacted for her by men and women assuming the roles of the king and his faerie queen, though the coming of the cult of the One God has banished this practice to memory. But Edain ruled as the queen of Erin at Eocaidhe Airemh's side; they loved, and from their love, Edain bore a daughter named Ess. They lived well and were happy, then one day Midhir returned, appearing to Edain in the guise of Ailill Anglonach, Eocaidhe Airemh's brother whom she had taken as a lover. Midhir came so to Edain and finally told her of her past and how he was her first husband and that she'd been lost to him. She remembered, but could not agree to leave with Midhir unless Eocaidhe Airemh consented.

'So Midhir went away and thought. When he returned, he challenged the king to a contest, and the king found himself unable to refuse such a challenge from one he saw as a god, especially since the terms gave the victor the right to ask whatever was in the loser's power to grant. They played at chess, and Midhir carefully lost at first. On his first victory, Eocaidhe Airemh ordered Midhir to clear these plains around Tara of rushes. On his second victory, Eocaidhe Airemh ordered Midhir to cut down the forest of Breag, and on his third, Midhir was ordered to erect a causeway over the moor of Lamraide, so that men might live more easily.

'But Midhir won the fourth game and told Eocaidhe Airemh that he wished but his arms about Edain, and a kiss from her lips. He left promising to return in a year to claim his prize.

'When the appointed day arrived, Eocaidhe Airemh welcomed Midhir into his house, but he ringed it with warriors and locked all the doors. The precautions availed him naught; as soon as Midhir clasped Edain, he lifted her up and carried her through the sky window of Eocaidhe Airemh's home. He cast the *feth fiada*, and they flew back to Bri Lieth in the forms of swans.

'Eocaidhe Airemh was furious. He gathered his druids and commanded of them the location of Bri Lieth and the secrets that would grant him entrance. He took his armies there and began to dig into the sidhe in search of Edain. Midhir came out and watched the destruction of his home with infinite sorrow and anger, and Eocaidhe Airemh agreed to stop on condition that Edain be returned to him. Midhir – the Tuathan lord – agreed grudgingly, but when he came again to Eocaidhe Airemh, he brought out a procession of sixty women, all of like form and raiment, and all appearing to be Edain. Eocaidhe Airemh had to choose, and his choice was as close to Edain as could be. He chose his daughter Ess and returned here to rule with a false queen. Midhir and Edain were reunited at last.'

Megan stopped speaking, drinking deeply from the flask.

'Beautiful,' Thyri whispered, her eyes now closed, her head back against the Lia Fail. 'But I don't understand, Meg.'

'Why I told you this story?' Megan smiled and stood. Swirls of magic began to flow from the ring. 'I feel stronger now,' she said. 'Come.' She began tracing the glittering edges of a gate in the air.

'Meg!'

The sorceress looked down, suddenly solemn. 'I told you because it is a tale of my people. But mainly I told you what you've ached to ask, but never have. Edain was my mother.' She paused, gazing out over Erin's four ancient kingdoms, lands that men could no longer find. 'She was my mother,' the sorceress repeated softly, her hand reaching down for Thyri's, 'by Coryn Kaerglen.'

Tana and Finaan

Awareness came slowly, filtered through a sea of malevolent, burning red, a red that haunted her vision even as she opened her eyes and painfully looked around. She was in a room, a circular chamber high in the west tower of the keep, she suspected. The only light came through two thin slats – perhaps as wide as her hand – in the wall near the ceiling.

Outside, it was day; here it was only dark and red; she was awake several minutes before realizing she wasn't alone. She crawled blindly across the floor, and her hand slipped in a slick pool of blood, cracking her elbow against the stone. She fell, then rolled against Finaan's still body. Patrick had imprisoned them together! She placed her ear against Finaan's chest; his heart yet beat, but only just. Struggling, she pulled his shirt and his rent mail over his head, then she gingerly traced his wounded stomach with her finger; the gash was deep and caked with clumps of dried blood. His breathing was shallow; she was surprised he still lived at all.

Slowly, she gained her feet, trying to shake the red shadows from her mind. What power did Patrick have with which to defeat her so completely? She could imagine only one source, but of it she scarcely dared to think. If the prince of Kaerglen had summoned the Prince of Darkness, then all hope was surely lost. The island, steeped in sorcery already, might very well sink under such an evil weight. She found the chamber's door and tested it, finding it locked. She whispered a charm and placed her hand over the keyhole, when the door suddenly burst open.

She had not caused this; Patrick's bulk filled the open

frame. His red eyes blazed into the room, turning Finaan's flesh the color of blood and his blood the color of coal. Tana backed away.

'Do you think your sorceries will work now, sister?' Patrick asked. Something had changed in his voice. It was deep and coarse, like the voice of an animal. She didn't answer; she just let him laugh. 'Yesterday, I allowed you power. Today I have taken it away. Your spells will not work, I'm afraid.'

'We need food and water, Patrick,' she said at last.

He grinned at her. 'If you are hungry, Tana, then certainly you should eat. Raw flesh should provide you a great deal of strength.' He laughed, and slammed the door shut.

Tana stumbled back to Finaan's side and fell to the floor, retching at the thought of Patrick's suggestion. Finaan was nearly dead . . . She too would die, but he couldn't expect her to – no. She took Finaan under his arms and pulled him away from the pool of his own blood, then she leaned back against the wall under the window and placed his head on her lap. There, in the dim light, she looked down into his face. It was pale and peaceful, free of all the demonic qualities she'd found in it in the past. She looked at it closely, running her fingers gently over his eyelids. She almost cried; she saw now what she'd desired to see the night before. As she gazed at him, she found within herself love, but not the love that she'd feared in his absence, that she might somehow have come to love *him*. Instead, she loved his life and knew at the same time that she'd won their battle, but if he lived, he could only be a friend, nothing more. Too much pain had passed between them for him to win her heart.

'Brigid,' she prayed softly. 'Let him live. Let us live in this dark place, let us defy my brother. We have no food and no water, so must I draw strength for us from the rock?' The hand on Finaan's brow – the hand with which she had held the wishing stones the night before – began to glow a soft blue as she spoke. So, Patrick had not stolen all of her power! She brushed this hand over Finaan's body, over the wound in his stomach. He stirred slightly under the sorcerous caress.

When she was done, she touched the hand to her lips and felt a wetness like water in her mouth. She touched her eyes and the last traces of red fled from her vision, then, with Finaan cradled in her lap, she drifted off to the borders of dream, keeping one eye slightly open lest Patrick should ever again open the door.

Wildfire

Between the worlds, Thyri and Megan suddenly found themselves fighting for their lives.

Always before, time had seemed scarcely to pass in the moment between entering the gates of Megan's sorcery and emerging on the other side, whether that be an inn on Kaerglen Isle, or the crest of the hill of Tara. Now, something had gone terribly wrong. Before them blazed an inferno, an immense tower of fire within which figures writhed and faces moaned and twisted into horrifying masks of pain. The fire burned Thyri's flesh (though she really had no flesh in this place) and her eyes (though she could not truly see). She felt Megan near her, but she knew not where, and the fire drew her in, like a magnet drew iron, like water drew rain. She tried to swim away, but she had no arms. She screamed, but heard no sound, and she even prayed – against all the wishes of her heart – for the beast to take her and free her from this prison that drew her relentlessly, moment by moment, nearer to its fiery heart, so great was the pain she felt in every part of her being.

Such agony – she would rather walk again the rivers of blood of her early nightmares. She would rather taste again the blood of a man, than endure this another moment. She screamed out to Megan, fearing the sorceress had abandoned her. Was this the price she must pay for doubting their love? Was this where her torments would end, in a caldron set on devouring her whole? The faces in the fire – she felt she knew them; she feared she was becoming a part *of* them. Perhaps it was her own face there, twisting before her.

After an eternity, silver erupted into her world, and she suddenly felt grass under her feet. Megan's body lay collapsed on the ground, and Thyri fell next to her, her blood pounding in her ears, her hand reaching out to Megan's, pulling her closer to her lover to make sure she was alive. Megan's head lolled slowly toward her. 'Must sleep,' she whispered. 'Was . . . mistake, I think, to gate for the castle . . .'

Thyri watched Megan's eyes fall shut before letting her own close. She quickly entered dream – dream that for a while remained haunted by the horrible fire that had almost consumed them both.

Patrick summoned his dark master to cast thunderclouds in to the bright afternoon, then he summoned his armies – his men of Kaerglen and Finaan's men of Erin – for his self-styled coronation. He was to have been crowned by the Priest Brenden, but he'd locked away the clergyman and assumed the burden of the ceremonies himself.

Under blackened skies they erected a pyre and onto the pyre, Coryn's body was laid, its pale flesh almost translucent in the dark light. The red burned freely in Patrick's eyes as he lorded over the assembly covering the entire hill below the castle.

Queen Moira, looking old and gray, stood crying at Patrick's side. She fretted about Brenden – whom she couldn't find – and looked nervously from time to time at her son. As the torchbearers approached the pyre, Patrick turned to her. 'Join him,' he said, pointing at her. 'In days past, queens ever died at the king's side!' She cried out in protest, but his red eyes locked on hers and her feet began to move of their own accord. Grumbles were heard throughout the ranks of the armies, but they stifled when Patrick's gaze fell down on the men. Slowly, Moira mounted the pyre and stretched out on the wood, next to her dead husband.

Patrick grinned and ordered the pyre set alight. Coryn yet wore his crown; as the flames shot high into the sky and the queen's screams grew piercing, Patrick walked through the fire and, unscathed on the other side, he placed the crown of Kaerglen on his own head. 'I am King!' he shouted, so loudly that all in the city and port heard his words.

Behind him, his mother's screams reached an ear-shattering pitch for a moment, then only the flames could be heard as Patrick stood there, gazing out over his kingdom.

Thyri woke near dusk, a wretched taste in her mouth and an ache in her heart, as if, in the ordeal of the gating, she'd been physically burned. She rolled over and looked up; the branches of bare trees hung overhead, and leaves blanketed much of the ground around her. Beyond the trees, the sky looked dark and stale, as if a storm threatened to brew, but a storm without the strength to bring rain. Megan lay still in the grass and leaves next to her. Not far away, Thyri heard the music of a running stream, and she began to crawl toward it.

As she drank the water – handful after handful – she wondered what had happened. What could have thwarted Megan's sorcery so? The last time she'd been here, the land had known but one threat, that of Pye, the wizard of the Blue Moon. But she had killed him – ten years before as time passed on Midgard. Ten years . . . That would put Seth and Tana in their teens; Moira would be old and frail, and Patrick would be in the prime of his manhood. And with Coryn's death he would be king.

Still, Thyri could make little sense of it. Why had Megan so desired to return? She cursed herself for not having questioned the hasty action; as it was, she'd hardly thought of it, hardly thought at all, so absorbed she'd been in her own plans. She'd followed Megan recklessly, like a child. She'd forgotten the dangers of such unthinking haste, and they'd nearly died because of it. Thyri shuddered, thinking back on that fire. Of all she'd suffered, that had by far been the worst. Who had the power to inflict such agony?

She emptied her flask of mead, filled it with water from the stream, and returned to Megan's side. There, she wet her hand and brushed it over the sorceress's face until Megan moaned, then she tilted Megan's head and let water from the flask trickle between her open lips. After a moment, Megan coughed and sputtered, opening her eyes. She took the flask from Thyri and drank deeply from it, and Thyri went to refill it and let Megan drink again before they spoke.

'Patrick,' Megan said, her thirst finally sated. 'Somehow – some way – that was Patrick's doing.'

Thyri listened; it was strange hearing the name of Kaerglen's prince on Megan's lips. Thyri had mentioned it in the past – talked of the time when the young whelp had tried to take her in the baths of the castle – and Megan had scarcely acknowledged knowing of the name. Yet Patrick was brother to her, if not in blood then by name. 'Megan Kaerglen,' Thyri whispered, testing the sound of it. If the tale she'd heard on the hill of Tara were true – and she had every reason to suspect that it might be – then much of her own past had suddenly and unexpectedly changed. All these years, she'd thought Megan a former mistress of Coryn Kaerglen, but never his daughter.

'The power of this land has been changed,' Megan said, sitting up. 'I can feel it.' She breathed in deeply, whispering words of enchantment under her breath and pointing at the leaves around her. Nothing happened until the silver of her ring flickered forth; only then did the leaves flutter and rise from the ground. 'I'm all but powerless,' Megan sighed. 'They've cursed all the land with the One God's blessing; only my ring has the power to overcome it, and I've spent most of its power over the past few days – much just in bringing us here.'

Thyri frowned; they'd faced this before – Morgana had sapped all of Megan's strength and left her near death for weeks on end. Yet Morgana had not had the power of that inferno. What had earlier seemed but a diversion from her quest northward now threatened to prove fatal if they didn't quickly change their tactics.

'Patrick,' she said thoughtfully. 'How much strength have you left?'

'For battle? I fear he's allied with the One God's enemy, Thyri. Against such darkness, I can do nothing.'

'Then don't try,' Thyri said. 'Can you learn for me the

truth? Who is where? Who fights for whom, and for what? Where the powers reside?'

'Perhaps, but not here. The One God's blessing clings well to soil, but not so well to stone. Find me a circle or a cave, and I will try.'

Thyri nodded and left, letting the senses of the beast rise within her as she scouted cautiously over the land.

As the night grew dark, she carried Megan to a cavern she'd found in a hill several hundred paces away to the south. To the north, she'd found Megan's old home, the little hut near the cliff's edge that looked out over the northern sea. She was glad Megan had not returned them inside the place, for surely their enemy knew of it no matter what the sorceress had done to grant them safe arrival. And she must have done something, else they'd have been slain in their sleep.

The clouds hung heavily above them as Thyri entered the cave and laid Megan down on her sable cloak. From there, the sorceress smiled. 'I could have walked,' she said.

Thyri smiled and kissed her. 'You need all your strength now.'

'You as well, white-hair.' Megan pulled her down, tears rising to her eyes. 'Don't forsake my love, Thyri. Whatever has come between us, it cannot be stronger than my heart.'

'Nor mine,' Thyri whispered. But so much had happened. 'It's just me, Meg. I feel so lost.'

'So you need battles? I think you've found one here . . . After my castings, you must leave me. I will be too weak to be of any use.'

While Megan prepared herself, Thyri hunted in the night, returning with two rabbits, which she butchered and wrapped tightly in cloth so that Megan would have food even if her legs failed her. She brought water also, and went to Megan's old hut, retrieving baskets which she filled with berries. All this, along with a neat stack of wood for fires, she laid near Megan's side.

Then the sorceress cast her magics, her ring blazing silver

that danced in the air above her. Thyri held her hand and sat alert, her sword ready, awaiting any threat from without. When Megan finally opened her eyes and spoke, she told her this: Patrick was indeed king, and his brother Seth had disappeared, though Megan would not name him dead. Tana, the princess, waned, imprisoned in the west tower of the keep, and with her was a prince of Connaught who had betrayed the king. The armies under Patrick's command comprised over ten thousand men, though many feared their king's unearthly power gained in a recent alliance with the One God's enemy. What resistance remained – what group of men still faithful to the old powers – had its greatest strength among the bandits in the forest, a half day's journey southward.

Nightreaver would arrive within three days. That was it; then Megan slept.

Changes

Thyri left after covering the mouth of the cave with a tangled mass of leaves and fallen branches. She assumed the sorceress had retained some defense against attack – her ring had kept a slight glow at least – but Thyri saw no point in allowing anything, man or beast, to happen upon Megan by chance. After constructing the barricade, Thyri went north to Megan's old hut where she rummaged through a trunk of clothes, emerging with a long, green, hooded cloak that hid her features well and would aid her in blending into the foliage of the forest. At her waist, she strapped her weapons belt with her sword on one side and a long, thin dirk – almost a half-sword – on the other. Thus armed and disguised, she started south.

She knew the lay of the land well; she'd wintered on Kaerglen that first years of her curse, and the trees around her reminded her of the interal battles she'd waged under the eye of the full moon. To a degree, she felt the pain again, but she'd since defeated much of the horror, and learned to accept something of the dark side of her fate. And the forest seemed to greet her with its memories, of paths she'd followed, of glades where she'd rested. She knew of the farmers and shepherds of these parts, and of the occasional stable where she might find a mount. She went first to the nearest of these, taking her pick of three horses while the owner – a wealthy mrchant escaped from the city, by the look of his house – slept, unaware of the pale, snowy-haired thief from the north.

Yes – snowy-haired. Time had passed, and each year had colored Thyri more pale and less the blond of her youth.

Each year had colored her more in the shade of the white beast within her.

On horseback, she sped southward, slowing only when she reached the dark forests where Megan claimed there were bandits. The quickest, surest way to find them, she knew, was to let them find her. So she kept her steed reined in to a steady, even pace.

As she rode, she again recalled Astrid. She'd spent little time on horseback since their days together; she'd either been at sea or on foot, in battle, in some wilderness, or in a city full of men. Sometimes, with Astrid, she would just ride, the miles dissolving effortlessly beneath pounding hooves, or afternoons melting away at lingering gaits with words seldom spoken – but a glance could betray her heart to Astrid. But it was while passing through a forest much like this that Astrid had come to her end. They'd left the road to slay a man-killing wolf, but instead Astrid had fallen, and Thyri had come by her curse. So the dark shadows began to leer at her anew with their memories, spectral wolves among the trees stalking her on either side, calling to her with deep, mournful howls – howls forged in her own mind, howls shaped like those of the beasts who'd loved her in the new land across the waters. Howls of her own making – there were no wolves on Kaerglen Isle.

No wolves but one.

The arrows came first, as she'd expected; she depended on the sorcery of her sword, which she held limply by its hilt, to send them astray of their mark. The fifth rune of Odin gifted her by Scacath had saved her before, as it did now. The arrows rained; Thyri didn't flinch though they came straight for her. Four of the missiles, though, thudded in near-unison into the flanks of her stolen mount. It bolted, and she leaped gracefully from its back, wishing it a safe journey under her breath as she stood to face her attackers alone.

For a few moments, the shower of arrows continued. She

stood patiently, her face hidden in the shadows of her hood, her sword held calmly in front of her. After a while, about ten men stepped out onto the road before her; she sensed an equal number did so behind her as well. One man stepped forward, drawing his sword, brashly approaching until he stood but three paces away. Under her cloak, she smiled, but he couldn't see it.

'This is our forest, stranger,' he said. 'Do you have sorcery to turn aside my blade as you have my bow?'

She chuckled. 'Only my own blade, if you consider that sorcery. Some have in the past.'

'It's but a boy!' someone behind the leader exclaimed.

Thyri heard footsteps behind her. 'Please have them stop,' she said. 'I don't wish to fight all of you.'

'Then you will surrender your arms to us.'

'I'd rather be a guest.'

He laughed. 'You're a brave lad to ride this wood. If not for the obvious value of your sword, I'd ask you to join us. Are you for the king, or against?'

'Which king? Coryn is dead.' Her remark drew the expected response; they had not yet heard, so how could she (he) know? She heard other words as well – the name of Seth placed on her from behind. This she hadn't expected; she weighed it a moment and considered it useful, at least a mystery she shouldn't discourage. And if they thought her the prince, then they couldn't know him for several reasons, the main being his age of fifteen. He would be almost a man, his voice deepened by now, not at all like hers.

'So Patrick rules –'

'Unfortunately,' she said, ending his absent reflection. 'I hope you don't think it good news, else I'll have to kill you.'

'Lad,' he laughed, 'you *are* a brave one. Lower your hood; show the face of one so brave as to threaten thirty men.'

'No,' she said. 'Not yet.'

He eyed her carefully. 'What brings you here? You rode from the north, where there is nothing – how is it that you know of Coryn's death, and we do not? How does a boy learn such things where they cannot be learned?' Behind him now, whispers that included Seth's name grew more frequent. Thyri smiled; again he couldn't see it. He only saw her shrug.

'Perhaps I'll answer you, if you'll tell me you oppose the new king.'

'It is Patrick, lad, that we've opposed all along. So you'll answer my questions?'

'In time,' she returned. 'I wish to speak to he who leads all of you. I need to know your strengths. What is his name?'

'Lugh,' the man answered sarcastically.

'Very well,' she said, chuckling. 'Keep it a secret – that's your right. But take me to him. You may call me a prisoner if you wish, but I will not give up my sword.'

He eyed her for a while, then sighed, almost smiling. She could see in his starlit eyes the same questions his men asked. Was this Seth before them? Had their true leader surfaced at long last?

'Come,' he said. 'Dawn approaches.' He turned to his men. 'It is well nigh time we returned to camp, is it not?' As they gave their assent, he turned back to Thyri and nodded. 'Let's go then.'

Ai'reth turned briefly away from Midgard and whispered charms against the realm of fire that tried, immediately, to suck him in. Such a realm he would not enter no matter how strong its call. He was Light, and it was not, though its seductions spoke sweetly and offered him power. He *knew* where the powers were. This place had changed, so suddenly that he could not have foreseen it, but he smiled nevertheless. He had done well so far, hiding Thyri and Megan from the darkness while they'd rested, while the sorceress had cast her own spells. Simple charms indeed could deflect the evil eye. True, the enemy of the One God was powerful, but his ways were more like the old ways, stolen from the darkest priests of the ages. Ai'reth knew many defenses.

Yes, he had done well. He had saved the true prince with the gift of the sword of power, though the princess deserved credit as well. Yet without the sword, the prince would have fallen quickly, but moments after the false prince's alliance.

So what now? The powers were safe, the helpless hidden, and the white-haired joined to an army. She would have to face the false prince; indeed, only she was equal to the task. And Loki would not threaten yet, not even should he escape his prison, not on this island claimed now by a darkness more dark than he.

Ai'reth sat, half in Alfheim, half on the border of Midgard. The princess – she suffered now. And she was a power as well – how had Midgard come to harbor so many powers in such dark days? She had not the mettle of the two he knew, though. She was too young, and could greatly use his help.

So he reflected, rising at last, skirting southward along the Midgard border, crossing through half-worlds where they would shorten his path. He would not risk any quicker means of movement, not this close to the fires; the sorceress had made that mistake and paid dearly for it. Ai'reth took the lesson to heart.

He approached the old fortress, passing through its walls, then fully into Midgard. All the words touching here grew hot from the nearby fires. He hid in shadows awhile, waiting to learn whether the false prince knew of his entrance. After a time, he turned his talent out, seeking the princess's light.

It was a strange quest, this one for Ai'reth. Castle Kaerglen reeked of hidden sorcery, the footfalls of ancient powers and the decaying glow of the Tuatha de Danaan, all of it subdued and shriveled up, however, by another light, the light of the One God's magic, the crosses of the sacrificed son he discovered at every turn, feeling more and more the weight of Klorista's words that day before S'kiri had died. Such simple spells they were, these that bound up the ancient mysteries and caused them to shrivel. He dared to touch one – just a small wooden talisman nailed to an oaken door – and it burned and numbed his fingers at the slightest of contacts. After that, he kept his hands close to himself, understanding all of Klorista's fears and praying ever more fervently that he had chosen the proper path, that Thyri and Megan might be the ones to save them all. Should they fail and their world suffer Surt's fire, what if the One God's enemy then directed his inferno there? And after that – if these simple talismans had such power – what if the One God himself came?

Such thoughts so darkened his mood that he scarcely noticed Tana's light at first. He followed it, reaching a door, guarded and warded by sorceries he understood, yet sorceries directed against she who was inside, not he, who wished to enter from without! So confident was this false prince. Ai'reth grinned – baring his sharp teeth – and pushed open the door. Her blue-white magic struck him in a soothing wave, and he revealed himself to her half-open eye.

'Hurry,' he whispered. 'Escape you can, but be quick!'

She looked at him oddly, started to speak, then looked down at the man she held in her arms. 'Did Brigid send you?' she asked.

'Ai'reth sends himself. Hurry!' He moved forward, examining the man's wounds. The princess had sealed them with her blue magic, but the life blood was weak within him . . . Ai'reth cursed softly, and took S'kiri's Queenstone from its pouch; he pressed it against the man's wound, digging in his claws around it, and incanting words of healing and life. After a moment, the man's eyes fluttered open. Would that the Queenstone could have revived S'kiri so easily. Too much life force in a felnin. The man's *yangi* began to shine with its normal, weak strength, and Ai'reth quickly returned the Queenstone to its pouch of safekeeping and glanced back involuntarily at the open doorway, for fear the false prince might have found them and shut it again. But no – it remained open. Perhaps they were more safe than he knew; perhaps the false prince was out, displaying his powers to others, forgetting his home and his prisoners there.

Ai'reth wondered on this; surely the One God's enemy could see them, so close to the fire as they were. Or could the fire's eyes be blinded, able to see only where it was invited to look? Whatever the reason for their safety, he was thankful for it.

Finaan stood with Tana's help. His eyes were a while adjusting to the light; by the time he could see, they were already moving – behind some creature that looked like a clothed, walking cat. As the image registered, he shook his head, but Tana held tightly to his arm. 'He is a friend,' she whispered. 'One of the elder races. Please trust him, Finaan. Our lives are in great danger.'

Danger, he thought. From Patrick? What on earth had happened to him? In the grotto, Tana had bewitched him, pitching him back into her past, making him feel all her pain, all Seth's pain, and then he'd returned to the present and found her gone. He'd sat on the rock and cried, understanding how he'd lost her forever on that day of youthful lust long ago. He'd fled to the shore below and spent hours in mourning, unable to decide anything, scarcely able to think. And when he'd regained the courage to climb back to the castle, to risk seeing her again face to face, he'd instead been drawn somehow to the roof of the east tower. There he'd found Patrick – a strange, changed Patrick – and they'd fought. He remembered a blinding red light, pain after that, then nothing.

Now Tana aided him. The pain – he'd felt it in his stomach. As they hurried along behind the cat-creature, Finaan explored his flesh. He had a long, deep scar across his abdomen, but it felt healed, ages past. The cross he wore around his neck was gone; his sword was gone, as was his shirt, but he wore the same pants he'd worn that last day of his memory.

He felt as if he'd been dead and brought back to life. In his dreams-near-death, he vaguely remembered Tana in them, but not the Tana at his side. In his dreams, she had tortured him, again and again, with the memories of her pain, taking pleasure in her revenge. When he glanced at her now, he found only concern in her eyes. Much had changed, and he had so many questions, but he asked nothing, for fear that the sound of his voice might spoil something, ruining their escape, or revealing it to be but another dream and thus end it. If this was a dream, he didn't want it to end.

After descending the tower stairs, they each took a hand of the felnin and passed through the stone wall of the castle. Outside, the morning sky was dark and brooding with only a paler tint in the eastern sky betraying the passing of a recent dawn. Then, their fingers still caught in Ai'reth's hands, they came into another world, an indistinct world of purple lights and uncertain winds, a border-world at the edge of Midgard. Ai'reth led them north, quickly, through half-worlds, in and out of the border as he had come there.

Tana marveled at the journey, while Finaan grew ever more fearful that he did, in truth, but dream.

They came into a northern forest before they finally stopped. Tana heard the voices of men nearby and pulled Finaan down into a crouch behind bushes.

'If she asks,' Ai'reth whispered behind her, 'was Brigid who saved you, not myself.'

'If who asks?' Tana turned around, but the felnin was already gone.

Warriors

The man who escorted Thyri to the main encampment of the bandits was named Ailill, a name which, once Thyri heard it, sent her thoughts back to the tale Megan had told her on the hill of Tara; such a misty, elusive tale it had been, with gods changing other gods to water, and gods changing themselves into flies. The way of the world when the Aesir and Tuatha de Danaan had both been strong. Thyri felt a sadness that she'd never asked Megan more of the gods of her people and a sorrow that Megan had seldom volunteered a tale in her desire for Thyri not to know the full truth of her past. Perhaps such tales were painful for the sorceress; she was apart from her mother's people, and yet not really a part of the world of men. In a way, this had unrooted Megan's life in much the same way Thyri's curse had unrooted her own.

Yet Thyri could do with more of such tales. As Megan had told it, Thyri had felt young again for a time, the way she had felt when as a little girl she'd heard the tales of her own gods from her father.

The leader of the bandits was absent upon Thyri's arrival, forcing her to endure the early morning in a tent alone with Ailill. The man was pleasant enough, but Thyri grew tired of talk and impatient of waiting. In time, when they were finally hailed outside, her spirits lifted when she saw the face of he she sought, a face she knew – not the one she'd most hoped for, though she knew Cuilly would be too old for this. It was Dearen, the man who had come to lead her charges after her departure from the Kaerglen Guard so long ago. She smiled under her hood as she approached him, then without warning, she threw the hood back. For a moment, he looked at her as if stunned, his mouth falling slightly agape, then he grinned broadly and let out a whoop that attracted the attention of all in the camp. 'Thyri!' he shouted then. 'The legend yet lives!' He came to her as if to embrace her, then caught himself, smiling uncertainly. 'You choose your moments, don't you?' he asked in disbelief. 'I have just learned from the south that Coryn is dead.'

'I know,' she said.

He shook his head, smiling at her, then turned to address his men. 'All against the new king!' he shouted out. 'Let Patrick tremble when he hears that she who slew the Blue Moon stands against him! All you too young to know the tales – this is no wench come among us, but the finest warrior by far these eyes have seen. And to all you who whispered Prince Seth as I entered the camp, hear this! I'd rather this one among us, than ten rightful kings of Kaerglen! Speak ill of her, and I'll have your head!' With that, he turned back to her and invited her to council, in the open air where they could keep an eye on the darkened sky.

With Dearen and his lieutenants, Thyri discussed Patrick and his dark alliance. It came as news to most, though Daren had heard something of it along with the news of the king's death. He told Thyri something she didn't know: Patrick had ordered Moira onto the pyre with Coryn. This disturbed Thyri deeply, driving home a new understanding of the dangers they faced. Before, Patrick had been Moira's pet, seemingly the only true object of her love. If he'd turned on her so easily . . . The darkness within him had to be strong indeed. Yet he was new to it from all accounts; they could use this to their advantage.

There would of course be a war. Though Dearen was pleased with Thyri's arrival in the camp, they yet sorely needed Seth, if he could be found. They needed the rightful heir to show to the people, else they'd be defeated quickly and all hope would be lost. With Seth, they might cause confusion and desertions among Patrick's ranks in the heat of battle. Otherwise, they were outnumbered better than ten to one; Dearen had less than a thousand men.

So they discussed the prince. Thyri could offer nothing but that he should still be alive. As the discussion prolonged itself, Tana chose her entrance. As if from the air itself – her sorcery fed by the faith in the old ways among all in the camp – she and Finaan stepped among them. 'My brother lives,' she said, 'and he is safe.'

As the shock of her entrance passed, cries erupted among those who looked on. 'It is Connaught! We are betrayed!' came the shouts, tens of fingers pointing at Tana's companion, as many arrows notching into suddenly battle ready bows.

Tana turned on them. 'No!' she declared. 'He owes his life to me, so that makes it mine to take or leave intact, not yours!'

Dearen, still seated, glanced at Thyri. 'If not a prince,' he said, 'it seems we have a princess.'

Thyri remembered Tana, the little girl who'd escorted her to Megan's bedchamber in the castle. She looked up at Tana now, the young woman whose fear of the situation was betrayed only by a slight trembling of her hand. Thyri smiled, doubting anyone else had noticed.

The council continued on through the day, Tana at Thyri's side. The princess spoke vaguely of the whereabouts of her brother, for how could she explain to them how he rode free on the wind? She herself was unsure in ways of what she'd done. With assistance, he might return to Midgard, anywhere at any time. But could he now if she called him?

Before they'd joined Thyri, she and Finaan had hidden while she'd attempted sorcery to call Seth back from the wind. Either her spells had failed, or he had not heard her. So what, in fact, could she tell them but that Seth was alive and safe for the moment from his brother?

In an act of humility and of his own accord, Finaan stood behind Tana, baring his naked torso for all to see until someone finally asked of the scar, and he replied the wound was Patrick's doing, and he would have his revenge or die in the process. Beyond that, the prince of Erin said little until the talks turned to discussions of Patrick's armies and his strengths. Only then did Finaan sit and become an equal among them; of the captains under the king's command, Finaan knew a great deal, perhaps even more than Patrick himself. And in the course of his contribution, Finaan pointed out that over half of Patrick's forces owed their primary allegiance to Connaught, not Kaerglen. Was he not, then, more valuable even than Seth? Might he not, in battle, turn over half the king's armies against the crown?

As Finaan said these words, Thyri laughed. He was right, and even she hadn't thought of it, though her lack of foresight had been rooted in ignorance of this aspect of the conflict. Dearen, however, cursed himself affably; he should have known, and he'd had ample time to beat Finaan to the observation. As the idea developed, Finaan stood, his self-assurance finally reemerging after all the trials of the morning. 'If any here still see treachery in my heart, he may kill me now.' He looked around, at the ragged crowd of men gathered around the central council. No one challenged him, and he spoke again. 'We may not have Seth, but if we attack quickly, before Patrick can fully turn my men against me – and he will surely attempt this when he learns of my escape – then we can defeat him. I have heard talk here that we should wait, redouble our efforts to find Seth, but such a wait could cost us dear. I regret that in past years I've sought the rightful prince's death, but were he to join us now I would rejoice with the rest of you. If the prince remains hidden, we yet have among us a rightful heir to the throne. Who here says Princess Tana could not be queen of Kaerglen?'

All eyes then turned to the young sorceress, and she felt the weight of their stares. She smiled for them, but inside she prayed fervently for Seth's return. Not once in her past had such a suggestion occurred to her, and the thought of the responsibility – the safekeeping of all on the island – made, moment by moment, each stare more heavy than the last. Under this weight, she couldn't flinch; she had suddenly entered an alien world – the world of battle and armies – but she knew enough of it to understand that showing her fear could cost them all the gains and hope of the day. Only yesterday, she had asked her father for hope, but she'd never considered that the hope might lie with *her*. She'd gained in strength, but had she the strength to challenge Patrick for the throne itself?

Shouts had arisen around her – distant shouts, as if the turmoil in her own mind pushed the external world ever away from her, forcing her to flee against the weak resolve of her reason. They were cheering her, these distant shouts, calling her queen, assuming the royal blood in her veins equal to the task. Even Finaan, for he led them in their shouts; and beneath his stare, he smiled at her. She wished she'd had the thought to speak of this to him before he could thrust her so in front of all, unprepared as she was. But she had failed to consider the eventuality, and she'd forgotten the nature of Finaan's essence. He was a man of power, used to wielding it, used to seeking it. Patrick's sword had only subdued his nature for a time; she'd failed to foresee its rebirth.

Something began to draw her back – Thyri's hand on her own. As she returned to them, she noticed the ache in her cheeks; her smile hadn't faltered. Her reason had forced the acquiescence of her body even while her mind had fled. But Thyri had sensed her failure in that moment.

'Do not despair,' the swordsmistress said softly, so that only she could hear. 'All things may be righted in the end.'

As Tana looked into Thyri's smile, she recalled the comfort it had given her long ago. It renewed her strength, returning her fully to the present. If necessary, she could bear the burden. This was the war, the conflict with Patrick she had to face in any event. Had she to assume the mantle of usurper, she would have to do so while Seth rode free on the wind. Thyri's smile revealed a hidden confidence, and Tana took it to heart. This was the woman who had once saved her father, delaying his death. And as her mind calmed, she remembered for the first time that day that Thyri meant something else. She was a friend to her sister. Surely the swordsmistress would have news of Megan . . . Tana ached to ask it, but held back the question before it could pass her lips. This was not the place; few on the island knew the name of Megan Kaerglen, and fewer still held it dear. Should she mention it, they might realize that yet another heir lived, an heir with an older claim to the throne than she. Should she mention it, they might take her words as a rejection of their allegiance, see in them her weakness and reluctance toward her heritage.

Thyri's hand remained on hers; the swordsmistress yet smiled, as if seeing into her thoughts. She spoke again, softly again: 'She lives,' she said, 'though she has aided already all that she might. We shall win this battle, Tana, and then you will meet her. Many things will change.'

Tana thought on that. Yes, things would change; things had already changed. There would be a battle, a war. She had seen but one in the past, and that only in her wind-dream on the hill below the castle. How had that one fared? For all she knew, the Tuatha de Danaan had all perished in their world away from her own. How much might their defeat change? Where would it lead? If the gods warred, what meant the petty wars of men?

The council went until dusk. As Dearen's men erected tents for those who had newly come among them, Tana found herself nervously facing Finaan. There were wounds she could see in his eyes, and the dark evil she'd grown so accustomed to finding there had fled. But would he renew to her now his pledges of love? Would he fall to his knees and plead with her to bed with him? Would he force upon her such questions? She couldn't read the answers in his face; the wounds of his eyes were too deep to allow any other feeling an escape.

So he gazed upon her and time passed in silence. He reached out to her and took her hand lightly in his own. 'Thank you,' was all he said, then he turned away, leaving her to watch him depart. At that moment, Thyri called to her, bidding her to come and sleep.

So Thyri and Tana came to share a tent over these days. It must be written that Thyri never once felt the lust for the young princess that she might once have felt in earlier years. Tana had many of the qualities Thyri desired in her lovers: strength of resolve, physical beauty, and the vulnerability of inexperience. Tana might have had the tranquil side of Pohati, the shy hesitancy of Akan, or the untapped tender passion of Megan reborn. But this speculation falls flat before the winds of reality. What happened at night in the tent they shared compared most to the nights Thyri had shared with Astrid upon first arriving in the world of Scacath, only then Thyri had had the questions and the other had had the answers. With Thyri and Tana, this was reversed. As they lay down to sleep, they would talk, slowly and quietly, Tana generally asking and Thyri answering, reassuring, complimenting, inspiring confidence or mystery as the questions required.

From time to time, however, the roles would reverse. As they rested, letting their talk grow softer and gentler with the approach of sleep, Thyri said to Tana, 'So Brigid did find you . . .'

The words puzzled the princess; she took them as some unexplained mystery concerning the appearance of the felnin in her locked room that morning. In fact, Thyri was remembering a night in the land of the Saxons, the night Gerald had led her to a place of power to summon Megan to her side. The place had been Brigid's, and Thyri had spoken long with the goddess. In this discourse, Thyri had told Brigid of Tana, and how the magic of the old ways was strong within her. The goddess had replied that the finding had already been done.

Tana answered a simple yes, ending, so far as she was concerned, all questions of her escape from her brother. Nothing more was said on that matter in any case.

Fire

The alliance led by Dearen, Thyri, Finaan, and Tana began its march southward the next morning. They moved as quickly as they dared without risking complete exhaustion on the dawn of the battle; it took them nearly a week to gain the southern reaches of the island.

They were a motley army, these bandits: ill-equipped, some carrying no more than a bow and a quiver of ten arrows. One day, Thyri took it upon herself to count the longswords among them, and they numbered less than two hundred. That explained, at least, Ailill's words concerning 'the obvious value of her sword' that night on the road in the forest. By confidence they were driven. Thyri would have held them back were there not so many unknown factors unsolved without the battle begun. She deeply desired to confront Patrick herself and see this new power of his through her own eyes. And if Finaan *could* bring half his army to their side, then this might become possible.

Patrick, in his arrogance, let them come, not bothering even to interfere with their swift passage, instead preparing his men to greet them; over these days of his waiting for the final defeat of his last enemies on the island, he moved his forces to the plain named Dagda, an ancient battlefield some two miles north of the city.

Before this, Rollo and *Nightreaver* arrived.

The voyage over the seas passed uneventfully, except for its speed, which often caused alarming creaks through *Nightreaver*'s hull and the unexpected illness of many of the veteran seafarers aboard. Gerald spent it deep in thought, his memories of The Emporium yet fresh in his mind. As for the sea – he recalled the name given it by the poets of his people. Whale's road, they called it. Yes, he realized, but *Nightreaver* traveled far more quickly now than any whale ever could. No leviathan of the deep stood a chance of hindering their journey.

As for Rollo, he had no problems with his new crew, the sorcery of the vessel bespoke all the power of its owners, such a power disallowed any thoughts of mutiny or any lesser disobedience.

The time, as well as the leagues, passed swiftly.

Megan's sorcery propelled them through the island's mists, then let the ship idle. Rollo would at least have the decision of where to land. It was late afternoon; in the distance those in the rigging could just sight the port. Rollo directed them north of it, putting *Nightreaver* to anchor in a cove five miles upcoast of Port Kaerglen itself. From there, he, Gerald, and Rui manned a landing craft with eight other men, and they put this smaller boat to water and headed south to learn the state of things on the island in a less conspicuous manner than docking *Nightreaver* at port, letting all witness its wolfshead prow and the uniform black of its wood.

The port they found seemed abandoned. Beyond it, the light of a huge bonfire blazed into the sky, at first seeming as if the city itself burned. Rollo led them cautiously onto the docks, then – having little inspiration concerning future courses that might reunite them with Thyri – he started them toward the distant, billowing clouds of black smoke.

As they passed the hovels and houses of the seamen and their wives the streets remained abandoned. Upon occasion, Rollo noticed faces disappearing quickly from open windows when he turned his head toward them. Something, surely, was amiss in the city. They came to the port wall and passed through its unguarded gate, then kept in a line toward the fire. From time to time, Rollo thought he saw a castle on the hill far beyond; the smoke was too thick to tell. As they grew ever more near, they saw the crowd.

The bonfire burned at the edge of the city, a sea of people surrounding it on all sides. Someone stood on stacked rock at the foot of the flames, clearly the figure of man cut into silhouette by the glow beyond. Rollo thought, even at this distance, that he could almost hear the man's words above the roar of the flames and the shouts of the mass of men. For the most part, they were armed men. Nearing them, he discerned a fanatacism in their eyes, another thing adding to his disturbing impression of the scene. He was unsure of the nature of the wrongness until they drew up and into the fringe of the crowd, and he saw a man he knew: Rorvald Arngrimson, a veteran of Guthrom's campaign against Alfred, a man who Rollo had once heard express a desire to abandon the Saxons and seek out the turmoils of Erin. Well, Rollo decided, he had obviously found them.

So Rollo approached Rorvald, placing a hand on his shoulder. The other Viking turned to him; in his eyes was the absence of sight, the vacancy of the blind, of the seer or invalid. Rollo cocked an eyebrow and greeted the man. 'Hail Rorvald!' he declared with a wink. There came no response. Every muscle in the Viking's body seemed to bid him to turn, to face himself toward the bonfire and the figure lording over it. Rollo could hear his words now; they were vile, repulsive words, but there was a sorcery within them, a sorcery that bid him listen, to look, to match their evil with whatever evil he might find within. He began to mumble to himself to shut out the sound.

A short distance away, the others waited. Several of the Vikings stared now at the bonfire; Rollo grabbed each and pulled him to the ground, bellowing into his ear until he was certain that he'd returned him fully to the present – his present, and, he hoped, Thyri's present. He gathered them all and spoke to them: 'For now, let us stay here. Stand and face the fire lest we become discovered, but don't stare. Keep your eyes moving. Trade tales with the man next to you. Talk of anything, but keep talking; there is a powerful sorcery here to which we must not succumb.'

'Then let's leave,' Gerald suggested.

'In time perhaps. I'm not yet certain what to do; what if Thyri is among them?' he asked, waving his arm at the crowd. 'I agree we should not stay long, but allow me leave to think. As we stand here, should the man next to you move forward grab him and throw him to the ground. We cannot lose a single man to this sorcery, else we all may be lost.' With that, Rollo spread them out, and he thought: It was true that they shouldn't stay. He could feel the call grow stronger the more he tarried. They could hide in the city, as some obviously still did, but perhaps those were only women, children, and old ones. This crowd before him was an army, mostly soldiers, but looking around he saw blacksmiths and weavers, tailors and fishermen. Those men of the city and port with the strength to do battle had been called. That could mean only that battle brewed.

Battle against Thyri? Or another? The swordsmistress had told him precious little before her sorcerous departure from their ship. All she'd said had hinted at an innocent, short diversion, not a conflict, certainly nothing like this. He wished he could approach the fire, if only to see for himself what sort of man controlled this. And then he was guessing it was indeed only one man; he didn't really know enough to be sure. But if all the folk of the city and port were already here – all the able bodied men – then there had been a sorcerous summoning, followed by a binding into this crowd. Perhaps it *would* be safe to hide now in the city; they had seen no riders there, no evidence of an ongoing search for more blood.

If this were true, what should be his decision? He needed the rest of his men in any case, and that meant sending the boat back to *Nightreaver* to bring them ashore. If Thyri was not in this crowd, then he saw no reason to stay. If she was, failing to find her soon would result in his own loss of himself to the dark power of the fire. So he thought.

At the bonfire, events moved on. Onto the stone platform, more stones were raised, cut stones, as of an altar. A bound man, robed in white, joined the master of it all, standing there as an object of the crowd's jeers. He was laid onto the altar, and the lord of the bonfire approached, touched him, then held up a bloodied hand for all to see. Though Rollo's mind was far away, Gerald's wasn't, and he couldn't resist peering intently at this new development. In the one man's hand, was the other's still-beating heart. Though none of *Nightreaver*'s crew knew this, the robed man was named Brenden, the priest of the One God Moira had brought with her to Kaerglen's shores. All his life, he'd striven to bring the island under the One God's care, and in addition, he'd acted as tutor to the children of the king. Patrick dispensed with him as easily and more cruelly than he'd dispensed with his mother.

When Rollo at last pulled back his men, shaking each to chase the absence from his eyes, he formed them for a stealthy departure. He made them crawl to the nearest building so that a watcher might not witness their escape, then he led them back through the city, through the port wall, and to an abandoned hostel near the docks. By this time it was dusk. He gave them rooms, and sent two men to return with the others from the ship.

As time passed, the weird assembly below the castle went on, its participants never seeming to falter, sustained by the same sorcery that held them in place. After another day and night of it, they began to move; Rollo had scouts follow their passage from a distance. He who ruled the fire led his army north to a plain and kept them there. Rollo began to see the battle looming ever nearer in the future. All this time, no one reported Thyri or Megan among the strange army's ranks.

The crew of *Nightreaver* followed, keeping a mile or more to the west; from the occasional absent-eyed scout that came plundering through the woods, they hid. It wouldn't do to kill and alarm the army of enemies to the west. Rollo camped them in the hills over the army's plain, and there they spent two nights awaiting the clash, enjoyable nights on the whole except for the frosts, which they could not risk countering with small fires. Rollo was certain that discovery now would mean their end. They'd been lucky enough to get this far. Instead, they drank. On leaving the city, they'd plundered the abandoned shops, departing with provisions enough to last them two weeks or more.

From time to time, Rollo worried about *Nightreaver*'s safety. He'd left no one to guard it, and while it usually went to anchor protected by the sorceress's charms of invisibility and more, this time no such protection had been granted it. After their first night in the hills, Rui Taichimi announced that he would travel to the ship to verify its continued well-being. Rollo spent much of that day in worry, worry only relieved when Rui returned near dusk to assure him that all was well.

During these days, Rollo sent out his own scouts. On their second day, one from the north returned to report sighting a small army moving toward them. Eiriksdattir strode at this army's head, but the servant girl (the sorceress) was nowhere to be seen. Even so, elation grew among Rollo's men, despite the scout's estimation of Thyri's meagre forces. Rollo thought on the news awhile, then sent the scout back with a message for Thyri. He had arrived, and awaited her orders. If need be, he could join her that night.

Her message came back thus:

> Wait. Watch the battle – we are sorely outmatched. Cut arrows for Rui, and choose a tree on the battlefield in which to place him, then plan to get him there and command the Norse swords to guard him and advance before him if possible. Cut him arrows, Rollo – as many as you can; you have seen the forces we face.
>
> There may be tricks in the heat of battle, but let's not depend on them. Their leader must be slain, though this may not be an easy task. But, be strong, and don't join me. Stay hidden. Choose carefully the moment of your attack.

Rollo heard the message and sent other scouts. From them, he learned of a low hill topped by three trees about a hundred paces ahead of the western flank of Kaerglen's horde. Their description of it puzzled Rollo; it sounded too round and flat to be natural. It was probably the cairn of some ancient, fallen king. Rollo hoped the dead would be in good spirits when battle came to disturb the peace. Assuming Kaerglen's army would charge, the little hill cairn would find itself in the midst of the conflict on the western flank.

They passed the rest of that day and early evening fashioning arrows for Rui. Before they slept, word came that Thyri had reached the south and camped on the northern edge of the plain. She expected battle at dawn.

The night left them huddled in their furs within hastily constructed shelters, each lost in his own thoughts. Just before sunrise, Rui stole away from the camp to take his position in the appointed tree. When Rollo wakened, a nervous Viking confronted him with this news and gave him the archer's message. Rui had seen the lay of the battlefield and wished to ensure his usefulness. During the charge now, he would be able to add his arrows to the rain of the others without being noticed.

Rubbing his eyes, Rollo stared at the man, saying nothing.

'He says he can kill fifty or more before sword ever meets sword,' the Viking continued. 'After that, he can keep the hill clear long enough for Thyri's forces to gain it and guard his position. Now we'll be free to join in whenever and wherever you choose, regardless of the archer. He also said you could kill him afterward if you wish, assuming you both survive.'

Rollo grunted. It was a good idea – good if Rui had indeed gained his post undetected. But the archer could at least have cleared it with him, if only because Thyri needed to know of it. After a moment, he told the man to get word to the northern camp.

'It's already done,' the Viking returned. 'Erling Hallfredson has gone and returned. Thyri knows.'

Rollo gave him a brief, twisted smile, then went to rouse those of his men still asleep for their short trek eastward.

And so the stage was set for the battle of Dagda's Plain.

Blood

They came in one massive, unthinking wave, with a fury that surprised even Thyri, though she'd considered over and over again the possibilities of the battle in recent days. Patrick had retained no commanders in the merciless process of indoctrinating his army, and they were more than the ten thousand reported by Dearen; they were well over fifteen thousand with the men of the city and port included.

They charged blindly, out of blind loyalty. Only one mind operated to capacity among the entire horde, and that was the mind of Patrick himself. Thyri found herself wondering whether he was so drunk with his power that he'd abandoned all his past knowledge of tactics to depend on sheer might alone. Perhaps the evil within him simply desired death, and the more the better, it mattering not whether the death came from his pawns or his enemies. In a way, this made sense; he'd had ample time and opportunity to undermine their rebellion in far more subtle ways. And it yet surprised her that Rollo had managed what he already had.

Patrick's charge began from his encampment in the southern half of the plain. Without this further description, the picture of the battle is incomplete: Though covered with heather, Dagda's Plain was scarcely featureless, and the hill from which Rui would launch his attacks was but one of many. In addition, in recent past the south had boasted a small village, at the center of which was a small chapel, built by Brenden and Moira in their crusade to take the One God's cult to the people. In his arrogance, Patrick had let the chapel stand so that it grew from the center of his assembled army like the last bastion of Light, a thing to be mocked and leered at by all nearby. It was a small building, able to hold but seventy worshippers at most, but it had sufficed for the villagers, and they'd built it on the site of an ancient temple to Manannan. It was of plain oak, and decorated all around with the crucifix talismans of the god to which it had been dedicated. Patrick had ordered those that could be moved be turned upside down; other than that, the upright crosses seemed to cause him no trouble in any case. Such were the mysteries of the One God's cult, and the cult of his enemy.

With this – the One God's edifice – as a backdrop, began Patrick's charge. The king himself kept to the rear, greedily anticipating the death to follow, urging his forces on with shouts and curses.

Thyri had formed her army in a great wedge, weighted to the west. As the charge unfolded, she sent a messenger to Rollo with new instructions, then she too ordered her forces forward.

She'd spent long hours on recent nights discussing Patrick with Finaan, hearing tales of her enemy's prowess, trying to piece them together with her memories of the impertinent adolescent she'd known ten years before. Through Finaan's words (and Tana's, to a lesser extent), she'd followed Patrick's growth, spending endless hours attempting to dissect his personality, to forecast his tactics, what he would do. This was how she'd been taught, by Scacath, to understand her enemies. Now, the entire effort seemed pointless, so changed had the king become. Patrick's only tactic now seemed to be control, a tactic that spelled trouble for their plans to rally the forces of Connaught against their former leader. Patrick's army would be lessened in its overall strength because of it, but it still outnumbered hers by fifteen to one, and when she considered the ill-equipped state of her men, matters became even worse.

As they moved forward, Thyri glanced at Finaan and saw his eyes. There, she saw thoughts identical to her own, though the consolation in this was questionable.

In her tactics, however, remained some small hope. For Finaan and Tana, she had chosen another, smaller hill – this one obviously a cairn – about forty paces north of Rui's position. Her wedge rushed forward, passing it, those skilled in the bow dropping to their knees as soon as the two armies came within range. She'd ordered them to stagger and time their shots, spacing them two seconds apart – Rui Taichimi's most comfortable, effective speed. They did this, notching arrows and firing by the beat of a drummer. Rui quickly caught the rhythm of it, and the front ranks of Patrick's charge began to fall, slowing the advance of his western flank.

Under cover of the archers, the point of the wedge and nearly all the forces behind it made it straight for Rui's hill. Finaan, leading Tana by the hand, gained the other hill Thyri had chosen for him. As Thyri passed, she had another reflective thought, unusual in that she generally left evaluation of conflicts until after they'd transpired: By rights, Patrick was the defender and she the challenger. By rights, the hills were his to claim and defend. By rights . . . In terms of the warrior, the new king of Kaerglen had lost all reason. It was a good thing, and she wondered how Rui had foreseen it. Had he not – had Patrick decided to man that particular hill in the night with his own forces, he would already be dead. Such, however, was not the case. Rui's bow rained death into the enemy ranks; given the time and arrows, he could slay them all.

When Finaan took Tana by the hand and split to the west with about fifty men, Thyri herself broke ranks with another fifty and headed east, leaving the bulk of her forces to form a thin wall that would stretch from about thirty paces south of Rui's hill to link with Finaan's. Her best fighters – led by Dearen – were at the point, to defend against a flanking maneuver that might break through to the west and surround Rui's hill. Her biggest worry was that such would happen, allowing Patrick to cut her forces in two, centered around each point of her defense. In such an eventuality, the sheer weight of his numbers would ensure his victory. She worried also for Tana; she'd wondered long on whether she should bring the princess into the fray at all, but the advantages – assuming the possibility that Patrick's unrelenting control on his forces might diminish – outweighed all other considerations. In one sense, if it didn't come to that, and events forced them to attempt a normal, military victory, they would fail and all end the day dead.

As Thyri split from the main wedge, she glanced westward to see Rollo's entrance upon the field of battle. The Norse – all brave, hardened veterans – raced for Finaan and Tana, to form a shield-wall of defense if they could make it in time. She smiled at Rollo's quick reaction to her last order. With him defending Tana, she could lay some part of her worry aside. And she knew that no matter the odds, the Viking would glory in the battle, instilling his bloodlust in all those around him. She wished him well and many more battles before his ascension to Valhalla, then turned her mind fully to the task at hand.

She went east, becoming the wildfire, the wild card, the unexpected thorn in Patrick's side. With her small wedge, she would meet Patrick's frontal assault, hold back his forces, deny him the advantage of flanking her army and coming back around to assault the western slopes of the hills from the north. The arrows of the archers slowed progress to the west, placing dead bodies in the paths of the attackers, obstacles to hinder Patrick's advance. And as the dead were overstepped, more fell on top of them, creating small mounds, further hindering the king's momentum. And much to Thyri's surprise, the missile fire was never returned. Patrick had armed his men with sword and mace, the weapons of eye-to-eye death, and little more. If they survived long enough, victory itself might become conceivable.

As it was, with Patrick's eastern flank unhindered by missile fire, Thyri was the first to meet the enemy with sword. Her attackers fell, left and right, their mindless assaults offering not even the slightest challenge to her blade, a weapon trained to defeat the most skilled in combat, a weapon that had tasted more blood perhaps than any other in all of Midgard. She plowed through them, never losing her stride, killing anything around her that moved. Unfortunately, her men did not fare as well. When Patrick's followers fell, no sound at all issued from their lips; it was as if they were already so close to death that all she did in killing them was to complete the transition. Her own dying, however, made their agonies known; the screams filled the air around her. She faced a truly relentless tide with fifty men. Before the battle had been joined, she'd wondered whether she should take a hundred; now she was glad she hadn't. Within minutes, she stood alone against the rabid horde. Even surrounding her, they posed no real threat. As she had when fighting Alfred and the Saxons, she became a machine of death, scarcely thinking, merely reacting. Bloodfang lashing out with death in all directions.

Just before this – in hearing the deaths of the last of her men – she hoped the west fared better.

Rollo shaped the shield-wall just after the battle was joined before the hill of Finaan. In the process, Egill Hakison fell, as did Hrethel of Vestfold, a Viking who had joined with Thyri because he knew Harald Tangle-Hair and had battled for him and been wronged by him in an uncertain affair involving a contest that by his telling he should have won. So Rollo formed the shield-wall with less than twenty men. Though he knew Gerald to be an able swordsman, he knew also that the Saxon was unversed in the Norse ways of battle, and he ordered Gerald up the hill, to be the last defense of the royal blood which they all fought to protect.

And the enemy came. Over the fray, Rollo could see the southern forces fared slightly better due to Rui's skill with his bow. The far southern line, though, looked to have fallen, and Rui's hill would soon be beseiged. Yet Rollo shortly had no time to consider the south. The weight of the enemy pressed against him, urged on by a tall, dark-haired whelp on horseback whose eyes glowed red and whose mouth had twisted into a permanent, grotesque, grinning leer – the lord of the bonfire. Rollo knew him with certainty though he'd never before seen him so close. With the presence of this leader, the fury of the attackers reached frenzied heights. One by one, the Vikings of the shield-wall began to fall. When a mace cracked suddenly against the head of Thormard Rurikson, the sound so loud that it rose above the din, Finaan of Connaught took Rurikson's fallen weapon and broke through the shield-wall from behind, entering the fray with a blade of blinding speed.

Rollo shouted at Finaan for a few moments – after all, what had they to protect if their charges abandoned their haven? – but then, seeing the prince's blade flashing red with fresh blood, seeing the enemy fall before him like wheat in a ripened field, he understood. As Rollo had heard Thyri's plans, the prince of Connaught – merely by his presence – should have turned some of the enemy to their side. That hadn't happened, and now the prince saw their defeat looming, all the while knowing the prowess of his own swordarm. He could have been Rollo himself, as well as he fought, and for this the Viking could fault him not at all.

But Finaan could not remain content to face the enemy and take down ten times his own number each minute. He carved himself a path toward Patrick, and the king did not flee – if anything he came closer, and when Finaan reached him he dismounted. All this time, but one image burned in Finaan's mind, one image of the many Tana had granted him, the image of Patrick's face, his cruel smile as he sat hunched on the rock of Tana's grotto, listening distantly to words coming from the mouth of the monster whose weight bore down on top of him and whose loins pounded into him with a frantic fury he could no longer stand. This image he had – it was the image of a sister looking pleadingly at her brother, her brother who sat by idly while she, only ten years old, was raped.

Amid this fury, Finaan's sword met that of her former friend. In the first moment of his attack, he caused his enemy to retreat, but then the red flashed once again in the eyes of evil and Finaan again felt the sudden, unexpected pain of iron piercing his flesh. This time, Patrick's blade found not his stomach, but his heart, and Finaan fell dead to the ground, unable to hear Tana's cry of despair behind him.

Changes

Thyri killed, Bloodfang biting into flesh and bone in all directions, sending streams of blood into the air as if she were the center of a bright, red fountain. Only when she'd cut her way through Patrick's ranks did she call to him.

Behind her, the flood had passed through the breach allowed by her fallen men. It had grown distant, begun to skirt around the north to come up on the far side of the hills as she'd feared. And from what she could see, the line between her two hills had broken, the defenders forced to guard the entire circumference of Rui's hill, though luckily the breach had been at the south end and Tana still had a good number of men to protect her. But as time passed, they wouldn't be enough.

Thyri let her voice erupt over the battlefield, a crackling, strangled voice, full of fury and hatred. 'You are nothing, little boy!' she screamed out. 'My sword is stronger than yours!' Her words were meant only for him, meant to recall for him the memories of his defeat long ago at her hands, the time in the castle when he'd tried to take her, and she'd instead mocked him. She laughed now, a demonic sound that managed to turn even some of the heads of Patrick's men. She berated him, cursed him, repeating over and over again the same words, the same laugh, until she spied him among those gathered around Tana. So deep was her fury that she scarcely noticed Finaan's absence from the hill. And now she called to him more strongly, 'Dog!' she cried. 'Face me now! Come and try to take my body! Have you no lust inside you! Has a king no loins? Where is your fire? Burn me, you son of Loki, if you can! If you dare!' So she went on, until at last he turned and stepped away from the battle so that naught but dead bodies lay between them.

Thyri moved like a cat, like a hawk against her prey. She gave him no time to think or consider; she hit him full force, her blade whirling, propelling him ever backward toward the south – if she could do anything, she wanted him well away from his men; if Tana's presence could mean anything, they needed Patrick well away from the fray. So Thyri fought him; he parried her attacks well, but after the first minute of their battle she had learned his every move, his every attack, his every counterstroke. All the while, the evil red sorcery burned in his eyes; she could sense its power without feeling it. She fought him, insulted him, and cursed him, the invectives rolling off her tongue to push his ire to furious heights. She insulted his swordsmanship, his manhood, and his cruel, twisted face. She knew him now, and she knew that she could kill him if only she could be sure she could slay the man within him without unleashing the evil source of his power.

That red evil became her true enemy, the man hosting it merely its tool. She didn't dare tempt it; with her curses and insults she fought to bring the man to the surface, to bolster the man's anger, to make him a crazed slave to his own pride. She fought, smashing him to his knees with one mighty overhand blow. In that moment she could have darted in with the dirk in her left hand; against a normal man she could have buried it in his heart, but she feared what the evil might do to stop her. Instead, she took a step back and ripped open the front of her shift, baring her breasts, running the blade of her dirk over her own flesh and digging it in slightly so that she drew a thin line of blood over her own skin. She laughed then, and skipped past him to the south, toward the small chapel at the center of what once had been a town. As she passed him, she spoke softly. 'Come, Patrick,' she said. 'Come show me your manhood. Take me on the floor of the house of the One God, he you've rejected. Show me your power!'

She glanced back only briefly to make sure he followed her.

Rollo watched Thyri's handling of their enemy with something akin to awe. With the king growing smaller and more distant, Rollo began to hope that the mindless assault against his shield-wall would lessen. But it did not; whatever distraction Thyri had provided, it was not enough. If anything, the fury of the assault increased. He was down to twelve men, and even with the others fighting on his side, there were places where only one man stood between the blood-thirsty mass and the princess behind him. He began to call out to Thor, to Odin, to whatever god would listen. He battled, his every muscle straining with the ache of it, and he did not intend to die this day. He had long since lost count of the number that had fallen before his blade.

Tana looked on, terrified, her heart still screaming after the death of Finaan. Next to her stood Gerald – to her but a strange Saxon whose eyes never left the fray below, whose body and sword shifted from side to side, dancing around her as he moved to cover one possible breach in their defenses after another. And then Patrick's men did begin to break through.

The Saxon leaped to her defense, cutting down one assailant only to find two more taking his place. The sides of the hill became slick with blood. When three men rushed at Tana at once, she grimaced as Gerald threw himself before them, gutting one, cleaving deeply into the next's neck, and feeling the bite of the third's sword in his side before running his Norse blade through the man's heart and pushing him down the hill, there to impede the progress of two others attempting to climb up. And as Tana looked away from this, her eyes found only the endless sea of their enemies. To the south, only a few she knew to be friendly remained. Among them was a strange, olive-skinned warrior, a man with a face like a cat's – Rui Taichimi he was, the archer, though the princess could not know this. Still, his sudden appearance in the battle with a sword in his hand was enough to turn her thoughts from disaster. By his looks he reminded her of the Tuathans and of the felnin who had rescued her from

Patrick's prison. She thought, and knew she had to revive her hope, else would it end like this? Would the red sea overwhelm them, slay them all? This Saxon who fought bravely now, one hand clutching at his side, the other guiding his sword to the heads and hearts of those who wished them death – would he die in vain?

At first, she shouted to them, calling out her name, calling herself queen, but they wouldn't listen, their mindless assault persisting. She began to despair, then caught herself. Holding up her hand, she whispered prayers to Brigid and called out the name of her twin. The blue sorcery of the wishing stones began to light the air above her. She called out to her twin and tried to feel the wind, to make it blow through her, to find Seth within its substance. All around her, the dam that held back the flood of death began to break. An attacker's blade cut through the Saxon's leg, and her defender fell to one knee.

Below, those Tana knew were far more dead than alive. Then, without warning, she felt the wind's answer. It came into her body through her breast and blew down her legs and up again, through her belly, back through her breast and into her shoulders and up her raised arm until it circled in her hand full of the sorcery of the wishing stones. She spoke other charms and ancient words until the wind emerged suddenly from her palm, and she felt like the earth, the wind a river and a waterfall cascading from the cliff of her hand. She dared to look to her side, and she found substance coalescing there, the wind gaining form; she turned back to the sea of madness below and shouted into it. 'Behold!' she cried. 'It is the true king come to cleanse Kaerglen. Behold him and know he is the true heir of Coryn.'

Before her, the Saxon painfully gained his legs to slay two others who had nearly reached her. He staggered a few more steps before falling and rolling slowly down the hill.

As she watched Gerald's descent, Tana suddenly heard a new voice – one she had lost to the distant past. It had grown deep and resonant, and it sounded out, a single word that rang out over the entire battlefield. 'Stop!' Seth cried, and all below fell suddenly silent.

Tana glanced at her brother, then turned suddenly away when a boot thudded heavily onto the earth on her opposite side. She turned to look into the gaze of a blacksmith, a man armed with a mace held high in the air, the weapon ready to fall and crush her skull. She flinched away; at the same time, the man shook his head, looked at her with suddenly focused eyes, and fell to his knees.

In the chapel, Patrick knew none of this. He had followed Thyri inside, leaving sorceries behind to bolster his army's resistance to Tana's call. But he had failed to think of Seth, his brother who had not died but had disappeared on the breath of the wind. So it was that, though the battle without had come to a sudden end, he and Thyri remained locked in their private duel.

For him, she had ripped open her shift. He intended to take her.

Thyri goaded Patrick to the altar, then again thrust her sword between them. The red yet burned in his eyes, but here she felt more safe to face it. Here was the house of the enemy of Patrick's ally, and here was the privacy to protect her from what she feared most deeply; here she could risk Patrick's death without fear that the wrath of his power might engulf the entire battlefield in flames, the terrible inferno she and Megan had just barely escaped. So she pressed him, displaying the true worth of her skill for the first time. Her attack bit deeply into his chest. To his credit, he moved quickly enough to avoid it landing on his neck. Her second thrust left him no such escape; her blade sheared through his shoulder armor and pierced his skin, and in that moment he realized his error and understood her ploy. In that moment, the red power of his eyes lashed out to consume her blade and toss it aside, parrying her stroke in the way that no normal weapon could. She had defeated him in the ways of battle, but he would yet have her. He had power she couldn't possibly resist.

Now *he* pressed *her*, wrapping his sorcery around her like a great, blood-red talon, lifting her from the floor, squeezing her so that her lungs could not inhale and her blood could scarcely force its passage through her veins. Thyri felt a sudden twinge in the back of her neck, and the lust of beast surged forth.

Could she *remember* it, the death of Patrick would have played much like the death of Erik. The wolf emerged, shaking off its red fetters in a matter of moments, brimming with the forces of Chaos and nightmare to meet the sorcerous attack with fangs and claw. When it was done, Patrick's body lay torn on the chapel floor, his blood flowing in slow streams to form a pool at the foot of the altar.

Idylls

Over those short, fateful days following the death of Coryn Kaerglen, the island endured its painful rebirth, a time that quickly became legend, haunting the songs of the people for years to come and immortalized in poems and sagas (as well as here). The queen few had known or loved was dead with the king. The priest of the One God named Brenden – who had come to Kaerglen to extinguish the ancient fires – was dead as well. Patrick had spilled Finaan's blood, Thyri had spilled Patrick's, and the island had a youthful, rightful king to help in forgetting all the death. Those pawns of Patrick who had survived until the end went back to the city and port, there to begin peaceful lives anew; even the warriors went to take up the trades left vacant by fallen craftsmen, merchants, and artisans.

Of the warriors: Dearen was dead, his skull crushed in the onslaught fueled by Patrick's lust. Rui suffered a long, shallow wound on his left shoulder, but otherwise survived. Rollo ended the battle drenched in blood, though none of it was his own. He had left, however, only five of the Norse come from the riverbank of the Franks.

Gerald lay near death, with wounds too many to count.

At battle's end, silence reigned – a silence split abruptly moments later by sudden screams from the south. Only when Thyri emerged from the distant chapel, raising her sword high for all to see, did the survivors of Dagda's Plain burst into cheers. They went to Seth and lifted him up, chanting songs of elation as they carried him southward, on toward his castle. They attempted the same with Tana, but the princess shrugged them away, ordering them back to clear her path. Then, unaided, she slid and stumbled down the blood-soaked hill to kneel next to the Saxon who had so bravely defended her life. His body was bent and torn; she began to cry and leaned close to him, praying that he yet breathed. When she heard the faint, labored efforts of his lungs, she summoned the blue power to her fingertips and touched each of his most mortal wounds, stemming the flow of blood from where it still came freely. After a time, she looked up and ordered a flat construction of wood, a construction on which to lay the Saxon to keep him still for a journey back to the castle.

When this was done, she went to Finaan, her tears finding a new life. She ordered him lifted from among the dead, to be buried that same day among the graves beside the chapel wherein Thyri had made final their day's victory. As for the rest of the dead, that very moment Rollo led a crew of fifty in digging graves around Rui's hill. Still, the work would take them days. The hill itself became known as Archer's Tower, the glory of the ancient king encrypted beneath long forgotten. Legend would quickly have it that, during the battle of Dagda's Plain, a foreign god had come to the aid of Kaerglen and, from Archer's Tower, slew tenfold more men than any mortal warrior that day save perhaps Eiriksdattir, the bane of the Blue Moon, the wildfire that would ever break loose and come to the aid of Kaerglen in its darkest moments. Or so it is said in the city and port.

Megan, wakened though yet weak, was brought south and welcomed back into the royal house by Seth and Tana. Only these three remained to carry on the legacy of Coryn mac Fain, the mortal of Erin gifted the island by Fand, wife of Manannan, nearly a century before. Under Seth, Tana, and Megan, the old ways were reborn, and those of the people in which the old flames still burned soon went to the wood and built new altars, havens of worship for the gods abandoned by their former king. During the ensuing weeks, Seth ordered a new circle of stones erected in the center of Dagda's Plain so that all in the future would know what forces had emerged victorious. And yet he refused a purging of the One God from the island. While in the port, he had come to know some who had made the One God their own and found a peaceful comfort with him. On the chapels built by Moira and Brenden, Seth decreed thus: Should those living near wish them burned, then they should be burned; should they not, then the buildings should survive. Too much blood had been spilled already, and the people, he said, had a right to their gods, whatever gods they might be. In any case, he decreed the chapel at Dagda's Plain should survive and be preserved as a monument to their victory.

But Megan returned. Thyri greeted her sadly, the swordsmistress's days haunted darkly by all that had transpired. She saw no room for love in this aftermath; she walked the halls of Castle Kaerglen a silent, grim ghost.

Tana, though, was too young to let war fully extinguish the fires of her youth within her. These fires she tamed, and she guided them all into the wounded body of Gerald. He should have died by virtue of his countless wounds, wounds so dire that no sorcery could quickly heal them all. Instead, Tana tended to him over the days, parceling out her magic (even refusing Megan's offers of help, though Gerald could not know this at the time), and spending long hours at his bedside, speaking to him tales and the hopes and dreams of one just entered womanhood. Over these days, Gerald came to know Tana more fully than any other, even Seth who had been her companion in childhood; often, the adult emerging from the child bears little resemblance to its past life, just as the butterfly emerging from its cocoon reveals no kinship to the leaf-eating worm in which it was begun.

And slowly Gerald recovered under the care of the princess sorceress. He became used to her smile, her soft voice, and her simple, flawless face framed by her flowing brown locks. He knew pain – terrible pain that would waken and cause him to scream out in the night. Even at such late hours, his calls would ever bring the princess, and he later learned that she slept alone in the room next to his so that she could always answer his calls. And when she'd come, his pains would lessen, her voice a soothing balm, her face like that of a goddess in the candlelight.

For Thyri, the days brought no such respite. Megan spent long hours with Seth, holding his hand through one royal decision after another in order to teach him to be just, to respect the thoughts of those both like him and unlike him so that he would never err and act as his father had. It came to pass that for the time being, he would have no other counselor. The decision on the One God's chapels, in fact, had been Megan's, and it must be written that the sorceress found great pleasure in these acts, for she had at long last regained her littlest brother who had been little more than an infant when she'd been banished to the north years past. And she'd regained as well the respect of the crown under which she'd been born.

To the slayer of Patrick, the sorceress yet swore her love, but the days left Thyri alone as she had no desire to use herself in the making of a new king. Had she interest in such things, she would have long before taken a kingdom of her own to rule, and if she was to involve herself in it, she would do so only in the north – in the north after she'd freed it from the shackles of Harald of Vestfold. She found some consolation in the presence of Rollo and Rui, but even that grew painful. On idle days, near Rollo, she could not shake the memories of their one afternoon of love from her mind. She would look at him and feel him inside her again, or rather feel the ache to have him inside her again, and these thoughts of lust she rejected, so strong remained the taste of Patrick's hot blood in her mouth. But with her, Rollo wished desperately to leave, to take to sea and continue Thyri's quest against Harald with their crew of five. Rollo's taste for battle had not been sated at Dagda, not because he hadn't exacted his share of death, but because he could not think it a real battle, it having been no more to him than a mindless slaughter of enemies driven not by noble purposes but by the absence of their thinking minds.

Once again, as events would have it, Thyri had found herself on Kaerglen with winter aproaching, confined to land while ice descended to lord over the seas. Even had they departed directly from the land of the Franks, they would have risked some ice in northern waters. Now after their delay, the northern approach would be impossible. So once again she was forced to winter there, though this time she hadn't a willing, undistracted lover to warm her nights. And amid all this, she had the full moon with which to contend.

Rollo brought *Nightreaver* to the port, and Thyri spent the first night of the next full moon in her captain's cabin where Megan had once conjured a mystical landscape on the wall, a gateway into distant, otherworld forests where she was free to roam and hunt far away from the realm of men. When the change came over her there, she entered the painting, only to find its forest burned, its life fled. Consumed by her hunger, she ranged far, and only luck allowed her to find and kill an old buck near midnight. The next night, and all nights of the full moon after that, she spent trapped on the island – not even daring to attempt the pathways between the worlds – preying in the north on wild boar and deer and the sheep of farmers when necessary. She grew detached, noticing but scarcely caring about the blade Seth now boasted at his side; to Thyri's mind, that Megan had never bothered to explain this only proved how far distanced they'd become. Beyond this, her mood grew so dark that she would sometimes make herself long absent from the castle, spending weeks and sometimes months of the winter alone in the northern woods, alone with her thoughts and the burdens of her curse. And there she began once again to dream.

She had dark dreams, dreams in which she slew all she loved, her fangs tearing out the throat of Megan, then moving on to Gerald, Rollo, Rui, Sokki, even princess Tana. Since Astrid's death, Thyri had never weathered well the idle days free of conflict; in the past, she'd survived only by taking a lover, but a lover now she refused to accept.

One dream, above all others, came to her again and again. She would find herself on a plain of ice, where the wind itself pounded her, forcing her to fight merely to keep her feet. Against this wind, she would walk, painful step by painful step, until the wind abated and she realized now that she walked as the wolf; the lust then in her heart would be great. She would walk, her claws digging into the ice until she came upon a frozen lake, and in the lake she would see faces, the faces of all those she'd ever known: Her mother, her father, Erik, Akan, and Megan . . . on and on until the faces became strange, became the faces of gods. And all these faces gazed at her with lifeless eyes, and the wolf within her would claw at the ice above them, at each in turn in this endless dream. The part that was herself would mourn the dead eyes, while the part that was the wolf would hunger for them, its fury growing ever wilder since, when her claws had cut deep enough to uncover flesh, the face would disappear, revealing itself as but a reflection or a trick of the ice.

In this dream, the last two faces were ever the same. First would come the sad face of Astrid, a face that even in death tried to smile at her. The wolf would dig, and Astrid would disappear. She'd move on, and the last face was her own. By now, the wolf's lust would allow no control, and it would dig quickly ever deeper, and at last reveal flesh bared to the hunger of the beast within her – she would always waken, her sweat like ice on her skin in the winter's cold, and she would lie sleepless then, until dawn.

When spring came, she departed on *Nightreaver* with Rui, Rollo, and the five surviving Vikings. Gerald did not go with them; he might have, had Tana not begged him to stay. He had become her sole confidant, and with her he felt more alive, more meaningful, for she ever asked his council and took it for wisdom. Among Thyri, Rollo, and Rui, Gerald lacked that gift.

On the docks of Port Kaerglen, Thyri bid Megan Kaerglen, sister to the king, a silent farewell. All the sorrow of their impending separation lived in their eyes. Thyri did not even ask Megan to join her; she knew the workings of Megan's heart and could not forget the tale she'd heard on the Hill of Tara. The sorceress had found again her family, her banished past, and Thyri could not bring herself to ask her lover to abandon it. But even so, she could not abandon the demands of her own history. As Thyri looked into Megan's eyes, she realized that their love was far from dead; it was merely wounded, and given time the wounds would heal. Given time, they would reunite, just as they had after Thyri had left before to travel west to where the sun spent its nights and had found instead the new land of the Habnakys and the Arakoy. On the docks then, she reached out and touched Megan's cheek with her silver gauntlet, then *Nightreaver* was set, once again, upon the seas and guided to its northerly course.

BOOK IX

EIRIKSDATTIR

As I write, this tale seems to race away from me, becoming its own creature as the tapestry of the Norns wraps more tightly about it, as surely as the entrails of Narvi, Loki's son, hardened and bound his father in the darkness of a cave where Loki's wife, Sigyn, held a bowl above his face to catch the dripping venom of the serpent bound above her husband.

All I have seen . . . All that I know. All these gods with their own fates bound to Midgard – the One God's inexplicable rise, the fading of all the rest. I still do not profess to understand, at least no better than I have learned through Megan's words from Klorista through Ai'reth. But in the nine worlds lorded over by Odin, all the prophecies of the Sibyl save the last have now transpired behind what I have written. So long ago, it seems, I wrote of Thyri's return from the new land astride Astrid's winged steed. During that flight, Astrid told Thyri of the death of Balder, the signing of the coming of the end. So it happened, and Fandis and others prophesied the coming of *fimbulwinter*, the prelude to Ragnarok. But more transpired.

I still do not fully understand Loki's purpose in his meddling with Thyri – his games. For him – by the Sibyl's reckoning – the events that followed Balder's death were tumultuous. And he never caused true harm to Thyri; not when he forsaw the demise of the Black Rabbit and caused the girl Elaine to be in its midst; not when, disguised as Al'kani, he tormented her; not even when he wakened Morgana. And the raft that turned into snakes before my eyes – that must have been some weak manifestation of his power, even though he was bound that very moment. What else might explain it, yet not explain it, if not the Trickster? Perhaps the raftsman had manifested the One God's enemy, though I find no sense in that thought. He never assailed us or hindered us, and without us, Patrick would surely have prevailed at Dagda. Perhaps, once again, I simply fail to understand; the One God's enemy does not seem to glory in worship, only in death. The lack of sense I see here comes from the means. The snakes and the laughter bore all the marks of Loki's nature, and it must have been him unless I'm further mistaken and the truth will have it the One God's enemy and Loki boast more similarities than I perceive.

But that set aside, by my reason, Loki has either sought Thyri's undoing, or he has sought in her an ally. The latter possibility puzzles: In past acts, he hardly wooed her; he only complicated her life, tormented her. Were his manipulations so subtle? Did he seek to torment her to draw her to his side solely by nurturing the darkness of the Chaos within her? As for Thyri's undoing – he hardly came close to success. But *were* that his goal, only another mystery could explain his failures: Odin, who seemingly remained ever distant, and yet might have watched over Thyri all the while, diluting Loki's influence while allowing her torment for reasons of his own. The keys to these riddles escape me. But I do know things. Even Odin was bound, in essence, to his foretold fate.

By the prophecies sung by the skalds of the north, a darkness hung over Asgard after Balder's death as all who lived there knew what it portended. Time passed, the gods mourning and Loki growing ever more confident and brash of his victory. He had his own prophecies, the Trickster did. He was part evil, part closed – part Chaos. He had his own prophecies that said that no prophecy could bind him, bind Chaos. So he battled on in his own inexplicable way.

It came to pass that all the gods went to Aegir's hall in the sea next to the isle of Hlesey for a feast. They went in friendship, wounded as they were by the passing of Balder. When Loki entered and saw that Thor had not yet arrived, he leered at them and began to insult each of them in turn, sparing none – not even Odin, whom he accused of being a witch. This went on and on, the gods growing enraged, and Loki's insults growing ever more sharp in their twists of spite. At last, Thor arrived, and Loki insulted him as well, though when Thor's anger grew and all the worlds began to tremble with his anger, Loki made a hasty retreat, fleeing to a remote haven in Midgard.

This must all have occurred while Thyri, Megan, and the crew of *Nightreaver* were trapped on the seas of Jotunheim. Deciding Loki's transgressions had exceeded the rights of his divinity, the gods pursued him, led by Thor and guided by Odin, who could see all from his seat of Valaskjalf in Asgard. They caught him, even though he nearly escaped in the shape of a salmon. In their vengeance, they took his two sons, Vali and Narvi, and put them together, working sorceries upon Vali to turn him into a monstrous wolf. The wolf Vali leaped at Narvi and tore him apart. The gods then took the dead Narvi's entrails with which to bind Loki in a dark cave, and they bound a serpent above him, there to drip poison down upon him until all fetters would break before the end of all things.

Already, Loki's other offspring – begat by the giantess Angrboda – awaited that same day, and powerful they were. Fenrir the wolf lay fettered like his father on the isalnd of Lyngvi. Jormungard the serpent lurked under the sea. Hel waited in Niflheim, where Garm lay chained, guarding the entrance to her world.

The other enemies of Odin and Asgard ranged free throughout Jotunheim and Svatalfheim, and even Alfheim and Nidavellir. Megan's people, the Tuatha de Danann of Alfheim, fought in vain all this while to stem the tide of warring giants marauding from one world to the next (as Tana saw well in her wind-dream). Meanwhile, the Norns relentlessly wove the inevitability of Ragnarok into their tapestry of life. Of these giants, the sons of Muspell, the legions of fire commanded by Surt, wreaked by far the most destruction. So it went on, intensifying on all worlds save Midgard as the *fimbulwinter* fell on Asgard and the Aesir saw the coming of the end.

What to write here of Ragnarok? This is how the skalds tell it:

The three winters with no summer between them – *fimbulwinter* – will fall upon Midgard, and mothers will seduce their sons, and sisters their brothers. Skoll will devour the sun, and Hati will devour the moon. All the stars will go out.

Great shudders will wreck the body of the earth, and no stone will survive without damage. Three great cocks will crow, alerting and awakening all the giants, all the warriors in Valhalla, and all the dead in Niflheim. All fetters will break: Fenrir will run free, Garm will stretch his horrible limbs and howl out in ecstatic, demonic freedom, and Loki will emerge from his cave and set sail for Vigrid, followed by all the legions of the dead.

Fenrir and Jormungard, Surt with his giants and his sword of fire, Loki and the dead, and army upon army of giants – all these will cross Bifrost, the rainbow bridge, and enter Asgard, the land of the Aesir. Bifrost will collapse behind them, wrecked by their immense weight.

Heimdall the watchman will sound his great horn, Gjall, and it will be heard throughout all worlds. All the gods, the Aesir, the survivors of the wars in Alfheim and Nidavellir, and all the warriors ascended to Valhalla – the Einharjir – will arise and go to Vigrid behind Odin to meet the invasion. As they clash, Midgard will shudder, and destruction will lord over it. Two humans – Lif and Lifthrasir – will see what happens and escape, and they will hide in Yggdrasil, clutching in terror as the great ash trembles and the battle goes on.

Odin and Thor will lead the charge of the forces of Light. The All-Father, wielding his great spear, Gungnir, will meet

Fenrir, and Thor, Jormungard. Then, immortals will begin to die. Heimdall will kill Loki, and Loki will kill Heimdall. Garm and the one-handed Tyr will kill each other. And Surt, with his flaming sword, will kill Freyr of the Vanir.

The greatest matches go on. Thor, the mightiest of all the gods, will kill Jormungard the serpent, but Thor will be poisoned, take nine steps back from his victory, and fall down dead. And when Odin witnesses the fall of his son, he will be overcome with grief and forget, only for a moment, the danger of Fenrir before him. In that moment, Fenrir will swallow the father of the gods.

The skalds tell this tale well. Over the centuries, all the world's shoesmiths have tossed aside scraps of leather for one purpose: For the shoe of Vidar. For as soon as Odin disappears into Fenrir's gaping maw, Vidar will rush forward and use this shoe to prop open Fenrir's jaws while he tears apart the wolf and avenges the All-Father's death.

Then Surt will burn all, setting all the worlds alight with his flaming sword. Everything will die, save Vidar and Thor's sons, Modi and Magni, and Vali and Vili and Ve and Honir. And Lif and Lifthrasir, the humans who had fled in time into Yggdrasil to hide.

So it will all end, leaving the seeds for a new beginning. Balder and Hod will come back from the dead, and the world will be a better place, for much evil will perish at Ragnarok on the plain of Vigrid.

Yes, that is how the skalds tell it. How it is told, as if it has yet to come.

Ice

The harsh, northerly wind whipped back Thyri's hair, pummeling into her face, which grew red as if burned by the sun. But it was the cold that dug into her, the newly cracked winter greeting her with its biting breath. Ice still floated in chunks on the water.

Had she cared, she could have avoided this by tarrying another fortnight on Kaerglen, but she'd refused to consider the thought. And the ear-blistering cold – she reveled in it, summoning it against her skin, seeking its frigid bite. She left it to Rollo to navigate the ship around the worst hazards. She didn't care; some madness inside her almost wanted her to jump in and embrace it all. She finally felt free from the shackles of winter. She had but seven men under her command, and she felt as if she commanded an army, as she'd not felt since she'd led the Habnakys against Aralak's hordes in that war across the great ocean.

Winter's end, traveling north – free of the dreams that had haunted Thyri's nights these past months. No nightmares could now intrude upon her will. She would go north. She would have Gyda's head before she returned to Kaerglen. Megan could no longer understand her . . . The objections in the sorceress's eyes, as they'd stood there on the docks, only proved how far apart they'd drifted. The thought left a bitter lump in Thyri's throat. She swallowed it and turned her thoughts outward, into the cold. Perhaps this was *fimbulwinter* bearing down on her from her homelands. Perhaps Megan's ravings of Ragnarok on Asgard alone were wrong. All these affairs of gods – what were they to her? *Nothing. Embrace the cold, Chaos. Take it inside of you. Make it your bones and your blood and your heartbeat. Your breath with which to burn all who stand against you.*

Behind her eyes, a great serpent rose up from the water. Jormungard, poison dripping from his fetid, gaping maw. He fanged the clouds, then swooped down over her, his sibilant voice oozing into her, through her eyes, not her ears. *You and I,* he said, *we ssshall desssstroy them all. With you at my sside, I might devour even the One God himssself. With our brother Fenrir, we sshall tear Midgard assunder, and people itsss fieldsss, my ssseed in your womb* . . .

The earth cracked, a horde of wolf-headed vipers rising from the depths. Behind them, fountains of blood spouted from the rock. The vipers grew wings and flew, dragons to lord the air above their father in the great sea that strangled Yggdrasil. Clouds of black poison washing through Alfheim, engulfing all in their path. The fall of the thirteen elven kings: the king over the mount, the lord of the golden briar and thistle, the standard bearer of the treedrytes, the king of oaks, the lord of the swallows . . .

Mad, Thyri thought distantly, *I'm going mad*. The shadow play of the apocalypse yet faded, in and out of her vision. Gods, she thought. Damn them all. The power surging within her was *hers*. She was a warrior, and she would have her battle. These visions tugged her this way and that, but never away from her sword. Odin had abandoned her long before. She may not serve him now, but neither did she serve another. Not Loki, not the serpent. Not the wolf with eyes like prisms and the fur of frost.

She still remembered the faces in the ice – they'd burned themselves into her waking mind. She could feel her claws digging in toward them; always before she'd fought the feeling, now she almost welcomed it.

By the stars, they came within a day of the northern reaches when all changed. It was just night, and the lights of the gods danced mysteriously in the sky above. Yet Rollo guided *Nightreaver* on, standing on the prow next to Thyri and peering ahead, his eyes picking out the great chunks of ice just in time to call out his orders to port or starboard.

Under the play of the heavenly lights, figures began to take shape in the air before them. At first, Thyri thought it another vision, but when gasps came from behind her and she felt Rollo stiffen, she knew suddenly the vision to be truth. The figures – wispy and ghostlike – coalesced, glowing like new stars in the heavens, their white armor and golden blades shining as brightly as the moon itself. They were the Valkyrie: Host Fetter and Shrieking, Spear Bearer, Might, and Shield Bearer . . . *Shield Bearer*, Thyri grunted, *Astrid.* Since leaving the new land, she had seen her cousin only in dreams. Now on the northern seas, the Valkyrie had returned.

'Hail!' Thyri greeted her. *Astrid, my love* . . . The Valkyrie were armed; on their faces she did not see welcome.

It was Astrid who spoke to her: *'You cannot pass, little one.'* Thyri glared at her, and tears came to her eyes. *'It is Odin's wish. You must turn back.'*

Thyri drew her sword and held it up in the air before them. 'I will not!' she shouted, full of madness. 'I am the wolf, and I will have my blood!'

'You are not the wolf, little one,' Astrid replied. *'Did Scacath not teach you well? Why do you lust to be named The Usurper? Wars rage among the gods, yet you wax insane, questing to bring new battles when the battles are nearly done.'*

'But it is Gyda, my love!' Thyri cried. 'Gyda who has caused the lands of the north to be soaked in blood. Once I abandoned them, but they are the lands of my birth, and they cry out for justice.'

Astrid looked at her long. *'Gyda is nothing,'* she said at last. *'Harald is nothing but that he has made small kingdoms, small jarldoms, into nations. And nations they need to be; Midgard changes, Thyri. One thing ends, and another begins.'*

'No! You speak like the dead king of Kaerglen who gave up his land to the One God because he feared the battle needed to stop him!'

'Then perhaps your dead king was right.'

Thyri waved her sword again in the air, then spun, pointing it at her crew. With the appearance of the Valkyrie, Rollo had ordered the sail slackened. Now she ordered it filled. 'Forward!' she commanded. 'Else I will have all your heads!' Yet despite the menace in her eyes, none moved. Next to her, Rollo gripped her shoulder, then moved on. He took the guide rope of the sail and made it taut, pulling until the sail filled and *Nightreaver* again moved forward. With the motion, Thyri turned again to Astrid and glared. 'We will reach Vestfold or die!' she shouted.

With that, the Valkyrie said not another word. Astrid broke from their ranks, her steed – named after Loki himself – carried her forward, and she raised her great golden sword into the air and brought it smashing down against the wolfshead prow, splitting through the wood, then shearing down through the hull itself, the ship screaming as the Valkyrie's sword tore the prow asunder.

Nightreaver lurched, then it pitched Thyri and her crew unceremoniously into the sea.

Magic

Rollo spat the brine from his mouth and clung to the side of the floating, icy island that held him above water. Rui had already climbed up onto its flat surface; the archer lay there, heaving softly, his bow gone, as was Rollo's sword.

Nightreaver sank behind them; as Rollo looked back, the last foot of the ship's stern slipped silently beneath the waters, leaving hardly a ripple behind. What moved on the surface of the sea was the work of the wind. Two other Vikings clung to a similar island – he could see them now on the other side of the ship – even so, as he watched, one slipped under and did not reappear. The other tried to grab him, failed, then saw Rollo and attempted to swim the distance through the freezing water. Halfway there, he too floundered and sank, and Rollo and Rui were alone. Their three other men had never surfaced – they along with Thyri – had been swallowed by the sea. And all this the fault of the Valkyrie. Rollo cursed them, damning them if they hadn't stayed in their spirit forms to escort his five fallen warriors to their rightful seats in Valhalla. This was not the way. Could Thyri have truly perished and he survived? He'd always imagined their last battles, his sword next to hers, his flesh always succumbing while her body churned on, one sword laying waste an army of thousands, man by man.

Now he froze. His legs went stiff with the cold. He tried to pull himself onto the ice as Rui had, but the cold had worked into his arms and they failed him. He cried – barked – out his pain, and after a moment the archer crawled to him and took his hand, pulling him up to safety – a freezing safety, though one much less quick and sure than the waters beneath. On the ice then, he and Rui collapsed against each other, and Rollo let the cold surround his head and steal away his thoughts at last.

He dreamed, he dreamed of lush, sweltering southern forests, places he'd never seen with his own eyes but had only heard whispers of in late-night taverns. In forests were trees the size of giants, and insects the size of birds. The birds themselves spoke – real words in a language he could not understand. And in all the trees – quiet kings of earth, greenery, and sky – were cats.

Ai'reth watched the moments pass with a deep frown cutting furrows into his forehead, The Valkyrie had had no right! Did they seek the downfall of their last wild champion? Had they sided now with Loki, even as he lay chained? From his haven next to Midgard, Ai'reth looked on; the white-haired power sank, then suddenly twisted away from Midgard toward him. So great was the fury in her eyes that he fled for cover, emerging only when he was sure she'd passed. By then, the mortals he could have saved had all perished. Except these two still on the ice, the two he knew better than the rest for their ties to Thyri were strong. He let them lie there, let them alone until sleep came to take their minds away. Then he cautiously stepped out into Midgard.

Even Ai'reth felt the bite of the north wind's breath. This was weather for ice giants, he thought, not felnins. He went quickly to them and dug his claws into their shoulders, then said spells to take them all away from the cold.

Once on the Midgard border, he carried them one by one to the safety of a half-world (where it indeed sweltered, and there were insects the size of birds), then watched over them awhile before taking up his finger drum and tapping a simple charm that would revive his low-born charges.

In his dream, Rollo suddenly wakened. But for Rui sitting next to him, shaking the clouds of sleep from his mind, Rollo would never have thought this place to be true.

Before them, tending a fire on which a haunch of wild

boar roasted, was a creature, half cat, half man. The creature looked at him and grinned, fangs bared in the light of the fire. 'I am Ai'reth,' the creature said. 'I am a felnin.'

Rollo cleared his throat. 'The ice?' he asked after a moment.

'It was cold, yes. No place for life to be left to perish. Your clothes have dried now – they are there, on that limb.' The felnin pointed to a nearby branch from which hung Rollo's furs and Rui's silken dress and cloak. Before seeing this, the Viking had not yet grown aware that they were naked. He rose unsteadily, then began to dress, glancing back at the felnin. 'Where – ' he began.

'It doesn't matter,' the creature interrupted him. 'Where you should not be. We must leave soon, else we'll attract powers you will be too slow to escape.' Ai'reth grinned again. 'And to the other question I see floating behind your eyes – the question you don't dare ask – I tell you she still lives. She you call Eiriksdattir. She lives.'

'Where?'

'Everywhere.'

The answer caused Rollo's ire to flare, his hand moving to his side where there should have been a sword but there was none now. 'I don't play games,' he said abruptly. 'With cats or anybody. Where is she?'

'On her own path,' the felnin answered. 'You cannot follow her now. She has moved beyond this, beyond her agonies of recent years. She walks a path only she can follow.' With that, the felnin took the pork from the fire, hacked away a chunk with a small knife and offered it to the Viking. Having nothing else to do, Rollo sat down to eat it.

Later, the felnin let them sleep again. On awakening, they were led on a curious journey, through wooded land, then charred forest. Over beaches that turned suddenly to gold-paved city streets and then back to forest. Time passed, and the felnin finally stopped them in a small stand of wood from which Rollo could hear distant laughter. 'Midgard again,' Ai'reth said with a smile, then he disappeared.

Following the laughter, Rollo and Rui came to a tavern. The night was late, and there were few guests within. Those there spoke the Frankish tongue, and Rollo cursed under his breath when he heard this. After all their travels, they'd but returned to the place they'd departed.

The guests – three drunken swordsmen who taunted each other continuously while pawing at the sole, homely serving wench – failed to notice the newcomers until they'd sat and ordered mead. Then they turned their insults in Rollo's and Rui's direction. Demon, they called Rui, and spawn of the devil and more. Rollo allowed such words to be said for only a few moments before he rose abruptly, went to the nearest man, and punched him heavily in the mouth before moving on to the next two. As the servant girl brought their mead, Rollo tossed Rui one of the fallen Frank's swords, took another for himself, detached three pouches of coins from three belts, and signaled his companion that the time had come to leave again.

Back in the night, armed and moneyed again, Rollo held a finger to the wind to test it, trying to grant moment to a decision that he knew no longer mattered. As they set off on foot, the two warriors each fell back to their own dark thoughts. As for Rollo, he could think of no future course, no direction that might be better than any other. His thoughts were filled with Thyri, and he was certain – so certain he could not entertain even the slightest hope or doubt – that he would never see her again.

Chaos and Rune

Along the pathways, Thyri raced. *I am the white beast,* she thought, *the mistress of this world*. She became the wildfire, the wolf, the heartbeat of Chaos. Through her mind tumbled the promises of Jormungard, those words he'd spoken to her before the death of her ship. She held them close, for if Odin had sent his Valkyrie against her – Odin who had allowed her torture and curse all these years – then who might she call a friend? She took Jormungard's words to heart and held them there. Behind her, she sensed the Valkyrie's pursuit. She would not think of them, only of her quest.

Thus she locked up her thoughts, fearing any digression, knowing the pain she would feel if she set her mind free. Astrid had been her first love, a love pure and never tainted by doubt or sorrow until the end. A love of youth, without the sorrows she'd come to find with Megan. She could not face such thoughts. She could not let the Astrid in her heart transform into the Astrid standing against her. She might have tried to think the Valkyrie's attack on her ship an illusion, a trick of some enemy, but she knew Astrid too well. No sorcerer in the world could show her an image of Astrid and trick her into believing the illusion. Their pasts had bound them too tightly together.

On the pathways then, she ran. The Midgard gate she sought came quickly, and she surged through it, Chaos bursting into the realm of Harald. The fires of his great hall burned in the distance, but she reached it in moments and barreled through the door, pushing servants aside, feeling every bit the wolf though indeed she had not changed form. Only her eyes held the beast's red hunger, like the eyes of Erik, the eyes of Patrick, eyes she had always despised.

In the depths of the hall, she did find Gyda, she who had once been princess of Hordaland, daughter to the king who had ruled Thyri's people. But the discovery was not made in Harald's private chambers; it was made in his hall of women. Thyri burst into it, sword in hand, and held herself back, so unexpectedly did the colors, the occupants, and the lay of the room strike her.

The place was large, almost a cavern, with a huge fire in its center around which girls draped in silks lounged, rubbing oils and perfumes over bare limbs, their own limbs and those of others. After a moment's pause, Thyri strode among them. The women, terrified, cleared out of her path, and when she whispered the name of her whom she sought, several terrified fingers lifted into the air to point nervously in the same direction, the direction Thyri then went. When she found the princess of her homeland, she found something quite different than what she'd expected. Sitting at a stool, the woman rubbed powders furiously into the wrinkled skin of her neck, cursing under her breath. Thyri saw her eyes first in the mirror she held before her. Gyda's eyes, even, had lost their life, and beneath them were dark purple patches, the heavy marks of the years.

As Thyri looked into the eyes, so did the princess turn to see Thyri. In that moment, Thyri knew that she could not be mistaken. This was, in truth, Gyda before her, but not the power-hungry vipress she'd hated all these years and resolved at last to hunt. Once, this woman might have been beautiful; now she'd fallen victim to the ravages of time. Her wrinkles did not stop at her neck; they spread out over her face, and her bare breasts hung limply on her chest, empty sacks with little power to stir the loins of a man, much less a king with all these women from which to choose. So Thyri stared at her, unable to speak, her sword dropping limply at her side.

Behind her then came a voice, one full of laughter. 'So

princess!' a harlot said. 'Here is another taking your place in the king's bed! How long has it been? How many years?' The voice did not wait for an answer; it melted quickly into laughter that echoed, never quite fading into silence.

Thyri turned and glared at the source, catching another glimpse of the female paradise in which she'd suddenly found herself, She'd heard long past that Harald had taken over seventy wives, and collected more each day, but she'd never imagined that Gyda would have been just one of them and not the highest of them all. In all these years, Thyri had misjudged this king – this ravager of all the north. And as for the wrinkled creature before her – what satisfaction might her death now bring?

Asking this question of herself, Thyri turned away. As she passed through the doorway, she again met Astrid, the Valkyrie's sword now sheathed. *'So now you have seen,'* Astrid said.

Thyri lowered her eyes, then Astrid reached forward, lifting her chin. *'You cannot usurp Harald to unite the north, little one. It is too late.'*

Thyri felt tears welling up in her eyes at the sight of the beauty of her cousin.

'Look,' Astrid continued, and she waved her hand; the air beneath it shimmered, and Thyri saw Harald, a king that she knew had to be Harald Tangle-Hair, though he was neat, and walking with another man who named him Fair-Hair. She could hear their words. *'So you will join me?'* the king asked. *'By Odin's beard,'* the other answered, *'I swear.'* Flanking each of the two men were Vikings – strong elite guards of their royal charges. The second man who spoke with Harald had a voice stained by the twist on Norse of the Danes. She witnessed an alliance formed here, an alliance forged by Harald himself. There was no belligerence; the guards of the two kings did not carry themselves warily. They joked with each other in fact, and several of them carried flagons of mead in their hands instead of swords.

'You see?' Astrid asked after the scene had played out. *'The union of the north has been Harald's from the start.*

Before my death, I was a fool to think otherwise. It is not your destiny to take his place, to renew the bloodshed.'

'Then what is my destiny, Astrid?' Thyri asked, finding her voice at last. 'Where must I go from here?'

Now the Valkyrie smiled but did not answer. Slowly, she began to fade.

'Astrid!' Thyri cried. 'Take me with you. I cannot abide by this world another day!'

'You can,' the Valkyrie answered distantly. *'And I cannot.'*

From the hall of Harald Fair-Hair, Thyri wandered, she as directionless as Rollo, full of mourning, of a lost possibility, of lost glory. She cried not where she went, yet her feet propelled her to the sea, and there onto a merchant ship whose captain gave her passage without question.

She did not speak words; she simply boarded the ship and sat, heedless of the crew's prodding, a prodding that ended abruptly when one among them suggested she could be the kinslayer of Hordaland, Thyri Eiriksdattir. Bloodfang – her name and deeds were legend. And so the ship set sail, Thyri ever distant. If she had a clear thought at all, it came when she saw, around the neck of one of the crewmen, a small talisman shaped after the crosses of the One God. At the sight, she spoke, asking the man why he would wear such a thing. Grinning, he told her how it was a token of his past, a part of his plunder on his one raid to the south. She asked him if he would so quickly display any of the symbols of Loki, and he gave her a curious look, but he did not cast the cross into the sea. Thyri said nothing after that.

They docked, and she wandered ashore, through a bustling port in which she heard no words of war, only talk of merchants' goods and travel. She wandered on, and once away from the docks, the land began to call her back. This was the land of her youth to which she'd come. This was Hordaland, where she'd grown as a girl, where she'd lived and learned from her father, where she'd played with Astrid and Skoll and then mourned Astrid's departure when she was but seven and left only with her wonder at the affairs of the gods.

On these roads, Thyri moved again, her feet finally finding direction. They carried her home.

Yrsa – her cousin, Astrid's younger sister – worked on tanning hides in the unkempt field before the hall of her youth. Thyri approached slowly, then stopped ten paces away, waiting for the woman's eyes to rise. Memories surfaced slowly – memories of rumor heard long past from Anlaf Olafson in the land of the Saxons. These fields had been burned, he'd said. Yes, she thought, noting a distant, charred tree, but they were alive again, and her elders' hall had survived. Was it a trick, or had Anlaf also told her that Erik had sought Gyda's hand for himself? Could that have been true, before he'd sought her death? She would never know.

'Begone phantom,' were Yrsa's words when she first sensed Thyri's presence.

'I am no phantom, cousin,' Thyri replied. 'But I am weary, and home at last.'

Yrsa stepped away from her work, squinting in the afternoon sunlight. 'If you be my uncle's daughter,' she said, 'then you are not welcome here.'

Thyri smiled sadly. 'Are they all gone?' she asked.

'All you knew? Those you did not kill? Yes – they are gone, all but me. And if you wish to kill me, do so quickly and be done with it. I have no defense. My husband, Leif Hallson, is away to the south on campaign.'

So the marauding yet continued, at least in part. 'I will not kill you,' Thyri told her. 'You are the last of my kin.'

'What of Erik?'

'Dead,' Thyri whispered, adding no more.

'Then leave. They call you kinslayer here; I will not have you in my house!"

Thyri looked at the trembling woman now brandishing a

tanning knife in the air. Yrsa was brave, as brave as she'd ever been. She knew the ways of the runes and had once attempted Thyri's death through them. But she had no real power – in their family, all that had been given to Astrid and herself. All others had been forced to live in their shadows.

She thought these thoughts, and she began to turn away. Yet as she did so, the afternoon seemed to fade into the distance, and on the road leading up to the hall, another approached. It was a stranger, a man draped in brown cloaks and sporting a wide, floppy hat on his head. Thyri abruptly stopped; the rider's steed walked on eight legs.

As the stranger approached and Yrsa saw what Thyri had already seen, she gasped, letting her tanning knife fall to the grass. She knew the lore well; only one rider in all the worlds boasted such a mount, and that rider was Odin, the father of all the gods, and the father, in the distant past, of them all.

The All-Father stopped time; the birds and insects of the fields ceased their chatter, and the sun grew more distant, though a warmth seemed to rise from the ground. He stopped before Thyri, paused a moment, then raised the brim of his hat. One eye was patched over, ruined ages past during his self-sacrifice as he hung from the branches of Yggdrasil. Thyri looked into the other eye, finding a gaze infinitely more fathomless than any she'd ever known.

'I end your pain,' the All-Father said. From his cloaks, he brought forth a golden ring and held it out to her. 'Wearing this, the moon cannot harm you.'

Thyri reached out hesitantly, taking the small band of gold. She realized in that moment that she had forgotten the passing of the days. Quickly, she counted them back; were she not mistaken, this very night the moon would again be full? 'Why not before?' she asked him, the question freeing itself before she could test its weight.

'We all must suffer,' he answered. In his presence, she could find no argument. By his patched eye, he proved wrong all she might say; as she knew the lore, from his sacrifice he had gained his runes of power, and she herself had lived through many a battle with the aid of but one of them – his fifth rune – the rune placed by Scacath on her sword that gave it power to deflect all missiles.

'It tests our mettle,' Odin added enigmatically. 'You are much more than you think, Eiriksdattir.'

'But what? What am I?'

'You will learn,' he said, then winked at her with his one eye and tugged at Sleipnir's reins, to head back down the road away from them.

Thyri knew not how much time passed before her thoughts turned outward. By the sky, dusk neared, and on her hand she felt the warmth of Odin's gift of gold.

In her other hand was Yrsa's. When her cousin saw the focus return to Thyri's gaze, she began to lead her, slowly, toward the hall.

Idylls

That night of the full moon, Thyri went out, laid her sable cloak down on the ground, and gazed up at the sky and the stars. The moon yet seemed to glare at her, but the ring on her finger – Odin's ring – felt warm and it sheltered her. Let the moon glare . . . The longer she gazed up, the more the warmth spread through her even as the chill winds of night began to whisper through the trees. The stars – she wanted to reach up, pluck them from the heavens, and draw them inside. She almost felt that she could. As Valkyrie, Astrid had flown among these stars; perhaps she, as well, would gain that privilege in time. All this became possible once Odin had come to her. But he had taken so long . . . Her wondering was idle; she'd nearly hated him over the years he'd shunned her, but she couldn't hate now, not after seeing him with her own eyes. And he had not spoken so darkly of the future. All of Megan's dark forebodings of Ragnarok fell before the power of the All-Father's visitation.

Thyri spent the entire night there, under the stars on her sables. Never had she known such peace. Though she thought of it – realizing the source of her past pains had been vanquished – not even her separation from Megan bothered her. She was happy to be alone here, to confront herself and her past, and Megan had no real place in it. Megan's presence would confuse her memories, distract her mind, fill her senses with something other than this quiet peace, a peace for which she had so desperately ached over the years, what she needed all along: solitude in silence, and a mind free of guilt, anguish, and doubt. The anguish was gone; the moon, above her yet powerless, was proof. And

Odin had taken from her the guilt, even the deaths she had inflicted on her family. He had not accused her; *he* had not named her kinslayer and demoness.

So the night passed . . .

Thyri thought back on that time in Alfheim, the night from which Megan's sorcery had shielded her memory. As she thought on it, it came back to her, a whole memory: her unease in the felnina, the arrival of Ai'reth, her confrontation with Erik, and his death. She could remember it all. Had Odin changed her so completely inside? Could she remember, and remember without pain? Even understanding? Megan had been right; with Erik, she'd done everything she could do.

But that was the guilt and anguish. Since that day in Alfheim, she'd tortured herself over her love for Megan, even doubted her lover's sincerity. And why? Lifted now of her curse, Thyri's doubts melted away into meaninglessness; something weak inside her had given birth to them, and she was stronger now. She'd imagined her love supported only by Megan's ability to give her pleasure in spite of the tragedies of her life, the curse in her blood, and thought Megan's love nothing but pity or some perverse attraction to Thyri's nature. No, love was much more than that. It had to be. She felt free now of everything on which she'd imagined their love was based, yet she could feel her love all the more for it. She had hurt her lover gravely. That would have to be repaired.

In time . . . right now she had this peace, and Megan still had the affairs of Kaerglen to manage. There was no need to hurry back. She decided, at least, to stay through the spring. Their reunion then would be that much sweeter. And Megan, no doubt, could find her if necessary.

And so Thyri came to stay in the hall of her youth. What it had been in the past was gone. To the little girl, the hall had seemed huge, almost a castle. When she'd returned from time to time after her training under Scacath – when she and Astrid had warred together under their king, Ragnar – the hall had grown smaller, though still spacious and always alive with activity and the heady smells of cooking and mead. After Astrid's death, it had all become like a foul, festering wound on her soul. Still later, when she'd returned after her first ordeal with the moon, when she'd killed her mother, her brother Halfdan, and her uncle Egill and found her father dead as well, the hall had hardly touched her, so consumed had she been with grief and hatred of her own very life. Yes, then it had been like a stark, bare dream – an empty shell, a house of weak, impotent ghosts, a thing with walls, a meaningless place defining only by chance the distinction between the warmth inside and the cold without.

Since then, when she'd happened to dream of the hall, she'd dreamed it as either pain or nothingness. Her dreams had never carried her back to the warmth of her youth. So now, returned home, her heart embarked on something of a rediscovery. Within the walls, she found comfort, like the contented afterglow of love. She didn't feel herself a child again; rather, she felt the child she had once been there with her, guiding her, showing her happy memories and simple thoughts.

The weight of her curse had been lifted.

As for Yrsa, who had borne over the years a hatred for Thyri akin to Thyri's long hatred of Gyda – the All-Father had torn down and rebuilt her world in a matter of moments. She cared for Thyri as she would care for any high-born guest of her husband. In Leif's absence, Thyri was all she had, and she insisted on playing the servant though Thyri refused to assume the mantle of master. In time, Thyri's calm eased her cousin's demeanor, and Yrsa began to allow Thyri to help in the kitchen when she prepared their meals, and they took to spending the evenings together, sometimes in silence, but often talking at length of their youths and their lives, Yrsa at once working diligently on her leather, and pressing Thyri for every detail of her past and Astrid's past, and Thyri asking Yrsa, with equal enthusiasm, of her own life, of her knowledge of the runes, of her husband, and even of the arts of shoemaking and of the kitchen.

Through Yrsa, Thyri began to regain something of the

normal, rustic life that might have been hers had Scacath not chosen to take her from her family and set her on a course far different from that she'd expected as a young girl.

Such was Thyri's last idyll, the meeting of her present with her past. Odin had gifted her with an eventless sort of serenity, all traces of the wolf whisked away, or, rather, hidden from her heart and mind by the power of his gift to her. But one event of note did happen there, an event of transcendence, of another kind:

One day, with Yrsa absent, gone into the village to sell the fruits of her labors, a young, would-be Viking came onto their land and bellowed out the name of Eiriksdattir.

Thyri was in the barn. 'Hail, stranger!' she called out. She waited for him to come to her.

He showed himself in the doorway. He was young, still a boy with but a wispy, downy growth for a beard. In his eyes, she discerned both determination and fear. He spoke abruptly. 'Eiriksdattir,' he said, 'I would battle with you!'

'I am Olga,' Thyri countered, looking puzzled. 'Eiriksdattir does not live here – she hasn't for many years.'

The boy, irritated, tossed a sword at her feet. 'You lie!' he insisted. 'I have heard whispers, that Eiriksdattir is returned to Hordaland. You must be she.'

'Why?'

'No more words! Take up that sword and fight me!'

Thyri bent, glancing up at him. 'Why would you battle Eiriksdattir?' she asked. 'She would kill you.'

He laughed. 'Then I would find Valhalla, wouldn't I? But perhaps I would kill you, no? Then my name would be known throughout the north as the slayer of Thyri Bloodfang.'

'I am not she.'

'Pick up the sword, or I will kill you without it!'

She grasped the weapon's hilt and stood. Years before, Thyri had been accused of being a wench impersonating a swordsman. Such an accusation had always pushed her ever more close to fury and battle; now she played the part willingly, becoming in her mind a milkmaid, a simple farmgirl. When she tried to heft the blade, her wrist collapsed under its weight. She dropped it, its point digging into the ground perilously close to her foot.

She jumped back and almost fell. She looked fearfully at the boy, then smiled. Instead of battle, she offered him her hand and seduced him.

That nameless young warrior had Thyri in a way that no man ever did, in the way that Gerald and Sokki – even Rollo – had dreamed. She fell back on the fresh hay, her hands, shaky and excited, running up her legs, hiking her shift up to where the boy could see the mound of her womanhood emerging slightly from the shadows. In her mind, all thoughts of swords and death and battle had vanished. She felt both innocent and wanton, as if she were still discovering the sensations of her flesh, as if she had had but a rare taste of love and wanted it again but knew only how to ask and not demand. When the boy knelt before her, the fear of innocence came into her eyes, and the nervous ecstasy of a virgin on her wedding bed washed over her loins as he kissed her thigh.

As his excitement mounted and he crawled on top of her body, she let him rip open her shift, savoring every infinite moment of anticipation before his lips touched her breasts. As he entered her, she clung to him, and only then did the past intrude dreamily on her thoughts. It flowed in almost magically, merging with the cascades of sensation that flowed from each caress: the boy became Akan, Rollo, Hugin, Munin, Gerald, Sokki – every man she had ever had, and every man who had ever wanted her. She gave herself to them, a sacrifice on this primitive rustic altar; she held them, together and separate, and she kissed them and wept, out of sad pleasure, out of joy and sorrow for the lot of men in this world, for their beauties and their lusts. She felt pure again, as pure as the blue of the sky, as the black of the night. Gyda, Yrsa, Odin – and now this boy – had made her clean. Stripped free of the stains on her soul, she could at last truly love.

All the while, Bloodfang hung in its scabbard on a peg

inside the room of Thyri's childhood. She hadn't seen it in weeks, and she'd almost forgotten it was there. While the boy labored above her, she nearly *believed* that she was Olga, and not Eiriksdattir at all.

When the moments of passion ended, the boy fell asleep in her arms and she held him until he wakened. Near dusk, he left, promising to return after the spring's campaign. He never did. Under Harald's banner, he was the first to fall in an assault on a renegade Danish reaver. As he died, he thought of his lover, the tender white-haired woman of the house of Eiriksdattir. Her name – Olga – was on his lips as the last of his blood spilled onto the deck of his ship.

Nothing else of much import transpired for Thyri until the end.

On Kaerglen, the making of Seth the king went on. Megan lectured her brother constantly on the arts of leadership, arts she herself knew mainly from Thyri. Though the sorceress busied herself all the more as time went by and still no word came of Thyri, her thoughts did begin to turn relentlessly back to her lover. She began to worry; through her sorcery, she lifted for a time the mists that shielded the island from outsiders, from foreign ships. Seth questioned her, and she knew not what to tell him, except the truth. She wanted contact – news from the outside, of the world, and possibly of Thyri. Her powers had not returned to her fully since their battle with Patrick, and she knew no other way. And even if she could, she told him, more powerful sorceries could draw to them, in these dark times, evil they were not prepared to face.

But she had to know, so she lifted the mist, though she did in her own way ask and receive the king's consent.

After but two days, a small ship came into Port Kaerglen. On board were Rollo Anskarson and Rui Taichimi. They went to Megan and told her what had transpired on the seas south of Vestfold. Astrid had crushed *Nightreaver* and they – and Thyri – had been pitched into the sea. They described their saviour and Megan immediately knew him, but what had finally become of Thyri, she could not know.

The news did little to improve Megan's mood. But she did know from Ai'reth through Rollo that Thyri had survived the Valkyrie's attack. Her thoughts turned ever more to her sorceries, even in these dark times. She'd regained some part of her strength, only it remained true that its use would not, and could not, be wise.

But if Megan knew her lover, she would have continued on; the loss of a ship deterring her not in the least. She waited impatiently for news, word from afar that Eiriksdattir, the berserk, had stolen Harald's kingdom for herself and now brought the northern fleets south to make all of Midgard tremble.

Meanwhile, came other news: There would be a wedding. More must be told: The love of man and woman grew finally between Gerald of Jorvik and Tana Kaerglen.

If indeed there was a day of transition, it came in mid-spring, when all the castle was alive with activity. The folk of the city and port roamed the halls freely as Seth had ordered the fortress painted white, inside and out. And with the common folk among them, gossip had quickly spread of the princess and the Saxon who was ever to be found at her side. On this day, the gossip was worst, as it was the day to paint the halls.

Before the decree, Tana had persuaded Seth to leave the depths of Kaeglen untouched, and on this mid-spring day, to escape the stares and the knowing smiles, she took Gerald by the hand and led him down to the grotto. There she showed him Fand's haven.

Of what transpired there, the writer will say little but that it was beauty reborn and that the love was untainted, a joyful love never marred, even by what was to come.

One month later, Gerald and Tana were wed.

Ragnarok

In late spring, Thyri awoke one morning with thoughts of deep reflection. At her bedside, she set to combing her hair, and when she was done, when her white locks shone with a tender glow, she began slowly to braid – a ritual she had long since abandoned. In her fingers, she held her rune-bead, and she did each braid carefully, recalling all of her victories of note and the lessons hidden within them. She braided knots she had never braided before, victories far in the past that had eluded her at the time, revealing themselves only now. When she'd finished this endless process, her braids were two hundred and thirteen. Finished, she affixed her rune-bead, and rose to retrieve her sword.

Yrsa saw her as she passed through the halls, moving like a serene goddess. She did not question her; the last woman of the house of Egill sensed a strange presence in the air; and she knew somehow that this, above all things, had been foreshadowed by the All-Father's gift to her cousin.

Yrsa did not know this – nor did Thyri – but Loki had burst free of his fetters a week past, and that night, just before the break of dawn, Heimdall's horn had sounded to alert all the worlds. Yet it had not been heard on Midgard.

This morning had been sent to Thyri by Odin himself, and it needed no explanation. The white wolf had to prepare. And Odin sent to her as well his last messenger – the last messenger he could trust as the warrior himself scarcely understood his purpose. But the messenger nevertheless was dispatched.

As Thyri donned her sword, Ai'reth stepped into Midgard before her. The felnin looked up at her with enraptured eyes, and it was long before he spoke. 'There is one who loves you, white-hair,' he said. 'One who needs you now, and you must come.'

'I am ready,' she said. Her gaze remained distant. He had the thought that he might have asked of her anything and had the same reply. Yet he didn't question her; he took her hand and led her onto the Midgard border. Once there, he started onto the pathways he'd planned – the careful ways that would hide from all eyes – when suddenly a sorcery erupted from the Queenstone in its pouch, throwing a gate before them which they had no time to avoid. They stepped through, into the grassy courtyard of Castle Kaerglen.

The sudden force of the sorcery rippled through the worlds to shake the trunk of Yggdrasil itself. On Bifrost, Loki's head turned, and he smiled. One power had been hidden from him these past months, but now, just before the battle could be joined, he sensed it anew. Ordering his forces on, he disappeared briefly from their midst.

Megan stood among the orchids, reflecting also on the past, when Thyri's presence struck her in an unexpected shower of magic. She turned to find her lover in full battle gear before her, the morning sun glinting off her unsheathed sword. Next to Thyri, the figure of Ai'reth shimmered, then faded into the next world and they were alone.

From a window above, Gerald witnessed Thyri's arrival, and he raced for the stairs, calling out the news to his wife.

Thyri came into the present, Megan before her. If anything, the beauty of the sorceress had grown, overwhelming all the wonders of Kaerglen's garden. In that moment, she would have taken Megan and sealed anew their love on the grass – just as they had on reuniting long ago in that place of Brigid near Jorvik – had another not suddenly appeared in their midst.

He was tall, draped in black, an evil, two-bladed sword

jutting from his gauntleted hand. Megan reacted immediately, a giant spear of her silver magic flying in a burst toward the intruder's face. He laughed at it once, then turned back the silver, striking it into Megan's chest without giving her a moment to scream. Ever slowly, to Thyri's heightened senses, the sorceress collapsed to the earth.

Eiriksdattir turned on the man, launching swiftly into the attack. 'I will fight you,' the man said, laughing, 'and best you as well.'

'I cannot be bested,' Thyri growled. 'Not since my youth has another blade found my flesh.'

'Mine will,' he replied, and she felt a searing pain in her arm. She fought harder; entering the mind-of-the-tyger, sequencing her attack to end in a crushing blow that could not be blocked by the best sword in Midgard. But block her the man did. They went round and round the garden, skipping over Megan's fallen body. Thyri thought of nothing but her opponent; against him she focused the very essence of her skill, the full force of her battle fury and her strength. She felt her mind fall away, the point in battle when only blood began to matter, when she would kill and kill again like a machine. Yet the man before her would not fall. She had not even scratched him, while she herself bore now countless wounds off his blade.

From the entrance to the courtyard, Gerald and Tana looked on in horror.

There was a way, Thyri knew. A way she could best this man, best any man, or any god – she had now guessed him a god, though his power would not let her see him as Loki. Still, even a god might fall before the hunger grown within her but leashed only by the ring she wore on her hand. She could not die this day, not with Megan already fallen, not after all the blood spilled to rid Kaerglen of Patrick's evil. If she fell, this evil would simply take his place.

Megan would die.

Seth would die.

All would be lost and meaningless.

Thyri launched a final assault with all her mortal fury, then backed quickly away and threw off Odin's golden ring. The beast surged already within her, and it took her more quickly than ever in the past. To Gerald and Tana, she became the beast the moment the ring left her finger. So it was. The white wolf leaped at Loki only to be engulfed by a terrible red fire. In the distance she heard laughter, laughter that rang and echoed off the walls of Castle Kaerglen. But when she landed, Midgard fell away from her,

From the portal Gerald crept hesitantly toward Megan. He lifted her under her arms and carried her back to the safety of the castle, all the while looking nervously askance at the monstrous white beast that lay motionless on the grass.

Chaos

She walked on Bifrost, her weight as great as Jormungard's and Fenrir's, they who came behind her. Her lover strode at her side; his tall dark body a part of hers. For him she would do anything. For him, she would now slay gods.

They descended to the Plain of Vigrid below, there to meet the assembled Aesir. So pitiful looked these gods, Odin with his dead men, the Valkyrie on their puny winged steeds, the pathetic little gods of Alfheim, most already dead, consumed by the hunger of the giants behind her, the Jotun who loved her and held her name on high, Surt with his flames and all those behind him. It would be an easy day. Her lover whispered to her the name of Thor, and her mouth watered at the thought of swallowing the thunder. She would devour him, and then feast on the legions of Odin.

With Loki she touched upon the ground of Asgard. The ranks of the gods awaited them in the distance, all but Heimdall who stood with drawn sword, barring their way. Beside her, her lover cursed and launched himself at the watchman of the gods, their blades crashed together while she led the others forward. On the Plain of Vigrid, the Aesir and their forces began their charge. Her lust for blood grew. Thor – her first enemy, her first meal – came in the forefront; she ran toward him, Fenrir who would destroy the All-Father running at her side. She watched Thor's eyes lock on Jormungard's, he who came behind her, more slowly. She would beat the serpent to victory. So consumed with her hunger did she become that she raced ahead, outdistancing even Fenrir himself. But together, at the forefront of their host, they made for Odin and his son, the leaders of the enemy. Together, they would die.

They grew ever near, close enough to see the faces of those they would devour. Her gaze bore down on Thor, but she turned it once toward Odin, and the All-Father winked, and she suddenly remembered that wink from her past. *What am I? You will learn . . .* The wink released her; her body, without warning, came to a halt.

Where was she? This all felt like a dream, yet never had a dream felt so real. She heard words in her head. Loki's voice: *Thor! Kill Thor!* Odin's voice: *Turn, white-hair! Behind you!*

Such a dream . . . She glanced back to see the Midgard Serpent, Jormungard, poison dripping from his great scaly jaws. In her mind then she heard Loki's scream as he fell before Heimdall, the saddest of all the gods.

In the distance, Thyri saw Scacath, the swordsmistress of all the Tuathans; she had survived all the battles before this. Thyri watched her use her sorcery to propel herself through the air, into the very midst of the ranks of the Jotun. The Valkyrie, too, flew ahead, diving down around the fiery head of Surt, using their steeds to dodge his deadly sword. Even as she watched, they began to fall, one by one.

And so Jormungard approached behind her and Thor came closer. Fenrir, now ahead of her, met Odin with force enough to shake the plain beneath her. She looked from them to Thor, then back to Jormungard, and snarled, turning suddenly on the serpent. Thor would have to find another fight . . . In one great leap, she landed before the serpent, he who had whispered seductions to her on the Midgard seas. She leaped again, onto his back, her fangs digging deeply into the place behind his head, where all his struggles couldn't turn his deadly head to attack her and free himself from her locks of her jaws.

And so did Chaos ride the monster whose thrashing tail swept over Vigrid, crushing whole legions of giants under its weight. Chaos dug in her fangs and held on, raking her claws forward, over his eyes, blinding them. She rode him until

Vidar, fresh from avenging his father's death by the fangs of Fenrir, came to cleave the head of the serpent in two.

Thyri released her jaws, feeling exhaustion wash through her every limb. She felt herself growing smaller, until she lay on the bloodied plain, scarcely able to move. But she was a woman now, and what was left of the war of the gods continued in scattered pockets. Before exhaustion finally overtook her, she saw Thor emerge from the fray, the smouldering head of Surt held high in his hand. This was a day of victory for the Aesir, and she had done her gods the highest honor of all.

Thor, proudly showing the head of the fire-gaint king to all – by the prophecies of the Sibyl – should have been a ghost. By the prophecies of the Sibyl, the Thunderer had died by the poison of Jormungard, and then at Ragnarok's end, Surt would have set all the worlds alight.

All the worlds, she heard whispered in her ear, *save Midgard*. She turned her head to see Megan stooping over her. The sorceress smiled and helped her to her feet, then she led Thyri over the battlefield, through the legions of the dead, even past Astrid's fallen body; before his death, Surt had exacted his toll.

As Megan led her away, Thyri could find no further mourning in her heart. To her, Astrid had perished long before. And if she'd died now, it had been in the only battle that mattered. Thinking this, in the distance she heard the elated battle cries of the Tuathans as the last of the giants fell before them. As with Astrid, Thyri could find no mourning if Scacath had fallen. This had been a day of victory; the battle had gone past dusk, and now the waxing moon shone brightly overhead. Odin had died, Heimdall had died, and so had Freyr and Tyr, yet the Aesir remained powerful under Thor and the end of all things had not come to pass.

Behind them, they heard a great crack as worlds split apart, no longer bound together by Odin's power. Megan put her lips to Thyri's ear. 'Midgard has fallen away now,' she whispered. 'Into the hands of the One God.'

So split finally from her past, Thyri walked, supported by the one she most loved, under the moon that had been her enemy. Her last thought, just before Megan cast a sorcery to carry them away where they might at last share solitude, concerned that moon:

If Skoll had swallowed it before Ragnarok, how then did it yet shine?

Thus was the truth of Ragnarok.

On Kaerglen, time passed, Rollo and Rui joining the watch over the fallen wolf in the garden, and Tana watching over the sorceress stricken by the force of her own magic. Near dusk of that day, Tana came to tell them that Megan had disappeared – not a mystery, but a fading she had witnessed with her very own eyes. The sorceress had gone, the reasons behind such a thing to remain obscured for a long while.

With this news, Gerald moved hesitantly for the wolf. He reached it, stooping down to touch its fur. In days past, he had heard Rollo's pained laments countless times over, that his life had no meaning without the white-haired swordsmistress of the north. With the body of the wolf at his feet, Gerald felt much the same.

I, GERALD

I

Here ends the tale of Thyri Eiriksdattir on Midgard, with Gerald of Jorvik stooped beside the body of a white wolf, and Thyri herself nowhere in sight, for she has departed, forever, from this world.

The tale, however, has not ended in full, for Gerald is there, next to the wolf, and he wonders and mourns. In his heart, he knows Thyri has departed, that this beast is no longer her but simply a part of her, the dark part, but dark no longer without her. He thinks the beast is dead, but on the contrary, as he reaches out to touch it, it rears its head and bites his hand, then races away, never to be seen again on Kaerglen Isle after Rollo and Rui step aside to allow it passage through the castle.

Gerald stays near the ground, holding his hand, a new terror filling his heart.

When writing of Gerald, I of course write of myself. I remember very well that day and the days that followed. The full moon was but a week away, and my hand bore the throbbing, painful mark of the beast's fangs.

The day before the first night of the next full moon, I traveled far from the castle, taking with me several large skins of wine, all of which I emptied into my stomach before dusk. As it was, I passed out before the sunset. Later, in the middle of the night, I woke to get sick and found myself in the arms of my wife. She had followed me; she admitted that she knew my fears and my intentions, but had stayed silent while I'd waited for the moon to go full because she knew I wouldn't believe her if she'd said I feared in vain. She'd known through her sorceries that my blood was yet clean. The wolf that bit me was no longer *were*.

Nevertheless, that bite was Thyri's, and it's stayed with me, as surely as if it carried her curse. In that bite, and the pain it's left in my hand, reside all the memories of the years I spent with Eiriksdatir, and, moreover, there is the lust there, the lust to know more. I felt it then as I still do now, though the telling is done. I must soon leave it, unsated.

So I bore her wound, and as time passed I realized fully that she, and everything she'd brought with her, was gone. I grew obsessed, testing Tana's love for me to its limits. Thyri's absence made her hold on me all the more strong; I had to have her back. I felt I couldn't live until I regained her, if only in part, and so my lust for more bid me leave, and in the still of the night, with Tana fast asleep, I set out on a quest of my own.

I wandered that night, coming first to a circle of stones. I sat in the middle holding my arms up to the sky, invoking every name of every god I knew or imagined. None heard me; only the wind answered. It seemed that an eternity passed, but when I finally rose, the night remained young. I moved on, reaching next the abandoned temple of the One God where Thyri spilled Patrick's blood.

As I entered, I could almost feel the fury of that battle anew – the screams outside, Patrick's fear, and Thyri's wrath. The Christ on his cross gazed down upon me with his tragic eyes, and I kneeled before him, pleading that he lift my agony, that he give me Thyri again, that he tell me all the things I never dared ask – yes, even that he make her return and love me at least once before her death. Once again, I had no answer. The Christ's eyes did not move. The cross would not bend and let him step down. In another corner, the Virgin beckoned to me and I knelt before her, pleading the same things, receiving the same silence. Again, eternity passed, but when I left, it remained night.

It was a night, somehow, that lasted forever. I wonder now whether it wasn't some spell, some dark spell cast upon me in the wake of Thyri's passing. But as I count my enemies, those who might have had the power, I count them all dead. Who knows? Perhaps it *was* that bite. In any case, I lived all this, though how or why I'm uncertain.

Exiting the One God's temple, exhausted from my pleadings, I thought to return home to my wife, to try to forget it all, to live out what years I had left in happiness. Couldn't I see that? Couldn't I let Thyri die and live my own life in peace, without her chaos, her adventure? I was no longer young, but I had a beautiful wife and we might yet have children. Might that not be enough?

I thought and wandered, away from the chapel and its graveyard – all those souls lost on Dagda's Plain. I had almost reached the road back to the city when I met the dark priest.

He was cowled; I could not see his face. He stood before me, and as he did I felt cold, as cold as I had that day when Morgana died, in her sorcerous, fierce winter. And yet I couldn't move, couldn't flee. He stood before me, dark, scarcely more than a shadow, and he spoke to me. 'Ask,' was all he said. His was a sibilant voice, the voice of a snake.

Without warning, all my pleading issued forth anew. I wanted to know all; I wanted Thyri's love, her memories, everything. The dark priest listened until I'd poured it all forth, and then he spoke again in that hissing voice: 'If you have all this, when it is done, will you give yourself to me?'

I stared into his shadows. 'Yes,' I said. 'If you can give all this to me, I will be yours.'

'Forever?'

'As long as I live.'

'Your life is much longer than you know,' he hissed.

I eyed him anew, but I heard my own voice, speaking as if it had a life of its own. 'As long as I live,' I repeated.

'Very well,' he said, and he told me the formula for the pool of blood, the liquid talisman that has granted me all the knowledge I wished, the source of my own sorcery, the thing I came to name after the dark priest, after reflection and discovery of his nature. The thing I call Satan's Chalice.

On that night, I stepped upon the path that led me here to this writing. All the while Tana has stayed with me, comforting me in the night, even asking how my work has fared. Honestly, I do not understand. She must have felt, often, that Thyri stole me away through this work like a lover, that my mere act of writing, not to mention the experiences of Thyri I had in my research, proved my unfaithfulness. No, I do not understand love – Tana's love and how it has kept her bound to me. Not that I would lose it; were it possible, I would burn this manuscript, all this work, if it might give me a day longer with her than I might be allowed.

But I feel drained. The tale, in truth, is done, and Satan's Chalice, in my final researches of Ragnarok, runs dry with only a thin layer of red powder on its walls to betray what it once contained. After following the dark priest's formula, I first used it to learn that Thyri had not, in fact, died, but had passed, willingly, with Megan into . . . whatever world the sorceress had chosen. My feelings on that day were those of great elation. Last week, I exhausted the pool looking at the same moments of Thyri's life, the moments of her final passing from Midgard. Somehow, it seemed fitting that the last blood of the pool reveal to me the same scene that I saw in the beginning of my sorcery. With that willful act of voyeurism, I brought the end back to the beginning. And I have few questions left that I would ask the pool, the main concerning Ai'reth. I cannot claim to know what became of him, only that he did not take part in Ragnarok. I lost touch with him after he brought Thyri back to Kaerglen. He seemed to disappear then entirely – at least to my sorcerous eyes – and perhaps the speculation closest to the truth might be that he was in fact a minor aspect of the All-Father's mind, and having performed his last useful act, he'd returned promptly to join with his source.

In any case, now I rest. All promised to me by the dark

priest has transpired but the act of love with Thyri herself. All this time, I have felt that one request of mine hanging over me, hanging over my bed while I loved my wife. All this time, of all that I asked, that is the one request I would have first taken back, but now, when I think of it, I feel a strange peace within it, perhaps the peace of my salvation. If the dark priest cannot deliver it – and with Thyri departed, it hardly seems likely he can – then our contract remains unfulfilled.

II

At night, howls from distant forests somehow rise high above the city to reach the walls of this castle. I hear them, though distant they are. Some nights I have stayed awake, straining to detect this distant howling of wolves.

Yes, they have multiplied again on Kaerglen Isle. I wonder whether that wolf Thyri left behind in this world has mothered them. But whence came the father? Some escaped pet of some trader? Some stowaway on an anonymous ship? Or were the consequences of Ragnarok more deep than I've described? Might another have been freed of the curse? My imagination has taken flight on those sleepless nights – after all I've witnessed, this puzzle of wolves where there were none smacks of mundanity, and yet . . . What if another were freed of the curse? What if that one were myself, created and freed in a moment when that which was once part of Thyri bit my hand? What if that part of Thyri has mated with a part of myself, and it is my children that I hear calling to me?

Such imagination . . . I cannot discuss such things with Tana. After all that has transpired, she says to me always, 'Have hope.' To speak this of the wolves – she would think me mad at last. Perhaps that is true; I have not discussed these howlings with anyone. Perhaps they howl only in my mind, a haunting from Thyri's past.

As I've reflected, I'm amazed to find my sanity relatively intact, so many pasts I've absorbed into my own. Occasionally, when some little thing – some noise or some smell – triggers a memory within me, I discover that the memory is not mine, but Thyri's or Rollo's. When this happens, it is fleeting the way that dreams are often fleeting in the morning. But it is a strange feeling while it lasts; should such memories come more strongly and more often, I fear I truly would become mad.

I feel a strange kinship with Thyri's brother Erik, more so him than Patrick, son of Coryn, though he as well certainly suffered the ultimate fate for which I am destined. Erik, however, was twisted by much the same forces as I. Erik's weakness was the history of his kin and the paleness of his own shadow next to those of Thyri, his elder sister, and Astrid, his elder cousin. Even his elder male kin – warriors all.

Twisted – when he was younger, he revered Thyri, so why did he become a tool of evil and seek to kill her? I wish now that I had researched this deeply; in this I can now see where my work has surely lacked, for my sorcerous omnipotence over it seems less omnipotent with each day, now that it is done. Yet I can imagine Erik's sleepless nights as if they had been my own (and I have had many!). His thoughts would have boiled with visions of his parents' deaths, the plague of his sister's curse that was responsible, and his own aching ambition to equal her. And this maelstrom of thoughts – might it not have attracted *temptation*? On a world defined increasingly by the lore of the One God, temptation in the form of Lucifer might have reached even one in the north, and then whispered promises into the chaos of Erik's mind. What might have been promised? Many things: That he might have vengeance on the curse that destroyed his family; that he might himself, rival its powers; even that he might, in killing Thyri, assume the mantle of her power for himself. All these whispers – and I stress that I only imagine them – might have tricked Erik into a contract like my own.

However it happened, he came to serve the same master as I, with his service rooted in the same essential reason: Thyri Eiriksdattir. Erik and I – we must both have lusted to possess, to change, even *to become*. Such lusts transform into a sort of madness when we have not the power to fulfill them. And our madnesses have led us to the same end. How many others have walked this path?

How many others will walk it?

The mists have lifted. Kaerglen now lies fully in Midgard. Tana says . . .

I'm sorry – something has happened and I am called away.

III

He has come. Too soon! Even now, Tana entertains him in the dining hall, for all that I know she is terrified by his very presence. She walks like a ghost these days, her sorceries fading noticeably between each dawn and dusk.

Last week we returned to the grotto, and she told me of all Brigid had taught her there. I listened, though I already knew the tale. I couldn't tell her that I knew, that I had spied on her through Satan's Chalice as surely as I had violated the intimate privacy of all whom I have loved. So she told me again and I listened. Then she cast spells, to call to the goddess. We had no answer.

And Tana – my beloved wife – she has sought gate upon gate into other realms where we might follow Thyri and escape. The gates are all gone now, eight of the nine worlds released from their bindings to Midgard. And, as written, what sorceries that still work here fade by the day.

The mists that hide Kaerglen from the world have lifted.

But Tana has been brave and fought to persevere. For a short while after I began this, I kept secret the pool and its power. The secret could not last long; when at last I told Tana of the pool's power, how it seemed to grow and not weaken at all, she even tested it. The visions did not come to her, and to her sorceries, it would reveal itself as nothing but a pool of blood. She told me that its magic was beyond her, and its power only mine to wield.

While she fades.

While the worlds shook at Ragnarok, splitting apart, the Aesir and the Tuatha de Danaan abandoning Midgard to the One God and his opponent.

My master.

The darkness in him – he does not shield us from its power as he hid it from me that night we met – is a void so black that the night outside, which I see through my window now, seems the most transcendent of dawns. I must cherish this pale night, burn it into my memory, that I might remember it in that void.

Too soon he has come! Tomorrow, Tana and I would have set sail for Tara and the Lia Fail, where Thyri and Megan rested on their journey here after Coryn's death. If a gate to other realms remains, it would be there, where all sorcerous pathways intersect. We cannot leave now . . .

But I am husband to the sister of the king!

Seth knows nothing of this – Tana forbids telling him.

The dark one – she speaks to him now.

I write in circles.

My mind burns; my hands shake.

He has come; even now his dark clouds fill my heart.

IV

I have slept. How long? I sit here, and find before me the pages penned last night. What have I written? My mind still burns, but I have dreamed a dream, a horrible dream, but one so real I felt I've lived it.

I must tell it. I must find in it a way out.

On a moonlit beach, black water coming in with the rising tide . . .

Do angels howl and leer? I saw them above me, a grotesque procession, a parody of the One God's host. They had faces like dogs and horns like goats. Their wings were white, but they had no feathers. They had the wings of huge, white bats. They howled a cacophonous dirge, their serpentine tongues dripping green and orange spittle down into the black water, where it burned and sputterd, releasing a stench beyond description. This procession turned, circling above me, coiling about itself like an endless snake until the highest disappeared into the night and I found myself at the bottom of this nightmarish, writhing, leering whirlpool of monstrosities. And all of them whispered my name.

Some force (Within myself? Without?) pushed me back to the sand so that I stared up at the stars and moon through this ghastly circle. Swirls of smoke, from where the stench rose up from the water, danced over me, penetrating my nose as if alive. I felt bound to the earth, unseen bonds strapping me to the sand. I could not lift even my head.

I wanted to run, to race down the beach, up a cliff, up a mountain, into the clouds, the heavens, the depths of the sea. Anywhere. I forced my eyes shut, and found another vision there, a vision of a burning cross, the cross of the Christ. Nailed to the wood was Thyri, her flesh aflame, and then the procession entered this vision as well! A leering parody of beauty with orange eyes and green fangs thrust unexpectedly before my eyes. I could smell its breath – more terrible even than the stench rising from the water. This face peeled away my eyelids as if they were merely the curtains of a stage. The whirlpool nightmare returned; the visions meshed and combined. Thyri hung there in the center, burning on that cross.

The whirlpool descended until its bottom tier reached the sand. Then it whirled tighter. I could feel them now, mere inches from my body on all sides. Just then, the cross began to spin, the flames giving way to spears of light. Faster and faster . . . It became a cloud, and the cloud pelted me with rain and hail, snow and ice. I grew cold and numb in an instant. The cloud became the sun, and it burned me, the lurid angels howling and weeping their delight. The closest began to lick the sweat from my skin.

Slowly, as the bile rose to my throat, the sun became the moon, and the moon became Thyri. Only now she was naked, glowing, as beautiful as ever I'd seen her, nay, more beautiful than ever. She walked down a silver ladder from the sky until she stood at my feet. And there, she began to run her hands over her body, over her breasts and thighs. Some of the dark angels broke ranks and surrounded her, kissing her, biting her, and she answered with caresses of her own and moans of ecstasy.

I still felt the bile in my throat. I still felt this horrible revulsion, but, just as some power pinned me to the sand, some darkness raised and hardened my manhood at this sight above me.

'He likes you, my pets!' Thyri said, grinning and falling before me to her knees.

I cannot write what came next, for never might I have imagined such horror and beauty possible in the space of a single moment. I endured, trapped in this nightmare. I endured, and felt pain and pleasure, attraction and revulsion, and everything – every feeling known to man – in between.

I yet shake as I think on it. I want to purge it from my mind, but it will not go away. And yet, though I know whence to seek relief, I cannot yet go. I know what power gave me this vision. That power is here in this castle, awaiting me, dark and patient, wielding its boundless, malicious evil. He toys with me, but he has tried to cheat me!

Yes! In this vision lies the seed of his defeat, for did he not promise me I would love Thyri? Is that not why he sent me this dream? Is that not why he made the dream so real and powerful? Yet it was but a dream; it wasn't real. He does not hold power over Eiriksdattir. Even should he argue that he transported me to that beach, that could not have been Thyri herself who came to me. That was not her, not her love I felt.

And that is what she promised me, her love. Her love as she shared with Astrid, with Munin, with Akan in her tent in the new land where they thought her akiya toyn, the wildfire, a goddess. With Pohati, gently, slowly, on furs as with Astrid. And with Megan, always with Megan – oh, Tana! Do not read this my love and hate me! It is you I want, but she is whom he promised me, and if he failed in this promise, then he cannot take me! Please understand!

V

I have played a game of words and lost.

'What is a dream?' he asked me, his voice a dark hiss under his cowl.

I was shaking, clinging to Tana's hand, staring into the darkness under that cowl. There was no face inside. Just black upon black. 'An unreal thing,' I answered resolutely.

'And what is a real thing?'

'Something that happened.'

'So dreams don't happen?'

I stared into his darkness, trying to calm my body. 'Yes, dreams happen,' I said, 'but the thing that is dreamed – that doesn't happen. It is an imagined experience, not a real one.'

'So what makes a real experience?' he hissed out. 'Something that you feel, taste, see?'

I nodded cautiously.

'But you feel, taste, and see in dreams, don't you? You must explain to me more clearly the difference between dream experience and real experience. This is very important with regard to our business, is it not?'

'Yes,' I said, clearing my throat. 'But in a real experience, you are *there*. It is happening around you.'

'But that's true also in dream. Come, you must tell me the *difference*, and it must make sense.'

I turned to look at Tana then, but her head did not move; she stared into his darkness, unflinching. I squeezed her hand more tightly, but she did not squeeze back.

From the darkness, came a soft laugh. 'She will not help you,' he said. 'I will not allow it, for this agreement we must settle between us, not her. What is the difference between dream and reality?'

My mind burned with a cold fire, for what could I answer? He toyed with me; he had taken Tana away for some reason. Could she answer better than I? Could she help me win?

What *was* the answer? *Simple*, the thought came into my mind. *Dream experience happens when the body is asleep.* That is what I told him.

'I agree,' he hissed at me.

'But will you agree that dream experience is not real?' I asked.

'For settling our agreement? Yes, I will give you that. Do you agree? This is very important, as you know.'

'Yes, I agree, and I have won!' I shouted, laughing.

'No,' he said, and the darkness flowed from his cowl, filling the room, then filling me with visions, of my past, of memories and things I have felt and seen.

Yes, he showed me again how I sat like a parasite inside Akan as Thyri loved him. And he showed me other times when I did the same, with other lovers. I felt again Thyri's touch, her lips and her body, and the thrill of joining with her. At the end, the darkness and the visions lifted, and my mind raced to understand, to reach a new battleground in this game, this dark and deadly duel that had suddenly trapped me. 'But I was not *there*!' I protested.

'I have given you all I promised,' he said, ignoring my complaint. 'Now you must settle our pact.'

'But I wasn't there!'

'Were you asleep?'

'No.'

'Then it was a real experience, based upon the terms that we just now defined.'

With that, he rose. 'You may go,' he said. 'My gifts have served you well, have they not? Do not despair. I am generous. I will give you until tomorrow night at dusk when the moon is full. I think that then will be a fitting time to consummate our contract.'

No longer able to bear looking at him, I nodded, I had lost. He lingered a moment, then left.

As I write, I turn that word game over and again in my mind. Could I have won? Could I have answered that real experience requires physical presence? Would he have accepted that, or would he have argued artfully until he forced me in the end to admit that, perhaps, no difference between dream experience and real experience exists at all? I think so. I think I was trapped before it had begun. That dream last night – the one he sent me of Thyri – that closed the trap. Had we argued until no difference existed between dream and reality, I might still have said that *I* must experience as *myself*. The dream covered that escape.

So I am lost to him, condemned to the company of Erik and Patrick and how many others? Tomorrow night, I must leave this world, and I will shortly set down this pen for the final time and go, to spend what time I have left in the arms of my wife. When all is done, she will have little more than these writings left of me; I would that I could have given her more of myself these past years. But I accepted this fate; it is my burden alone to bear.

As I write these last words, I am filled with a distant sort of hope. I have learned that immortality is fleeting, and eternity meaningless, for I know that even immortal gods can perish. These new lords over Midgard, this One God and his opponent – how long might they last? A hundred years perhaps? Two hundred?

I will wait. This Satan must perish as have other gods before him. Then, at last, I might be free.

Author's Note

This story was translated from an untitled manuscript uncovered by Lord Basil Horning during excavations he made before World War II. His notes describe its origin as a dark drywell in what was once a shrine to the Celtic goddess Brigid. In addition to the manuscript, he uncovered several jewel-inlaid human skulls. The discovery was kept secret from the archeological world – it seems Lord Horning was involved in occult researches and cared little for the methods of the hard scientific community of his day. Recent attempts to find the site of his investigations have failed.

In 1982, I was in the air force and stationed in San Angelo, Texas. A friend called me and, knowing of my interest in the legends of the darker ages of Europe, told me of this manuscript and that he had come into possession of it. He refused to tell me how, but he invited me to his home in Florida to examine it, so I took a week of leave. I drove to Dallas and got lost in the crush of international jet-setters at the airport. When I finally reached Florida, I was cursing my friend. But he gave me that which I had come only to see. He asked me to take it, read it, study it. So long as I respected the necessity of secrecy – not of the story, but of specific occult formulations contained therein – I could sate my curiosity, then return the bundle to him.

My friend would not tell me why parts were secret. I knew that he also had embarked upon various occult researches, and I assume that he'd copied the specific passages down, else he would never have given the thing to me. In any case,

I've not heard from him since that weekend, and his family believe him dead.

I've respected his desire for secrecy; in fact, I superstitiously avoided even reading the parts he'd singled out. The story alone fascinated me. At one university, I had fragments of the fibery parchment carbon-dated to circa 900 A.D. This meshes roughly with the times of which Gerald writes: the battle of Ethandune, the seven hundred-ship assault of the Norse up the Seine, and the reign of Harald of Vestfold all occurred historically in the late ninth century. The script itself was in a free-style dialect of the more formalized Old English found in the Anglo-Saxon Chronicle penned under the direction of Alfred the Great, and a kind professor from another university that shall remain nameless assisted me in unscrambling some of the more hastily scribed passages.

The adaptation to modern English, however, is mine and mine alone. Some of the names and some entire passages are modernized, some are not. Where the prose turns to modern forms and phraseology, I take full responsibility. I feel I am justified – my task was to retell Gerald's story, not to provide a literal transcription.

After much wrestling with my conscience, I burned the original manuscript. For one thing, my friend's death was surely related to his possession of it. For another, I am a novelist. Who would believe this story is true?

MDW

Danville, Virginia

10/88

THE HEAVENLY HORSE FROM THE OUTERMOST WEST

MARY STANTON

The Heavenly Horse is the Dancer, an Appaloosa stallion, first of all the horses in the Army of One Hundred and Five, guardian of the Courts of the Outermost West.

But the Dancer is under sentence of death. Anor, servant of the Dark Horse, is the appointed executioner. But between them stands Duchess, last true mare of the line.

When Duchess, ill-treated and ill-tempered, arrives at Bishops' Farm, only El-Arat, Story-Teller and Dreamspeaker among the horses, understands that she is unique.

Then the Dancer arrives. Duchess, along with the brave mare Suzie and Cory the devoted farm dog, runs away with him to face a winter of terrible hardship and danger. For now Duchess' foal is the last hope for the breed and Anor with his harrying hounds are closing in on them.

'A surprisingly powerful fantasy'

Orson Scott Card

'Exciting, poignant and big-hearted. It deserves to be read'

Stephen Donaldson

VALE OF THE VOLE

PIERS ANTHONY

It all started when Metria, the shape-shifting demoness, took up residence in Esk's secret tree house.

Esk *needed* his hideaway. When your mother's a nymph and father part-ogre, you have to be able to get away from it all now and again. But Metria was determined to force him out. She tried violence, threats, wheedling and seduction. Seduction nearly did it.

So it was that he set out through the Kingdom of Xanth, to find and ask help from the Good Magician. Travelling the enchanted pathways, first he saved Chex, winged she-centaur, from the overheated attentions of a small but nasty dragon.

And then they met Volney the Vole, who had a real problem. And so one thing just kept on leading to another . . . and another . . .

HODDER AND STOUGHTON PAPERBACKS

WHITE MARE, RED STALLION

DIANA L. PAXSON

The Lady of the Ravens

Maira lived in the land that someday would be called Scotland, in a time when magic hung heavy on the hills and the Old Gods were revered with pageantry – and with blood.

The soldiers of Rome had claimed the island for their own, but the Celts would never surrender their homeland for they were a fierce and warlike people. When they were not warring against mighty Caesar, they warred against each other.

Daughter of a chieftain, Maira was as fierce and proud as any Celt, trained in the arts of war as well as the mysteries of women. She was of the White Horse clan and her beauty shone like the sun itself. Carric had loved her since he'd first seen her. Even though she was of an enemy tribe. Even though she had vowed to kill him . . .

HODDER AND STOUGHTON PAPERBACKS

LADY OF LIGHT, LADY OF DARKNESS

DIANA L. PAXSON

The four Jewels of Power had been created by a priestess in the days when the Covenant between the people and the Guardian of the land had been threatened. The heirs of her line held the Jewels – one for each of the sovereign elements – and through them, ruled Westria.

And in the sixth century of the Covenant, the Estates of Westria petitioned the King to marry, so that he might have an heir. So the King and his companions set out to find a Lady for Westria – a woman who would become both the mistress of his heart and the Mistress of the Jewels . . . Queen . . . Healer . . . Sorceress . . .

'This might be an authentic legend of another time and place. Truly it holds one spellbound in the old meaning of that word'

Andre Norton

HODDER AND STOUGHTON PAPERBACKS

THE CLAN OF THE CAVE BEAR

JEAN M. AUEL

First in the celebrated Earth's Children series continued in the bestselling THE VALLEY OF HORSES

Here is a novel of awesome beauty and power, a book that transcends time and space, a moving saga about people, relationships and the boundaries of love. Swept back to the dawn of mankind, we meet a very special heroine, Ayla, who takes sanctuary with the Clan of the Cave Bear. At first the men and women of the Clan mistrust this tall, blonde and very intelligent girl but gradually Ayla wins their confidence. And as she leads them in their struggle for survival, the Clan comes to worship Ayla. For in her blood flows the future of humanity.

'Beautiful, exciting, imaginative'
New York Times

HODDER AND STOUGHTON PAPERBACKS

THE MAMMOTH HUNTERS

JEAN M. AUEL

Ayla's story began with THE CLAN OF THE CAVE BEAR and THE VALLEY OF HORSES. This is the magnificent sequel.

Leaving the Valley of Horses that had become her home, Ayla embarks on a momentous journey. It will lead her to the Clan of the Mammoth Hunters – a people at first hostile and disturbingly different. With her is Jondalar, the handsome man she has nursed back to health and come to love. But as she gradually settles into this strange new life Ayla finds herself irresistibly drawn to the magnetic Ranec, master-carver of the Mamutoi. Ultimately she is compelled to make a fateful choice between them . . .

The third volume in the celebrated EARTH'S CHILDREN series.

'The authenticity of background detail, the lilting prose rhythms and the appealing conceptual audacity continue to work their spell'

Publishers Weekly

HODDER AND STOUGHTON PAPERBACKS